THE
INITIATE BROTHER
DUOLOGY

DAW Books by Sean Russell:

The Initiate Brother Duology
THE INITIATE BROTHER
GATHERER OF CLOUDS

Moontide and Magic Rise
WORLD WITHOUT END
SEA WITHOUT A SHORE

The River into Darkness
BENEATH THE VAULTED HILLS
COMPASS OF THE SOUL

SEAN RUSSELL

THE INITIATE BROTHER

DUOLOGY

THE INITIATE BROTHER
GATHERER OF CLOUDS

DAW BOOKS, INC.

DONALD A. WOLLHEIM, FOUNDER
375 Hudson Street, New York, NY 10014
ELIZABETH R. WOLLHEIM
SHEILA E. GILBERT
PUBLISHERS
www.dawbooks.com

First Printing, July 2013

1 2 3 4 5 6 7 8 9

DAW TRADEMARK REGISTERED
U.S. PAT. AND TM. OFF. AND FOREIGN COUNTRIES
—MARCA REGISTRADA
HECHO EN U.S.A.

PRINTED IN THE U.S.A.

INTRODUCTION

The Initiate Brother was a strange hybrid in its day. The book grew out of my love of Tolkien, my fascination with T'ang dynasty poetry (and thus the period), and my newly discovered interest in the court writings of tenth-century Japan, especially *The Tale of Genji*. It was also deeply influenced by Chinese history and the great wars of succession. It was not the first "Asian Fantasy," but I believe it was the first successful one. I was determined at the time to distinguish my book from all the vaguely medieval, Norse-saga fantasy that was being written at the time. An Asian based fantasy seemed to be one way to do it. The problem was—and I had no way of knowing this—that publishers were still looking for more of the same.

The Initiate Brother had no wizards, elves, dwarves, or even "magic" as it was understood. In fact, it read more like an historical novel than a fantasy, yet it was set in a non-existent kingdom that combined elements of ancient China and Japan. No one really knew what to make of it. The letters that came back from editors were confusing to a neophyte writer. On the one hand, several editors appeared to love the book, but they didn't know what the market might be for a book that fell somewhere between an historical novel and a fantasy. Who would read it? What shelf did it fit on? One British editor wrote my agent to say that she didn't think they could sell *The Initiate Brother*, but she thought I might be a major writer one day and would we please send her anything else I wrote. It was like good news/bad news. Love the book—can't publish it.

It began to look like *The Initiate Brother* would be confined to that odd little category of good books that just didn't fit into the publishing paradigm. That was until Betsy Wollheim came to the rescue.

Betsy was the part-owner and one of the two senior editors at DAW Books, a company started by her father, Donald A. Wollheim. One of the things about Betsy's position was that she could buy a book without having to get half a dozen other editors on board. I remember the day Betsy called me—at work (I still had a day job). I had the flu and was actually on my way out the door, heading for home, when someone caught me to say there was an editor on the phone wanting to talk to me. I scurried back to my desk, answered the phone, and that moment aspiring writers dream of occurred. A woman with a slight New York accent told me she loved my book and wanted to buy it. I always remember what Betsy said: "I don't know if we can sell it, but it's too good a book not to be published." I thanked her profusely, went home, and threw up. Not really the way it's supposed to happen, but we don't get to write our lives.

I was terribly intimidated by Betsy at first. After all, I had wanted to be a writer from the age of ten, and here was my chance. "Don't screw it up" was my main thought. Over the next few months, though, we became friends. We were the same age, had come of age in the sixties, liked the same music and books. Despite the fact that she grew up in New York (Queens, actually) and I grew up in small town Ontario we had a great deal in common, and she was a dedicated editor. At the time I had nothing with which to compare this editorial experience, but having worked with countless editors in the subsequent twenty-three years, I have learned that Betsy is an editor from the old school. She edits. She loves the job, loves the books she works on, and is utterly determined to make the books better. And she did, too. Betsy is the only editor I've ever had who asked me to make a book longer!

I attended a couple of "cons" the year the book came out and was welcomed into the world of writers. People like Tad Williams, Stephen Donaldson, Pat McKillip, Neal Stephenson, and Sean Stewart became friends and have, over the years, supported me both personally and professionally. It is no exaggeration to say that *The Initiate Brother* changed my life.

I have noted recently a number of fantasy novels drawing on cultures other than northern European, and even heard an interview recently where someone asked if this was a new trend. Considering that I started writing *The Initiate Brother* in about 1984, this made me smile. *The Initiate Brother* might have more "mysticism" than "magic" (it is more like the film *Crouching Tiger, Hidden Dragon* than *The Lord of the Rings*) but I still think it has that "feel" that made fantasy such a popular genre. It is epic in its scale, filled with intrigue and characters that match the scale of the world. And it has action— lots of action. I still get letters from readers asking me if I ever plan to write a third book in the series. (My answer: "Never say never.")

I look back at the last twenty years of my writing career and am firstly rather surprised that it has been that long—I still feel like a new writer with much to learn. And secondly I can't believe what a crooked path I have followed. Certain books stand out as having shaped some part of my writing life. *The Initiate Brother* began a period of fantasy writing for me—nine books in total. More recently, *Under Enemy Colors* turned me into a writer of successful historical novels. Even more recently I have written a mainstream novel with an elderly Huckleberry Finn as the main character. Rather ironically, editors are again saying, "We love this book, but what is it? Who will read it? What shelf does it go on?" I have somehow cycled back to the beginning—to an unusual book that does not fit into the publishing paradigm. Here we go again.

Writing is rather like marriage, I think—it is not for the faint of heart. It requires persistence, yes, but more than anything it requires an enormous amount of love. You have to want to do this more than anything else. I still get up in the morning and feel blessed that all I have to do that day is write. I am one of the fortunate few. For this I have to thank editors, publishers, agents, friends, family, and most of all readers. I get letters from readers almost every day, and it is one of the great pleasures of my morning to read them while I drink my coffee. I never forget that it is these people who have allowed me to do what I do for a living.

I am delighted that Betsy and DAW have decided to bring this book out again. I don't know if we could call it "groundbreaking," but it was certainly unusual in its day. To those people who ask "What is it? What shelf does it belong on?" I say it is a novel. You can put it on any shelf marked "Fiction." Readers write and tell me they have put it on the shelf reserved for their favorite books. That is the shelf writers long to have their books on. To those readers I say, "Thank you."

Sean Russell
2013

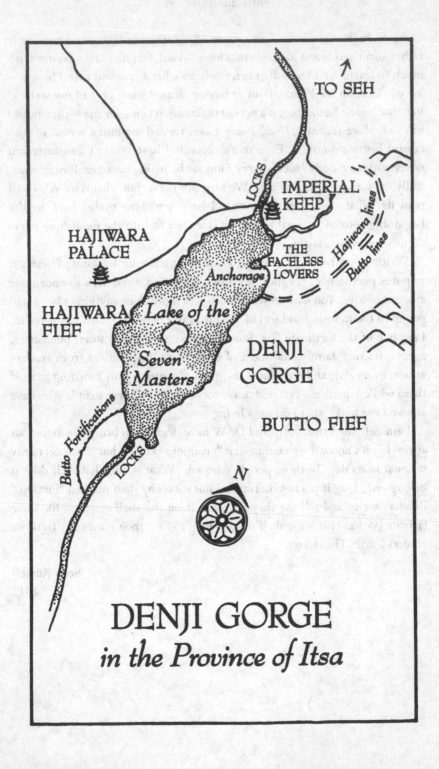

TO SEH

LOCKS

IMPERIAL KEEP

HAJIWARA PALACE

Hajiwara lines

Butto lines

Anchorage

THE FACELESS LOVERS

HAJIWARA FIEF

Lake of the

DENJI GORGE

Seven Masters

BUTTO FIEF

Butto Fortifications

LOCKS

N

DENJI GORGE
in the Province of Itsa

EMPIRE OF WA
during the Reign of Akantsu II

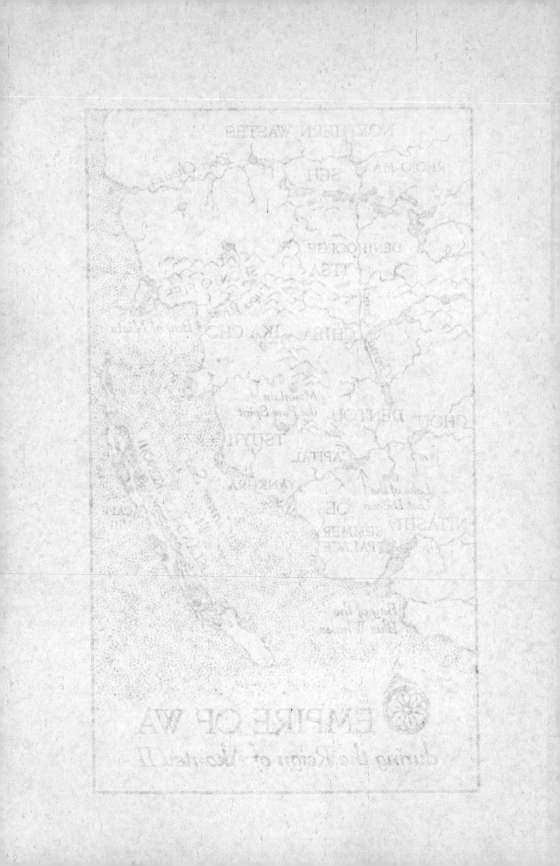

The Initiate Brother

DEDICATION

This book is dedicated to my grandfather, Stan Russell, in his ninety-fourth year, and to the memory of my father who loved books.

ACKNOWLEDGMENTS

I would like to thank my family and friends who supported my efforts tirelessly and more selflessly than anyone could have a right to expect.

As one reads the history of our Empire, it becomes apparent that we have always had a preoccupation with our past. For two thousand years we have written the chronicles of our dynasties, histories that reach back into the distances of time to the Kingdoms of the Seven Princes. It is interesting to note that we are taught to value all of these works equally. Yet, as we read back through them, each successive chronicle seems less factual and more storylike. When one has studied the writings of antiquity, it can be seen that history and fantasy become indistinguishable.

The Spring Analects;
Hakata.

One

T**HE PRACTICE OF** condemning messengers, the Supreme Master thought, had not developed without reason. The old man looked down at the scroll he had received from the Floating City that very morning and he shook his head. A lifetime of dedication and effort and still he received messages like this. It seemed a great injustice.

Brother Hutto, the Primate of the Floating City, wrote that Botahist Brothers were being accosted on their travels by criminals and ruffians: accosted by the people of the Empire!

The Supreme Master slowly began to roll the mulberry paper scroll. The attacks were not the true problem—one would have to search a lifetime to find someone more able to defend himself than a Brother of the Faith—it was what these attacks said about the situation in the Empire and the attitude of the new Emperor. This was the Supreme Master's real concern.

He set the scroll on the corner of his writing table. Brother Hutto had written that several of these robbers had been injured recently, but this did not seem to be a deterrent. If anything, the attacks were increasing. The old monk reached for the scroll as if to read it again, but stopped himself. There could be no doubt of what it said.

If only the Emperor would turn his attention to the roads! That would be an indication that this new dynasty was capable of something more than ambition.

The Supreme Master took a deep calming breath. Emperors, he reminded himself, come and go; the Faith is eternal. It was important to keep the proper perspective.

Of course, Brother Hutto had recommended that a *display* might be appropriate. It was an old solution but one that had not been employed for many years. The Supreme Master lifted the scroll again and hefted it as though it were Brother Hutto's suggestion he weighed. Perhaps a Brother of the Faith *should* enter the Emperor's kick boxing tournament during the River Festival.

Yes, the Supreme Master thought, he would allow a monk to enter, but not a senior Brother; no, that would not have the desired affect. He would allow a junior Initiate to compete—the smallest, youngest looking Initiate that could be found. That would be a message neither Emperor nor subjects could mistake, a message to spread down all the roads of the Empire!

Fortunately, it appeared that finding the boy would not be difficult. The Supreme Master felt satisfied with this idea. Not only would it fit his purpose, but there was historical precedent for such an act. The Lord Botahara himself had first been a warrior and, in his time, had entered the Emperor's tournament—though the other fighters would not compete against him.

Lord Botahara had crossed the cobbled courtyard to the fighting ring and the cobbles had *broken* under his feet. The story was no longer believed by the population at large, such was their lack of faith, but the old monk knew it to be true. The Supreme Master himself could. . . . Well, it was wrong to be proud of one's accomplishments—after all, what were they compared to the Enlightened One's and he had overcome pride altogether.

Addressing the problem in Brother Hutto's letter had been the first difficulty of the day. Difficulty two had just disembarked at the monastery's wharf. Sister Morima; Botahist nun, acquaintance of forty years (could it be that many?), would grace him with her presence as soon as she finished her bath. Days like this were sent to try him! The Supreme Master had always hated surprise visits. That was one of the many beauties of the monastery on the island. There were almost no visitors at all, let alone any coming unannounced.

His mind drifted back to the report from Brother Hutto. What was that ass of an "Emperor" up to now? The old fool had lived on past all predictions. It happened sometimes, and not always to everyone's advantage. The only benefit of this Emperor's long life was that he did not leave a mere child to follow him, which invariably meant succession struggles. But then, the heir was no prize either, and not friendly to the Botahist Order. Well, the Brotherhood had plans and plans could be adapted to changing situations, just as one adapted one's strategy at the gii board. Botahara taught patience as a principal virtue and the Supreme Master adhered to the principal virtues whenever possible.

The old monk let his eyes drift over the design set into the opposite wall in polished woods. Such a perfect pattern—abstracted from the blossom of the Septfoil, one of the ninety-four healing herbs. Seven petals within a septilateral, within a circle, the design intersected by the seven lines of power. So simple. So complete. The work of Botahara was a constant source of joy to him.

I am a fortunate man, he thought, and then realized that someone was approaching down the hallway. Sister Morima.

There came a tap on the frame of the shoji.

"Please enter," the Master said, his voice the model of quiet dignity.

The shoji slid aside, revealing the great bulk of the Botahist nun. She was dressed in a long, unpatterned kimono, in a most unbecoming shade of yellow, gathered at the waist with the purple sash of the Botahist Orders. Her hair was cut short like a boy's, offering no softness to relieve the square line of her jaw. She was, the Supreme Master noted, tanned like a peasant.

"Sister Morima. We are honored that you would come so far out of your way to visit us." He rose from his cushion and bowed formally. The nun returned the bow, though only equally.

"The honor is mine, Brother Nodaku. To visit the monastery of your *sect* is a privilege granted to so few . . ." She stopped, as if at a loss for words.

As he had planned earlier, the Supreme Master moved his writing table aside, but the nun did not apologize for interrupting. He offered her his cushion and took a second one from a wall closet.

"I bring you greetings and wishes of long health from Sister Saeja," Sister Morima said as the Supreme Master seated himself opposite her.

"And how is Sister Saeja? Well, no doubt?" Brother Hutto's report had mentioned that the head of the nun's Order had recently returned from her annual pilgrimage to Monarta, the place of Lord Botahara's birth, and the old nun was slowing down noticeably.

"She is as constant as the river and as supple as the willow wand, Brother Nodaku, a continual inspiration to us all."

He always found this ploy of hers—using his common name—disconcerting, as though the Initiate Nodaku had suddenly been caught impersonating the head of the Order.

"That is good news, Sister. Do you have other news you can share? We are so isolated here!"

She flashed an amused smile. "I've just returned from the island of the barbarian, Brother. I'm sure your news is more recent than mine." The Supreme Master remained silent, but the nun offered nothing more.

Lifting an ivory hammer that sat before a polished bronze gong, the monk asked, "Cha?"

"Thank you, yes, Brother, and some food, if it is not too much of an imposition." She bit off the last words.

The Supreme Master almost laughed as he tapped the gong. He knew the nun's weakness. *Brother Nodaku*, indeed! Footsteps sounded in the hall and then, as a knock was heard on the screen, a second set of footsteps joined them.

"Please enter," the Supreme Master said with understated authority. The face of Shuyun, the senior Neophyte who was causing all the fuss, appeared and before the Supreme Master realized what was happening, the face of the Neophyte servant came into view also. The two boys were startled by the unexpected presence of the Botahist nun. For an instant they stood in awkward silence and then they both bowed, bumping each other in the half opened doorway.

"Do you need me to serve you, Supreme Master?" the second Neophyte asked.

"That is why I sound this gong," the old monk said evenly. "Please, bring cha for Sister Morima and me. And some food. The Sister has not yet eaten due to an unforgivable lapse in our manners!"

"Immediately, Supreme Master." The boy bowed and hurried off.

"Shuyun-sum?"

"Excuse me for interrupting, Supreme Master. I was told to come here at this time to discuss my Seclusion."

The Supreme Master had forgotten.

"Have you completed your term, Initiate?" Sister Morima asked suddenly.

Shuyun bowed to the nun, while watching his master out of the corner of his eye. He decided it would be impolite not to answer.

"I'm only a senior Neophyte, honored Sister, but yes, I have just finished my Seclusion."

"Good for you, senior Neophyte. Did you stop the sand?" She smiled as she asked this question.

"No, honored Sister," the boy said, his tone serious, "I failed to stop the hour glass from measuring time. I can count the grains and name each one as it falls, but that is all."

The Botahist nun was unable to hide her surprise.

By the Lord Botahara, the Supreme Master thought, what karma has arranged for the Sister to be here now!

"Shuyun-sum, Sister Morima has graced us with her presence, so our interview must be postponed. I will call for you at another time."

Shuyun knelt, touching his head to the floor, and backed out of the room. "Thank you, Supreme Master." Then, suddenly emboldened, he asked, "May I join the junior Initiates in chi quan? They're about to begin."

The Supreme Master nodded his assent and made mental note to speak with the boy about addressing him after being dismissed.

As soon as Shuyun was out of hearing, the woman asked, "Is this true?"

"Yes, Sister, the junior Initiates train in chi quan every day at this time."

"You know what I mean, Brother!" She allowed impatience into her voice. "Is his chi ten ability so far developed?"

The Supreme Master shrugged. "I have only spoken to him just now."

The nun adjusted her posture, sitting more erect, forcing herself into a studied calm. "I believe he was telling the truth." She drew a deep breath and then almost whispered, "By the Lord Botahara!"

The sounds of the chi quan class drifted in from the courtyard and filled the silence in the study.

"And what do you plan to do with such a one, Brother?"

"If he learns to walk the Seven Paths, he shall serve Lord Botahara, as do all of our Order."

"Which is to say, you will indenture one with such abilities to some power-hungry lord, and draw him into the intrigues of the Empire for your own gains."

The Supreme Master was surprised by Sister Morima's sudden attack, but forced himself to remain calm; his voice, as always, was controlled. "We should not forget that the Lord Botahara was a peer of the Empire, born a 'power-hungry lord,' as you say. The political intentions of our Order, such as they are, have always been aimed at maintaining a climate in which the following of Lord Botahara can grow. We have no other purpose. *Your* Order benefits as much from our "intrigues"—which amount to nothing more than giving sound advice—as does my own, Sister Morima."

"I am not a Neophyte in need of instruction, Brother Nodaku. I choose my words with great care. So, you will take this boy and thrust him into a society of decadence where even the best training may not save him? Three of your Order died of the Great Plague—don't deny it! Botahist monks *died* of disease! Could you really be willing to risk one with such talent? What if he could learn to stop the sand?"

The Supreme Master fought to maintain his outward calm. How did she know about the plague deaths? Everything possible had been done to keep them secret. What a world! Spies everywhere! "To serve a peer of the Empire is a great test, Sister. If a member of our Order cannot pass it . . ." the old monk shrugged, "that is his karma. Stopping the sand is much more difficult than serving among the peers."

"Who was this one in his former life?" Sister Morima asked, pushing what she sensed was an advantage.

The Supreme Master shook his head. "We do not know."

"But he was a monk or perhaps," the nun touched her tongue to her lip, "perhaps a Sister?"

"That seems probable, Sister Morima."

"He chose from among the objects offered?"

"Yes, of course."

"And you say it is *probable* that he was a monk?"

"Wouldn't you agree?"

"Huh."

The Supreme Master realized he was revealing more than he intended. The truth was that he had no idea who the boy had been in his former life. As a child, when Shuyun had come to the Order he had been tested in many ways. One of these tests was to choose, from among a random array of objects, those commonly used by members of the Order. Shuyun had chosen all the correct objects—a feat almost unheard of—but subsequent tests to discern who the boy had been were unsuccessful. This had never before happened. Perhaps Shuyun *had* been a Sister! The Supreme Master found this thought unsettling.

"When will you give up this meddling in the affairs of the world, Brother, and concern yourself with the perfection of the spirit, as my own Order does?"

"I assure you, Sister Morima, that we are as concerned with the spirit and its perfection, as you are."

"But you are more concerned with perfecting the spirits of the wealthy, yeh?"

"Our temples and retreats deal with the less fortunate also, Sister, or have you forgotten? It was our Order that found the cure for the Great Plague, saving peasants, merchants, and peers alike."

Footsteps sounded in the hall, and then came a tap on the shoji.

"Please enter."

Two Neophytes bowed and came into the room carrying trays.

"I will serve the cha," the Supreme Master said.

A small wooden table was moved to the center of the room. The servers moved with studied precision, anxious not to bring shame to the Supreme Master or the monastery.

The Supreme Master prepared the tea according to the practices of a thousand years, while the servers laid small platters of rice and vegetables on the table.

"Please, serve our guest first," the ancient monk instructed, and then, with fascination, he watched the nun select from each dish offered, her pupils wide with pleasure. Such a foolish weakness, the Supreme Master thought. If she were a Brother of our faith, she would be required to live on water and air three days out of seven for the rest of her life to show mastery of her desire. He dismissed the servers and poured the steaming cha, offering the first cup to his guest.

"I am not deserving, Brother. Please take this cup yourself."

"Your presence honors me; please, I insist." He proffered the cup again and this time she received it with a bow which he returned. Outside, on the small, private porch, a cricket began to chirp. The chi quan training continued in the courtyard. The Supreme Master poured his own cha and tasted it. Perfect! The cha leaves were grown in the monastery's own garden and overseeing the cultivation of the cha plant was one of his continuing pleasures. He ate a small portion of rice, to be polite, and watched the nun as she tried to hide her gluttony . . . and failed.

The Supreme Master knew that, when the food was gone, Sister Morima would reveal the true reason for her visit—and he wouldn't need to guess what that reason was. He sipped his cha.

He could hear the swallows building a nest under the roof of his balcony. They would make a terrible mess, but he loved to watch them and make friends with them. Such beautiful fliers!

Looking at the running time glass on its stand, the Supreme Master began to exercise chi ten, stretching his time sense until the sand appeared to slow as it fell. He looked down at the steam rising from his cha in languid swirls, like impossibly fine curtains moving in a breeze. He smiled inwardly.

What if this young one *could* stop the sand, as the nun had asked? What if he could do more? Since Lord Botahara, no one had stopped the sand—not in a thousand years! Why did they all fall short of the Perfect Master? The old monk's own teacher had had more highly developed chi ten abilities than any of his students and he had claimed to have fallen short of *his* Master.

The Supreme Master felt the warmth of the cha bowl in his hands. Such a simple pleasure! He pondered the secret that, for so long, only he had known, and wondered who else might have this knowledge now. The sand, the sand. He turned his gaze to watch the grains as they fell.

Lord Botahara, the Perfect Master, through the discipline of chi ten, had learned to control his subjective sense of time until the world slowed around him. All Botahist monks could do this to greater or lesser degree. But the Enlightened One had gone far beyond this. It was written that Lord Botahara would meditate upon the running sand until it not only stopped but, to His eye, it ran backward. The mere idea awed the Supreme Master. It was said that Lord Botahara could *move through time like a swimmer through water.* The monk had meditated upon this every day for as long as he could remember, but still, the meaning of it eluded him. He knew that it had been wise to make this part of the *secret knowledge* to be passed from one Supreme Master to the next. How was he to explain what even he could not understand? There was no answer.

Sister Morima had finished eating, and he noted how well she hid her sense of shame. The Supreme Master lifted the lid of a porcelain bowl and offered her a steaming, white cloth. She took one to clean her mouth and hands.

"More cha, Sister?"

"Please, Brother Nodaku. The food, by the way, was delicious."

He poured, holding back the sleeve of the long kimono worn by all Botahist monks. Loose fitting pants that came to mid-calf, sandals, and the purple sash of the Botahist Order completed their clothing.

Sister Morima took a sip of her cha, replaced the cup on the table, and composed herself. The moment had come.

"Sister Saeja has again instructed me to ask you, in all humility, if members of our Order may come to study the scrolls written by Lord Botahara."

The Supreme Master stared into his cha, turning the cup slowly on the table. "Sister Morima, I have assured you that the scrolls you study are the same as those studied by my own Order. The last time we spoke I offered you my personal scrolls and I offer them to you again. The words you have are the words of Botahara as transcribed by the most well versed monks of any age. They are, I assure you, the most perfect copies possible."

"We don't doubt, even for a moment, the abilities of the scholars who have transcribed Lord Botahara's words, Brother. For us, this is a matter of spiritual interest only. You have come to be the guardians of this treasure, yet it is the legacy of all of Lord Botahara's followers. We wish only to look upon the words of the Enlightened One, as you have. We don't wish to remove them from your excellent care, Brother, but only to send a delegation— perhaps two or three of our most learned Sisters—to examine the scrolls—under your supervision, of course. There is no reason for you to protect the scrolls from us. We revere these treasures as do you."

"Sister, the scrolls, as you know, are very old. They are handled but once in a decade, when we unseal them to inspect for the slightest signs of degeneration. They are resealed almost immediately. All of us make do with our transcribed copies. *All* of us. I can say nothing more. I have an oath and a sacred trust which I will not violate. Please do not ask me to waver in this area of duty, Sister Morima."

"I would never ask that you break your trust, Brother, but you . . . you are *Supreme Master*. You may alter decisions that were made when the world was not as it is now. This is wisdom. Botahara taught that change was inevitable and to resist it, folly."

"Perhaps two or three of my sisters could be present at the time of one of your examinations? We would not hinder you in your duty, I assure you. Certainly it is allowed for the followers of the *Word* to attend this ceremony?"

Cunning old cow! How, the Supreme Master wondered, was he to get around this? "Let me consider your words and take counsel with the seniors of my Order. To do as you suggest would be to break the practices of a thousand years, Sister Morima. You must realize that such a decision cannot be made quickly. I will say no more and, please, understand that I can promise nothing."

"Ah, Brother Nodaku, your reputation for wisdom is indeed well deserved. I thank you, a thousand times over! You honor me to listen to me for so long." She bowed to him. "If you were to decide to allow us to be present at a time of examination—and I realize you have not promised this—but if; when would this be?"

The Supreme Master looked up for a second as though he needed to calculate when such a momentous day would come.

"It will be nearly nine years from now, Sister Morima."

"A short time, Brother, the days shall fly!" She clapped her hands together like an excited child. "How close to nine years, Supreme Master?"

He paused again. "Eight years from now on the seventh moon."

She drained her cha and then said with emotion, "May you attain perfection in this lifetime!"

And may you attain perfection *tonight* that I might be done with you, the Supreme Master thought.

"The ship did not have a large cargo to unload here, Brother, I'm sure they must be waiting for me. May I ask one more thing before I leave? When might we expect a decision on this matter?"

"I cannot say, Sister."

"Perhaps you could give me some estimation, that I might allow my Sisters a time to which they may look forward?"

"I cannot say, Sister Morima," the monk repeated, a hint of annoyance in his voice.

She bowed. "As you say, Brother, it was not my intention to impose upon you." She rose from her cushion with surprising grace and bowed again, the old monk rose with her and bowed simultaneously.

"I have kept you too long, Brother. You have honored me with this interview. I am in your debt."

"It is I who am honored, as your visit has graced our monastery. There can be no debt in such a matter."

The nun bowed a last time and backed out of the room. At the door she stopped for a second, catching the Supreme Master's eye. "What if this young one develops a perfect ear for truth?"

The Supreme Master ignored what was implied in this question, answering without hesitation, "Then he shall see not only the truth of Botahara's words but also the truth of our sacred work."

A senior Neophyte came down the hall to escort the Sister through the maze of Jinjoh Monastery. She nodded as though acknowledging the wisdom of Brother Nodaku's answer, turned on her heel, and was gone.

The Supreme Master stood for a moment, staring at the closed shoji, and then slid aside the screen that opened onto his private porch. A swallow flitted off the almost completed nest, protesting the intrusion in a high voice. The Supreme Master did not step out onto the wooden deck but instead hung back in the shadow provided by the roof. In the courtyard below he could see the junior Initiates practicing the Form. He took a half step forward, bringing more of the courtyard into view, until he could see all of the students, each standing in his own Septima—the geometric design identical to the one set into the Supreme Master's wall.

The instructor moved slowly and with perfect grace before the rows of pupils. They had come to the end of the sixth closure now and most of the students were faltering, though an untrained eye would never have been aware of this. Shuyun was in the second row, conspicuous for his small size and for his confidence. The boy's movements were precise and flowing, executed without hesitation.

Sotura-sum had not exaggerated. The senior Neophyte's form made the more advanced students look clumsy; indeed, he rivaled the instructor in his control. The Supreme Master watched, fascinated by the spectacle.

"Never before have I seen such a sight," he whispered. "Who could this child have been?"

Beyond the courtyard wall, of white plaster and wood, he could see Sister Morima being escorted down to the waiting ship. She moved with a light step for one so large of frame. The woman was far more clever than he had given her credit for. He would have to be more careful in the future—far more careful.

He had no intention of letting her, or anyone else, see the scrolls. Not now, not in a hundred years. The matter was no longer within his control. He felt his body slump, ever so slightly, and he fought this sign of resignation. How could this have happened? he wondered for the ten thousandth time. Every precaution had been taken. Every precaution! But it didn't matter now. Nothing mattered. The scrolls were gone. Stolen from under the sleepless eye of the Sacred Guard of Jinjoh Monastery.

The twenty junior Initiates, including one senior Neophyte, came to the end of the seventh closure and stopped, absolutely motionless, in the ready position. The senior chi quan instructor stood looking at the students before him, all of them barefoot and stripped to the waist. When none of them wavered in their stance, he nodded, satisfied.

"Take a partner," he said quietly. "We will spar."

The boys broke into pairs and resumed the ready position.

"Shuyun-sum," the instructor beckoned. "You have never sparred?"

"No, Brother Sotura, senior Neophytes only push-hands."

The instructor seemed to consider for a moment. "You will learn soon enough. Today we will both watch. Begin!"

Sotura walked among the combatants, stopping to watch each pair. The sparring started slowly, following the stylized movements of the form and then gained momentum until all movements became a blur, as each student sought a point of resistance against which he could push or to which he could deliver a blow.

Shuyun began to stretch his time sense, practicing chi ten to allow him to analyze the sparring as it increased in speed. The motions of the combatants became fluid and endless, each movement leading into the next without hesitation.

Brother Sotura held up his hands suddenly. "Cease!" he ordered, and walked to a position in front of the class. The silence was perfect.

"I see that some of you still believe that you can gain an advantage by using bone and muscle. Perhaps you secretly wish to be kick boxers?"

"To move within the form is not enough. You must become insubstantial. No one can kick the wind. No one can push water. It is of no value to make even the most perfect soft-fist if, at the moment of impact, you tighten the muscles. Chi is the source of all of your strength—direct it into your hand as it is needed. Remember that you hold a caterpillar in your curled fist. Its hairs tickle your palm." The monk paused as a tiny, blue butterfly drifted by and settled on Shuyun's shoulder. The instructor smiled. "I will demonstrate."

He took a step forward and reached out to Shuyun, gently removing the butterfly from his shoulder. Closing his hand over the insect, the instructor moved to the wooden gate that led into a walled garden. Pausing for a split second to take a stance, the monk suddenly drove his hand through one of the gate's thick planks, which splintered and broke with a loud *crack*. Pivoting gracefully, Brother Sotura held his hand out to the class—a perfect soft-fist—and then released the butterfly, unharmed, into the air. All of the class knelt and touched their heads to the stones.

"That will be enough for now. Go and meditate upon chi. Try to become a breeze so soft that even a butterfly would be unable to perch on your will."

Shuyun opened the gate with its broken board and went into the large garden beyond, a garden known for its many paths and private bowers overlooking the island and the sea. He found a nook formed by flowering rhododendrons and settled cross-legged onto a flat stone. For a moment he contemplated the display of his chi quan instructor—basking in the perfection of it.

The boy, Shuyun, had emerged from his Seclusion that morning and felt both a vast sense of freedom and at the same time a loss of freedom like none other he had known. Perhaps at no other time in his life would Shuyun have the opportunity to spend so much time totally alone. The Supreme Master had been right; six months could be a lifetime. A lifetime alone to meditate upon the Word of the Perfect Master.

The routine of his Seclusion had been relentless. Rise with the sun and practice chi quan on the pattern set into the floor of his one-room house. At midday he took his only meal and was allowed to meditate or compose poetry in the enclosed garden. Then came an afternoon of chi ten. Sitting within the Septima, concentrating all his being upon the Fifth Concurrence where the sand glass sat. Then, again in the afternoon, chi quan practiced before his wall-shadow until dark, followed by meditation on the Seven Paths. He was allowed three hours' sleep before sunrise.

Each afternoon Shuyun had sat, as he was sitting now, on the pattern and practiced the discipline of chi ten. Controlling his breathing, feeling chi drop to his *Ooma,* the center of being, he had reached *out* with his chi, sending it into the lines of power in the pattern. And each day the sand ran more slowly in the glass as Shuyun learned to alter his subjective time.

The ability to alter one's perception of time was not unknown beyond the walls of Jinjoh Monastery. The kick boxers could do it, to a degree, and some of the best tumblers and dancers spoke of it. Shuyun wondered if perhaps everyone experienced the stretching of time in brief moments of complete concentration. But only the Botahist Orders had discovered the keys to its mastery: chi quan and chi ten, the disciplines of movement and meditation represented in the pattern of the Septima, the Form which taught perfection of motion and total concentration.

"Entering the mind through the body," Lord Botahara had called this. Shuyun was beginning to understand. It was as though he had finally begun to do that which he had only understood before in words.

Sitting on the rock overlooking the sea, Shuyun felt chi drop and he began to push it out from his body, imagining that it rushed out into the infinite space around him to slow all motion.

A leaf fell from a ginkyo tree and spiraled endlessly downward. Anxiety touched the young monk and he felt his focus waver, but the leaf kept falling ever so slowly and Shuyun's confidence returned. He was able to concentrate on the play of sunlight on the planes of the leaf's surface as it fell against the background depths of a blue sky. Finally it touched the surface of a small pond and sent ripples out in perfect circles. Shuyun counted the tiny waves and named each one after a flower as it died at the pond's edge. A poem came to him:

> The spring has blossomed
> Yet a ginkyo leaf
> Falls endlessly
> Into the lily pond.

Shuyun released a long breath. Relief swept through him and it felt like an endless, powerful wave. Twice during his Seclusion he had lost control, or so he thought. Twice his altered time sense had seemed to distort and he had found himself somewhere . . . somewhere he could not describe. And when he had returned to the usual perception of time, it was with a crash which he knew indicated loss of all control. His teacher had never warned him of this and the young monk felt a strong fear that he was failing to learn what he must learn to become a senior of his Order.

He had intended to speak of this with senior Brother Sotura but did not, deciding it would be better to wait. And he felt now that he was gaining control. There had been no reoccurrence of this strange experience in several months.

A memory of the time before his Seclusion came to him: kneeling before his teacher, listening.

"You must always move within the pattern, you must even breathe within the pattern. Chi will strengthen in you, but you must never try to become its master. Offer it no resistance, only allow its flow. Chi can never be controlled. You can only make your will synonymous with it."

If his master had not said this, Shuyun would not have believed it possible. But now that his Seclusion was complete, he began to understand. He also began to see the wisdom of his teachers.

I must meditate upon chi, Shuyun thought. I must become a breeze so soft that even a butterfly cannot push against me.

After a timeless time a bell rang and Shuyun brought himself out of his meditation. He rose and walked calmly through the garden. It was time to bathe in the hot spring and then partake of the evening meal.

He paused at the gate to look again at the splintered board and his earlier joy at his teacher's demonstration became complete. The shattered board had been replaced and into the new board a monk had carefully cut a hole the shape and size of a butterfly. From his position, Shuyun could see the blue sky through this hole. With a last look, the young Neophyte hurried off. All the senior Neophytes would want to hear about the butterfly-punch which he alone among them had seen.

Brother Sotura, chi quan master of Jinjoh Monastery, mounted a stairway which ended in a hall leading to the Supreme Master's rooms. He had bathed and changed into clean clothes, taking time to compose himself before meeting with the head of his Order. The instructor knew of the nun's visit and was concerned.

He tapped lightly on the shoji of the Supreme Master's study and waited.

"Please enter," came the warm voice Brother Sotura was expecting. He slid the screen aside, knelt, and touched his forehead to the grass mats. The Supreme Master sat at his writing table, brush in hand. He nodded, as his rank required, and then began to clean his brush.

"Come in, my old friend, and sit with me. I have need of your counsel."

"You honor me, Supreme Master, but I fear that in the matters you consider, my counsel will be of little value."

"Take a cushion and dispense with this fear. I need you. That is that. Do you desire food?"

"Thank you, but I have eaten."

"Cha, then?" He reached for the ivory hammer.

"Please, cha would be most welcome."

The gong sounded and immediately there were footsteps in the hall.

"Please open," the Supreme Master said before the knock came. "Cha for Sotura-sum and me. And please, see that we are not disturbed." The boy bowed and slid the screen closed without a sound.

"Well, Sotura-sum, I had a most interesting visit this afternoon with the old cow." He paused and smiled, then shook his head. "She very nearly extracted a promise from me that certain members of her Order would be allowed to be present at our next examination of the scrolls."

The chi quan master remained silent.

"Very nearly but not quite. I told her I must confer with the senior members of my Order, which is what I am doing now."

Brother Sotura shifted uncomfortably. "It seems they will plague us until they have seen the hand of Botahara. I hesitate to suggest this, Supreme Master, but under the circumstances it may be wise to satisfy this curiosity. We have in our possession very ancient scrolls, perfect copies in fact. There are none living but perhaps four members of our own Order who could possibly know they are not real. I realize this is hardly an honorable path, but . . ." He shrugged.

"Honor is a luxury we may not be able to afford at this time, Brother." The Supreme Master looked down at his hands, examining them as though they were mysteriously changed. "We dare not raise suspicions about the scrolls . . . not now. I will consider your counsel, Brother, I thank you."

The server approached, though he had barely had time to go to the small kitchen and return. The Supreme Master cocked an eyebrow at the other monk.

"They have begun to anticipate me. Have I become old and predictable? That would be a danger. Do not answer, I shall meditate upon this."

The cha was served, its bitter-sweet aroma filling the room.

"Do you still think it is possible that the Sisters have the scrolls, or did your visit with Morima-sum do away with that path?"

"I can't say. Sister Morima may not be party to such knowledge. But if she is, and came here only to blow smoke in our eyes, she did admirably. I believe that she did indeed come to try again to gain access to the scrolls—but of course, one can never be sure. Sister Morima is an accomplished actress and no fool."

"So, we have not eliminated a single possibility?"

The Supreme Master nodded and sipped his cha.

"Did Brother Hutto's report offer anything?"

The old monk shook his head. "Robbers have begun to accost members of our Order on the highways of Wa. He recommends a *display* to curb this. Another Initiate has disappeared—Brother Hutto suggests that he is a victim of robbers. I can't believe it! The new Emperor has consolidated his power almost entirely, with one curious lapse—he has allowed the old Shonto and his family to live."

"How is this?" Brother Sotura rocked back on his cushion. "He cuts his own throat! What deal could those two possibly make? Shonto is absolutely loyal to the old Imperial line."

"Yes, but the Hanama line is no more. It is true that there are others with a claim to the Throne at least equal to Lord Yamaku's, but they failed to join against the Yamaku until it was too late. There is no help for them now. The old Shonto was betrayed and captured during a battle he may well have won. Lord Yamaku, or should I say Akantsu the First, Emperor of Wa, allowed him an honorable death—the two old foxes had fought side by side in the past. Lord Shonto composed his death poem, and when the Emperor heard it he relented and lifted his sentence on Shonto and his family!"

"The old fox has taken leave of his senses! Next he will set the *wolf* on the throne beside him. What was this poem, did our Brother say?"

The Supreme Master reached for the scroll and unrolled it.

After a lifetime of battle
And duty,
At last!
A moment to write poetry.

The chi quan instructor laughed with pleasure. "I commend them both for their wisdom. Only a fool could destroy one so clever."

"There is more," the Supreme Master said. "A week after the stay of execution, Lord Shonto's heir, Motoru, announced that he had married Lord Fanisan's widow and adopted her daughter. The two women emerged from hiding under the roof of the family the Emperor had just spared."

"The Shonto have always been bold. My concern for their Spiritual Advisor, Brother Satake, has been misplaced. Again the Shonto survive the jaws of the dragon. Had Lord Fanisan already fallen to the Emperor?"

"He fell to the plague first, poor man, leaving the Emperor in the awkward position of not being able to do away with the Fanisan women openly. Lord Shonto's son has saved them from an assassin, I'm sure. At least for now."

"So, young Shonto will marry off this adopted daughter to the Emperor's son, legitimizing the Yamaku claim and tying the Shonto to the new dynasty. The entire family has genius!" The instructor's voice was full of admiration. "And what of the plague, Supreme Master, have there been recent outbreaks?"

"We seem to have been successful. There has not been a single case reported in three months. But all the damage has been done. When the plague fell upon the Imperial family, Lord Yamaku mobilized. It was a great risk, but the confusion in the Empire gave him the only chance he would ever have. And now we have a blood-sucker on the Dragon Throne."

Neither man spoke for a moment. The room darkened as the sun set. The Supreme Master lit an exquisite porcelain lamp.

"The Emperor still does not require the services of a Spiritual Advisor?"

"No, Sotura-sum, he still fears our influence. We must watch this one carefully as he is very dangerous to us. His son will be no better. These will be difficult times for our Order. We must all flow like water and wind or we will be damaged—not destroyed—but years of work hang in the balance."

The Supreme Master poured more cha. "Senior Neophyte Shuyun was sent to me today and arrived during the Sister's visit—a terrible mistake. He was indiscreet."

"How so, Supreme Master?"

"She knows of his chi ten ability."

"Unfortunate, but she cannot begin to suspect his true potential. I feel I'm only beginning to realize it myself. Shuyun joined the junior Initiates at chi quan, today. They were clumsy beside him!" He looked up at the older monk. "What will we do with him?"

"He will, no doubt, become a Spiritual Advisor to a peer of the Empire and spread the teachings of Botahara."

"Shuyun would make a perfect advisor to an Emperor, Supreme Master."

"A very remote possibility. Other things seem more likely and almost as useful. We must intensify Shuyun's training without making him appear too special. I want to know his potential. He has never sparred, has he?"

Brother Sotura shook his head.

"How long would it take to bring him up to a level where he could win the Emperor's kick boxing tournament?"

"He could win it today, I'm sure, but I think he should train more specifically for such a test. Not long—perhaps two months."

"Begin his training tomorrow. I have a feeling that you and he will make a journey to the River Festival in the autumn." The old monk stood and moved to the open balcony screen. He stared out into the open courtyard for a moment. It was lit only by starlight and the shadows played tricks on the eyes.

"You have doubled our security?"

"Yes, and I check the guards personally every night."

"You are indispensable, Sotura-sum." The Supreme Master finally asked the question that each of them carried with him day and night. "If the Sisters do not have the scrolls, who else would want them?"

Brother Sotura was quiet for a moment as he considered his answer. "Their value is inestimable, for that reason alone anyone might want them. But no thief could effect their sale and remain unknown—word would surely get out. The greater possibility is that someone has stolen them for political reasons. Anyone who would benefit from a secure hold over the Botahist Brotherhood is suspect."

"The Emperor?"

"He would earn my first suspicion. He does not love us. There are no monks in his household to keep such a secret from and he is one of the few who could accomplish the theft."

"Who else?"

"Lord Shonto, Lord Bakima, Lord Fujiki, Lord Omawara, perhaps half a dozen others, and the magic cults, though I don't believe it was them."

"And we still don't know when they were stolen?"

"Sometime in the last ten years."

The Supreme Master shook his head. "All of the guardians of the Urn have been questioned now?"

"All but two, Supreme Master."

"And they?"

"They died of the plague."

"Huh."

The lamp flickered in a draft from the open screen.

"If the scrolls have been taken to blackmail us, why haven't they approached us with their demands?"

"Perhaps the time is not yet right for their purpose, whatever it might be."

"There is another possibility, Sotura-sum. What if the scrolls have been destroyed?"

"I refuse to believe anyone could perform such sacrilege!"

"The followers of Tomsoma?"

"They are bunglers and fools! They could never have accomplished the theft."

"I'm sure you are right, Sotura-sum. We have spies in their midst?"

"Yes, Supreme Master, and we have contacted them. They report nothing out of the ordinary."

"You are thorough, Brother Sotura."

The Supreme Master stood for a moment more and then turned from the open doorway. "Thank you, my friend, you have been most helpful."

The chi quan master rose and bowed before backing out of the room.

"Sotura-sum," the Supreme Master said, stopping the monk at the door. "I saw your instruction of the junior Initiates today." The Supreme Master bowed deeply to the chi quan instructor. Words were unnecessary. From the Supreme Master, there was no greater honor.

two

FROM WHERE HE stood by the steps to the quarter deck, Kogami Norimasa could see the Botahist monk silhouetted against the stars as he leaned by the rigging that supported the main mast. Kogami had been watching the young Brother ever since he had boarded the ship, though the sight of the monastery where the Perfect Master had begun writing his great works had begged his attention.

Very few had seen Jinjoh Monastery and Kogami counted himself fortunate to be among the few in yet another way. For too long he had been among the many—just another in the legion of faceless bureaucrats who served the Dragon Throne. And a very remote throne that had seemed!

As an Imperial Functionary of the Fifth Rank, Kogami had not caught even a glimpse of the present Emperor. Yet, whether the Son of Heaven knew it or not, Kogami had been of immense benefit to him, though of course the Functionaries of the Fourth and Third Ranks had received the credit.

But this injustice was about to be rectified. Kogami Norimasa's abilities had finally been recognized, and by no less a figure than Jaku Katta, the Emperor's Prime Advisor and Commander of the Imperial Guard. Such incredible luck! Such amazing good fortune! Kogami's wife had burned incense at the family shrine every day since then, despite the cost.

After so many years of laboring to make the Emperor richer, Kogami Norimasa would now see the rise of his own fortunes—Jaku Katta had promised him this. Kogami Norimasa, Imperial Functionary of the Third Rank.

Not since the fall of the Hanama had Kogami dared to even dream of rising to such a position. And that was not all! Jaku Katta had granted him an Imperial Writ which would allow him to participate personally in trade outside of the Imperium—in a limited way, of course—but still, it was a privilege granted so few outside of the aristocracy. Kogami Norimasa was exceedingly clever with money and now he would have a chance to prove it beyond a doubt, on behalf of both himself and the Emperor.

This would help compensate for the shame he felt at not having become a soldier as his father had wished. But he wasn't made for military life; that had been apparent from his early youth, to his father's lasting disappointment. His father had been a major in the army of the last Hanama Emperor and had died resisting the Yamaku entry into what was at that point an almost empty capital. That was the cause of Kogami Norimasa's stalled career.

If the plague had not decimated the Imperial Capital and, with it, the bureaucracy that made the vast Empire run, Kogami knew that he would never have been allowed to keep his head, let alone swear allegiance to the new Emperor. But now, after eight dark years in which he had risen only from the Sixth to the Fifth Rank, he was moving again! The papers had been delivered to him by Jaku Katta's own brother, papers that bore the stamp of power; the Dragon Seal of the Emperor of Wa. It was as if the gods had decided to once again grant Kogami a future.

The ship was only two days out of Yankura now, perhaps less. He prayed the winds would remain fair. Two more days of watching this young monk and then he would be back in Wa and his new life would begin.

Kogami looked again at the Brother who stood motionless on the rolling deck. He had been there for hours, dressed lightly but not seeming to feel the night's chill. They were all like that, Kogami thought. The monks who had been his teachers when he was a child had felt neither the heat nor the cold—or anger or fear for that matter. They remained enigmas, always. Even after seven years in their charge Kogami knew so little of them. But the Brothers had left their mark on him, and he knew he would never erase it.

Despite his feelings about the Brotherhood, Kogami did not object to his wife keeping a secret shrine to Botahara—though it was really against his better judgment to allow it in their house. This was not something that was disallowed; in fact, many families he knew did the same, but, like Kogami Norimasa, they wisely kept their beliefs within their own walls. The Emperor had turned his back on the Botahist faith and any who expected to rise in His service did the same, at least outwardly. Of course, this went against the teachings of Botahara, Kogami realized, but his wife was doubly pious for his sake. The monks themselves did not follow the teachings of the Perfect Master, as Kogami understood them, for the Brotherhood meddled in politics and acquired property and wealth. Kogami sighed. What a complicated world. Time would take care of it all, though, and the Faith would still exist when Emperors and monks had passed. It had always been so.

Outside the Imperial Service, people worshiped as they pleased and, despite the Emperor's hatred of the Botahist faith, he had not made the mistake of openly offending the Brotherhood. The Botahists held a great deal of power in the Empire and the Son of Heaven was too aware of this.

Kogami shifted his position to try to gain more shelter from the wind. The dark form of the monk remained unmoving at the gunnel. Perhaps he meditates upon the full moon, Kogami thought, and felt a twinge of guilt as he looked up at the pure, white disk of the autumn moon.

I have done nothing wrong, he told himself. To watch is not a crime. That was undeniably true, but there was a slim possibility that he might be required to do more. The words of Jaku Katta came back to him again and he analyzed them for the thousandth time.

"You will assist Ashigaru, if he requires it, though this is unlikely, otherwise you are just to observe. Get to know this monk. Buy your way into his favor if you must, but find out everything you can about him."

Assist Ashigaru? Assist in what? Kogami had not asked. Somehow he knew that to ask that question was to put his new future in danger. Kogami Norimasa, Functionary of the Third Rank, had pushed these thoughts from his mind.

So far, the man Jaku spoke of had not required Kogami's assistance—he prayed it would remain so. The priest, Ashigaru, was below decks with Kogami's wife and his daughter who was suffering from a sickness of the sea. Kogami had disliked the priest from the moment the man had boarded the ship from the island of the barbarian.

A large man with wiry hair and beard, Ashigaru had the look of the religious fanatic—as though he'd been out in the sun far too long. He had the habit of repeatedly tugging the lapels of his robes as he talked, pulling the material closer around him, protecting himself from a cold that no one else perceived.

For the first few days of the voyage, Kogami had spoken to the priest only in passing, just as Jaku Katta had instructed. But since his daughter had fallen ill, he'd exchanged words with Ashigaru often. This, of course, was entirely natural and should raise no suspicion; still, Kogami was most concerned about such matters, for his entire future depended on how well he performed his duty on this voyage.

He marveled again at his good fortune. Of course he had been a perfect choice for this matter. He had traveled several times to the island of the barbarian on business for the Emperor, always posing as a vassal-merchant for some minor lord. The Son of Heaven would never have it known that he participated in trade like a common merchant! So Kogami had become a trader and traveler and, except for the time away from his family, he had come to find pleasure in this life. But on this journey Jaku Katta had asked him to take his family with him. It was not an uncommon thing for a vassal-merchant to do, especially one who was adding to his personal income on the side, as more and more seemed to be doing. Jaku had thought the family would add to Kogami's appearance of innocence, so his wife, daughter and maidservant had accompanied him—at the Emperor's expense, of course.

Kogami had found much amusement in watching the reactions of his family to the absurd customs of the barbarians. They had laughed about it in private. What fun they had mimicking the things they'd seen! But now his daughter had fallen ill and Kogami had asked the priest, Ashigaru, to see her, as the members of religions were all more or less skilled in the practice of healing.

A gong sounded and sailors began to emerge from below for the change of watch. Silently the crewmen went about their routine of examining all critical parts of the ship's running gear. The rigging was checked briefly, but expertly, except for the shrouds where the silent Brother stood. The captain of the watch motioned toward these, shaking his head; and the sailors passed them by, leaving the monk to his meditations. The Botahist Brothers were invariably given such respect, even by those who did not love them.

For his part, the silent Brother stood by the rail, thinking about a woman he had never met. Her name was Lady Nishima Fanisan Shonto and she was the adopted daughter of Lord Shonto Motoru—the man Shuyun journeyed to serve. Shonto's previous Spiritual Advisor had left a most complete report detailing everything his successor would need to know about the House of Shonto and though Shuyun had only needed to read it once to be able to recall every word, he had read the section dealing with the Lady Nishima twice, as if to reassure himself that it was true. The words of Brother Satake, Shuyun's predecessor, revealed the man's great affection and admiration for the young woman. Shuyun felt that, in this matter, the old monk had come very close to losing the Botahist Brother's eternal objectivity. This made the woman even more intriguing.

Satake-sum was not a man to be easily impressed, indeed he had been one of the most renowned Botahist Brothers of the century, a man who surely could have become Supreme Master if he had so desired. Satake-sum's talents had been legendary, for he had attained levels of accomplishment in several endeavors that usually required the single-minded dedication and study of a lifetime. And, in many ways, this young aristocrat had been his protégée.

Lady Nishima Fanisan Shonto—Shuyun liked even the sound of her name. Already she had gained fame for herself as a painter, a harpist, a composer of music, a poetess—and these, if Brother Satake's report could be believed, were merely the most visible facets of a personality of even greater cultivation. It was no wonder she was so sought after. A woman of such unusual talent, the only remaining heir of the powerful Fanisan House. What other woman of the Empire was so entirely blessed?

Shuyun contemplated the perfection of the moon as he thought of this matter and a poem came to him:

I am drawn always toward you,
Your delicate and distant light,
Face which I have never seen.

The poem seemed to release him from thoughts of Lady Nishima, at least momentarily, and he was left with memories of his earlier trip to Wa. That had been a truly exciting journey. Shuyun had lived in Jinjoh Monastery from such an early age that he had formed no clear memories of the Empire, just as he had no recollection of his parents. On that first voyage, the River Festival had been his destination and Brother Sotura, the chi quan master, had been his companion. The newly initiated monk had struggled to contain his excitement and maintain an appearance of decorum, lest he bring embarrassment to the Botahist Order.

Though eight years had passed since that journey, Shuyun could still recall the trip in vivid detail.

They had been like wanderers from a far land, cast up on an unfamiliar shore. And there, before them, lay all of Wa, compressed into a space that could be walked in a day. The River Festival, lit by ten thousand lanterns, attended by uncounted people; an endless ebb and flow of humanity along the banks of the moving waters.

To have come to this from Jinjoh Monastery. . . . It was as if Shuyun had completed his meditation in a barren, silent room, opened the screen to leave, and there, where a tranquil garden should have been, twenty thousand people milled and laughed and danced and sang. To the boy from the island, it seemed that unreal.

Shuyun had followed his teacher through the crowds. Lanterns of all colors hung from the trees, and where there was no lantern light, moonlight seemed to find its way. Shuyun had seen ladies of high birth carried through the crowds on sedan chairs, smelled their perfume as they passed, laughing and hiding their faces coyly behind fans. And the next moment he had stepped over wine victims lying in their own disgorge. Fascination had caused him to pause beside the tumblers and jugglers, forcing Brother Sotura to return and find him raptly watching every movement, every trick, lost in the slow-time of chi ten.

Shuyun and Brother Sotura had passed a tent with beautiful young women beckoning at its door, and though the women had made signs to Botahara as the monks passed, the youngest of them had tried to flirt with Shuyun and had laughed when he looked away.

Brother Sotura had led him over a footbridge into a park, and Shuyun felt as though he had entered another kingdom. The riotous noise quieted, and the pungent smoke of cook-fires was replaced by the delicate aromas of cut flowers and rare perfumes. Drinking and laughter continued, but those drinking and laughing were dressed in elaborate silks and brocades, unlike any the young monk had never seen. Shuyun was certain Sotura had sought this place out, yet he did not know why.

They had passed by a group of people whispering and gossiping at the edge of a circle of willows, and had come upon a stage lit by lanterns. A woman sat on cushions at the edge of the stage and read from a scroll to a silently attentive audience. Her voice was as clear as winter air, yet the words she spoke were weighty and formal. Shuyun had realized that an ancient play was being performed, and had recognized the language of antiquity, understandable, but charged with vowels that rolled oddly off the tongue.

Sotura had settled down on a grass mat, motioning for his student to do likewise.

"Gatherer of Clouds," the master had whispered, and Shuyun had recognized the title from his studies.

As the play unfolded, Shuyun had become entranced by the portrayal of a central character who was an eccentric Botahist monk, a hermit unconcerned with the day to day lives of the other characters but deeply committed to the esoteric, the intangible. It was the first time Shuyun had seen a monk depicted by someone outside his Order and he found this a fascinating if not a reassuring experience.

It was hours before Shuyun emerged from the world of the stage and he found himself deeply moved by his first encounter with theater.

Two days later the kick boxing began. The official who registered Shuyun for the tournament could barely hide his amusement when he realized that it was not the chi quan master but the boy who accompanied him who would compete. The politely disguised smiles quickly disappeared as Shuyun won his first contests with an ease that surprised everyone but Brother Sotura. Of course, his first opponents were not highly skilled by the standards of kick boxing, so the small monk, though he gained some respect, was still not thought to present a threat.

It was on this journey to the Empire that Shuyun first encountered violence. Though he had trained in chi quan for many years, the young Initiate had never seen a man consciously try to cause another damage. Among the kick boxers were those who had forsaken honor for cunning and brutality.

But Shuyun did not lose his focus. And Sotura showed a careful confidence in him.

As the two monks observed other bouts, it became apparent that two men fought outstandingly and were favored to win: an Imperial Guardsman named Jaku Katta, and a lieutenant of the Shonto family guard. Shuyun saw the Imperial Guardsman fight, though briefly, and it was easily apparent why he had earned the name "Black Tiger." Jaku Katta was not only strong and fierce, but he was exceedingly clever and possessed a sense of balance which was almost uncanny. He was almost twice Shuyun's size.

As Shuyun faced opponent after opponent, he began to feel chi flow through him with a strength and power he had never known before. He came to realize that the violence of his adversaries enabled him to draw from an unknown reservoir of power—a well which could be tapped only when he faced true danger. Boxer after boxer was forced from the ring. Crowds began to follow Shuyun's progress.

As they prepared for the bout with the Shonto lieutenant, Shuyun noticed his teacher glancing at the gathered crowd. Following his instructor's gaze, Shuyun saw a group of guards in blue livery surrounding a man, a girl, and an old Botahist monk.

"Beware of this one," he said as Shuyun stepped into the ring, "it is impossible to know what training he has had."

Shuyun obeyed the instructions of his teacher and approached the match with extra caution, but Sotura's concerns proved unfounded. The man was as good if not better than any the young monk had yet faced, but he was still a traditional boxer and knew only the path of resistance.

There was only one more contest after that, the one in which Shuyun faced the Imperial Guardsman. Shuyun knew that the man was physically impressive, he towered over the diminutive monk like a giant, but as Shuyun entered the ring he momentarily lost focus. For, like the tiger he was named for, Jaku Katta had gray eyes. The young monk had never before seen a man whose eyes were not brown.

It soon became apparent that Jaku would have bested the Shonto guard. He was faster than all the previous fighters Shuyun had faced, much faster. And he thought as quickly, changing an attack in mid-strike—moving with the perfect balance of a cat. Still, Shuyun turned all blows aside, all kicks. And Jaku kept his distance, dancing away after each onslaught. He had obviously studied Shuyun in the ring and purposely drew the contest out, hoping the monk would make a mistake. No one should test his patience against that of a Botahist monk.

Jaku was the one to err in the end, suddenly finding himself in a corner. But he would not surrender and wildly fought to gain an advantage, desperately using every bit of skill and strategy known to him. In the midst of a complex series of punches and kicks, Shuyun deflected a blow, and even as he did, he knew that *something* had happened, something unique. There had been no feeling, no touch. It was almost as though he had deflected the punch with chi alone!

And Jaku faltered. Only one with an altered time sense could have perceived it, so quickly did it pass, but Shuyun did not fail to mark it. The Black Tiger had *faltered!*

Surprise paralyzed Shuyun for a split second, and in that time his opponent recovered. The contest did not last long after that. Jaku's motivation seemed to have abandoned him.

Shuyun knew he had won a victory for his Order and hoped that it would restore respect for the monks of his faith as it was intended to do. He felt no personal pride in this, as was only proper. But his training could not stop him from feeling terrible doubts. What had happened in the ring with Jaku Katta?

It was not till several days later that Shuyun brought up the subject with Sotura. "Is it possible to deflect a blow with chi alone—without making contact with the body?"

The chi quan instructor had considered for a moment, as though the question was only of theoretical interest. "I do not know if it is possible. No such incident has been recorded, not even by the Perfect Master. This would seem to make it unlikely, Shuyun-sum. It is a good question for meditation, however."

Shuyun realized his perceptions must have been colored by the intensity of the moment. His teacher would certainly have noticed anything unusual.

Yet after this journey, Shuyun noticed that Sotura's attitude toward him had changed. He was still a junior Initiate, but he was treated differently somehow, as though he had earned greater respect. Shuyun found this both gratifying and, at the same time, unsettling.

A flock of water birds skittered away from the ship's bow, their sleep interrupted by the passing behemoth. Shuyun turned his mind from his memories, which he found endangered his sense of humility, and watched the clouds pass in front of the moon.

He voyaged again toward the Empire, this time to serve the man that Brother Satake had described as ". . . endlessly complex, as full of possibilities as the third move of the game of gii." The description would have applied to any number of Shonto lords back into antiquity when the House had first emerged as the *Sashei-no Hontto.* But by the time the Mibuki Dynasty had united the Seven Kingdoms the Sashei-no Hontto had become the Shonto, and they had begun what would become one of their consistent practices—they had married their first daughter to the heir of the Mibuki Emperor.

Hakata the Wise had been an advisor to the fourth heir of the Shonto House and had dedicated his great work, *The Analects,* to his Shonto liege-lord. The history of the Shonto continued in the same vein through all the years. Other Houses appeared, flowered and then wilted, often within a single season, but the Shonto endured. Certainly they had times when they seemed to be in disfavor with the gods, but these were short-lived and the House invariably emerged, stronger and richer than before. Of the Great Houses of Wa, very few exhibited such resilience.

The words of the Mori poetess, Nikko, came to him:

The dew becomes frost
On frightened leaves,
And the seasons turn
Like a scroll
In the hands of the Shonto.

Lord Shonto Motoru was presently without a wife, though he did maintain consorts, but by and large, the Lady Nishima had taken over the duties her mother had once so ably fulfilled. The Shonto household continued to run smoothly and their social events were still noted for their elegance and imagination.

A cloud obscured the moon from Shuyun's view and the wind seemed to ease a little. The island of Konojii was not far off and fear of the pirates that infested the coastline would begin the next morning and would not abate until the ship rounded Cape Ujii and entered the Coastal Sea.

From below, a woman emerged, her steps silent on the wooden deck. She was dressed in the manner of the women of the middle rank, yet she had a dignity and bearing that often comes to those who have suffered great loss or hardship and survived. Given a change of dress and a smile that appeared more easily, she could have been the wife of a minor lord. But her smile had been forgotten and she had been the spouse of Kogami Norimasa for seventeen years.

The match had been made when his future had looked very bright indeed. He, the scholar who had just passed the Imperial Examination, and she, the daughter of a minor general—that gentleman, at least, had seen the rightness of Kogami's career even if his own father could not. They had all had futures then, when the Hanama ruled, when the Interim Wars and the Great Plague were just muddled riddles that, only later, the soothsayers would claim were clear omens.

"Nori-sum?" she said as she approached her husband in the moonlight.

"How is she, Shikibu-sum? Has the priest eased her pain?"

"He has given her a potion that has made her drowsy." She reached out and found her husband's hand in the dark. Her voice quavered. "I wish we had asked the monk to see her. She is very ill. I have seen this before. I don't believe this is her spirit out of balance with her body. This pain and swelling on the side of her abdomen, it is poison collecting, I'm sure. I'm afraid for our daughter."

Kogami felt a growing sense of alarm. Ashigaru had assured him it was only a sickness of the sea and Kogami had believed that—he had needed to believe it. But what if the priest was wrong? What if this *was* poison collecting, as his wife said, and his daughter needed more help than this Tomsoian priest could give?

Ashigaru was the Emperor's man, as was Kogami Norimasa. And the monk, if not the Emperor's enemy, was at least perceived as a threat—though in some way that Kogami did not understand. There was no love between the followers of Botahara and the followers of Tomso. Kogami knew that the priest would be more than insulted if he suddenly were to ask him to step aside so that the monk could practice what the followers of Tomso called "heretical medicine."

"We must give the priest a little time, my faithful one," Kogami whispered. "If there is no improvement, we will ask the monk to see her."

"But . . ." Kogami held up his hand and his wife choked back a sob. "I apologize for this lack of control. I am not worthy of your respect. I will remove myself from your sight and sit with our daughter."

She turned to go, but he stopped her, his voice soft. "If she grows worse . . . send the servant to inform me."

He was alone again in the moonlight. The sea had eased its motion since the wind had abated, but Kogami did not notice—inside of him a storm grew.

The moon emerged from behind an almost perfectly oval cloud and took its place among the stars. The constellation called the Two-Headed Dragon appeared on the horizon, first one eye and then the other, peering out above the waves. A sail began to luff and two crewman hurried to tend it. Men went aloft to set a tri-sail as the wind fell off and a reef was let out of the main. The ship began to make way at renewed speed.

Around the iron tub that contained the charcoal fire, men gathered to brew cha. When they spoke at all, it was in whispers, the formality of cha drinking reduced, of necessity, to mere nods and half-bows aboard ship. In a most deferential manner, a sailor went to offer a steaming cup to the Botahist monk, but the young Initiate shook his head. If he spoke at all, Kogami could not hear him.

Kogami had approached the monk himself, earlier in the voyage, and had met with a similar rebuff. Having known the ways of the Botahist Brothers since his earliest days, Kogami had sought out the monk at a time when they could not be overheard and offered to make a "contribution" of fine cloth to the Brotherhood in return for a blessing. There was nothing uncommon in this and if the offer was made with tact (one did not go with the gift in one's hands), a refusal was unusual. Yet when he had finished his carefully worded speech, the monk had turned away, leaving Kogami in a most humiliating situation. Then without even looking at him, this boy-monk had said, "Give your fine cloth to someone who has need of it, then you will be blessed."

Kogami could not believe he had been witness to such a display of bad manners! He had been forced to walk away, his parting bow unreturned. What if that had been observed! He had never known such anger and shame. Even now he felt the humiliation as he recalled the event. The Botahist Brothers were capable of such hypocrisy, Kogami thought.

Botahara had taught that humility was the first step on the path to enlightenment, yet the monks who professed to walk this path displayed an arrogance that would shame a Mori prince. It was clear that this young monk needed some education, away from the confines of Jinjoh Monastery, for he did not yet understand the practices of his own Order.

Kogami tried to calm himself. Anger, he knew, would affect his ability to perform his duty to the Emperor, and he could not let this occur.

Kogami's anger was soon dissolved and not entirely as a result of his own efforts. His childhood teachings, learned at the feet of the Botahist Brothers, could never be entirely forgotten and a single phrase surfaced from his memory though he had tried to suppress it: "Give to those who have need and you will be blessed." So Botahara had answered a great prince who had come offering a gift in exchange for a blessing—a gift of cloth spun of gold.

Ashigaru appeared in the hatchway, his breathing loud as he labored up the steps from below. The smell of sanja "spirit flower" preceded him, its sickly-sweet aroma causing a chill of fear to course through Kogami. The dried petals of the sanja were scattered over the dead or those thought to be near death, to drive away evil spirits.

Kogami Norimasa's mouth went dry and his hands shook.

"Is she . . . is," his voice failed him and suddenly he found it hard to breathe. Reaching out for the rail, he steadied himself.

Ashigaru looked solemn but not at all hesitant. "She is in the hands of the gods. Whether they choose to take her now or return her to this plane is their matter. I have scattered the blossom of the sanctified flower around her. No evil spirits can possess her no matter what occurs."

"But *you* said it was only a sickness of the sea! You said it was *nothing*." Kogami spoke too loudly.

The priest drew himself up. "Don't tell me what I said or did not say! Do you not know your place? I have protected your daughter from spirits that would torment her for all eternity. Could you save her from this fate?" The priest tugged at his robe and glared off into the darkness. Yet he did not walk away as Kogami expected. Instead, he stepped closer. "Listen, Norimasa-sum," the priest said in a lowered voice, "we must not argue. We do *his* work, yeh?" And Kogami knew the priest was referring to the Emperor, not to the Father of Immortals. It was the first time either of them had acknowledged their true reason for being aboard.

"He can be generous . . ." Footsteps sounded on the stairs and the priest fell silent.

Kogami's wife stepped into the broken moonlight that fell between the rigging and the sails. Across the distance that divided them, Kogami tried desperately to read his wife's face but could not. She looked at the two men— and she hung her head. Then a sound, which neither man could hear, came to her from below and she raised her head, meeting their eyes.

Her face was beautiful in the moonlight, Kogami thought, beautiful and strong. She turned on her heel and strode across the deck to where the Botahist monk stood at the rail. Kogami Norimasa made no move to stop her, even though he felt his future slipping away like daylight over the horizon.

She cannot understand what this act will mean, Kogami thought. Even so, I bless her.

"What is she doing?" Ashigaru demanded.

"She is asking the Botahist monk to attend to our daughter." Kogami was gratified that his voice sounded calm. The Fates have decreed this, he thought, it is karma. One cannot fight the Two-Headed Dragon.

The Initiate monk, Shuyun, heard the woman's footsteps behind him and turned slightly. He had been expecting her to come—or her husband, the trader in cloth. It depended on how ill the daughter was. He had overheard the crew talking of the young woman's sickness and knew the Tomsoian priest had been asked to see her. So Shuyun had waited, knowing that if the girl were truly ill the parents would put their religious scruples aside and come to him, the only Botahist monk on board, the only person who understood the secrets of the body.

"Pardon my lack of manners," the woman said, an obvious forced calm in her voice. "I apologize for interrupting your meditations, honored Brother, but it is not for my sake that I do so." She bowed, formally. "I am Shikibu Kogami, wife of the merchant Kogami Norimasa-sum."

Shuyun nodded. "I am honored." He did not give his name as it was assumed that everyone aboard would know it.

"My daughter is very ill. She suffers from the gathering of poisons. The right side of her abdomen is afire with the signs of this. She is unable to move from her bed. Honored Brother, could you see her?"

"Is she not in the care of the Tomsoian priest, Shikibu-sum?"

"He has scattered the petals of the spirit flower over her and commended her into the care of the Immortals." She looked down at the deck. "He can do nothing for her. I am a follower of the True Path, Brother Shuyun, and say my devotions daily. She is my only daughter. I . . ." The woman's voice broke, but there were no tears.

"I will come," the monk said, looking into the woman's careworn face.

Descending into the dull lamplight of the aft cabins, Shuyun was confronted with the overpowering scent of the spirit flower. The Botahists always took this smell as a bad omen.

On deck a mere zephyr touched Kogami's neck and somehow that reinforced the tranquillity that had come over him when he saw his wife walk across the deck toward the Botahist Brother.

"The currents of Life cannot be refused. They are the only course possible. The most powerful Emperor may choose at what hour of the morning he will rise, but whether his spirit will slip away before the dawn, this he cannot order." So the teachings of Botahara read. Kogami felt every muscle in his body relax.

The priest grabbed his shoulder roughly, "You must stop her!" he hissed as the monk disappeared below.

"I cannot," Kogami said quietly, not even struggling to free himself. "You have given my daughter into the hands of the Immortal Ones. She is no longer your charge."

"Nor is she that monk's! You damn her for eternity. Do you not understand that? They defile the sanctified human form. Her spirit will be cursed and condemned to darkness!"

"But I can do nothing, Ashigaru-sum. The monk has been asked to attend her. I will not humiliate my wife by ordering him away."

"You will not humble yourself, you mean. You fear the boy: How could Jaku Katta-sum have chosen a coward for this matter?"

"And what of you, Ashigaru-sum? Will you defy the young Brother? Or has Jaku Katta chosen two cowards?" Kogami snorted, unable to contain his contempt for the priest any longer. He realized that the crew was watching, wondering what would happen, but it no longer mattered.

I cannot sacrifice my daughter to the Emperor's intrigues, he thought.

Unseen by the priest and the bureaucrat, a sailor slipped below to the captain's quarters.

The priest pulled himself up to his full height, staring down at the small man dressed like a successful trader. He gathered his robe about him and walked away with exaggerated dignity to the aft companionway.

Kogami Norimasa made no move to follow. The currents swirled about him, he would not struggle.

In the woman's cabin, the Botahist monk knelt in the lamplight beside the bed of the stricken girl. She lay, obviously drugged, yet still in considerable pain, and though she made no sound her eyes screamed with the effort. The maidservant had opened the girl's robe, shaking off the petals of the sanja flower. Shuyun could see the swelling—red, and radiating heat. The mother had understood, even if the fool of a priest had not.

"You must be still," Shuyun said, his voice strong and assured like one much older. "I will not hurt you. You need not worry."

She managed half a smile that dissolved into a shudder of pain.

The monk took a small crystal from a gold chain around his neck and held the cylinder lengthwise between his thumb and forefinger. A pale, green light seemed to come from within the polished stone, though it may have been only refracted moonlight. Moving the stone above the girl's skin, Shuyun slowly followed the lines of her life-force radiating out from the afflicted area, the stone amplifying his chi sense like a water-finder's rod.

The monk did not flinch when the door banged open, revealing the half-lit form of the Tomsoian priest. The women gasped and the girl flinched in fear, causing a new spasm of agony to course through her.

"You damn your daughter to eternal darkness!" the priest accused thickly, ignoring the monk who had risen fluidly from his knees and half-turned toward the door.

Shuyun spoke quietly to the two women so the girl would not hear. "I must have the ebony chest from my room *immediately*. There is little time."

"He will desecrate the sacred body. There is no forgiveness for this," the priest said, his voice rising.

No one moved. Shuyun glanced down at the girl who was bathed in sweat and shaking uncontrollably. It was almost too late for her. But there were edicts within his own Order forbidding any monk to do violence to a member of another church except in self-defense.

A sailor's face appeared in the dim passage behind the priest and Shuyun addressed him, ignoring all formality, "I must have the ebony chest from my quarters, immediately."

The man gave a quick bow and was gone. The priest and the monk stood facing each other across a space of two arm's lengths. One man's eyes burned with the fires of fanaticism and fear—the other's watched and measured. There was no fear.

The sailor appeared, carrying the dark wooden box, but the priest stood his ground and would not let him pass.

"I must have my trunk. Stand aside," Shuyun said, his voice still quiet, emotionless.

"You do not order *me!*"

From the hallway the captain's voice was added to the confrontation. "Ashigaru-sum, please, do as the Brother asks. I do not wish to have you removed."

The priest glanced over his shoulder, "To threaten me is to threaten my church. We bask in the light of the Son of Heaven. Already you have earned his disfavor, as has this *heretic,* this defiler of the spirit's vessel."

The captain did not respond. At sea his word was law, but he was no fool and knew that it was never wise to earn the Emperor's disfavor—not *this* Emperor.

The situation was in danger of losing all motion, and Shuyun knew he couldn't allow that, couldn't wait for the captain to weigh the situation. He took a step forward, his eyes never leaving the large man blocking the door. The priest's eyes flared and his hand moved imperceptibly toward his left wrist, a subtle motion, almost impossible to see in the dim light.

Yes, Shuyun thought, that is where the knife is. He changed the position of his hands to counter this threat and sank lower on his leading leg. They were an arm's length apart now and Shuyun altered his time sense, slowing the world around him.

But the priest suddenly froze in his place, like a man who has seen a sand-cobra rise before him, and the monk stopped in mid-stride.

"Stand aside. I must have my chest."

"You dare not," the priest hissed, the air rasping out of constricted lungs. There was sweat on the man's brow, though the night was turning cool.

"Now," Shuyun said, his voice calm in the room charged with tension.

The older man felt his pulse begin to race out of control.

"I have the Emperor's protection!" he almost pleaded.

In the dim light, the monk's movements were barely seen. There was a sound of cloth tearing and then he stood with the priest's knife in his own hand. Through the scent of sanja flower, he could smell the poison on the blade's tip. The priest had lost his balance as he stepped back, now totally overcome by fear. Hands caught him, taking his arms. He gasped but could not find air. He did not notice when a second knife disappeared from his sash. He was half-carried, half-dragged onto the deck. For an instant his eyes met Kogami Norimasa's. The trader did not look away to spare the priest from embarrassment. Kogami Norimasa smiled openly.

He gloats, the priest thought, unable in his state to feel anger. Two sailors held him as he leaned over the rail and was violently ill, completing his public humiliation. Ashigaru sank to the deck in a heap, his beard and clothing soiled. His mind whirled. The monk must die, screamed his thoughts. The trader must pay! May this ship and all aboard her be swallowed by the ocean!

For a moment he fell into utter darkness, and when he returned to his senses he was sure that the monk had opened him with his own knife, releasing his spirit which had then appeared in a hall before the seated form of Botahara. The Enlightened One had barely looked at him before pronouncing him unfit to return to Life as a human. Botahara had turned over a sand glass on a stand and the grains had fallen like feathers through the air—so slowly. Ashigaru's new life would be thus—interminable, without event.

The priest shook his head to clear it. The deck hurt his back and his leg lay twisted under him where he had fallen like a drunk in his own vomit. The sky spun overhead when he moved, so he lay still watching the masts sway among the stars. The air was cool and the moon stared at him openly, unmoved by his fall. Soon the anger would return, the hatred.

More lamps had been brought to the cabin and the mother asked to leave. Shuyun raised the empty cup that sat beside the bed. He smelled it.

"Was this the only thing the priest gave her?"

The maidservant nodded. Shuyun set the cup back in its rack. For a change, one of the priests had not done his charge irreparable harm. Loda root, the sleeping draught. The girl would survive the potion's after-effects, which were considerable.

Several wide sashes had been used to restrain the patient, but they did not stop her from shaking or reduce the pain. Shuyun held her head gently and opened one eye to the light. He nodded. The maidservant knelt to one side, ready to assist him without question. She was a good choice, the monk realized. She had all the signs of one who had seen many births and had nursed countless of her charges through their childhood illnesses. She also had utter faith in the Botahist trained.

From a silk case, Shuyun removed needles of silver and gold, sterilizing each one before carefully inserting the point into the girl's skin. The chi flow of her body was interrupted, and suddenly there was no pain. The girl's face softened, and her breathing became regular, almost normal.

The edge of the tiny knife was unimaginably sharp. When Shuyun drew it across the girl's skin, she felt nothing. The monk was not a second too soon.

The priest Ashigaru mounted the steps leading from below. He ignored Shikibu Kogami seated on a cushion outside her cabin door. Ashigaru had washed and changed, and though he still felt weakened and unwell his anger carried him onto the deck. Ignoring the staring eyes, he crossed immediately to Kogami Norimasa who still held his position by the rail. All caution was abandoned now. The priest didn't care who saw them talking. He had decided on his course of action.

He grabbed Kogami's sleeve, roughly, and spun the smaller man around. "Now, Kogami Norimasa, you will earn your rewards." The man's voice was a hoarse whisper.

"Everyone watches," Kogami protested.

"Let them watch and damn them for it!"

"Ashigaru-sum, please!" The trader was alarmed by the man's manner and by the frenzy in his voice.

"Listen to me, Kogami," the priest spat out the man's name, "Jaku Katta will hear of your treachery. You have my word that if you do not follow my instructions now, you will not pass beyond the docks with your head on your shoulders. Katta-sum has no patience with failure and I do not intend to try *that one's* patience."

"But I . . . I was only ordered to observe, to report. I . . ."

"You lie, Kogami Norimasa. You were ordered to assist me and assist me you will. That, or you will lose more than your recent promotions. Do you understand?"

The smaller man nodded, unable to answer. The hand that held him shook with anger, and the priest's eyes were wilder than ever.

Looking around him for the first time, the priest caught the stares of the crewmen, even as they turned away to avoid his eyes.

"Take this," Ashigaru said, slipping a small packet into Kogami's hand and closing the unwilling fingers around it. "When the young Brother has finished damning your daughter to the Netherworld you must take him some cha. No doubt he will be grateful. Make sure the cha is strong and that the contents of the packet which I have given you are stirred into it.

"Your head hangs in the balance, Kogami Norimasa, *Functionary of the Second Rank.* The monk need only drink the cha. No one will know it was poisoned. You will not be held accountable by the Imperial Courts, I guarantee it. After all, the monk has saved your daughter. How could you wish him harm?

"Remember Jaku Katta of the flashing sword and let the memory of such a worthy general bring you strength."

The priest bowed formally to Kogami Norimasa who returned the gesture as if in a dream.

He felt himself being swept along on the outgoing tide, beyond safety, beyond hope. He gripped the wooden rail with both hands and stared down into the rushing water. A glowing path of phosphorescence stretched out along the ship's wake. He felt the tiny package in his sleeve pocket as it brushed against him. I am going to take the life of a Botahist Brother, he thought. What karma will I acquire! It will not matter that I am not blamed. He tried to work some saliva into his mouth but couldn't.

I have no stomach for murder, he thought, no stomach at all. How could my life have come to this?

"Pride," a small voice said from within. "Pride has brought you to this. Your life was good and yet you walked around as if under a dark cloud. Always wanting more. Humility, Botahara taught, humility."

I will not face Jaku Katta, his mind screamed! He could see the point of Jaku's famous sword arcing toward him.

And so he stood at the rail in the moonlight, a soft zephyr caressing him, Kogami Norimasa, the Emperor's servant, the Brotherhood's student—a man entirely at sea. Before him the Two-Headed Dragon had risen and stretched its wings across the southern sky. I am doomed, Kogami thought, and knew it to be true.

The monk emerged from below and spotted Kogami Norimasa leaning against the rail. He crossed the deck to where the man stood, and the trader jumped when the monk cleared his throat.

"May your harmony return within the hour, Norimasa-sum. I believe your daughter will recover entirely, though she will be very weak and should not be moved any distance for several days after we have docked. You may look in on her, but do not wake her."

Kogami Norimasa put his hand to his face and seemed close to breaking down but took a series of deep breaths and regained a semblance of control.

"I do not know a way to express my gratitude for what you have done, Brother Shuyun. Nothing one such as myself can do would begin to repay the debt I owe to you."

"I am a student of the Great Knowledge. How could I have done otherwise?"

Kogami Norimasa bowed deeply. "It moves me, Brother, to find one who follows the Way so completely. To meet you is a great honor." Kogami, the bureaucrat, was shocked by the sincerity of his own words.

Shuyun bowed slightly in return. He realized now that the trader had at one time been a student of the Botaharist Brothers. The signs were all there, the inflection and the careful choice of words. The posture, the mixture of fear, awe, and suppressed resentment that so many students developed. Yet the man wore no prayer beads or icon to Botahara and he associated freely with the Tomsoian priest. *A lost one,* Shuyun concluded.

"If you wish to see your daughter now, you may," Shuyun repeated thinking the man had not understood.

"First, allow me to bring you some cha," and before Shuyun could answer, the trader in cloth was on his way to the charcoal fire amidship.

Shuyun watched the man go, but his attention was diverted by the sight of the priest who was seated, almost hidden, in the shadow of the foresail on the ship's bow. That priest bears watching, Shuyun thought. A man who feels he has been humiliated is a dangerous man. But he was confident that the priest was a physical coward. Ashigaru would never confront him again. Even so, Shuyun regretted the incident. If the girl's life had not been in danger, he would not have allowed the confrontation to develop. There was enough tension between the two faiths as it was, and though everyone believed that the Emperor's interest in the Magic Cults was for purely political reasons this still gave the Tomsoian priests an advantage. The Emperor was unpredictable and could use an incident between the faiths as an excuse to try to suppress the Botahists. For this reason, the Botahists restricted their activities and waited. It was only a matter of time. The followers of Tomso were without discipline or patience and their use to the Emperor was limited.

Shuyun could see Kogami's back as the man bent over his cha preparation. He was taking unusual care, it seemed. Gratitude, Shuyun thought.

Finally the trader rose and started across the deck, which now barely rocked on the quiet seas, yet Kogami stared intently at the two cups he carried as though spilling a drop would mean the loss of all his family honor. The moon was obscured again by clouds and Shuyun had trouble making out the trader's face as he approached, but Shuyun sensed *wrongness* in the man's carriage. All his years of training came suddenly to focus on the man before him. Shuyun knew the feeling well and had been taught to trust it completely. He controlled his breathing and took the first step into chi ten—

time slowed and suddenly the trader seemed to float toward him, each step stretched to many seconds.

It is there, Shuyun thought, in the voice of his body, the wrongness. The monk waited now, waited for the knowledge that would come from his focus. He made himself an empty vessel, easier for the understanding to fill him.

And so it arrived, not like a flash, but like a long-familiar memory, one that had no surprise attached to it—and no doubts. It was there, in the merchant's right hand, the wrongness, like a knife concealed in a sash. Yet it was only a cup of cha. Shuyun could smell the herb in the air.

The merchant came floating to a stop like a man in a dream, while everything about him screamed fear and guilt and sorrow.

Is it possible that anyone could not see this, Shuyun asked himself? Can people be that blind? The man's fear was more obvious than the look of a lover for his beloved. Shuyun could smell the fear in the man—a pungent tang coloring his sweat. But it was not the monk that the merchant feared— at least not entirely—Shuyun was sure of that. But what was it?

"My daughter has been . . ." the merchant started, words coming with great difficulty, "the greatest source of joy in all of my life, though I have not always known it. I can only offer you this small token, for there is no way that I may express the gratitude which I feel." The merchant bowed and proffered a cup to Shuyun, but it was from his *left* hand!

Shuyun did not return the bow but nodded at the cha Kogami still held. "Why have you chosen this?" The smell came to the monk now—faint, so faint—the poison.

The merchant fought to maintain his control. Without answering, he began to raise the cha to his mouth, but the monk's hand was there, stopping him. The fingers rested so lightly that Kogami could barely feel them, yet he could not raise his arm. His hand trembled with the effort.

"Why have you chosen this?" Shuyun asked again.

"Please," the man whispered, his dignity beginning to dissolve, "do not interfere, Brother."

But still Shuyun restrained the man, seemingly without effort. "But that cup was to be mine."

The merchant's eyes widened and he shook his head choking back a sob. "Not now, not now. . . ." He stared down into the steaming cup. "Karma," he whispered. Then he looked up to meet Shuyun's eyes. "It is not the place of a follower of the Way to interfere in a matter of . . . continuance. It is the law of your Order."

The monk gave a slight nod and his hand was gone from Kogami's arm.

The merchant released a long sigh that rattled in his throat. "Listen, Brother, here is my . . . death poem," he said, forcing the words out.

"Though long veiled by clouds
And light,
Always it has awaited me,
The Two-Headed Dragon.

Beware of the priest, Brother. Beware of his master."

The man drank off the poisoned cha and dropped the cup over the side. The desperation in his eyes was replaced now by utter and total defeat.

"May you attain perfection in your next lifetime," the monk whispered, and bowed formally.

Kogami Norimasa crossed the deck and seated himself in a position of meditation in the shadows. He composed his mind, hoping that, in his last moments, the poison would not rob him of all dignity. He tried to fill his mind with the presence of his wife and daughter, and when the end came, these were his final thoughts.

Three

LORD SHONTO MOTORU was in a state of extreme harmony with both himself, which was usual, and with the world, which was less common. He rode in a sampan sculled by four of his best boatmen and guarded by nine of his select guards. Ahead of him were two identical boats and behind three more. All had a large man and an elegantly kimonoed young woman seated inside, only partly visible through side curtains.

The canal they moved along was lined by high walls of plaster and stone, broken only by the arched entrances onto the waterway. Each entrance had solid gates extending to the water from which point metal grillwork descended to an underwater wall. Behind these well guarded facades stood the residences of the hereditary aristocracy of the Empire of Wa. Out of the walled gardens drifted occasional strains of music, laughter, the acrid odor of burning charcoal, perhaps a hint of perfume.

"I thought you said you were feeling secure, Uncle?" the young woman said. She was, in fact, his legally adopted daughter but had called him uncle from the day she could form the word and still persisted in its use, sometimes even in public.

"I am feeling secure, Nishi-sum, which is to say that tonight I'm not concerned about what the Emperor may be plotting. He needs me, for the moment. As to any others who may wish me short life—I'm a little more cautious. Thus the decoys, if that is why you ask. Security, as you can see, is a relative term." He laughed.

"I think you are only happy when you are going off to war," Nishima said.

Pulling the curtain aside slightly, she peered out to assess their progress, and there, riding the surface of the canal, was her reflection, wavering like a flame. My eyes are too large, she thought and closed them slightly, but it then looked as though she were squinting so she gave it up. Her long, black hair, worn up in a formal style, was held in place by simple, wooden combs, inlaid with a motif of fine silver. She took one last look at herself, sighed, and jerked the curtain closed. The Lady Nishima Fanisan Shonto did not agree with the general assessment that she was a great beauty. To her eye, the bones of her face were too strong, her eyes the wrong shape, and, worst of all, she was too tall. She did not consider the mirror her friend.

"How long will this campaign against the northern barbarians take?"

"Not more than half a year, though I will stretch it out to the tenth moon. It is always dangerous to be too successful in battle. The Emperor is not too secure himself, yeh? But for now he needs me and we both know it."

"It would be good if your Spiritual Advisor would arrive in time to accompany us. That would be a great help, yeh?"

"Ah, I have not told you? He came to Yankura this morning. I received word from Tanaka. He calls our new Brother 'a fine young colt in need of breaking.'"

"The monk has been sent to the right liege-lord then, Uncle. Do you know anything about him?"

"I have a full report. He seems to be somewhat special, even for a Botahist Initiate, very skilled as a doctor, very learned. I have a letter from him—the brush work is superb! I must show it to you." He paused to pull a curtain aside a fraction of an inch to check their progress.

"Tell me, Nishi-sum, do you remember going to the River Festival in the year I married your mother?"

"Oh, yes, I could never forget that festival, Uncle, we had been in hiding for so many long months and then suddenly we were secure. What a beautiful autumn that was."

"I seem to remember that as being the year the young Botahist Neophyte bested some of the strongest fighters I have ever seen, including one of my own lieutenants on whom I had bet heavily."

"Yes, I remember. I wanted you to bet on the monk because he was so small and showed no fear, but as usual you ignored my excellent advice."

"You were precocious even then. Well, I may be wrong, but I believe that boy is our new advisor. *Brother Shuyun,* does that sound familiar?"

"Shuyun . . . yes, that could be. If it is the same monk, you will have to rebuke him for causing his liege-lord such a great loss of money." They both laughed, and then fell silent, lost in their memories.

When Nishima resumed the conversation, it was on a more subdued note. "What of Lord Shidaku, Uncle, now that he has failed to contain the barbarians?"

"Lord Shidaku is a great administrator and a terrible general. The Emperor sent him to Seh to deal with the problems left by the old bureaucracy, before the raids began. He was never meant to be a military leader. The Emperor acknowledges this and has transferred Lord Shidaku to his personal council. Lord Shidaku has thus been honored and his failure to contain the barbarians . . . overlooked. The Emperor is seldom so wise—good administrators are rarer than good generals, if the truth be known."

The sampans turned into another canal, and the wall of the Emperor's palace grounds appeared on the left. Guards on regularly spaced towers saluted as the water-borne entourage passed.

"Ah, you're a governor now, Sire, see how they honor you."

Shonto grunted, refusing to look.

"So, Nishi-sum, how will the Emperor entertain his guests tonight?"

"Dancers, certainly. They are his favorites, for obvious reasons. Perhaps a short play. The finest foods, of course. Music. Maybe a poetry contest, which you will not be allowed to enter because of your esteemed father's reputation."

"Good. Unlike my father, I could not win the Emperor's poetry contest if my life depended on it. But you, my only daughter, are the one who should not be allowed to enter! I will bet on you if there is a contest." He checked their progress again.

"Which of the Emperor's sons will pay court to you tonight, Nishi-sum?"

"You tease, Uncle. The sons of the Emperor will not notice such a plain-face as me. Nor would I want them to. Boors! All three of them!"

"But Nishi-sum, I have it on good authority that Prince Wakaro holds you in high esteem."

"Oh, Uncle, you must be teasing. You know I aspire to the life of a painter, or perhaps a poet. I would be miserable married to an insensitive oaf!"

"Oh, you are too great an artist to marry an Emperor's son?"

Nishima colored. "Certainly not now, but who can tell what the future will bring. Women produce all the finest art in the Empire, no one can deny it. Don't laugh! I challenge you to name seven great male artists."

"Haromitsa, Nokiyama, Basko . . . Minitsu made some fine paintings . . ."

"Already you are grasping at shoots. You see, it could be a crime against our culture to make me a wife!"

Shonto laughed derisively. "I am your *father* and your *liege-lord*. If I decide that it is in your best interest to marry someone as *unworthy* as an Emperor's son—someone who could himself be Emperor one day—then you will do so!"

Lady Nishima lowered her head. "Yes, Sire. Please excuse my bad manners. I have acted in a manner unworthy of your respect."

"I will consider this apology."

They sat in silence until the sampan turned into the palace gate and then Nishima spoke. "Satsam, Rhiyama, and Doksa the print maker."

"I was getting to them."

"Yes, Sire." Nishima tried to hide her smile.

The sampans docked at a stone stairway and the boatmen scrambled off to hold the craft steady. An aide to the Emperor hurried down the steps. Lord Shonto held the curtain aside so the guards could see that no one was hidden inside.

The aide bowed as Lord Shonto and his daughter stepped ashore. They were escorted up the steps by the black-clad Palace Guard to a large open house with a massive, winglike tile roof set on carved, wooden posts. Shonto removed his sword and handed it to one of his own guard, for no one went armed into the Emperor's presence except select members of the Imperial Guard. Assassination had too long been a tool of aspiring sons and ambitious peers for those who sat on the Dragon Throne not to have learned caution.

The sound of flutes and harps came from one of the gardens and kites of every shape and color decorated the wind.

"The Emperor is receiving his guests in the Garden of the Rising Moon beside the Seahorse Pond. Would you like an escort, Lord Shonto?"

"I know my way, thank you."

The aide bowed and Shonto nodded in return. They walked under a long portico built in the same style as the gate house. To their right, a glimmering pool descended in three falls—the Pool of the Sun—full of flashing sunfish.

Beyond this stood the most intricate hedge-maze in the Empire, planted by the ruler Shunkara VII nearly four hundred years earlier.

The Island Palace was the Emperor's primary residence and it was impressive not only for its size but for the astonishing beauty so many centuries of royalty had created. Originally built at the beginning of the Mori Dynasty the Island Palace had been razed by fire and rebuilt three times in six hundred years. The buildings were from five distinct periods yet placed in such a manner that harmony was never broken. The finest artisans, in a culture rich in artisans, had wrought and painted and carved and sculpted in an attempt to create perfection on earth.

At the end of the portico was a terrace of colored stone which looked southeast into the Garden of the Rising Moon. The Seahorse Pond bordered the garden's farthest edge. A wooden stage had been erected on the pond's shore and within viewing distance in front of it stood a raised dais under an ornate silken canopy. A line of guests moved past the dais beneath which the Emperor sat, now hidden from Shonto's view.

Perhaps two hundred Imperial Guards surrounded the Emperor on three sides, kneeling in rows that radiated out from the jade-colored canopy. A dragon design was woven into this semicircle by the clever placement of guards in crimson to form the spread Dragon Fan of the Imperial family.

His Imperial Highness, the Most Revered Son of Heaven, Exalted Emperor of the Nine Provinces of Wa and the Island of Konojii, Lord of all the World's Oceans, Akantsu II was a small, dark man of fifty-two years.

His father, Akantsu I, had founded the Imperial line of the Yamaku when he had ascended the throne during the chaos of the Great Plague that had decimated the population a decade and a half earlier. The former Imperial family, the Hanama, had fallen victim to the disease as it swept through the capital and there had been no hesitation by any number of pretenders, both legitimate and not so, to take the fallen family's place.

The struggle for the Dragon Throne had been short and brutal, and the outcome as much a matter of chance as martial skill. In the end, the faction that lost the fewest men to plague emerged victorious. The civil war lasted little more than three years, yet it was long enough to shake the Empire to its ancient foundations. Minor families rose to the status of Great House overnight, because of their role in a single key battle. Foot-soldiers became generals and generals peers, as the rigid social structure of the Empire crumbled.

After two hundred and fifty years of relative peace and economic prosperity under the Hanama Dynasty, the line had ended in disease and flame. A third of the population had died before the Botahist Brotherhood found the key to both immunization and cure. The social fabric of Wa had been torn beyond restoration and, under the Yamaku, order wasn't a priority. The roads beyond the inner provinces were unsafe to all but the largest parties; pirates infested the coastline and private wars abounded—and the Emperor obviously believed this state of affairs was to his advantage.

In constant fear of being deposed, the Emperor had devised a number of methods to keep the aristocracy resident in the capital where the Imperial troops were supreme. By dividing the year into four "Social Seasons" the ruler could then "invite" the lords he most feared to attend whichever seasons he chose, being careful to separate any potential alliances by keeping some members isolated in the provinces. Refusing the Emperor's invitation was an open act of treason, and staying in the capital when your presence had not been requested led to immediate suspicion on the part of the Emperor's guard.

To further his control, Akantsu II had disallowed the use of any harbor but Yankura, the Floating City, for the importation of trade goods and made death the penalty for smuggling. All trade could then be easily taxed by the Imperial customs officials as well as monitored by the ever present Imperial Guard. This way, other harbors—traditionally under the control of a single powerful lord—could not be used as an excuse to create large armed forces for "security" reasons. The Emperor was thorough in his bid to hold all the reins of power.

Despite his lavish parties and his love of the social life, Akantsu II remained an enigma, even to those closest to him. His unpredictability did not win him friends, as he was known to ignore acts of loyalty as often as he rewarded them. The physical life was what drew him—hunting, hawking, dance. He sponsored kick boxing tournaments often and was known to be a fine swordsman and without fear. He had once dispatched an assassin, unaided, and then personally beheaded all the guards on duty for their failure to protect him. Like his father, Akantsu II was a formidable man.

As Lord Shonto and Lady Nishima descended the stairs, they could see the Emperor seated on a cushion, talking with his guests. His kimono was Imperial crimson belted with a gold sash, and he held the sword of his office across his lap in a jeweled scabbard. The Empress was conspicuously absent, and though she was said to be ill it was well known that she was out of favor. A young and exquisitely beautiful Sonsa dancer was the Emperor's current mistress—that is, she was preferred among a half-dozen.

"There is your cousin, Kitsu-sum," Lord Shonto said as they crossed the garden.

"Oh, good. I must talk with her."

"She is your competition for the Emperor's sons, I think."

"Thank you for pointing that out, Sire."

"That is, unless I marry her first. She's not very pretty, but I have great affection for her."

"She's the most beautiful woman either of us know, and you dote on her." Nishima chided.

"Huh! I'm far too old to indulge such weaknesses."

The Lady Kitsura Omawara saw them coming across the garden and favored them with her famous smile. Numerous hearts began to flutter. She walked toward her cousin and Shonto. Her kimono, a print of butterflies in flight, hung perfectly, the long sleeves swaying as she moved. Silver combs with jade inlay held up her dark hair and her eyes were highlighted by the most subtle use of makeup. She was a woman used to the sound of flattery.

"Kitsura-sum, you are the reincarnation of all the Empire's great beauties!" Nishima said, taking her cousin's hands.

"Lord Shonto," Kitsura said, bowing. "Cousin, how lovely you look. And, Lord Shonto, I believe you grow younger by the day."

Shonto bowed lower than his position required. "I was just telling Nishima-sum that your kimono is ill-fitting, you're skinny for your age and you walk like a boy, but because I am so fond of you, I will offer to take you from your father's house."

Both women laughed. Kitsura bowed deeply. "You do me too much honor, Sire. I think you try to turn my head with flattery. Truly you are your father's son. But I am too naive and inexperienced for a man like you. I would not allow my father to take advantage of your kind nature."

"It is a small thing. My house is full of stray cats already. Look at Nishi-sum. Ungrateful daughter that she is, I have affection for her all the same. Charity toward the undeserving must be a weakness of mine."

"You see what I must live with, Kitsura-sum? I think the Emperor would reward us if we pushed his new governor into the Seahorse Pond. Otherwise he will bankrupt the province of Seh by filling the Governor's Palace with 'stray cats.'"

"We will have to ask the Emperor's permission in this matter." She turned to look at the dais, but then became more solemn. "I think the Emperor will request that you play for his guests, Nishi-sum. I have already been asked, and could not refuse. I hope you won't be angry, but I suggested you might consider a duet with me?"

"Oh, no! I have not practiced. What will we play?"

"Play the 'Song of the Enchanted Gardener'" Lord Shonto offered.

"You and your *Enchanted Gardener*, Uncle. Don't you ever tire of hearing it?"

"Can one tire of perfection?"

Nishima rolled her eyes. "Now we will receive a lecture in the philosophy of aesthetics. Run, Kitsura-sum, I will try to hold him!"

They laughed as they crossed the garden toward the receiving line. A gong sounded, announcing the hour of the cat. It was near dusk and servants began lighting colored lanterns.

Lord Shonto and Lady Nishima stopped several times to greet guests and exchange news.

At one point Nishima touched her uncle's arm and whispered to him, "There is Lady Okara, the painter."

The woman stood among a throng who seemed to be her personal court. It was obvious that they hung on her every word.

"She is almost never seen at social gatherings. I must try to work up my nerve to meet her."

"I will introduce you, Nishima-sum, she is an old friend."

"Don't tease me, Uncle, this is a serious matter. She is the most accomplished painter of the century! I have admired her work for years."

"I do not tease. Come, flutter your eyelashes at the Emperor and then I will introduce you to your goddess."

The line moved along very slowly, the guests trying to hold the Emperor's attention as long as they could, thus signifying to what degree they had the ruler's favor. In their turn, they knelt before the dais on a grass mat and touched their heads to the ground. The Emperor never rose or bowed to his subjects but nodded slightly to recognize their presence. Lord Shonto and Lady Nishima were announced by an aide and bowed low, remaining in the kneeling position.

"Lord Shonto, Lady Nishima, I am honored that you have come."

"The honor, Sire, is ours entirely," Lord Shonto answered for both of them, as his position required.

The Emperor turned his attention to Nishima as if there was a matter of great importance that demanded immediate attention. "Lady Nishima, I wish to ask you a great favor."

"Name it, Sire, and I shall comply."

"We have already asked Lady Kitsura if she would play for our guests and she has honored me by agreeing. Would you accompany her?"

"I am hardly a musician of sufficient skill to perform for such an esteemed audience, but as the Emperor asks, it would be my honor to do so.

"I must apologize though, Sire, for I failed to anticipate this request and did not bring an instrument."

"One shall be found for you, then, one that I'm sure will be to your liking. What will you play, Lady?"

"Certainly we would allow the Emperor to make that decision if the selection is within our skills."

"Wonderful! Do you know the 'Song of the Enchanted Gardener'?"

"Yes, Sire. A lovely melody and a fine choice."

"Good, good!" He broke into a toothy grin which disappeared just as quickly.

Turning to Lord Shonto, the Emperor changed his tone of address and immediately had the attention of all those around him.

"Lord Shonto Motoru, Imperial Governor of the Province of Seh, as I have invested you, when do you leave to protect our northern border?"

"Within the week, Sire. My household and my forces prepare."

"You are efficient as well as courageous. How long will it take to teach the barbarian rabble proper respect for the Emperor of Wa?"

"I have sent my son ahead to assess the situation and have not yet received his report but, even so, I hope the campaign will be short."

"The barbarians are poor students, but I send them my best teacher. A year, then?"

"A year should be adequate. Lessons learned too quickly are most easily forgotten."

Rising to his full sitting height, the Emperor said, "Do you hear? The new Governor of Seh will cleanse our northern border of the barbarians in one year!" He bowed slightly to Shonto and said, his voice surprisingly cold, "I salute you, Lord Shonto."

The assembled guests followed the Emperor's example and also bowed to the kneeling lord. The gathering became unnaturally quiet, and Lord Shonto felt a sudden chill.

Nishima became aware that she was being stared at and noticed out of the corner of her eye that Prince Wakaro, the Emperor's middle son, was kneeling at one side of the dais. She was careful not to meet his eyes.

The Emperor raised his hand to an aide. He did not bother to look at him, and the man hurried forward carrying a silken pillow across which lay a sword in a very old scabbard. The Emperor took the weapon, unsheathing it and examining it with an expert's care. Shonto felt the skin of his scalp tighten.

"Do you know this blade, Lord Shonto?"

"No, Sire," Shonto said, his voice perfectly calm. Conversation flared suddenly, then quieted at the sight of the weapon.

Looking up from the sword, apparently satisfied, the Son of Heaven smiled, but his eyes were hard. "This sword belonged to the famous ancestor for whom you were named, Lord Shonto Motoru, who gave it as a gift to the Emperor Jirri II, his close friend. The Emperor and Shonto Motoru later fought and conquered the northern barbarians in the time of their greatest power, as you no doubt know. Sadly, Lord Shonto was killed by an arrow in the final battle." The Emperor tested the sword's edge with his thumbnail. "This is a gift to you, Lord Governor." The Emperor's expression was unreadable.

The aide came forward again, taking the sword from his master and placing it on the mat before Shonto.

"This is a great honor, Sire. I will always endeavor to be worthy of it." The ritual words seemed strangely hollow to Lord Shonto.

"See that you do. Put it in your sash, Motoru-sum. You may wear a sword in my presence."

Shonto bowed his head to the mat before taking up the weapon. "I will wear it always for the Emperor's protection, Sire."

"We must speak again later." Around them the sound of conversation resumed. "Lady Nishima, we look forward to your recital."

Lord Shonto and Nishima bowed once more, rose, and backed away. A young man dressed in the black kimono with the Dragon Fan of the Emperor's staff stepped forward.

"Lady Nishima, I have an instrument for you, and the Lady Kitsura awaits. May I escort you?"

Nishima touched her uncle's arm. "Remember, you promised me an introduction." There was much unsaid between them as she turned to join her cousin.

Shonto watched his daughter as she disappeared into the crowd, her long sleeves dancing as she moved. She is precious to me, he thought, and this is a dangerous time for such feelings.

He turned toward a table laden with food, his hand resting on the unfamiliar hilt of the ancient sword of his namesake. Lady Okara appeared among the river of passing faces. She bowed to Shonto, who returned the formality with equal courtesy. Without any discussion they began to walk toward the edge of the garden, away from the press of people.

Large, flat stones had been arranged along the pond's shore in a pattern of studied randomness, asymmetry being one of the laws of Waian art. Stepping out onto these islands of granite the two old friends were alone.

"So Mito-sum, I have just watched as you were honored and threatened at the same time," Lady Okara said. She was a tall woman with immense dignity and presence and Shonto admired her greatly.

"It was quite a performance." Shonto seemed to consider for a moment and his body visibly relaxed. "No matter. Tell me, Lady Okara, how has the Emperor tempted you to one of these—what is the term you use?—social dog fights?"

"He used the greatest of all coercions—he appealed to my vanity. The Lady Okara is here to be honored, and one does not refuse to be honored by one's Emperor.

"He has had my *Twenty-one Views of the Grand Canal* set to dance. I admit to being curious as to how this has been done. I might add that I'm more than a little suspicious. Art is not something that the Yamaku have ever shown an interest in." She reached out and the hand which squeezed Lord Shonto's was cold. "What possible use can he have for me, Mito-sum?"

"I can't imagine, so perhaps the compliment is real. You richly deserve it, you know."

"Even you have become a flatterer!"

"I see your lovely daughter is with you, Mito-sum. You've waited a long time to find her a husband, yeh?"

Shonto shrugged.

"Perhaps the Emperor will choose his heir soon and that will help you with your decision?"

"That doesn't seem likely." Lord Shonto sighed and looked over his shoulder. "He doesn't think that anyone is fit to replace him on the Dragon Throne, including his sons. This makes all of them somewhat less suitable as husbands."

"But if one of these sons had a good advisor, he might last long enough to pass the Throne to *his* son, making the mother very important."

"The Shonto family have never had designs on the Throne, Okara-sum, everyone knows that. I don't think my grandson will carry the Sword of Imperial office, and that does not concern me.

"Finding Nishi-sum a suitable husband, without insulting the Imperial family—*that* is my real problem."

"She carries too much of the old Imperial blood for her own good. If you marry her to the Yamaku, you strengthen their claim, and if you marry her elsewhere her sons will always be a danger to the Emperor. I don't know anyone who has enough power to risk having her as a bride."

"You're right, Okara-sum, there's no one—not now."

"Poor girl." The woman's voice was sad. "She is a soldier on a vast gii board."

"She is the *Empress,* but refuses to recognize it. Nishima-sum would like nothing better than to marry a poet and spend the rest of her life pursuing art—but this is not possible."

"A life in art is not as easy as it sounds, Mito-sum. I know."

They turned away from the Seahorse Pond after allowing themselves one last moment to enjoy its reflecting beauty. Their conversation turned to less private matters as they rejoined the other guests.

"I must introduce you to Nishima-sum. She idolizes you."

"Best she meet me, then, and learn that I am human—I would be happy to receive her."

Servants were spreading straw mats and cushions on the lawn before the stage and the guests had already begun to seat themselves in anticipation of the night's entertainment. Shonto and Lady Okara chose a position off to one side nearer the back. Better places were available for people of their rank, but Shonto wanted to be able to watch both the stage and the Emperor. He had not survived as long as he had by missing opportunities to scrutinize those in power.

Cushions were arranged on the stage and a harp of carved ivory set before them. When everyone was seated, a man of the Imperial court, a scholar of some note, appeared on the stage and bowed twice—once kneeling, for the Emperor, and once very low but standing, to the audience. The first full moon of autumn showed its copper rim on cue.

"Honored guests of the Emperor of Wa," the scholar began, "the Emperor has asked the Lady Nishima Fanisan Shonto and the Lady Kitsura Omawara to honor his assembled guests with a recital of the 'Song of the Enchanted Gardener.'" The man bowed to the curtain from behind which the Ladies Kitsura and Nishima emerged. They bowed twice and took up their places before the attentive audience.

In her hand Kitsura held a silver flute almost half her height in its length and Nishima sat poised behind the harp. They began.

The flute and harp followed each other in delicate measure, through the three movements without hesitation or error. It was clear the cousins had played this piece together many times. Out of the corner of his eye Shonto watched the Emperor. He could see the middle son sitting to one side of the dais watching the performance raptly. Yes, Shonto thought, I have a problem. He looked back at the Emperor and realized that the father was equally captivated. I hope it is Kitsura that he desires, Shonto thought. He gazed up at the young flutist and felt a stirring himself. And to whom, he wondered, will Lord Omawara marry his daughter? He put the question aside for further consideration.

With a moving crescendo in intricate counterpart, the "Enchanted Gardener" drew to a close and the music was over. The applause was more than polite.

The courtier returned to the stage. "It is the Emperor's wish that these instruments, which once belonged to the courtesan Ranyo, be presented to Lady Nishima and Lady Kitsura in gratitude for their performance."

The members of the audience bowed as the players left the stage.

"She plays very well, Mito-sum," Lady Okara said. "Who was her teacher?"

"My formal Spiritual Advisor, Brother Satake. He was a man of many talents. I miss him."

"They are a charming breed, the advisor monks. Do you think they are educated to be that way?"

Shonto shrugged. No, Oka-sum, he thought, what they are taught is *focus*. It is the source of all their abilities—and what I wouldn't give for that one skill!

Nishima was making her way through the crowd toward her uncle and Lady Okara, her progress slowed by the need to stop and acknowledge each compliment. She stopped and bowed at almost every step.

"Nishima-sum," Shonto said as she slipped off her sandals before stepping onto the mat, "The 'Enchanted Gardener' has seldom known such enchantment." He bowed deferentially to his daughter. "I must say that the Emperor's musical tastes . . ."

"Are exactly the same as yours, Uncle," she leaned toward him to whisper, "and nothing to be smug about, let me assure you."

Shonto turned to his friend. "Lady Okara, may I introduce you to my impertinent only daughter, Nishima-sum."

"I am honored, Lady Okara. I have long been an admirer of yours, and if my secretive uncle had told me before this evening that you were friends, I would have asked him to introduce us long ago."

"After listening to your performance, I must say the honor is mine. How lovely you play, my dear. If you paint as well as your father assures me you do, then your talent is prodigious indeed. You must come and visit me in my studio one day."

Nishima broke into a smile, "I would be glad to, Lady Okara. Thank you."

The moon had now risen sufficiently to cast light into the garden where it made a path across the Seahorse Pond, and mixed with the colored light from the lanterns.

The courtier came out onto the stage again and bowed twice before speaking. "Tonight the Emperor asks that we pay honor to Lady Okara Haroshu, whose series of woodblock prints, *Twenty-one Views of the Grand Canal*, has, at the Emperor's request, been set to dance by the Sonsa Troupe of the Imperial City."

He turned and bowed toward the curtain from behind which the first dancers would emerge. Unseen attendants shaded the lamps and cast the stage into comparative darkness. Dew glistened on the lawns and a warm breeze came in off the nearby lake.

Wooden drums began a low, syncopated rhythm and a single lantern was unveiled to reveal a group of dancers, dressed as peasants, stooped under invisible burdens in the predawn. A flute began to mingle with the drumming, the notes fluttering like a butterfly on a breeze. The half-dozen dancers, wearing the loose fitting clothes and the flattened, conical hats of field workers, began to drop their burdens and dance along the tow path. More lanterns were unveiled illuminating the backdrops, which were painted in a style similar to Lady Okara's, though greatly simplified. The dancers began a series of pantomimes of courtship and revelry, the suppleness that came from long years of Sonsa training captivating the crowd. A young woman stepped forward to dance a solo and Nishima touched her uncle's arm.

The Emperor's new lover, Shonto thought. Of course Nishima had never seen her before, but he was sure she was right. And yes, the woman was beautiful. Even in her peasant costume the perfection of her dancer's body was obvious.

Dance your best, Shonto thought. The Emperor is not always kind to those he discards. Your only strength then will be your talent, because no one will dare to take you to wife.

But she could dance! She was not just some flower the Emperor had plucked and set in the sunlight. She was a talent. Perhaps this would protect her. With some effort he turned his eyes away to study the Emperor. The ruler's admiration for his Sonsa was absurdly blatant—no more subtle than the emotions of a child. She is in no danger from him tonight, anyway, Shonto thought, unless his lust is to be feared.

The drumming returned to its original cadence, then stopped abruptly, the dancers frozen in the poses of the peasants in Lady Okara's print, *On the Tow Path at Dawn*. On top of the curving bridge the Emperor's lover balanced, her arms thrown out gracefully and one foot in the air as if she had just jumped for joy. The lanterns were shaded as the applause began. The guests near Lady Okara bowed to her and paid her compliments.

Six more of the *Twenty-One Views* that made up the Grand Canal sequence were performed, each as clever as the first, four featuring the talents of the Emperor's lovely Sonsa.

How he flaunts her, everyone thought, but what will become of her, poor child? She was not of a good family, as everyone knew, a vassal-merchant's daughter, and therefore not entirely without education, but still. . . . There was no denying her talent, though. Breeding or no, she would have been a marvel during any dynasty.

The dancing came to an end and received prolonged and enthusiastic applause. Lady Okara was surrounded by bowing guests, all of them wishing to be seen with anyone so honored by the Emperor.

Lady Okara rejoined Shonto and Nishima as her admirers wandered off to eat and laugh and court and gossip.

"Oh, Mito-sum, this isn't good for a person, all of this." She waved her hand to encompass the garden in general, at a loss for words. "I must pay my respects to the Emperor before I leave."

"Okara-sum, don't be in such a rush to go. The worst is over. You have survived! Let me get you some wine so that you may begin to enjoy the rest of the evening." Shonto smiled at her, his voice full of affection. He was touched by his friend's discomfiture.

"Well, one cup and then I must go," Lady Okara conceded.

Shonto left his friend in his daughter's care and set off to find a servant. One came to his aid before he had gone far.

"Lord Shonto," an unfamiliar voice called. A young man who looked vaguely familiar strode toward Shonto across the lawn. The lord sent a servant hurrying off to look after Lady Okara and turned to speak to the young man.

"Excuse my bad manners, Lord Shonto," He bowed. "I am Komawara Samyamu."

Ah, yes, Lord Shonto thought, the same slim build and the long thin nose. If this youth is anything like his father, his apparent lack of muscle is deceptive. The old Komawara had been a strong swordsman and lightning fast.

"I am pleased to meet you, Lord Komawara." Shonto returned the man's bow. "I met your father several times when I was young. He was an impressive man."

"Yes, a great loss to us all, I'm afraid. I honor his memory." He caught Shonto's eye and hesitated briefly before he went on. "I understand that you will come to Seh as our new governor. It is about time that the Emperor sent us a soldier! I mean no disrespect to Lord Shidako—he has admirably resolved the problems left by the corrupt Hanama bureaucracy." He let the statement hang in the air, but Shonto didn't take the offered opportunity to either criticize the Hanama or to praise the Yamaku.

The young lord was obviously unnerved by Lord Shonto's lack of response, and his resolve seemed to flounder momentarily. "Your daughter plays very well, Sire. The Shonto continue to produce artists, to the good fortune of the rest of us. I have recently read your father's memoirs—what a delightful approach he took to his life!"

Shonto nodded, letting the man ramble on, wondering what this young lord's purpose was.

Lord Komawara's eyes hardened and he regained his determination.

"Will you come to Seh soon, Sire?"

"Yes, very soon."

"That is good. Perhaps you will get to the bottom of these mysterious raids."

"I didn't realize that they were thought in any way mysterious, Lord Komawara." Politics, Shonto thought, everyone must have a theory.

"It seems, Sire, that only I find them unusual. May we speak privately, Lord Shonto?"

"Certainly, I am most interested." Shonto pointed off to their left where they could talk without being overheard. He had liked the old Komawara immensely, though he'd been a man doomed by his refusal to change with the times.

"As a native of our northern province, Sire, I have had first-hand experience of the ways of the barbarian tribes all of my life," the young man began, the tones of his father's voice occasionally echoing among the words. "I have traded with them when we were at peace, and fought with them the rest of the time. I have to say that in both areas they are formidable and have no code of honor whatsoever!

"Through all the years that we've warred with them, though, two things in their behavior have remained consistent. They are always bold. Bold beyond anything *these* people would imagine," he waved a hand at the assembled guests with a slight disdain, "and, whenever it is possible, they take our women. This never fails! It is more than just the fair skin. One of our servant girls is valued above the daughters of their most powerful chief! A woman of Wa is the greatest prize a barbarian can have. Of course this has always been their undoing. The men of Seh cannot live with this dishonor, so we cross the border and burn their villages, driving them back into the barrens—for a time.

"This game of raiding our villages and estates always has the same end, yeh? But recently, Lord Shonto, the behavior of the barbarians has changed.

"It has always been their practice—for hundreds of years—to press their attacks with total commitment and when our reinforcements arrive, to either stand and fight or, if they are vastly outnumbered, to wait until the last possible second before they retreat. This is the kind of bravura I expect from them. They despise cowards more than anything. But in these new raids they don't risk a single man! They are always gone before our reinforcements arrive and they seldom even break through our stockades. I know them, Sire, I have watched them all my life. This is not proper barbarian behavior!

"This is why I consider it to be a mystery. These attacks make no sense. Even in barbarian terms they are without purpose. They have taken very little plunder and no women though they have had opportunities. Yet I seem to be the only one who thinks the barbarians are acting in an unusual manner. It is said, though not to my face, that my odd ideas are the result of my youth. So you see, you may have wasted your time listening to the babblings of a child." Komawara laughed nervously.

"And what do those who are not hampered by youth say?"

"They say the barbarians become weaker and more cowardly every year and that soon they will be afraid to even cross our borders. The men of Seh believe that their prowess as warriors has the barbarians cowering in fear."

"Ah. And from your position of relative inexperience, what do you recommend?"

"So far we have not taken a single captive. The barbarians are too cautious. I recommend a quick sortie into their lands with the express purpose of taking prisoners. I have often found that when two men speak from their hearts, much can be learned. But no doubt this is an immature view that I will soon grow out of."

"I, for one, value the opinions of the young. They are not informed by long experience, but they are also not the result of mere habit. I shall consider your words with great care, Lord Komawara, I thank you."

"It is my duty, Lord Governor. I am honored that you have listened."

"Now tell me, what is it that brings you to the capital when Seh is in such danger?"

"Unlike most of my neighbors, my lands are well guarded and fortified. My father believed in spending more on defense than on trade, yeh? In this way he was a bit old-fashioned. The result of his belief is that, though the Komawara are not poor, we have not the position we once had. To my everlasting shame, my father sold part of the family fief before he died. It is my hope to buy this land back and to restore the good name the Komawara once had."

"Everyone knows the name of Komawara to be ancient and respected. I'm sure you will have even greater honors under the new dynasty."

"I hope you are correct, Lord Shonto."

So, Shonto thought, this is what the young one desires—a return to former power. It was an old story and Shonto had heard it many times before. Most of the secondary Houses in the Empire had the same dream, though in many cases the former power was mythical. But not so with the Komawara. They had once been the true rulers of the north—and long before the Imperial Governors had been created. At times the Komawara had even rivaled the Imperial family in military strength. More than one Komawara daughter had been a bride to an Emperor—but that had been long ago; their power and influence had waned in the early days of the Hanama.

During the two hundred years that sea trade had developed, the House of Komawara had slowly declined as had all the clans that clung to the past. The old Komawara had seen the error of his ways, and before his death had sold some of his fief to raise capital for his heir to start trade. This had been a great sacrifice on the part of the old lord, one which had saved his son from the stigma of having sold family lands.

Virtually all the old noble families had made the transformation to merchant families, yet they still clung to the fiefs as they always had because to lose them was to become merely merchants. The past was gone, but the habits remained—the merchants were traditionally disdained. This, of course, didn't stop most peers from having their own vassal-merchants whose positions and rewards went far beyond those of other servants. Occasionally vassal-merchants gained real power in Houses with weak rulers— some even began trading for themselves or bought their freedom from their lords. The latter was a new development that had been illegal in the past and some thought it should be illegal again.

"Lord Komawara, tomorrow my vassal-merchant Tanaka will arrive with my new Spiritual Advisor. My merchant is a man of some skill in the world of trade, perhaps our Houses could enter into a venture that would be of mutual benefit. I would be pleased if you could share a midday meal with us tomorrow, if that would be convenient."

"The honor would be mine, Lord Shonto." The young man's face betrayed his surprise and pleasure.

He will learn, Lord Shonto thought. "Good. Come along and meet Lady Okara and my daughter, Lady Nishima."

In the colorless moonlight they found the two women with Kitsura, drinking wine and giggling. Kitsura fanned herself furiously as the men approached, as if that would take the blush off her face.

"Allow me to introduce my friend from Seh, Lord Komawara," said Shonto, giving the youth much more importance than his age and status deserved.

"We wondered where you had disappeared to, Uncle. The speculation, in fact, has completely occupied us," Nishima said, sipping her wine casually. Kitsura covered her mouth with her fan.

"Yes, I can see how it would," Shonto said. "Lord Komawara has been advising me as to the present situation in Seh, and we have been discussing other business."

Kitsura composed herself and fixed the young lord with a cool eye. "Lord Shonto is shrewd beyond compare in affairs of state. You must be wise beyond your years, Lord Komawara, to offer him advice." She smiled her disarming smile.

Be nimble, Shonto thought. She will not hesitate to find you wanting. A woman in her position does not need to reserve judgment.

Komawara shrugged. "One does not go to the gii master expecting to equal him, Lady Kitsura, it is enough to simply learn. I have only presumed to provide Lord Shonto with some small measure of information that I believe to be accurate. The conclusions that Lord Shonto draws will, undoubtedly, be very instructive."

Lady Kitsura raised her fine eyebrows, the look of the skeptic.

"What brings you to the capital?" Lady Okara asked pleasantly, turning the conversation abruptly—a comment on Lady Kitsura's behavior.

Lord Shonto smiled. Thank you, Oka-sum, he thought. I don't wish to offend Lord Komawara. I must have all the allies in Seh that I can. Even this boy may prove to be important. Who can tell? Only a fool discards an ally unnecessarily, no matter how insignificant.

More wine was served and the conversation returned to its earlier gaiety. Lord Komawara proved able to hold his own in conversation, both in knowledge and wit, giving Nishima hope that the court in Seh would not be of as little interest as she had imagined. She had never traveled to the outer provinces and, like most residents of the capital, felt that even the wealthiest peers of the outer regions must be dreadfully parochial.

For their part, the peoples of the outer provinces, especially in the north with their history of barbarian wars, felt that the residents of the inner provinces were decadent and soft. To their lasting satisfaction there seemed to be some evidence in history to support this thesis. Virtually all of the long-reigning Imperial dynasties were founded by families from the outer provinces. The Hanama were a case in point, coming from Chou, in the far west, where they had long been influential.

Shonto's fief lay on the edge of the "civilized" inner provinces along the central sea coast, so he was claimed by both southerners and northerners alike—a state of affairs he did much to promote. His was a good fief of moderate size in the Empire's temperate belt. The land was exceptionally fertile and, because it was bounded by mountains and the Fuga River, easily protected. The Shonto House had long prospered in these lands and their capital was known as a center of culture and learning.

An aide from the Emperor's staff interrupted their conversation, bowing low to Lord Shonto. "The Emperor wishes to know if he may have the honor of your company—all of you."

"Of course," Lord Shonto answered. "When should we attend him?"

"Now would be convenient, Sire."

"Certainly. Please tell the Emperor that we are honored by his request."

The aide made his way through the crowd, Lord Shonto and his party in tow.

He needs me, Shonto thought, he knows that. Putting a hand on the unfamiliar sword hilt, Shonto tugged to see how tightly it sat in the scabbard. It slid with ease.

They joined the throng surrounding the Emperor's dais while the Son of Heaven spoke pleasantly to a man and woman kneeling before him. The courtiers followed the conversation closely, laughing politely at the appropriate times or nodding their heads in silent agreement, their sensitivity to their master's requirements sharpened by a lifetime of study. The Emperor gestured to the audience mat before him, and nodded to Shonto and his companions. All of them knelt and touched their heads to the mat.

"I am pleased you accepted my invitation so quickly," the Emperor said, and then before anyone could respond he gestured to the dais. "Lord Shonto, Lady Okara, please join me. We must make room for these fine young players and their companion."

There was more bowing and polite exchange, for to be seated on the same level as the Emperor was almost unheard of. Servants hurried forward with fine silk cushions for the Emperor's guests.

"I hope, Lady Okara, that you felt tonight's performance was an acceptable translation of your work?"

"Far more than acceptable, Sire, inspired I would say. I do not feel worthy of such praise."

"Ah, but it is never for an artist to judge her own worth, that is for those of us of lesser talent. Is that not so, Lord Shonto?"

"Talent comes in a myriad of forms, Sire. To be able to recognize great art is a talent all its own, I think."

"You see, Lady Okara, it is the role of the Shonto family to teach the Yamaku appreciation of art. Do not protest, Lord Shonto! Your father once taught mine a most unforgettable lesson in poetics and now his son offers me instruction in the appreciation of art. I bow to you, Lord Shonto. You are right that a talent is needed to recognize great art. Perhaps I should create an office of Aesthetic Judgment to which I would appoint Lord Shonto, for the betterment of the Empire." There was general laughter and nodding of heads. Shonto tried to maintain an outward calm, not sure where this was leading.

The Emperor seemed to remain genial. "It is fortunate that in my Empire there are many people with this talent Lord Shonto mentions, for everyone recognizes the beauty of your art, Lady Okara. So you see when Lord Shonto corrected me a moment ago, he also complimented me and everyone in the Empire simultaneously. What am I to do with one so clever?"

The courtiers nodded agreement, apparently vastly amused by the Emperor's logic.

"I will have to give this great thought," the Emperor said, contemplating Shonto. He turned again to Lady Okara. "For too long now the Yamaku have been neglecting their responsibilities to the artists in our Empire. A culture is only as great as its existing arts, don't you agree, Lady Okara?"

"Wholeheartedly, Sire."

"This very night I intend to begin to rectify my family's neglect of our responsibilities toward the artists of Wa. Those of us who can should support the cause. Don't you agree, Lord Shonto?"

"Absolutely, Sire," he answered, reserve obvious in his voice. What is this about, Shonto asked himself? He had a growing fear that whatever the Emperor planned, the entire evening had been staged for this one purpose. But where did Oka-sum fit into this? It was out of the question that she would conspire with the Emperor against him. Or was it? His mind raced. Every faculty was in full operation trying to provide him with a single clue that would allow him to sidestep the Emperor's thrust when it came.

"Lady Okara, perhaps with your assistance I will be able to help the worthy artists of our land. I propose an Imperial Patronage, a generous patronage, I might add. I want to encourage our best artists to take on a talented young apprentice. Lady Okara, I would be honored if you would be the first to accept." He smiled warmly.

The artist tried to hide her shock. "The honor, Sire . . . is mine. It . . . I accept, certainly, but I don't feel worthy! I feel there are others more deserving."

"Ah, Lady Okara. As our friend, Lord Shonto, has said, perhaps I have a talent for recognizing great art. Let me be the judge in this matter. Do you accept?"

"I do, Sire. I thank you." She bowed low. Applause broke out at Lady Okara's acceptance.

"Now we must find you a worthy apprentice—one of whom you approve, of course." The Emperor paused as if deep in thought. Too late, Shonto realized what lay ahead.

"Lady Nishima," the Emperor said, addressing Shonto's startled daughter, "if it is mutually acceptable to both you and Lady Okara, I name you to be the first apprentice of the Imperial Patronage." The Emperor smiled broadly, pleased with himself. The courtiers masked their shock at the Emperor's bad manners.

It was unheard of to put anyone in a position where they must accept or reject another in public. All such arrangements were traditionally done in private, through a third party, so that no one would lose face in the event of a refusal or rejection. All eyes were turned to the two women to see how they would resolve such a dilemma.

Lady Nishima, despite her youth, had the benefit of a lifetime of Shonto's training. She responded at once. "Sire, this is a dream come true. I will immediately gather together some of my work and send it to Lady Okara so that she may make a decision in this matter. And to be fair, Sire, perhaps other artists should be given the same opportunity? An artist of Lady Okara's importance should not expend her efforts for any but the most deserving. I'm sure all would agree." The entire speech was delivered in a most humble tone, the Lady Nishima's gaze cast down.

The Emperor's face contorted in annoyance—he was not used to having his wishes thwarted. He regained control almost immediately.

"Lady Nishima, your fairness is a credit to you, but you must allow me to be the judge. It is my talent to recognize art and artists, yeh? Lady Okara, I ask you to accept Lady Nishima as your apprentice. Her talent, I must tell you, is beyond question."

Shonto watched with a sense of helplessness—the struggle was entirely in the hands of his daughter and Lady Okara and he could only pray to Botahara for assistance.

Nishima was to be a hostage. That was what the Emperor desired, to keep her in the capital, isolated from Shonto and his army. She was a prize. The Fanisan blood and the Shonto name and power. Which son did he want her for? Would it be the heir? Yes, Shonto thought, that would make the most sense, but there were also reasons to wed her to the least powerful son—an attempt to nullify Shonto. Which son would be heir?

Lady Okara swallowed in a dry throat, visibly shaken at suddenly finding herself cast into the center of the Emperor's designs. Court intrigue was the one thing she had avoided all her life.

"I trust your judgment totally, Sire. I would be honored to give Lady Nishima the benefit of my limited expertise, *whenever* it would be convenient to her." This was her only card and she cast it out, desperately hoping Nishima would pick it up.

"It was my intention," the Emperor said, "to invest the patronage on an annual basis, starting immediately. I trust that will be convenient."

"Excuse me, Sire. I don't wish to sound ungrateful," Lady Nishima said in her quiet way, "but I am now torn between my duty and this dream you have offered me. My father and liege-lord is about to undertake a serious campaign on the Emperor's behalf. It is my duty to Lord Shonto—and to you, my Emperor—to give the head of my House every assistance possible. As my father has no wife to run his household, I am more necessary than a daughter would normally be." She looked up suddenly, meeting the Emperor's gaze. "I have always been taught that duty takes precedence, it is our way. I do not know how to resolve this problem."

The Emperor was unable to hide his frustration. He looked around, struggling with his rage, looking for someone to vent his considerable temper on. He was being outmaneuvered by a mere girl. He hadn't expected her to hesitate for even a second—he had been assured that the bait was perfect.

"Lord Shonto, certainly there are members of your personal staff who can carry out Lady Nishima's duties for you. Not as well, no doubt," he hurried to add, "but can't you live without her for a while?"

"No sacrifice is too great, Sire." Shonto answered without a second's hesitation, much to his daughter's dismay. "A warrior can live without everything but weapons, if need be. I can certainly survive if my household is less efficient than I am used to it being."

The Emperor smiled broadly. "It is settled, then. The arts shall flourish again as they did in the time of the Mori!"

There was loud applause. Several of the wealthiest lords present, inspired by the Emperor's example, offered to invest patronages of their own. If there had been any aspiring artists in attendance they would, no doubt, have found themselves suddenly able to live in a manner they had never dreamed possible.

Having accomplished his immediate purpose, the Emperor turned his attention to Lady Kitsura with whom he spoke in a most flirtatious manner, forgetting himself completely. This was the Emperor at his social best, entirely engaging, and Lady Kitsura was equally charming and many times more attractive. Lord Shonto watched the play between them with great interest. Twice he politely tried to draw Lord Komawara into the conversation, but the Emperor brushed these attempts aside as if he hadn't noticed. Shonto noted the young lord's neck becoming increasingly red, though his face remained calm, a slight smile crossing his face now and then at a remark or quick response.

The autumn moon had moved far into the western sky by the time the party began to break up. The Dance of Five Hundred Couples had been performed on the lawn, the long-sleeved kimonos creating the illusion of water flowing in the moonlight. Poems had been composed and recited. Assignations arranged, plots hatched, betrayals conceived, and large quantities of food and wine consumed. For those not singled out by the Emperor, it had been a most satisfying event.

Lady Nishima, though, was truly desolate. Even her harp, which had once been used by the legendary courtesan Ranyo to pacify the Mad Emperor, gave her little solace.

"I have failed you, Sire," she said once the sampan was out the palace gate. "I stepped into the Emperor's trap like an uneducated serving girl. All of your trust in me has been misplaced."

Shonto grunted, it was not his place to make excuses for the failings of either his children or his vassals, so he let Nishima continue, barely listening to her as he pursued a tiny thread in the evening's conversation. His fine memory led him back through every turn of the conversation that his intuition told him held the key to his problem. Finally he laughed loudly and slapped his daughter on the knee, making her jump.

"I don't see how there can be humor in this, Uncle! I am to be hostage within the city while you are at the other end of the Empire!" She was close to tears.

"Nishi-sum, I will tell you this only once, because if you do not understand it now, you never will. All plans have flaws—without exception! The trick is to find the flaw before the trap closes. In this case the trap is not yet closed, and I have found the flaw." He laughed again, immensely pleased with himself. Shonto, like his father, loved to lecture. He continued. "This is why I always beat you at gii, I don't wail and tear my hair when things go against me. You must always remember when setting a trap that it is not enough to know your opponent's weaknesses, you must also have made a careful study of his strengths. Half-wisdom is the most dangerous foolishness.

"Console yourself, Nishima-sum. You did the best that could have been done under the circumstances."

Nishima brightened a little. "Tell me, Uncle, what is the flaw? I cannot see it."

Shonto pulled the curtain aside to check the boatmen's progress, grunted and refused to say more, leaving his daughter to ponder the problem perhaps in the view that it might be instructive to her. There were many things to occupy his mind, preparations to make, his Spiritual Advisor to train, information to gain, and false information to spread. But something that should not matter at all kept returning to his mind.

The Emperor's lovely Sonsa had brought Lady Okara flowers, thanking her for the inspiration that had shaped the evening's dance. The exchange had been polite in the extreme, though the young dancer's very real shyness and infectious laugh soon won over Shonto and his companions. She had surprised Shonto by asking him to be her partner in the Dance of the Five Hundred Couples. He had been thrilled by her Sonsa skills as she moved through the measures of the ancient dance. As the music ended and the applause began, she had leaned close to him and whispered, "Good fortune in Seh, Lord Governor. Sleep lightly, there are always greater dangers than the barbarians." Then she was gone, leaving Shonto with only the lingering scent of her perfume.

Why, he wondered, had the Emperor instructed her to say that? Surely he did not think he could throw Shonto off balance with a few simple feints?

"Strange, yeh?" he said aloud.

"Pardon, Sire?"

"Strange young man, Komawara, yeh?"

"He seemed quite normal to me, Sire, and not very experienced. You should advise him to return to the outer provinces as soon as possible. He is a lamb among wolves here in the capital."

"Nishi-sum, have I ever told you that you place too much value on those qualities that are the most superficial?"

"It is my evening to fall short of your expectations, Sire. I apologize most humbly."

"Social bearing and wit, it is true, are not as highly developed in the outer provinces as they are here but, contrary to what most people think, that is because the residents of the outer provinces have better manners."

"Oh, Uncle, you romanticize the country folk like a bad poet," Nishima objected.

Shonto snorted. "What I've said is true! The *veiled barb* has never become the *art form* it is in the capital, for the simple reason that, in the outer provinces, insults are answered with swords. I always find my dealings with the people of the north most refreshing. A man only needs to keep his sword arm free and his tongue in check to enjoy the social life of a place like Seh. I much prefer that to the insignificant concerns of the Imperial courtiers!"

Yes, Shonto thought, a stay in the provinces would do Nishima good.

Four

SHONTO'S PRIVATE GARDEN was small but entirely exquisite. The designer, Shonto's former Spiritual Advisor, had joined all of the garden's elements into a delicately balanced whole that expressed both unity and diversity without losing the composition's harmonious sense. Shonto thought of the garden as a fine piece of music wherein all of the elements complimented each other, while the underlying structure was one of tension. The garden was widely thought of as a work of high-art and was much copied throughout the Empire. The present gardener's major problem was to maintain the essence of the original design while allowing the garden to grow, for it was, after all, a living thing and to stultify it would be to initiate a slow death.

Shonto knelt next to the babbling stream that fed the small pond, and pulled his sleeve back before plunging a hand into the cool water. He groped around in the shallows until he found the large stone he searched for and then raised it, dripping, into the sunlight. After a moment's contemplation, he replaced the rock farther upstream, so that it now rested half exposed in the miniature rapids. The lord listened intently for a few moments and then adjusted the rock slightly, listened again, and nodded, satisfied.

He rose and walked back toward the house, stopping every few paces to listen to the results of his efforts. Stepping out of his sandals, he seated himself on a cushion on the low veranda and listened to the sound of the breeze through the bamboo stands, the buzzing of insects, and the rippling rush of his stream.

"Better," he muttered, nodding.

Recently the stream had lost its clarity and for several days, Shonto had spent some time each morning trying to regain it, though not always to the delight of his gardener, who felt that such matters should be left to those properly trained.

The day was new, the sun not yet over the wall, and Shonto had slept only a few hours after the Emperor's party, but he felt relaxed and refreshed. The events of the previous night were still strong in his mind.

Almost soundlessly, servants appeared from the inner apartment and set a low table before Shonto. A square covered bowl, which held steaming cloths, and two other bowls, one of peeled and sliced fruit and one containing a hot grain mash, were arranged on the table. A light mead was poured into a cup and offered to the lord, who received it with a distracted nod. He listened to his garden. A single servant remained, kneeling behind him in utter stillness.

An almost imperceptible tap sounded on the shoji and the servant opened it a crack, to listen to a whispered voice.

"Your pardon, Lord Shonto," the servant said quietly, "it is Kamu-sum. He feels it is important that he speak to you immediately." Shonto waved his hand to have the man allowed in. Kamu, Shonto was well aware, never interrupted him without real purpose. The man was Shonto's steward and had served his father before him. He was old now, gray-haired and wrinkled like the face of a storm cloud, but his knowledge of the affairs of the Empire was invaluable and he was conscientious—one might even say meticulous—in the extreme. He still appeared vigorous and strong and he had long since learned to compensate for the right arm he had lost in battle.

The steward came in and knelt easily, bowed his head to the mat, and remained kneeling without a sign of impatience.

After a moment Shonto spoke. "I have adjusted the Speaking-stream, Kamu. Does it seem more focused now—sharper perhaps?"

Kamu bowed his head slightly and closed his eyes. After a few seconds he nodded. "The clarity is improved, Sire. To my ear it sounds sharper."

"Too sharp, do you think?"

Kamu bowed his head again. "Perhaps, Sire, but it may be that the water flows too rapidly."

"Hmm. I have wondered that myself. Perhaps if the bamboo were thinned, then the sharpness of the water would not be so obvious."

"The bamboo is a little heavy, but in the fall winds the leaf-sound will be higher."

"Huh," Shonto said, still concentrating on the garden music. "Tomorrow I will slow the water somewhat and see.

"Now, Kamu, what is it that could not wait?"

"Jaku Katta is here, Sire. He arrived unannounced and requests an audience on the Emperor's behalf."

"Unannounced." Shonto made a long face. "Unusual, yeh?"

"Most, Sire."

"I will see him here. Station guards out of sight. He must come alone. That is all."

The old warrior bowed and rose. He was not surprised that Shonto had chosen to meet Jaku in the garden. Staging was very important in these matters. To receive Jaku in the garden would make it very clear that Jaku had interrupted the lord at his morning meal, which would put the visitor at a disadvantage. It would also make a young upstart like Jaku aware of just how much a lord of Shonto's stature could afford to indulge himself—the garden would make that point perfectly.

Shonto heard the sound of men moving into position around him and then the garden was peaceful again. He turned his attention to the problem of Jaku Katta, the Emperor's prime advisor and Commander of the Imperial Guard. Jaku was the Emperor's eyes and ears throughout all of Wa and controlled the vast spy network that the Son of Heaven felt was necessary to maintain his rule. At the age of thirty-five, Jaku Katta was known to be one of the most powerful men in the Empire, and one of the most ambitious. The son of a small land holder, Jaku had first come to the Emperor's attention as a kick boxer, champion of all of Wa for almost a decade before his duties to the Emperor took precedence.

Shonto searched his mind, dredging up odd facts and stories about the man who was about to join him. Jaku Katta was not married and was an almost legendary womanizer. His memory was apparently prodigious and his mind supple and cunning. He was, in fact, the kind of man Shonto would have trained himself—had he discovered him first—but then there was the issue of Jaku's ambition. Shonto wondered how great the man's loyalty was to any but Jaku Katta—and perhaps the two brothers, who were his immediate lieutenants.

Jaku, Jaku, Shonto thought, now I will have my chance to measure you.

Reaching behind him Shonto moved his sword, which stood upright on its stand, to within easy reach. He ordered the servant to bring more mead and a second cup. He smiled broadly. It was going to be a long, full day and Shonto relished the thought of it. So much to do, so much to prepare for! He joined his hands, back to back, over his head and stretched his upper body like a young sapling growing toward the sun. Jaku, Jaku, Shonto thought, what fun we shall have!

Without any noticeable signal, the servant moved to open the shoji. Inside the opening, Kamu bowed low.

"General Jaku Katta, Lord Shonto."

Shonto nodded and Jaku stepped through the doorway dressed in the black uniform of the Imperial Guard, on his right breast, the Dragon Fan of the Imperial House, surmounted by the six small crimson dragons denoting a general of the First Rank. Under his right arm Jaku carried a finely crafted dress-helmet, reminding Shonto that the general was left-handed.

The general knelt and bowed surprisingly low to Shonto and remained kneeling, refusing the cushion that the servant offered.

"This surprise visit honors my House, General," Shonto said, bowing slightly. "Please, join me in some mead."

"It is my honor to be received, Lord Shonto," Jaku answered, without apology. His gaze was drawn out from the veranda into Shonto's garden. "It is as everyone says, Lord Shonto. This garden is the pattern of which all others are but imitations."

Shonto gave a half nod, "It was designed to be neither too elaborate, nor too ostentatious—as I prefer all things—so the essence is not masked in any way but only enhanced."

Neither man spoke for a moment as they contemplated the garden. The servant leaned forward unobtrusively and filled porcelain cups.

"I have been trying to bring the water sound back into harmony with the rest of the garden, Katta-sum. Tell me, does it seem too sharp to you?"

Jaku Katta closed his eyes and listened, without moving. Shonto studied the man's face, which was strong featured, especially the jaw and the high forehead. The eyelids were heavy, almost sleepy, under dark brows. Jaku's thin lips and wide mouth were not quite hidden by a magnificent, drooping mustache. Just above average height and perfectly proportioned, Jaku knelt across from Shonto with an easy, relaxed poise which was also present in his movements, and the lord remembered that the other kick boxers had named him the Black Tiger, after the steely-eyed cat.

Jaku's eyes were aberrant in color—a light, icy gray rather than the al-most universal brown. Both his brothers were green-eyed, which was also unusual, though somewhat more common. The eyes were just another factor in Jaku's mystique—"the entirely uncommon man."

"I feel the stream is perfectly in balance with the whole. I would not touch a pebble of its bed," Jaku said opening his tiger-eyes.

"You do not think the bamboo should be thinned?"

Jaku listened again. "No, Lord Shonto, I think that it's perfect. I have never in my life heard nor seen such a beautiful garden."

Shonto nodded, "I thank you for your opinion, Katta-sum. So, General, tell me. What is it that brings you here so early?"

Jaku set his cup carefully on the fine wooden table and composed himself before speaking. He met Shonto's eyes and the lord was startled by their intensity.

A mark for you, Jaku, Shonto thought, you understand the power of this gift.

"The Emperor has asked me to express his concern for your safety, Lord Shonto."

"Ah. I am touched by his concern, but the Shonto have long since learned to take precautions and, of course, I will take more now that I represent the Throne in Seh."

Jaku continued to hold Shonto's eye. "Your new Spiritual Advisor arrives today?"

Shonto almost laughed. You cannot throw me off so easily, my friend. We *both* have been keeping track of his progress.

"I have been expecting him for the last few days. Why?"

"The Emperor has reason to believe that this monk is a threat to you, Sire."

"I see. And is this so, General Jaku?"

Jaku looked down at his strong hands at rest on his thighs and then he met Shonto's eyes again. This tactic, Shonto realized, would soon lose its impact.

"We have reports on this young monk that we find . . . disturbing, Lord Shonto."

"Can you elaborate, Katta-sum? Nothing about the young man seems at all out of order to me."

Jaku cleared his throat quietly like the bearer of some bad news, news that it would pain him to reveal. "We have received reports that this monk—

this Initiate Brother Shuyun—has been given a great deal of special training, the nature of which is not entirely known to us. During his year in Wa as senior Initiate he was apprenticed to the most accomplished Botahist Brothers who treated him almost with deference. The entire time he was in Wa the Botahist Sisters spied on him and even tried to maneuver a young Acolyte nun—in disguise, of course—into his company. They were, by the way, unsuccessful.

"It seems that this boy-monk possesses powers that are unusual even for the Silent Ones," Jaku spoke the term with distaste. "And he has been chosen for you, Lord Shonto, the Emperor's most trusted governor.

"We fear that there is a plot against you or against the Emperor or both. The Botahist Brotherhood can never be trusted. They have strayed far from the teachings of Lord Botahara and have meddled in the affairs of the Empire far too often. I cannot believe they have changed in this regard, despite the platitudes of their current leader." Jaku fell to silence and Shonto could see that he was controlling his anger in the manner of the kick boxers—his breathing became even and his face almost serene. The fighters always looked so before a contest.

Shonto listened again to the sound of his garden and wondered if Jaku, with his boxer's sense, was aware of the guards nearby. He would, no doubt, realize that they must be there—being trained to stillness could not prevent that.

"It seems to me, Katta-sum, that the Brotherhood has been most obliging, in fact unusually so, to our Emperor. Did they not make a present of the land that the Emperor wished to purchase from them not more than a year ago? Have they not blessed the Son of Heaven and his line, thereby assuring the support of all the followers of Botahara? No small thing!

"There are rumors that they have offered the Emperor greater services than this and he has refused."

"They offer nothing without its price! They are merchants of the human soul, trading their so-called enlightenment for power and gold. They are hypocrites, without loyalty to anything but their own aspirations."

Ah, Shonto thought, did not Botahara say that we hate in others those things which are the least admirable in ourselves?

"So, Katta-sum, I don't understand what it is the Emperor wishes of me. I can hardly turn away my Spiritual Advisor now. That would be out of the question! I have made an agreement. Besides, I have paid very handsomely for this monk's service—gold in exchange for the knowledge of the soul, as you have said. Perhaps you have come merely to warn me of the Emperor's suspicions in this matter?"

"The Emperor thinks you would be well advised to send this monk back to his teachers, Lord Governor."

"General Jaku," Shonto said in his most patronizing tone, "I cannot do that on the scant information you have given me. Our family has employed Spiritual Advisors continuously for *over five hundred years*. It is a Shonto belief that we have profited from these arrangements. I can hardly believe that the Botahist Brothers would send a monk who was a threat to the Emperor into the Shonto House. It would make no more sense than sending such a one to Jaku Katta!" Shonto laughed and motioned to have their cups refilled.

"It is as the Emperor said: you will oppose him in this matter," Jaku said coldly, ignoring the laughter.

"Kattu-sum, the Emperor is an intelligent and reasonable man. He cannot expect me to turn away my Spiritual Advisor and insult the Botahist Brotherhood on so little evidence. If you have more information, enough to convince me, well, that would be different. Can you tell me why the Sisterhood was following this young monk? This is very unusual, yeh?"

"In truth, Lord Governor, we don't know."

"Huh. So I have been warned. I will watch this monk with great care. There is little else I can do, yeh?"

"There is *one* thing." Jaku turned his eyes on Shonto again, but the effect was gone. "The Emperor has suggested that a servant be assigned to this monk. A servant who is trained to watch and report. I have such a servant. If there were any danger to you, Sire, he would see it."

"He would report to Jaku Katta, yeh?" Shonto could not help but smirk.

"All of his reports would go through you first, Sire."

"I see." Shonto swirled the contents of his cup. "The Emperor does me great honor with his concern, but it is unecessary. I am Shonto and do not need to have a *boy* sent to look after me. I will deal with this monk in my own way. If there is cause for concern, I will send word to the Emperor himself." Oh, Jaku, Shonto thought, you must truly believe that you have leverage or you would never suggest a plan so transparent. But Nishima will be safe, he told himself, as he had so many times since yesterday evening, I will see to that.

Jaku turned his gaze back to the garden. "As you wish, Lord Governor," he said, but his voice did not ring with resignation.

Yes, Shonto thought, this is a man always to be wary of. The Black Tiger—someone who could explode out of darkness without warning.

"The Emperor has given your daughter great honor, yeh?" Jaku asked suddenly.

"He has honored my entire household with his concern and generosity," Shonto said almost by rote.

"This is so. It is good to be in the Emperor's favor, yeh?" Shonto didn't answer, so Jaku went on. "I have been instructed to tell you that the Emperor will see to your daughter's safety while you are in Seh. He is very fond of her, and who could not be? She is lovely, talented, and possessed of great charm—such a rare combination."

"The Son of Heaven need not trouble himself. Lady Nishima will be well guarded."

"To guard Lady Nishima is not *trouble,* Sire, it is an *honor.* I would perform this duty to our Emperor personally, if I could." Jaku turned to Shonto and lowered his voice. "But as it is, my reach has grown long. Many blows can be warded off by *anticipation*—this is an essential skill of the kick boxer. It is the skill that makes me valuable to the Emperor."

Shonto listened to this performance, fascinated. He almost forgot to respond.

"And what danger do you anticipate for my daughter, Katta-sum?"

"At the moment, none, but I rule out nothing. I want you to know, Lord Shonto, that I think your daughter a person of far too much importance to be under threat by anyone—*anyone* at all."

Ah, Jaku, it is as I suspected, your loyalty is the servant of your ambition. And now you aspire to too much! This long reach of yours may yet leave you with empty hands. But what a fine animal you are, Jaku! Such amazing *hunger!* Yet you think this hunger is your strength, when it is your weakness. You must learn to control your desires. Ah, I lecture, but of course you cannot hear.

"You know, Katta-sum," Shonto said turning and looking out into his garden. "Sometimes I think that there are forces outside these walls that are causing an almost imperceptible but continuous change in my garden. Like a man's spirit, yeh? If he allows the outside world to breach his inner walls, his clarity will be lost. One must always guard against this, don't you think, or we may lose our tranquillity?"

"I'm sure you are right, Lord Governor," Jaku answered, but his voice suddenly seemed far away.

Shonto watched while Jaku again relaxed his muscles as the kick boxers did—a settling of the body, as though it had just made contact anew with the earth. He seemed to have turned his attention elsewhere, toward the garden, and he had achieved perfect stillness, eyes closed, his hand at rest on his sword hilt. Shonto said nothing, fascinated by the great cat before him as it sank into total concentration.

Yes, even the sound of my garden is that beautiful, Shonto thought, just as the shoji to Jaku's right exploded toward them. One of Shonto's personal guard swept the remains of the screen aside as he came through, face impassive, his sword beginning a tight arc toward Jaku Katta. *Chaos* erupted all around them!

Magically, Jaku Katta seemed to be in the air from his kneeling position, his sword in hand, even as Shonto reached for his own blade. The shoji to the inner house jerked back at the same instant that Jaku's right foot caught his assailant's forearm, spoiling the blow aimed at Jaku's torso. Two guards burst through the bamboo stand as Jaku's sword flashed. The assailant smashed the low table as he fell, dead, and Jaku landed on his feet beyond the veranda's edge, his sword at the ready, his stance strong.

"No one moves!" Shonto yelled from his position, standing, his back against a post, sword out. The young servant stood, unarmed, between his lord and the shattered wall, prepared to intercept anything that might come. The sounds of men running and shouting came from every direction.

Kamu appeared, pushing between the guards at the door, but stopped, stricken by the sight of the dead guard in Shonto livery. Behind him stood Jaku's lieutenant whose eyes darted everywhere as he assessed the danger.

Shonto dipped the point of his blade toward the corpse, "Who is this, Kamu?"

The steward turned to a lieutenant who stood in the frame of the shattered shoji.

"Tokago Yama, Sergeant of the Guard, Sire." He bowed to Lord Shonto but kept his eyes fixed on Jaku Katta.

"He attempted to assassinate his liege-lord," Jaku's voice sounded strongly, imposing itself over the confusion, "but fortunately Jaku Katta was in his way. I saved Lord Shonto from having to clean this one's blood off the Emperor's gift."

"Kamu," Shonto turned a cold eye on the steward, "all of the guards in this garden are now foot-porters. You will break their swords personally. A

guest in the house of Shonto has been endangered. This is unacceptable!"
Shonto paused, regaining control of his anger. "Where is the captain of my
guard?"

"He comes now, Sire."

"Good. Send for my worthless gardener and assure Lady Nishima that all
is under control."

Shonto turned his back on the scene and stepped off the veranda. He nodded to Jaku who followed the lord into the garden. Both men kept their
swords in hand.

"Katta-sum, I can never apologize for this occurrence. *Never* has such a
thing happened while I have been head of this House. I owe you a great
debt."

"I did what any man would have done in my place, Sire. I ask for nothing
in return except that you consider the danger around you. To bring one of
these treacherous monks into your household now, I'm sure, is a mistake. I
beg you again to reconsider."

"Your concern honors me, General. Certainly I will consider your
words."

The captain of Shonto's guard and the chief gardener arrived at the same
moment. Both knelt and touched their heads to the ground, showing none
of the fear they felt.

Shonto motioned the gardener to follow but ignored the captain. Crossing
to the far wall the lord stopped before an exquisite chako bush. The shrub
had been shaped by an artist of some accomplishment and was beautiful even
to the most uninformed eye.

"This is a present to you, Katta-sum. It is a piece of my inner harmony,
yeh? A token of gratitude for today. Shall I send my gardener to choose a
place for it in your garden? I believe he is the best in all of Wa."

"That would be a great honor, Lord Shonto. But my humble garden is not
worthy of such beauty. Now it is I who am in your debt."

Shonto turned to his gardener. "You will accompany General Jaku to his
home and consult with him and his gardener in this matter. You will prepare
this chako immediately." Shonto turned back toward the porch.

"Every man must have the best garden he possibly can, Katta-sum. It is
essential to the human spirit. When a man has as much to do as you and I,
he needs a sanctuary, yeh? A place which nourishes the soul. Don't you
agree?"

"I do, Sire."

They passed the kneeling captain again and proceeded to the veranda. Servants were just in the process of replacing the ruined shoji and already the grass mats had been changed and a new table set with cups.

Shonto handed his sword to his servant who sheathed it and returned it to its stand.

Both men sat on the veranda edge while servants washed their feet, for they had gone into the garden barefoot.

"Again I thank you, Katta-sum. I will consider what you have said with great care."

Jaku nodded. "Your chako will be the centerpiece of my garden." Jaku came to his feet on the veranda and paused. "I thank you for your time, Sire. To have seen your garden has been a great lesson. Unfortunately, the Emperor's business calls."

A servant brought Jaku his helmet. Shonto and his guest exchanged parting bows and Jaku was gone, escorted by Shonto guards. The shoji closed and Shonto was alone with his servant and the Captain of the Guard who still knelt in the garden's center. Except for the trampled bamboo, there was no sign of the attempted assassination. The garden was again tranquil.

Shonto tapped the table impatiently. "Where is my fruit?" he demanded. The servant bowed quickly and turned to crack the shoji. Shonto gestured to have the cups filled and the boy leaned forward to pour.

"Fill them both," Shonto instructed. Raising a cup, the lord turned to face his servant. "A toast," he said. The boy was confused but looked attentive all the same.

"You cannot toast without a drink," Shonto nodded at the second cup. The servant still hesitated and then realized what honor his lord offered him. He reached for the second vessel.

"To your new position—junior assistant to Kamu. You have studied arms?" The boy nodded as if in a dream. "Good. You will begin tomorrow. What is your name?"

"Toko, Sire."

"So, Toko, you were brave today and quick. These are important qualities. You may do very well if you pay attention and learn quickly. Drink." Shonto looked at the boy as if seeing him for the first time. How long had he been one of Shonto's personal servants? The lord did not know. The boy was no more than sixteen, so he could not have served long. Certain qualities were looked for in servants; physical competence, a softness of voice, attractiveness, and an inner stillness that made them totally unobtrusive. Toko exhibited all of these.

The boy touched his head to the mat, "This is too great an honor, Sire."

"We will see. But today you are still a servant and I am waiting for my fruit."

The boy turned to the shoji, opening it a fraction, and then placed a bowl on the table.

"Kamu-sum is here, Sire," the servant said softly.

The lord nodded and turned back to the garden and began popping segments of a peeled orange into his mouth. The old man was there, bowing, waiting in silence. Shonto finished his orange, savoring each segment, having so recently been reminded of how easily it could be his last.

"So, Kamu, a morning of surprises, yeh?"

"I feel nothing but shame, Sire. This lapse in security is my responsibility entirely. An assassin among your own guard. . . ." He shook his head in disbelief. "I . . . I grow old and forgetful, Sire. I am no longer worthy to serve you."

"I will decide that. Has our young Brother arrived?"

"Not yet, Sire."

"So," Shonto nodded toward the Captain of the Guard, "I will talk with this one now."

Kamu rose and went to the single step off the veranda where he cleared his throat. The captain raised his eyes for the first time since entering the garden. Kamu nodded, commanding without words in the manner of those accustomed to power.

The steward turned to leave, but Shonto raised his hand and Kamu returned to his place and his silence.

The Captain of the Shonto House Guard walked toward the two men sitting on the veranda. He had no doubt about who was to blame for the morning's incident and he had no doubt of what the result of it would be—and that, the captain believed, was justice. For this reason he remained entirely composed and Shonto had a second of admiration for the man's unruffled dignity. It would not sway him in his judgment, however.

Rohku Saicha had been the Captain of the Guard for a decade. He was forty-seven years old. During the time of Shonto's father, the captain had been a renowned soldier and had risen through the ranks during the Interim

Wars that led to the establishment of the Yamaku Dynasty. It was said that when it came to intrigue Rohku could uncover a plot before it had been spoken. This had made him the perfect choice for Captain of the Guard—until today.

Rohku Saicha stopped before Shonto and took the sheathed sword from his sash, laying it carefully on the gravel border before the veranda. He bowed his head to the ground and spoke without looking up.

"I return this gift to you, Lord Shonto. I am no longer worthy of it."

Shonto nodded. The immediate responsibility for any breach in security belonged to the Captain of the Guard and though he was of lesser rank than Kamu, the captain's will prevailed in matters of security. Below the lord himself, the ultimate responsibility for anything occurring within the Shonto domain rested with the steward and he could therefore be held to blame, though this would not be usual—at least not in Shonto's House. He was not known for the irrational purges of his staff that other lords indulged in.

"So, I ask you both. How is it that this assassin, this Tokago Yama, came to be in my personal guard?"

The Guard Captain spoke. "Tokago Yama is the son of Tokago Hideisa who was a captain in your father's Fourth Army. Hideisa-sum was killed in the battle in which your father was betrayed, I honor his memory. The Takago have served the House loyally for seven generations, though Yama-su . . . Yama has brought them eternal shame.

"He was assigned to your personal guard recently, Sire. I did this at his request because he said," Rohku stopped and spoke slowly, recalling the words with care, "that guarding his lord required utter concentration and took his mind away from his grief. I was swayed by this, Sire. His wife and son were drowned not long ago aboard a boat proceeding from the Floating City.

"Yama was always an exemplary soldier, Sire. I misjudged him entirely." The man's shoulders sagged, but his voice remained calm and respectful.

So, Shonto thought, no one knows but me. How strange. They let their sense of failure cloud their thinking.

"There was no indication of Yama's change of loyalty?"

"Since the loss of his family, Yama has been withdrawn—as one would expect. Of late, he has gone off by himself whenever he could, but in his duties he has always been most conscientious. I valued him, Sire, and I believed he revered you."

"I remember the accident," Shonto said, "a river junk, yeh? Was it ever found?"

Kamu spoke, quietly. "No, Sire, it disappeared beyond Yul-ho. Strange, because the river there is shallow and easily navigable. It never reached the light-boat at Yul-nan, disappearing with all hands and a valuable cargo."

"We did not consider piracy?"

"On the river, Sire?"

Shonto shrugged and went on, "So, how is it that a man who, I'm told, revered me became an assassin, Kamu?"

"His grief, Sire. It must have driven him mad."

Shonto grunted. I'm surrounded by romantics, he thought, *Botahara save me!*

"So. A perfectly good soldier, from a long line of Shonto retainers, is driven mad by grief at the loss of his family and attempts to assassinate his liege-lord during a meeting with a representative of the Emperor—a man who just happens to be one of the most formidable fighters in Wa?"

The two men before Shonto made no sound, as indeed they would have made no sound if he had whipped them.

"Has it not occurred to you that Yama could have chosen a better time? He had great opportunity, yeh? One of my personal guards?"

"Excuse me, Sire, but that is why madness makes sense. Why else would he choose to assassinate you at . . ."

Shonto slammed his fist on the table, his patience at an end. "He was *not* trying to assassinate *me!*"

The wind played in the bamboo, the stream burbled. There was no other noise.

"I was not here at the time, Sire," Kamu said in a small voice, "but I was informed that Yama had attacked you and that Jaku Katta stopped him."

"Yes, Kamu, and who told you that?"

"A lieutenant of the guard, I believe."

I'm sorry, Kamu, but you deserve this. "Toko," Shonto said over his shoulder, surprising Kamu by knowing the servant's name. "Can you remember who gave Kamu this information?"

"Jaku Katta," the boy answered quickly, embarrassed that he was being used to shame Kamu.

"I do not understand, Sire," Kamu said, all traces of his normal ease of manner gone.

Well, I won't shame you further by having the servant explain things, Shonto thought.

"Tokago Yama was trying to kill Jaku Katta." Shonto said, and he was sure the boy behind him nodded. "Jaku blew smoke in your eyes, Kamu."

"But why? Why would Yama try to kill Jaku here, in your house? And what would make Jaku say the attack was aimed at you?"

"I can think of a hundred reasons. They could all be wrong."

"Perhaps," the captain paused to gather his thoughts, "perhaps Yama believed his wife and child to be still alive. Taking hostages would explain why the ship was not found. Stranger things have happened." The Guard Captain seemed relieved to learn that his lord's life had not been in danger. Of course, this made no difference to his failure of duty. "It becomes a question of who would want Jaku killed in the House of Shonto at the hand of the Shonto guard. The Emperor would have no choice but to respond. Two birds with one stone, yeh?"

"Jaku has many enemies," Kamu said.

Yes, and Shonto has enemies, the lord noted.

The servant moved to answer a tap at the shoji, and then whispered to Kamu who moved to the opening. There was more hushed conversation, which Shonto ignored.

"Excuse me, Sire," Kamu said. "Guards have just found Yama's brother, Shinkaru. He has fallen on his sword in the back courtyard."

The Captain of the Guard shook his head sadly, "Shame," he whispered without meaning to.

"Huh," Shonto grunted and then addressed the sky. "Does no one in my House know his place? I would have talked with this brother before he *indulged* himself!" The lord drank off the rest of his mead in a single swallow and immediately the servant replenished the cup.

"Did we question the keeper of the light-boat at Yul-nan?" Shonto asked suddenly.

"He was questioned by the Imperial Guard as soon as we reported the boat missing."

"But we did nothing?"

"The Imperial Guard administer the waterway, Sire."

Shonto stared into his garden for a long while. Then he spoke, his manner suddenly light. "We need to find out why Yama tried to kill Jaku Katta and we need to know immediately. We will spare no energy in this matter. If the wife and child didn't drown, we must know. We will talk to everyone who would have had reason to be on the river that night. Perhaps the Imperial Guard will learn of our inquiries and lead us to someone with knowledge.

"The second thing I want is *Jaku Katta's soul!* I want to know everything about him—everything! He must be watched always. When he sleeps, I want to know his dreams. And his immediate lieutenants—these green-eyed brothers—watch them also. Have we anyone in the general's house?"

Kamu shook his head.

"Then get someone. If Jaku can infiltrate my house, then I can infiltrate his." Shonto's mind was racing now, each thought seeming to lead to a dozen others. "All care must be taken. No one else—I mean no one!—must learn what Jaku's true intention was. The Black Tiger must never know that we have seen through his charade—if he even suspects that this is so, our advantage will be lost. He has saved Lord Shonto from an assassin. No one inside or outside of this garden should hear otherwise. We do not know who else Jaku may have in this house." Shonto cast his eye on each man in turn. "Is this understood?" All nodded. "Good." Shonto looked out into the garden, thinking.

"The Emperor's Sonsa—find out what you can about her also. There is much to do. The Shonto have been inactive too long. It is a mistake to believe that because we threaten no one, no one is threatened by us."

"Captain." Shonto surprised the guard by using his rank. "You are in charge of these matters I have just spoken of. Also, you will be responsible for Lady Nishima's safety while I am in Seh—we will discuss this later. If you perform these duties successfully, you will have redeemed yourself. You may go."

"But Sire . . ." the captain stammered, "they will say you have grown soft!" He was obviously shocked at how lightly he was being treated.

"Good! Let Jaku Katta think that I am soft. The truth is I need all of you. I can afford no more indulgences among my retainers. Go."

The man bowed and rose, crossing the garden on unsteady legs. He left by a concealed gate, his mind in turmoil. He could not overcome the shame he felt at being allowed to live.

Shonto reached into the fruit bowl distractedly.

"Are you sure, Lord Shonto?" Kamu said, hesitation in his voice. Only his age and position gave him the privilege of asking such a question. "The captain is right, the entire Empire will hear of this."

Shonto glared at the old man. He was tempted to dismiss him, the question ignored. "No, Kamu, it is not wise, it is an impulse. A message for Jaku Katta to ponder. What is done is done. We are in a much better position now than we were an hour ago. Jaku Katta has revealed that which he meant to hide. For this knowledge I could forgive Rohku almost anything."

Kamu shook his head forlornly, and spoke to no one in particular. "It is perhaps time for me to retire. I no longer see the things that my position requires me to see. I am adrift in all of this."

"You were not here during the attack, so you could not have seen what I saw. The Black Tiger was *prepared* for the assault! He knew it was coming. Only after Yama was certainly dead, did Jaku claim this was an attack on me.

"I am amazed by this, Kamu. Two possibilities seem clear to me: someone wanted Jaku dead in my house by the hand of a Shonto guard—someone who was both an enemy of Jaku and mine—but Jaku got wind of the plot and decided to use it to his own advantage. It appears that he has saved my life, yeh?

"The second possibility is that Jaku planned the whole thing to unsettle me, to make me believe that Jaku is an honorable man or a thousand other reasons. Until we know more, it would be foolish to say."

"Should we not ask ourselves if Yama had his own reasons for wanting Jaku dead?"

"This does not seem likely. A Shonto House Guard and the advisor to the Emperor? If Yama did have private reasons for wanting to destroy Jaku, then it would seem unlikely that the general would know about them or that Yama would do it here, where the Emperor would certainly hold me responsible. Everyone who knew Yama must be questioned; perhaps that will give us a clue."

Shonto sipped his mead and stared into the void. "There is something else I need to know, Kamu. Quite recently, within the last two years, the old Komawara of Seh sold a piece of his fief. I need to know how much was paid for this land and I need to know today, before the midday meal. I will have Lord Komawara as a guest and we will share our fare with Tanaka and perhaps the young Brother. We will see. Have they arrived yet?"

"They are expected within the hour."

"Good. I will meet with them as soon as they have bathed and refreshed themselves. Open the upper reception hall to the sun. That will be formal enough. You may go."

The old warrior bowed and rose, backing out through the shoji the servant opened behind him.

"Oh, Kamu." The steward stopped. "You will take Toko here as an assistant. Train him, and if you feel he is of any value then see what he can do, yeh? That is all."

Shonto was alone, his mind racing to try to make sense of all the information the morning had provided. His thoughts settled on Jaku Katta.

That man, thought Shonto, is cunning beyond belief and willing to take great risks. But he is rash! Oh, he is rash! He believes this display will win me to his side. Jaku the brave, Jaku the prescient, yeh? Who could not want such a formidable man for his ally—or for a son-in-law? Shonto truly believed that Jaku was capable of precipitating a crisis in Wa in the belief that one as nimble as the Black Tiger could only gain by it. So he thinks that he can hold the Emperor in the palm of one hand and Shonto in the other, but he holds a *scorpion* and a *wasp*. Shonto smiled broadly. What fun we had today, Jaku! Don't make too many mistakes too soon; we can have more fun yet. Shonto laughed aloud and banged the table with the flat of his hand, completely unaware of the servant kneeling behind him.

So, Shonto thought, I go to Seh and the Emperor believes this fits his plans, while Jaku thinks my journey is to his benefit. The game begins in earnest now. The board must be turned around so that only Shonto will benefit from Shonto's moves.

There was one last piece of information that Shonto had that he was sure Rohka's inquiries would not reveal. Jaku Katta had only once lost the kick boxing championship of Wa and that had been eight years earlier. If Shonto was right, the Black Tiger had been defeated by a young Botahist Neophyte. Shonto rubbed his hands together. What, he wondered, were the Botahist Brothers sending him?

The lord's attention was drawn back to the garden. Cocking his head to one side he listened, then suddenly he laughed long and loud. The trampled patch of bamboo now whispered with an entirely different voice. The garden had regained its harmony.

Five

ONLY THE EMPEROR'S most trusted advisors were received in the private Audience Hall off the Imperial apartments. Only the most trusted advisors and spies.

The man who bowed his head to the floor before the Most Revered Son of Heaven had at one time served as a spy but had risen to the rank of general and Commander of the Imperial Guard.

"Be at your ease, Katta-sum," the Emperor said, gesturing for the general to raise himself and kneel in comfort.

"Thank you, Sire."

Kneeling before the dais in his black uniform, the Commander of the Imperial Guard seemed entirely relaxed, and that could be said of few who came before the Emperor.

"The autumn trade winds seem to have taken a deep breath, Katta-sum. It will be good if they carry with them all that we need to fill the treasury."

"I'm sure they will, Sire. All the reports indicate that this will be an exceptional year."

The Emperor nodded, waving the Dragon Fan in a gesture of salute. Voluminous robes of gold bearing the Imperial Dragon seemed to increase the Emperor's size three-fold, making his sword of office, which stood to one side on a stand, seem insignificant.

"So tell me, General," the Emperor said, snapping his fan closed, signifying an end to the polite formalities, "how was your visit to the esteemed Lord Shonto?"

"It was as you said, Sire." Jaku shook his head slowly. "This young monk has some special significance attached to him. Shonto was unmoved when I told him of your displeasure at his decision to employ a Spiritual Advisor. A hint that his daughter could be vulnerable while he was in Seh was ignored, and when I informed him that you, Sire, were considering halting all sea traffic out of Yankura, to 'starve the pirates,' he merely shrugged as though it wouldn't cost him triple to transport his goods in and out of his fief by land. There was no moving him, Sire."

The Emperor's smile disappeared to be replaced by a scowl. "These treacherous Brothers are up to no good, Katta-sum. They plot with the cunning Shonto, I know it. This stir over a young monk it is most uncommon." The Son of Heaven shook his head. "What can be so unusual about a young Initiate? Something is very wrong here, I feel it."

"I fear you are right, Sire. But soon we shall know more. The ship bringing Shonto his monk has docked. A messenger is coming, even now."

"That fool Ashigaru? What can you expect from that fanatic?"

"Nothing directly, Sire. He will certainly fail, but the attempt will have been made by a Tomsoian priest. That will throw the Brotherhood into an uproar. And the one I sent to watch is most observant. I chose him personally. We will know the details of Ashigaru's failure and that will give us a measure of Shonto's monk."

The Emperor snorted. "It were better if the ship and all aboard her went to the bottom. Then we would be rid of this Botahist thorn forever."

"If the ship *could* be sunk, Sire. There's an excellent captain in charge of a fast ship. A Shonto man, undoubtedly. He will not come by the usual sea lanes, and once he rounds Cape Ujii we dare not touch him. The traffic is too great and the act would be known.

"I think this way is best. We send Shonto and his Botahist servant north together. We keep the Lady Nishima here in the capital, and Shonto's son will be sent to administer the family fief. The family will be spread throughout the Empire. Shonto will get no warm reception in the north, this being the slap in the face we intend. The northern lords are proud and will not take kindly to the suggestion that they cannot guard their own border against the degenerate barbarians. Shonto's time in the north will not be pleasant, I assure you, Sire."

The Emperor laughed. He nodded. "I am too impatient, Katta-sum. You do me good. Your foresight is most appreciated."

Jaku bowed his head. "You do me too much honor, Sire. I am not worthy."

The Emperor raised his eyebrows at this. "So what is this story of an assassin in Shonto's garden?"

If Jaku was surprised, he showed no sign of it. "I was about to tell you, Sire."

"Of course."

"It was really a bungled attempt on Shonto by one of his own guards. He would not have fallen to it, he is too quick. It seemed appropriate that I dispatch the assassin, thereby curbing any suspicion that the Throne was behind the attempt. It was an embarrassing situation, Sire, Shonto threatened by one of his elite guards and the murderer stopped by your servant. The whole Empire will know of it by week's end. Shonto will look the fool—and we send such a one north to save the men of Seh!" Jaku smirked.

"Don't be so smug, General. It would take more than that to damage the reputation of Shonto Motoru. He is a shrewd man and you would do well not to underestimate him."

"Of course, you are right, Sire. I apologize for my lack of humility." Jaku touched his head to the mat.

"Shonto must be kept off balance and must never know what is afoot, Kattu-sum. He is too masterful a player and we cannot afford a single error."

"Everything goes as planned, Sire. In three days Lord Shonto will depart for the north, leaving Lady Nishima here in the capital. Everything we had hoped for has been arranged in Seh—everything and more."

"We still have concerns, Katta-sum. Promising the governorship to two different parties is a great risk."

"But neither of them can speak of it openly, Sire. If Shonto were to hear even a rumor that someone was preparing to take his place with your approval—there would be no hope for the man. Shonto has never hesitated to eliminate a rival, nor has he ever failed. We must have at least two parties working against Shonto, Sire, and two will be just sufficient.

"In the off chance that Lord Shonto does find out about the plot . . ." the general shrugged, "we know nothing of it."

"It is still a great risk! If our hand is seen in this, Shonto's suspicion may turn to us entirely. That would be disastrous!"

"Shonto suspects everyone, Sire—everyone at all times. And after today he even has his own staff to fear." Jaku smiled coldly. "We cannot fail, Sire, I am sure of it."

"We hope you are right, Katta-sum. Others have thought they held the Shonto in their hands and have been cruelly surprised. Such surprises are not appreciated." The Son of Heaven banged the heels of his hands together with force. "*Damn* my fool of a father! If he had done as I advised, he would have done away with the old Shonto when he had the opportunity!"

"But then the son would have sought revenge, Sire," Jaku reminded him.

"Yes, and we would have fought him then as we fight him now! I see no difference. We cannot sit securely on the Throne while the Shonto live. They have too much power, too much ambition, and this Fanisan daughter—she is the eye of the storm that threatens to overwhelm us. If Shonto gives her to a Great House, then there will be war. There will be no choice. And oh, how he bides his time! Whom will he pick as ally? Whom?

"*Damn* that superstitious fool! *Damn him!*" the Son of Heaven banged his fist on his armrest and cursed his Imperial father with passion.

"Perhaps your father did you a favor, Sire," Jaku said tentatively. "Now you fight Shonto Motoru on your terms and not on his. And this time there is no soothsayer secretly in Shonto's pay to strike fear into our hearts if we move against the Shonto clan. Things are very different."

"Yes, Katta-sum, you are right. I know you are." The Emperor's fit of anger passed as though it had never been. "We must talk again tomorrow. I wish to be kept informed on this matter at all times. And I'm still expecting a written report on the situation in Seh, Katta-sum, you haven't forgotten?"

"It can be in your hand within the hour, Sire."

"Good. Tomorrow, then."

Jaku Katta touched his head to the mat, palms flat on the floor, then rose and backed out, leaving the Emperor alone in the heavily guarded Audience Hall.

The Emperor stroked his mustache and smiled, the heavy lines in his face disappearing. He laughed.

The Son of Heaven ordered food and ate, attended by several servants, his mood improving by the moment.

You are almost in my hands, Shonto Motoru, I can feel it! And I keep my hands very strong in anticipation.

He laughed several times during the meal for no apparent reason, which startled the servants who were unused to gaiety in their master. It unsettled them considerably.

After he had eaten and finished a lingering cup of cha, a retainer knocked and announced Lieutenant Jaku Tadamoto, younger brother of the esteemed general.

"Ah, my report," the Emperor said, waving the servants out. The lieutenant entered—a tall, slim version of his famous brother. But Jaku Tadamoto had none of the physical presence of the champion kick boxer and could be as inconspicuous as a servant—until he spoke. Not that his voice was unusual; it wasn't that, it was his use of words that commanded one's attention, for he used them, not in the offhand manner almost universally heard even among the educated, but like an artist used a fine tipped brush—with infinite discretion and precision.

Jaku Tadamoto was also a scholar of some accomplishment and possessed a fine critical mind. His interest in the past gave him a much broader view than his older brother who, though brilliant in his own way, tended to concentrate on the immediate at cost to the future.

The Emperor had only come to realize this through a spy he had placed in Jaku's midst—a master spy to watch the spy-master! So despite Kattasum's attempt to keep his younger brothers in the background, the Son of Heaven had skillfully arranged to meet the young men by demanding that messages passed between the general and the Emperor never be delivered by a lackey, no matter how trusted. So the two brothers became messengers and the Emperor came to know them. He realized immediately that one was of no consequence, a common, unexceptional soldier, while the other, Tadamoto, was brilliant.

Jaku Tadamoto prostrated himself before the Emperor.

"Be at your ease, Lieutenant," the Emperor said, with warmth.

"Thank you, Sire. I am honored that . . ." He went through the formalities the situation required and the Emperor let him do so, not yet ready to allow the familiarity that he granted Jaku Katta.

Finally the Emperor gestured with his fan. "Have you something for me from your esteemed brother?"

"I do, Sire, the report he promised you this morning."

"Excellent. Please leave it here." The Emperor pointed with his fan to the edge of the dais. As he had ordered all the servants out for the sake of privacy, there was no one to carry the scroll and it was out of the question that the Emperor would receive it himself.

"May we enquire into the well-being of your family?" the Emperor asked.

"I am honored that you would ask, Sire. My wife and son are healthy and dutiful and ever grateful for the honor the Emperor has given our name. My brothers . . ." He broke into a smile. "Excuse me, Sire, but how can they be anything but blissful at their good fortune in being allowed to serve our revered Emperor?"

"Ah. And what of your brother's concerns? Is he still troubled by the unfortunate woman and child he had taken under his roof?"

"They trouble him no more, Sire."

The Emperor waited.

"They have departed this plane for the time being."

"How sad. An accident?"

"The woman took her own life and that of her son, Sire."

"So tragic, yeh? After all your brother had done for them?"

"Most certainly, Sire."

"And you still don't know who she was, this woman?"

The brother of Jaku Katta shifted uncomfortably and the Emperor fixed him with an intense stare.

"It seems possible, Sire, that this woman had been at one time a very minor lady-in-waiting to the Lady Nishima Fanisan Shonto. Though it seems more likely that she was a favored servant."

The Emperor moved, placing an elbow on his armrest and leaning his chin on his fist. He showed no other reaction.

"How kind of your brother to take in a woman who had fallen from such a position. Few would have such compassion. And to tell no one! Modesty, no doubt. Very noble of him. Of course, we will say nothing of this to him. It shall be his secret, but we must admit that this act of kindness has affected us greatly."

There was silence while the Emperor digested this new information.

"So, the Lady Nishima. Hmm. I wonder if this unfortunate woman would have provided Katta-sum with any information about the great lady?" His eyebrows rose, punctuating the sentence.

"It seems possible, Sire. Information about the Shonto is crucial to the Imperial purpose at this time."

"Ah, yes, the *Imperial purpose.*"

"My brother would never bother the Emperor with mere speculation, Sire. I'm sure if he can verify any information he may have received, then he would report it."

"I don't doubt it for an instant, Lieutenant, so say nothing about this conversation. I would never have a man as proud as your brother think that I doubt him. Not for a moment."

"As you wish, Sire. You can count on my discretion."

The Emperor nodded his thanks. "The Lady Nishima is a desirable woman, yeh?"

"I agree, Sire."

"Unfortunate that Katta-sum does not have the rank to merit such a woman. Most unfortunate."

Jaku Tadamoto said nothing.

"And what of my lovely Sonsa, Tadamoto-sum? Have you done as I asked? I wish to be reassured that she is in no danger."

"I assure you that she is not, Sire. And her devotion to you seems unquestionable. She lives only for dance and for her Emperor."

"Huh. I am truly fond of her, Tadamoto-sum, but," the Emperor paused as though searching for words, "I am an Emperor, after all, and she . . ." He let his open hand drop. "But I would like to see her happy and settled."

Ah, I have your attention now, young Jaku, the Emperor thought. "I must consider this. An Emperor must always be fair, yeh? Just as he must reward loyalty. I will consider this."

Jaku Tadamoto nodded agreement.

"Yes," the Emperor said distractedly, then he turned his attention back to the man sitting in front of him as though seeing him for the first time. The Son of Heaven smiled broadly.

"I thank you for discussing these things with me, Tadamoto-sum. I worry about your brother. He is so dedicated in his duties and takes so little time for himself, yeh? We must talk again. There are other matters we wish to discuss with you. We value your counsel, and your loyalty has not gone unnoticed. We will talk soon."

Jaku Tadamoto backed out of the Audience Hall, his heart soaring.

A look of confusion came over the Emperor's face as the doors closed. He shook his head. How could such an intelligent man allow his desires to set his course, the Emperor wondered? Strange. Well, perhaps he *would* give Tadamoto-sum the girl at some future date. No one else would dare to court her. The Emperor smiled at the thought of the previous night. Tadamoto-sum had not earned her yet.

Such strange brothers. So Jaku Katta desires Lady Nishima. The Emperor snorted. Had the general taken leave of his senses? The entire family will bring ruin upon themselves over women! Lady Nishima! Jaku must realize how impossible that is. The Black Tiger plots—but what? A secret alliance with Shonto? To deliver me into Shonto hands? Perhaps he plots with one of my useless sons. Is it possible that Jaku could be truly smitten with Shonto's daughter—endangering himself like a lovesick fool?

The Emperor reached behind him and took the ancient sword of his office from its stand, drawing it half out of its scabbard, without thinking.

And what of this woman and her son, he wondered? A maid of Lady Nishima, huh. I'm willing to wager a province that she was connected with the attempt on Shonto's life. If that is indeed what it was! Oh, Katta-sum, what a disappointment you are to me. This throne infects everyone around it with the desire to possess it. Worse than any woman, yeh? He laughed bitterly. The difference between us, Katta-sum, is that I possess this most desirable of women, the Throne, while you never shall.

There came a knock on the screen to his right and a servant opened the private door revealing his Sonsa mistress, a questioning smile on her face, her head cocked to one side showing the fine curve of her neck.

"Ah, Osha-sum!" He broke into a toothy grin as she came toward him, seeming to float as all the Sonsa did. The shoji closed behind her as she crossed the room, without a bow, directly into his arms in one lithe motion, seeming to curl all of herself against him at once. His face flushed and his pupils went wide with pleasure.

"How good to touch you, Sire. My body misses you."

"Since this morning?" he teased.

"Oh, yes. Certainly. It missed you as soon as we parted and gave me no peace all through my training. I danced so badly, completely unable to concentrate as a Sonsa should."

He kissed her neck and she arched it with pleasure. The fine silk of her kimono seemed almost as soft as her skin as he touched her. The bow of her sash came undone easily as soon as he pulled it and the Emperor realized it had been tied in a "lover's knot." He laughed at this discovery.

"Oh, ho! The servants will have noticed," he teased.

"Oh, no. It isn't possible, I can tie the knot perfectly. No one can tell the difference. I have practiced for you."

"You have so many talents that are never seen on the stage. Are all the Sonsa so talented?"

Her outer robe of sky blue fell open to reveal her three inner kimonos and these he opened slowly, kissing her shoulders, thrilled by the softness of her skin. Her breasts were tiny; he had never known a woman so small.

"The light in my chamber is beautiful this time of day," he whispered to her, his breathing already heavy. She took his face between her hands and kissed him passionately.

A shoji behind the dais opened into a hall that led to his sleeping chambers. Sunlight poured into the room through paper screens set high in the walls, a beautifully filtered light like the sun falling through forest leaves. A massive, low bed lay bathed in this light, its coverlets of flower patterns resembling the forest floor. They sank into this softness.

She did not find him unusual as a lover, this man who commanded so huge an Empire. In fact he would have been quite ordinary but for the passion he had for her which seemed boundless. And he was *strong*, stronger than she would have guessed and the Sonsa were usually unerring judges of the human body. The Son of Heaven knelt slowly, lifting her with him, supporting her with little effort.

When they finished, he was like a man who had fought a battle. He lay on top of her completely spent, his breathing deep and languorous. At that moment she always felt amazing abandon, and her mind wandered in the most surprising manner, leading her to wonder about other men, many of them, like the tiger-eyed Jaku Katta whom she had seen earlier as he came from his audience with the Emperor. And Lord Shonto, with whom she had danced the night before. She laughed at herself for these fantasies, calling herself "the secret Yellow Empress" after the Empress Jenna, who, it was said, had known a thousand men while she controlled her son on the Dragon Throne. It was even rumored that she had known her *own* son. Amazing!

Yes, she thought, that is me, the secret Yellow Empress, desiring every man who catches my eye. She laughed inwardly, desiring them but making love to them only when she danced, and making them want her in return.

Osha thought of Shonto as she lay warm and still aroused. She had brushed against him as they had danced the Dance of the Five Hundred Couples. A certain amount of flirtation was expected in these dances, but she had been *shameless* and had learned that he was hard-bodied, like a much younger man, and fluid in his movements for one with no training. The famous Lord Shonto, the man her Emperor hated. Osha had been so curious to know who this man was when the rumors were stripped away. But of course there had been no time for them to speak, not there. All she had learned was that he was quick of wit, which she had expected, and that he seemed to enjoy the company of younger people, surrounded as he was by his daughter's friends.

Why did the Emperor hate this man? Most curious. But he would never discuss Shonto with her, never Shonto. So very odd.

She drifted off into a soft dream, the *Yellow Empress* inside her given full rein. Osha smiled as she slept.

LORD SHONTO SAT on a low dais in the upper Audience Hall leaning on his armrest, chin in hand. He gazed out at the long, empty room and watched the dust particles turning slowly in the sunlight that streamed through the open wall. On the straw-matted floor a pattern of large rectangles glowed golden in the light that fell between the posts. The autumn day was warm, the air rich with the smells of the season.

Shonto consciously controlled his breathing and tried to empty his mind of all its noise. He needed time to think after the visit of Jaku Katta. The lord sensed danger. Things were happening too quickly, becoming a rising wave of events that he neither controlled nor understood.

No one realized how much hope Shonto placed on the coming of his Spiritual Advisor, and now that the hour of their meeting had arrived he felt sudden, and unexpected, doubt. This was not Brother Satake returning; this was a very young man, a stranger of questionable loyalty with a lifetime of Botahist dogma behind him . . . and little experience of the real world—the very unspiritual world of Wa. Over the years Shonto had grown used to the quiet opinions of his former advisor, and relied heavily on the old monk's penetrating insight—and that was what bothered Shonto. Satake-sum had had long years of experience that the lord, his junior by several decades, had been able to draw upon. But his new advisor was almost as many years his junior as Satake-sum had been his senior.

Shonto drummed his fingers on the armrest. The attack in the garden had affected him more than he liked to admit. How could such a thing have happened in his house? Oh, Jaku, my sixth sense tells me that you were behind this "assassination attempt." If so, I will soon know. Even a Black Tiger can place a foot wrongly. Even a Black Tiger can be hunted.

A tap on the shoji brought Shonto back to himself. The face of a guard appeared in the doorway.

"Tanaka is here, Sire," the guard said quietly—not "Tanaka-sum," just "Tanaka," the merchant, technically a servant.

Shonto nodded and the guard pushed the door aside, allowing a corpulent man in a dark robe of the merchant class to enter. Shonto did not smile, though Tanaka's "disguise" always amused him. In Yankura, the Floating City, where the merchant oversaw Shonto's vast trading interests, he was known for the quality of his clothing and his penchant for hats in the latest fashion. But here, before his liege-lord, he was somber and dressed in a far from new, traditional robe of his class.

The merchant bowed his head to the floor in the most humble manner and then sat back, saying nothing. The shoji closed behind him.

"Come forward," Shonto said, gesturing to a place before the dais.

Tanaka walked forward on his knees, stopping several paces away from his lord. Shonto regarded the merchant, a man who had served his father. A loyal man. Tanaka's intelligent face stared back at him and Shonto realized that the merchant was making his own assessment of his liege-lord. Shonto smiled.

"It is good to see you, old friend," the lord said, paying the older man greater respect than the use of the honorific "sum" could ever convey.

Tanaka bowed. "I am honored that you receive me, Sire. May I say that it is good to see you looking so well. I was most concerned when I heard of the events of this morning."

Shonto nodded, not surprised that the news had reached Tanaka. The merchant had his own sources in Shonto's staff, all well meaning, and impossible to purge for that very reason.

Except for the Lady Nishima, Tanaka was the closest thing to a friend Shonto had, and, in a way, their difference in rank was what allowed their friendship to exist—in Wa equals too often had conflicting interests. But the difference between Shonto and his merchant could never be bridged—master and servant always—and so the understanding between them, out of necessity, never seemed to breach the conventions of the society. But it was an association that both men valued and protected with all of their considerable powers.

"And how are things in the Floating City?"

"The Floating City seems to be floating these days on rumor and intrigue and an army of Imperial Guards dressed as anything but Imperial Guards."

"This is unusual?"

"Not perhaps unusual, Sire, but 'escalated.' This young Brother seems to have the servants of the Emperor most concerned."

"The actions of the servants of our Emperor can never be explained. Does your work go well?"

"Very well, Sire. This should be the most productive year ever. May I ask if you have heard the rumor that his Imperial Highness, in his wisdom, is considering outlawing coastal traffic in an effort to 'combat the pirates'?"

"I have heard this, though Jaku Katta-sum was here this morning and said nothing of it. Do you think it's true?"

"I hope not, Sire. It would have a great effect upon you and your allies. I believe that the Province of Seh would also feel the effects of such a law. Strange that this single action could be so entirely selective in whom it affects, yeh? Of course, we could survive it for a year, but even that would begin to tax us, and your allies—they would either be ruined or no longer allies. Personally, I believe we should consider other methods of dealing with this situation, if it arises."

"Other methods? Please continue, Tanaka-sum."

The merchant looked steadily at his lord for a second before speaking. "I make it my business to watch out for merchants who represent . . . powerful factions in Wa. If your interests are affected, I personally believe it would only be karma if these merchants I refer to were to be affected equally.

"If the pirates are deprived of coastal traffic to prey upon, they will no doubt be forced to turn to sea traffic. More difficult for them but not impossible, especially if they were to have certain intelligence, yeh? And there are ways of importing goods other than those sanctioned by the Son of Heaven."

"But those are outlawed and the penalty is death. Dangerous, yeh?"

"If you or your representative were to do so, Sire, certainly that would be dangerous, but others have their own business, their own karma."

"And how soon could these other methods be employed?"

"Tomorrow, Sire."

"Ah! So you have been anticipating this change in Imperial policy, old friend."

"It is my duty to guard your interests to the best of my ability, Sire. To that end, I make sure I hear rumors at their origin."

Shonto laughed and clapped his hands once, loudly. A screen opened to his right. "Bring cha for my guest and me.

"You are a most valuable man, Tanaka-sum. I think you should have a large estate on my fief to retire to when you are ready to rest. And your young son, the one with all the curiosity, if you approve, he shall go into my officer corps."

The merchant bowed formally, overwhelmed by the suddenness of these gifts. "Agree? Of course! How could I refuse these honors. I accept on my son's behalf. He shall make a fine officer, Sire, I'm sure of it. Thank you."

Shonto shrugged. Cha arrived in steaming pots and separate tables were set for the two men, a servant kneeling by each, but Shonto waved them away. "We will pour for ourselves."

When the shoji closed, Shonto leaned toward his guest. "So tell me about our young Brother."

"Ah." Tanaka lifted the lid of his tea pot to smell the steeping herb. "He is indeed something special, something out of the ordinary. You received my report of his sea crossing?"

"I read it while you bathed."

The vassal-merchant shook his head. "Strange, the man committing suicide like that—the Emperor's man. He had nothing to lose offering the poison to Shuyun-sum, yet he chose not to." The merchant looked up, catching the lord's eye. "He is a magnetic young man, Sire. He has that quiet strength all the Brothers have . . . but to a greater extent. He has . . ." Tanaka groped for words.

"*Tranquillity of purpose.*"

The merchant stopped short. "*Tranquillity of purpose*; yes, Sire.

"He met with Brother Hutto when he arrived in Yankura. I had no instructions, so I allowed him to do so."

"You acted correctly. How was the old monk?"

"I didn't go myself but sent guards as escort. They reported that Brother Hutto treated Shuyun-sum with great respect—almost as an equal."

"They exaggerate, surely! I would be surprised to hear that Brother Hutto thought the Emperor his equal."

"I was not there, Sire, but I believe the reports to be accurate."

"Huh. Did the two of you talk?"

"Some, Sire. He is like most Botahists, difficult to draw out, but even so I managed to find out a number of things."

"Such as?"

"He is well informed, Sire. The Brothers appear to have excellent sources of intelligence and obviously they have been preparing your advisor with care. His knowledge of the powers-that-be within Wa is good; his view of the political situation, broad; and, I must admit, he even has a working understanding of our economy, which I believe I have added to."

"No doubt. Did you talk of Seh?"

"Yes, and again he knew who the strongest lords were and what the history of their alliances has been. He knew who had married into which family and who could be considered as a possible ally. He views the entire endeavor with suspicion, though he said you were undoubtedly the finest general in Wa and the logical choice to send to Seh.

"Shuyun-sum also said something else, Sire, something I had not considered. He seems to think that there is a historical pattern in the barbarian wars, and that pattern, he believes, has now been broken." Tanaka paused as if gauging his lord's reaction, but Shonto said nothing so the merchant went on. "Shuyun-sum thinks that there is a twenty-five-year cycle in which the last seven years see an escalation which may or may not then lead to major war depending on the situation of the barbarian tribes. Our young Brother thinks that certain factors are critical at this point—the economy of the tribes, the strength of their leaders, the quality of the resistance they experience in Seh, and also the effects of the climate on what *they* call *agriculture*. All of these things affect their ability and their desire to mount a major campaign against the Empire. Shuyun-sum has pointed out that it has been over thirty years since the last Barbarian War."

"Interesting. Do you think this is his own observation?"

Tanaka stroked his beard, his gaze far away. "A good point, Sire, I don't know."

A message, Shonto wondered, is this a message from the monks? He poured his cha and Tanaka did likewise. The lord began his habit of turning the cup in his hand as he stared into its depths, looking for answers, for questions.

"Did you ask him how he will resolve the conflict between his service to the Shonto and his allegiance to the Brotherhood?"

"I did, Sire. He said the interests of the Brotherhood and your interests were not in conflict."

"I see. And?"

"He seems to believe it, Sire. He is young despite his abilities—only time can erase naïveté."

"His answer is not good enough, though it will do for now. Even the Botahist trained are not beyond influence . . . we shall see."

A swallow swooped through the open wall and out again, landing on the porch rail where it sat regarding the two men. Shonto watched the bird for a few seconds then said, his voice betraying a trace of weariness, "I heard a nightingale three evenings past, singing in the moonlight . . . it would be good to have peace again, yeh?"

"It would, Lord Shonto."

The two men sipped their cha and looked into the garden.

"Have you heard the most recent pronouncement of the Botahists' Supreme Master, Sire?"

Shonto turned his gaze from the swallow. "What now?"

"The Botahist Brothers have decided that though it's true women cannot attain enlightenment because they are too attached to the cycles of the earth, they can attain much greater spiritual knowledge than was formerly believed. Apparently they still think that women must finally be reborn as men before they can attain enlightenment. That point, they have not given up."

Shonto shook his head. "So, the celibate Brothers have finally realized that women have souls." The lord snorted. "How can such intelligent men suffer under so many delusions? If Brother Satake had become Supreme Master, he would have united the Sisterhood and Brotherhood and done away with this squabbling."

"That is one of the many reasons Satake-sum could not have become Supreme Master, Sire."

"True, my friend, true."

"The activities of the Botahist Brotherhood in the past years have begun to intrigue me, Sire. Their policies seem suddenly out of character, inconsistent."

Shonto's interest rose immediately, "I have thought the same thing, Tanaka-sum. The Brotherhood has never been known to ingratiate itself with anyone in the past, but now they recognize the Yamaku Dynasty of their own volition, receiving nothing in return but the Emperor's scorn; they gift the Son of Heaven valuable land, again receiving nothing in compensation; and now this sop to the Botahist Sisters. I believe that even I have been treated unusually. Kamu-sum arranged a most reasonable price for the services of our young Brother. He was full of suspicion afterward."

Tanaka shook his head, causing a golden drop of cha to fall from his mustache onto his dark robe. "The Empire is in the grip of some strange magic, Sire. I would have said that the Botahists would never lose their arrogance, their nerve, yet look at this! I do not understand. They must know that, despite his own convictions, the Emperor could never touch the Brotherhood without bringing about his own downfall. His own soldiers would take his head if the Guardians of Botahara's Word were ever threatened. I am less and less sure of what transpires in the Empire. Excuse me, Sire, I don't mean to sound pessimistic."

"Good, there is enough pessimism among my retainers over this appointment to Seh, and then this omen, this 'assassination attempt.' Huh!"

"It is only concern for their liege-lord, Sire. There is more to this appointment to Seh than meets the eye. Everyone feels that. We all fear treachery from this family that calls itself Imperial. We all fear the Yamaku trap."

Shonto's nostrils flared. "I've been in and out of a dozen traps in my time and have only wisdom to show for it. Have my own retainers come to doubt me?"

"Never, Sire! Their faith in you in unshakable, but they are concerned nonetheless, because they honor you, and the Shonto House."

Shonto sat for a moment staring into his cha. A knock at the entryway seemed loud in the silence. The screen slid open and a guard's face appeared.

"Excuse me, Sire. Kamu-sum has sent the message you requested."

"Ah. Enter."

The servant, Toko, who had earlier in the day become an assistant to Kamu, knelt in the doorway and bowed. Shonto motioned him forward and he moved, kneeling, with the grace of one who has performed this act countless times. Removing a scroll from his sleeve and setting it within Shonto's reach on the dais, he bowed again and retreated the appropriate distance.

Shonto checked the seal on the scroll and then broke it, finding Kamu's spidery brushwork inside. "You may go," he said to the boy. When the shoji slid closed behind the servant, Shonto turned to his merchant. "After I have met with Shuyun-sum, you will join me in a meal with the young Lord Komawara. You remember his father?"

Tanaka nodded.

"The old Komawara sold a piece of his fief before his death, undoubtedly to allow the son to begin trade; so the new Lord of the Komawara is here to begin this endeavor. He will need guidance." Shonto consulted the scroll again and quoted a substantial sum in Imperial ril. "I wouldn't think he has the entire amount available, but we will assume he has a good portion of it. Do you have some venture he could invest in that would prove profitable?"

"For a knowledgeable man this is a time of great opportunities. I'm sure we can get the young lord started, but truly he should have his own vassal-merchant, Sire."

"But finding or training such a man takes time and I want him in Seh, not here."

"In that case I believe I can accommodate him until a suitable vassal-merchant can be found. I may be able to locate an acceptable person myself, if this would serve your purpose, Lord Shonto. But, Sire, surely you should assess him some part of his profit otherwise he will feel it is charity—a proud man would not allow that."

"As always, your advice is sound, Tanaka-sum. What would be appropriate in such a case?"

Tanaka caught the corner of his mustache between his teeth and worried it for a second, making his lord smile.

"Eight parts per hundred would be too generous, Sire . . . twelve parts would be fair."

Shonto smiled again. "Ten, then. I will suggest it over the meal. I want this young man treated with respect, old friend. He is not powerful in Seh, but he seems knowledgeable and that will be just as important."

"And he is the son of your father's friend," Tanaka said.

"Yes. He is the son of my father's friend," Shonto repeated.

Tanaka nodded and filed the figures away in his fine memory. Even as he did so, the merchant found himself observing his lord carefully. He had watched Shonto all the nobleman's impressive life—had watched the precocious child grow into the strong-willed young man, the young man become the head of one of the most powerful Houses in Wa. It had been an inspiring process to witness. Tanaka, though fourteen years older, had had his own education to concern him in those days, but still he had come to know Shonto Motoru—had come to admire him. The man Tanaka saw before him now looked like the gii master that indeed he was—a man who surveyed the board in all of its complexity without thought of losing. A man who came alive to challenge.

Tanaka had often played gii with Shonto when they were young; the lord had learned the game too quickly and left the merchant-to-be far behind, but still he remembered the Shonto style forming—bold and subtle in turns. Equally strong on defense or offense. Shonto would understand the traps Tanaka laid better than the merchant understood them himself, sometimes stepping into them with impunity and turning them against their surprised designer. Yet the peaceful life of the gii master was not possible for the bearer of the Shonto name and the lord had indulged his passion for the game for only a short time. In the end he had made gii subservient to his larger needs—using his skill at the board to make a point to any of his generals who questioned his decisions too often. The military men prided themselves on their ability at the gii board, yet few in all of Wa had the skill to sit across the board from the Lord of the Shonto as an equal.

"It seems a long time since the days when we played gii, Sire."

Shonto smiled warmly, "We still play gii, my friend, but the board has become larger than we ever imagined and now we share the pieces of the same side. Individually we are strong, together we are formidable. Don't ever think I'm unaware of this. The world has changed, Tanaka-sum; for better or for worse doesn't matter, it has changed irrevocably and therefore so must we. A strong arm and a sharp sword are not what they once were. We play a different game now, and in the next exchanges you will be a general in your own right. The Shonto interests must be protected at all costs. They are the basis of our future strength. Never forget that."

The merchant nodded and then, emboldened by his lord's confidence, spoke quietly, asking the question that weighed on him, "Why are you going to Seh, Lord Shonto?"

Without pause Shonto answered, "Because my Emperor commands it and therefore it is my duty."

Tanaka's eyes flicked to Shonto's sword in its stand and back to the lord. "I heard of the Emperor's empty threat at his party. He cannot possibly believe you will fail?"

"No, I'm sure he doesn't. The barbarians are already beaten." Shonto paused and tapped his armrest with his fingers. "And who else could he send to Seh that has my battle experience? Jaku Katta? No. He likes to keep the Black Tiger close to him, and not just for his protection. Lord Omawara is dying, I'm sad to say. There are a few others who have the fighting skills but would not command the respect of the men of Seh. The plague and the Interim Wars have destroyed a generation of worthy generals, Tanaka-sum. I am his only choice and yet . . . he thinks I am his greatest threat. So, until the barbarians are put down, I believe I am safe from whatever the Emperor plots. I have a year—an entire year—that must be long enough."

The two men were silent then. Lord Shonto poured more cha, but it was overly strong so he let it sit and did not call for more.

"I am ready to meet my Spiritual Advisor now. Perhaps my spirit has need of this, yeh?" He clapped his hands twice and servants scurried in to remove the tables and the cha bowls. The guard opened the shoji at the far end of the hall. "Please bring in Brother Shuyun and the honored Brother."

Shonto felt his fists clenching involuntarily and he forced them to open, assuming a posture of studied ease. In the back of his mind he heard his own voice saying that Brother Satake would not have been fooled by this act. Satake-sum had missed nothing—not the tiniest detail.

Guards opened the screens at the end of the hall to their full width and a young monk, accompanied by a senior Botahist Brother, stepped inside. Yes, Shonto thought, he is the one, and visions of a kick boxing tournament years before flashed before his eyes.

The two men bowed in the manner of their Order, a quick double bow, low but not touching the floor, a gesture reserved only for the seniors of their faith or the Emperor.

Shonto stared at the small monk, ignoring his companion. Young, the lord thought, so young. Yet he seemed calm under this scrutiny. But was it real, Shonto wondered, was it that same inner stillness that his predecessor had possessed? Brother Satake had been a man who had not been in a perpetual state of reaction—constantly vibrating with the motion around him. With Satake-sum, there had been only stillness and silence—what the old monk had called "tranquillity of purpose," something Shonto had been able to achieve only to the smallest degree. "I offer no resistance," Satake-sum had answered when Shonto had questioned him, and that was all the explanation the lord had ever received.

Now Shonto found himself staring at this young man and trying to detect this same quality in the first seconds of their meeting.

He nodded and then spoke formally, "Come forward, honored Brothers, I welcome you to my House."

The two monks stopped within a respectful distance of the dais, Shuyun kneeling so that the shadow of a post fell in a dark diagonal across his chest, leaving his hands and his face in golden sunlight.

"Brothers, I am honored by your presence as is my House."

The older monk spoke in a soft voice that rasped deep in his throat. "The honor, Lord Shonto, is ours. I am Brother Notua, Master of the Botahist Faith, and this is Brother Shuyun."

Shonto nodded toward his Spiritual Advisor, noting the fine structure of his cleanly shaven face, the perfect posture without trace of stiffness. But the eyes unsettled him—the eyes did not seem to belong to the face. They were neither young nor old, but somehow ageless, as though they viewed time differently, and remained unaffected by it. Shonto realized that everyone was politely waiting for him to speak.

"Your journey has not been uneventful, I am told."

The young monk nodded. "There was a sad occurrence on board ship, Lord Shonto, but it found resolution."

"And the young girl?"

"She was well at the time she was taken from the boat, but understandably unhappy."

"I am curious about this incident, this merchant Kogami. He was a servant of the Emperor?"

"It would appear so, Sire."

"Did you realize that, Brother?"

The older monk observed this exchange carefully. He was surprised that Shonto had gone into this incident so soon, almost before it was polite to do so. Of course what was polite for a Botahist Brother and what was considered so for the Lord of the Shonto were different things.

"I thought it was so. The priest invoked the Emperor's protection during our confrontation . . . and then there was the poison. Such treachery is the way of the priests."

Shonto was silent for a moment. "And the priest, what happened to him?"

"He was met in the Floating City by Imperial Guards dressed as followers of Tomso." He said this with assurance and the lord did not doubt it was the truth.

"Huh. In the future you will not go beyond the walls of a Shonto residence without guards. The Empire is yet unstable and dangerous even to the disciples of the Perfect Master." Shonto looked around suddenly as if something were missing. "May I offer you mead, Brothers?"

Servants appeared at Shonto's call, and tables, laid with cups and flasks of fine mead, were set before the guests. Polite inquiries into the health of one's family would normally have followed, but Shonto turned again to the young monk. "Brother Shuyun, you should know that you replace a man I esteemed above all but my own father. You take up a difficult position."

"Brother Satake was an exceptional man and as honored in our Order as he was in your House, Sire. I'm sure he was irreplaceable. It is my hope that I may be of equal value to you in my own way."

Shonto nodded, seeming to find this answer acceptable. He hesitated a moment and then said, "Brother Satake, in an uncharacteristic moment, once demonstrated what he called 'Inner Force' by breaking a rather stout oar that had been placed across the gunnels of a sampan. He accomplished this by merely pressing down upon it with his hand without being able to bring the weight of his body to bear, for he was sitting at the time. None of the oarsmen could do this, and they were as strong as any of their profession, nor could I, and I was a younger man then. Do you know how this feat is performed, Brother?"

Shuyun shrugged slightly. "I am Botahist trained," he answered simply, and Shonto saw the young man's eyes dart to the table before him.

Shonto clapped and servants slid aside the shoji. "Remove these things from Brother Shuyun's table."

After doing their master's bidding, the servants bowed and backed toward the exit.

"No, stay," Shonto said on impulse. I will have all the servants know of this, he thought. Then, committed to this course of action, Shonto clapped his hands twice and ordered the guard to enter and observe.

Brother Notua cleared his throat and then spoke in his soft voice, the rasp more pronounced than before, "Excuse me, Lord Shonto, but this is most . . . unexpected."

Shonto drew himself up and answered, enunciating each word with care,

"Is it not the custom that I should test the monk who is to be in my service *for a lifetime?*"

"It is, Lord Shonto. Excuse me if I appeared to criticize." The old monk smiled sweetly. "It just seemed to me . . . Shuyun-sum has so many talents," the monk looked up at the fire in the lord's eyes. "Of course, this matter is for you to decide, excuse me for interrupting, I . . . please excuse me." He fell silent.

Shonto turned to Shuyun, "Do you have objections to this test, Shuyun-sum?"

"I am ready to begin, Sire, if that is your wish."

Shonto paused, deciding. "Begin," he said. He watched as the young monk entered a meditative state, slowing his breathing, his eyes focused on something unseen. Glancing at the older monk, Shonto realized that he, too, had begun to meditate. Strange, Shonto thought, but his attention was taken up by the younger monk.

Shuyun focused his being on the table in front of him. Time slowed and he followed the pattern of his breathing, a pattern as familiar to him as the halls of Jinjoh Monastery.

The table before him was beautifully made of iroko wood, a wood so dense that it would sink in water; "Iron Tree" it was called by the peasants who cut it. The top was twice the thickness of a man's hand, two hand lengths across, and stood at a convenient height for a person kneeling. Shuyun knew the table's joinery would be flawless and each plank selected for its strength and beauty—there could be no weakness in the structure, so there could be no weakness in his will.

In the sunlight streaming into the room, the monk's face appeared as peaceful as the face on a bronze statue of Botahara. Very slowly he drew his hand in a low arc and placed it, palm down, on the center of the table. The tight grain of the wood felt warm against his skin. Sunlight illuminated the fine hairs on the back of his hand and forearm. *He pushed.*

There was no visible change in the young monk's body, no sign of strain. And the table stood as solid as if it were carved from stone.

Botahara forgive me, Shonto thought, I have set him a task at which he must fail. Memories of an oar shattering came to him. Shonto cursed himself for this ill-considered act. Hadn't the old Brother tried to warn him?

Suddenly there was a sharp *crack*, and slivers of dark wood flew in all directions, spinning in the sunlight. The old monk drew back like one who has been brutally awakened by a slap, and on his face, clear for all to see, was a look of fear. The table had not buckled, it had exploded.

Guards and servants stood in the hall like statues of stone. The table lay smashed in the center like an animal broken under its load. Shonto slowly picked a sliver of iroko wood off his robe and turned it in his hand as though it were entirely alien material. No one else moved, no one spoke, preserving the moment as long as possible. Then Shonto bowed low to his Spiritual Advisor and everyone in the room followed his example.

Shuyun watched through his altered time sense as Lord Shonto bowed, watched the ripple of muscle that showed even through the man's robe.

Slowly Shonto returned to a kneeling position, his awe apparent, even to those not Botahist trained. But there was more than awe, there was wonder—wonder at what he had seen in the old monk's face.

Shuyun bowed in response as deeply as the shattered table would allow. He began the return to real-time; the sound of the birds changed tone, he watched Lord Shonto blink and the movement took only a fraction of a second.

Shonto nodded to the guard and the servants, dismissing them. "Shuyun-sum, my steward Kamu will take you on a tour of the grounds and give you the passwords. Please join us for the midday meal with Lord Komawara. Thank you." Shonto nodded to the monk, again with deference. "Brother Notua, please leave your papers with my secretary. It has been an honor."

The two monks bowed again and Shonto was sure that the older monk faltered almost imperceptibly as he rose but caught himself and backed from the room with dignity, leaving the lord in a state of confusion.

Shonto and Tanaka were alone again, but neither of them spoke. Before them the table lay broken, and Shonto noticed for the first time that the legs were pressed through the thick floor mats. He turned to Tanaka who was plucking a spear of iroko wood from his beard. Like his lord, he examined it carefully, as though it had a secret to reveal.

"How much weight would that table bear?" Shonto asked.

Tanaka shook his head and shrugged. "The weight of five large men?"

"Easily," Shonto shook his head. "Impossible, yeh?"

"According to my understanding of the principles of nature, yes, Sire. Even if it were possible for him to bring his entire weight to bear from a sit-

ting position, he should have merely pushed himself away from the table."
He shook his head and turned the sliver in his hands again. "I'm glad I saw
this with my own eyes, otherwise I would not have believed it."

Shonto said nothing for several long moments. He considered asking
Tanaka if he had seen the old Brother's reaction but something stopped him.
Finally his eyes came back into focus and his face brightened. He smiled
broadly. "A most interesting morning, Tanaka-sum! I wish to refresh myself
before Lord Komawara arrives. Please join us later, in the summerhouse in
the main garden."

He clapped his hands twice and spoke to the guard and servants who appeared. "See that no one disturbs this." He gestured to the broken table.
Rising, the lord turned to leave by his private entrance, a servant rushing to
take up his sword and follow.

Tanaka bowed but did not move until Lord Shonto was gone, then he
went closer to the table, full of curiosity. The guard, who had positioned
himself inside the door, cleared his throat. The merchant looked up. "Amazing, yeh?"

The guard nodded but continued to stare at Tanaka.

Suddenly the merchant realized that he still held the shard of iroko wood.
He raised it. "What shall I do with this?"

"Lord Shonto ordered that nothing was to be disturbed."

"Ah, I see." Tanaka looked suddenly puzzled. "But as this clung to my
beard, and I don't think Lord Shonto wished me to remain here until he has
made a decision on what he will do with this table, I am puzzled."

The guard realized that Tanaka was having fun with him and despite the
fact that Tanaka was a servant and the guard was an officer, there was no
doubt in the man's mind that Tanaka was far more important to Lord Shonto
than any legion of soldiers. "I think it should stay in the room, Tanaka-sum,"
the guard said, using the honorific.

"But anywhere I put it will not be its natural place and, therefore things
will be disturbed, yeh?"

The guard felt his temperature begin to rise, but he remained outwardly
calm. If the merchant forced him to go to Shonto to clarify what should be
done about a sliver of wood, the lord would be furious. The guard shifted
uncomfortably.

"Perhaps," Tanaka offered, "I could place it near where I sat and that will
be the best we can do, yeh?"

The guard broke into a grateful smile. "Yes, I agree. That would be best. Thank you, Tanaka-sum."

The merchant returned the smile and set the piece of iroko wood on the floor in the agreed position and then swept out of the room with as much grace and confidence of manner as a lord.

Neither guard nor merchant was aware that a servant watched all of this through a crack between shojis, and that when he repeated the incident to Kamu, who had him repeat it to Shonto, the lord laughed and banged his fist on his armrest with pleasure. The servant was greatly surprised by this reaction. Humor was sadly lacking among Shonto's retainers.

Seven

> *The canal beyond my garden*
> *Is like a dark vein,*
> *And yet I cannot*
> *Take my eyes from it.*
> *Where has he gone this long night?*
> *And why does the canal*
> *Flow so loudly?*

Origin unknown but attributed to
the poetess, Lady Nikko,
or one of her students

LORD KOMAWARA SAMYAMU, the ninth Komawara Lord to be so named, watched the bustle on the canal's edge as his boatmen deftly guided his sampan among the throng of craft that filled the waterway. He had chosen to pass through a commercial area where cargo from the Floating City arrived, not because this was the most scenic or the quickest route to the House of Lord Shonto Motoru, but because Komawara wanted to see the variety and volume of trade—to see the commerce of the capital with his own eyes.

Soon, he thought, soon Komawara goods will arrive at these very quays and then there will be a change in the Komawara fortunes.

The young lord's sampan was preceded by only a single boat, in which rode his guard, and neither craft was of the ornate variety commonly seen in the capital. Komawara's steward had pressed him to hire more boats of better quality so the young lord would not arrive at the Shonto estate looking like a country pauper, but Komawara had decided against this. Shonto, he knew, was too clever a man to be impressed by appearances and it was also likely he would have made himself familiar with Komawara's exact situation. Shonto would be able to acquire such information with ease, and would do so, of course, with a new associate.

Yes, Komawara thought, and it is likely that no one, not even the Emperor, knows the scope of Shonto's holdings. I would look the fool to arrive in hired sampans, to wear a lie.

I am of an ancient House, he reminded himself, as ancient as the Emperor's. I have fought twenty skirmishes with the barbarians, a handful of duels, and I taught those cattle thieves, the Tomari, that the boundaries of my fief cannot be encroached upon. Shonto is a general of great renown; he will judge me by what is important, I need have no doubt.

Yet the Lord of the Komawara did have doubts. He was on his way to meet the Lord of the Shonto, and who knew who else, for a meal. The Shonto! A family with a history unlike any other's. To think that Hakata the Wise, upon whose teachings were based all the principles of the Empire's government and law, had been a retainer of Shonto's ancestors. Generations ago a Shonto lord had sat with Hakata himself and discussed justice and moral philosophy as today people discussed the thoughts of the Wise One at their own tables. It was a Shonto lord who had the writings of Hakata inscribed upon the One Hundred and Three Great Stones that lined the Walk of Wisdom in the Shonto garden. The One Hundred and Three Great Stones at the Emperor's Palace and at the Imperial Academy were but copies of the Shonto originals.

Yet the man Komawara had met at the Emperor's party had not seemed at all impressed with his own greatness. In fact, he had seemed very direct, a man who had no time for vanity and who spoke from the heart. Komawara had liked him immensely.

And the daughter, Komawara thought, a smile appearing involuntarily. But then he shook his head and the smile disappeared. She is to be an Imperial Princess, perhaps an Empress, and I——I am the poor Komawara from Seh. My family is ancient enough, but my holdings are nothing. He sighed.

And the cousin!——she is even more beautiful. But she is also more dangerous. Even the cold-fish Emperor becomes a boy in front of her. With a wife like that I would be lost. I would abandon all the pastimes of true men and do nothing but write love poems and court. What a fool I would become! Ah, well, there is little danger that I will wed Kitsura Omawara, so I need not lose sleep in worry.

Komawara gazed at the scene around him. Ships of all sizes, though of common design, lined the quay—the shallow draft river junk with its high stern and blunt prow. The bargemen, many bare from the waist up even on this cool autumn day, worked quickly, swinging cargo ashore with booms and tackle. The smaller junks of the river people swept past in every direction, without course or thought to safety, whole families sculling with all their strength and yelling at every boat within range as they moved goods out to the inns and the myriad shops and private homes of the Imperial Capital. Komawara reached out and trailed his hand in the cool water.

He marveled at how clean the canals were. The Imperial Edicts governing the waterways forbade the dumping of refuse, dunnage, or human waste into the canals. The penalties for doing so were severe in the extreme. Yet, Komawara thought, perhaps they need not be so. Human waste was used to fertilize the rice fields of the great plain and the capital provided the majority of that most essential material—he had seen the dung barges early that very morning. Beyond that, the people of Wa were never wasteful and always fastidious by nature. But, the lord thought, the waterways of Wa are the veins and arteries of the Empire and we would die without them. Their preservation cannot be left to chance.

They passed out of the main canal and down a byway lined with prosperous inns and tea houses. Traffic on the waterway thinned. Along the stone quays lining the canal walked merchants and minor peers, landholders, and not a few soldiers—among them Komawara thought he saw the blue of Shonto livery.

Areas such as this attracted him, they were perfect places to gather gossip. He had spent a good deal of time on this trip sitting in tea houses and frequenting inns, listening to conversations, asking questions, enjoying the role of the naive young lord from the outer provinces. He had learned a great deal. For instance, that very morning he had overheard two Imperial Guards whispering about a failed attempt on Shonto's life!

He also knew, as did most of the population, that Shonto had paid the Botahist Brothers for the services of a Spiritual Advisor. The Emperor,

Komawara thought, will not be pleased. Yet it might be worth the displeasure of the Son of Heaven to have one of the Botahist trained in your service. But what a price it must be, he thought. How many could afford the cost of such an advisor? No, it wasn't the money that made the Botahists' services prohibitive—it was the greater cost—the displeasure of Akantsu II, Emperor of Wa. Very few could pay that price, very few indeed.

They turned again, into an area of residences this time—not the residences of the great, they were further toward the outskirts. Komawara himself might afford a home in this area one day soon. He admired the houses set in their small gardens, half hidden by walls, and imagined himself as prospective buyer, choosing among the better locations, imagining which garden received the afternoon light. He laughed at this fantasy, and turned back to his thoughts.

So Shonto will come to Seh. When he sees the truth of my situation there, will his interest in me disappear? He had no sure answer to this question. All he could be certain of was that Shonto was known for his loyalty, and their fathers had shared a mutual respect. My fortunes can't help but rise with the good will of the Shonto . . . as long as the Son of Heaven does not become too disaffected by Shonto's independence. Perhaps I should advise the lord against taking on this monk? Komawara rejected the thought immediately. Shonto, he knew, had advisors of great renown—he must be careful not to presume too much.

It is not my place to advise Shonto Motoru, he thought, not yet. Though when he comes to the north, Shonto will need all the support he can arrange. The men of Seh do not take kindly to the suggestion that they cannot deal with the barbarians themselves.

He pondered again the behavior of the savage people and found it, as usual, unexplainable.

Ah, well, Komawara thought, if all goes as I hope, I will have a powerful ally, an ally who will soon be the Governor of Seh. So few days in the capital and already my fortunes have begun to rise! But perhaps I should be careful not to alienate the Son of Heaven entirely. It has been nine generations since a Komawara resided in the Governor's Palace in Seh. That, he thought, is too long.

Beyond the garden of Shonto Motoru were arranged the other gardens of the estate. Some, like Shonto's, were small, enclosed and private, while others were open, with large areas of lawn for outdoor entertainment. Pathways bordering ponds wove in and out of the stands of exotic trees, then ascended to the next terrace into a garden with a different theme, another purpose.

Streams meandered, seemingly without design, among arbors, under the arches of bridges, and through stands of cherry and willow and pine.

Lord Komawara could not help but compare these gardens with his own in Seh—the comparison was humbling. And this, the lord realized, was Shonto's secondary residence!

He followed Shonto's steward down a long, tiled portico. The steward, Kamu, had met him at the gate and despite the young lord's lack of entourage, had greeted Komawara like an old and honored friend of the Shonto family. Komawara knew of the one-armed old man by reputation. In fact, his own father had spoken of him often, for Kamu had been a great swordsman in his day—a man around whom legends had grown. In Seh such a man would have been made a minor peer, but it was known that Kamu felt it a greater honor to serve the House of Shonto than to be a lord in the outer provinces. There were many who would make the same choice.

Turning a corner, they came at last to a gate, which Kamu opened before standing aside to allow Komawara to step through. The old man bowed as he passed. "Lord Shonto awaits you, Lord Komawara. May your stay with us be pleasant."

Komawara Samyamu bowed and went through the gate. A set of steps, made of stones set into the bank, led the lord up into a stand of pines. The aromatic scent was strong on the breeze and reminded Komawara of the forests of Seh. The path branched, and on the walkway which turned left, a fist-sized stone tied with a thong of softened bamboo marked the way he should take.

Intentionally, Lord Komawara slowed his pace and began to observe the details of his surroundings. It was possible that the path left unmarked was the more direct route to the place where he would meet Shonto, but this way had been chosen for him, perhaps for a certain autumn flower that bloomed there, or because there was a view Lord Shonto wished his guest to see. There could even be a message on this pathway, and if that were so, he must not miss it. Lord Komawara opened his senses and breathed as if in meditation.

The path rolled down a low hill, the large flat walking stones, like footprints disappearing among the pines. Rocks, forming a grotto, grew up around him, and then, a few paces on, he was again in a pine arbor. Moss carpeted the floor, thick and green in the sunlight that filtered through the branches. The path forked once more and again the walkway to his left was marked. This footpath also wove its way down, giving him the illusion that he descended into a valley.

The notes of a flute carried to him on the breeze and he paused to listen. The tune was unfamiliar, melancholy, haunting. Komawara thought for moment of the beautiful Lady Nishima and wondered if this hidden musician could be her.

He went on, not wishing to keep Lord Shonto waiting, while still taking the time appropriate to the enjoyment of the walk his host had planned for him. He came to a small arched bridge crossing a stream where the water babbled among sounding-stones, and then the path turned to follow the water course a few paces through lime trees. The branches parted to reveal a pond—a pond carpeted in yellow water lilies, the favorite flower of his father.

Lord Komawara sat on a boulder of coarse granite and gazed out upon the lily pond. "I knew your father," the message said, "he was an esteemed friend. Here we may honor his memory, in this place he would have loved." Komawara Samyamu looked down at his sandaled feet and there, beside the boulder grew the flower of his House, the pale mist-lily. And there, the blossoms appeared at the bowl of a weeping birch, a tree which symbolized purity of purpose; close by, the shinta blossom, symbol of the Shonto House, was planted between carefully arranged stones—the symbol for both hardship and loyalty.

Lord Komawara's hand fumbled for the familiar feel of his sword hilt, but it was not to be found, for it had been left in the care of Kamu. He rose, not quite sure where he was going. Inside him he felt his spirit swelling, the memory of his father seemed to inhabit him and he felt strangely at peace with himself, with his surroundings.

Setting his feet before him, he turned back to the path though his body moved as if it were without weight. The way rose up again among birch trees whose leaves had begun to yellow with the autumn. Up, until the pond of lilies lay in a pattern below, like embroidery on a woman's kimono. Rising behind the pond, he could see the borrowed scenery, blue mountains, far off, maned white like the ghosts of lions.

Here on this rise he found a tiny summerhouse of rustic design and the plainest material. Through the round "window of the moon" that overlooked the pond, Komawara could see the silhouette of a sitting man. Lord Shonto Motoru.

As he came around to the open side of the structure, Komawara saw that Shonto sat before a table studying a large map. The young lord bowed formally. Shonto looked up, and he smiled and nodded in return.

"Lord Komawara. Please join me." He gestured to a cushion to his right and Lord Komawara stepped out of his sandals and entered the summerhouse.

Through the window of the moon, the lily pond and the rest of the grounds spread out below with the mountains behind providing both balance and contrast. The view from the adjoining open side was of the hills northeast of the city with the Hill of Divine Inspiration, and its several large temples, off in the distance.

On a small, round stand, below the window of the moon, a plain vase held an arrangement of pine boughs and branch-maple, the leaves red with the passing season while the pine symbolized constancy of life. It was a simple arrangement, elegant and carefully executed.

The map before Lord Shonto covered the areas from north of the capital to the northern steppes, the point where Seh ended and the lands of the barbarians began. Komawara glanced down upon it expectantly, but Shonto acted as though the map were not there.

"Would you care for mead or rice wine? Cha, perhaps?"

"Thank you, wine would be perfect."

"You enjoyed your evening at the palace?" Shonto asked as he raised his hand, turning it slightly in signal to an unseen servant.

"Yes, it was most enjoyable. I must say that your daughter plays beautifully."

"Lady Nishima will be pleased to hear you've said that. Perhaps she will join us later," Shonto said and saw Lord Komawara's pupils go wide with pleasure. "It is unfortunate that on such short notice I could not have invited Lady Kitsura also. She is such pleasant company, don't you think?"

Komawara laughed. "Yes, most certainly. But if you surround the table with such beauty, I would be unable to concentrate on anything else. Even now, this view and your perfect garden call for my attention. But of course, you are a more disciplined man than I, Lord Shonto. I see that you can concentrate on the task at hand," Komawara gestured to the map, "without falling prey to distractions."

Shonto smiled. A servant arrived and poured wine in silence.

"Do not confuse lack of choice with discipline. I am forced by circumstances to contemplate the details of my pending journey to Seh." Shonto sipped the cool wine and looked down at the map before him. "Did you encounter any difficulties on your journey south?"

Komawara followed the lord's gaze, tracing the route he had taken from Seh—seven hundred rih along the Grand Canal. "I traveled with a moderately large force, my own guard and a group of other travelers. We saw no sign of bandits, though we heard many stories of others who were not so fortunate. Here," Komawara placed a finger on the map about halfway to Seh, "I was delayed by the Butto-Hajiwara feud, but we were eventually allowed to pass when it became apparent that we were no threat to either side. I paid no bribe myself—I refused!—but others paid rather than wait. That is their business. The Hajiwara delay everyone, hoping to see profit from those whose time is of value. They are just short of levying a tax for passage, but I believe that would finally stir the Emperor to some action."

"Huh, an unfortunate situation, this feud."

"Yes and it should not be allowed to continue. A war that disrupts traffic on an Imperial waterway is unacceptable! The Butto and the Hajiwara are virtually demanding tribute from those foolish enough to pay. And the Emperor allows this!" The young lord took a drink of his wine, embarrassed by his outburst.

"I am concerned about this situation myself. I do not wish to be delayed on my way to Seh. Do you recall the manner in which the battle lines were drawn when you passed?"

Lord Komawara set his cup down and began to study the map, placing an elbow on the table as he bent over the intricate cartography. He began to massage his brow in a manner Shonto realized was reminiscent of his father.

The area that had become the center of the dispute between the Butto and the Hajiwara was a gorge on the Grand Canal, surrounded by high granite cliffs. On the map the gorge appeared as a swelling in the canal, with a small, almost round, island in its center, making the gorge look like an eye with an island pupil—the eye of the storm that raged around it. At either end of the gorge, locks were situated and these were held by the opposing armies, which possessed fiefs on either side of the river. Only at the captured locks did either family have a foothold on the other's land.

Komawara Samyamu, as a warrior and native to Seh, the only province in the Empire forced to defend its borders, had taken an immediate interest in the war, and it was this perspective that Shonto valued.

The young lord placed his finger on the map. "The southern locks are held by the Butto and all along their flank they have established earthworks on the Hajiwara lands. These fortifications were not built overnight and have been planned with skill using the natural terrain to its best possible advantage." Komawara ran his hand in an arc along the west bank of the river. "The outer fortifications, which consist of earthen and reinforced siege walls and trenches, run from the cliffs above the river, here, to an outcropping of granite that I would place here." The long finger tapped the paper. "The inner fortifications are strongly built of wood and are protected from behind by the cliffs. A bridge across the canal has stone palisades guarding either end but on the eastern shore, the Butto side, there are no fortifications, though the guard towers placed along the canal bank are only a stone's throw apart.

"The Hajiwara have not had to prepare in quite the same way, as they took the Imperial guard tower situated beside the northern locks. This tower sits on an outcropping, which forms a large natural, and quite unassailable, fortress. Whether the Son of Heaven was involved in this is a point that many still debate, though I myself doubt this theory. I believe the Hajiwara took the castle through the simplest tactic of all: bribery. It is their way. From the tower they have managed to push their front out across the plain as far as these low hills. Here the Butto have contained them and the battle lines remain static."

"What is your opinion of these palisades? Could they be breached?" Shonto asked.

Komawara looked at Lord Shonto, wondering if the great general was patronizing him but decided this was not so—the Lord of the Shonto had no need to do that. Komawara also realized that Shonto would already have thorough intelligence on this situation—so he must be testing the younger man, finding out what he knew, how he thought. Komawara forced a calm over his mind, realizing that much of his future would depend on his answer.

"The fortifications have no apparent weakness that I know of and both have a very great advantage in that their backs are protected by cliffs and, across bridges, the opposite shores are entirely in their control for many rih.

"To overcome either stronghold, it would be necessary to cut the bridges and isolate them. A massive frontal attack and sustained siege would no doubt be effective in time, but this would take months. The bridges could possibly be rebuilt during that time, and this would almost certainly save them." Komawara realized he was speaking his thoughts, wondering aloud, but no inspired answer came.

"Stealth," he said finally. "Stealth and surprise. I know no other way. The bridge would have to be taken or another way found to enter either fortress. It would be difficult, perhaps not even possible, but it is the only way." Komawara stopped again, his mind racing, realizing that he had no solution, nor any way of finding one so far from the fortresses that guarded the canal. I have failed the test, he thought, and tried not to show this feeling of failure.

Shonto nodded, not taking his eyes from the map. "My generals all say the same, but as of yet we have no solution to the problem. Perhaps we will not need one. I thank you for your counsel." Shonto nodded, as though satisfied, and began to slowly roll the map.

The next signal Shonto gave was so subtle that Lord Komawara did not see it, but Shonto turned to him suddenly and asked, "I would be honored if you would take a moment to meet my vassal-merchant; you may find what he has to say of interest."

Shonto said all of this in a tone which indicated how trivial a matter this was to lords of their stature, but they should indulge this man whose concern was money, as one would indulge a very old relative.

"I would be honored, Lord Shonto. I would not think it an interruption at all." Komawara answered, copying Lord Shonto's manner of amusement and politeness.

And at this, the merchant Tanaka appeared, coming up the rise. He was dressed in clothes identical to those he had worn earlier and he walked in the manner of a servant, eyes down, his face serious, all of his motions subdued. After the story he had been told about Tanaka's interchange with the guard, Shonto almost laughed to see the merchant looking so subservient. I hope he doesn't overplay this, the lord thought, feeling sudden misgivings.

Tanaka came up to the summerhouse and knelt in the fine gravel before it. He bowed, careful to keep his eyes cast down.

Shonto stared at his merchant and suddenly a weariness came over him. There is enough intrigue around me, he thought, enough falseness.

"Tanaka-sum," Shonto said surprising the merchant by using the honorific before a stranger. "Come, we have no time for this charade. Lord Komawara understands the importance of your position. Join us." Shonto gestured for the servants to bring another table. There, he thought, this young one should know the truth of the times. I was right this morning, I have no time to indulge children.

If Komawara was affronted by this, he managed to hide it.

"Lord Komawara, it is my honor to introduce you to Tanaka-sum, my valued counselor. Tanaka-sum, you have the honor of meeting the son of an old friend and ally of the Shonto, Lord Komawara Samyamu."

The two men bowed, Tanaka purposely deeper than the lord, and then he rose and joined Shonto and his guest in the small house. A table arrived for him and mead was poured into his cup.

"We have just been discussing the journey to Seh. Lord Komawara has recently traveled south along the canal."

Tanaka set his glass down. "Ah, and will you return north with Lord Shonto?"

"I had not considered this. I do have to return to Seh soon. The situation there is so unsettled. I don't wish to be away any longer than I have to be."

"You would be most welcome to journey to Seh with us, Lord Komawara," Shonto said, "though I intend to leave within a few days and will have little time for leisure. Perhaps this wouldn't allow you time to complete your business in the capital?"

"This is a generous offer, Lord Shonto. I will certainly see if it is possible."

"Please do, your company would be most welcome." Shonto signaled again and a servant appeared to refill the cups. "Tanaka-sum, tell us about this venture you mentioned to me, I think it would interest my guest."

Tanaka set his cup down, and cleared his throat quietly. "At Lord Shonto's request I contracted to purchase all of the corrapepper of a grower who has his fields on the southernmost of the islands of the barbarian. Due to the disfavor of the gods, the other islands were struck by an evil storm which ruined the corrapepper harvest. This terrible misfortune has left us in control of virtually all the surviving corrapepper crop.

"Due to the unfortunate circumstances I have described, there will certainly be inflated prices for corrapepper this year—of course, we shall have to pay more to protect our crop from theft by the unscrupulous barbarians, but still, if Botahara wills it, our profit should be great."

Tanaka glanced at Lord Shonto, and then continued. "The investment in this venture has been large, so on the advice of Lord Shonto, I sought partners to share the risk . . . and the profits. Due to family matters, one honored friend has been unable to continue in our venture. It could not be helped," Tanaka hastened to add, "and we feel his conduct has been beyond reproach, but his withdrawal has left us with an opening for a new partner or partners, as you can see."

"I don't know your plans, Lord Komawara," Shonto said, "but this would seem a good opportunity for you and we would welcome your involvement. You could invest whatever you wished to risk, up to . . ." He looked at Tanaka.

"Perhaps 200,000 ril."

Lord Komawara shook his head. "But certainly this is too generous, Lord Shonto," he protested. He meant to go on but could not marshal his thoughts.

"Of course," Tanaka hastened to add, "you would be assessed some part of your profit, Lord Komawara." He pulled awkwardly at a ring on his little finger. "Let us say twelve parts . . . no, ten parts per hundred."

The young lord paused to contemplate. "It must be twelve, then, if I am to agree."

"Certainly ten would be customary, Lord Komawara," Shonto said, eyeing his merchant, but Tanaka would not meet his gaze.

"I am honored by your offer, Lord Shonto, but I think you can understand that I cannot accept it unless I am sure it is not charity." Why, Komawara thought, why would someone in Shonto's position do this for someone of as little concern as I? Did he really hold my father in such high esteem?

Shonto seemed to consider Komawara's words for a moment, but it was the young lord's assessment of the barbarian attacks that kept coming to mind. Yes, Shonto thought, what he said about the barbarians rang with truth. None of my generals saw mystery in the attacks.

"Lord Komawara, it is not my intention to offer you charity, which obviously you do not require, but only to offer you this small service in return for something I need. Something I need now. I require your counsel—I realized that when we first spoke. I also value Komawara loyalty—it is a trait that your family is known for and it is beyond price. If you wish to begin trade in the name of Komawara, I give you that opportunity. In return, I hope you will journey with me to Seh to give me the benefit of your knowledge of the north."

Komawara said nothing. He appeared to be weighing Shonto's words as though they were made of nothing but insubstantial air. But he could find no trace of deceit in them. I bind myself to the Shonto and Shonto destiny with this, he thought, and he found the idea somewhat disturbing. Reaching out, he took a drink of his wine, and then, setting his glass down, he said, "I accept this offer, Lord Shonto, Tanaka-sum. I am honored by your words. I only hope my counsel will prove worthy of your investment." There, Komawara thought, it is done.

"I don't doubt it for a moment." Shonto signaled for more wine. "We must eat—it is our most common form of celebration, is it not? Tanaka, will you join us?"

The merchant seemed to struggle within himself for a moment. "I am honored by your invitation, Sire, but there are so many things to attend to before your departure. . . ."

Shonto turned to Komawara. "I cannot even tempt my retainers from their duties. Is this a common problem, do you think?"

"It is a problem most lords wish they suffered from, Sire."

"Tanaka-sum, I bow to your sense of duty. Another time."

Tanaka bowed to the two lords and took his leave, walking away with the quiet dignity Shonto admired.

"So, Lord Komawara, I'm sure the two of us can enjoy our food as much as three?"

Komawara nodded. Servants brought the midday meal—simple but delectable fare, elegantly served in the summerhouse overlooking the pond of yellow water lilies. Under the influence of the food, the fine wine and Shonto's conversation, Komawara achieved an almost euphoric state. Being a Shonto ally looked less daunting than it had seemed earlier.

"The food, Lord Shonto, was of a quality that would satisfy an Emperor."

Shonto bowed slightly. "You are kind to say so. Cha?"

"Thank you, that would be perfect."

The rustle of silk was heard from the path below and then Lady Nishima appeared, on cue, followed by two of her ladies-in-waiting and a young maid. If Komawara had found her enchanting in the moonlight, he realized that the sunlight brought out her true beauty, as it did the flower of the morning-vine.

Dressed in a robe of spring green embroidered with a pattern of falling ginkyo leaves, the Lady Nishima Fanisan Shonto seemed to shine among her companions, as though the sunlight did not bless them with its warmth. She stopped and bent down to examine a bush by the edge of the walk, and the gold of her inner kimonos appeared at the nape of her fine neck. Lord Komawara felt both thrilled and terribly nervous.

At the sight of her uncle, Nishima smiled with unconcealed affection. She handed her parasol to the maid and stepped out of her sandals before entering the summerhouse. The two lords returned her formal bow.

"Nishima-sum, how kind of you to join us."

"The kindness was yours in inviting me, Uncle." She took a fan, shaped like a large ginkyo leaf, from her sleeve pocket and waved it open in an easy gesture. "Lord Komawara, how pleasant to see you again so soon. Did you enjoy the Emperor's party?"

"Entirely. I have had the sounds of your music with me ever since and it has made my day most pleasant."

"You are too kind," she said, but she was not displeased by the praise.

"Have you met our new Spiritual Advisor?" Shonto asked.

Nishima turned her attention to her uncle now. She examined his face, looking for signs of the attempt on his life, but she saw no concern or anxiety. Indeed, he seemed entirely relaxed—she glanced at his companion out of the corner of her eye.

"I have not, Sire, though I understand he is to join us."

Shonto nodded toward the pathway and Nishima saw a young monk of the Botahist Order walking toward them.

Yes, Nishima thought, *that is him,* I remember. And the diminutive monk in the kick boxing ring became clear in her memory. The other fighters had appeared so massive and the boy-monk had seemed so small . . . yet completely calm. The same calm was somehow still apparent in this Brother, and as she watched him approach she was overcome with an unexpected emotion. Suddenly, the Lady Nishima wanted to hide. She looked around almost in a panic, then her years of training took charge and she regained her composure. But she was disturbed by this sudden surge of emotion, left shaken by it.

The monk, Shuyun, stopped at the entry to the summerhouse and bowed to his liege-lord and his guests.

"Brother Shuyun, please join us." Shonto said and gestured to the servants. A table large enough for four was exchanged for the individual tables and this gesture surprised Lady Nishima, for such an arrangement was usually reserved for immediate family only.

Brother Shuyun was formally introduced to Lady Nishima and Lord Komawara, neither of whom betrayed a trace of the intense curiosity they felt for this young Initiate. Lady Nishima was especially intrigued after the report she had received of the monk's display that morning.

The utensils for the making of cha came and Lady Nishima, as one of the most famed hostesses in the capital, took charge of the preparation. At the same time she guided the conversation deftly and with great charm, impressing Lord Komawara, who was intimidated by the urbanity of the women he met in the capital.

The drinking of cha, like every activity of the aristocracy, was formalized and governed by its own particular aesthetic, though among the aristocrats, it had not taken on the aspects of ritual that it had among certain sects within Wa. In its existing state of formality, Lady Nishima was able to bring her considerable imagination to bear upon the social aspects of drinking cha. Today she had it in mind to do something different, something that she knew no one present would associate with cha. How to introduce it in a manner that seemed natural, that was her problem.

"Will you come to Seh with Lord Shonto, Brother Shuyun?" Komawara asked. He has having trouble not staring at Lady Nishima, though his warrior's discipline was just barely winning.

"It is for Lord Shonto to decide," the monk said, and offered no more.

Lady Nishima felt sudden resentment toward the Botahist monk and his cold manner. It is their way, she thought. But still it annoyed her. Looking at the monk kneeling across the table from her, she searched for the man behind the mask. This had been an obsession for her with Brother Satake, their former Spiritual Advisor. With Satake-sum she would stoop to almost any ploy to see him laugh or grow impatient—anything that seemed a human emotion. It had been a frustrating campaign, for she had seldom been successful.

When the tea had been poured and offered in its proper way, Lady Nishima began to ask Lord Komawara questions about Seh and about the barbarians and their motives.

Lord Komawara answered her, being careful not to let the conversation stray too far from the approved tone for such occasions. "Their motives are not the same as ours, Lady Nishima. You cannot understand them in our terms. As to what will happen, who can say? I cannot tell the future, and for this I apologize." He bowed with mock sincerity.

"Lord Komawara, there is no need to apologize to me for not being able to predict the future. I am quite capable of doing *that* myself."

Knowing his daughter's humor, Shonto took the bait quickly, "Nishi-sum, how is it that I have not been aware of this talent? Or was it simply lost among your myriad of other gifts?"

"Not at all, Sire, it is as you say. You are far too perceptive not to have noticed such an ability in your favorite daughter. The reason that you have not, until now, been aware of this skill is that I myself became aware of it only this morning. In fact it was just after sunrise. I sat combing my hair when suddenly I was overcome by . . ." her eyes went wide, "Deep Insight! Yes, and I thought immediately, I must tell all of those around me of their futures. They will find it most useful."

"Ah," Shonto said, keeping a straight face, "Deep Insight! Do the Botahist Brothers have experience of this phenomenon, Shuyun-sum?"

"Certainly, Lord Shonto, and it is well known that it is most often experienced while combing one's hair. That is the reason Neophyte monks must shave their heads—so they don't experience Deep Insight before they are prepared for such a momentous occurrence." As he finished saying this he smiled, causing a thrill to course through the Lady Nishima.

The man behind the mask! she thought, but then the smile was gone and across the table sat one of the Silent Ones, unmoving, without apparent emotions.

"Well, Lady Fortune Teller, I, for one, would be interested in seeing what can result from Deep Insight, if you would so honor us." Shonto said.

"Gladly, Sire, but I must warn each of you . . . I can take no responsibility for what you may learn of your futures, either good or bad."

"Agreed," Komawara said, "only the gods will be held responsible." And then remembering the Botahist monk, "Botahara willing," he added.

The assembled guests acted as though they had not heard the reference to the gods, the mythological beings that the Botahist religion had replaced, but Shonto found himself thinking, Well, it is true, he *is* from the provinces.

From her sleeve pocket Nishima took an ornate canister of black leather decorated with a pattern of white wisteria. She shook it and the jangle of coins caused everyone to laugh for they all knew the sound—the coins of Kowan-sing.

Kowan-sing was one of the innumerable methods of divination popular in Wa. Almost every possible object had been used at one time in an attempt to foretell the future: bones, the lines of the face, stones, crystals, entrails, cards, even the gii board. Kowan-sing, though, had history to lend it credibility, for it was thought to have been practiced by the indigenous people. The people who had been displaced by the Five Princes so long ago that the histories could not agree on a time.

"Who shall be first?" Lady Nishima asked, rattling coins again.

"Lord Komawara must have that honor," Lord Shonto insisted.

Cups were moved aside so the coins could be cast.

"Are you ready to know your future, Lord Komawara?" Nishima asked.

Lord Komawara nodded, and in one fluid motion Nishima spread the seven silver coins across the table.

All heads bent forward to examine the arrangement of the coins.

"It is clear that the pattern here is *The Boat*, Lord Komawara, symbol of both travel and prosperity." Nishima said, not raising her eyes from the table.

"With the slight movement of two coins it could easily be *The Cloud*, could it not?" Lord Shonto asked.

The Cloud was the symbol for romance, as all knew, and Lord Shonto's comment caused Komawara some discomfort.

But Lady Nishima did not seem embarrassed by what Lord Shonto implied. "As you say, Uncle, but *The Boat* is too clear for *The Cloud* to be influential here, excuse me for saying so."

"I bow to your superior source of knowledge," Shonto said, nodding to his daughter.

"Here, Lord Komawara, it can be seen that one coin spoils the line of the keel." She touched the coin with a long finger, careful not to change its position. "It indicates a danger to you, something you should beware of, perhaps, as *The Boat* indicates, on your return journey north. But also, prosperity may hold some danger for you. And again here, the coins that make the mast show that it is falling, indicating that there is danger in your immediate future. Only you could know what this might be." She touched another coin, the only one that did not bear the outline of the *Mountain of Divine Inspiration*. "Here, the Prime Kowan is temptation; the open fan. Only time will tell what is hidden by the fan. All that can be said with certainty is that temptation will figure in your future, possibly related to prosperity, I cannot be sure. But temptation can be dangerous." Nishima looked up and the serious faces of her companions reminded her that she had meant this to be fun.

"You seem to attract danger, Lord Komawara," she said in a whisper. "Perhaps it is unwise for us to sit so close to you." She looked about with wide eyes, as though something terrible was about to fall on them from the sky. Everyone laughed in appreciation. And then, in the voice of an old crone, "you must keep your sword sharp, young Sire. The great world is full of . . . danger! You must watch behind you . . . and in front of you, not forgetting either side. Danger, danger, danger . . ." Her voice trailed off and her companions broke into applause.

Water arrived, and Lady Nishima took a moment to prepare more cha.

"Now, Uncle, I believe you must be next."

"I am honored."

Lady Nishima collected the coins and shook them again in their leather canister. Twice she removed the top and was about to cast them when she stopped, as though inspiration had fled. But then she looked up, a mischievous grin on her face.

"You do enjoy tormenting me, don't you," Shonto said.

And his daughter laughed and cast the coins of Kowan-sing, her long sleeve streaming behind the graceful sweep of her arm.

Shonto put his elbow on the table so that it hid the coins from the young woman's view. "Ah, Nishi-sum! This is most interesting, most unusual!"

Laughing with the others, she snatched his arm out of the way. "Ah, Uncle, this *is* interesting. Who would think that your pattern would be *The Dragon*? It is not as clear a pattern as Lord Komawara's, but the eyes are certain, and here," she pointed, "is a curving tail. *The Dragon* symbolizes both power and mystery."

Nishima paused then, examining the coins with complete concentration. In the distance, a flock of cranes passed south over the plain, unnoticed by the occupants of the summerhouse.

"Mystery and power are the keys to your future, perhaps there is a power that will affect you and your endeavors, yet the source of this power will be unknown. The body of *The Dragon* itself seems to be twisted in an unusual manner, as though the power will appear in an unexpected form. Here," she touched a coin, which this time had landed with the fan down, exposing the other side: the *Sheathed Sword*, "the Prime Kowan is the hidden threat. It cannot be known if the sword is sharp or dull, but it is always a danger and must never be ignored. The sheathed sword also indicates treachery— danger from an ally perhaps."

"Can it not also indicate peace?" Shonto asked.

"It can, Sire. But in combination with *The Dragon*, this does not seem the most likely interpretation. Excuse me for saying so."

Shonto shrugged. "It is you who speak from Deep Insight."

"Perhaps, Sire, you should seclude yourself for the remainder of the year in our summer palace." Nishima smiled. "I believe I deserve a reward for my work. Cha. Does anyone wish to join me?"

Cha was brewed again. Secretly, Lady Nishima wished to cast the fortune of their new Spiritual Advisor, but would never suggest this, being unsure of his opinion of such frivolity. Yet she was curious to know what the coins would tell about this quiet monk who was now a member of their inner Household. She was curious, not least of all because she felt there had been some truth in what she had told the others. Some of the things she had said she had felt certain of in some inexplicable way.

Do I grow superstitious? she wondered, but Shonto interrupted this train of thought.

"Nishi-sum, it seems unfair that we have received the benefit of your Deep Insight, and yet your own future remains unknown to you. This cannot be correct." Shonto watched Komawara out of the corner of his eye but realized the young lord was too shy to take up the suggestion himself. Ah, well, Shonto thought, I have started this and now I will have to carry it through.

"I believe what Lord Shonto says is true, Lady Nishima," Shuyun said in his quiet tones. "It is only proper that you should know what the future holds for you. I would be honored to cast the coins for you, though I cannot claim to have your skill with them."

No one showed the surprise they felt at the monk's offer. Komawara immediately regretted his hesitation to make this proposal himself, for Nishima obviously was immensely flattered.

"I could never refuse such a kind offer, Brother Shuyun."

Collecting the coins in the canister, Lady Nishima passed it to Shuyun, but as she did so she was seized by a desire to fling them into the garden, as though what her future might hold was too frightening. But she did offer them and the monk shook the canister, producing what suddenly seemed an ominous rattle.

As deftly as Lady Nishima, Shuyun spread the coins across the table and as they came to rest Nishima could see that her fears had been groundless. They were only the coins of Kowan-sing, familiar, worn, in need of a polishing. What she had expected she did not know—something disturbing— coins she had never seen, bearing haunting images and an unwanted message.

She closed her eyes and felt relief wash through her. It is the curse of my blood, the name that follows me like a banner. May it never become the rallying point for the war that so many desire. She shuddered involuntarily. Opening her eyes she tried to smile.

"Are you well, Lady?" Shuyun asked, his eyes searching her own.

"Well?" she said. "How can I be well. Look at this pattern. Is it not *The Mountain*, the symbol for calculated waiting and enlightenment." She laughed. "I have no patience whatsoever, it is my shame to admit. If I am to have enlightenment I would like it to arrive by sunset at the latest." She laughed again, a delightful laugh.

Shuyun smiled. "But Lady Nishima, I may be wrong, but I believe this is *The Crane*, symbol of the aesthetic, of beauty and art."

"Botahara has guided your hand, Brother." Shonto said.

The monk nodded. "Your reputation as an artist has reached even the Oracle, Lady Nishima. yet here *The Crane* stands erect, waiting. Patient, as you must be patient, even though you claim not to be. It is this waiting that makes a great artist. And look, your Prime Kowan is also the open fan. As you have said, this is the symbol for temptation, but it may also indicate that the artist cannot hide behind the painted fan. The artist must show herself. Part of her inner beauty must appear in her work. Of course temptation should not be ruled out, perhaps temptation that is related to the aesthetic or to beauty, I cannot say." He bowed toward her and again fell silent.

"I thank you, Brother Shuyun. It will be an honor to have your wisdom in the Shonto House."

After more mead, Lord Komawara offered to recite a poem he had just composed. All assented readily for poetry was common, even expected, on such occasions. Komawara had hesitated only because of Lady Nishima's reputation as a poetess.

> *"A crane waits, staring down at*
> *green water.*
> *Is it drawn to a reflection?*
> *Does it watch for movement*
> *In the still waters?"*

There was silence for a moment, as was the custom, so that the poem could be considered.

"You have been hiding your talent as a poet from us, Lord Komawara," Nishima said, and there was no doubting the sincerity of her words.

Komawara bowed. "Knowing of your skill, Lady Nishima, I thank you for your words, which are more than kind."

"Nishi-sum, you must have a poem for us," Shonto said, "You are never without inspiration."

"You embarrass me with your flattery, Uncle. Please allow me a moment to consider." She closed her eyes for only a few seconds before speaking.

> "The crane stands,
> White in the green pond.
> Does it see the water's
> Stillness as illusion?
> But wait,
> Is it a crane or
> The reflection of a passing cloud?"

"Ah, Lady Nishima, your fame is more than well deserved," Komawara said. "I am honored that you should use my simple verse as the beginnings of such masterful display."

Now Nishima bowed in thanks. "Your poem was not simple, Lord Komawara, and my verse merely tried to reflect its meaning, yeh? Look into its depths."

A final cup of cha was brewed and the conversation returned to a more relaxed tone. Seh was again a topic of discussion and Lord Komawara was given an opportunity to exhibit his knowledge.

"Brother Shuyun," Komawara addressed the monk, "I am not familiar with your name. Does it have significance in the teachings of Botahara?"

Shonto was glad the question had been asked, for he had been searching his memory of the Botahist texts trying to find it, assuming that, like most monks, Shuyun's name had originated there.

"It is adapted from the tongue of the mountain people, Lord Komawara, so it is not recognized in Wa. *Shu-yung*: he who bears, or the bearer. It is a name for the humble carriers. A name which does not encourage pride."

Huh, Shonto thought, unlike the name Shonto or Fanisan or Komawara for that matter. Why does such a one consent to serve among the prideful? Of course, the lord thought, he did not consent, he was ordered by his superiors and obeyed without question. Brother Satake had done the same, once.

"Kowan-sing is also of the mountain tongue, is it not, Brother?" Nishima asked.

"It is from the archaic form, Lady Nishima, from a time when it is assumed the mountain dwellers lived in the plains and along the sea coast. Many place names remain from the ancient tongue; *yul-ho, yul-nan;* even Yankura derives from the same source, *Yan-khuro,* dwelling by the water. It was a beautiful tongue and only a few dialects remain among the mountain people to remind us of it."

A bell rang the hour of the tiger and it seemed a signal to everyone in the summerhouse, a reminder that each of them had much to do and that, despite the illusion of timelessness created in the garden, the day wore on.

Lord Komawara took his leave, needing to prepare for his journey with Lord Shonto, though he found the presence of Lady Nishima made it difficult to think of anything other than her lovely eyes and graceful movements.

Lady Nishima's ladies-in-waiting and her maid returned to accompany her through the gardens. She went in a rustle of silk, leaving only the scent of her perfume lingering in the summerhouse.

Shonto went to consult with Kamu on the preparations for the trip to Seh, leaving Shuyun unattended in the garden. For a few moments Shuyun sat listening to the sounds, appreciating the subtlety of the garden's design. This will be my home, the monk thought, or one of them. He looked around him. What wealth! How easy to forget the life of the spirit here. Yes, how easy.

Rising, Shuyun made his way slowly down from the summerhouse, planning to return to the apartment Kamu had had prepared for him. Everywhere he looked, the details of the garden seemed to call for his attention, slowing his progress.

As he bent down by a low wall to admire a climbing vine, Shuyun stopped as though he had seen a spirit. He cocked his head, listening to a sound that seemed almost to blend with the sounds of the breeze, but it was there, unmistakably, a sound he had heard far too often to not be absolutely sure. He felt his heart begin to race and quickly controlled it. What is this? he wondered. The sound of movement, the swish of soft material and the hiss of controlled breathing. He knew it like the sound of his own voice.

I must see, he thought, and began to examine his surroundings looking for observers. Shuyun realized he was taking a chance, but it could not be helped. What if he were seen?

He stepped back along the path a few paces and bent to examine the leaves of a chako bush. From this position he could see the windows of the main house. There was no movement, but it was difficult to be sure as they were all shaded.

He stepped carefully off the path behind a pine that hid him from view. Glancing around the garden again, afraid that Lord Shonto was having him observed, Shuyun reached up and tested the strength of the vines that climbed the walls. Hoping that, at least for that moment, he was not seen, Shuyun quickly clambered silently up the branches. He raised his head above the wall and his grip tightened on the vines. There, in a small enclosed garden, dressed in loose cotton robes, Lady Nishima moved through the measured dance of the Form—chi quan! As he watched, she reached the fifth closure and proceeded with confidence. It was almost beyond his ability to believe—*one of the uninitiated practicing the Form.* The key to the Secret Knowledge of the Botahist Orders.

He lowered himself to the ground, his heart pounding in a most un-Botahist-like manner, and continued down the path attempting to appear composed.

Brother Satake, the monk thought, the renowned Brother Satake. It could have been no one else. But why? Shonto's former advisor had been almost legendary, a man held in the highest regard by the most senior members of his Order. A man Shuyun had tried to emulate in his own learning.

The monk walked on, his head spinning. What shall I do? he thought, this is unimaginable! By the Nine Names of Botahara, *we have been betrayed!*

Eight

WALLS, SISTER MORIMA thought, they are the "Significant Pattern" of our Empire, and the fact that no one notices them speaks of their complete acceptance by the entire culture. Here we draw the stylus and there is division—the Son of Heaven on that side and all of Wa on the other. We draw the stylus again and Lords of the First Rank make their position clear, they on one side and all of society on the other, and so on down to the paper screens of the poorest street vendor. Last of all we have the beggars and they can erect no walls at all.

Walls: they were everywhere and everywhere they went unnoticed—not that they weren't respected, that was not the case—they were simply not considered for what they were; the Significant Pattern.

But it had always been so. Even a thousand years before, the Lord Bo-tahara had spoken of walls: "Between themselves and the weak the strong build walls, fearing that the weak will learn of their own strength. So it is that the poor are shut out into the wide world with all of its uncertainty but also with all of its purity and beauty. Whose palace garden compares to the wild perfection of the mountain meadows? So, thinking to shut out the poor and the weak, the strong succeed only in walling themselves in. Such is the nature of illusion."

Sister Morima walked stiffly up the graveled roadway that led along the base of the wall surrounding the Priory of the First Awakening—the Seat of her Order. Shielding her eyes, she looked up at the white stone rampart and wondered what the Enlightened One would think of a religious Order, based on his teachings, that hid itself behind walls. The Significant Pattern, she thought again, it was a Sister who had first spoken of the concept, another Sister who had written the definitive work on the idea.

I grow cynical, she thought. The Sisterhood needs the walls to protect itself from those who have not yet developed their spirit sufficiently. She looked around her at the pilgrims who crowded the roadway. Tired, covered in dust, poor for the most part, some with the eyes that looked beyond the world—yet all of them seemed to exude a certain air of barely controlled passion, of deep unrest. "May the Lord Botahara bring you peace," she muttered under her breath.

Yes, it felt good to be returning. Her time among the Brothers had left her feeling . . . tainted. She shuddered involuntarily. I have much to tell you, Sister Saeja, she thought, much that I don't understand.

She walked on, staring at the road before her feet, listening to the sounds of the pilgrims walking, to their mumbled prayers, the coughing of the desperately ill. The morning air was fresh, still retaining a trace of the night's chill, but the sun was warm. The autumn seemed to have attained a point of balance; like a gull on a current of wind, it seemed to hang in the air for an impossibly long time. Each night you expected the balance to have been lost, but each morning the sun would rise, as warm as the day before, and the smells of autumn would return with the heat. It was as though time had slowed—leaves floated down without hurry, flowers blossomed beyond their season. It was uncanny and very beautiful.

The gate to the Priory of the First Awakening loomed up as she rounded a corner and the usual horde of Seekers surrounded the Sisters of the Gate. Sister Morima could see the desire on their faces, each of them hoping to be allowed entry, to be housed for a few evenings, to attend services or vespers, perhaps to hear a few words from the Prioress, Sister Saeja, who, they all knew, was coming close to her time of Completion.

Slowly Sister Morima moved through the throng, the pilgrims making way for her.

"Allow the honored Sister to pass."

"Make way, brother, a Sister comes."

"Intercede for us, Honored Sister, we have come all the way from Chou to hear a few words from the Prioress. All the way from Chou . . . Honored Sister?"

The Sisters of the Gate greeted her warmly, their eyes full of questions for they knew from where she returned. She passed through into the outer courtyard of the Priory, into the company of the privileged Seekers, those allowed through the main gate, their way eased by an introduction from a Sister in their home province, or by a donation to the worthy causes of the Sisterhood—or in some cases, simply because the pilgrim would not go away. The press of the crowd was gone here, the privileged few moving about in blissful silence.

Sister Morima prostrated herself on the cobbles in front of the statue of Botahara before she entered the second gate that led to the inner courtyard. Only robed Sisters and young Acolytes passed her here and the noise of the crowd outside was completely muffled by the high walls. She breathed a sigh of relief. I do not bear my burden well, she thought, but soon I shall share it. This did not gladden her as she hoped, for what she had to share was disturbing indeed.

The Acolytes who accompanied Sister Morima were anxious to be released, to bathe and to rest, but she said nothing and they continued obediently in her wake. They must learn, she thought, our way never becomes easier, there is no reward of respite, not in this life.

A senior Sister came toward her across the cobbles, obviously intending to meet her. The face was not familiar immediately, but then she realized—*Gatsa*, Sister Gatsa. So, the vultures gathered. The representatives of each faction would be here, then, waiting, plotting. A surge of fear passed through her. No, she told herself, she knew the Sisters on duty at the gate, if Saeja-sum had arrived at the point of Completion they would have warned her. But still the vultures circled, and this one was about to land.

"Go and assist with the pilgrims' meal," she said, turning to the Acolytes who attended her, and watched the disappointment and resentment flare in their eyes. Then it was gone.

"Immediately, Sister Morima, thank you for this opportunity." And they hurried off, burdens in hand.

Sister Morima nodded, satisfied; they understood, they would do well.

"Sister Morima, how pleased I am to see you. I did not know you were expected," and Sister Gatsa bowed to her.

Letting the lie pass, Sister Morima returned the bow and walked on, letting her fatigue show. Gatsa fell into step beside her. She was a tall woman, Sister Gatsa, somewhat regal in her bearing and in her speech, an odd manner to find in a humble servant of the Perfect Master. She was square jawed, but this harshness was relieved by a lovely mouth and eyes that seemed to dance with the pleasures of being alive—no staring into the great-beyond for this Sister. Her eyes were focused on the world around her, and they missed very little.

"I trust your journey has been productive?" Sister Gatsa said.

"Most pleasant. You honor me to enquire," Morima answered in her most formal tones. They turned inside an arch and continued down a wide portico.

"Then you actually *saw* the scrolls of the Enlightened One?" She turned and examined Sister Morima's face, awe apparent in her voice.

Sister Morima did not answer immediately and then looked away as she spoke. "I saw the Brothers' scrolls."

"And?"

"And what, Sister?" Morima asked.

"You saw the scrolls of the Lord Botahara and this is all you can say?" The tall Sister sounded annoyed.

Again Sister Morima hesitated, then released a long sigh. "It is not an experience words can convey, Sister." She paused and reached out to steady herself on a post. Sister Gatsa regarded the large nun who looked as if she would burst into tears, but then Morima regained control. "You must excuse me, but I . . . I must meditate upon the experience. Perhaps then I will be able to explain my reaction."

Sister Gatsa took Morima's arm and continued along the walk. "I understand, Sister, it must be very moving to look upon the hand of Botahara. I do understand."

Nuns nodded to them as they walked, and, as the two passed, eyes followed. This is the Sister who was *chosen*, they thought. She has attended the ceremony of Divine Renewal. Whispers passed through the Priory like quiet breezes.

"She is back! Sister Kiko has seen her."

"And?"

"She is transformed, Sister! Morima-sum glows with inner knowledge. Yet she seems disturbed also."

"Who would not be—to look upon His words. Remember, too, that she has spent many days in the company of the Brothers. Would you not find this disturbing?"

"Your words are wisdom, Sister."

The two nuns came at last to the door Sister Morima sought. The door that would lead to her quarters. But Gatsa was not ready to release her yet, and Morima felt the tall nun's grip tighten on her arm.

"Much has happened in your absence, Sister Morima," Gatsa said, lowering her voice. "The Prioress has become weaker. I tell you this to prepare you, I know how close you are to her. There will be a Cloister before the year's end, I fear. We both know how large a part you will play in the Selection. The Empire changes, Sister, we must not be the victims of the change. The work of Botahara is all-important. You must feel that more than ever after what you have just seen. I know we have opposed each other in the past, Morima-sum, but I believe there may be a way to resolve our differences. This would be good for the Sisterhood and good for us also. Please consider my words. We can discuss this when you are rested." She let go of Morima's arm and stood facing her, eyes searching. "But don't wait too long, Sister." She bowed and swept off down the long portico, bearing herself, as always, like a Lady of the Emperor's Court.

A young Acolyte attendant met Morima as she mounted the stairs to her quarters.

"I have run your bath, honored Sister," the girl said bowing to her superior. "I am to tell you that the Prioress will see you when you are refreshed." She fell into step behind Sister Morima who nodded as she passed.

Yes, Morima thought, the Prioress will see me, but what am I to tell her? She rubbed her brow with a hand covered in dust. The question was one she had asked herself repeatedly since leaving the Brotherhood's Island Monastery. Still she had no answer. What do I know that is in any way certain? the nun asked herself again. Nothing, was the answer and she knew it, yet the feeling would not go away. There was something wrong in Jinjoh Monastery; all of her instincts told her so.

The bath the Acolyte had drawn was like a healing potion. Sister Morima sank into the steaming waters like a marine mammal returning to its element. She closed her eyes and allowed her shoulders and forehead to be massaged. To compose herself for the coming interview, she began to meditate. A calm began to flow through her body, the turmoil in her mind was pushed back and partially silenced.

Later, as she dressed, she pushed the screen aside and stood looking out from her small balcony across the plain. In the distance the Imperial Capital shimmered in the rising waves of heat. The palace of the Emperor wavered in the unstill air, white walls seeming to change their shape before the eye, one surface joining another then separating itself again. The harder she looked, the more difficult it became to be sure of the palace's true shape.

An endless line of Seekers moved along the road that meandered up the mountain to the Priory. Dust seemed to enclose them like a skein of silk— red-brown and drifting slowly to the north. The pilgrims, too, were caught in the rising waves of heat, their bodies distorted, billowing, insubstantial.

I am in the Priory of the First Awakening, Sister Morima told herself. I am a senior of the Botahist Order. Beyond the rice fields lies the Emperor's city. Its walls are white and quite solid. Down there are the Seekers—poor, hungry, and often quite foolish. That man among them in the blue rags is a cripple, and it is only the effect of the warm air that seems every so often to straighten his limbs.

Pulling the screen closed, she turned and went out to meet the head of her Order.

The nun who was the Prioress' secretary smiled with real warmth when she saw Sister Morima. "How glad I am that you have returned, Sister," she said. "Our prayers have been with you."

"And my prayers have been with you, Sister Sutso. Your concern honors me." She bowed. "Tell me quickly, how is our beloved Prioress?"

The secretary lowered her gaze and shook her head. "She is an inspiration, Sister, but she is not well."

Morima reached out and touched her Sister's shoulder. "She can go only to a better life, Sutso-sum. Is she able to see me now?"

The secretary nodded her head. "But you mustn't tire her, Sister. She needs constant rest." She shook her head again sadly. "May Botahara smile upon her, she is so old and has served Him so well."

They walked down the hall that led to the apartment of the Prioress, both of them taking care to make as little noise as possible. Sister Sutso tapped lightly on the frame of the screen and then cracked it open ever so slightly. Her face lit up. "Ah, you are awake. Sister Morima is here to see you, Prioress. Shall I allow her entry?"

There was no sound from within, but Sister Sutso opened the screen and stepped aside, nodding to Morima.

Taking a deep breath and releasing it as she had been taught long ago, Sister Morima entered the room, feeling her tension flow out with the outgoing breath. She knelt inside the door and bowed to the mat, hearing the Shoji slide shut behind her.

"Morima-sum, it is always such a pleasure." Sister Saeja said, her voice a whisper.

"I am honored that you receive me, Prioress."

"Yes, I know. Come closer, my child, I cannot see you so far away."

Sister Morima moved forward on her knees to within an arm's length of the old woman. Sister Saeja, the Prioress of the Botahist Sisterhood, sat propped on embroidered cotton cushions near an open screen that let onto a balcony overlooking a view much like Sister Morima's own. She was a tiny woman, wrinkled and thin, but she had the kindest face Morima had ever seen. The ancient eyes regarded her and the gentle face wrinkled into a beatific smile.

"Ah, you are thin, Sister Morima. Has this been a difficult task I have set you?"

"I am anything but thin, Prioress. And the task . . . is done."

"The task is never done, child, not for those such as you—those with special abilities, but we can talk of this later." She reached out a thin hand and touched the younger woman's arm, but then let her hand fall. "You have already spoken with our good Sister Gatsa, I am told." The old woman's eyes seemed alive with humor. "I awake each morning and wonder if I awake on my pyre, such is their haste. But there are tasks to be completed before I am truly done, Morima-sum. We both know this. There will not be a Cloister as soon as they would wish." She laughed a small laugh. Reaching out again she took Morima's hand in her own. "Tell me of your journey, my child, I sense that something troubles you."

Old, yes, Morima thought, but the eyes still see. "The journey itself was uneventful, Prioress—no storms no pirates, only a calm sea and fair winds."

"Botahara protects you, child."

"The Brothers were no more arrogant than usual. For ten days prior to the Ceremony of Divine Renewal I fasted, as is the custom of the Brothers. The Ceremony of Purification took three days and was performed by their Supreme Master himself, the doddering Brother Nodaku. During this time, I was kept apart from the rest of the Monastery and was unable to observe any of their secret trainings or teaching.

"The Ceremony of Divine Renewal takes place at sunrise and is performed by seven senior Brothers. The Urn is removed from the altar by the

Sacred Guards and set on a special stand. Unsealing it is a lengthy ordeal, as every precaution is taken to protect the scrolls from deterioration." Sister Morima fought hard to keep her hands from trembling. *How do I tell her?* she asked herself. She saw fatigue in the Prioress' eyes and felt the grip on her hand lessen. She seemed so frail.

"Are you well, Prioress?"

"Yes, go on," she whispered.

"The scrolls are removed from the Urn by the Supreme Master as the sun rises, and laid upon the stand. Outside, every person in the monastery chants thanksgiving." Sister Morima swallowed hard.

The Prioress had closed her eyes and Morima peered at the ancient nun, but again the whisper came, "Go on."

"The scrolls are then unrolled, one by one and examined with extreme care. I was allowed to watch though I could not touch them."

"Something was wrong?" Sister Saeja said, not opening her eyes.

"Yes!" Morima said hiding her face in her hands.

"Tell me, child."

"Prioress, in preparation for this event, I studied every known reference to, and every copy of our Lord's writing. I cannot explain what I saw there . . . They were very old scrolls, I'm sure but . . . I believe, *no*, I am *certain that those were not the scrolls written by our Lord Botahara in His own hand*." She took a deep, uneven breath and looked at the face of her superior.

The old nun nodded almost imperceptibly. "Of course," she whispered and fell into a deep sleep.

Nine

*The purpose of the move must not
be merely hidden within another
purpose.
It must be concealed entirely,
lost within the complexity of a
plan that is even more plausible
than the real one.*

Writings of the
Gii Master Soto

SHONTO'S FLEET ROUNDED the Point of Sublime Imperial Purpose
and entered the Grand Canal, the ancient waterway which spanned the
Empire from north to south. It was an impressive fleet that began the journey north, made up largely of flat bottomed river barges rowed by muscular
oarsmen, but there were swifter craft also and not a few that had been armed
for the journey.

It said much of the Empire under the rule of Akantsu II, that an Imperial
Governor took measures to defend himself from robbers while traveling
from the capital to his province. The truth was that Shonto could not have
been more satisfied with the situation. It allowed him to arm himself openly,
which meant he could protect himself more easily from those he saw as a real
threat.

One of those Shonto felt threatened him stood on a guard tower watching the fleet through a narrow opening in the stone wall. Jaku Katta leaned on the worn sill and examined each ship as it passed, assessing Shonto's strength with professional deliberation. Nearby stood his youngest brother, the lieutenant Jaku Yasata, who waited obediently for the general to complete his surveillance. Occasionally Yasata cast a glance down the walkway toward the door where he had posted soldiers, but he did not really fear interruption here—the tower was an Imperial Guard stronghold and had been for centuries.

Jaku Yasata shifted his substantial weight almost imperceptibly back and forth from one foot to the other though his face betrayed no sign of his impatience. The youngest of the three Jaku brothers, Yasata had neither the martial skill of Katta nor the intellectual brilliance of Tadamoto. He was a soldier of no special merit other than his unquestioning loyalty to his elder brothers. This one trait, though, was enough to make him immeasurably valuable to both his brothers, which indicated the amount of trust they were willing to place in those around them.

Jaku Katta stared at length as each of the river craft passed and he was reassured by what he saw. It proved that his informants were performing their function and indicated, too, that Shonto went off to the north without suspecting the real dangers that lay in his path.

Jaku caught himself gloating and suppressed the emotion. The Emperor is right about one thing, Jaku thought, I must not become overconfident. It is a great weakness. But look how the great Shonto goes! Burdened down with the poorest travelers, luckless merchants, and near bankrupt peers. Everyone has sought his protection for their journey north and Shonto has refused no one. Jaku shook his head. He had expected more from a man of such renown. He felt a momentary flash of pity for Shonto Motoru, but then Jaku laughed. Soon, so soon. Everything goes as it should.

An image of Lady Nishima appeared in his mind—a very grateful Nishima—and this thought excited him.

"Less than five thousand troops," Yasata said peering over his brother's shoulder.

Jaku did not turn to answer him but nodded. "Yes, and half the sycophants in the Empire." He pointed through the opening in the stone wall. "Look at them all! Huddled together under the banner of the Imperial Governor—as though that would protect them." He dropped his hand to the window ledge and leaned forward as far as he dared.

Yasata peered over his shoulder. "I see no special preparations. He seems to go without suspicion."

"Shonto goes nowhere without suspicion, Yasata-sum. Do not be fooled. But this time his suspicions have been drawn from the true threat. He has special preparations, be sure of that, but for the wrong contingencies."

"The false-trap?" Yasata ventured hoping to learn some of his brother's plans.

"It is not *false,* it is *secondary*—but it is where Shonto's focus has been drawn. And when he falls, the great general will take others with him. Yasata-sum, but not the Jaku. The Jaku shall *rise.*" He turned and clapped his brother on the shoulder, surprising Yasata with his speed. "And that means you, Colonel Jaku. Yes! I make you a colonel. I must prepare you. I will have even greater need of your service in the future, you and Tadamoto-sum."

Yasata looked for words to thank the general, but Katta had already turned back to the window.

The general looked down on the canal as the last barge passed. A smile appeared on his face. No, Emperor, you are wrong, it is not I who am over-confident.

Ten

Our boat of gumwood and dark locust
Her paint scaling like serpent's skin,
Sets forth into the throng of craft
On the Grand Canal.
Uncounted travelers,
Uncounted desires
Borne over blue water.
Only the funeral barge
Covered in white petals
Appears to know its destination.

"Grand Canal"
From the later poems of
Lady Nishima Fanisan Shonto

THE MOTION OF the river barge, and the crying of the gulls seemed to lighten Lord Komawara's spirit. He had been too long in the Imperial capital for a country lord and now his spirit had need of the wider world. I belong in Seh, he thought, I am not made for this courtier's life of careful condescension. He took a deep breath of the fresh country air. The beginning of the journey, he thought, how the heart lifts at the beginning of a journey.

Along the riverbank entire villages of peasants gathered to show respect for the Imperial Governor's progress. They bowed low as the flotilla approached and did not move again until it was past. Komawara saw an old man push the head of a curious child down into the dirt and hold it there, teaching the young one proper respect.

The riverbank was low here, only the slight swelling of a grass-covered levee between the water and the fields. Far ahead, around a bend in the canal, Komawara could see the first boats in the fleet and he began to count. Thirty to the barge he was on, and he had no idea how many more followed behind. It is not often that such a progress is seen, he thought, except when the Son of Heaven moves to his Summer Palace.

So many craft and who is aboard them? Soldiers, musicians, merchants, magicians, potters, swordmakers, scholars, smiths, fortune-tellers, swindlers, gamblers, Botahist Sisters, courtesans, priests. There is a representative of every part of our world, all gathered together aboard these ships. He thought a poem might be made of this, but the words would not come.

It had been a somewhat smaller flotilla that had brought him south. Of course, that had been before his attendance of the Emperor's party, before he had met Lord Shonto. Strange how karma worked. He had gone hoping to gain the Emperor's favor and had been ignored by the Highest One. Then, somehow, he had caught the attention of the man the Emperor felt was his greatest threat. Now here he was, returning to Seh in the entourage of the new governor.

He wondered, again, why Shonto had requested his presence. It seemed the new governor had time for many tasks. Most lords of Komawara's acquaintance would be completely overextended in an endeavor such as this, yet Shonto seemed to proceed as though nothing in his life had changed. He has an excellent and loyal staff, Komawara thought, not all lords could say this. I have the good fortune of the same blessing, I thank Botahara and my father's wisdom.

A member of the Komawara House Guard cleared his throat behind his young lord. Komawara looked over his shoulder.

"The sampan is here, lord."

He walked, on newly caulked planks, across the deck to the waiting boat. Crewman gathered amidships to raise the single sail, for a fair wind had come up aft of the beam and the oarsmen would get a rest. Two sailors lowered a ladder over the side and held it in place for him. Their muscled torsos glistened from the labor of rowing and Komawara had no doubt that they would take his weight with ease.

A small boat, manned by Shonto House Guards, lay alongside the barge and Komawara clambered down to it with characteristic agility. The Shonto guards and the crewmen who bowed as he passed, knew him, though he was not aware of it—*the son of the swordsman,* they thought as he passed. Yet he appeared young to all of them, with that wiriness and length of limb one expected in a colt. But he is the son of the father, the guards thought. What a man to have had as swordmaster! And then there were the duels. Young Komawara was known for the duels he had won—several already—and it was said he feared no one.

Oblivious to all this, Komawara took his place in the boat feeling some-what uncomfortable. The role of Shonto ally was disconcerting to him. His awe of Shonto Motoru was too great for him to see himself as in any way necessary to the Shonto purpose. Somehow it all seemed like a mistake that would soon be discovered. Perhaps this thought, which he realized was en-tirely without honor, was what made him apprehensive about meeting with Shonto.

Sculling up through the line of boats, the guards came skillfully alongside a large, ornate barge. Komawara stepped out onto the boarding platform and the guards there bowed to him with respect. It was strange the way the soldiers could do that, Komawara thought. A person of rank would receive a bow that was flawlessly polite, but a person of equal rank who was also a fighter would receive a bow that unquestionably conveyed more respect, yet Komawara could not say how it differed. He only knew that it was so.

Mounting the stairs to the main deck Komawara began to loosen the strings that held his scabbard in his sash, but as he reached the deck he met Shonto's steward Kamu, and the old man gestured to Komawara's sword.

"My lord asks that you wear your sword, Lord Komawara," he said bow-ing formally.

Komawara bowed equally in return. "I wear it always for his protection, Kamu-sum."

Kamu's face registered his approval. "Lord Shonto asks that you join him on the quarter deck, Sire."

Komawara nodded and followed the steward to the barge's stern where he could see Shonto sitting under a silk awning. The lord bent over a low table, brush in hand, and his secretary knelt in attendance to his right. The rattle of armor as guards bowed to Komawara caused Shonto to look up and his face creased into a smile of warmth.

"Lord Komawara, I am honored that you join me."

Bowing with formality, the two lords made the polite inquiries their strict etiquette required. Cha was served and the lords amused themselves by watching children on the barge behind as they threw scraps to the crying gulls. Only the occasional offering would land in the water, so quick of wing were the small, river birds.

The mid-morning sun was warm, casting a soft, autumn light over the lush countryside. Leaves drifted south in procession on flowing waters, as the flotilla made its way slowly north. A swift Imperial messenger swept by, the powerful oarsmen sending it shooting ahead with each stroke of their long, curved blades.

Shonto watched the messenger glide by. They report our progress to the Emperor, he thought, knowing that the farther from the capital he traveled, the closer he came to the Emperor's purpose.

"Will fourteen days see us in Seh, Lord Komawara?"

"If the winds remain fair, Sire. But we must expect at least some delay from the Butto-Hajiwara feud."

Shonto nodded. "Delay, yes," and he gestured to a guard who placed a tightly rolled scroll on the table before them. Shonto examined the seal carefully before breaking it and then spread the thick paper across the table. It was a detailed map of the area disputed by the warring families. All of the fortifications were drawn in, as well as the troop placements and the strengths of each garrison.

"If it is not an imposition, Lord Komawara, I would ask you to look at this map and verify its details to the best of your ability. Please, do not hurry."

Komawara bent over the map, examining each placement, each notation. He searched his memory and asked for the help of Botahara. Finally he raised his eyes from his task. "It seems to be correct in every detail, Lord Shonto."

Shonto nodded, "It was made up from the combined information of several spies." He rolled the map again and it was taken by a guard. "The words of spies should never stand without verification."

Lunch was served and this brought to Komawara's mind thoughts of Lady Nishima gracefully serving cha. The conversation strayed through an array of subjects before settling on the lords of Seh and how those of note would react to Shonto's arrival. It was a topic that Shonto and his advisors had discussed almost endlessly, but they knew that it was all speculation—nothing was sure.

Aware of the secretary who knelt beyond the awning, obviously waiting, Lord Komawara excused himself as soon as he could politely do so.

Shonto watched him go, watched the way the young lord carried himself. He will be tested severely within the year, Shonto thought, though he did not know where the thought came from.

From his sleeve pocket Shonto removed a small scroll that had come that morning, smuggled through the disputed area by a Shonto soldier disguised as a fish buyer. He unrolled it and again read the strong hand of his son. The words themselves were innocent enough. It was the message within, the message in one of the Shonto ciphers, that concerned the lord. There were two sentences that begged his attention again: "The Butto-Hajiwara feud is stable, the lines of battle have not changed in several months—I do not anticipate any problem there," and, "The barbarian problem is, as you expected, comparatively minor and the reports you received about large buildups on the border are certainly false."

Shonto read the characters again: ". . . the lines of battle have not changed in several months . . ." The feud was stable. So what do they wait for? Shonto wondered. Do they wait for the other to make a mistake or is it something else altogether? Do they wait for Shonto? And if so is it the Butto or the Hajiwara, or both, that I must fear? "I do not anticipate any problem there." Which, in cipher, meant BEWARE.

He misses very little, this son of mine, but he does not know the real danger or he would have written of it.

And the barbarians, that situation was not as it seemed either. Shonto had received no reports about a buildup of barbarian fighters along the border and he knew his son was aware of this. So Komawara had been right, Shonto had sensed it immediately; there was more to the raids in Seh than the northern lords were willing to see.

Shonto rolled the scroll and put it back in his sleeve. May Botahara smile down upon me for I sail toward the abyss. Yet had not Hakata said: "Only from the abyss can one turn and see the world as it truly is." Then soon I shall see.

From his son, Shonto's thoughts turned to Lady Nishima, alone in the capital. If it is my enemies' hope to distract me, they could not have chosen a more effective ploy, he reasoned. Lady Okara is the key to Nishima's safety—if she will agree to my plans. I must make no mistake in monitoring the situation in the capital. He thought of the distance to Seh. Fourteen days, though the Imperial messengers covered the distance in only seven.

Thus occupied, Shonto sat on the quarter deck of the Imperial Governor's barge and, to anyone watching, it would have seemed that he was enjoying the passing countryside and attending to the correspondence his position required.

It did not appear so to Shuyun, who emerged from a hatch on the fore-deck and stood for a moment looking at his liege-lord. Shuyun was aware of the lord's concerns, both from his discussion with Brother Hutto, and from what he was able to learn from Tanaka and Shonto's steward, Kamu.

Shuyun had spent his short time in the Shonto household meeting as many of Shonto's staff as was possible. It was as his teachers had said—the Shonto had an unerring sense of a person's abilities. This seemed to be coupled with insight into where a person's talents could best be employed and an ability to inspire great loyalty.

If there was to be criticism of Shonto's staff, it would be that many of them were older, with the inherent weaknesses that age brought. Shuyun wondered if this was just the "prejudice of the young" his teachers had warned him against. He must consider this in his meditations.

To the degree that he had been able, Shuyun had talked and listened to Shonto's guards and soldiers and, more importantly he had watched them, gauging their attitudes by the thousand minute actions which spoke to his Botahist training. Everything he saw told him they had utter faith in their lord, but even so, all of them went to Seh with misgivings.

Shuyun turned his gaze from Lord Shonto to the canal bank. A tow path ran along the shore, though it was only used in the spring floods when the river craft could not make way against the strong currents. Several Botahist neophytes from a nearby monastery bowed low to the passing lord. In the fields behind, as far as the eye could see, peasants stopped their work and bent low until the progress passed. We minister to them also, Shuyun found himself thinking, but still the obeisance caused in him a feeling of discomfort. This is not the world of the spirit, he told himself, it is my task to dwell here while keeping the goal of the spirit at the center of my being.

Yet, as he said this, a vision of Lady Nishima, laughing in the summer-house, came to him unbidden, and he could not easily push it from his mind.

Eleven

The cycle of the rise and fall of
dynasties seems to be the reverse
of the pattern which affects the
flourishing of art. For at the end
of a dynasty, art is invariably at
its most vigorous, while it is at
its crudest at the outset of a new
political era.
One of the contributions
of Lady Okara, and her few
students, was the preservation of
the Hanama aesthetic through the
early days of the Yamaku.

From Study of Lady Okara
by Lady Nishima Fanisan Shonto

LADY NISHIMA LOOKED again into the mirror of polished bronze and
felt nothing but dissatisfaction with the image she saw. "I am plain," she
said in a whisper. "I am without talent. Lady Okara wastes her time with me.
Oh, if only the Emperor had not forced me to take his patronage! Lady
Okara would not be burdened with someone so undeserving of her attention, and I would be in Seh, away from the Emperor and his weakling sons.

Close to my uncle, who may need my assistance." She worried about Lord Shonto, gone now three days. *He is strong and wise,* she told herself for the thousandth time, *I can help him by avoiding any further traps the Emperor may lay.*

The water clock in the courtyard rang the fifth hour and she knew it was time for her to leave. A boat waited. The Guard Captain himself had insisted upon accompanying her with a large escort, but she had refused, knowing this would only draw attention to her going to the Lady Okara—only draw attention to her shame, for that is what she felt. Shame that she was being forced on so great a painter, and only to fulfill the Emperor's hidden design. She felt anger and frustration boil up in her. And worse—she felt trapped.

Forcing an outward calm over her emotions, Nishima went out into the hall and down the wide stairs into the main courtyard. Rohku Saicha, Captain of the Shonto House Guard and the man charged with her safety, met her as she crossed the tiled enclosure.

"Your sampan awaits you, Lady Nishima," he said bowing. "I hope you have reconsidered. I do have orders from your father to . . ."

"I will take the responsibility, Captain Rohku, please be at your ease," she said, nodding but not stopping.

He fell into step beside her. "All well and good, my lady, but I'm not sure my lord would accept that if something were to happen."

"Shall I put it in writing, then?"

"It isn't that, Lady Nishima. I am concerned about your safety."

"And what do you foresee happening to me in the capital in broad daylight?"

He shrugged his shoulders. "I do not know, Lady Nishima."

"You have assigned guards, that will be adequate. The Shonto must not go about as though the wrath of the gods were about to fall upon them. Where is the dignity in that?"

"I understand your point, Lady Nishima . . ." he meant to say more but they had reached the stairs to the small dock the Shonto family used and she had given him her hand to assist her in boarding the sampan.

She looked back at him from her seat. "You have done all that is required, Saicha-sum," she said, chiding him, "I will return by late afternoon or send a message if I am detained. Do not be concerned." She motioned to the boatmen and they pushed off—three sampans, two as escort and Lady Nishima's personal craft.

Outside the gate, Nishima felt a pang of guilt at having thwarted the captain's precautions. Uncle would be furious if he knew, she thought. Ah well, it was done.

Her thoughts turned again to Lady Okara. Despite her guilt she felt excitement at the idea of seeing the great painter's studio. She cannot know how much I admire her, Nishima thought, and she is so modest, so unassuming. How can she be so, when everyone agrees that she is the most important painter in three generations? I must try and learn this modesty myself, she thought. I am too vain about my meager accomplishments. Already she had forgotten her session in front of the bronze mirror.

The escort took the sampans by a preselected route that would be reasonably quick while not subjecting Lady Nishima to the cruder areas of the city. Large residences passed on either side, partially hidden by their walls. Few of them were mysteries to Lady Nishima, though, for she had been to social functions in many of the more important homes in the capital.

At last they came to the island on which Lady Okara resided. It was one of the dozen islands on the edge of the city where the homes overlooked the Lake of the Lost Dragon and the rolling, green hills beyond. An attendant of Lady Okara's met Nishima at the dock, a man of middle age whose smile was as disarming as a child's.

"Lady Nishima, it is a great honor that you choose to visit. Lady Okara awaits you. Her home is nearby, but a hundred paces—do you wish to ride?" He gestured to an open chair and four bearers who bowed before it.

"It is a good morning for a walk," Nishima said and waited for the attendant to show them the path.

They started along the narrow cobbled street that led up the hill from the dock, the attendant and his bearers, the empty chair, Lady Nishima and her escort.

"I have never been here before. Are there many homes on the island?" Nishima asked the attendant who walked beside her shading her from the sun with a parasol.

"Perhaps a hundred in all, Lady Nishima, though most are on the other side closer to the capital. Only those who choose a quiet existence live here on the lake, though as you can see, it is very pleasant."

Nishima looked around her and had to agree. The vine-maples had turned a bright crimson and the cherry trees lining the street were turning their own, darker reds. Fall flowers fell in drapes over the top of a low stone wall, and behind them the lake lay shimmering in the sunlight, white sails cast across the surface like petals in the wind.

They turned into a tree-lined lane and in a few paces crossed a small bridge over a gurgling stream. Beyond this stood a wooden gate set into a sun dappled stone wall.

Entering the courtyard Nishima saw a medium-size residence built in a charming country style she had always admired. From the upper terrace Lady Okara saw her guest arrive and she descended a wide stairway to greet her.

"Lady Nishima, I am honored that you are able to accept my invitation so soon." The two women bowed to each other.

"I . . . I wish it were only that, Lady Okara, but I come with some embarrassment. We both know why."

"We won't talk of that, Lady Nishima. Our families have had too much in common in the past for us to be concerned by such things. It is long past time that I took an interest in you. I had heard of your talent before, you should know. It is only a reflection on my terrible manners that I had not invited you here long ago."

"You are too kind, Lady Okara."

The great woman smiled warmly and gestured for Nishima to accompany her. "Tell me of your father, Lady Nishima. Did he set out as he'd hoped?"

The two women turned and walked back toward the stairs. "He is gone three days now, Lady Okara. I received word from him this morning. They make excellent time and all goes well." Nishima paused. "If I am not being too presumptuous, Lady Okara, I would be pleased if you would call me Nishima-sum."

Lady Okara smiled. "You could never be too presumptuous with me, my dear, I have known Lord Shonto for over thirty years. I was also an acquaintance of your mother's—did you know that?"

Nishima shook her head in surprise.

"It was long ago, when we were younger than you are now. You look a great deal like her, you know, though you are more beautiful, I must say."

Lady Nishima went almost as red as the vine-maples. "That can't be, Lady Okara, I have seen the portraits of my mother in her youth and she was a great beauty."

"Nonetheless, you are more beautiful than she. Please call me Okara-sum; I too, would be honored."

The two ascended the stairs to the terrace where cha was served in steaming bowls.

"The view is breathtaking, Okara-sum, it must be very peaceful to live here." Nishima said as they sat taking their leisure in the warm autumn sunlight.

"It is, both beautiful and peaceful, but nothing is a fortress against the world, Nishima-sum. It is a good thing to remember."

"I worry about Motoru-sum and this appointment to Seh," Lady Okara said suddenly. She touched Lady Nishima's arm, "I don't mean to cause you anxiety. He is wise, your father, and far more clever than anyone realizes."

"You don't cause me anxiety, Okara-sum. It is true that he is wise, but he is also without fear, and that is what concerns me."

"He has always been that way. All the years I have known him. His father was no different. It is in the blood."

Yes, Nishima thought, it is in the blood and I do not share that. My blood is Fanisan. Inside her she felt her resolve suddenly strengthen and she thought, But my spirit is Shonto.

"Would you like to see my studio?" Lady Okara asked.

"Oh, yes. I would be honored." And they rose from their cha and walked down the terrace toward the studio doors.

A breeze had sprung up by the time Nishima left the home of Lady Okara and the lake had developed a short swell before her boat was into the system of canals of the Imperial Capital. Opening the curtains of the sampan, Nishima saw small whitecaps sweeping across the lake and suddenly the sailboats seemed to be hurrying on their way.

The experience of seeing Lady Okara's studio still excited and deflated her. What a wealth of talent! The decades of hard work showed themselves in the fine detail and control apparent in all of the paintings. It is as Shuyun said, Lady Nishima thought, a part of Lady Okara's inner beauty goes into each work. She does not hide herself in her art. Strange, for she obviously tried to seclude herself in life. But perhaps that was only to allow her time to work. Someone of her fame could be interrupted continuously if she were not careful.

The paintings Lady Nishima had seen appeared before her mind, all of them so perfect. One, an unfinished view of the lake from the terrace, struck Nishima particularly for its beauty. Yet when she said this to Lady

Okara the painter had answered, "Oh, that. I started it years ago and was never happy with it. I don't think I'll finish it now." And she had gone on to something else.

Nishima was left feeling very humbled—she *dreamed* of starting a painting of such mastery and here Lady Okara abandoned such a work as though it were a mere trifle.

Lady Okara's life had immense appeal to Lady Nishima—the freedom, the removal from the social whirl and the responsibilities of one's House. It seemed the perfect life.

The artist had taken time to look at sketches Nishima had brought with her and had been most complimentary.

She is an old friend of my uncle's, Nishima thought, she could hardly say anything else. Yet a part of her wanted to believe Lady Okara's words and a few moments later she had convinced herself that Lady Okara was too honorable not to have told her the truth. An instant later she was sure this could not be—Lady Okara was simply being polite in her comments, as any person of breeding would do.

As she swung back and forth between her secret hopes and her lack of confidence, the boats rounded a corner into a larger waterway and were immediately confronted by a dozen craft waiting to pass through an Imperial Guard blockade. She heard her own guard on the escort boat in front of her begin to shout. "Make way for the Lady Nishima Fanisan Shonto! Make way! Make way!" How inconvenient, she thought, settling back into her cushions, and then her instincts told her to beware.

It was too late to turn back now—to avoid a blockade was forbidden, and her guards had announced her presence. Already, they had moved to the head of the line. She could hear the lieutenant of her escort talking to the Imperial Guard now. Her name was mentioned several times with the emphasis on *Shonto, Governor* Shonto. Yet they did not move.

Her sampan swayed as someone boarded it. The Shonto lieutenant bowed to her as the circumstances would allow. "The Guard wish to detain us, my lady, it is not clear why. They are claiming 'orders.' They wish to speak with you personally. I have told them it is out of the question, yet they insist and will not let us pass. I shall send a boat to the palace immediately, but it will take time. I apologize for this inconvenience, Lady Nishima."

She considered for a moment, controlling her fear. "Do they doubt that it is me here?" she asked.

"That does not seem to be the case, Lady Nishima."

"Huh. Tell them I will complain of their actions *directly* to the Emperor and see what effect that has."

The lieutenant bowed quickly and went forward again. Nishima pulled the curtains, leaving only a slit through which to watch. She could see the lieutenant draw himself up into a suitable posture of outrage as he approached the guards, but she could also see that they were not going to allow themselves to be intimidated. They argued back and forth for a moment, voices becoming louder on both sides. Without bowing, the Shonto guard turned and came back across his boat and stepped now onto hers.

"They refuse to let us pass," he said bowing, and she could see that he fought to control anger. "They are intolerably *insolent,*" he spat out suddenly. "Excuse me, Lady Nishima, pardon my outburst."

She said nothing, not seeming to notice his apology. The situation was becoming dangerous, and she could see the anger rising in the other Shonto guards. Do they seek to provoke us into violence? It could serve no purpose. She had never been put in a situation like this before and did not know how to deal with it. Rohku Saicha would be furious when he heard, she thought.

"Tell them I will speak with them," she said suddenly.

"Are you certain, my lady?" the lieutenant was obviously shocked by her decision.

"I am certain," she said forcing confidence into her voice. I am Shonto, she told herself, they dare not interfere with me.

The lieutenant crossed the boats to the Guard again, obviously feeling humiliated that they should be in such a situation. Nishima watched as he nodded to the Guard commander and explained his lady's decision. She could not quite hear the words, but suddenly the lieutenant went rigid for a split second and then reached for his sword. Imperial Guards jumped forward to protect their officer and Shonto guards did the same. The lieutenant came to his senses before a melee erupted, though, and ordered his men back. He turned, again without bowing, and returned to Lady Nishima, his face scarlet with rage.

Lady Nishima's heart was pounding with fear.

"The officer in charge refuses to come to you, Lady Nishima. He insists that you come to him. I'm sorry. I have demanded that he take us to his commander, but he refuses. This is intolerable, I have never witnessed such lack of respect. These are men without honor. I apologize, Lady Nishima, but I don't know what we should do. We cannot go back, other Guards block our way." He cast a glance behind him. "I am entirely at fault and dishonored." The man bowed his head in shame.

Nishima realized that Lord Shonto would agree with the man entirely, but she felt sympathy for him. It is not his fault, she said to herself, though his own code says that it is.

"Tell them I will come to them," she said.

"My lady, it is out of the question! These are not even soldiers of rank!"

"It doesn't matter. There is no choice but violence, and we are few while they are many." She turned to the crewmen. "Boatmen, move me forward."

Slowly, boats parted and Lady Nishima's sampan pushed through the crowd. Rivermen and their families stared at the spectacle. They are so close, she thought, never have I been so vulnerable. She was not afraid of the rivermen, who were hardworking and honest, but this was a perfect place to hide an assassin. She cursed herself for ignoring Rohku Saicha.

Finally she came up to the Imperial Guard's boat which blocked the canal. She could see the Emperor's soldiers now, dressed in their black armor. Their commander was only a Guard Captain, and a huge man he was. He leaned silently back on the boat's small cabin, his arms crossed before him casually. He chewed something as he waited, perhaps oona nut, she thought. It was terribly bad manners.

When her sampan was ten feet away, Lady Nishima pulled the curtain back fully and stared out coldly at the Imperial Guard Captain—the soldiers with him, she ignored entirely.

"I am Lady Nishima Fanisan Shonto, why am I being delayed?" she demanded.

"You are being delayed because I am an Imperial Guard and I choose to delay you," he answered without hesitation.

Again her escort reached for their swords, but she stopped them with a gesture.

"This is unpardonable insolence, Captain, I warn you. Give me your reason for this delay or let me pass immediately!"

"I must see your papers before I will consider whether you will go on or not," he said.

There was a buzz in the surrounding crowd now, they had never seen such a thing, not with the Shonto! Could it be that such a family was in disfavor with the Son of Heaven?

"*Papers,* Captain? Could it be that you believe the Shonto carry *papers?* Perhaps you think also that I sell *fish* from my sampan?" she said, gesturing to her elegant craft.

The crowd laughed and the Guard Captain stared them into an abrupt silence. "If you can produce no papers, then you will accompany me to our keep. I have my orders."

Lady Nishima went on to her next ploy without hesitation. "You," she said, addressing the captain's second in command, a tall, young sergeant. "Your captain has taken leave of his senses. He endangers your future if not your lives, for the Emperor is not tolerant of fools. This man is unfit to command. Relieve him of his position and you may yet save yourselves."

The captain turned to stare at the younger officer, but the man looked only straight ahead as though he had not heard Lady Nishima's words. But as the captain shifted his gaze back to Lady Nishima, the sergeant looked out of the corner of his eye at two guards directly behind the captain. They nodded almost imperceptibly and shifted their positions slightly. Other guards seemed also about to act. Lady Nishima's hopes rose.

An uproar exploded to the right, beyond the boats of the river people. Shonto guards drew their swords and formed a protective barrier before their mistress. The crowd of onlookers parted as if by invisible command and more Imperial Guards rushed across the decks down the corridor they created. Lady Nishima's view was blocked, but suddenly a voice she recognized rang out over the din. The voice of Jaku Katta.

The Emperor! Nishima thought, unable to believe that this could have been done so boldly—in the capital in broad daylight with a hundred witnesses.

"*You!*" It was the voice of command and Nishima could feel even her own escort harken to it. "*Captain of the Guard. What is this you do?*"

Anger! Lady Nishima heard anger in the general's voice. Her hopes rose. Jaku Katta jumped from a barge and landed on the deck of the Imperial Guard boat. The Guard Captain bowed, a look of confusion on his face.

"I follow orders, General Jaku," he said defensively.

"You have orders to harass the Lady Nishima Fanisan?"

The guard's mouth worked, but no words came.

"I'm waiting, Captain."

"I was ordered to . . ." He did not finish. The back of Jaku's left hand smashed across his face. The guard reached for his sword, but Jaku's was out of its sheath before the captain's hand had found the hilt.

"Do you not bow to your commander, Captain?"

The man looked around him and realized he was the only one on the barge who had remained standing. Slowly he knelt, his hand to his bleeding mouth, his eyes riveted to Jaku's sword.

The general seemed to hesitate for a moment and then he sheathed his sword. "This man is your prisoner, Sergeant. Report yourselves when you return to your keep. All of you will face a Court of the Imperium's Military."

Giving a hand signal to one of his own elite guard to clear the area, Jaku Katta turned back to Lady Nishima's escort. He bowed to the Shonto lieutenant.

"I apologize for this incident, Lieutenant. It is unforgivable, I realize. I will inform the Emperor at the earliest opportunity. Would you ask if I may extend my apologies to Lady Nishima in person?"

The Shonto guard bowed in return. "Certainly, General. But please, before I do, I must inform you that the insult inflicted upon the House of Shonto and the honor of my mistress by this barbarian in Imperial Guard livery is beyond tolerance. I, too, feel that I have been dishonored by this man. I cannot accept this."

Nishima watched all of this through her partially drawn curtains. The words drifted to her only in part, but it was easy to guess what was being said. I am rescued yet I do not feel the danger has passed, she thought.

Jaku Katta shook his head in sympathy, one soldier to another. "I understand completely, Lieutenant, but is it not enough to know that his punishment will be . . . *extreme,* at the hands of the Court of the Military?"

The Shonto lieutenant seemed to weigh his words, but then asked, "Would you accept this insult, General?"

Jaku Katta considered this for only an instant, and then shook his head. "I would not." He turned to his second in command. "Clear a place on the quay and give the captain his sword. Be sure no one interferes." He turned back to the lieutenant. "Take two of your guard as witnesses." He bowed. "You choose the course of honor, Lieutenant. May the gods stand at your side."

The lieutenant bowed in return and relinquished his command to his second, a young captain with the face of a scholar. This young man went immediately to convey Jaku Katta's request to Lady Nishima.

"Is there to be a duel?" she asked as soon as the Shonto captain approached.

"It is unavoidable, Lady Nishima. I would have given the challenge myself if the lieutenant had not taken it up, as was his right."

"But the Imperial Guardsman is huge!" She raced through several arguments in her mind. Honor, she thought, this is about honor, not about fear. I must appeal to that. "Does not the lieutenant endanger the Shonto name more if he is to fail?"

"He will not fail, Lady, though I fear the cost may be great." He turned back to the quay where a crowd gathered to witness the conflict. The sight of the general reminded him of his duties. "General Katta has asked if he could convey his apologies to you in person, Lady Nishima."

"Of course, yes. Bring him to me." She could see the fight was about to begin, and there on the quay the difference in the size of the two men could truly be seen.

"General," Nishima said as Jaku approached. "Can you not stop this senseless fight? Will not the Imperial Guard be held responsible for his actions as it is?"

Jaku bowed low. "I tried to dissuade your lieutenant, Lady Nishima, but it is his right. He felt Shonto honor had been put in question. I am sorry."

Swords rang out in the silence that had settled. Lady Nishima hid her mouth behind an open fan, but in her eyes there was anguish. This is my fault, she thought. If I had listened to Rohku Saicha, this would never have happened. Or would it? Something still told her there was more to the situation than met the eye.

"Do you wish to move along the canal until this is completed? You can do nothing for your lieutenant here."

"Yes, please," she said. Anything to be beyond the sound of the swords.

Jaku signaled to her boatmen who obeyed him as though he were their commander. They rounded a corner and settled close to a stone quay.

Jaku broke the awkward silence first. "Please allow me to apologize for the actions of my guards, though I know they were unforgivable."

Lady Nishima interrupted him. "You need not apologize to me, General Katta. I remain indebted to you for your act of bravery in our garden. You saved my lord's life. This is a thing for which I can never repay you."

Jaku shrugged in modesty, then turned his tiger eyes on the young woman. "It was an honor to serve the Shonto, Lady Nishima, an honor which I would gladly repeat." He let the statement hang in the air and then turned his eyes away. "I have assured your esteemed uncle that you are in no danger while he is in Seh. Excuse my presumption, but I have been concerned about your safety since the . . . incident in Lord Shonto's garden."

"Your concern flatters me, General Jaku, but it is not the Shonto way to allow ourselves to be in another's debt."

"Debt? It is I who am in your debt, Lady Nishima, that you have not called me a presumptuous fool."

Lady Nishima nodded to Jaku for his kindness, but the ringing of swords, loud and frenzied drew her gaze away. There was silence then.

Jaku Katta cocked his head to one side concentrating on the distant sounds. "It is over, Lady Nishima. We may hope honor has been restored." He stood as an Imperial Guard came running up.

"The captain has fallen, General."

"And the Shonto lieutenant?"

"He lives, Sire, but his wounds are severe. We have taken the liberty of removing him to a doctor's care."

Lady Nishima hid her face in her hands for a second but then regained control.

The general nodded, dismissing the man. "I'm sorry, Lady Nishima, but he could not be dissuaded. I will see to his medical care myself and inform you of his condition."

"There was nothing you could do. Please do not feel the blame is yours. Pardon me, General, but I must continue, if I may."

Jaku bowed quickly. "Of course, I did not mean to detain you." He stepped off the boat onto the quay. "Perhaps we will meet at the Emperor's celebration of his Ascension?"

You are bold, Nishima thought. "Perhaps."

He smiled and fixed her with a parting glance.

The cold eyes of the predator, Nishima thought, as the general turned away. But still she felt stirred by his presence. Had he not saved her uncle? Had he not rescued her from this impossible situation?

Her escort returned and the boatmen pushed off. A voice inside spoke, saying that despite all appearances, something was not right. What was it Jaku had said to the Imperial Guard captain when he appeared?—"You have orders to harass the Lady Nishima Fanisan?"

That is how he sees me, she realized suddenly, *Lady Nishima Fanisan—a daughter of the blood.* She felt the island of Lady Okara slipping away, and the life she desired gone with it. "I can never escape it," she said in a whisper, "though I would not choose it if offered a thousand times. My blood, I cannot change my blood."

As the dusk settled in the capital of Wa, the Lady Nishima rode toward her destination feeling, more than ever, that it had been chosen by forces beyond herself.

Not far away, Jaku Katta boarded his own sampan and signaled his boatmen to take him to the Imperial Palace. Once in the privacy of his craft, Jaku could not help smiling with satisfaction. She is not as unattainable as I had been led to believe, he thought. Oh, but she was no fool! Almost she had convinced the guards to mutiny against their captain! He shook his head in disbelief. If he had not appeared when he had . . . well, it was done now, and that fool of a captain would never tell what his orders had been. That had been a close moment, and the lieutenant was so small! Jaku had feared he would not be able to perform the deed. He should not have been concerned— Shonto men were trained to be the best and, except for Jaku's elite guard, they were.

The Emperor's general leaned forward as if to hurry his boat along. Battle had been engaged and now everything hung in the balance. Only time would tell if his plans were adequate. And the time would be short.

Only one doubt nagged at the Commander of the Imperial Guard. He knew it grew out of something that could almost be called superstition, but he could not reason this doubt away.

Jaku Katta could remember failing to accomplish something once in his life and the person who had brought about that failure had returned, and slipped through an assassination attempt already.

The famed kick boxer closed his eyes and rubbed his brow as if in sudden pain. It was not a memory that brought him comfort. Not one of the thousands of people who watched had seen what had occurred. But it had marked Jaku and he could not erase that mark.

A small Botahist monk had stood before him, utterly calm after deflecting a blow that had all the power of Jaku's huge frame behind it. Deflecting it, yet Jaku knew there had been no contact between them. He had felt the power though, the unheard of power. To turn a blow without touching the assailant. . . .

Jaku shook his head to free himself of his memory. He looked out to the banks of the canal and saw the people bow as he passed. Drawing a long breath, he forced a calm over himself. They no longer stood in the limited arena of the tournament ring. Here, the boy was hopelessly beyond his depth, there could be no doubt of that.

The boat rounded into the Canal of His Highest Wisdom, the widest canal in the capital, and there, at its end, the white palace of the Emperor seemed to glow in the failing light. It was Jaku's destination.

Twelve

THE BOTAHIST ACOLYTE, Tesseko, knelt by the charcoal fire that burned amidships. The motion of the river junk was less noticeable there and her sensitive stomach appreciated that. A wind fanned the coals and smoke curled up to sting her eyes, but she did not seem to mind—it was a fair wind and it hurried them on their way to Seh.

She chanted the glory of the Perfect Master silently as she worked, knowing that this helped speed the time during the performance of menial tasks. (Glory, glory to His wisdom which leads me.)

She glanced up as she cooked and saw the people on the canal bank kneeling as the Imperial Governor's progress passed. She, herself, felt awe to be part of this procession. As she had thought herself immeasurably fortunate (Glory to the Seven Paths) when she was selected to accompany senior Sister Morima on this journey. Sister Morima, the woman who had looked upon the *Hand of Botahara* with her own eyes! Yes, she had felt fortunate.

Junior Acolyte Tesseko bent over the food she prepared, vegetables, steamed rice—the simple fare of the ascetic. Into this she mixed a secret blend of herbs, for Sister Morima had been taken ill, or so it seemed. Since they had set out from the Priory of the Divine Awakening, seven days past, Sister Morima had become more and more withdrawn. Her face had become pale and her skin waxy. This will set her to rights, Tesseko told herself.

She felt a certain disappointment at Sister Morima's silence. She had hoped to learn more; after all, Tesseko was almost ready to become a senior Acolyte—and she was only eighteen—she had hoped the Sister would take her more into her confidence, there was so much Sister Morima could teach her. But she realized now that it was not to be so.

Tesseko did not even know the reason for this journey. Of course, she had not dared ask—the Sisterhood did many things in secret—it was the place of a junior Acolyte to serve. But still she could not help but wonder. She had begun to observe Sister Morima carefully, yet all she could learn was that there was a certain Botahist Brother, the Spiritual Advisor to the great Lord Shonto, that Sister Morima seemed to be very interested in. She watched him secretly, and Acolyte Tesseko was certain she wrote her observations down in a cipher. It was all very mysterious and exciting, she thought.

She tried to imagine why Sister Morima watched this young monk. Was he secretly a spy for the Sisterhood, living in the midst of the aristocracy and privy to the secrets of the Botahist Brothers? She did not know. All she knew was the young Brother was thought very gifted—she had heard much in her short time aboard—and he had greeted her with respect when they had met by accident, in the small town where the fleet had stopped two days previously. He seemed most kind. That was all she knew.

Perhaps she expected too much; the honored Sister was not herself, with this sudden illness taking hold of her as it had. Sister Morima had had fevers and delirium in the night, Acolyte Tesseko knew, for she had been forced to listen to the Botahist nun in the darkness of their shared cabin. It had frightened her to hear the Sister rant. And she had said such things! (Glory to His name, eternal glory.) Well, she did not want to think about the things Sister Morima had said. She shuddered involuntarily, for Acolyte Tesseko had seldom heard blasphemy before and certainly not from the mouth of a senior Sister.

She removed the food from the coals and served it into porcelain bowls, which she set on a bamboo tray. (Glory of His words, their perfection, glory.) Crossing the deck she noticed a sailor watching her. Often, she had been told she was pretty, though she could not imagine why anyone would think that—her black hair was cropped short and her robe was shapeless and unflattering. It is wrong to think of such things, she told herself. (Glory of His vision, highest glory of His vision.)

The steps to the cabin were steep and difficult, but the training of the Sisterhood had given her suppleness and strength beyond that of most inhabitants of Wa. Not using even a hand for balance, she descended with ease. She tapped on the screen to their cabin, but there was no response. Sliding the shoji quietly, she entered the darkened room. Sister Morima lay in a low bed, set against one wall. Tesseko could hear her labored breathing.

"Sister Morima?" Tesseko said as she crossed the room. But there was no response. She set the tray on a small, fixed table, and knelt beside the bed.

"Sister Morima?" she said again a bit louder, but still there was only the sound of the Sister's breathing. She felt the nun's brow and found it hot and clammy. Poor Sister Morima, she thought. It was then that she noticed that her superior was dressed in her outer robe, she could see her shoulder protruding from beneath covers. Has she been out of bed? Tesseko wondered. I should have been here to assist her.

The young Acolyte moved away, deciding to let the nun sleep, and was about to rise when something assailed her nostrils. She turned her head to each side, testing the air for the source of the odor. This cannot be, she thought. It seemed to come from under the low table. She bent down to look and could not believe the evidence of her eyes! There, pushed out of sight, was a plate, and on it the remains of a meal of *flesh!* Bones and pieces of disgusting fat. Acolyte Tesseko felt immediately ill. *May Botahara save her,* she thought, Sister Morima has eaten of the *flesh of an animal!* She turned and fled from the cabin.

The boatmen guided the sampan with deft strokes, moving it quickly against the canal's current. Acolyte Tesseko sat in the prow watching the large junks and river barges as the sampan glided past them. It was another fine day in what seemed like an endless autumn. She breathed the spiced air in careful rhythm, as her instructors had taught her, forcing a calm over her body and mind. Acolyte Tesseko had been distraught, almost in a panic, since her discovery of the day before. Now she felt closer to being at peace. She was aware of the slight time-stretch that the Sisters spoke of, felt the chi-flow in her body. She wondered again if it was true that the Brothers had mastered their sense of subjective time?

This brought her back to the reason that she was aboard the sampan and shook the feeling of confidence she was trying to create, for the truth was, she was not sure that what she was about to do was correct. But were they not both followers of the Great Way? She could not believe that this young monk, Lord Shonto's Spiritual Advisor, was evil, as the Sisters said all Brothers were. Her instincts had told her immediately that he was good, a follower of the True Faith. Some of the Sisters believed that this strife between the Sisterhood and the Brotherhood went against the teaching of Botahara, for the struggle was centered on power, and the followers of Botahara renounced all claim to power as they renounced property and the desires of the flesh.

The desires of the flesh, well, she must not think of those. (Glory to the Seven Paths, glory.)

If what these Sisters believed was true, then it would be correct for her to speak with this Brother—whose name, she must remember, was Shuyun.

And besides, Tesseko realized, there was no one else she could discuss her problem with. Who else was there who understood the divine secrets of the human body? Sister Morima, in her few lucid moments, absolutely refused to be taken off the junk (they must get to Seh!) and there were no other Botahist Sisters in the flotilla. What I do is correct. In my soul I do not doubt.

They came abreast of the Imperial Governor's barge and Acolyte Tesseko was allowed to wait on the boarding platform while a guard went to find Shonto's steward.

It took only a moment for the guard to return, accompanied by a one-armed old man. He bowed to her formally.

"I am Kamu, Steward of Lord Shonto Motoru. Excuse our precautions, Sister, but is it true that you wish to see Lord Shonto's Spiritual Advisor?" He said this calmly, as though he were merely verifying information. He showed no surprise at the request.

"Please, Steward Kamu, it is most important."

He said nothing for a few seconds but then asked, "May I tell Shuyun-sum the reason that you wish to see him?" When he saw the pained expression on her face he raised his hand. "I will speak with him." He disappeared onto the deck and left Tesseko in the company of the Shonto guards who, though stationed to watch her, seemed to be staring off at something in the distance, as was only polite.

A moment later Kamu reappeared. "Please, Sister, would you come with me?" He gave the guards a hand signal that the nun memorized. She would report it to her superiors. They recorded these things and, over a period of years could sometimes break a family's code altogether.

She crossed the deck in Kamu's wake and followed him to the bow. Out of a hatch emerged the monk she had spoken to in the town. He nodded to Kamu, who bowed respectfully.

"Acolyte Tesseko, I am honored that you visit me. Perhaps this is a sign of what will happen in the future between our faiths." He bowed politely and she returned his gesture.

"Perhaps, Brother Shuyun, though I must tell you that I am here on my own initiative, not on behalf of my Order."

Shuyun nodded and motioned to the bow area where they could speak in privacy. He leaned against the low rail and regarded the Acolyte. She was fine of form, he thought, and tall. Under the flat, conical hat, her eyes were guarded, she seemed to be suppressing agitation. She had not yet mastered the technique that would allow her to do this, for he could see tension there, in the tightening of the skin around the eyes and the redness of the tear ducts.

"Would you care for cha, Acolyte Tesseko?" he asked, following the etiquette of the situation.

"It is kind of you to offer, Brother, but I have other duties and can only speak with you briefly."

He sensed the urgency in her voice. "Perhaps it would be best if we did away with formality, and spoke openly, Acolyte Tesseko."

"I agree, that would be best." She took a breath in preparation but could not begin the speech she had rehearsed. Suddenly, she wondered if what she was doing was right.

"If it will make it easier, Acolyte Tesseko, I will swear by the Perfect Master that your words will not go beyond me."

She nodded. "I have come for advice, Brother, medical advice. I travel with a senior Sister who is very ill. I have not seen these symptoms before, Brother, I am most distressed."

"She would not consent to see me?"

"No, it is out of the question." She put a hand to the rail and turned to stare off across the canal.

"Can you describe these symptoms, Acolyte?"

"She is fevered, often at night. But in the day she seems distant, as though she were in the grip of fever, yet she is not. She eats, some days, in excess, while other days she cannot bear the sight of food. All of her behavior is uncharacteristic. I am not sure what should be done, Brother."

"It is unfortunate that she will not see me. Is there anything else you can tell me."

Tesseko looked off into the distance again, watching a swallow play with a feather. The tension around her eyes increased, and Shuyun wondered if she would be able to go on.

"There are other things . . . Brother. She speaks in her deliriums. She frightens me."

"Frightens you, Acolyte?"

"She says things that—it is only her illness—but these things endanger her spirit. They must. And Sister Morima is such an enlightened woman."

Sister Morima! Shuyun remembered her—the large nun in the Supreme Master's audience hall. ("Have you learned to stop the sand, Initiate?") Yes, he knew her, knew that she had been selected to witness the Ceremony of Divine Renewal.

"Tell me of these things, Acolyte, it may be important."

"I . . . I cannot repeat them, Brother, they are *blasphemous.*"

"Can you tell me something of their nature without repeating them, Acolyte?"

"She speaks of the Word of Lord Botahara, the actual written Word."

"I know that she attended the Ceremony of Divine Renewal, Acolyte Tesseko."

She nodded but continued to look away. "She says—she seems to say that the words of Botahara are not his words."

"She seems to say this? What do you mean."

"Over and over she repeats," the Acolyte half covered her mouth with her hand, " '*lies! all that we have learned is lies!* '" Tesseko closed her eyes tightly for a moment. "There is more. Sometimes in the darkness she yells: '*These are not the words of truth! These are not our Lord's words!*' I cannot say any more. I am most concerned, Brother."

"Yes," Shuyun said, and it was almost a whisper. She had started now, she would not stop until she had told all.

"When she eats, she gorges herself, entirely without discipline, and sometimes—I don't know where she gets it—she eats *flesh,* Brother!"

She covered her face completely now. Her shoulders shook, but there were no sobs. Shuyun let her cry, he had no experience in comforting women, and he was afraid anything he said would cause her embarrassment. The monk did not show the shock that he felt. *A Sister eating the flesh of animals!* It said so much. He felt a deep sense of revulsion.

Acolyte Tesseko regained her self-possession, though her hands still shook and she tried to hide them. "Pardon me, Brother, I do not deserve your respect after this display of weakness."

"Please, do not think of yourself this way. It must be difficult to see a Sister behaving in this manner. I am honored that you would choose to come to me with this. You must feel no shame.

"What you have described to me, Acolyte Tesseko, I have heard of before. I believe that Sister Morima suffers a crisis of the spirit. Her apparent illness is only a reflection of her inner sufferings. Why this is . . ?" he shrugged, "It seems to be connected with seeing the scrolls of Botahara. Perhaps she was not properly prepared for such an experience.

"You must not leave her, Acolyte, but word must be sent to your Order. They must know as soon as it can be arranged—a messenger tomorrow at the next stop. Do you have a cipher?"

Tesseko nodded.

"Good. Keep this as secret as possible. And you must stop her from eating flesh! Shame her if you must. Tell her everyone aboard speaks of it as scandal. It may well be the truth.

"Tell me what herbs you have given her." He saw how she hesitated. "It does not matter. I will tell you what I would treat her with and you may make a decision from that knowledge. In all likelihood what you have given her would be the same. Root of menta, steamed not boiled, mixed with tomal. Every fourth hour will be often enough. But it would be even better if you could convince her to meditate and to do chi exercises. How far north do you travel, Acolyte Tesseko?"

Again she hesitated, which he found strange. "We go to Seh, Brother."

"Then perhaps you should send a message ahead also. Your Sisters will know what to do, I would not fear. If you need to speak with me again, I will leave word with the guard to allow you through."

Tesseko bowed to him, formally. "I am indebted to you, Brother. I must return to Sister Morima now." She turned to go but stopped and smiled at him over her shoulder. "I thank you for your counsel, Brother Shuyun, it has been an honor meeting you."

He watched her go, a tall young woman in the yellow robe of the Botahist Sisters. He tried to make his mind address this new information but he could not.

The Scrolls, he thought. *The Scrolls of our Lord! The Sacred Scrolls.*

All of his years of training, and yet his mind refused to focus.

Thirteen

A moth in the dark,
Searching among the mulberry leaves,
And honor is so
Easily lost.

Jaku Tadamoto

THE WALK OF Inner Peace was a long, covered hall, open along one side, high in the Palace of the Emperor. It looked east, over the vast gardens, toward the distant hills, with their large temples and monasteries—white walls stark against the dark green. Jaku Tadamoto strode along the walk, his keen mind examining the latest information he had received. His brother Katta surprised even him with his audacity. This report of the Imperial Guard Captain who had interfered with Lady Nishima, it had the signature of Jaku Katta brushed upon it. He shook his head in disbelief.

The Lady Nishima! What was his brother thinking? It could not be an alliance with the Shonto, that would be unthinkable. The Shonto were too strong. Katta would not take the chance of having allies to whom he would be secondary. It was something else, something more.

It was this "something more" that frightened him. The Jaku had risen beyond anyone's most secret hopes, did that *fool* Katta wish to endanger this now? Tadamoto increased his pace. In his sleeve he carried a written report from Katta to the Emperor. It seemed to lay there, heavy with purpose, waiting.

It was very early morning, too early for the great numbers of people who, each day, sought time to stroll the Walk of Inner Peace. Jaku Tadamoto was surprised, therefore, to see a solitary figure, half hidden by a column, near the far end of the walk. Golden robe, rich material (as all material worn in the palace was rich). A woman, he decided. A Lady of the Court, returning from an assignation? A courtesan who had pleased the Emperor? He walked on. But then, as he drew closer, his heart lifted. He recognized her—*Osha, the Emperor's Sonsa dancer!*

He approached so quietly that he startled her.

"Oh, Tadamoto-sum," she put her hand to her heart, "I was so far away."

He bowed to her. "I apologize for destroying your harmony, Osha-sum. I was surprised to find anyone here at this hour and was most inconsiderate of your presence."

She smiled at him, a lovely smile, though somehow full of cares. "Please, do not apologize. I am honored to have your company, it is so seldom that we speak." She held his eye for a second and then turned to the view over the grounds. She seemed to be inviting him to share this with her. Looking up and down the hall, Tadamoto moved to the low wall beside her.

Wisps of cloud still glowed faintly with the colors of the dawn.

"Is it not beautiful?" Osha asked.

"It is," he agreed.

"But so brief." She did not look at him. "Why is it that things of great beauty seem to come into this world for only an instant?"

Tadamoto shook his head. "To remain always a rarity, is that not part of their beauty?"

She turned to him then, seeming to search his eyes for the source of these words. "I can see why the Emperor values you so, Tadamoto-sum."

He nodded modestly, embarrassed by her flattery. Yet she had said this so strangely, with such an emphasis on "you."

She turned back to the scene which spread out below them, the vibrant colors of autumn scattered among the greens and browns. She seemed sad somehow, and this pulled at Tadamoto's heart. He wanted to take her in his arms to comfort her, but he knew he dared not. A sound almost caused him to whirl around, but it was only a dove cooing softly.

"Does our Emperor seem . . . distant to you, Tadamoto-sum?" she asked suddenly. The moods of the Emperor were a highly sensitive subject, and Tadamoto was honored that she would trust him enough to ask.

"I have not found him so."

"Ah," she said, and nodded, "I have wondered."

She glanced back along the hall herself now, but still no one was there. "Tadamoto-sum, there is something I need to discuss with you. I would not ask you if I did not know how loyal you are to our Emperor."

"Of course."

"But we cannot talk here." She looked behind her again. "Could you meet with me? Do I ask too much?"

"You could not ask too much of me," he said.

"There is a place in the east wing. A Hanama shrine to Botahara. No one goes there now." She turned to him then, her eyes full of anguish. "Tonight, could you come tonight?"

He nodded, saying nothing.

"The hour of the owl," she whispered and suddenly brushed by him and was gone. He was left with the touch of her hand on his arm and the memory of silk brushing against him. His heart beat out his excitement.

Why did she wish to meet him? Was it truly something to do with the Emperor? Or did she wish only to meet with Jaku Tadamoto? He prayed that it was so—and that it was not so.

Her hands shaking with the danger of what she had just done, Osha slipped quietly into her own rooms. Cracking a screen on the far side of the room she said, "cha," to an unseen maid. To stop her hands from trembling, she clasped them to her breast.

What choice do I have? she asked herself, what choice?

She dropped her knees to a pillow. The Emperor was growing cold toward her. She put her hands to her face. It was all so sudden. Only three days ago he had seemed totally enamored of her. She shook her head. *I don't understand!* she whispered. Was it because the Empress would soon return from the Summer Palace? It could not be. He hated her openly, Osha knew. She had seen the way the Empress tried to keep her hold on him. She was a woman without dignity.

This will never happen to me, she told herself. But she was not convinced. Osha was aware of how far a mistress of the Emperor could fall when she earned his disfavor. *Earned!!* What had she done to earn his disfavor? Nothing, she said, he has simply grown tired of me, as he did of the others before me. I thought I would be different. I thought I could hold him. A sob escaped her, but she fought the tears.

A maid entered with cha, but Osha sent her away as soon as the hot liquid was poured. She wanted to be alone.

This is more than love-pain, she told herself. With whom would she dance when it became known that she was in disfavor with the Emperor? What troupe would risk offending the Son of Heaven by presenting him with someone he did not wish to see?

"I was a fool!" she said aloud, surprising herself with the outburst. She sipped slowly to calm her nerves.

She would need an ally, that was the decision she had come to. If she were to fall—and that had not happened yet—she would need a powerful supporter, someone the Emperor valued; as he valued Jaku Tadamoto. She knew this because the Emperor had spoken to her about this young man on more than one occasion. He had described Tadamoto in very flattering terms.

Osha had also considered the elder Jaku—Katta—but he would demand too much of her and then, no doubt, cast her aside. No, she was safer with Tadamoto; he was not as handsome as his older brother, but he was a man of honor and there was much to be said for that.

So, she was committed to this course, and the plan was simple. With the right ally she could dance again. She could keep her place as the preeminent Sonsa in the capital, and in time she could free herself of the need for others. She would live without a patron.

Setting her cha down, Osha went to change into her dance costume. She must dance now. Dance until every movement she made was flawless. Her world had changed. There would be no room now for mistakes.

The mats felt cool against his forehead as he bowed before the Most Revered Son of Heaven. Almost, he could have stayed there, eyes closed, feeling the cool grasses against his skin—it felt so safe. But he rose and faced the Emperor, and his green eyes did not waver.

"I understand that you are addressed now as 'Colonel'?" the Emperor said.

"This is true, Sire."

"Well, Colonel Jaku Tadamoto, I congratulate you. It is no more than you deserve."

"I am honored by your words, Sire."

The Emperor nodded. He sat upon the dais, his sword of office held across his lap. Tadamoto thought the Highest One looked as though the concerns of his Empire weighed upon him. Age seemed to show in the Emperor's face, and he kept pulling his sword half out of its sheath and then pushing it back, as though the sound gave him comfort.

"You have a report for us from your esteemed brother?"

"I have, Sire." Tadamoto removed the sealed scroll from his sleeve and placed it on the edge of the dais. The Emperor paid no attention to it.

"I have difficult decisions to make, Tadamoto-sum," the Emperor said suddenly.

"If I am not being presumptuous, Sire, I would be honored if I could assist in any small way."

"You are kind to offer, but these are decisions about my sons, Colonel."

"I understand, Emperor."

"Do you?" he asked, fixing Tadamoto with a searching gaze.

"I understand that these would be difficult decisions, Sire."

"I see," the Emperor said, pulling the sword half out of its sheath and pushing it back with a "click." He looked off, his eyes losing focus. "One of my sons must marry the Lady Nishima. You understand that, don't you Tadamoto-sum?"

"I do, Sire."

"The problem is many-faced. The Lady Nishima is the loyal protégée of Lord Shonto, a man who plots to gain control of the Throne, yeh?"

Tadamoto nodded agreement.

"And there are other problems with the Lady Nishima. Oh, she would be a perfect Empress, that is not in doubt. But she is strong and my sons are weak—it is the fault of my useless wife, she raised them to be fools and effetes." (*click*) "So, we have a problem. One must wed the Lady Nishima, and another," he paused, "another must become . . . an example. For the one who weds must be educated to his responsibilities. So, one will go to Seh to share in Lord Shonto's fate—do you understand what that means, Tadamoto-sum?"

"I do, Emperor."

"I appreciate how quickly you see things, Colonel." (*click*) "Who would accuse us of plotting the great lord's fall when our own son falls with him?" The Emperor was silent for a moment. "I wish it were otherwise, but my sons do not serve the Yamaku purpose well, and the one that is to wed must understand that he is not, not . . . *inexpendable*." (*click*)

"Katta-sum has been like a son to me." He pulled the sword half from its sheath, "yet he begins to disappoint me also. This interference with the Lady Nishima. . . ." The Son of Heaven shook his head sadly. "His appetite for ladies from the Great Houses is a terrible weakness, Tadamoto-sum. Perhaps you should speak to him about this—you are wiser than he—Katta-sum listens to your counsel.

"Your brother has been of great value to us, Colonel, so we have indulged him—it is not always good to indulge a son, if your desire is that he will grow strong, yeh?"

The Emperor looked around the room as though something were missing, but before he discovered what it was he again became distracted and began to toy with his sword.

"It is a time of decisions, Tadamoto-sum, it is also a time of focus. The stars align for great occurrences—all of the seers agree. Houses may topple, Empires could be shaken. There can be no mistakes on our part, I hope your brother understands this. If there are mistakes, the whole Empire will be plunged into war. The Yamaku waited a thousand years for our Ascendancy. If it is endangered now. . . ." (*click*) The Emperor shrugged. "Speak to your brother, Tadamoto-sum; tell him how much his loyalty is valued."

Suddenly, the Emperor became present, as though he had just walked into the room. He smiled at Jaku Tadamoto. "We do not wish to burden you with our problems, Tadamoto-sum."

"I am honored that you would speak of these things to me, Sire, and certainly I will talk with my brother immediately."

The Emperor waved his hand as though this was understood, a small matter. "You have kept a watch on Osha-sum, Colonel?"

"As you have commanded, Sire." Tadamoto said too quickly. He was careful now to meet the Emperor's eyes.

The Emperor looked up to the heavens. "I have too many decisions. May the gods help me. She does not seem to understand my responsibilities, Tadamoto-sum. It is hard for someone in her position." He gripped his sword as though he would wring water from it. "Ah, well." He smiled at Tadamoto.

"We must speak again, Colonel, it helps to restore my harmony." He nodded to Tadamoto who touched his head to the mat and backed from the room.

The Emperor watched the young man go. Will Osha have him? he wondered; it would be difficult after an Emperor. Ah, well, it hardly mattered. She served to keep the young Jaku loyal to his Emperor. He pulled his sword free of its sheath and hefted it, cutting across the air in front of him. Yes, he thought, Osha must be settled soon. She was delightful, it was true, but the Emperor had come to a decision—something he had told no one. He laughed to himself. I am not as old as everyone seems to think! They will soon see. He laughed again. Ah, how we will surprise them! He returned the sword of his office to its scabbard. I will have a new wife! *That* will give my scheming Empress and her useless sons pause to think.

He weighed the question again. Lady Nishima was Shonto—in spirit if not in blood. It would not be wise to have her too close to him, not wise at all. But her cousin, the Lady Kitsura Omawara! His blood *sang* at the thought. Well, he had made no decisions, but there were more paths open to him than those around him realized. Many more.

All that remained to be done was to rid himself of Shonto Motoru. And then the problem of the Fanisan daughter could be dealt with in any number of ways. Once Shonto was gone, there would be no one left in the realm strong enough to raise the great lords against the Throne. He could do what he pleased.

His mood of gaiety passed when he thought of his new governor. We cannot fail, he said for the thousandth time. We cannot.

But was Shonto not ever resourceful? He touched his palms to his forehead and felt the dampness on them. Everything goes as planned, he told himself, I must remain tranquil. I must wait. I must.

Fourteen

THE SMALL STREAM which branched from the Grand Canal lay still in the gathering dusk. Willow trees hung over the bank dripping leaves into the dark waters. Hidden along the bank, Shonto guards waited for the boats they knew would come. A whistled signal went from sentry to sentry as their lord's sampan passed—the sound of a night bird calling in the dusk.

The flotilla had been left alongside the stone quay of the nearby town, the crews allowed a few hours ashore—"a break from their toils." The truth, though, was that the Imperial Governor wished to pay a visit to a very old man who had once been his gii master.

Shuyun was surprised at this whim of Lord Shonto's. It was apparent to the young monk that more than just the currents of the canal swept Shonto toward Seh. Other forces, too, powerful forces, propelled the lord north—toward what, Shuyun did not know. Yet Shonto had somehow slipped aside, sloughing off the grip of the currents, to steal down this backwater on an endeavor that seemed merely sentimental.

The Lord of the Shonto sat beside his Spiritual Advisor in the sampan, saying nothing. Shuyun wondered about this Shonto predilection for loyalty. It had been loyalty that had allowed the first Yamaku Emperor to trap Shonto Motoru's father—and on that occasion the Shonto had almost been entered on the long scroll of names of Great Houses that were no more.

This trait of the Shonto, it is both a strength and a weakness, Shuyun thought, so it must be watched, and watched carefully.

The boats pushed out of the stream onto a small lake, released from shadow into the last of the day's light. The colors of evening spread in a wash across the western horizon, running from cloud to cloud. There wasn't a breeze to stir the surface of the lake and the sky seemed to lie on the water like a perfect print of the unfolding sunset.

On the far side of the lake, smoke curled out of the trees, and, as Shonto's sampan approached, a dock came into view, seeming to detach itself from the shadow of the bank. And then, behind it, the outline of a roof appeared. The boats of Shonto's guards lay drawn up on a narrow, sand beach, and the soldiers stood watch from the shadows of ancient trees.

As they approached the small wooden dock, a captain of Shonto's elite guard gave the "all clear" handsign from the wharfhead and the sampan slipped alongside. The guards knelt as Lord Shonto and his Spiritual Advisor emerged from their craft.

Raising his head, the captain nodded to his lord.

"Yes?" Shonto said.

"Excuse me, Sire," and he gestured toward the nearby point.

There, in the shallows under the branches of a tono tree, a tall bird stood silhouetted against the sunset in the waters.

"An autumn crane," Shonto whispered, his pleasure evident.

"A good omen, Sire," the guard said.

Yes, Shonto thought, and his mind went back to the coins of Kowan-sing— the crane had been the pattern cast for his daughter. Nishi-sum, the lord thought, you will be safe, I will not fail. He stayed for a moment, watching.

The crane stood, unmoving, and as the dark flowed out from among the trees and across the lake, it became easier to believe that the great bird was nothing more than a bent branch emerging from the waters. Just as Shonto was no longer sure of what he saw, the crane struck, coming up with a wiggling fish in its bill. It took two steps to the sand, disappearing into the shadows and then, an instant later, it emerged on the wing, sweeping across the water in slow powerful strokes. Where the wingtips touched, perfect rings appeared in the water's surface.

Shonto nodded to the captain and then turned toward the shore, Shuyun a step behind.

The lord had said very little on the short trip from the town, and he did not seem to want to break that silence now. Shuyun had expected to learn something more of the man they went to visit, but this did not happen. A favored teacher of the Shonto and a famous gii master, that was all the information he had—except for the man's name, Myochin Ekun, and that Shuyun recognized from his own study of the board. The games of Myochin Ekun were among those chosen as exemplary, by the teaching Brothers. These were then examined by the Neophyte monks, who were taught to play gii so that they might learn to focus their young minds.

Myochin Ekun. Shuyun felt as if he was about to meet someone from the past, a legend in fact—Myochin Ekun: gii master of gii masters.

How is it that the Shonto drew such people to them? Shuyun wondered. The answer was almost too obvious—they were the Shonto. And now he had come to them, Initiate Brother Shuyun. This thought left him with nothing but questions.

Unlike the Lady Nishima, Shuyun thought, I cannot see the future. My history will be bound with that of the Shonto or I will be unknown. It does not matter, he reminded himself. One's karma is not dependent on one's service to the Shonto.

They approached the house in the trees. Shuyun could make it out now, a low building with a simple tile roof. There was no garden wall, though a sparse garden had been arranged around the porch.

An old man who does not take an interest in his garden, Shuyun thought, how odd.

Servants knelt beside the walkway to the house, most of them older. They smiled with great pleasure as Shonto passed, and Shuyun was surprised by the lack of respect this showed. But then, Shonto stopped before an old woman who glowed like a proud mother.

"Kashiki-sum, you grow younger by the year." The lord smiled, almost boyishly.

The woman laughed, the laugh of a girl, musical, light, without cares. "It is the waters, Sire, we all approach the Immortals here. But it is you who have remained young." She broke into a large grin. "Young enough to take another wife, I'm sure all would agree."

Everyone laughed, Shonto harder than the rest.

"I am waiting until I am older, Kashiki-sum, I must slow down somewhat before a young woman will be able to keep up with me." Shonto bowed to the woman and, as he did so, gave a hand signal to a nearby guard. "I have brought you something from the capital. Something for each of you."

The staff bowed their thanks and Shonto went on.

Of course, he knows all of these servants, Shuyun realized, perhaps they helped raise him as a child.

There was only a single step to the porch and here knelt the senior member of Myochin Ekun's staff.

"You honor us with your visit, Lord Shonto, Brother."

"The honor is ours, Leta. Where is your master?"

"He awaits you inside, Sire." The man rose, and taking a lantern from a hook, led them into the darkened house. It was a small and comfortable home, open on three sides where screens had been pushed back. The servant held the lantern aloft to light three wide steps that led to the next level. There, in the gloom, Shuyun could just make out the form of a man, sitting, bent low over a table.

"Master Myochin?" the servant said in a loud voice.

The form straightened, surprised by the sound.

"Your guests are here, Master."

He turned to them now, long white hair in confusion, framing a face old with the whiteness of age, skin as translucent as the wax of a candle. Shuyun was startled by the man's eyes, porcelain white, pure, unmarred by the dark circle of a pupil.

He is blind, Shuyun thought, he has been blind all of his days.

This apparition in a white robe smiled as benignly as a statue of Botahara.

"Motoru-sum?" came a soft voice.

"I am here, Eku-sum."

"Ah, what pleasure your voice brings. Come. Bring light for our guests, Leta. Come, Motoru-sum. You are not alone?"

"I am with my Spiritual Advisor, Brother Shuyun."

"I am honored. It is always a pleasure to have a pilgrim of the Seven Paths in my home. Do the young monks still play gii, Brother Shuyun?"

"They do, Master Myochin. And your games are chief among their lessons."

"After all these years?" His already apparent pleasure increased noticeably. "I do not deserve to be so honored. Still play my games? Imagine."

Servants brought lamps and mead for the gii master and his guests. It was a most pleasant house, warm with the colors of rich woods. The scent of the nearby pines traveled freely through the open walls and an owl could be heard, calling softly over the lake.

Lord Shonto and his teacher talked briefly of Shonto's staff, the old man asking specifically after several people, Shonto's son and Lady Nishima first among them. To be polite to Shuyun, the conversation then turned to other things, the old man impressing the monk with his knowledge of the affairs of the Empire. It was hard to imagine how he received his information, the lake seemed so far removed from the rest of Wa. But the truth was, it was close to the canal and, as an Empress had once said, "if we could tax the rumors traveling the Grand Canal, we should not need to bother with the cargo."

"So you have taken this appointment to Seh, Motoru-sum?"

"I had little choice."

The old man nodded, a gesture Shuyun knew he could never have seen.

"I suppose that is true. Sometimes you must step into the danger. You are too strong, Motoru-sum, he cannot abide that," the old man said in his soft voice. He seemed to pause for a moment, listening. "We must accept certain inevitabilities. You will never make peace with the Emperor as equals. Do not imagine it, Motoru-sum. That is the real trap for you, but it can never be. There is only one winner at the gii board. Do not have false hopes that Akantsu will come to his senses. He will not."

"I have thought the same thing." Shonto said.

The old man broke into a smile. "Of course you have. I did not waste my time training you!" He laughed.

As they spoke, Shuyun noticed that Lord Shonto's eyes were repeatedly drawn to the gii board set on the nearby table. Finally the lord could no longer contain his curiosity. "I see you cannot give it up entirely." He reached over and tapped the wooden table.

"Ah, well. It is the habit of a lifetime and I must do something to fill my days. Do you know, I have found a third solution to the Soto problem."

"Really?" Shonto's interest rose immediately.

"Yes, I was as surprised as you."

"I know the Kundima solution." Shonto said.

"Yes, my own teacher."

"And the Fujiki solution," Shuyun offered.

"Ah, Brother Shuyun, you do know the game."

"But a third . . ." Shonto said, again looking at the board.

"Perhaps you can find it," Myochin Ekun suggested. "Consider it while dinner is prepared."

The board was brought closer for Shuyun and Lord Shonto. The pieces were already arranged for the classic problem, contrived, more than three hundred years earlier, by the gii master, Soto. Obviously the old man had been awaiting an opportunity to share his discovery.

Lord Shonto and his young advisor both stared at the board, but their companion had turned away, turned so that the small breeze, coming through the open screens, caressed his face.

"I could advance the *foot-soldier* in the fifth rank. This would put pressure on the keep." Shonto suggested.

"Huh." The old man considered this for a moment. "If I were defending, I would answer with the *swordmaster* to his own seventh file and you would be forced to retreat and cover. In the end this would cost you dearly in moves lost."

Shonto moved the two pieces accordingly, that he might examine the new position. "I understand." He said at last, and returned the pieces to their places.

"You must look deeper," the gii master said in a whisper. "You will come to the disputed lands soon, will you not?" he asked suddenly.

"What? Oh, yes, yes, of course."

"A puzzling situation," the old man said, and Shuyun was not sure what he referred to. "The solution, if I may give you some indication, is entirely unconventional. It came to me like a revelation, something I'm sure you can appreciate, Brother."

"Any obvious attack has been explored a thousand times," Shonto said, thinking out loud.

"More, I would say, Motoru-sum."

Suddenly Shonto looked up. "If I do not attack, what will you do?"

"An important consideration." The gii master sat with his blind eyes closed, turning his face slowly from side to side, enjoying the feel of the breeze. "I am much like any other Emperor; it is my purpose to win."

The two guests looked long at the board, hoping it would reveal its secret to them.

"We must attempt to draw you out of your keep, Master," Shuyun said, "but your position there is strong."

"That is true. I cannot be drawn out by a simple ruse."

Shonto moved a piece. "We could sacrifice a *dragon-ship*."

"I could refuse it."

Shonto considered this. "Huh," he said, and returned the piece to its position.

"A sacrifice is not effective unless your opponent has no choice but to take it." Myochin quoted from Soto's treatise on gii.

"It is a dangerous error to rely on your opponent's stupidity," Shuyun added, quoting the same source.

The gii master nodded agreement. "The Butto and the Hajiwara have reached an impasse, I understand," the old man said, changing the subject again.

"So it would appear, Eku-sum."

"Hmm. Good for them but not necessarily good for you."

"How so, Eku-sum?"

"You step into a situation without momentum, yet movement will be required. It is easier to redirect something that is in motion than to move something which is still. Is this not true?"

"So you have always said, and I must admit it has proven to be so."

Silence fell again and Shonto did not take his eyes from the gii board.

"Are you ready to give up now?" the old man asked suddenly, sounding somewhat annoyed.

Shonto laughed affectionately. "Give us a little more time, Eku-sum. Even you did not find the answer with only a few moments' contemplation."

"It is true, my lord. I grow less patient with others as I grow older. Ah, well." He paused, seeming to contemplate his statement. "I have said that you must look deeper, but remember, it is not enough to look deeper into the game, you must look within, also. It is always there that you will find the resources needed."

After a moment's more contemplation, Shuyun said, "I would move my *guard commander* back to the first rank."

The old man nodded again. He smiled. "An interesting thought."

"But you would open your flank to the wing of his greatest strength, Brother," Shonto said.

"Yes," the monk answered.

"What will you do when he attacks?"

"I do not know, Sire."

The old man laughed. "You see, Brother Shuyun, Lord Shonto has always played with his mind and never with his greater powers. He is a master of the game, certainly, but this is his limitation. You, on the other hand, have been taught all of your life to draw upon other strengths. What makes Lord Shonto unique is that he recognizes his weakness. For this reason it has been arranged that you serve him. Did your teachers tell you that, Brother?" When Shuyun did not respond, the old man said, "I thought not.

"You see, Motoru-sum. Our young Brother has made a leap beyond logic. He knows that there is a solution—I have told him so. He knows that he must draw me from my keep—upon that we agree. Once he has come that far, he has let his instinct dictate the next move, an instinct that he trusts implicitly. His move, by the way, is correct, though the rest of the series is equally difficult. Ten moves to forced surrender." He rose slowly, but without assistance. "If you will excuse me, I must go out and feel the night for a moment, and then, if you will, we shall dine."

The gii master, who had never in his life seen a gii board, walked out onto the porch, down the steps and into the garden. His white hair and robe could just be seen, fluttering in the breeze.

"Remarkable, yeh?" Shonto said, taking his eyes from the board.

Shuyun nodded. "I am honored that you would bring me to meet him, Lord Shonto."

Shonto shrugged. "My instincts, which I have never been able to apply to the gii board, told me that it was important that the two of you meet. It gives me pleasure to watch someone who is truly able to appreciate what he has accomplished. Did you know that he was the Champion of all of Wa six times!"

Shuyun shook his head.

What is remarkable, the young monk thought, is that he accomplished this without Botahist training. Shuyun pictured the gii board in his mind, the pieces arranged for the Soto problem, and began to explore the possibilities of the first move he had made. He took the first step into chi-ten, and felt his sense of time begin to stretch. In his mind he moved the pieces through a hundred permutations, all at what seemed a normal speed. He held his focus and followed what came of it, move after move. In a matter of minutes he had found the third solution to the Soto problem. He opened his eyes to find Lord Shonto staring at him.

"Show me," Shonto said simply.

He has had a Brother in his house before, Shuyun reminded himself and let no sign of surprise show at Shonto's request.

He controlled his time sense now, but still, he moved the pieces through the solution too quickly. Shonto did not grasp it for a moment, it had been done so fast, but then his face lit up.

"Yes, yes! That is right, of course." He nodded, a slight bow, to the monk. "It is sad that I could not have been trained in your way when I was young."

"You cannot be a servant of the Perfect Master, Sire, and a lord also," Shuyun said, but immediately he was reminded of Lady Nishima, practicing chi quan in her private garden. Did Lord Shonto know, he wondered? Was it Brother Satake who had taught her? Shuyun could not say.

Shonto shrugged. "It seems to be true."

Myochin Ekun returned to the room. "You will have to take the problem of the third solution with you to Seh, Motoru-sum. I was going to show you, but it will give you something to do during the winter rains." He chuckled. "Yes, that will keep you occupied. Ah, Leta, where is our dinner?"

The meal was served, accompanied by hot rice wine and spiced sauces. Warm robes were brought for the gii master and his guests, for the night grew cooler, yet no one wanted to shut its beauty out.

Talk turned again to the Shonto household, as was perhaps inevitable, and Shuyun was the willing audience of the older men's favorite stories. Food and drink were accompanied by much laughter.

"You were an impossible student, sometimes, Motoru-sum, I have not forgotten. I often envied Brother Satake's manner with you, I don't know what his secret was, but you listened to him without your attention wandering all over the wide world."

"He did have his way, didn't he?"

"Yes. Yes, he did. It has been so long, how is Satake-sum?"

Shonto paused before answering quietly. "Brother Satake is gone, Eku-sum."

The old man shook his head. "Of course, I . . . how could I forget?" He muttered something more, that Shuyun did not catch, and went back to his food. Lord Shonto gazed at the old man for a moment, sadness apparent in his face, then he, too, returned to his dinner. An attempt was made to resume the conversation, but it faltered and failed.

Shojis were set in place to create rooms for the night and beds were made, as was the custom, on the straw mats. Shuyun occupied the room in which the dinner had been eaten, but he did not sleep. He thought of the young Acolyte and the story she had told him. He thought of Sister Morima and the Sacred Scrolls.

It seemed odd to him that Myochin Ekun had forgotten the death of

Brother Satake—a man who was still capable of finding a third solution to the Soto problem. It seemed very odd.

Outside the house, a large tulip tree surrendered to the increasing night breeze, and released its leaves to the wind. They fell in a slow rain, blowing into the house and scattering across the floor. Shuyun lay in this shower of leaves, entirely awake, until dawn slipped into the night sky. When he looked outside, the tulip tree was all but bare.

Fifteen

THERE WAS NO moon, though it would rise later, a waning disk floating in the morning sky. The quay and the cobbled square seemed to be
made up of shades of gray, lines of black. Shapes that suggested things to the
mind, things that moved and changed and flowed.

If Tanaka had not known the area, he would not have understood what it
was he looked at. Across the square there was an inn, he knew it well, and
to his left an Imperial customs house, its large doors darker rectangles in a
dark wall. A line of ships rode quietly against the quay, tugging at their
moorings—massive spice-traders and warships—single lights illuminating
the quarter decks for the night watch.

Opposite the spice-traders, shops and the large Trading Houses stretched
along the stone quay—the first building would belong to the Hashikara, and
next to it, the Minikama, the Sadaku, and then the giant Sendai warehouses.
None of these great families would allow their names to be attached to their
trading concerns, but it did not matter, Tanaka knew them all, knew the
vassal-merchants and which Houses each silently represented. Yankura was
his city and little passed in it that he did not soon learn.

From the balcony of the inn, on which he waited, Tanaka could see all
three roads entering the square, black mouths yawing, the glint of starlight
on cobbles. Nothing moved there but a stray cat that searched along the wall
of the inn, looking for a way to the food it no doubt smelled.

The old man who stood in the dark beside the merchant did not move. In
fact, he hardly dared breathe, he was so frightened. It shocked him that he

should react so. In his younger days he had served in the army of Lord Shonto Motoru's father. Once, the great lord had given him the Dagger of Bravery for his part in a battle against the Yamaku's allies. It was a memory he cherished, a story he had told his grandchildren a hundred times. But his days of being a warrior were long past, and tonight he felt fear as he could never remember feeling fear before. The apparent calmness of the vassal-merchant shamed him and made him determined to show none of what he felt. If only his stomach and bowels would cooperate! They churned and writhed like a dying serpent.

Neither man dared speak his thoughts, there in the shadow of the building which sheltered them. They remained as still as the shadows themselves. They listened.

Have I come on a fool's errand? Tanaka asked himself. Has this old man fallen into a fantasy that he can again play a part in the struggles of the Empire? He felt pity for the old man if that were so. It was hard to imagine, looking at the old man now, but he had been a full captain once, a good and competent man. Long ago, he had served on Tanaka's own guard. But tonight the merchant wondered if the retired captain was slipping into a sad state of senility. They had been standing in the dark for over three hours. The hour of the owl had just sounded. I believe I am wasting my time, Tanaka decided, and a certain relief accompanied that realization.

He was just about to put a hand on the old man's shoulder and take his leave when he heard, or thought he heard, a sound. But then there was nothing and Tanaka wondered if he was beginning to suffer the same fate as the old man. Again! A sound, so familiar, a sound he had heard since childhood. The sound of armor—leather creaking, the muffled jangle of metal rings. Tanaka pushed himself closer to the wall behind him.

Now he regretted coming without guard. If the captain had not insisted he would never have considered it, but the old warrior had been adamant. Tanaka pushed back and felt the wall, solid against his taut muscles. He tried to wrap the shadow around him like a cloak. *Breathe,* Tanaka ordered himself, *breathe.*

The sound came again, and suddenly there, by the fountain in the middle of the square, there was a dark form—a man. Tanaka could see him turning slowly, searching the shadows with his eyes. How long had he been there? The merchant fought panic. We cannot be seen in this darkness, he told himself—*breathe!*

A second man came into view, silhouetted for an instant against the reflection on the fountain's surface. The captain did not lie, Tanaka thought, they are Imperial Guardsmen. If we are found now, we are lost. *Breathe, breathe slowly.*

A third guard crossed the square almost silently, making his way toward the quay. He stopped before crossing the last stretch of cobbles, but when he was sure there was no activity along the waterfront he trotted directly to an Imperial Warship. The ship's lone watchman did not offer challenge but instead lowered the gangway. Tanaka could hear the creak of the ropes and the dull "thump" as planks hit stone. On deck the light was extinguished.

Again there was a long silence. The merchant peered into the shadows until he thought he saw guards hovering everywhere. He felt completely trapped. There was nothing to do but remain still and pray to Botahara to hide them.

The black rectangle of the customs house door began to change shape suddenly, and Tanaka realized it had opened without a sound. The hinges had been greased, that was certain. More guards emerged—ten? twelve? more?—Tanaka could not be sure. It was then that he heard the breathing of someone below them. The scrape of a sandal on wood. Stairs led from the square to the balcony on Tanaka's right. He turned that way, staring at the blackness.

If we cannot avoid discovery, he thought, I will smash through a screen into the inn and hope to lose myself in the confusion this act will cause. He braced himself and listened for a foot on the stairs.

The guards from the customs house hurried across the square. They could not hide their noise completely now; there were too many of them. And they carried something, Tanaka realized, a box the size of a traveling trunk. It hung between poles and guards carried it. Imperial Guards carried it!—not bearers. Tanaka almost stepped forward, such was his surprise. They struggled with it, too, he could see that even in the dark. Eight men struggled with this burden!

He swallowed in a dry throat, it had not been just a story, then. The old man's nephew had indeed given him valuable information. The merchant wondered if the nephew could be among the guards below? Another reason that they should not be caught.

Tanaka glanced over at the dark form of his companion. The old man had shriveled into the wall, pulling his robe high to hide the lightness of his skin. The old warrior has not forgotten his Shonto training, Tanaka noted.

The stairs creaked! Or was it someone moving inside? Tanaka stared into the dark square of the stairwell until he could no longer discern anything at all. His muscles ached from the effort he made to be still.

Across the square, the guardsmen reached the Imperial Warship and began to load their burden. It went over the side quickly on tackle, but Tanaka could see nothing on the deck. There were more sounds, the sounds of men emerging from the ship's belly. Then they moved back across the square, fanning out, searching the periphery of the area.

There were sounds on the stairs—footsteps!—but then they seemed to hesitate. Tanaka looked wildly around—where would he hide? It was then that he saw the old man was gone! It hit him like a blast of cold wind—*I have been trapped,* the merchant thought.

Tanaka began to edge along the balcony toward the nearest shoji. It was his only hope. The footsteps approached now. He could hear breathing and the sounds of armor—an Imperial Guardsman, undoubtedly. A shape appeared in the opening, dark against the darkness. Tanaka tensed, ready to spring, wondering if it was too late to reach the shoji now. The guard set a foot onto the balcony.

He looks right at me, Tanaka thought. It was in that instant that the merchant saw them—on the balcony behind the guard—two figures, seeming to take form out of the shadow. One held a knife. The merchant stood frozen, watching.

But then the two figures seemed to melt into one and slump into the darkness of the floor. The guard stopped, Tanaka could see the glint of light on his chin strap, he turned slowly about and then, almost silently, descended the stairs.

I have not been seen, Tanaka thought. Thank the darkness, thank Botahara!

In another instant the guards were gone. The Imperial Warship slipped its lines and began to recede into the darkness. Tanaka told himself to breathe again. But still he dared not move. Out of the black pool of the floor a figure rose, small, catlike in its movements. It faced him on the dark balcony. It spoke.

"Do nothing rash," came the soft whisper. "He would have betrayed your presence." The figure motioned to the floor. "He will awaken soon. Then you must go."

Tanaka blinked, trying to focus. The figure evaporated, the merchant watched it happen, but his eyes would not believe it. He shook his head to clear it, but nothing changed. There was a sound now. In the darkness on the floor, something stirred. He heard a soft moan.

Tanaka went immediately to the sound. The old captain lay on the rough planks, his dagger by his head. The merchant put his fingers to the man's lips. "Make no sound. You are safe."

He propped the man's head up in his hand and listened, waiting for the old one's breathing to become regular. He felt the old man touch his arm and nod. Helping him to rise, Tanaka returned the captain's blade, and steered him toward the back stairs.

When they were around the side of the inn, the old man put his mouth close to Tanaka's ear. "What happened?"

"We were saved," Tanaka answered and said no more. When they reached the alley, the man who had once been a warrior reached into his sleeve and removed a small leather bag and placed it in Tanaka's hand.

The merchant hefted it once, then leaned close to speak. "I will tell our lord." He lifted the bag again. "This will not be forgotten."

The two men parted, going silently through the streets of the Floating City. Tanaka felt more exhausted than he would have thought possible. His head spun with the significance of what he had just witnessed.

As soon as he had entered his own residence and assured his guard that he was, indeed, well, Tanaka pulled open the knot that closed the leather bag. Whatever was inside, had come from the trunk carried by the Imperial Guard. By the light of a single lamp he emptied the contents onto a table.

The merchant sank back on his heels. "May Botahara save us," he muttered. Before him, glinting in the lamplight, lay five square gold coins, unmarked but for a hole in the center of each. They bore no stamp of official coinage, yet, clearly, they were newly minted.

"My lord does not imagine his danger," Tanaka said to the room. "I must warn him."

As he reached for his brush and ink, the merchant recalled the figure in the dark—his savior. Tanaka smiled to himself. He had never known praying to Botahara to have such a direct effect, for unless his age had overtaken him entirely, what Tanaka had seen in the dark was an Initiate of the Botahist Order.

"Impossible," he whispered. "Impossible. The Botahist Brothers endanger their Order for no one!" He could fashion no explanation for what had occurred, though something told him it was not Tanaka the Brothers wished to save, nor even the Lord Shonto Motoru—no, he was sure, it was a young monk they were concerned with. A young monk who Tanaka had seen perform an impossible feat. Yes, he thought, Lord Shonto must be warned.

Sixteen

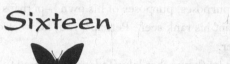

The smoke-flowers turn,
Deep purple.
And the dew lies upon them
Like cold tears.

It is said the Emperor
Is entertained by a young Sonsa.
Does she dance well
I wonder?

From "The Palace Book"
Lady Nikko

A GONG SOUNDED—THREE TIMES, a pause of two beats, and then a fourth deep ring. The sound echoed through the Palace of the Emperor, down long hallways and among the many courtyards. Then all was quiet again, all was still. In the cycle of the lengthening and shortening of the days, the hour of the owl never saw the light of the sun, and perhaps in balance, it never missed the moonlight. The autumn moon waned toward its last quarter, now, and its light seemed to take on the coldness and purity of the night air.

Jaku Tadamoto walked silently down an empty corridor, his sandaled feet making no sound on the marble floor. He wore the black uniform of the

Imperial Guard, though without the insignia of a colonel on the breast, and he carried in his hand a bronze lantern.

It was not unusual for a colonel of the Imperial Guard to be walking the palace at night; security was, after all, their duty, but it was somewhat less common that a colonel would not display his rank. It indicated that he had other purposes, purposes of his own—perhaps a test of security—and did not want his rank seen. Perhaps, too, he went on an errand for his famous brother.

The truth was that Jaku Tadamoto wanted to reduce the chances of being recognized, yet he wanted the freedom to roam the palace that the black uniform would provide.

He walked on, confident that his knowledge would allow him to avoid the guards on their rounds. Coming to a junction in the halls, the young colonel stopped to light his lantern from a hanging lamp. Once sure that it had been lit and would not die, he closed the lantern so that no light could be seen. He removed a single iron key from his sleeve and, without hesitation, crossed to a large, hinged door.

The lock turned without sound and Jaku Tadamoto was immediately inside a darkened room. It was a cluttered place, he knew, one that he would not attempt to negotiate in the darkness. Opening the lantern for a brief second, Tadamoto examined his surroundings. He was in the Hall of Historical Truth, which in fact, was made up of twenty rooms of similar size. It was here that the scholars labored on their great work, the history and assessment of the Hanama Dynasty. Tadamoto knew much about this because the work fascinated him, and he came here often to speak with the historians.

Closing the lamp, he crossed the room, by memory, to the far shoji. The screens opened onto a balcony, lit only by light from the waning moon. Staying back in the shadows, Tadamoto went silently to the balcony's end parapet where he stopped to let his eyes adjust to the night. Far below, in a lantern-lit courtyard, the Palace Guard was changing. Tadamoto could hear the sound of muffled armor. Somehow this made him aware of the madness of what he did, yet the pounding of his heart was not from fear. The thought of Osha waiting for him caused a thrill to course through him.

We will not be found, he told himself, and wondered if his judgment was entirely clouded by his passion.

When his eyes had become accustomed to the darkness, Tadamoto leaned over the parapet, gauging the distance to the next balcony. Two arm's lengths, he decided—he did not even consider the distance to the stone courtyard—the darkness below him seemed endless. There are safer ways, Tadamoto told himself, but I might be seen, and that would not do. I must cross here—it is an easy jump, a child could do it. It is only the thought of height that makes it difficult.

He climbed up onto the parapet's wide top and balanced himself in the darkness. But still he hesitated. He bent his knees, flexing them for the leap, but then he straightened again. His palm, against the cool bronze of the lantern, was slippery with sweat.

Katta is the adventurer in our family, he told himself. So, he thought, perhaps I could have him come and carry me across to my assignation with the Emperor's mistress! He took a deep breath then, and jumped into the darkness. His foot landed squarely on the parapet of the next balcony and he let the momentum carry him farther. Landing on his feet on the tiled floor, he let out a low laugh and shook his head. It had been ridiculously easy, as he had known it would be.

"The mind must control the fears," he whispered to the night, and he turned to the nearest shoji. On an "inspection tour" earlier that day, he had left it unlatched and he found that it had not been discovered.

The east wing of the Imperial Palace had contained the private apartments of the Hanama before their fall, but now it was inhabited only by the royal ghosts. No one went there if it was not required of them.

Tadamoto did not let the fear of spirits overcome his very rational mind. He stepped into the room and pulled the screen closed behind him. Feeling his way, he crossed the wide floor before he dared let even a slight glow escape from his lamp. He breathed deeply to calm himself, but his lungs were assaulted by the mustiness of the unused rooms. The air seemed to smell of the past.

He opened a screen onto a large hallway, anxious to be moving, to leave the presence of the Hanama behind. His lamp picked out the wall paintings and the fine carvings in both stone and wood. The Hanama had exhibited much more refined tastes than their successors. Their art had been simple and elegant, with a subtle use of color, yet the court painters of the Yamaku were not required to execute such cultivated work.

Tadamoto came to a wide flight of stone stairs which rose up into landings on the next three floors. He stopped to listen for a moment but all was silent, all was dark.

He went up, his thoughts turning now to the Sonsa dancer. How had she come to this place? Had she been seen? Was she not afraid? A vision of her filled his mind, a memory of her hand on his arm.

At the second landing he turned down the hall, his lantern casting a warm glow over the floor and walls. Finally, at the end of the hall, he came to a set of large doors, ornately carved, painted with gilt. Depicted in this relief, were the Door Wardens—the giants who guarded the sanctuary within from entry by the spirits of evil. The door on the right was slightly ajar. Tadamoto reached out and grasped the bronze handle and pulled it toward him. It started to move, but then came to a stop. He pulled harder; it gave but then stopped again.

"Who dares disturb the sleep of royalty?" a voice hissed from the dark.

Tadamoto let the door go and it closed with a bump.

A voice came to him again, a woman's voice. "Tadamoto-sum?"

He almost laughed with relief. "Yes. Osha-sum?"

The door swung open now, and in the light from his lamp Tadamoto could see the lovely Sonsa step back into the shrine.

"I . . . I was afraid you would not come," she said in a whisper.

"I would not miss an opportunity to see you," Tadamoto answered, and with that he opened the cover of his lantern. Osha wore an elegant kimono of the finest silk, blue like the morning sky, with a pattern of clouds. Her sash and inner robe were of gold. Around her, the gold of the ornate Botahist shrine seemed to take up the colors of her dress and reflect them, as though she were part of this sacred place—a priestess, an Initiate of the Way. She moved back across the floor, seeming to glide in her steps, coming to a stop in the center of a septilateral set within a circle on the floor.

"It is said that the Brothers dance in patterns such as this and that it is the secret of their power," she said suddenly. And then she began to move—flowing, effortless movement like the Brothers performed in their defense, yet unlike this. Osha danced. She turned slowly in the half light, her hands suggesting the movements of resistance, yet they enticed, they called to Tadamoto's senses as he had never felt before. In a final lithe motion, Osha sank to her knees, eyes cast down, and she remained thus for a long moment, unmoving.

At last she spoke in a forced calm. "I am no longer the favorite of our Emperor, Tadamoto-sum."

The young colonel did not know what to answer. He began a step toward her, but she looked up and something in her gaze stopped him.

"Is it justice that I will never dance again?" she asked.

"Why do you say this? You are the foremost Sonsa of our time."

"It means nothing, if to have me dance is to risk the displeasure of the Son of Heaven." She said this without bitterness, a mere statement of the obvious.

"Displeasure? Our Emperor shows nothing but the highest pleasure whenever you perform."

She sighed at this. "I fear that this will no longer be so, Tadamoto-sum. And there is the *new favorite*—she will not wish to see me, that is certain."

Yes, Tadamoto thought, that may be true. But the Emperor seemed to express so much care for her, for her happiness, would he not wish her to dance if that is what created her happiness? "The Emperor is too pleased by your . . . dancing to wish that you stop. And if that were not true, which I'm sure it is, there are places, other than the Imperial Palace where one may dance."

"If it were only the palace, I would not be concerned, but it is the capital we speak of, the capital and perhaps all the inner provinces. I would be exiled to the north or to the west. . . ." She shook her head. "After all my years of training, how could I accept this?" She looked down at the pattern around her. "It is not *right* that this should happen to me!"

Jaku Tadamoto sank to his knees before her. "It need not be as you say, Osha-sum. The Emperor is fair to those who are loyal, the Jaku know this." He reached out tentatively and took her hands. She returned his touch. "If I do not presume too much, when the time is right I would speak to the Son of Heaven on your behalf."

She looked up now and held his eyes. He felt her take both of his hands between hers and, with a pressure so slight he may have imagined it, she drew him toward her. She kissed his hand. "You are a man of honor, Jaku Tadamoto-sum. I was a young fool to allow myself to be ensnared by the Emperor and his promises."

She raised his hands and the warmth of her cheek against his fingers thrilled him. Jaku felt weak as his desire grew stronger. He bent down to her and their lips met in the most tentative kiss. Her breath was sweet, warm. Their lips brushed again, more certainly. He traced the curve of Osha's neck with a finger and she sighed and pushed her face into his chest. He held her there, close to him, certain that she could feel the pounding of his heart.

"Come with me," she said rising and drawing him to his feet. She swept the lantern up off the floor and turned, not releasing his hand, to lead him back into the small shrine. A hidden screen opened into a hall that ended in a flight of seven stairs. Osha led him up, hurrying now, and then through another screen into a dark room. In the lamplight Tadamoto could see the form of a large, low bed under a protective cotton cover; the room seemed to contain nothing else.

Osha turned now and kissed him, with longing, with promise. But then broke away, and, going to the far wall, unlatched a shoji, opening it wide to the night. And the moonlight fell upon her like a caress.

"The chamber of the Empress Jenna," she whispered, and laughed, a warm laugh. "What could be more fitting?"

"You are not as she," Tadamoto said.

"In my actions, no, I am much more circumspect. But in my soul?" Again she seemed to glide toward him. "In my soul, I am reborn the Yellow Empress Jenna." Taking his hands, she pulled him lightly toward the bed.

They removed the cotton cover and under it found rich quilts and pillows of the finest quality.

Kneeling on the bed, they kissed again, touching gently. With patience, Tadamoto unwound Osha's long sash and opened her silk robes. Her outer robe slipped from her shoulders and she was left with the thin, gold fabric of her inner kimono clinging to her skin. He kissed her breasts shyly, the beauty of her dancer's form stirring him. A shiver ran through Osha's body and she pushed him down into the quilts, falling lightly on top of him. She untied his sash and he felt her skin soft against his own.

They made love until the sky showed signs of morning, each bringing all of their skills to their tryst, each bringing a strong passion. If anyone passing below had heard, they would have been certain it was the moans, and sighs of the Hanama ghosts who were known to walk the halls still; ever restless, ever dissatisfied.

Seventeen

T HE BRUSH WORK was rather plain, but strong and clear. Nishima took it up from the table and looked at it again. The mulberry paper was of the best quality, almost heavy, and colored a pale, pale yellow. An arrangement of green autumn grain had been attached to the poem, a symbol of growth, while yellow was one of the traditional colors of fall.

> *Autumn settles*
> *Among the fall grains,*
> *And they wait*
> *Only for a sign of spring.*

Lady Nishima set the letter on the table again and turned back to the view of the garden beyond her balcony. She wondered if Jaku Katta had written the poem himself. The brush work was his, no doubt, but the poem? This revealed another side of him if it was, indeed, his composition. The verse was not terribly sophisticated, but it was not marred by the overornamentation that Lady Nishima believed was the major flaw in the court verse of that time. It did contain the obligatory reference to a classical poem; in this case to "The Wind From Chou-san."

> *Her heart is as cold*
> *As the wind from Chou-san,*

Yet the fall grains appear
In the fields.

He is bold, Nishima thought, and she was not entirely displeased. The contradiction that was Jaku Katta confused her thoroughly—the incident on the canal still seemed odd to her. And yet *it was possible* that such a thing could happen.

It was Jaku Katta who saved my uncle, she told herself again. And it can never be forgotten that he has the ear of the Emperor. Perhaps this would prove important to the Shonto in the future.

She took up her brush and wet her inkstone for the fourth time.

Cold is the wind
That rattles my shoji,
Yet I am told the fall grains
Need little encouragement.

She set the smoke-gray paper down beside the letter from Jaku Katta and examined the brush work critically. As modest as she was, the lady could not deny the great contrast between their hands. He is a soldier, after all, she thought, but still, she could find little to admire in Jaku's brush work once she had set it beside her own.

Lady Nishima read through her poem again and decided that it was exactly the tone she was looking for; discouraging, but not entirely so. She attached a small blossom of the twelve-petaled shinta flower to it—the symbol of the Shonto House. That would remind the general that the House of Fanisan was no more. She tapped a small gong to call a servant. The note must go off immediately, she had much to do to prepare for the Celebration of the Emperor's Ascension.

The Lady Kitsura Omawara passed through the gate into the small garden attached to her father's rooms. The sound of water was a subdued burble and, beyond the high wall, a breeze seemed to breathe through the last leaves of the golden lime trees. The young aristocrat was dressed in a formal robe of pale plum, with the hems of her four under kimonos in the most carefully chosen colors, revealed properly at the sleeve and the neck.

She slipped her sandals off as she stepped onto the porch. A harsh cough came from behind a screen set on the porch and pain flashed across the young woman's face as though the cough had been her own.

"Father?" she said softly.

A long breath was drawn. "Kitsu-sum?"

She could almost see the smile of pleasure and, as though it were a mirror, her own face also creased in a warm smile. "Yes. It is a perfect evening, is it not, Father?"

"Perfect, yes." There was a pause as the lord caught his breath. Kitsura examined the design on the screen, a stand of bamboo beside a tranquil pond.

"Did you see the mist . . . in the garden . . . this morning?"

"Yes, Father, I did. But you should not have been up, breathing that cold air."

He laughed, almost silently, and to his daughter it sounded like a far off echo of his old laughter. "I cannot give up . . . the world just yet . . . Kitsu-sum." The clear, autumn air rattled in his lungs like dice in a cup and he fell to coughing terribly. The young lady cringed, closing her eyes as though this would block out the sound.

"Should I call Brother Tessa, Father?" she asked, referring to the Botahist monk who acted as the Omawara House physician. He was unable to answer her, but just as she rose to summon a servant, he spoke.

"No. I will stop in a . . ." He coughed again, but then the fit ended and he lay gasping. His daughter waited, staring at the screen that allowed her father to maintain his dignity in the face of an illness that was certainly draining him of all life. If only he could be transported to the place I see on this screen, Kitsura thought. It looks so peaceful. May Botahara grant him favor for all that he has suffered in this life.

At last Lord Omawara lay quiet, and just when his daughter was sure he had fallen asleep, he spoke again. "Will you . . . go to the palace . . . for the Cele . . . bration?"

"I will, Father. I intend to meet Nishima-sum and we shall attend the festivities together."

"Ah. Take her . . . my highest . . . respects."

"I will, Father. She has often expressed a desire to visit you and asks always after your well-being."

"She is . . . kind." There was a long silence punctuated only by the lord's fight for air. "You must . . . assure her . . . that . . . my affection . . . is undying. . . . But to . . . see her . . . would be. . ."

"I understand, Father. I will explain this to my cousin."

"What of . . . Motoru-sum? Has he . . . gone . . . to Seh?"

"I will speak to your staff who are not to worry you with such things."

The echo of laughter came from behind the screen.

"But, as you know so much already, yes, Lord Shonto left for Seh some ten days ago."

"I am . . . concerned."

"He is wise, Father. Lord Shonto Motoru should never be a cause for worry."

"There is more . . . than the eye . . . sees . . . Denji . . . Gorge, Seh." He fell into silence.

"Lord Shonto goes nowhere without the greatest care, Sire. Our concern would be better placed elsewhere."

"Wise . . . Kitsu-sum. . . . Your mother?"

"She is with you, Sire. This is her happiness. How could she be cause for concern?"

"She . . . does not rest. . . . Worries."

"But she is not happy otherwise, Father, you know that."

"She worries that . . ." he coughed again but weakly, "that you are unmarried."

"Father. I am hardly an old maid!" She laughed her infectious laugh. "There will be time yet."

"Yes . . . but Kitsu-sum . . . the Emperor has . . . three sons only."

"What a pity. If he had had a fourth, perhaps he would have a son worthy of consideration!"

The laughter echoed, ending in a wheeze. "I have . . . raised you with expectations . . . that are too high."

It was Kitsura's turn to laugh. "Why do you say that? Because I consider an Emperor's son beneath me? Well, to be honest, I would not let any of them marry my maid!"

"Ah. Then . . . the Princes . . . must have . . . cluttered rooms," the lord said.

Kitsura laughed. "I tire you, Father. I will have Brother Tessa lecturing me again."

"Yes. I am . . . tired."

"I must go, Father."

The curtain in the screen moved slightly, and a pale, withered hand pushed through the opening. Lady Kitsura reached out and took the cold fingers within her own. It was all she had seen of her father in over four years.

From the balcony, Lady Nishima could look down upon the celebration, a mass of swirling color, as the courtiers and other nobles moved through the three large rooms and out onto the open terrace.

The Emperor could be seen on his dais, surrounded by lords and ladies known for their discerning taste in the area of music. The Highest One involved himself in the judgment of a music competition.

Very close by, on the edge of the dais, sat Lady Kitsura Omawara. She had been invited to judge the music and was now the object of much of the Emperor's attention. Nishima could see her cousin struggling to remain polite, yet still keep her distance from the Son of Heaven. Nishima found the Emperor's behavior shocking, yet there was nothing she could do to help. Already the Empress had retired from the gathering, and the Emperor did not seem to notice. Somewhere in the halls, Nishima had seen the young Sonsa dancer who had been the object of the Emperor's affections so recently. Tonight, however, she was being entirely ignored and looked as one does in such circumstances. Lady Nishima stood at the rail thinking longingly of the quiet life of Lady Okara—if only. . . .

Young peers presented themselves before the distinguished judges and offered their very best compositions. The prizes for the winners would, no doubt, be lavish and the guests at that end of the large hall sat listening in complete silence. Strains of music drifted up to the Lady Nishima, but somehow this did not lift her spirits as it usually did.

In the next hall, the Hall of the Water's Voice, Chusa Seiki sat with a group of her most promising students and a few courtiers, composing a poem-series. A wine cup was set floating down the artificial stream and as it passed, each participant in turn would pick it up, drink, and recite a three line poem which echoed the verses before, incorporated a reference to a classical verse, and also added something original. Nishima had been asked to participate, but seeing that Prince Wakaro was one of the poets, she had politely declined. Besides, her mind was on other things and she did not feel

that she would live up to her reputation. The subdued lamplight of the Hall
of the Water's Voice did not draw her tonight, as it often did.

She was about to turn and rejoin the gathering when a man's voice came
from behind her.

"The wind that rattles
Your shoji
Seeks only the lamp's warmth.
Winter gives way to
Other seasons.

"I thank you for the shinta flower, Lady Nishima."

"Not at all, General.

"The wind through the shoji
Causes the lamp to flicker,
I fear that I shall be left
In darkness."

She could feel his presence behind her, the Tiger in the darkness. Her
breath quickened and she felt the nerves in her back come to life as though
she expected to be touched at any second.

"I remember that we spoke of gratitude," he said.

Nishima almost turned toward him, but stopped. "Perhaps gratitude
means different things in different circles, General Katta."

"Please excuse me, I did not mean to suggest what you seem to think. It
was I who was grateful and who continue to be." He stopped as though to
listen and then whispered. "I have information that may be of use to those
who grow the shinta blossom."

Nishima nodded, staring down at the scene below.

"If I am not being too bold, Lady Nishima, please join me on the balcony
for a moment." And she heard him retreat toward the open screens.

She stood there briefly, gathering her nerve, making sure that she was not
watched, then she turned and went out into the light of the crescent moon.
The night air was cool. Soft-edged clouds traveled across the sky, now covering the Bearer, now the sliver of the waxing moon.

No one else had ventured out onto the balcony, either because they were drawn to the entertainments inside, or because the air was too chill.

"This way, my lady." Jaku's voice came out of the darkness to the left and Lady Nishima could just make out the shape of a large man in the black of the Imperial Guard. She turned and followed.

At the end of the balcony a short set of steps led to a second balcony, though this one was small and secluded, no doubt attached to private rooms. Jaku knelt on grass mats here, his formal uniform spread out around him like a fan. Nishima could see his face in the moonlight, the strong features, the drooping mustache, the gleam of the gray eyes. She knelt across from him on the soft mats.

"I am honored that you place such trust in me, Lady Nishima.

The shoji opens and
The light within
Warms even the night."

"Did you say you had information that may benefit my House, General?"

The Black Tiger nodded, surprised by her coolness. "I do, my lady. Information of the most delicate nature." He stood suddenly and went to the shoji, opening it and looking carefully inside. Satisfied, he beckoned Nishima to come with him. She hesitated but then rose and entered the chamber. Jaku did not close the screen entirely and they sat close to the opening, still lit by the moon.

"I have information about plans that will affect your uncle, Lady Nishima. I only wish that I had received the information earlier." He paused as though waiting for a response, but Nishima listened in silence.

"I do not know everything yet, but there is certainly a plot against your uncle that has its origins very near the Dragon Throne."

Still, Nishima said nothing.

"I take great risk telling you this. I hope that you will see it as a token of my good faith." He said this with difficulty, as though it was not usual for him to be in a position of trying to please another.

Nishima produced a fan from her sleeve, but instead of opening it she began to slowly tap the palm of her hand. "As you have conveyed this, it is hardly news, General Katta. Do you know more?"

The Black Tiger did not answer immediately and Lady Nishima suppressed a smirk. Oh, my handsome soldier, she thought, you expect so little of me. Should I throw myself into your arms in gratitude?

"I have heard more, Lady Nishima, but I wish to be certain of my reports. I would not want to give you false information."

"I shall pass this on to my uncle, though he must be almost in Seh by now.

"A single warm night
Autumn lingers beyond the walls,
The fall grains
Bend in the breeze.

"The shinta blossom is also endangered by the cold, Katta-sum. It is a matter of great concern to me, and I am grateful."

The warrior bent his head toward the mat, more than half a bow, and when he rose he was closer to her. He bent toward her, and she returned his kiss, though she was not sure why. Jaku reached for her then, but she easily eluded him and was on her feet and at the door before he realized what she had done. She stopped for an instant and spoke quietly in her lovely, warm voice. "We cannot take too much care, Katta-sum, you know that. But we must find a way to discuss the welfare of the shinta blossom further."

Slipping out the door and down the steps, Nishima found that she was nearly quivering with excitement and tension. Her head spun with questions. Was it possible that Jaku Katta could become loyal to the Shonto? What a coup that would be!

Lady Nishima returned to the entertainments and easily won a poetry contest. Many noted how lovely she looked that evening, how fully she laughed, and how engaging was her conversation. Among the ladies of the court this became the cause of much speculation.

Nishima ladled cha into a bowl for her cousin and then offered it, as etiquette required. It was, of course, refused, but then taken, after being offered the second time.

The two women sat in a small chamber in Lady Nishima's rooms. A charcoal burner glowed under the table, countering the slight breeze from the two screens that remained open to the garden. The moon was about to set and the stars were magnificent. A ground mist drifted in the garden, making dark islands of the trees and rocks.

"I don't know what I shall do!" Kitsura said. "It was all so entirely unexpected. What could the Emperor possibly be thinking? He cannot believe that I would consider becoming a secondary wife!"

"Perhaps it is time for the Empress to retire to the quiet life of the nun," Nishima offered.

"Even so, I have no wish to be his principle wife either!" Kitsura seemed entirely desolate, her face contorted into a near grimace. "Oh, Nishi-sum, what am I to do?"

"It is indeed difficult. If one had known this would occur, it would have been possible to take steps to avoid any embarrassment. But now," she shook her head, "it has become a matter that, perhaps, no amount of delicacy may resolve." She looked concerned, yet her cousin could not help but notice that there was something about her—an air of heightened being, almost—and a smile seemed to be about to appear on Lady Nishima's face at any second, despite the seriousness of the conversation.

A servant, hearing the voices, knocked on the screen and delivered a message to her mistress—a letter on embossed rice paper of dusky mauve. Attached to the carefully folded message was a fan of autumn ginkyo leaves. Nishima put the letter into her sleeve pocket, but not before Kitsura had seen it, and the look of pleasure on Nishima's face.

"I see we have different problems, cousin," Lady Kitsura said dryly.

Nishima laughed, but kept her silence on the matter.

Later, alone in her rooms, Nishima examined the note. To her great surprise and disappointment, it was not from Jaku Katta! Amazed that she would have another suitor, one that she was unaware of, the lady turned up the lamp and unfolded the letter on the table. And it was from Tanaka! There was no mistaking his elegant hand. This was most irregular. To make matters even stranger, there were two unmarked gold coins attached carefully inside. She bent over the small script and began the laborious work of deciphering one of the Shonto codes.

When she had transposed a complete copy she sat up straight, staring at the wall, her face suddenly pale. "May Botahara save us," she said aloud. "He is entirely mad."

Gold! Gold going secretly north. Tribute? Bribe? Payment? And who received it? Who was it the Emperor enriched in his effort to bring down the Shonto, for there was little doubt that this was the purpose. She pushed her hands to her eyes as though it would help her to see the meaning of this discovery, but her head seemed to spin. Picking up the coins, she rubbed them between her fingers as though she could divine their origin. Would Jaku be able to find out the destination of this fortune? But were there not Imperial Guards involved in its transport? She read the letter again. Yes. Did this mean that Jaku was party to it? In her heart she hoped this was not so. Oh, Father, what danger you journey toward.

Eighteen

AS A WARRIOR, Lord Komawara did not like his position. He stared up at the high granite cliffs of Denji Gorge and counted the archers looking down on the ships below. We are vulnerable, he thought.

Ahead of his own barge, the first ships were entering the locks. It would take two days for all of the fleet to be locked through. The House of Butto had, after three days of delay, finally allowed the Imperial Governor and all those that accompanied him to pass through their lands. The depth of their suspicion had surprised even Lord Komawara, who had been expecting difficulty.

In the past four days the young lord had attended many councils with Shonto and his military advisors. Komawara's head spun with the mass of details, the thousand lines of speculation. The warriors who were Shonto's advisors ignored no possibility in their analysis. When Komawara thought of his own councils he was embarrassed at how inadequate they seemed in comparison.

The position of the Komawara has long been less complicated, he realized, but now that he was a Shonto ally, all would change. He must learn all he could from these meetings with the Shonto staff. These were men to be respected, and he felt honored to be among them.

Komawara left off counting the archers on the cliff top—there were many beyond many, that was certain. The barge that preceded his, and the three craft immediately behind it, were moving into the first lock now. Despite having been through locks on many occasions, Komawara was always amazed by the process, and his admiration for the ancient engineers who had built them never diminished. They had known so much then, he thought; today this would be considered an undertaking of immense difficulty and colossal scale.

They passed the giant bronze gates now, half as thick as Komawara's barge was wide. Butto soldiers were everywhere. Komawara tapped his breast with his hand, reassured by the feel of the armor hidden beneath his robe. The young lord was uncertain of the bargain that Shonto had struck with the Butto but, no matter what the details, they would not have satisfied him— he did not trust either of the feuding families, and that would never change.

The gates began to close, swinging slowly on giant hinges, their hidden mechanisms moving them inch by inch, as the lock-men allowed the water to flow through the wheels that powered the gates. So slow was their movement, that there was no sound as they came together.

Around his barge the water began to swirl and boil. The sun lit the white foam as it danced across the surface and, almost imperceptibly, the river barges began to rise. Three of Komawara's guards moved closer to him now, shielding him from the Butto archers as the ship rose toward them.

They will not care about me, Komawara thought, and then realized that, as a Shonto ally, his position in the world had taken on new significance. He chose to stay on deck. We are in the party of the Governor of Seh. We travel the Imperial Waterway, where all have the protection of the Son of Heaven. What these families do here is against the law of the Imperium and should not be countenanced. He planted his feet against the motion of the ship, crossed his arms, and stared at the bowmen on the walls.

The waters grew tranquil and the gates to the next lock began to open. The barges moved forward, towed by teams of oxen, and the process was repeated.

At last Komawara's barge passed under the narrow bridge that spanned the gap from the Butto lands to their placements on the Hajiwara fief. The walls of the Denji Gorge opened up around them as they slipped into the Lake of the Seven Masters, named for the giant sculptures of Botahara, carved into the cliff. Two of them could be seen now—a Sitting Botahara, and the Perfect Master in Meditation.

Komawara wondered what Brother Shuyun could tell him about the massive figures, for their history was clouded by rumor and time. The images were said to have been carved in the two hundred years after the passing of

Botahara by a secretive sect that later fell during the Inter-temple Wars. This was before the Emperor, Chonso-sa, fought the Botahist Sects into submission and forbade them ever to bear arms again.

Strange, Komawara thought, followers of the Perfect Master who warred across the Empire when their own dogma forbade the taking of life except in the most extreme cases of self-defense. No doubt, they justified it somehow though the historians believed it was merely a struggle for power, nothing more, even as this ill-considered feud was a struggle for supremacy.

Crewmen took up their positions now, and started the boat forward with long sweeps of their oars. The seven rih to the anchorage near the lake's northern end went by quickly, though by the time Komawara's boat arrived the sun had traveled far enough that they moored in the shade of the western cliff.

An image of Botahara that was considered heretical dominated the section of the cliff above the anchorage. It depicted the Perfect Master in a state of conjugal bliss with his young wife, though the faces of the figures had been erased more than a thousand years before. What remained had the oddest effect—two anonymous bodies of cold stone entwined in the most intimate embrace, yet where the faces should have been, showing signs of their ecstasy, were two utterly blank sections of gray wall. It was as though the act of love itself had been rendered impersonal, an act of the body not participated in by the mind. Somehow, it seemed to Lord Komawara this was more obscene than any "erotic" drawings he had ever seen. The act of love without humanity. He shook his head, yet he did not look away.

Not far from the barge bearing Lord Komawara of Seh, Initiate Brother Shuyun stood on the deck of a similar barge looking up at the same image. To him the stone relief represented something quite different. It spoke of a schism in the Botahist Brotherhood over basic doctrine. The sculpture had, before its erasure, depicted the Lord of all Wisdom, in the act of love, with the rays of Enlightenment shining out from his face—Botahara enjoying the pleasures of the flesh after his Enlightenment. This was heresy of the worst kind!

In this very valley, in ancient times, a sect who believed themselves followers of the Perfect Master, had practiced their doctrine of the Eightfold Path, believing that enjoyment of the flesh was the eighth way to Enlightenment.

The Botahist histories told how overzealous followers of the True Path had destroyed the Heretical Sect in a great siege. This act had brought the Brotherhood into open conflict with the Emperor, Chonso-sa, who didn't realize that it was not the Brotherhood, but a group of their followers, who had destroyed the sect of the Eightfold Path.

We have survived many times of hardship, Shuyun thought, yet Botahara had taught that the True Path was fraught with difficulties and deceptions.

All this, Shuyun had been taught; it was only now, after the words of Acolyte Tesseko, that it occurred to him that these teachings might not be inspired and divine truth. It was only now that he considered the possibility that there might be an element of self-interest in the purposes of his own Order.

Once given information, the mind that solved the Soto Problem could not easily be deflected. The Lord Botahara had sought the truth above all things, and for this He had known the displeasure of the religious leaders of His time. As a follower of the teachings of the Enlightened One, Shuyun wondered if he could do less if that was what the truth required of him.

He stared up at the figures above him, locked in an embrace no Brother could know, and the thoughts this image brought to his mind stirred him in a manner he had always before resisted with all the discipline he had been taught. But now these thoughts would not leave him in peace.

Lord Shonto was not concerned with questions of history or doctrine as he regarded the stone lovers, it was the Hajiwara soldiers who stood in the openings cut into the granite relief that begged his attention. He clapped his hands and a guard immediately knelt before him. "I wish to speak to my Spiritual Advisor," the lord said. The guard bowed and was gone.

Shonto could see soldiers in the livery of his House being sculled ashore to the gravel bar behind which the ships had anchored. It was one of the few places in the gorge where men could actually land, the cliffs rose so abruptly from the surface of the lake. Beyond the gravel bar and the scrub brush that clung to it, the cliffs climbed up, fifty times the height of a man, solid and unscalable, yet Shonto still felt it prudent that the beach be in his control and not a base for spies or Hajiwara treachery. He would receive a report from the shore party as soon as they had secured the area. He looked up again and saw two Hajiwara men, in a dark granite window, pointing down at the beach. Yes, Shonto thought, they will see everything we do . . . by daylight. That cannot be helped. We will thank the gods for the darkness.

Shuyun mounted the steps to the quarter deck and the guards bowed him through to Lord Shonto. He knelt before his liege-lord, bowed his double bow, and waited. Shonto regarded the young man kneeling before him. "So, we have come through the first obstacle," he said, ignoring all formality.

"It is as your advisors believed. The Butto, no matter what their designs, would have to let us pass into Denji Gorge—it is the only way they could be sure you would not escape."

"Then you do agree that this is, indeed, a trap, and we will not be allowed to pass unscathed."

"I do, Sire," Shuyun answered evenly.

Shonto turned and looked up at the stone figures. "Tell me of these windows that look out from the bodies of the Faceless Lovers."

The monk did not answer right away, but gazed up at the cliff face as though the answer would be written there. "Several of the images carved here were also fanes for the followers of the Eightfold Path. Behind the figures lie tunnels and chambers for both worship and for living. It was an effective way to defend themselves from their enemies. The windows we see are just that, openings to allow the entry of light and air. During festivals, the figures would be decorated with cloth of purple and gold which would be hung in place from the windows. Sometimes there were narrow ledges that could also be used for this purpose, though it has been so long it is doubtful that more than a trace of them remains."

"Huh." Lord Shonto rubbed his chin absentmindedly. "Where are the entrances?"

"Commonly there was only one." Shuyun pointed to the cliff top. "There are stairs down the face of the wall. They are narrow and enter a door equally narrow. High above the door is an opening large enough to pour boiling liquids from. It was an entrance easily defended."

Shonto considered this for a moment. "How did they draw their water?"

"A shaft was sunk below the level of the surface of the lake and then joined to the water. There has been much speculation about how this was done, but to this day it remains one of the secrets of the sect. To the best of my knowledge, they had no other source of water so it was crucial that this supply not be cut."

"They were thorough."

"It was a time of danger, Sire."

Shonto nodded. "It has not changed a great deal. Thank you for this information. I shall gather the council after dark. We would be pleased if you would join us, Brother Shuyun."

The Botahist Brother bowed and backed away, leaving the lord surrounded by his guards . . . alone.

Nineteen

LAMPS SWUNG FROM bronze chains, moving almost imperceptibly as the ship rocked on the quiet waters. Shonto's nine senior generals sat in orderly rows before a dais in a chamber below decks. To the left of the dais sat Brother Shuyun, to the right, Kamu and Lord Komawara.

No one spoke as they waited; indeed, no one moved. They stared straight ahead at the silk cushion, armrest, and sword-stand that had been placed on the dais. The sound of water lapping the ship's planking came in through an open port and the lamps flickered in a slight draft. All were left with their private thoughts, their search for solutions to their situation.

A screen to the right of the dais slid open without warning and two of Shonto's personal guards stepped into the room, knelt, and touched their heads to the floor. The members of the council did the same, remaining thus until their lord had entered and seated himself. A guard hurried to place Shonto's sword in its stand.

The generals raised themselves back to their waiting position, but Shonto did not speak. Instead he seemed to be lost in thought, unaware of the others around him. For an hour he remained so, and during this time none of his staff moved. No one cleared his throat or shifted to become more comfortable. The lamps continued to sway, the water lapped the hull.

At last, Shonto turned to his steward. "Report our situation at the Butto locks."

Kamu gave a brief bow. "All of your troops and staff have locked through, Sire. The last of the barges bearing them come up the lake now. On the craft remaining, perhaps thirty boats, there is no one of importance to our purpose." Kamu paused to gather his thoughts. "The Butto still do not know if you have passed through their hands or not, though by now they must suspect you have. The large number of people in our fleet and the use of doubles have caused them great difficulty.

"Our information about the Butto has proven accurate—the father is old and no longer takes part in the ruling of his fief. Of the two sons, the younger is strong while the older is weak. There is no split in the Butto staff, though. All support the younger brother, which shows that there is wisdom among them. It is said, and I believe truthfully, that the older son is dissatisfied with his position. But it does not seem that he would be vulnerable to Hajiwara intrigue against his brother—he shares all of the Butto hatred for the Hajiwara House.

"The Butto give no indication of their true purpose in regard to you, Sire, but it is as you suspected—whatever their designs for the Shonto, their true hatred is for the Hajiwara, and, therefore, that is the key to their cooperation."

Shonto nodded and again silence settled in the room. "General Hojo Masakado, what has happened in your dealings with the Hajiwara?"

The general, a man of Shonto's age, though prematurely gray, bowed to his lord. "I have today requested that the Imperial Representative for the Province of Seh be allowed to pass into the upper section of the Grand Canal. The Hajiwara say they are willing to comply but, because of the special conditions which exist here at this time, they wish to confer personally with Lord Shonto. They insist that this meeting take place on their land, as is their right in this situation. I have told them that Lord Shonto is temporarily unwell and under the care of Brother Shuyun. The Hajiwara representative expressed concern and retired to report this to his lord. We have not yet received an answer from them.

"All evidence supports our information that this Hajiwara lord is not the man his father was, Sire. Though it is said he leads men well in battle, he constantly ignores his advisors and in the areas of state he is very weak.

"Reports from our spies say that every person passing through the Hajiwara locks is seen by two scholars who have met Lord Shonto in person. All craft are being searched in a most thorough manner—they do not seem sure that Lord Shonto has not secretly left his flotilla. This would seem to indicate that they have no spies close to our center."

Shonto shook his head. "So, they dare not make a mistake. To let the Lord of the Shonto escape while they fall upon innocent passengers on an Imperial waterway." He shook his head again. "This would be fatal. The Emperor would risk open war with the Great Houses, and this he fears."

"It does seem to be so, Sire," General Hojo said. "The Emperor has chosen wisely. There would be few others in all of Wa foolish enough to move openly against the Shonto. Does not Hajiwara realize what this will mean? Can he not see that the Emperor will be forced to act against him?"

Shonto shrugged. "The Emperor can be a most convincing man when he wishes to be. I'm sure this Hajiwara has ignored the counsel of his advisors and listened to the wisdom of his own desires."

"Pardon me, Sire." Bowing low, another general addressed his lord. "I feel it may be dangerous to assume the Emperor, and no other, has contrived this situation."

Shonto stared at the man stonily. "Who, then?"

The general shook his head. "Anyone who is jealous of the Shonto."

"If I fall to the plot of another House, the Son of Heaven will have no choice but to destroy that House—it would be the only way he could disassociate himself from their action. He fears to be seen as the predator, falling upon those he hates. He knows this would lead to his downfall. The Great Houses have never allowed such an Emperor to stay upon the Throne. History tells us that. So I ask you, who, other than a fool, would attack us knowing that the Son of Heaven, despite any secret agreements, would be forced to eliminate them?"

The general was unable to answer.

Shuyun bowed quickly. "A House that thinks they can eliminate the Shonto and, in the same action, turn the Great Houses against the Emperor."

Surprise showed on Shonto's face as he turned to his Spiritual Advisor. He nodded, almost a slight bow. "Ah. This is truth, Brother, but neither the Hajiwara nor the Butto could rally the Great Houses around them—they have not the strength. The Emperor would have them."

"I agree, Lord Shonto, but they may act as agents for another House, yeh? Their rewards would be great."

"Who would be so daring?"

"The Tora," offered General Hojo. "They feel they have as great a claim to the Throne as the Yamaku."

"The Senji, perhaps. The Minikama."

"The Sadaku," offered another.

"The Black Tiger," Kamu said, and his face twisted as though he had known a sudden premonition.

"Jaku Katta could never sit on the Dragon Throne." Shonto protested. "It is not possible, he has not the blood. . . ." Shonto stopped in mid-sentence and turned to a guard. "Prepare our fastest boat to return to the capital. Immediately! Call for my secretary. No. Bring me brush and paper."

Kamu bowed again. "Lord Shonto, such an action will only alert our enemies. 'While they do not suspect that we know their secret design, we are strong,'" he added, quoting the gii master, Soto.

"But Lady Nishima must know," Shonto protested. "If what you say is true, she is in grave danger. Jaku must not use her to seize the Throne. In all probability he will fail, and Lady Nishima will pay for that failure." A daughter of the blood, Shonto thought, a great prize for the bold man. He cursed himself now for keeping his true thoughts concerning the incident in the garden from Lady Nishima. It was overly cautious of him.

"But Sire," Lord Komawara said, speaking for the first time, "you must fall before Jaku could act and, for the moment, that cannot happen."

"What Lord Komawara says is wisdom, Sire," Shuyun said quietly. "Lady Nishima's safety can be assured most effectively by Lord Shonto escaping from this situation."

Shonto nodded. "But if I fall, Jaku will raise my allies against his own Emperor." The lord closed his eyes. "Jaku, who it appears so recently saved my life—for which my allies, not to mention my own daughter, are no doubt grateful. I have underestimated him entirely." Shonto banged his fist on his armrest. "Is this truly possible?"

"It appears very possible, Sire," Kamu said evenly. "And even if it is someone other than Jaku Katta who moves the pieces, the game would seem to be the same."

"Then I bow to your counsel," Shonto said, nodding to the assembled group. "I will send an encoded message by the Imperial carriers, addressed to a friend. It will reach Lady Nishima in less than three days. I will not fall before then." He searched the faces before him. "But now we must find a way to extract ourselves from this situation." Shonto looked around the room as though the walls were the cliffs of Denji Gorge. He waited, but no one spoke.

Kamu's quote from the gii master took Shonto back to the house by the lake, back to the peace and the quiet conversation.

"We must draw them from their keep," Shonto said, quietly. "We must offer them a sacrifice."

"Sire?" Kamu leaned forward.

"It is obvious. Our forces are small, while their positions are strong. To draw them from their castles we must offer them a sacrifice they cannot refuse."

"But what?" Kamu asked.

"*Each other,*" Shuyun said with finality.

Shonto smiled for the first time since entering the room. "Of course." He gripped his armrest. "We shall offer to deliver the Hajiwara to their mortal enemies, the Butto. And we shall offer to deliver the Butto into the hands of the Hajiwara. Each House may also believe that they will gain an advantage over the Shonto, who are trapped and helpless at the bottom of Denji Gorge. Thus, they eliminate their rivals and capture the Shonto for those for whom they act as agents—if that is indeed their game.

"Two things become apparent. Our offers must be flawless and entirely believable. And we must find a way out of the gorge. Shuyun, how were the Sects in these temples taken?"

"They were starved, Sire."

"An admirable tactic, but one we don't have time for."

"We must scale the figures to the windows, Lord Shonto," Shuyun said. "There is no other possibility."

"How do you propose this be done?"

Shuyun bowed quickly, and Shonto suspected he had entered a meditative trance, like the one he had seen at the home of Myochin Ekun. "I have taken the liberty of examining the figures on the cliff, without going close enough to arouse suspicion. The lower section, ten times the height of a man, is impassable, so we must find a way to raise a man above it. Once on the figures, there seem to be cracks and areas of broken stone. It is possible that they could be scaled to one of the lower openings. All must be done in stealth, the guards must be subdued without a sound. If it is accomplished as I have said, it would allow access to the plain inside the Hajiwara defenses." Shuyun bowed.

The generals exchanged glances and the senior member, Hojo Masakada, was silently selected as their spokesman. "Sire, it is a bold plan, and one which should receive consideration, but it has some weaknesses. The cliff must be scaled in the dark, which would be very nearly impossible. And if the climbers are detected, any other plans we have would be rendered useless—the Hajiwara will only be caught off guard once. The plan we select must not have so weak a link. And also, there is the matter of the cliff itself; who among us has the skill to climb such a face?"

"I would climb it, General," Shuyun said.

"Not alone, Brother," Lord Komawara said. "I would climb with you."

"Your courage is to be commended, Brother, Lord Komawara—and never to be doubted. But the danger of your failure is not confined to your-selves. All would fall with you."

Looking out at the faces before him, Shonto saw resistance, resistance to this new advisor. It will not do, the lord thought. They fear to look less skilled than this new one, this boy-man.

Shonto turned to his Spiritual Advisor. "Could you climb this cliff, Brother?"

The monk answered so quietly that all present leaned forward to hear his words. "I am Botahist trained," he said.

"Yes," Shonto said, nodding, "I have seen."

He turned back to his generals and spoke quickly. "We must draw the Hajiwara from their defenses and then they must find the Shonto army be-hind them. We need the cooperation of the Butto—this I'm sure we can achieve. But we must find a way out of Denji Gorge."

Shonto rose suddenly, a guard rushing to take up his sword. "I will hear your alternatives to Brother Shuyun's suggestion when I return."

The screen closed behind Lord Shonto and the room returned to perfect silence. The lamps swayed. Water lapped the hull.

Twenty

THE MANSION OF Butto Joda sat upon a hill looking west across the slopes that swept down to Denji Gorge. It was not coincidental that this situation also provided a perfect view of the lands of the Hajiwara. The fortifications surrounding the mansion were designed and built to be the strongest and most modern defenses possible, yet aesthetics had not been ignored entirely. The palisades and towers were of the finest local material and constructed in the sweeping style of the Mori period.

Kamu mounted the steps to the high tower, accompanied by Butto guards. Much negotiation had preceded this meeting with Butto Joda, the younger son of Lord Butto Taga, for Kamu had insisted that the meeting take place in privacy, away from the prying eyes of Joda's older brother.

A day had been lost in these arrangements, and Kamu knew he had no more time to lose. The bait must be offered and the Butto must take it without delay. Outwardly, Kamu maintained the serenity one would expect from a warrior who had seen many battles, yet this was a serenity that did not come from within. So much depended on this meeting—everything, in fact.

At the top of the stairway, guards flanked large painted screens depicting the Butto armies in victory over their rivals. The guards bowed low, showing respect to the representative of the great Lord Shonto Motoru, but also honoring the famous warrior, Tenge Kamu.

The screens slid aside, revealing Lord Butto Joda, sitting on a dais at the end of an audience chamber of modest proportion. Entering the room,

Kamu knelt and bowed respectfully. The lord nodded, and Kamu was again surprised by his youthful appearance. Even Lord Komawara seemed older than this pup, yet Butto Joda was not to be taken lightly. For three years, he had directed the battles against the Hajiwara, and the Hajiwara House was headed by a man twice his age.

"It is an honor to receive you again so soon, Kamu-sum. I have looked forward to this private discussion with great anticipation. Tell me, has your lord's condition improved?"

"I thank you for your words, as does my lord's House. Lord Shonto recovers quickly and sends his regrets that he cannot meet with you in person. It was his wish that he could pay his respects to his old friend, your honored father. May I enquire after his well-being?"

"The Lord Butto will be most pleased to hear of your kind concern. He grows stronger and I hope he will soon take his place in our councils again— a place I hold by his wish, until his recovery." Polite enquiry followed polite enquiry until the host deemed it proper to discuss other matters. "Is there some issue that Lord Shonto has instructed you to convey to my father? If there is, I would be pleased to be the bearer of such information."

"You are most perceptive, Lord Butto, for indeed my lord wishes to ask the boon of advice in a matter which he deems most sensitive"

"Please, Kamu-sum, it would be our honor to comply, though it is difficult for me to imagine a lord as famed for wisdom as Lord Shonto requiring our humble counsel. Please go on."

"As I have said, it is a matter of great sensitivity, and Lord Shonto would not speak of it if it were not of present importance." Kamu stopped as if what he was about to say was terribly embarrassing to him. "The problem my lord wishes your opinion on has arisen in his dealings with your close neighbors, the House of Hajiwara."

"Ah," the youthful lord said as though he were surprised but understood.

"I am not sure how best to explain this, Lord Butto, I don't wish my words to reflect badly upon a family you have, no doubt, been associated with for generations."

"I understand, Kamu-sum, but the Shonto are also our friends, please . . . speak as though you were in your own chambers."

Kamu bowed in thanks. "I am honored that you think of the Shonto as your friends, for so Lord Shonto regards the Butto." Kamu smiled warmly at the boy before him. Oh, he is bright, the warrior thought. No more than eighteen years old, and listen to the way he speaks! In ten years he will be a force to be reckoned with. "It has become apparent, in our short time here, that the Hajiwara have arrogated onto themselves powers that are the strict and exclusive domain of our revered Emperor. I hardly need to describe these to you, Lord Butto, for it is obvious that the Hajiwara control, for their own benefit, the traffic of the Imperial Waterway. As a representative of the Throne, Lord Shonto is most concerned by this situation."

The young lord nodded as Kamu spoke, a look of grave concern on his face. "For this very reason, and others also, my own House has been at odds with the Hajiwara for some length of time. In fact, I will tell you as one friend to another, this is only the most recent of a long history of such actions by the Hajiwara."

"Ah, Lord Butto, do you then share Lord Shonto's concern for this situation?"

"I hesitate to speak for my esteemed father, but I think I may say that this situation has been an insult to many Houses in this province that are loyal to the Son of Heaven, rather than to their own profit."

"What of the governor, then?"

Butta Joda laughed aloud. "Pardon my outburst, Kamu-sum. As you no doubt are aware, the Governor of Itsa Province is Lord Hajiwara's son-in-law, and loyal to the intentions of his wife's father." He said this with a trace of bitterness.

"I would not say this elsewhere, Lord Butto, but the Emperor has not paid close enough attention to your difficulties in Itsa."

The young lord nodded, but said nothing.

Kamu hesitated before speaking again. "It seems that a representative of the Throne should deal with this problem, and soon." He watched Butto's expression carefully as he said this.

The youth did not hesitate. "How could this be done, Kamu-sum?"

Yes, the old warrior thought, he is interested, but is he brave enough? "It is the opinion of some members of Lord Shonto's council that the actions of the Hajiwara are outside of the laws of Wa and therefore subject to sanction. As the governor of the province, the Imperial representative has broken his oath of duty to allow his wife's family to disregard the edicts that govern the canal, it may be necessary for another to enforce those laws in his place."

"What you say is wise, Kamu-sum, but the governor is still, despite all, the representative of the Throne. To oppose him is to defy the Emperor."

"This is true, Lord Butto, but it is not necessary to oppose the governor. To do his proper duty for him, that is what I suggest. I would also suggest that another Imperial representative could take the initiative in this, thus making it clear to the Son of Heaven that this was not merely a jealousy between rival Houses."

"What you say would, no doubt, be of interest to my father, but before I approach him with your words, I cannot help but wonder where such a willing representative of the Throne could be found. The only person in Itsa with such a title is Lord Shonto, and is his fleet not trapped in the Denji Gorge by the very family we discuss?"

"Lord Shonto is an Imperial Governor; he may go where he pleases."

"Ah. Then I have misunderstood. I was under the impression that the Hajiwara . . . *hindered* Lord Shonto in his progress north."

Kamu touched his hand to his chin, considering these words carefully. "Hindered would seem a good description, Lord Butto, yes, but my lord is a most resourceful man and has found a way out of this predicament."

"This I am most happy to hear. Will he go on his way soon?"

"Not," Kamu said, "until he has dealt with this situation to his satisfaction."

"May I ask how Lord Shonto will accomplish this? I have lived beside Denji Gorge all of my life, and I confess I don't know how this could be done."

Kamu folded his hand in his lap. "It has been said that if one separates true lovers, they will find a way to surmount all difficulties that hold them apart. My lord is like this—there is no difficulty he cannot surmount."

The young man broke into a boyish smile. "The Butto are fortunate to have such a friend. My father is a loyal subject of the Emperor and willing to help his delegates in any way. Is there some specific task the Butto could perform that I may discuss with my father?"

"It is kind of you to enquire. There is something you could do which would be a great service to the Son of Heaven. . . ."

Twenty-one

THE CHAIR HOJO Masakada rode in had once belonged to Chakao Isha, a famous general of the Dono Dynasty. Chakao Isha had been a forebear of the House of Hajiwara, so it was a great honor that they carried the emissary of Lord Shonto in such state.

Hojo Masakada thought it unfortunate that the Isha blood had been wed to, and finally found its end in, this House. He looked around at the green-liveried Hajiwara guards that accompanied him and could not tell that they were not farmers in costume.

They are a minor House in a small province, he told himself, and little different from any other in the same position. I must not forget that, at the moment, they have power over us.

The procession proceeded along a narrow road that led under long rows of peach trees. The sun cast the shadows of the almost bare, twisted branches onto the white gravel of the road, so that it appeared his bearers walked through a dark and tangled pattern.

Behind General Hojo came thirty Shonto guards in full armor and the blue livery of their House. It was a small retinue for such an occasion, but it had been calculated to appear so—an admission of the circumstances in which the Shonto found themselves.

Walls appeared at the end of the corridor of trees, the walls of a fortress, granite, like the walls that formed the famous gorge. As he drew closer, the general could see that it was a typical fortified dwelling of the country type, surrounded by a wide moat—though it appeared that this moat was not purely decorative. Unlike most other dwellings of its kind, this one was accessible only by drawbridge. It said much when a lord's home, only seven days' journey from the capital, had need of such defenses.

Hajiwara guards knelt in rows along either side of the wooden bridge as the procession passed, bowing carefully. The general wondered if the description he had read of Lord Hajiwara Harita would match the man he was about to meet. Shonto intelligence was seldom wrong, but when it came to men, Hojo liked to make his own assessments.

The Hajiwara steward received the Shonto emissary in the most formal manner. "General Hojo, my lord welcomes you to his house. His family is honored to receive you. Do you wish to refresh yourself before your audience?"

Audience? Hojo asked himself. Does this country lord think he sits on a throne? "I am honored that your lord receives me. The journey has been short, and I do not wish to detain your lord. If it is convenient, I would meet with him as soon as possible."

The steward bowed and the Shonto general was led up a wide flight of stone steps and through a gate. The garden they entered was of the middle Botahist period, sparsely planted, with large expanses of raked gravel broken by careful arrangements of stones—a type of garden once thought to be ideal for meditation. Behind a sculpted pine tree was a small summerhouse, and, as they rounded it, General Hojo could see, sitting inside, the large figure of the Hajiwara Lord. Hojo Masakada bowed to him and in return received a nod.

So it begins, the general thought, and entered the summerhouse.

The lord who sat before him had seen perhaps thirty-five summers, yet his face was lined like a much older man's. His hands, too, seemed to show more age—the large, tanned hands of a veteran campaigner. Yet, in contrast to this, he wore a robe of the latest and most elaborate fashion which, General Hojo thought, looked entirely out of place on the man's immense frame.

The lord welcomed him in a slow, deep tone, enquiring into the health of Lord Shonto. Cha was served and the two warriors discussed the unseasonal weather and the hunting in Itsa Province.

When the cha was gone, and the stories of hunting exhausted, Lord Hajiwara said, "I look forward to a meeting with Lord Shonto upon his recovery. I'm sure it is out of the question to move him while he is ill."

"My lord has instructed me to discuss this with you, Sire. He feels the need to continue on his way as soon as possible. He has a duty to the Emperor that cannot be ignored."

"Lord Shonto must not let duty endanger his health. It would be better for the people of Seh if their new governor would arrive with all of his strength. I'm sure the Son of Heaven would agree. Let us not speak of it any more."

The general almost smiled at this. Yes, my friend, he thought, you will have few surprises for us. "I am sure my liege-lord will be most grateful for your concern. He, too, has expressed concern for your own position, Lord Hajiwara."

The lord raised his eyebrows. "Pardon me, General—*my position?*"

"Your military situation, Sire. All of your efforts brought to a standstill, as they have been."

"Perhaps Lord Shonto is not truly aware of the situation, General, having only recently come to Itsa," the lord said, mustering all possible dignity.

Immediately, Hojo looked contrite. "I'm certain that is the case, Lord Hajiwara. It is never good to listen to the gossip around the Imperial Palace. I'm sure your position is not understood in the capital."

"They speak of my position in the capital?" The large man flushed now.

"Sire, I'm sorry to have mentioned it. You know the gossip that one hears from idle courtiers and Imperial functionaries," the general paused, "and ministers and generals."

The lord's eyes went wide. "What is it they say, General Hojo?"

"Pardon me, Sire, I do not believe what they say for a moment but . . . . in the capital they say you are being mastered by a boy."

"*What!*" The lord wheeled on his guest, knocking the cups from the table. "Who dares say this? Who?"

The general began picking up the cha service hurriedly, all the while shaking his head. "Please Sire, pay no attention to this. These Imperial Guards know nothing of what happens in the provinces, truly."

The lord smashed his fist on the table. "Guardsmen! How dare they speak thus of me!"

Hojo observed every minute detail of the lord's reaction, just as Lord Shonto had instructed him. Hajiwara had responded to the mention of Imperial Guards just as Shonto had thought he would. Interesting.

"It is a despicable situation, Lord Hajiwara, and one my lord is equally offended by. So offended, in fact, that he has instructed me to relate a proposal that he believes would change your position entirely."

The lord sat upright, straightening his robe. "I do not need Lord Shonto's assistance." But then Hojo's words seemed to register. "What do you mean, *change my position?*"

"Well, if I have not been misinformed, have not the Butto established a fortress on your own fief, a fortress that has been there for several years? Has not your offensive been thwarted—for some time now, I believe. As a warrior, of course, I understand that these are only appearances, but others who are less well trained. . . ." The general gestured with an open hand. "Lord Shonto was only hoping to assist in a small way in your efforts against the arrogant Butto. Our passage through the Butto locks was hardly arranged with the honor due to an Imperial Governor! I see that it must be a constant insult to have to deal with this House headed by a boy."

"Huh! This will not continue. The Hajiwara will triumph!"

"I'm certain that is true, Sire. The information Lord Shonto had thought to offer you would probably not change the final outcome." The general shrugged.

"But I do not wish to offend the great lord," Hajiwara said warmly, "if he has seen fit to send you with advice, then I would not think of ignoring it."

Hojo paused, thinking a long time before answering. "It is more than advice, Lord Hajiwara. Lord Shonto has intelligence that may prove of great benefit to you."

The lord assumed a posture of attentiveness. "Ah. The Shonto are known for their wisdom. I would be honored to hear Lord Shonto's words."

The general swept a drop of cha from the table absentmindedly. "If you were to know a time when Butto Joda was inspecting his defenses before the fortifications you have established on the Butto fief, would this be information you would deem useful?"

"*Indeed,* I believe it would. Do you know when this will happen?"

"We shall, Lord Hajiwara, we shall." The general regarded his companion closely.

"I see."

Neither man spoke, each hoping for the other to break the silence.

Finally, the Shonto general took the initiative. "Perhaps you should consider whether such information is of use to you, Sire," Hojo said, smiling and sitting back. He looked around him as though searching for his guard.

"This information, would it also include troop strengths and the number of Lord Butto's personal guard?"

"Of course."

"I see." The lord was deep in thought now.

General Hojo interrupted him, pressing, "This would be valuable knowledge, yeh?"

"It could be, General, it could be."

"Some would be willing to pay a great price for such information."

The lord seemed to shake himself out of his thoughts. "What you say is true, if the information were to prove correct."

"Of course, information from Lord Shonto would be above suspicion?"

"Certainly. But many things may happen between the time the information is received and the time it is to be acted upon."

"Ah. It would be best, then, if there could be mutual assurance in this matter, so that there will be no misunderstandings."

"How would this be arranged, General?"

"Half of our fleet would lock through upon receiving the information. The other half would lock through upon the fall of Butto Joda, providing he does not escape through a military error."

"I see." The lord rubbed his forehead. "For this to be truly effective, Lord Shonto must not leave the gorge until after the Butto Lord has fallen."

"It was assumed that this would be the case. His troops will stay with him, of course."

"Certainly."

"Except for those who accompany you against Butto Joda, those who will act as your personal guard."

The lord looked at Hojo in disbelief. "This cannot be, General! I have my own guard. I go nowhere without them."

General Hojo pressed his palms together, touching the fingers to his chin. "Despite your doubts, I think you should consider our proposal. It may prove very beneficial—your name will again be spoken with respect at court. The thorn will finally be drawn from your side. Speak of it with your advisors, with your kin. But do not wait too long, Lord, or the opportunity will be gone." He opened his hands to Lord Hajiwara, empty hands.

Twenty-two

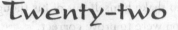

I T WAS NOT an auspicious night, the night of the first-quarter moon. Dark, starless, clouded. A cold wind swept down Denji Gorge from the north, pushing the first sting of winter before it.

Shuyun ignored the chill of the wind, which tore at him as he clung to the rigging of the river junk. The ropes bit into his hands and feet, even through the strips of cotton he had wrapped so carefully around them.

The ship swayed in the darkness, buffeted by the winds that deflected off the high granite walls. Somewhere, near at hand, the cliffs lay hidden by darkness, and the ship sailed blindly toward them. Lookouts in the bow whispered anxiously among themselves, but their voices were carried off into the night. At least the Hajiwara soldiers would hear nothing over the voice of the Wind God.

The ship pitched, causing Shuyun to hug the rigging to him with all his strength. Below him, in the blackness, Lord Komawara waited, no doubt suffering the same discomfort, the same misgivings. Rain, Shuyun thought, will it rain? It was the only thing that would, with certainty, destroy their plans, leaving Lord Shonto trapped by the feuding houses. A blast of wind seemed to fall on them from directly above, shaking the ship as though it were but a floating leaf. And then it was gone, soaring over the wave tops.

Shuyun peered into the night, willing his eyes not to play tricks. Was that something there, off the starboard bow? The wind howled off the rock, like an evil spirit screaming into his ear. That sound . . . we must be close. Yes! There! He reached down with his foot until he felt Komawara's cold hand. The young lord understood—the monk felt him move up another step.

Shuyun remembered the resistance this plan had provoked among Shonto's generals and he wondered now if he had been wrong to recommend it.

The wall of stone seemed to draw closer, though in the dark it was difficult to judge—dark against dark.

Shuyun moved up the rope steps one by one, careful not to lose his grip. The pitching of the ship was amplified more with each step. When he reached the top of the mast, he knew it would be describing a long, quick arc. The ship altered to port now, the sailors hoping to ease alongside the wall—without becoming its victim. The sculling oar pushed them on, rags silencing its inevitable creaking. Shuyun moved up again as he felt Lord Komawara stop at his feet. He is strong, the monk thought, but he is not Botahist trained. He did not scale cliffs as a child to learn to control fear, to learn focus.

The walls were there now, solidly unmistakable, yet the distance to them was still not clear. Shuyun began searching for signs of the sculpture above him. His examination of the Lovers had revealed that there was a ledge, or so it appeared, at the bottom of the stone relief. How wide it was could not be seen, but it was there that they must begin the climb. In the darkness below, Shuyun could sense the presence of the sailors ready to carry out their orders.

A gust of wind seemed to counter the motion of the ship, and Shuyun used the few seconds of reduced pitching to move up to the top of the mast. He was high above the waters now, ten times the height of a man at least, and the motion was terrible. Encircling the mast with his arms, Shuyun held tightly to it; the wood was cold against his face. All the while he tried to feel rain in the force of the wind.

They were parallel to the cliff face now and the helmsman, the best in Shonto's fleet, edged them closer. The swell running in the lake was not large, but the winds coming from all directions defied any attempt to compensate for their effects.

Shuyun tried to penetrate the darkness, looking for the ledge he knew must be there.

"The gunnel of the ship almost scrapes the stone, Brother." Komawara's voice came to him—a whisper out of the darkness, out of the wind.

Yes, Shuyun thought, now is the time. And, as though his thoughts had been heard, the men below began to ease the lines they had set to the mast-head. The spar, steadied by many guy lines, leaned toward the cliff face. It will work, Shuyun told himself, if we are not dashed against the rock.

He braced his foot on the mast and turned toward the cliff as best he could. He felt along the coil of rope over his head and shoulder to be sure that it would not snag as he jumped.

But still the cliff face seemed blank, featureless. The pitching of the boat threw the mast toward the rock and Shuyun braced himself for the impact—but it did not come, not this time.

There! A change in the blank stone, a shape that he could not be sure of—a curve, an area of gray. There was nothing else it could be. The sculpture was the only feature that broke the uniformity of the granite. The ledge should be directly below, Shuyun thought, and he prepared to leap, using every sense his teachers had trained, trusting them, for it was a leap of faith he would make, he had no doubt. He contolled his breathing, stretching his time sense, and felt the motion of the boat slow. The mast heaved toward the rock again and Shuyun focused all of his consciousness on its path.

There will be a split second when it stops, he thought. Then I must jump without hesitation or it will return and my jump will become a fall.

The huge spar seemed to attain an even greater speed, careening toward the granite wall, and then, just as quickly, it stopped. Shuyun leapt, crouching like a cat tossed by a child.

His feet and hands hit the shattered rock of the ledge and he was thrown, shoulder first, into the cliff face. I am not injured, he told himself, and was up, feeling his way along the ledge in the direction the ship moved. He could hear nothing above the howl of the wind, the crash of the waves.

His hands groped before him, feeling the way. Thank Botahara, the ledge is wide, he thought as he went, and indeed it was, as wide as a man's shoulders, But it was broken and sloped and littered with moss and fallen stone. He scrambled on as quickly as he dared. Where was Komawara?

Suddenly his senses warned him, and he dropped flat to the stone as a body crashed into the rock above him. He made a desperate grab as the figure fell past and caught Komawara by his robe. The young lord lay half off the ledge now, dangling out over the dark waters, but he made no move to save himself.

Dazed, the monk thought. He felt himself slipping over the stone, Komawara's weight pulling him toward the edge. His hand scrabbled along the back of the ledge for a hold to pull against. His fingers curled around the stem of some stunted brush and he heaved against the dead weight of the young warrior.

Let it hold, Shuyun prayed. Komawara stirred, trying to pull free, but then he came to his senses and his hand grasped the monk by the back of his neck. He made a feeble effort to pull himself up. The bark of the bush began to slough off, letting go of its own stem like the skin of a shedding snake. Shuyun gripped it tighter, trying to bend it back on itself. Slowly Komawara came up over the edge, using the monk as a ladder. And then he lay on top of him for a long moment, gasping for breath.

"Are you injured, Lord?"

"No . . . I don't know, I'm. . . ." Komawara shook his head. He moved his left arm. "I am unhurt, Brother." He pushed himself off the monk and into a sitting position against the wall, the sword strapped to his back digging into his muscles.

"We must continue," Komawara said.

Shuyun sat also, concerned, afraid that the young lord was not telling the truth about his injuries. Knowing also that Komawara was right.

The wind screamed at them for a long moment and neither of them moved or tried to speak. When it abated, Shuyun stood, running his hands along the rock face. "We must determine our position," he whispered. Moving to his left, he continued, testing the ledge with his feet, running his hands along the stone wall. Komawara followed him as he went, though the lord did not rise to his feet, preferring to keep himself close to the rock.

After a moment of exploration, Shuyun felt the granite swelling out toward him, reducing the width of the ledge. It is the foot of Botahara's Bride, Shuyun realized. So it was still a good distance to the cracks he had seen in the stone that would, he hoped, offer them purchase on the sheer face.

Shuyun reached as far as he could around the smooth projection. Wide, it was wide. Here, on the rock itself, he began to get a sense of the true scale of the carvings. The foot was probably three times the height of a man, and all else was in proportion to that.

He knelt down then and leaning out precariously, he explored the narrowing ledge, testing the stone, brushing it clean of debris. It was then that the Wind God struck, attacking the poorly balanced monk without warning. Shuyun's supporting hand came off the ledge and he pitched forward, but then he felt a pull on his sash, and he was safe. A voice close to his ear said, "My debt is repaid, Brother." And Komawara let the monk go.

Pushing the coil of rope over his head, Shuyun passed it to his companion before tying the end around his waist. This time he felt the tautness of the rope Komawara held as he leaned out to run his hand along the ledge.

Narrow, it became very narrow—no wider than a man's hand was long. He came back onto the ledge, another gust of cold wind tearing at them.

"We must not hesitate, Brother. There is the smell of rain in this air."

Shuyun nodded to the darkness. "If I slip, you must not fall with me. Let me go if you must."

"I understand," Komawara answered.

On his feet again, Shuyun moved to the narrowing of the ledge. He paused for a moment to push himself farther into chi ten; a blast of wind struck the ledge, but Shuyun seemed to have so much time to counter it.

Komawara's voice came to him, as though from the bottom of a pit. "Are you ready, Brother?"

"Yes," Shuyun answered, and stepped out onto the narrow edge. Against his hands the rock was smooth, featureless. He felt with his feet, edging along the shelf, testing each step. He faced the rock, careful to keep his body out, balanced over his feet. The sound of the waves echoed up from below, reminding him of what lay beneath, wrapped in darkness.

Shuyun came to the widest point of the giant foot and the ledge disappeared. He stopped and balanced himself. Reaching up with his left hand, he searched the stone for any irregularity, any break in the granite. There was nothing. He could hear Komawara shifting impatiently. I must be bold, Shuyun thought. He stretched to the limit of his balance and found a tiny edge—half the width of his fingertip, but an edge. Bracing himself, he tested it. It held. He risked a little more weight on it.

Yes, Shuyun decided, it will do. He pulled some rope from Komawara so he would have no resistance to work against, and then swung out into space. His left foot scrabbled on the hard stone, desperately searching. It was only then that he realized he could not return—there was no way to pull himself back to the ledge!

I am in the hands of Botahara, he told himself, and let his right foot slide off the safety of the ledge. He hung there by one hand, trying to reach around the swelling in the stone with his foot.

"The ledge must go on," he told himself, and brought his right hand up to the tiny edge to which he clung. There was only room for two fingers, but that would do. He called chi into his hands and took his weight on the two-fingered hold. In a smooth easy motion, his left hand moved in an arc out to his side. Yes! There, a vertical crack that took his fingers to the first knuckle. He pulled himself left, searching with his foot until he found flat stone. In one quick motion he pulled himself onto it, his breathing still even, unlabored.

"Praise to my teachers," he whispered, as he began exploring the rock with his hands. Following the crack up, he found it formed a cleft in the rock. He ran the rope through this natural groove, and began to draw it in. When he had taken in all the slack, he signaled his companion with two light tugs.

It was impossible to tell Komawara how he had found his way around, but with the rope positioned as it was, Shuyun felt confident that he could hold the young lord in case of a fall.

Shuyun tried to guess Komawara's movements by what happened to the rope. It slackened slightly, and Shuyun pulled it taut, taking it around his waist, sure that his companion was out on the narrowing ledge now. More rope came free and he gathered it in. He will come to the end of the ledge in another step, Shuyun thought. The rope stopped. The monk kept a light but positive pressure on it, reading Komawara's progress as though the line were a nerve connecting them.

He cannot find the way, Shuyun realized. He waited, willing the lord to reach out, to push himself. But there was no change in the tension on the rope. If he stays too long he will grow tired, his focus will waver, and he will lose his nerve.

Another moment passed, and Shuyun decided he could wait no longer. Slowly, but with great strength, he began to take in the rope. It will pull him up and to his left, the monk thought. Will he understand?

The wind continued its shrill chorus, whipping dust up from the ledge and shaking the monk's robe like an untended sail. There was only the same resistance on the rope, no sign that Komawara moved on. Then there was a sharp tug, then another. Shuyun answered it. He braced himself, and felt the increase of weight as the rope bit into his muscles. There was another tug and Shuyun realized that the warrior had not found the handhold, but instead was using the rope—climbing it hand over hand. Shuyun wrapped the rough fibers of the line tighter around him and waited. A second later,

Komawara swung smoothly onto the ledge. Even above the sound of the wind, Shuyun could hear his ragged breathing.

Fear, the monk realized, and its odor was carried to him on the air before it was swept off into the night.

"Can you continue, Lord?" Shuyun asked.

Komawara fought to control himself. "Yes . . . don't be concerned. We must go on." He rose to his knees and began to coil the rope.

Shuyun waited a moment and then, tugging at Komawara's sleeve, he led on. The ledge did not change for several paces, but then they found some loose blocks of stone that the elements, ice and wind and sun, had pried from the solid cliff. Shuyun rocked the first block and decided it would hold. The others were much the same, though several small pieces had fallen away and others of similar size were ready to go. The two men picked their way across the rubble, realizing that even the storm would not hide the sound of sliding rock.

Again they came to a place where the stone seemed to swell out from the face of the cliff, though not as dramatically this time. The hip of the Bride, Shuyun thought, and the image on the wall seemed almost to taunt him. Shuyun felt along the walls here, looking for the cracks that he had seen running up the length of the relief.

In the darkness on the lake the lights of Shonto's fleet could be seen bobbing and swaying in the waves. They seemed far off now, far off and very small. He is a great general, Shuyun told himself; everything that could be done to insure our success has been done. If only the others do not fail. The plan depended on so many different elements, so many different people.

Shuyun pushed these thoughts from his mind as he came to the point he had looked for. He explored the cracks as far up as he could reach. They were smoother inside than he would have expected, older and more worn, but they were wider than he had dared hope. He thrust his hand into one and found it as wide as his fist and quite deep.

Now, Shuyun thought, we will see if the long hours of discussion with Lord Komawara will have been worth the effort. Shuyun retied the knot around his chest and made sure that Komawara had untied his. Taking a moment to compose himself, Shuyun searched his inner self to be sure that he had, as his teachers said, tranquillity of purpose.

He began to climb, twisting his cotton-wrapped feet and hands into the crack, forcing himself up the fracture in the stone. The rope was the length of twenty-five men, as long as he dared carry without fear of tangling, and Komawara carried a similar length. If the window they climbed toward was higher than their estimate, they would be unable to drop the rope back to the waters. Shuyun climbed, emptying his mind of such doubts, filling it with the convolutions of the stone, with each measured movement.

The wind tried to grasp him, but he could not be pried loose. The skin on his knuckles tore and both his ankle bones seeped fluid from their contact with the stone. Shuyun felt as though he climbed up into the spirit world, and though he did not consider himself superstitious, he felt a presence, as though the long vanquished Brothers hovered about him, still clinging to the earthly plane.

There, there is our enemy, they would say. *He climbs across the hip of Botahara's Bride as though it were not sacrilege to do so! May he fall into eternal darkness!*

The rock canted in slightly as he crossed the cold stone hip and he stopped to rest a moment before going on. A lifetime of Botahist training came into play, chi flowed into his arms and legs and, even against the unpredictable winds, his balance remained perfect.

He reached the point where the bodies of the Lovers joined. No amount of training had prepared him to meet this sight on such close terms.

"Heresy," Shuyun whispered to himself.

The very rock seemed to be stained with this crime. And yet he clung to it for his life.

It was only then that he realized he had stopped climbing, and this lapse shocked him. In his mind he began a chant to Botahara, attempting to regain his focus. The life of my liege-lord depends on my success, he told himself, and the lives of all his retainers and family.

"Lady Nishima." The whisper came to his lips unbidden. He leaned his head against the cold stone. I am unworthy of the efforts of my teachers, he thought. He began his chant again and started up the crack that led over the hip of the figure of the Perfect Master. In his mind he measured the rope that he had used and guessed that Lord Komawara still held half of it. The crack suddenly became deeper and wider, and Shuyun found that he could sink his arm in to its full length. It continued to grow as he progressed upward and he pushed his shoulder into the crevice.

Wind seemed to funnel down this widened fissure—a cold hand pushing him down—and he fought against it. Finally, after a long struggle, his fingers found the top of the stone hip and he realized then that it was formed by a narrow ledge. He pulled himself up onto it, struggling against the rock which seemed to clutch at his clothes and snag the rope.

Peering into the darkness, Shuyun tried to follow the path of the ledge. The gray line of its edge seemed to rise up on a steep diagonal, but then it blended into the colors of the night and Shuyun was unsure of its direction. He searched his memory of the relief, but it made no sense to him. The back of Botahara? Could it be? What else could be rising at that angle? He had crossed the sculpture at its thinnest section, so it was possible. The window they hoped to enter was almost directly above him now, but perhaps this ledge offered unexpected possibilities.

Bracing his feet against the ledge, Shuyun wedged himself back into the crack and began to take in the rope. When he reached the end, he gave it two light tugs and waited to feel Lord Komawara begin his ascent.

The wind did not seem about to abate, but continued to scream and fly in every direction like a mad dragon. Komawara was only a few feet below Shuyun before the monk heard the sounds of his approach. It had seemed to take Komawara an age to reach the ledge, but Shuyun had not once felt the weight of the warrior on the rope.

With some difficulty Komawara found his way past Shuyun's feet and levered himself onto the ledge. He fought to regain his breath and his muscles were trembling with the exertion.

"Where?" Komawara said, finally.

"You sit astride the back of the Faceless Lover," Shuyun whispered.

"But what is this ledge?"

"The arch of His back. A ledge used long ago to drape material for festivals."

"Does it lead to a window, then?"

"It is not likely, Sire, the ancient monks were too careful. The ledge would have been reached by ropes or ladders. There should be an opening below us, though farther to the left. It is a question of whether it will be easier and quicker to continue up as we are or to cross the ledge and lower ourselves to the opening which we shall have to find in the dark."

Komawara was silent, thinking. "Surely, Brother, this opening to our left will be closer to the water and therefore will make an easier ascent for Shonto's soldiers."

Shuyun realized that in this darkness it was impossible to know which route would be easier. There was something attractive about the ledge, it was there and substantial, and somehow not as intimidating as climbing up again into total darkness.

"I think we should explore this ledge, Lord Komawara. It is as you say; we shall be lower this way, and there is little doubt that our ropes will reach."

With that, the monk stepped over his companion and set out along the ledge. He moved on his hands and knees at first, but as the ledge narrowed he dropped to his belly. The surface beneath him continued to shrink and Shuyun was forced to hang his leg and arm over the side. He crawled on, his eyes closed against the dust whipped off the ledge by the wind. Twice he was forced to climb past areas where the stone had cracked and fallen away, but these only slowed his progress and tested his skill.

The ledge ended abruptly in a small platform, confirming Shuyun's theory that the monks had gained access to them by ladder or rope. Searching with his bleeding fingers, he found a crack that ran along the back of the ledge, but nothing wide enough for him to use as purchase or into which he could jam a knot.

Komawara will have to make the traverse alone. I cannot save him if he falls, or I will be swept from the ledge myself. Untying the rope from his chest, he pulled in the slack and gave Komawara the signal they had agreed upon—two tugs, a pause, and then one more. A second later the rope went slack, Shuyun took it in carefully, arranging it so he would not be tangled in it should Komawara fail.

Twice the intake of rope stopped, as Komawara found his way past the breaks in the ledge, and each time Shuyun controlled his urge to take the line around his waist. But then the line came in again as it had before.

They hardly dared speak when Komawara arrived on the platform, they were so unsure of the location of the opening they sought.

Komawara put his mouth close to Shuyun's ear. "Is it not directly below, Brother?" Even in the darkness Shuyun could tell that the lord rubbed his eyes, trying to free them of the dust.

"I cannot be sure," Shuyun whispered back. "It should be nearby, perhaps three heights below, but to the left."

Komawara leaned over the edge, feeling with his hand. When he sat back he again whispered into the monk's ear. "The rock seems sheer—without holds. How?"

Shuyun felt again into the crack along the wall. "Your sword, Lord

Komawara, it must be the anchor." He took the young warrior's hand and showed him the opening.

"*We must think of something else!*—my *sword!* It was my father's—I cannot leave it."

Shuyun put his hand on the other's arm. "We have nothing else."

The wind whirled about them, buffeting them on their small ledge. Deliberately, Komawara began to undo the harness that held his weapon. In a moment he had the sword and scabbard off and handed them to Shuyun without a word. Using the tip of the sheathed weapon, Shuyun explored the crevice, probing until he found the deepest spot, and here he pushed the scabbard and sword in the length of a man's hand. He tied the rope carefully around the weapon, working the knot down as far as he could.

"It is best that I go first, Sire. Perhaps, without a weapon, I will have an advantage." Not waiting for a reply, Shuyun took the rope around his waist and slipped over the edge of the rock.

The wind seemed far greater on the exposed face of the cliff. He put his feet against the stone and leaned back, but the wind seemed to rock him, pushing him first one way then another. Letting the rope slip slowly across the cotton wrappings on his hands, Shuyun swung himself downward, placing each foot with care.

The window must be nearby, Shuyun thought. He tried to peel aside the layers of darkness, but his eyes told him nothing. A smell came to him on the wind—salt, sweat, and oil. He turned his head, searching for the source of the scent. There! He smelled it again. Moving to the left, Shuyun tried to trace the odor. Yes, he thought, it comes from over here. He moved a step farther, but his foot began to slip and then stopped. As he moved off to the side of his point of attachment, like a pendulum he would tend to swing back toward the center. He forced himself over two more steps, but could go no farther. Was that a line there in the darkness—a hint of light?

Suddenly a voice drifted to him, though it might have been a trick of the wind. Lower, the monk thought, and let some rope slide through his hands. Again! He could almost make out the words now. He lowered himself farther, trying to grip the granite with his feet, forcing himself to the left.

"There is much movement on the plain tonight." The voice seemed almost at Shuyun's elbow!

"It is to do with Lord Shonto. Perhaps he will help our lord rid this land of those cattle thieves."

"Huh! It will be a warm winter when the Shonto and the Hajiwara become allies."

"Well, it has been a warm autumn, until today. Perhaps that is a sign. Please excuse me, I have duties to attend to."

Shuyun could almost hear them bowing in the dark. He realized that he must go lower, but first he must return to the center of his pendulum.

It would not be possible to move across as far as the opening without chancing a slip which could alert the Hajiwara guard to his presence. There was only one sure way to reach the window.

Shuyun moved to his right, away from the opening, pushing himself as far as he could. And then he waited for the Wind God to favor him. He chanted silently and prepared himself as if to spar. What is good for the Shonto will be good for my Order, he told himself. Yet he felt apprehension—not fear, but an anxiety that he would be forced to do battle in earnest. May I be forced to hurt no one, he prayed. The Brotherhood has fought battles before, Shuyun told himself, and though they were to insure the safety of the followers of Botahara, this is no different. Lord Shonto supports the Botahist religion against the wishes of the Emperor and therefore he deserves our complete loyalty.

Shuyun had no way of knowing where the guard would stand, or if he was in the opening at all. It seemed likely that the weather would force him back into the rock as far as duty would allow.

He braced himself, feeling the wind backing. When it favored him entirely, Shuyun ran across the face of the rock, becoming a human pendulum. He judged his distance to the window by his steps, steps which seemed unbelievably slow to his altered time sense. The stone seemed rough against his foot, rough and cold. His momentum grew until it carried him far into the arc.

The door should be here, the monk thought, and there in the dark rock a line appeared. He grasped the line—a hard edge of stone, and pulled himself into the opening. He hit the stone floor and careened across it into the other side of the window. The sound of a sword coming out of its scabbard brought him to his knees. He could see the guard silhouetted against a dull glow that came from somewhere inside. Reaching out, Shuyun grasped the soldier by his armor, and, in one smooth motion, pulled the man toward him. The soldier fell forward, the blow he had aimed going wild, and then he was in the air. A scream seemed to come out of the wind, and the man was gone. There was only the noise of the waves below. May Botahara have mercy on him, Shuyun prayed, and on me.

Shuyun crept back into the light of the tunnel. It opened into a large room with a high, round ceiling that had the signs of a typical guard station—the remains of a meal, weapons neatly arranged, a single lamp on the table. There was no one there. Shuyun went to the door carved into the back wall and found an unlighted stairway that led upward. He heard no sound but the rushing of the wind as it funneled through the rock.

The rope! He had lost his grip on the rope! It was gone, lost in the darkness where Lord Komawara awaited his signal!

Shuyun ran back to the window. The wind made his eyes run with tears and he tried to shield them with his hand. In the darkness he could see nothing. Komawara must have my signal or it will be impossible for him to make a decision, Shuyun realized. He will not know if I have fallen or been taken.

Returning to the chamber, Shuyun looked for something, anything, that would help him reach the rope. A long spear with a barbed tip leaned against the wall. He took it up and felt its weight. Yes, he thought. A noise came from the stairway and Shuyun crouched, listening, ready to strike. It is only the wind taunting me, he thought.

Crossing to the window, he leaned out, blinded by the force of the wind. He realized he had no time to spare, not knowing when the guard might be changed. When the wind veered toward him and he judged the rope would blow nearer, Shuyun reached out blindly with the spear. Something soft seemed to roll under the shaft as he pulled it along the rock, but it did not catch on the barb. Again the wind offered him a chance, but this time he did not feel the rope at all. If it catches on a projection, I am lost, the monk thought. Forcing a calm over himself he waited, dividing his attention between the direction of the wind and the stairway.

The fifth time the Wind God favored him, he felt the rope snag on the tip. Slowly and with great effort, Shuyun brought the rope toward him, never easing the pressure of the spear against the wall. Suddenly it was in his hand and he grasped it as though it were his line to life. Shuyun was about to signal Komawara but stopped. He laid the spear across the opening and tied the line to it. Back in the room he found a strong dagger in a sheath, and he tied it to the rope. He signaled his companion to take in, and then waited, keeping the bitter end in his hand.

When Komawara finally descended, Shuyun braced himself against the stone and pulled the lord across the cliff to the safety of the tunnel.

Feeling his feet on a solid stone floor, the young man clapped the monk on the back in a most disrespectful manner. "I shall tell Lord Shonto of your bravery, Brother. Never would I have climbed here alone. *And my sword . . .*" he bowed deeply. "I thank you." He glowed with the elation of one who has risked great danger and survived.

"There will be time later for discussion, Sire, but you must guard the door while I make the sign."

Komawara's face changed at the monk's words. He nodded, and drawing his weapon he went to the stairs.

Shuyun took the shield from the lamp and went to the door. May the watchmen be alert, he thought. Careful not to allow the wind to kill the flame, Shuyun gave the signal and waited. The lights on the lead ship died altogether as though the wind had had its way.

Now, Shuyun thought, we must lower the rope and hold this room at all costs. He returned to the chamber.

"They have seen," he told Lord Komawara.

It was in the hands of Lord Shonto's boatmen and soldiers now. The sound of the wind and the waves beating against the rock did not change. It is not done yet, Shuyun thought. He waited by the window, ready to pull up the rope ladder. The wind moaned all around him, and it was almost a moan of pleasure.

Twenty-three

DRESSED IN FULL armor, with helmet and face-mask, Lord Hajiwara crossed the small yard of the keep accompanied by six Shonto officers and an equal number of his own guard. The rattle of armor could be heard everywhere in the dim light, as fifty Shonto soldiers prepared to escort Lord Hajiwara into battle.

The sound and smell of horses permeated the cool air and a shrill wind whistled among the towers, causing the many banners to flutter and crack.

The Shonto general, Hojo Masakado, almost ran to keep up with the giant stride of Lord Hajiwara.

"There must be no time wasted, General Hojo. None at all."

"My men await you, Sire."

They came to a stone stairway which they mounted two abreast. At the top, a platform looked out across the plain, yet in the storm and the darkness, nothing could be seen. Dust, collected by the dry autumn, filled the air and stung the eyes.

"Damn this wind!" Hajiwara said.

"It shall be the perfect mask, Sire," General Hojo said quietly.

"Yes, but it will also be the perfect screen." He stared out into the darkness, into the cloud of dust. "So, Butto Joda, you think to hide behind the skirt of the night." He banged a gloved fist against the stone parapet and then turned to his aides who dropped to their knees.

"All is ready, Sire," a senior officer reported.

"Then we must not hesitate," Hajiwara said, and strode across the platform to another set of stairs.

General Hojo jumped to his side. "This is not the way, Sire! My men await us here." He pointed back to the courtyard. A Hajiwara guard stepped between his lord and the general and swords were drawn all around. Hajiwara guards seemed to materialize out of the shadows and the Shonto men found themselves surrounded.

Drawing himself up, the general stared at the Hajiwara lord. "This is treachery," Hojo almost hissed. "Lord Shonto is not a man to trifle with. I strongly advise you to reconsider." The Shonto officers formed themselves into a tight knot around their commander.

Hajiwara stopped at the head of the stairway. "*Treachery*, General Hojo?" His voice sounded unreal through the metal of his face-mask. "These are strong words. I do this to assure myself that there will be no treachery. If the information your lord has provided proves to be true, then you shall be freed and your lord sped on his way. You may be sure of this. I take only the precautions any man would take—any man who was not the fool I seem to have been taken for. Be at your ease, General. You shall be treated with all due respect. Please see that your men cooperate." The lord gave a quick nod and disappeared down the stairway.

The Captain of the Hajiwara guard stepped forward and nodded, pointing with his sword to the stairs the men had ascended. Not exposing their backs, the Shonto soldiers passed down to the courtyard where their fellow soldiers waited.

So, General Hojo thought as he assessed the situation around him, Hajiwara is not the fool we had taken him for. Why, then, is he out chasing phantoms in the storm, while I am here, at the heart of the fortress that controls the locks to Denji Gorge?

Butto Joda dismounted and his horse was led away by an armed aide. The sounds of horses, stamping in agitation, mingled with the wail of the storm.

The Dragon Wind, the young lord thought, but who will it assist tonight? He sat upon his camp stool and a guard handed him a war fan bearing the Butto seal. Senior officers knelt waiting in the dim light of torches.

From this position on the hilltop the young lord could see the many fires of the two armies that faced each other on the broad plain. Far off, the lights of the Imperial Guard Keep, now occupied by the Hajiwara, were just visible, and to their left, the long black line of Denji Gorge bordered the entire plain.

If only we can trust the Shonto, the lord thought. They have lied to one or the other of us, there is no doubt of that. I pray to Botahara it is as I believe and removal of the Hajiwara is their true goal. He touched his forehead in the sign of obeisance to Botahara.

A senior general came forward and knelt before his young lord. "An army moves over the plain, Sire, though it is difficult to know how large a force it is. Our spies tell us that, even in this storm, it is clear the Hajiwara soldiers make preparations."

The young lord nodded, deep in thought. In his armor, laced in black and Butto purple, Joda looked even smaller and younger than usual, yet his generals showed no sign of lack of confidence in their lord. All waited, ready to carry out his orders without question.

"And what of the Butto, have we made our preparations?"

"The armies await your commands, Sire," the general said. "And the *goat* has been staked in the field. We wait only for the *leopard*."

Butto Joda nodded. "Our soldiers must be patient yet. The *leopard* comes to us. The Hajiwara will attack first, they must. And we will pull back in disarray, drawing them farther into Butto lands. A single battle stands between us and the victory we have so long prayed for. Bring me good news to take to your lord, my father. Let it be said that, in his lifetime, the Butto finally had retribution for generations of compromised honor."

The wind curled and howled around them, making speech impossible, but then it seemed to rise and throw itself at the sky. "It is a sign!" Butto Joda said. "The Dragon Wind comes to aid the Butto, have no doubt!" The young lord reached up and tightened the cord on his helmet, and all of his retainers did the same.

Horses pawed the ground and snorted as the dragon howled around them. Their manes streamed in the wind, dancing in the torchlight. And then soldiers pushed the torches into the sand and the darkness was complete.

The hundredth Shonto soldier scrambled over the ledge, clawing his way up the cargo nets that had been made into a giant rope ladder. He nodded to Shuyun, observing some formality even in such circumstances.

Can they not come more quickly? Shuyun wondered, though he knew there really was nothing that could be done about it. Holding a boat next to the cliff was an almost impossible task in this storm. Two soldiers had been lost already—swept under by the weight of their armor when the boat lurched.

Leaving the soldiers to tend to their arriving companions, Shuyun entered the chamber of stone, and signaled Lord Komawara. They crossed to the stairway. It was time to see what lay ahead. The monk had a rough idea of what to expect in such a temple, for all Botahist fanes had certain things in common. But he also realized the sect that had dwelt here so long ago would no doubt have had their own needs.

The walls of the stairway had once been painted with elaborate figures, many in the act of love. They were difficult to discern now, for the centuries had not been kind to them. Ancient written characters left Botahara's word carved into the rock, but painted over them in many places were the blasphemies of heretics and nonbelievers.

The stairs seemed to twist up into the rock of the cliff so that soon the little light that came from below was gone. Komawara chanced a slight opening of his bronze lantern, but this showed no change—the stairs continued their long spiral. The two climbed on, making as little noise as they could, which slowed their progress painfully. Around the next corner a dull glow seemed to come from above and the warrior and the monk slowed their pace even more.

The stairs ended at a door in the rock and it was from here that the light came. Komawara drew his sword, but Shuyun stepped past him to approach the opening. Stopping to listen, he pushed chi through his body and slowed his time sense; when he moved again, Lord Komawara was unable to believe the speed of his motion.

The door opened into a corridor wide enough for four men abreast. The sound of the storm was less here, but the air still rushed and funneled through the doors and tunnels.

This will be the level of the three windows, Shuyun thought. I am in the hall that connects them. He stepped farther into the corridor, looking toward the source of the light. An eerie wail came from behind and Shuyun whirled toward it . . . but there was nothing there except the wind.

The voice of the dead Brothers is still in the wind, the monk thought, and he turned back to the light. It seemed to come from a door on the right. An inner chamber, Shuyun thought, and signaled Komawara to wait while he investigated. The lord took up a position in the doorway where he could watch the hall at the monk's back.

Shuyun moved forward, seeming to flow like a Sonsa. His bare feet made no sound on the cold stone.

As he came close to the door, there was a noise from the hallway's end— footsteps and the rattle of armor. A light illuminated the opening and Shuyun could see stairs. He stepped back, ready to run, but realized there was no time. A soldier appeared, lamp in hand, his eyes fixed to the floor in front of him. He was three steps into the corridor before he looked up and saw the monk crouched in the halflight.

The soldier's eyes went wide and he stopped. *"Spirit-walker!"* he whispered and turned and fled.

Alerted by the noise, a second soldier appeared in the door to the right. He, too, recoiled in shock at the sight of the monk and Shuyun used the second of surprise to drive a soft-fist into the bridge of the man's nose. There was a "crack" like the sound of a breaking board and the guard fell to the stone in a heap. Shuyun jumped into the room and with a sweeping motion of his left hand deflected the blow of a second guard. Stepping aside, the monk found the center of resistance in his opponent and easily propelled the man across the hall into the solid granite wall. He fell and did not move.

Komawara was beside the monk now, sword in hand.

"Did one escape, Brother?"

Shuyun nodded as he knelt to tie the guards.

"Then we are discovered! He will sound the alarm." The young lord's face twisted in what seemed like pain. "We have failed."

"I don't think we have, Sire. The guard is sure he saw a Spirit-walker—a ghost of the dead Brothers who once dwelt here. No doubt he is frightening his companions with his tale even now. I think no one will venture down here while this storm lasts. But we must be sure this level is secure so that no one escapes with the truth."

The lord nodded and was off to the other doors without hesitation, moving with the assuredness and grace of a falcon about to strike.

Shonto slid his brush carefully across his inkstone and went back to the paper he worked on. *No man knows the weaknesses of his own child,* the lord wrote. *And no man knows the strength of the tree by the shape of the seed.*

It was an exercise Shonto had done a thousand times—ever since he was a child, in fact. He formed each character with the utmost care, focusing all of his attention on every stroke of the brush. *To exist beyond the world, beyond the emotions, in the purity of the act itself, that is tranquillity of purpose.* He inked his brush again and stopped to examine his effort. Was that the slightest sign of a shake? Had his attention wandered?

He set his brush to paper again, recopying the line that dissatisfied him. There was no reason for the brush work not to be perfect. The plan would work or it would not, and if it did, the fleet would be in the locks before dawn. Then, and only then, would Shonto have things to deal with. Until that time, thinking of what might or might not be happening was of no use.

Speak carelessly and your orders will be followed in the same spirit. The brush moved on the paper without sound, and the lord bent over his work in total concentration.

A horse galloped up the hill, rising with such speed it seemed as though it were borne by the wind itself. Lord Hajiwara listened to the sound as though he would tell the news by the haste of the rider. It was the hour of the dove, he guessed as he gazed up. The sky was broken and ragged, clouds sailing like a fleet before the wind. The quarter-moon glowed from behind a cloud on the western horizon and in the east there would soon be the beginnings of dawn. Around him, on the shoulders of the hill, Hajiwara could see the signs of battle—fallen soldiers and horses—though the color of their livery was not visible.

"Who wins the battle by night?" Hajiwara said to himself, posing the question from an old adage. *"Those who see the day break."*

The wind had not fallen and its howl mixed with the sound of the battle that was still raging. It was a strange, unsettling storm and none the less so for being dry. No rain had fallen and now the clouds broke up and scattered as though they had accomplished their purpose.

The horse slowed at the outer ring of guards and then raced on to the hilltop. Reining in his mount, the rider appeared in the torchlight, a lieutenant attached to the lord's staff. He dismounted as a guard hurried to take the bridle, and then went directly to Lord Hajiwara. He bowed without any sign of haste, and then pulled open his face-mask. His mouth was surrounded by a black ring where dust had stuck to sweat.

"Lieutenant?" the general at Lord Hajiwara's right prompted.

"Sire, I come to report that we have taken Lord Butto Joda."

Lord Hajiwara nodded and opened his face-mask. His staff knelt around him, bowing as the lord offered his thanks to the gods.

"Where is the vanquished lord?" Hajiwara asked. "You say you have 'taken him'?"

"Sire, he was captured unharmed and has been brought safely through the lines, though not without pursuit. I came ahead to allow you time to prepare."

The lord nodded and then he and his staff sat without discussion or sign of impatience. They noted the beauty and tranquillity of the moon in contrast to the sounds of battle. They reflected upon the state of their own spirits at that instant. The Hajiwara had waited generations for this; they intended now to make the moment perfect.

Horses galloped, a resonance like a heart pounding out of control. Twenty men slowed for the guards and then pushed on. In the half light the Hajiwara green was visible and, as the riders grew closer, purple on one horseman no bigger than a child. They reined in and untied the child from the saddle. He was forced to his knees before Lord Hajiwara, arms tied behind his back.

"Do you not bow, Lord Butto Joda?" Hajiwara asked quietly.

The figure in black and purple made no move but remained still and, somehow, dignified. Hajiwara gave a signal to his general who nodded to a guard who stepped forward and removed the young lord's face-mask and helmet. He pushed the boy's face down to the ground and then stepped back.

"Look up, young lord, see what your family's pride has brought you."

Slowly, ever so slowly, the boy rose until the flickering light of the torches illuminated his child's face. Hajiwara was on his feet, his sword half out. He glared at those around him like a crazed man who has discovered that everyone is a traitor. And all of the faces went pale with the realization.

"*Get him out of my sight!*" Hajiwara screamed.

"Sire, we did not know. . . . We thought . . ." The lieutenant fell silent and then rose and dragged the false Joda off into the night.

The hammer of horses' hooves came from behind. The Hajiwara staff closed around their lord as the riders approached, but then relaxed as they saw the green lacing.

The senior officer of the group, an old captain, dropped to his knees before his superiors.

"Captain?" the general asked.

"Sire, there is an army on the plain at our rear."

This time Lord Hajiwara did draw his sword as he rose. "An army! This is not possible! How could the Butto penetrate our lines?"

"They do not seem to be the Butto, Sire."

"Not the Butto! What colors?—what colors do they show?"

"Blue, Sire."

Spinning, Hajiwara sliced through the pole of a torch, sending it rolling down the slope. "Shonto! It cannot be!"

"They are on foot, Sire. Yet they still come quickly. If you are to escape, you must go now."

Hajiwara's senior general took charge, ordering horses, setting guards off with the Hajiwara banners in a different direction. Torches were pushed into the dirt. The lord set out east, hoping to skirt the Shonto army and to gather reinforcements from the Hajiwara perimeter.

The sounds of battle did not diminish and no one noticed as the moon disappeared behind the hills. In the eastern sky, morning stained the clouds with its pale dye.

An arrow sparked off the stone above General Hojo's head, causing him to crouch as he leapt. The first Hajiwara guard went down to a single stroke and the second fell back, parrying madly, before he slipped from the walkway to his end.

Hojo Masakada moved quickly toward the tower now, not allowing himself to run. A dozen elite Shonto guards followed behind him. It had all been easier than he had hoped. His assessment of the Hajiwara men had been correct—no match for the Shonto trained. But then the men Hajiwara had left in the keep were the weakest of his soldiers. He must have truly believed the Shonto guards would sit meekly and wait for his return. The general almost laughed.

The main gate was open now, and Shonto soldiers poured in from the plain. He would bow low to Brother Shuyun and Lord Komawara when he saw them. He had not truly believed they would succeed.

In the darkness he saw figures pull back into the tower door. Let them hide there awhile, he thought. It does not matter. The bridge was open to them now. Only the locks remained. He hefted his sword; it was good to find that he was still a warrior. It was very good.

*   *   *

On the hillside, a mist hung in the branches of the northern pines. A hawk's call echoed across the slopes and mixed with the creaking of leather saddles. A flight of wood-crows went excitedly from tree to tree, watching the activities of man, eyeing the carnage. A line of riders passed under the hill, banners waving, but they were of no interest to the crows for they posed no threat and were strong and very much alive.

At the head of this column of soldiers, Lord Hajiwara entered the keep. It was early morning. His wrists were raw where the cords cut into them, but he ignored the pain. There was no sign of a Hajiwara soldier within the walls, though the evidence of battle was everywhere. High above the tower the Shonto banner, white shinta blossom on a blue field, fluttered in the falling wind. Hajiwara looked at it for only a second and then turned his gaze to the cobbles.

Two Shonto guards pulled the lord from his saddle, not roughly but with little sign of respect. They moved him to the center of the courtyard and made him kneel. A noise on the stairs alerted him and he looked up. Lord Shonto descended, deep in conversation with General Hojo. He was followed by a monk, an old man with only one arm, and a young lord not wearing the Shonto blue. Shonto did not even wear armor, though he carried his own sword.

At the bottom of the stairs Shonto stopped to complete his orders to the general, and then, finally, he turned to Hajiwara. He regarded the lord carefully, but without apparent emotion, as though the nobleman were a horse he might purchase. A stool was brought and Shonto sat, holding his sheathed sword across his knees.

" 'An act of treachery: a victim of the same.' Is that not the saying, Lord Hajiwara?" Shonto asked. The lord said nothing.

"It is close enough, though you say nothing. Yet you must speak, Lord Hajiwara, and it is treachery you must speak of, yeh?"

"The treachery I am aware of was not of my making," the kneeling lord spat out.

Shonto smiled openly. "Look around you, Lord Hajiwara—no, look! Do you think I have taken your stronghold and captured you this easily by being a fool? It seems that the mists cloud your sight, if that is what you believe. Yeh?" The kneeling lord maintained his silence and Shonto continued to regard him.

"So, Lord Hajiwara, let me tell you something of the message I am about to send to the capital. I intend to say in this letter, that you and your son-in-law, the Imperial Governor of Itsa, have conspired with a certain . . . officer in the Imperial Guard to end the life of Lord Shonto Motoru in such a way as to make it appear that the Dragon Throne has condoned, if not directed, this plot. This would have had the effect, had it been successful, of turning the Great Houses against the Throne, creating a situation that could have proved very advantageous to the officer I have mentioned." Shonto regarded Lord Hajiwara. "Even if I am not to use the name of this Imperial Officer, I think the Son of Heaven will quickly guess the name for himself. Do you still prefer to remain silent?" He waited for a long moment, but the lord said nothing.

"Lord Hajiwara, you disappoint me. You do not think the Emperor would have been involved in such a clumsy attempt do you? Was it not the *tiger*, the *tiger that speaks,* who came to you?"

Hajiwara glowered at the stones in front of him.

"Kamu," Shonto said addressing the aged steward.

"Sire?"

"In your dealings with Lord Butto, did you agree to pass Lord Hajiwara into Butto hands?"

"That is correct, Sire."

"Ah. Perhaps we were hasty. Lord Hajiwara, excuse me if I explain something that is already clear to you. The Butto army rages across your fief as we speak. You are captive without hope. Below us, my fleet passes through locks that are controlled by Shonto guards. Your son-in-law, the governor, has resigned his position and gone into hiding. Nothing remains to you: not family, not allies, not troops, not land, not even honor. Do you wish to suffer the humiliation of being the captive of a child whose name is Butto?"

Lord Hajiwara did not look up, but he shook his head slowly and with what seemed like great effort.

"Then it is perhaps wise that you speak to me of treachery. If you do so, and your words are deemed worthwhile, you will be given a sword. It shall be said that you died in battle, honorably. This is your choice, Lord Hajiwara, but you must make it now."

The kneeling lord closed his eyes, his body rigid with anger. "Do you give your word that I shall have the sword?"

"On the honor of my family. Bring Lord Hajiwara his weapon," Shonto said, then nodded to the man on the stones before him, an order to begin.

"It is as you said. Jaku Katta approached us through his youngest brother. It was he who arranged that the Hajiwara take this keep and he encouraged our just war with the enemy of our family. Jaku promised us that, in return for our services, he would, in time, give us the Butto and their fief. But this was all done in the name of the Emperor, not in the name of Jaku Katta, as you suggest. The service the Black Tiger wished performed, was the . . . interception of Lord Shonto at the locks." The lord fell silent, seeming to contemplate the stone in front of him.

" 'Interception,' Lord Hajiwara? Please explain?"

The kneeling lord met Shonto's eyes, but he paused before speaking. "He wanted you dead, Lord Shonto."

"Huh. Brother Shuyun?"

"I believe he is telling the truth, Sire."

"You have earned your sword, Lord Hajiwara," Shonto said. He rose and walked away.

Twenty-four

THEY HAD ENTERED the province of Seh before dawn and few but the night-watch had seen the border markers pass. Late morning still found the air cool, though the sailors did not complain for it filled the sails and gave them rest from their toil.

On the bow of the river barge Shuyun watched the passing landscape, wondering at the change of it. They had left the canal and locks for a quicker passage and were in a true river now, a river that wandered across the countryside and among the hills like the tail of a sleeping dragon. The shores broke down into long gravel banks which then rose again in great steps of gray-white stone.

Stands of pine and cedar scented the breeze. And then the boat rounded a bend to find a whole hillside atremble with ginkyo, leaves turning to copper-gold in the late autumn sun.

Shuyun had never known a place that felt so pure and alive. The very air seemed light and newly created, a sharp contrast to the capital where the air tasted as though it had been too long in too many lungs. Here the air caressed him.

As the day passed, Shuyun began to sense the pattern of Seh, began to discern a deeper design. Seh was a land frozen in the midst of great motion, as though Botahara himself had stopped all movement. And this stillness was balanced by the sense that motion could begin again at any instant.

Hills rolled and folded, and ran their crests off into the far distance, their sun greens turning finally to silhouettes of blue. Field and pasture, irregular in shape, appeared among the forests and pushed their way up hillsides and along valleys to end abruptly at walls of fall-turning trees.

Here and there, as random as only the earth could be, great fractured blocks of stone pushed through, as though the ruins of some mammoth fortress lay hidden beneath the land. The gray-white stone was layered in thick bands and broken into blocks of enormous proportion as though it were the stone work of a giant race, its mortar worn away through the ages of wind and rain. Moonstone, this was called, and it seemed ancient despite the freshness of the land.

Along the river's course, cliffs of great scale would suddenly rise up and echo the voices of the water back and forth until men would hear words and even their own names spoken among the tumult.

Shuyun rode the prow of the boat as it plunged down into a steep gorge and he felt as though his heart had been opened and his spirit exposed to beauties so great that he ached with the power of them. Never before had he risked his life; he did not know that many a man who had fought the Haji-wara and scaled the rope ladders into the ancient fane above Denji Gorge felt much as he did now. But unlike Shuyun, most had felt the shock of powerful emotions before. The young monk was alone in his experience, with nothing to compare.

They were swept into the white foam roar of the gorge and boatmen fought their steering oars to stop the barge from making a fatal broach. The tiny, pure white tinga gulls screeched their high notes and knifed into the whirlpools and crests as though they had made a pact with a river god to allow them passage.

The rushing of the water became deafening and the speed of its flow truly frightening when, with a sudden final drop, the boat shot out onto a lake as clear as air and as tranquil as an enlightened soul.

Seh, Shuyun thought. I have been swept up and carried by the great river into the far reaches of the north, borne on waves of cloud, and tossed out onto the still surface of a great mirror. Seh, where my liege-lord has come to wage a war that he can never name, for it is not the barbarians we have come to challenge. Seh, where I become the Imperial Governor's Advisor and bring honor to my teachers or shame to my Order.

The monk looked down into the waters and it was as if he looked into the infinite depths of the sky. Illusion he thought, it is the purpose of my life to dispel illusion.

There in the depths of the sky he saw clouds sailing east in great billowing fleets.

"I am the Gatherer of Clouds," he heard himself whisper. Clouds that change and grow and become dragons and sprawling lands and shape themselves into birds and mice and women of great beauty. I will gather them all.

An hour passed during which Shuyun had pushed himself deep into meditation. Footsteps sounded on the deck behind him. General Hojo, Shuyun thought without turning, he has strong chi for one untrained. Pulling himself up out of his meditation, the monk turned and bowed.

"General."

"I hope I do not interfere with your contemplation, Brother Shuyun."

"I spend too much time in contemplation and not enough studying the wisdom of my lord's advisors."

Hojo gave a slight bow. "I am honored, Brother, but it was I who argued against scaling the walls of Denji Gorge. Fortunately I was not listened to."

Shuyun felt embarrassed by the officer's words. "General, you were listened to and your council was wise. No one knew if Lord Komawara and I would succeed, and if we had failed?—as you said, this would have had disastrous consequences. There was great risk, but Botahara smiled upon us."

The general gave a slight bow again and then looked out at the shore, ready to change the subject. "I have read that you can only experience something for the first time once. Yet each time I come to Seh, it is for the first time."

"All that I had read and been told did not prepare me. . . ." Shuyun trailed off, at a loss for words.

The two men stood, watching the passing land for a long time without speaking. Finally Hojo broke the silence.

"It must be disconcerting for our lord to come to Seh knowing that his famous ancestor's name is so much a part of the history."

"This is true," Shuyun said. "The first Shonto Motoru: is his shrine not close to here?"

Hojo nodded without looking away from the scene. "Yes," he said quietly, "quite close, but difficult to reach from the river." He paused. "So a Shonto lord comes again—even bearing the sword his ancestor gave to his Emperor. If I were a man of Seh, this would affect me."

Hojo shook his head. "Of course, the situation is not at all the same. That was the time of the barbarians' great power. And this Emperor . . ." he held up his open palms, "he is not the poet Emperor Jirri was."

Shuyun smiled at the joke.

They fell silent again and Hojo's remark caused Shuyun to remember his reading of the history of the Shonto family. Many poems had been written of the great barbarian war. Lord Shonto had been celebrated in songs and poems and plays. Many besides Emperor Jirri had set their brush to paper, many of the great poets of the Empire.

Broken stone.
As far as all horizons
Walls lie in terrifying ruin.
Everywhere one looks
The eye is pained.
Each report bears worse news,
The smoke of burning villages
Charcoaled across bitter winds.

Seh
In all her beauty
Is in flames.

Drums roll
Like the pounding of hearts,
Pipes call retreats that cost
Uncounted sons.

When a battle takes a lifetime
War is endless.

Hunger's forays
Leave as many in the field
As any battle,
Women, children
Fall to their silent enemy.

It is a whisper
From foot soldier
To horseman.
Shonto has come
Riding at the Emperor's side,
Shonto
And soldiers begin to sharpen swords
Despair had long left untended.

Shuyun looked up at a hillside that spread itself in crimson and yellow across the western horizon. Seh, he thought, in all her beauty. . . .

And Shonto has come.

twenty-five

A BRONZE BELL RANG in the darkness, echoing across the water and returning again from the far shore of the slowly moving river. Brother Sotura could see the light-boat itself now. "Yul-sho," he whispered. The Floating City should appear by midday.

Releasing the rail he began a series of intricate finger exercises, the movements hidden in the long sleeve of his robe. His focus, however, was elsewhere: larger issues concerned him.

He had known the Supreme Master for twenty-two years, had been the senior monk's closest advisor for perhaps half that time, and never had he seen the Order's most senior Brother despondent—until now. It was the Supreme Master's misfortune to bear the great responsibility of his position at a most difficult time in history.

The plague had devastated the Empire of Wa and though the Brotherhood had finally found a cure, uncounted lives had been lost. Yet all of the senior Brothers were aware that if they had found the cure earlier, the Interim War would never have occurred. This weighed most heavily on the Supreme Master. Had the Hanama Imperial family not died of plague the Yamaku would never have seized the throne, and there would still be a Botahist Brother advising the Son of Heaven and the Order would have retained its place of power in the Empire.

A tiny spark of light grew until it became the bow lantern of a river scow being rowed out toward the sea; current behind them, wind against them.

Sotura watched the boat pass, until even the sound of oars disappeared into the darkness.

The Supreme Master, Sotura realized, bore a harsh burden. But even more than the situation in the Empire, which Sotura was sure patience and time would change, it was the missing scrolls that destroyed the Supreme Master's tranquillity . . . and Brother Sotura shared responsibility for that loss.

The situation was so delicate that the Brotherhood had been forced to react to this blasphemy with the utmost secrecy. The scrolls of the Perfect Master contained much that was unknown outside the Botahist Orders; much that Sotura himself knew nothing of. Information that the Supreme Master was certain would endanger the Botahist Brotherhood's place in the Empire, if not its existence.

And yet they heard nothing! No demands for gold, not even a rumor that the scrolls were gone. Nothing.

Perhaps this inability to understand the thieves' motives was the most unsettling part. Where did one start to search for the scrolls when one did not even begin to know why they had been stolen? If it were for profit, that would be one thing. Stolen to blackmail the Brothers, that would be another. He would at least know where to start looking. But as it was. . . .

Perhaps his meeting with Brother Hutto would suggest a place to begin.

Meeting Brother Hutto would no doubt be a risk, but he could see no alternative. At least three days would be taken up arranging such a meeting. Three invaluable days.

The monk shifted his weight from one foot to the other and felt the unfamiliar robe move with him. After a lifetime in the garb of a Botahist monk he would never adjust to another form of dress. Yet the disguise seemed to be working. He was just another Seeker returning from a pilgrimage, even associating with the other religious fanatics on board, though he found their company oddly depressing. All the same, Brother Sotura, the chi quan master of Jinjoh Monastery, had not been recognized.

If he could just get through this meeting with Brother Hutto. It was a problem. The Honorable Brother was watched too closely—the price he paid for being Primate in Yankura. Not that there was a better place for him—that was not the case. A man of Brother Hutto's talents was a necessity in a place like Yankura—but it was difficult to be there and not attract the attention of . . . certain people. Sotura could not afford to become an object of their curiosity, this was certain.

The ship came abreast of the light-boat and seemed to hover there, making almost no progress against the current. Sotura shook his head. Perhaps it would have been better to take passage on a faster boat—but he had deemed this one less likely to attract the attention of the Imperial Guards.

Luckily it was a dry autumn. If the rains had started, the old barge would never have made headway against the current. Patience, he reminded himself, Botahara rewards the patient. He continued his finger exercises, coming to the first closure and beginning the isolation series.

It had been a long time since Sotura had visited Wa and he wished now that it was daylight so he could see the country in its autumn beauty. All of his years on the island of Jinjoh Monastery had left him with the most romantic view of the Empire of Wa. He shook his head. He could not help it—the countryside seemed unimaginably beautiful to him.

He turned his gaze to the shoreline and his imagination swept the darkness aside as though it were a wind gathering up a black mist. A village spread its bone-bleached walls across the side of a hill like the skeleton of some mammoth beast that had fallen in the middle of a giant stride. Above the village, a small copse of pine and sweet linden stood in silhouette, dark against the starlit sky. Rice paddies fell in irregular terraces, their dikes tracing a blue-green web down the dark hillside.

The harvest would all be in now and the time of the peasant celebrations was near. Sotura thought it unfortunate that he had missed the River Festival. He had always had an affection for this celebration, despite its pagan origins.

This thought seemed to break a spell and the darkness returned, pushing the shore into the distance despite all powers of the imagination.

The River Festival had been his destination on his last journey to Wa, eight years earlier. That, too, had been a journey with a political purpose, though he had not been forced to bear the indignity of a disguise.

The young initiate monk, Shuyun, had been his charge; there to compete in the Emperor's kick boxing tournament. On that journey Sotura had come as a teacher—to remind the people of Wa of the power of the Botahist monks. He had come as a teacher but had learned more than he taught.

Shuyun had been the perfect instrument for the lesson the Brotherhood needed to teach. In an Empire that was still unstable from the years of plague and the Interim Wars, respect for the Botahist monks was restored—again they could travel the roadways of the Empire without interference, though the same could be said of no others, except the heavily armed.

The second lesson they had hoped to teach had not been so successful. Shuyun had humiliated the Emperor's favorite, the arrogant Jaku Katta, but this only served to make the Emperor more wary of the Brotherhood, when the monks had hoped the Son of Heaven would see the value of taking a monk into his service.

So much for lessons taught.

The lesson Sotura had learned was more difficult to describe, for he had not been directly involved. In truth, he learned it only with the assistance of Jaku Katta. In the midst of the fight Sotura had seen Jaku lose all focus and, for an instant, entirely let down his guard. What Sotura had read in the kick boxer's reaction was *awe!* And yet nothing had occurred that Sotura had noted, and Sotura missed very little.

It was a strange and incomplete lesson. The chi quan instructor had watched Shuyun carefully after that. Had even sparred with him on more than one occasion, and though Shuyun was skilled far beyond his years, Sotura could detect nothing that would cause a kick boxer of Jaku's skill to stop in awe.

Perhaps Jaku had reinforced the Emperor's fear of the Botahist Brotherhood, it was impossible to say. The entire incident had been a sad miscalculation and a serious one.

The problem with the present Emperor was that the Brotherhood knew so little of him. No monk was allowed near the Son of Heaven and so he remained a mystery which no amount of analysis seemed to unravel.

Of course, he was a highly unpredictable man, the Emperor, but even so, Brother Sotura was surprised at how unsuccessful the Brotherhood was at anticipating the Emperor's plans. It was most unsettling—sometimes Sotura found himself wondering if his Order had somehow earned the anger of heaven, such was their lack of good fortune—but, of course, this could not be.

The chi quan instructor finished his finger exercises and began a stillness meditation. Several hours later daylight found him standing on the prow of the ship; a strange figurehead dressed in a ragged robe that the wind could not leave alone.

The Jade Temple was the most ancient of the buildings that stood in the old section of the Floating City. Over the seven hundred years the temple had stood, its position on a rocky island had saved it from the not infrequent flooding that Yankura experienced. Botahara, it was said, protected it from fire.

Inside the walls that surrounded the temple grounds clustered other buildings constructed in the style of the early Botahist period, all arranged around courtyards and gardens of meditation. The Jade Temple was the destination of many of the pilgrims who traveled the roads and waterways of Wa, so beyond the walls of the temple there were large buildings to house the many Seekers who arrived without bedding or coins, all having taken a vow of poverty.

Brother Sotura lay on a wooden bench in the darkness in one of these dormitories, ignoring the cold that seemed to seep into his body like spring-water. Around him he could hear the sounds that men made in their sleep—not all of them healthy sounds—and the noises of men too troubled to find the peace of unconsciousness. Voices whispered in the darkness, and beyond the thin shutters Sotura could hear that familiar mumbling of someone in the garden intoning a long Bahitra; a prayer for forgiveness.

For the hundredth time an old man coughed harshly and then sighed in despair or relief—it was impossible to tell which.

Brother Sotura lay on his side pretending to be asleep, avoiding the constant trap of conversation—seeking the truth of Botahara did not seem to do away with many men's loneliness and they looked always for their own kind.

A temple bell sounded the hour of the owl and the sound was answered a dozen times throughout the crowded city. Waiting a moment, Brother Sotura rose noiselessly. It was a skill of the Botahist monks to be able to move without sound and now Sotura brought his training into play, stepping among the sleeping pilgrims with care. At the end of the dormitory he slid a screen aside.

A sliver of moon cast shadows at the foot of buildings and trees and shimmered off the surface of a small pond. Avoiding a path of gravel, Brother Sotura crossed an opening between buildings and stepped onto a low stone wall.

At the end he found the higher wall of the temple itself. Here the monk stopped and examined his surroundings, searching the shadows for any sign of movement, stretching his mind, searching for presence, for a sense of chi that would mark someone hiding in the dark.

Finally satisfied that no one watched, Brother Sotura stepped down onto a cobbled walkway and took three steps to a door half-hidden by a Tenti bush. In the darkness he ran his hands over the metal sheathed wood looking for a handle. When he found it, he pulled toward him and the door moved silently—but then came to an abrupt halt.

A deep voice whispered from the darkness beyond the door. "What is it you wish?"

"I have come to consult with your Master about the Master's words." Brother Sotura answered quietly. He heard the sound of a chain being released and then the door swung out toward him.

"Please enter," came the deep voice again and Sotura stepped through the opening into the inner grounds of the ancient temple.

The door closed silently behind him. "Please, Brother, follow me." And with a quick bow the dark form of a Botahist monk turned and stepped into the shadows of a nearby wall. Sotura was quick to follow and before they had gone twenty steps the monk opened a lamp slightly and Sotura could see a hint of the man's appearance.

"Brother Shinsha?"

The monk turned to him and Sotura sensed more than saw the smile.

"Brother Shinsha, and honored to be your servant, though excuse me for not speaking your name." The voice was as deep and resonant as the darkness itself.

"The night hears all things," Sotura muttered and saw the lamp jiggle as his guide chuckled silently.

They mounted a stone staircase that led to a covered veranda at the rear of a residence. Inside the walls, the sounds of the busiest city in the Empire could not be heard and Brother Sotura found this oddly comforting. His guide slid a screen open and stepped into a wide hallway. A few paces farther, they again mounted stairs which took them up four levels to another long hall. Two Brothers standing guard outside carved double doors bowed with deference to the older monk and the unkempt Seeker. Without knocking, Brother Shinsha pulled the doors open. Bowing to the chi quan master as though he were an honored stranger, Brother Shinsha stepped aside.

Sotura entered the room and there, in its center, sat Brother Hutto, Primate of Wa, hunched over his famous double-sized writing table, scroll in hand.

"Ah, Brother Sotura." The old monk said, looking at the other monk's dress. "You should not be such a follower of fashion, Brother, it will endanger your spirit."

The Primate did not smile at his own joke—a habit that Sotura had once found disconcerting. That was before he had realized Brother Hutto enjoyed watching people decide whether it was appropriate to laugh. It was also a display of Brother Hutto's considerable intelligence and, once understood, not a small part of his charm.

"I shall heed your kind advice in this matter, Brother, though that is not what I have come to hear."

Hutto nodded and stroked his chin. He seemed to be staring into Brother Sotura who showed no signs of discomfort at this examination.

The Primate was a tiny man with a face that could appear either very old or surprisingly young depending on his mood. He had large features, like a peasant, yet his eyes were small and almost inky dark.

Brother Hutto stopped stroking his chin. "Words have never satisfied you, Brother Sotura. Please sit with me." He gestured to another cushion and as he did so he pushed the writing table away. One of the monks who had been guarding the door entered with a cha service on a lacquered stand. Setting this between the two men, he checked the fire in the iron kettle before leaving.

"You have word from our Supreme Master?" Brother Hutto asked. He had a way of stressing long vowels, stretching them out almost musically as though they had slipped out of a chant and into his conversation.

"He sends you his deepest regards but did not include a written message for fear that it would be discovered. I have many things to discuss with you, though, in his name."

"And what is it the Supreme Master thinks I am not telling him?"

"I am not aware of anything, Brother Hutto," the chi quan master said evenly.

"Ah. Then you have come only for the pleasure of the Jade Temple's bells?"

"No, Brother," Sotura said, and then hesitated before going on. "I have come to discuss the sacred scrolls of Botahara."

Brother Hutto made a sign to Botahara. "Then speak quietly. My hearing is not yet old."

The chi quan instructor looked down, rubbing his fingertips in a circle on the grass mats. "We received your report. The Supreme Master praised your forethought at having the Shonto merchant watched. Yet what was observed in the dark has raised many questions." Sotura let the statement hang in the air, waiting to see what the other would do with it.

After a prolonged silence, Brother Hutto spoke. "I assume you are asking if I know more?"

"Not at all, Brother; the Supreme Master is interested in your opinion of this matter."

The Primate adjusted the flame on a lamp. "And I am interested in Brother Nodaku's own thoughts. If what was being so secretly spirited away were the scrolls that you—that we both seek, then I would think the Supreme Master might tell me. Where else would the scrolls be taken by sea except to Jinjoh Monastery?" Brother Hutto fixed his dark liquid gaze on the larger monk.

"The whereabouts of the scrolls is still a mystery, though it pains me to say this."

"Huh. I almost wish you had told me it had all been done behind the sleeve and the scrolls were back where they belong." Brother Hutto paused to serve cha. "I fear I must disappoint you. I do not know what it was the Imperial Guards were transporting. A box the size of a small traveling trunk. It was apparently very heavy. I say apparently. Could it have been the treasure we seek?" He shook his head sadly and offered his guest a bowl of cha. "I do not believe so. To think that they are gone. . . !" he exclaimed and then recovered his control immediately.

Somewhere below them, deep voices began a long melodic chant and the two monks made signs to Botahara. A gong sounded four times, then echoed through a long pause—sounded thrice more and was still. Into the stillness a single voice poured like liquid into an empty bowl. It was a beautiful, clear voice and the melody was lyrical, haunting. Slowly the other voices returned, soft and powerful.

Sotura took a long breath and offered a silent prayer.

"Forgive me, Brother, but I have little time." At a nod from the Primate, Sotura continued. "The Initiate who witnessed this incident—did he not hear anything the vassal-merchant said?"

The monk shook his head. "Tanaka and the old guard watched in silence and, I am told, fear. They did not speak. I know nothing that was not included in my letter to the Supreme Master."

"I hesitate to speculate, but it does seem obvious that what was being done so secretly was of great importance to someone of consequence. The presence of Shonto's vassal-merchant suggests that this occurrence was also of interest to the Great Lord. Perhaps it is dangerous to carry the thought too far?"

"I have observed the merchant Tanaka for many years and have learned much that surprised me. Perhaps it is most telling to say that, in private, Lord Shonto will share a table with his merchant and calls him *sum*. This man is one of Shonto's most valued advisors, not just in the area of trade. To risk himself on a dark night, with only an old man for a guard? Whatever was in the trunk was of great concern to the Shonto House.

"But who arranged for this trunk to be moved? Jaku Katta? The Emperor? Or perhaps one of the younger Jaku brothers? And where was it sent?" The old monk shook his head.

"It is most curious that Tanaka was interested in this affair, most curious. So where could this valuable trunk be going that it would be of interest to the Lord of the Shonto? The obvious possibility is that it went where the lord himself has gone." Brother Hutto closed his eyes and sipped his cha and his face became the face of a delighted youth. "As to the contents of the trunk. Gold. Silver. Jade. A payment to Shonto's enemies . . ." He opened his dark eyes: "Or those who would become his enemies. All possibilities you have discussed with the Supreme Master, I am sure."

"It is good to hear your words, Brother Hutto. We are so isolated in the monastery that we have grown concerned that we have not explored all possibilities. But I am still concerned that it was the treasure we seek that was being moved, or perhaps even delivered to our enemies."

"It seems that you assume the Son of Heaven is the thief?"

"He is the obvious choice and he has in his service Katta, a cunning man who has his own reasons to hate the Brotherhood." Sotura tasted his cha, breathing in its rich perfume.

Brother Hutto laughed bitterly, surprising his companion. "Is it not ironic that we speculate in the dark like men who have lost their faith?" He turned his dark eyes on his ragged companion. "Look at you. Do you not laugh when you see yourself? A Botahist Master reduced to running around in costume like a courtier at a party." He laughed again and leaned forward, whispering, "I feel panic in you, Brother. Though you hide it well, still I feel it. And it is not just you, it is in all of us who know. Soon it will be felt by others in our ranks—an unknown, unnamed panic—and then the speculation will begin. Do you realize what that will mean?" The old man took a deep breath and let it out slowly. "And I, too, panic. Please, excuse me."

"Brother Hutto, this is the reason we must find the scrolls. Nothing is more important, nothing."

The two men fell silent, sipping their cha. A breeze slipped in through a half open shoji and with it the scent of fallen leaves. Brother Sotura turned his attention to the screens painted the length of the two-span hall. They showed the Perfect Master giving the Sermon of Silence in which he told his disciples that he would speak to them of their desires and then he said nothing, rising finally at nightfall to go to his prayers. Yes, Sotura thought, we wear our desire on our faces even as His disciples did.

"Brother Hutto, I cannot stay long and there are things I must ask you. What of the Emperor and Shonto?"

"Yes. I neglect my duty." He paused to refill their cha bowls. "It is no secret, the Emperor's fear of the Shonto. Yet suddenly the Emperor treats Shonto as an old friend and charges him with the safety of the Empire. It is very strange. Some see it as a sign that the Emperor is maturing and losing his fear of the strong. Others are deeply suspicious. I would put Shonto himself in this latter group. The Emperor has gone to much trouble to separate the family—Shonto's son to their fief, Lady Nishima in the capital and Shonto himself in the north fighting a war, and who knows what can happen in a war? Even a general can fall to a stray arrow. How much gold is needed to hire a skilled bowman?

"If the Emperor plots against Shonto, then I suspect that Jaku Katta has contrived something more subtle—he is a consummate swordsman and would never finish a man clumsily. Shonto, of course, realizes the possibilities of his situation; so we watch as though it is a game of gii. The great families wonder who will be next if indeed the Emperor plots Shonto's fall—many would then question the wisdom of allowing the Yamaku to stay on the throne. But with Shonto gone, who would be strong enough to create an alliance that could defeat the Yamaku? It is a problem."

"No doubt the Emperor has his Imperial Guards close around him—a questionable tactic. There are rumors—and this I have not told the Supreme Master—that Katta may be in disfavor. They are only rumors, but if they are true . . . by Botahara! Jaku will not fall without a struggle. He will remain a fighter to his last breath." The Primate sipped his cha, excitement apparent in his voice.

"I have also discovered that the Lady Nishima has been an object of Jaku's attention."

Sotura snorted. "His appetite is too large!"

"Unquestionably, though his charm is legendary. But is it not strange?—the Commander of the Imperial Guard and Shonto's daughter? The Lady Nishima is a threat to the Yamaku, and you may be certain the Son of Heaven's sleep is troubled by this knowledge."

"Why does he not marry a son to Shonto's daughter and avoid this stupid feud?"

"They are weak young men, Sotura-sum. They did not have the benefit of a Brother Satake to teach them. The daughter Fanisan would overwhelm any of Akantsu's sons, that is certain."

"So Jaku Katta pursues the Lady Nishima. But she is no fool. Perhaps she turns the Emperor against his own creation?"

The Primate's face became suddenly youthful. "Ah, Brother Sotura," he said without a trace of a smile, "what a delightfully suspicious nature you have."

The chi quan master laughed. "I, too, have had excellent teachers. Have you received word from my young protégé?"

"Initiate Brother Shuyun is probably in Seh with his liege-lord, or at least well on his way. There is a good chance that the Butto-Hajiwara feud is a trap for Shonto, but, if so, those who have laid the trap will get the measure of their opponent. Shonto is too much the gii master to step into such a situation with his eyes closed."

"The young Brother is all that you have said, Sotura-sum, I met him." The monk nodded to the chi quan master, a bow of acknowledgment. "Even the Sisters seem impressed, for they follow him to Seh, though I confess I am not sure why." The Primate examined the face of his guest now, looking for an answer.

They had entered into a game of trading, a game they both knew well, and information was the coinage.

"Karma manifests itself strangely, Brother Hutto. A Sister, one Morima, was present in our Monastery several years ago. Through lack of knowledge, Shuyun was indiscreet and this Sister learned something of his true abilities. The Sisterhood has taken an interest in him ever since."

"Huh. Most unusual, Brother, the boy is gifted, yes, but that does not warrant this degree of interest."

"I agree, Hutto-sum. The Supreme Master also concurs. It is his contention that the Sisters think Shuyun was not a Brother in his past life."

"Ah. So this is their secret desire! We do well to learn this, Sotura-sum. But still it is a mystery what the Sisters hope to gain by following your student."

"You are keeping Shuyun and the Sisters under observation?"

"As I can, from the other end of the Empire."

Brother Sotura pulled at his whiskers. "Perhaps we need to do more."

"Excuse me, Brother, I don't understand."

Sotura cleared his throat. "The Supreme Master wishes us to redouble our efforts to find the scrolls."

"This would be more easily done if I knew what efforts to double, Brother," the Primate said dryly.

"The Way is difficult, Brother."

"So I have read."

"I am to go north to Seh, Hutto-sum. It is clear from our meditations that many things seem to center around Lord Shonto and our young Brother. There is a focus on these two, as though suddenly all meridians connected in this one place. The Brotherhood cannot ignore this."

Brother Hutto sipped cha that had gone cold in its bowl. He considered a long time before speaking again. "It would be better if Shonto lived and the Emperor fell, would it not, Brother?"

"Hutto-sum, these are dangerous words."

"With the Yamaku on the Dragon Throne, we will always be in danger."

Sotura changed the subject. "What of the barbarians, does your intelligence extend to them also?"

"Among the barbarians I have no one, but the Brothers in Seh cross into the wastes as they can and they are concerned, as no doubt we would be if we lived under threat of constant attack. There are rumors again that the Golden Khan has come—at least the fifth time in my short life this has been said. Seh, sadly, is far away. I will be interested in your assessment of the situation."

"And the Emperor, what of him?"

"It seems likely that he will ask Lord Omawara for the hand of Lady Kitsura." Brother Hutto enjoyed the look of shock on his companion's face.

"Truly?"

Brother Hutto nodded once.

"So, the Empress feels a need to retire to a life of spiritual contemplation. I did not imagine this, not at all. More Imperial progeny. Now we shall see a House divided!" Brother Sotura fell silent, contemplating this new information.

"The Supreme Master will be most interested in this. The Lady Kitsura Omawara!" Brother Sotura shook his head. "What of the Sisters? Does their internal struggle continue?"

"It does, Brother, but we must not be deceived. It is not the Prioress, Sister Saeja, who is occupied with this problem—it is the faction that opposes her. The old nun keeps an eye turned outward. Events in the Empire do not escape her, even a talented young Brother is worthy of her attention."

"So there is no indication of who will win the struggle when she is gone?"

Brother Hutto shrugged. "Perhaps you should consult a fortune teller. I would not even begin to guess."

"Then no one can know, Brother."

"Shall I order more cha, Sotura-sum?"

"I am honored that you ask, but it grows late. I must return to my brethren. If you could include your thoughts about these matters in your next report to the Supreme Master, I'm sure his harmony would be enhanced."

"I would deem it an honor if I could assist our Brother in this way," the Primate said, bowing to his guest. "There is something else, Brother," Hutto said as the chi quan instructor stood.

Sotura stopped, almost crouching. "Yes."

"Another Brother, senior Master Den-Go, has disappeared."

Brother Sotura straightened. "I have forgotten, Brother; how many is this?"

"Twenty-two."

Sotura expelled a long controlled breath, and put his hand to his brow as though there were sudden pain. "In all our history I know of nothing as strange as these disappearances."

"There is one other thing, Brother." The Primate paused, watching Sotura's face. "I have not yet confirmed this, but I have received a reliable report from Monarta . . . it is said the Udumbara has blossomed on the slopes above the Perfect Master's shrine."

The chi quan master sank back to his knees. "This cannot be true. It isn't possible."

Neither man spoke for several long minutes.

"Who could it be?" Sotura whispered finally. "Even among our most Enlightened Brothers there is no one who has progressed so far. No . . . it is not possible."

Hutto nodded. "Perhaps you are right." But the old monk looked like a man whose soul was overcome by doubt.

Brother Sotura felt his heart racing while some calm part of his mind noted that this had not happened since he had been trained in the ways of the Brotherhood.

"An Enlightened Master," Sotura heard himself whisper. It could not be.

Twenty-six

The west wind blows
And the grasses bow to my passing,
Perfect golden grasses
What do they know of my thoughts?
Or of the heart
They have torn asunder.

The Empress Shigei

AS DAYLIGHT APPROACHED, Lady Nishima was barely able to hide her impatience. In the privacy of her rooms, she paced up and down the matted floor, regretting that Kitsura had gone. Not that she would necessarily have shared the information she had received from Tanaka, but still, it would have been comforting to have company.

Beginning a simple series of exercises taught to her by Brother Satake, Nishima attempted to subvert the thoughts that distracted her and pulled at her consciousness. With a great effort of will, she fell into the almost trancelike state the exercise required and began to feel the strange sensation of time slowing. It was only for an instant, a feeling so fleeting that it might have been imagined. But Nishima knew it was not. She opened her eyes and let out a long sigh. If only Brother Satake had been able to teach her more.

A light tap on the shoji reminded her of the things she had pushed from her mind, and it all came rushing back—the Emperor, Katta-sum, the message from Tanaka. The screen slid aside at a word from Nishima and a maidservant entered carrying a folded letter on a small silver tray. Lady Nishima controlled an urge to leap to her feet and snatch the letter. Instead, she sat staring at an arrangement of flowers set into an alcove in the wall.

"Please excuse me, my lady. I did not mean to interrupt your meditations."

"You have acted correctly, Hara."

The maid knelt and set the tray carefully on the writing table. "Would you care for your morning meal, Lady Nishima?"

"Not now, Hara, I will call."

Nishima reached forward for the letter but stopped when she realized that her maid had not moved to leave.

"Hara?"

The maid nodded and drew in a sharp breath. "Excuse my boldness, Lady Nishima . . ." she began, and then stammered to a halt.

"What is it, Hara?" Nishima asked, keeping impatience from her voice.

"I fear I have conducted myself in a manner unworthy of your trust, my lady," the young woman said in a near whisper.

Now what is this? Nishima wondered. An indiscretion, no doubt. That handsome assistant to Kamu I would wager, but why tell me? "The Shonto value the truth, Hara. Please go on."

"During my retreat to the priory at Kano I met a senior Sister, a highly respected member of the Order, Lady Nishima." The young woman glanced up at the eyes that studied her and then back to the floor. A blush of crimson spread across her cheek. "I spoke with her several times. I . . . I was flattered by her attention. . . . She seemed very impressed that I served the Shonto House and, my lady, she praised you very highly. I did not mark it at the time, but she was very curious about the Shonto and as she was a Sister of such high standing . . ." her voice became suddenly thick, "I was perhaps less discreet than I would otherwise have been." The woman took a deep breath and it escaped from her in a half sob. She did not raise her eyes.

"I see." Lady Nishima folded her hands in her lap. "I must know how indiscreet, Hara. It is important that you leave out nothing."

The maid nodded quickly, obviously frightened, which in turn made Nishima fear the worst.

"She asked about our lord, about his character and his habits. She wanted to know if he was a good master or if he beat his servants."

"And what did you tell her?"

"My lady, I have nothing but praise for Lord Shonto."

"I see. Go on."

"The honored Sister asked about our lord's friends, though of course this is no secret and certainly many people know who frequents the Shonto house." She paused as if to gather her thoughts. "She asked me if I knew when Lord Shonto had left for Seh, which again was no secret. She asked who among Lord Shonto's staff were loyal followers of the true path. Also, she asked many questions about our new Spiritual Advisor, but of course he was here such a short time I could tell her little."

"Did you tell her of Brother Shuyun's display when he shattered the table?"

The maid nodded her head silently, knowing by her lady's tone that it was as she had feared—she had been played for a fool.

"Continue."

"She asked also about Brother Satake though I could tell her nothing, for I did not know him."

Lady Nishima put her hand to her face as though she would hide how pale she had become.

"She had great praise for Brother Satake, as does everyone." She fell silent again, searching for words or for courage. "Something else she asked, though I did not understand what she meant. This seemed important to her, though I do not understand why. She asked if you danced secretly, my lady." The maid looked up, curiosity as well as fear in her eyes.

Lady Nishima dropped her hand back into her lap, fighting now for control. How could they ever know? she wondered, and felt her breath begin to come in short gasps. Closing her eyes, Nishima forced herself to breathe normally. How could anyone know?—she was so careful. The Sisters? Nishima had no contact with them—no contact with them at all! Opening her eyes, Nishima forced herself to focus.

"Did this Sister . . . did she explain what she meant by this, Hara?" Lady Nishima asked evenly.

" 'Danced secretly,' were her words, Lady Nishima. Is that not strange?"

Nishima shrugged with an ease she did not feel. "Was there more?"

"The Sister also asked about Jaku Katta-sum; if he came here often and if

I had heard the story of the Bla . . . of Jaku Katta-sum saving Lord Shonto. Of course I had, it was common knowledge throughout the capital. I told her that Lord Shonto had honored the general with a gift from his private garden." The maid kept her eyes cast down. "That is all, Lady Nishima."

"Are you certain, Hara?"

The maid closed her eyes, hesitating and then nodded.

"Hara?"

"Please, my lady . . ." A tear appeared at the corner of each eye.

"You must tell me," Nishima said softly.

"Yes, my lady. The senior Sister wanted to know if you had . . . lovers." She whispered the word, her eyes still closed and her face distorted by the effort to hold back her tears.

"I see."

"She seemed to suggest that it would not be uncommon . . . that it would be . . . as Lord Shonto was not your blood father, that . . ."

Nishima felt the sting of her hand striking the maid's face before she realized what she had done. The young woman lay stretched out on the floor like a pile of scattered clothes. She did not move.

Nishima froze, horrified. She looked at her hand which she held away from her as though it were something dangerous, something not part of her.

Oh, Satake-sum, you taught me too well and too little. She slid across the grass mats to the unconscious maid and felt for a heartbeat. Yes, it was there, thank Botahara! Rising to her feet, Nishima slid the shoji aside and was relieved to find the hall empty. Rohku Saicha should be told of this, she thought. But what of these questions? Dancing secretly! How would she explain that?

Nishima closed the screen quietly. Why were the Sisters suddenly interested in her? I am Shonto, she thought, that is reason enough. But still, the Sisters? She shook her head. What will I tell Captain Rohku? She leaned her forehead against the shoji's wooden frame. Behind her the maid stirred and moaned softly.

Nishima crossed the room and took the young woman's head in her lap.

"Hara?" she said quietly.

"Lady Nishima?" the maid mumbled. "What. . . ?"

"Shh. You are unhurt. Be still now."

"But what happened?" The woman tried to sit up, but Nishima held her gently.

"I don't know, Hara. Be still. Don't struggle."

"But I was struck, my lady. I . . . it felt as though I were struck. May Botahara protect me. What happened?" She began to weep softly.

"Shh, my child. I don't know, it . . . it was terrible." Nishima fought her own tears. "Take long breaths, like this. Do as I do." Nishima led her through a simple breathing exercise, all the while stroking the young woman's brow.

"There, now, is that not better?"

The maid nodded. "Thank you, my lady. The gods are angry with me. I don't know what I shall do!"

"There are ways to appease the gods. Of course there are." Nishima thought for a second. "You must burn incense at the Seven Shrines and take a vow of silence for one year. You will be forgiven, but you must observe these things and not falter."

Hara nodded. "Thank you, my lady. I am not worthy of your attention."

"Shh. Tomorrow you will begin your vow of silence. The gods will forgive you, Hara."

"I pity the enemies of our lord, my lady."

Nishima nodded. "Yes," she said in a whisper. "Yes."

After a few moments the maid was able to stand without help, and when Nishima was sure she could manage, the woman left quietly. "Not a word of this," Nishima said as the maid left and she received a bow in answer.

When she was alone again, Nishima sat with her fingers pressed to her eyes. I struck someone! I struck her in anger. She shook her head in disbelief. What a terrible, terrible thing. It was this situation, Nishima told herself, it must be. Caught in the city while her uncle went off to the north without knowledge of things that put him in great danger. And this madness for an Imperial Guardsman! She buried her face in her hands. It was all more than she could bear.

Closing her eyes, Nishima began a long prayer for forgiveness, and felt somewhat better. I am Shonto, she told herself, and forced a calmness over her fears and confusion. My lord's life may depend on my ability to make clear decisions. Tranquillity of purpose, she heard Brother Satake say. Tranquillity of purpose.

We will survive, Nishima told herself, only if our course of action comes from the very center of a pure and tranquil spirit. She composed herself then and again practiced a breathing exercise to bring a stillness to her spirit.

When she was done, she opened her eyes and looked around as though she had been transported to a new place and she was seeing it for the first time.

Daylight could be seen filtering through the screens and Nishima was glad. She leaned forward and blew out the lamp. It was then that she remembered the letter. She took it up—a tiny branch of slip-maple attached to a letter of deep purple mulberry paper.

It was folded in the most conventional manner, and not particularly elegantly. This cannot be from Lady Okara, Nishima thought, it is not possible. Spreading out the paper she took a second to recognize the hand. Katta-sum! He had taken his time, she thought, but then, considering his literary abilities, she was not surprised.

Moving to the outside screen, Lady Nishima opened it a crack and the cold air of morning seemed to flood in like water into a lock.

A whisper in the darkness,
The breeze speaks
In the voice of the poetess.
This cannot be the wind
From Chou-San?

   There is much to say, my lady.

Nishima read the poem through again. It was much better than she would have expected. Was it possible Jaku did not intend the double meaning of his final line? No, it was too obvious, certainly it was intentional.

The reference to Seh unsettled Nishima. Oh, Uncle, she thought, will the gods strike your enemies as Hara thought they had tonight?

She smoothed the paper on the small table, recalling the kiss she had allowed Jaku. The memory was almost as thrilling as she had found the kiss itself.

Nishima pushed the screen closed. This is foolish, she told herself. I have much to do. Decisions to make! When will I receive an answer from Lady Okara? It is only sunrise, Nishima told herself, I am too impatient.

Taking up a resin stick, she began to rub her inkstone rhythmically. I must answer Katta-sum, she thought, it will fill the time. But I must not rush the answer back to him, it is important that he not be overconfident. From an envelope she chose a piece of pale green paper, the color of fall grains, and a reminder of spring.

She wet her brush and began:

> *The wind whispers its secrets*
> *To so many,*
> *It is difficult to tell*
> *From where it blows.*

> *Perhaps it is loyalty we should speak of.*

There, she thought, blowing gently on the fresh ink. She held the paper up to the light and examined the writing. It was not the work of Brother Satake, but he would have approved. Certainly it would have the desired effect on the impetuous Katta—I am from a different station in life, my handsome general, mark this well.

She laid the poem carefully on the table and began to fold the fine paper, her long fingers seeming to have knowledge independent of her mind. It was done in a second, but she knew it would take Jaku Katta a few minutes to find the key to unfolding it.

She set the letter aside to allow herself time to consider what should accompany it. Perhaps a leaf of laughing poplar? She would see.

Nishima rang a small gong on her writing desk and a maid appeared almost without sound. "I wish to see Lady Kento and I will have my smaller meal."

Lady Kento, Nishima's senior lady-in-waiting, arrived almost immediately. Senior in this case was a relative term, Kento was only three years older than her young mistress. Nishima had an obvious partiality to Lady Kento which caused a certain amount of jealousy among the other ladies-in-waiting. But it couldn't be helped; Kento was simply more joyous than the others as well as being brighter. It was true that others surpassed her in many ways, Lady Jusha was a superb yara player, and the young Lady Shishika was never wrong in her advice on matters of ceremony and propriety, but they were not really close to their mistress. Their souls were not akin to hers.

The tiny Lady Kento knelt and bowed, her attractive round face beaming even though it was composed in the most serious manner.

"Will you join me for cha, Kento-sum?"

"I would be honored," she answered as though it wasn't an established morning ritual.

"Kento-sum, before we go on to other matters, I must tell you of something I have learned. I have found that Hara has been gossiping, not in a harmful way, but this is not acceptable."

"I will speak to her at once, my lady."

"It is not necessary. I have already spoken with her. But I want her sent to the country. She could be given a position that is not sensitive. I don't imagine that she would do this again, but I will not take the chance. Hara has taken a vow of silence for a year. For someone with her weakness that will be punishment enough."

"I will see this done as you wish."

Nishima nodded. A servant brought cha and a light meal for one and then was dismissed before she could kneel nearby, ready to serve.

"Kento-sum, I need your assistance in a delicate matter."

"I am your servant, my lady."

"I must leave the capital very soon, perhaps even tomorrow. Of course, I have been honored by the Emperor with an Imperial Patronage so it would be impossible for me to leave without gravely insulting the Son of Heaven. Nonetheless, I must go. It will be up to you to preserve the appearance that I am still in residence here. It will not be easy and naturally I don't expect such a charade to go far without being uncovered. But I must have five days. Ten, if Botahara will allow it. Is this clear?"

"It is, Lady Nishima." Lady Kento offered her mistress a steaming cloth and then ladled cha into bowls.

Lady Nishima wiped her hands and face, realizing suddenly that she had not yet slept and still wore the formal robes she had worn to the palace. I become more like my lord each day—caught up in the world around me, not sleeping, forgetting meals. It is the way of our House.

"There is more, Kento-sum. I have written to Lady Okara. This ruse can hardly be accomplished without her cooperation, though I am asking more of her than I should ever presume to ask." She sighed. "I have no choice. I must go to Seh, I cannot tell you why. You must trust me. Lady Okara will certainly think her friendship has been misplaced, but it should appear that the Lady Nishima still visits the great painter. I will understand if she refuses to become involved, but if she will not help me then your task will be more difficult, if not impossible."

"Perhaps the lady's friendship with your esteemed father will be of help in this matter."

"Oh, yes. I presume on that, too. It will be hard for her not to say yes, though it will not be what her heart desires."

"Excuse me, my lady, but it is as Brother Satake always said: Each name brings its own obligations."

A fleeting smile crossed Nishima's face. "You know me too well, Kento-sum. And I consider it very unfair of you to quote my mentor." Nishima smiled again and turned her attention to her food but gave up the pretense of eating in a few seconds.

"Is the preparation not to your liking, my lady?"

"No, Kento-sum, it is good, really," she said, but pushed the tray away from her all the same. "There will be another problem." Lady Nishima blushed ever so slightly. "I have been corresponding with the Imperial Guardsman, Jaku Katta. It is important that all of his letters are answered. He is hardly a scholar, Kento-sum, so you need not worry about the quality of the poetry, but it must be obscure, and not too discouraging. The Black Tiger may yet have a place in our lord's plans. Can Shishika-sum copy my hand?"

"I'm sure she can approximate it, Lady Nishima, though your hand is very distinctive."

"No matter, if she can come close, it will be adequate. I will copy out all of the poems we have exchanged so you can refer to them and Shishika-sum can examine my hand."

"Have you discussed these arrangements with Rohku Saicha, Lady Nishima?"

Nishima shook her head. "No. I need time to consider how best to approach him."

"He has been in an uproar since the incident with the Imperial Guards, my lady. The men at every gate have orders to detain you if you attempt to leave without his express permission."

"He has given orders to detain me?" Outrage was not masked in Nishima's voice.

"Excuse me, my lady. I should have told you sooner, but I did not wish to precipitate difficulties unnecessarily." The woman bowed low.

"It is not your fault, Kento-sum. The captain has much to atone for which affects his decisions. And, as you say, there was the incident on the canal."

Nishima fell silent, lost in thought, and her companion waited with no sign of impatience.

"That is all for now, Kento-sum. We will discuss arrangements for my departure after I have talked to Rohku Saicha. You may send him to me now. Oh, and Kento-sum, please have a maid bring me some small sprigs of laughing poplar."

"Certainly, Lady Nishima. The weeping birch still retains its leaves, if that would be appropriate."

Nishima laughed. Of course, Kento had seen the carefully folded letter on the table. "Perhaps not in this case."

"As you say." The small woman bowed and slipped out of the room. Almost immediately a maid came in to clear the morning meal away.

Nishima was left on her own. She suppressed an urge to open the letter she had written to Jaku and instead took Jaku's own letter from her sleeve. In doing so, she caused the coins Tanaka had given her to ring against each other.

"Uncle," Nishima whispered to the empty room, "do not be too bold yet. There are things even you do not suspect."

Nishima pushed open the screen to her garden and walked out onto the veranda. A ground mist still wrapped itself around the bushes and boulders even though the sun was quickly burning off the thin cloud layer. Nishima leaned against a post and unfolded the letter from Jaku Katta. She found that reading it gave her a lightness of spirit that she could not suppress. This is foolish, she told herself. Jaku is certainly beyond redemption—a womanizer and an opportunist.

Yet despite these thoughts the lightness she felt did not disappear.

A tap on the screen caused Lady Nishima to bury Jaku's letter in her sleeve. The face of Lady Kento appeared in the opening. "Rohku Saicha, my lady."

"I will speak with him out here."

Almost immediately, there was a bustle of servants as mats and cushions were laid out on the low veranda. Lady Nishima seated herself and nodded to a servant.

Rohku Saicha entered the room from the hall, wearing the light armor of a guard on duty. This was a statement for Nishima and she did not fail to notice it. Crossing to the veranda, he knelt and bowed in the most rigid and military manner, setting his helmet carefully beside him.

He is determined, Lady Nishima thought. This will be difficult. The stocky frame of the Captain of the Guards betrayed his resolution. He would not easily allow his young mistress to have her way again—not after what had happened with the Imperial Guards on the canal.

"Saicha-sum," Nishima said warmly, "it is a pleasure to have your company."

"It is I who am honored, Lady Nishima." Rohku answered formally. "You wished to speak with me?"

"Yes. How is your son, Saicha-sum? Does he prosper?"

"He has journeyed to Seh in Lord Shonto's guard." Rohku kept his eyes cast down, as though he were not on less formal terms with Lady Nishima.

"I shall worry less knowing this," Nishima said. She was about to go on in this vein when she realized that Rohku Saicha sat before her as unmoving as a stone Botahara. He would not be swayed by anything but an irrefutable argument.

"Saicha-sum, I have received information from Tanaka that is of crucial import to Lord Shonto."

"What information, my lady?"

Nishima struggled within herself, was about to tell him, and then shook her head. "It is information of such a delicate nature that if I were to tell you it would then be dangerous to our lord for you to remain in the capital. It is better that you do not know."

Rohku nodded his head. "Then it is unsafe for you to remain here?"

"That is true."

"Yet you are the student of Lady Okara who has received an Imperial Patronage to educate you. To leave is to insult the Emperor. This is a difficult situation."

"Saicha-sum, I cannot stay. The information I have is too significant; it is only a matter of time until it is discovered that I possess this knowledge. If the Emperor were to find out what I know, he would assume that my father had the same information and this would mean open war between the Yamaku and the Shonto. You must believe that."

"Lady Nishima, I would never doubt your words. It is your response to this information that I question, as is my duty. I believe you will now suggest that you must go to Seh, taking this information to your father."

"It . . . it is the only course possible, Saicha-sum."

"While I, who am to guard you, will be forced to choose between my duties in the capital and my sworn duty to protect you. Either choice will mean that I have broken my vow to my liege-lord."

"But when I explain, Lord Shonto will understand. He does not value obedience to the point of stupidity. Our lord understands that situations change and, to survive, we must change also."

"Lady Nishima, what you ask is impossible. I cannot allow it. You will not only offend the Son of Heaven by your absence, but you will put yourself at risk, risk that I have sworn to protect you from. And there is more. Before your father left for the north, he told me that it was possible that he would send for you. He did not say why, but he did tell me that I was not to let you leave until I received an order from him. Perhaps our lord anticipated this information you have received, Lady Nishima, in which case it would be unwise to act before Lord Shonto orders us to."

"Captain Rohku, let me assure you that my father could not have anticipated this information. Of this I entertain no doubts. If, as you say, Lord Shonto plans that I shall join him in Seh, then it is only a matter of timing. I shall go now with information that may save his life."

"Lady Nishima there are other ways to send information secretly, even across the Empire."

"Other ways, yes, but for other information. This will travel only in my head. I will accept nothing else." Nishima reached out as though she would touch the soldier but instead she gripped the rail of the banister. "Saicha-sum, you endanger your lord's life with this obstinacy. You know that there is a plot against Lord Shonto. I have crucial information about this. You are letting what you think of as your recent oversight cloud your eyes. But our lord trusts no one more than you or you would not be sitting before me. He values you for your judgment. Do not lose faith in it. What I say must have the feel of truth to it, I know it must."

The guard still avoided her gaze. "I cannot, my lady, I. . . . Too many things argue against this. What of the Emperor. . . ?"

"He need not know, Saicha-sum, but if it is discovered that I am gone, the Son of Heaven will be forced to act as though I left with his blessing. He will choose to save face, Saicha-sum—what else can he do?"

Rohku Saicha looked at his young mistress. "For such an insult, he could turn his back on the Shonto."

"Saicha-sum!" Nishima said in exasperation. "He is our lord's mortal enemy! He plots against our House and you are worried that he will scorn us?"

"Lady Nishima, you need not lecture me. What you say is the whispered truth, but the spoken truth is that the Emperor honors our lord and trusts him with the security of our Empire. One cannot insult an Emperor who honors your family and, indeed, honors you with his patronage."

"Now it is you who lecture me, Saicha-sum. You must understand that the risk of the Emperor's displeasure in this matter is of no consequence compared to the risk of me remaining in the capital and of Lord Shonto not receiving this information."

"Lady Nishima," the Captain threw up his hands. "This is easily decided. We will ask Lord Shonto."

"But Saicha-sum, how can that be done? The reason I must travel to Seh cannot be trusted to a letter. It is not possible. Only the Imperial Messengers would be fast enough, and that is out of the question!"

"I have my orders from our liege-lord," he said, the emphasis on "our." "I will not break them, nor will I willingly insult the Emperor, thereby giving him reason to act against my lord's House. I am sorry, Lady Nishima, but without word from Lord Shonto you must stay in the capital. If you do not struggle against my precautions, I believe you will be safe here."

Nishima reached into her sleeve pocket and felt the coins she had received from Tanaka. It is no good, she thought. If I show these to Rohku, he cannot stay in the capital either. It can only be a last resort.

"Is this your final word then, Captain?"

"It is, Lady Nishima. I apologize for opposing your will in this matter, but I feel it is my duty to do so."

"Then you will excuse me, Captain, I have other things to attend to."

Rohku Saicha bowed and was about to rise but stopped. "There is one other matter, Lady Nishima. I am aware that you have received correspondence from the general, Jaku Katta. I must tell you that the general is an object of interest to Shonto security."

"Oh, really, Captain?" Nishima said innocently. "An advisor to our much revered Emperor is an object of our suspicion? Aren't you concerned that the Benevolent Son of Heaven will be offended by such an attitude?"

"Lady Nishima, there is nothing to be gained in fighting me," Rohku said seriously.

Lady Nishima raised her eyebrows. "Huh," she said, in imitation of her father. "It was only recently that General Katta was honored by my father for saving my father's life, just as the Emperor honors my father for his bravery in meeting the barbarian threat. It can hardly be indiscreet for me to correspond with a friend of Shonto—a friend who has the ear of the Emperor." Nishima had drawn herself up to full sitting height. "Captain."

Rohku Saicha seemed to struggle with himself for a split second, but then he bowed and began to rise.

"I don't remember giving you permission to rise in my presence."

The guard's mouth almost fell open, but he recovered instantly and dropped again to his knees. Bowing low, he backed across the veranda and through the inner room without rising.

Nishima fixed her eyes on her garden though in fact she saw nothing. The inner shoji closed with the slightest noise—Rohku Saicha was gone.

There, Nishima thought, I have acted like a spoiled child. She pushed her fingertips to her temples and closed her eyes. If I had not forced my way out of here without proper guard and ended up in that embarrassing situation on the canal, Saicha-sum would not be reacting as he is. I have taken advantage of his affection for me and now he has hardened himself to resist me, no matter what. He punishes himself for his perceived failures this way, earning coldness from me for doing what he sees as his duty. Yes, he hurts himself. I have known him many years and now I see him becoming a martyr to his duties. Poor Saicha-sum. Does he not know that he lets what happened in Lord Shonto's garden control him? This would be a great danger—he would be reacting only to his sense of failure rather than to the situations he encounters. This is something that could be easily exploited. I could exploit it.

Nishima stood and reached a pair of sandals on a high shelf, slipping them on as she stepped into the garden. I will not let Rohku Saicha stop me from traveling to Seh. If he cannot be made to change his mind by tomorrow evening, then I shall find a way to leave without his cooperation. If I leave with Saicha-sum's assistance, there is a good chance that Lord Shonto will accept this decision as necessary once he sees the letter from Tanaka. If I am forced to deceive Rohku so that I may leave, it will be the end of our good captain. Lord Shonto would never forgive him for stupidity. I hope he will see reason.

Lady Nishima stopped and took a deep breath of the morning air. It still went cold into the lung, but already the sun was having its effect; the sky cleared and the light fell warm into her small garden. It was a morning to gladden the heart and Lady Nishima found herself turning gracefully in the steps of a courtier's dance. Ah, see, she thought, I do dance secretly, and she laughed. Clapping her hands twice, she took a last look at her garden and then turned as a servant knelt on the edge of her veranda.

"Prepare my bath, and please have Lady Shishika lay out robes for me to choose from."

When the servant was gone, she again found herself dancing. We are in terrible danger, she told herself, how can I be light of heart at a time like this. She did not admit to herself that it was the poem in her sleeve that made her so. But when she swept her arm in a graceful circle and heard the jingle of coins, she stopped. Shaking her head as though she had just heard a lie, Nishima turned and went to her bath.

The wind came up out of the east and even a hundred miles inland, in the capital, it was called the "sea wind." When it heralded a storm, the big gulls that sailed the river as far as Yankura drifted into the capital like refugees driven before an advancing army. Nishima could hear their throaty calls even now.

The wind hissed through the plum trees outside her rooms sending a draft between the shojis, yet the sunlight still filtered through the screens oblivious to the changing weather. Fingers of steam rising from the bath wove among the shafts of sunlight as though they were strands of silk on a loom.

Nishima slipped out of the cold air into her bath. The water was deliciously hot and Nishima let herself sink down into it as though it were sleep itself, for the night had been long and without rest.

She closed her eyes and the patterns of color formed by courtiers' robes swam in her imagination. The celebration of the Emperor's ascension had been full of surprises. Poor Kitsura, she thought, I'm sure she never dreamed that such a thing could happen. The Emperor desires her, there is no doubt of that; and we know what Botahara said of desire.

She ran her hands up from her stomach over her breasts and then crossed them at her neck, pushing her breasts flat with her arms. So the handsome general courted her. Or was it her name that fascinated him? She felt nothing but confusion when she considered this question. It seemed that her usual womanly senses had deserted her in this matter.

"If the mind is too full of facts there is no room for knowledge," Satake had told her, yet she could not cast out the facts.

A knock on the shoji brought Nishima out of her reverie. "Yes?"

"I have your robes, my lady," came Kento's soft voice.

"But where is Lady Shishika?"

"Pardon me, Lady Nishima, but I have taken the liberty of replacing her so that we may speak. Rohku is having your rooms watched and I will appear less suspicious if I come to help you dress."

"There is no end to foolishness!" Nishima said, bitterly. "Enter."

Nishima's favorite swept in, a number of inner robes of the sheerest silk folded over her arm. Stopping far enough away that Nishima could see without moving, Kento displayed each robe in turn.

"No, too dark—there is enough darkness. No Kento-sum, lighter still. Pure white is what I want. Bring me a robe made of the snow itself."

The lady-in-waiting bowed and hurried out in a swish of silk. Nishima closed her eyes, and ran her fingertips over her thighs, falling back into thoughts of the poem she had received that morning. The hot bath seemed to hold her, easing her tensions. She knew she was exhausted, yet she could not sleep.

Kento returned, seeming to Nishima to bring the world with her in her concern for her lady's dress.

"Ah, yes. Now that is closer. Yes, that one. And the other, a shade darker. Perfect. Leave them, I will dress and come out to you."

Maids hurried in bringing towels for their mistress, but Nishima sent them out and dried herself with the narrow lengths of rough cotton, rubbing briskly as though the roughness would bring her mind back to matters at hand. From a shelf she took an ornate lacquered box of turquoise and azure which bore a pattern of white warisha blossoms—the symbol of the ancient House of Fanisan.

The jewelry box, and much that it contained, had belonged to Nishima's mother and the young woman treasured it for more than its perfectly wrought contents. She twisted the handle in the special way and the lid popped open without a sound. Just the sight of what lay within gave her deep pleasure. Her long fingers caressed a set of silver bracelets and then a smooth jade pendant and a string of black pearls.

Lifting out a small tray, Nishima uncovered Tanaka's letter and her own decoding of it. Beneath these lay the coins. She examined them again carefully, looking for signs of their origin. They had been struck with great skill even though they appeared very plain. She turned them over on her palm, each coin about the size of her thumbnail and unmarked but for perfectly round holes in their centers. As Tanaka had written, they could well have come from the Imperial Mint, but there was nothing specific about them that would prove this true.

Taking a length of mauve silk ribbon, Nishima strung the coins along it, the metal catching the sunlight and seeming to gain depth as only true gold could. Wrapping this around her naked waist, she felt the cold metal warm to the soft skin of her stomach. Nishima slipped the robes over this, being certain that no signs of the coins could be seen. Once dressed she knew that the many folds of her sash would conceal secrets far greater than this.

Nishima slid open the shoji and stepped into the next room where her lady-in-waiting had several wooden wardrobes open and an array of kimonos displayed according to color and formality.

"A letter has arrived from Lady Okara, my lady."

"Ah. Let me see it." Nishima said quickly.

A tiny branch of sweet smelling lintel herb, a vine often found growing on old stone walls, was attached to a fine cloth paper of pearl gray.

Lintel herb, Nishima thought, used to purify water. She dropped to her knees on a cushion, forgetting entirely about the kimonos spread about her. The letter was folded in the manner called "Gateway" though it scarcely resembled this, but Nishima noted it duly. Such things were invariably part of the message or added an additional level to it. For a second she was disappointed by the simplicity of the hand and then she smiled. It was absolutely correct for Lady Okara and on closer inspection she realized that "simple" was not an adequate description. "Pure" would perhaps be a better word.

> I have read your letter through now several times, Nishima-sum. And though I do not know your reasons for this proposed journey I do trust you. I can't help feeling that this situation you find yourself in is my fault and I feel great resentment over being used in this way. Not toward you, my dear, but to others. There is only one solution to our problem; I will travel to Seh with you. In this way you will not incur the displeasure of the Son of Heaven, for the Emperor said nothing of us staying in the capital to pursue your studies. I have not seen the great canal in many years and I cannot imaging a more suitable place for us to consider the essence of our artistic endeavors.
>
> The white blossoms
> Of the lintel vine

Are scattered by the winds.
They flow north on strong currents
Like the crests
Of a thousand small waves.
How will we open the gates
Now that the arches crumble?

Nishima read the letter again and then refolded it as it had come. Suddenly she felt an overwhelming need for sleep—she could, now. Rohku Saicha would have no argument against this!

May Botahara bless Okara-sum, Nishima thought, I am going to Seh.

Twenty-seven

THE EMPEROR REALIZED he was pacing and felt his anger return again. He crossed to the dais and looked down on the pile of scrolls and letters scattered across the mats. All of this, he thought, and no news to gladden the heart. Without warning, he kicked a silk cushion across the room. Its collision with the shoji brought a horde of guards and attendants rushing in from all sides.

"Yes?" the Emperor said loudly. "Did I call any of you? Get out! You!— bring me my cushion. Now get out."

He slumped down on his newly returned cushion and regarded the yards of paper spread around him. "May the gods take Jaku Katta. I *need* that young fool!" Reaching for the letter he had received from Lord Shonto, the Son of Heaven read it again carefully, looking for any sign that Shonto lied—that the lord pointed a finger at Jaku only to take away the Emperor's valued servant.

Sire:

By now the Emperor knows of my difficulties at Denji Gorge but I have taken the liberty of writing, briefly, my impressions of what occurred there.

The northern locks of Denji Gorge have, for some years now, come under the control of the Hajiwara and during this time the Hajiwara House has used this control to increase their fortunes at the expense of the Imperial Treasury. The Hajiwara financial records I have sent to Your Majesty will show that this is true.

The Hajiwara have accomplished this theft by controlling the Imperial Keep above the northern locks with the unspoken approval of the Imperial Governor, the Lord Hajiwara's kinsman.

As I refused to pay a tithe to the Hajiwara, I was held in the Gorge for several days and prevented from fulfilling my duties to my Emperor. This situation was intolerable and an affront to your Majesty, so I arranged to take the locks from the Hajiwara forces and return them to the control of Imperial Authorities. Unfortunately, in this struggle Lord Hajiwara and his family died. This I regret for I will miss the pleasure of seeing the Hajiwara before an Imperial Court.

It seems that an Imperial Messenger, one Jaku Yasata was sent to Itsa some months ago, no doubt to deal with this situation, but such was the arrogance of the Hajiwara that Lieutenant Jaku was ignored—in fact the situation grew worse after his visit, as all Imperial Representatives were disallowed entry to the lock areas and were deprived access to the lock records.

I believe, Sire, that I have acted as the situation dictated and to restore respect for my Emperor. In this matter I was aided greatly by Lord Butto of Itsa whose bravery and loyalty were readily put at the service of the Throne.

I remain Your Majesty's servant,
Shonto Motoru

The Emperor realized that his palms were damp and he wiped them unceremoniously on his robe. Shonto must believe it was the Emperor who arranged this stupid escapade. All of the effort and cost that had gone into sending Shonto to the north and now this! If the lord had held any doubt that Seh was a trap, that doubt was gone now.

I am in danger, the Emperor thought. Shonto and his one-armed advisor and that accursed monk plot even now—I can feel it. Katta, you fool! You have placed me in danger when every effort had been made to hide the hand that held the knife. Fool! Stupid fool! Now what would he do? Be calm. His father had always remained calm and it had won him a throne. Akantsu stared down at the pile of reports as though they were responsible for his loss of tranquillity.

He tossed the letter back onto the pile.

There was a similar letter from Lord Butto or, more correctly, from his youngest son though under the old lord's signature. What a fiasco! And this visit by Yasata. The Emperor massaged the temples of his throbbing head. Jaku had long recommended that this stupid feud be allowed to continue as it weakened those involved which, he argued, could never be to the Emperor's disadvantage—but it now appeared that he might have had other reasons for his recommendations. What could he have been thinking?

Picking up a long scroll, the Emperor began to read the report prepared for him by his own agents—as if they could be trusted! He read each word looking for hidden meanings, seeing the hand of a traitor everywhere.

> The brief war that has taken place in Itsa is a continuation of the feud between the two chief Houses of this province with one significant difference. In these last battles Lord Shonto Motoru has sided with the Butto, no doubt planning all of the actions with his own formidable staff.
>
> Lord Shonto's reasons for involving himself in this affair seem to be self-interest only—he was being prevented from continuing his journey north—though it is almost certainly true that the Hajiwara plotted against him, no doubt as agents for another party.
>
> The Governor of Itsa is presently traveling to the capital to lodge official complaints with the Imperial Government and no doubt to plead his innocence to any charges that he has misappropriated funds destined for the Imperial Treasury—a blatant lie.
>
> There is as yet no evidence of who the Hajiwara served in this matter and we are endeavoring with all haste to discover this while it may still be possible to do so.
>
> There is one other note that should be recorded. Shonto found a way to move an army out of Denji Gorge without the assistance of the Butto. This was formerly believed to be impossible. We have not yet determined how this was done.

The Emperor found his heart was beating too quickly, and he put his hand to his chest to try to calm himself. This escape from Denji Gorge was what unsettled him. How had Shonto managed that? The Emperor knew the gorge from personal experience, knew its high barren walls. It must be a trick, he thought, the army must somehow have come across the land. It isn't possible for a single man to escape from Denji Gorge, let alone an army. But the Emperor knew that this was the lie and that the truth was Shonto had escaped from an impossible situation. This knowledge did not bring Akantsu II comfort.

The Emperor began rolling the scroll, keeping the paper tight. So much hangs in the balance, he thought, and now this? Who hid behind the screen of this feud and whispered the orders to Hajiwara? And who would be so stupid as to believe that fool Hajiwara could outmaneuver the Lord of the Shonto? Could it be, as Shonto implied, that Jaku Katta had arranged this entire escapade?

Katta, the Emperor thought, you have been like a son to me, and now, like a son, do you grow impatient for the father to pass on?

A quiet knock on the shoji interrupted the Emperor's thoughts. A screen slid aside and an attendant knelt in the opening.

"Yes?"

"Sire, Colonel Jaku Tadamoto awaits your pleasure."

"Ah." The Emperor gestured to his reports. "Have this arranged and then I will see the colonel."

Two servants rushed in and began rolling scrolls and picking up papers. "Leave them with us," the Emperor ordered, "and give me my sword."

Doors at the end of the audience hall opened, revealing Jaku Katta's younger brother, a tall, slightly built, handsome man who looked to be the scholar he in fact was. He knelt outside the doors, his head bowed to the mat.

"You may approach, Colonel."

Jaku Tadamoto came forward on his knees, stopping a respectful distance from the dais.

"It gives me pleasure to see you, Colonel."

"I am honored that you feel so, Sire."

A half-smile crossed the Emperor's face at Tadamoto's words, but then it hardened into the look of a man with many things weighing upon him. "Tadamoto-sum, events in our Empire have made me aware again that the throne draws to it traitors of all kinds. There are so few we can trust, so few whose loyalty is not a mask for private ambitions."

"It grieves me that this is so, Sire."

Nodding his head sadly, the Emperor rubbed his hand along the scabbard of his sword as though it were a talisman. "But you, Tadamoto-sum, you, I think, are different. Is that not so?"

"I am the Emperor's servant." Tadamoto said simply.

"Ah, I hope that is true, Tadamoto-Sum, I hope that is true." The Emperor paused, staring directly at the young officer. "Have you heard of these events at the gorge in Itsa?"

"I have, Sire."

"And?"

Tadamoto cleared his throat. "Excuse me for saying so, Sire, but I have long advocated putting an end to that feud and reestablishing Imperial Law on the Grand Canal."

"So you have. Tell me again your reasons for this."

"Sire, it is the lesson of history. Those Emperors who have offered stability have had the fewest internal problems to deal with. The canal has been unsafe ever since the Interim War, yet this canal is our link with half of the Empire. All of the provinces reached by the canal feel they are being ignored by the capital, they grow resentful, and soon there are problems resulting from this. I have never supported the policy of allowing the Empire to remain unstable, there is no evidence in our histories to support this idea."

The Emperor nodded. So, and it was Jaku Katta who recommended that I not allow the Great Houses to return to complete peace. Have I listened to the wrong brother all along?

"What you say has the sound of truth, Tadamoto-sum. But tell me what you think of this situation in Itsa."

"Sire, it is clear from the reports that Shonto used the Butto to push his way through the Hajiwara armies, though it is not yet known how this was done. The situation in Itsa was so contrary to the laws of the Imperium that Shonto was willing to take the situation into his own hands without fear of Imperial reprisal. No one in the Empire will feel that Shonto has acted without honor and respect for his Emperor. He has at once done the Emperor a favor while at the same time making it clear how inadequately the government has tended to certain of its duties. The Hajiwara were no match for the Shonto and I would not be surprised to learn that Lord Hajiwara thought he had come to an agreement with Lord Shonto that was to his advantage . . . only to learn that the Shonto never make agreements that do not favor them."

The Emperor caressed his sword again, with a certain compulsion. "I see. So what is to be done now?"

Tadamoto nodded, a quick bow, almost a reflex. "I believe, Sire, that you should seize the initiative in this situation. The Throne should restore order on the canals and the roads of the Empire. It will be costly to begin with, but once law is established then it shall become less so—and I fear the costs of not doing this will be much greater. There is much support for what the Lord Shonto has done in Itsa—he is the hero of the Empire for the moment—but there would be equal support for this action if it were undertaken by the Imperial Government."

"But would we not simply appear to be finishing the work of Lord Shonto, scurrying about after him like servants?"

"Sire, I believe it is only a question of making enough noise. Form an Imperial Triumvirate to deal with the problem of the roads and canals. Send out Imperial Functionaries and large forces of guards with power to do your bidding. Have edicts read in the capitals of all the provinces and then parade the robbers and embezzlers through the streets. It will soon be forgotten that it was Lord Shonto who took the first steps."

"Ah, Tadamoto-sum, I value your counsel. Others give advice only to further their own aims but you . . . there is indeed an echo of Hakata in your words."

The young colonel bowed his head to the mat. "I am more than honored by your words, Sire."

The Emperor nodded. "I do not think my praise is misplaced. We shall see."

"There is another matter, Tadamoto-sum." The Emperor lowered his voice. "A matter we have spoken of previously. Your brother, in his zeal to ensure our safety, has surrounded us with many who report to him personally. I understand this is for reasons of security, but it is more than is necessary as I have said to you before. Have you managed to discover who these people are?"

Tadamoto nodded once, not meeting the Emperor's eyes. "I have, Sire."

"And you have made a list?"

Again Tadamoto nodded.

The Emperor smiled. "Leave it with us, Tadamoto-sum. I will speak with your brother. Taking such precautions is more than is necessary, even for one as conscientious as Katta-sum.

"What of the followers of Tomsoma?" the Emperor asked, his voice suddenly cool. He went on before Tadamoto could begin to answer. "This attempt to cause more tension between them and the Silent Brothers was foolish. The Brothers are treacherous, but they are not fools. Has that priest . . . what was his name?"

"Ashigaru, Sire."

"Has he surfaced?"

Tadamoto shook his head. "He has not, Sire. I don't think the Emperor need be concerned. The magic cults have begun to realize that there is no hope of converting the Imperial Family. They are resentful, Sire, no doubt, but so far they are silently so."

The Emperor shook his head. "They have been of little use and demanded much." He turned his gaze on the young officer then, and there seemed to be great affection there.

"And did you ever discuss the Lady Nishima with your brother, Tadamoto-sum."

"I did, Sire."

"Ah."

"He felt it was a service to his Emperor to observe the Lady Nishima, Sire."

"Of course. And does he continue to see the lady?"

"He has not met with her, to the best of my knowledge, Sire."

"Perhaps he has reconsidered the nature of his duties. That would be wisdom. There is a duty I would ask you to perform, Tadamoto-sum." The Emperor did not wait for Tadamoto to answer. "Osha is unhappy with her situation, as you could understand—perhaps it would cheer her if you would escort her to the Ceremony of the Gray Horses."

"I would, gladly, Sire. May I say that I am touched by your concern for those of humble station."

The Emperor nodded modestly. "We shall speak again soon, Tadamoto-sum. Very soon. There are other matters in which we would value your counsel. We shall see."

Tadamoto bowed low and backed from the room. Alone, the Emperor reached for the list Tadamoto had left, but he did not read it immediately. "The Shonto never make agreements that do not favor them," he whispered. "Never."

The two men circled each other slowly, each matching the other step for step. They wore the black split pants and white jackets of traditional Shishama fighters, and one, the designated aggressor, wore a red band of silk wrapped above cold gray eyes. A sword flicked right and down in the beginnings of "swallow flight," but the other countered quickly and the swords went back to the guard position. The aggressor, Jaku Katta, slowed his circling, then stopped, planting his bare feet firmly on the stone floor. His sword went high to the "falcon dive" position, causing the other to step back and parry. Swords flashed in the sunlight, too quick for the eye to follow and then in the clash of metal Jaku's blade found the other's sword arm just above the elbow and it was over. The man bowed deeply, his hand moving to massage his arm.

Jaku Katta bowed also. "I hope I have not caused you harm?"

"The stroke was most controlled, General. It has been an honor just to stand against you. I thank you."

"The honor was mine, Captain." The two men handed their blunt practice blades to waiting attendants. "Again, perhaps?"

"Certainly, General." The man bowed again and Jaku nodded turning to a waiting guard. "Yes?"

The guard knelt quickly. "General Katta, your reply from the office of the Emperor." The guard offered a folded letter to his general.

Jaku took it and continued toward the nearby door that led to his private quarters. The exercise had felt good; it never failed to restore his confidence and now he basked in that warm afterglow poets called "the sun within." Slowly he unfolded the letter and as he stepped up onto his veranda he began to read. Two steps farther, on he almost stumbled and then stopped. He read the letter again:

> General Jaku Katta, Commander, Imperial Guards:
> Your request for an audience with the most revered Son of Heaven has been denied. His Majesty trusts he will have the honor of your presence at the Celebration of the Gray Horses.
>
> > Lord Bakai Jima,
> > Secretary.
> > For His Imperial Majesty,
> > Akantsu II

Jaku almost sank to his knees but reached out and gripped a post. The letter had taken him like the stroke of a sword—suddenly it was over. One could not take back the mistake, the misplaced foot, the weak parry.

Ever since he had received the report from Itsa early that morning he had known a sense of foreboding. If he could see the Son of Heaven, explain to him—Jaku had no doubt of his influence over his Emperor—then he could redeem himself. But now this. He would not have a chance to give his carefully prepared speech; a speech that could be his salvation.

The explanation he had prepared was clear and simple; just the way Akantsu preferred things to be. Jaku Katta knew it would be foolish to deny his involvement in the attempt on Shonto at Denji Gorge, there were too many ways the Emperor could have found out otherwise. No, Jaku's plan was simply to take responsibility and claim there were reasons of security that had necessitated his secrecy.

The failure was something else altogether. Shonto had not only escaped the trap, but he had embarrassed the Throne by removing those parasites, the Hajiwara, from the Empire's main artery—parasites that were there with tacit Imperial approval. And this due to counsel from Jaku himself. The Black Tiger shook his head and proceeded to his bath.

Servants scrubbed him thoroughly before he lowered himself into the steaming water. And now what? He had never received a denial of a request for an audience before. Never. The significance of this action shook him. He felt like a man who had fallen off a ship in the night and now watched it sail away into the darkness. It couldn't be happening. Yet it was. It had, in fact, already happened.

Somehow, Jaku felt a sense of injustice as though his plans, no matter what they may be or who they might involve, deserved to succeed for no other reason than that they were his.

Was it not he who had contrived the entire plan to rid the Emperor of the constant shadow of Lord Shonto? Had he not performed a thousand deeds for his Emperor, many at great personal risk? Things could not be as they seemed. Jaku would go to the Imperial apartments and demand to see the Emperor on a matter of security. All of the men who surrounded the Emperor were Jaku's men, they would let him through without question. It could be done. He would yet take back the mistake.

Jaku shifted in the water, laying his head back and closing his eyes. Yes that was what he would do. Once he was before the Emperor, he would hold sway. Whoever conspired against him, and he had no doubt that someone did, could not know the key to Akantsu II as Jaku did. The Emperor was, at heart, a soldier and he respected only those whose spirit was as his. And Jaku was the essence of the fighter, the raw matter distilled down until it was as pure as the spirit of the wind. Jaku was the warrior of all warriors and the Emperor knew it.

Jaku's thoughts shifted inexplicably to Lady Nishima, to the poem he had received from her only an hour before. Her reticence was only an act, he knew. Jaku had seen it before in other well born young women. But her eyes told him the truth, and the truth was she was smitten with him. There was no question of it; this was one campaign Jaku had won. It had not even been difficult. Jaku laughed bitterly.

Everything had fit into his design until Shonto had reached Itsa. What had really happened there? Jaku stretched his muscular arms above him, letting the water splash back onto his face. The plan had been without flaw—but then Hajiwara was a fool, there was no doubt of that. Jaku laughed again. All was not lost. He would recover as a fighter did, turning his enemies' thrust to his own advantage. He was still strong. The Lady Nishima would come into his plans soon enough and the Emperor, the Emperor who refused his audience, would understand that Jaku Katta was something more than he had ever realized.

Jaku rose and stepped, dripping, from his bath. Servants entered with towels to dry him.

"Bring my duty armor and helmet," he ordered an attendant. It was time to see this reticent Emperor. Time for a bold stroke. Jaku dressed slowly, enjoying the feel of his light armor, admiring the artistry of its maker.

"General Jaku," the attendant began. "General, there are servants and guards outside awaiting your orders."

"What?" Jaku picked up his helmet and started for the door.

The man bobbed in a quick succession of bows as he rushed along beside his master. "They do not understand, General. They have been sent. You must see for yourself."

Jaku preceded the attendant to the door and as it opened he was greeted by a gathering of faces, all of which he recognized. The servants of the Emperor. Jaku stood without speaking, the eyes of this desperate gathering turned to him, the faces registering a depth of fear that unsettled him so that he found himself taking a step, unbidden, back into the protection of his rooms.

The Ceremony of the Gray Horses was performed in the central courtyard of the Island Palace, a place well known for its view of the setting sun. Garlands of autumn flowers graced the columns of the nearby porticoes and autumn leaves and petals had been scattered on the ponds and streams. The many trees in their autumn colors needed no artistic assistance, and it was from their autumn palette that other colors were drawn, including the robes of the courtiers and officials gathered for this ancient ceremony.

Directly across from the gate of the inner spirit the dais and Throne of the Emperor had been situated, and there the most revered Son of Heaven sat with the members of the Imperial family arrayed about him, including a sullen Empress. The Major Chancellor and the Ministers of both the Right and the Left sat in their appointed places, while to each side of these the ranks descended from the First to the Third, the lowest rank allowed to attend such an important ceremony. Even so, the numbers reached to several thousand men and women, all dressed with an acute awareness of the appropriate colors and degree of formality so that the overall effect was without a single point of disharmony in the entire composition.

Seated among those of the Third Rank of the Left, Jaku Katta assumed the attitude of the other courtiers—respectful anticipation—but he watched the Emperor's every move, searching for a sign of his intentions. Yet he saw nothing, and there among the many, Jaku did not draw a nod from his Emperor.

It is as though I have ceased to exist, Jaku thought, as though I am already dead. He caught the eye of a young woman who smiled demurely and then hid her face with a fan, yet this hardly registered in his mind at all. What shall I do? Jaku asked himself. Everything I have planned falls around me.

The subdued excitement of the crowd was almost tangible and seemed to flow like chi along all the meridian of the whole. A love of ceremony that was almost an obsession had long been a prominent feature of Waian court life. All waited for the signal from the Emperor.

Being semi-divine, the Emperor was expected to intercede for the people of Wa with his ancestors and the gods. Even the advent of Botahara a thousand years earlier had affected these rites in only the smallest ways—a thin veneer of Botahist doctrine layered over the rites of the ancient pantheism.

The story of the Gray Horses originated at the time of the establishment of the Seven Kingdoms which later became the central provinces of the Empire of Wa. It was said that Po Wu, the father of the gods, gave the Gray Horses to his sons, the Seven Princes, who then drove the barbarians out of the lands of Cho-Wa and planted the seeds of civilization.

The gray steeds were imbued with magical powers by Po Wu and could not be injured or die in battle. From their running hooves came a thunder which shook the earth and split the hills, scattering their enemies before them like gulls before a storm.

The Gray Horses of the ceremony were said to be descendants of Po Wu's steeds, bred generation after generation and carefully guarded by the Emperor's staff.

At a nod from the Emperor, the ceremony began with the beating of drums like the sound of thunder and then the airy voice of a thirteen pipe flute. From the Gate of the Inner Spirit the clatter of unshod hooves striking stone seemed to blend with the rhythm of the music and then the horses appeared—seven pale gray mounts, groomed until they glinted in the sunlight.

The riders were the best in the province; two Imperial Guards, the sons of three lords, a Minor Counselor and a hunt master—all dressed in Imperial crimson and seated on saddles of gold and deep green. The horses were arrayed in headdresses of gold and black and the contrast of these strong colors with the pale tones of the audience had an almost startling effect.

The riders moved their horses through carefully coordinated exercises of great intricacy, and all with commands so subtle that none could see them. A story grew out of these exercises, the story of the Seven Princes and their magical horses. Dancers joined in dressed as foot soldiers and barbarians, yet there was never a confusion nor loss of focus to the movement.

After sweeping the barbarians from the field, the seven equestrians wheeled and paraded slowly before the Emperor, and as the living descendant of Po Wu he rewarded them for their valor with generous gifts.

The riders all bowed their thanks and led their horses from the courtyard to the buzzing of the courtiers' praise. A silence settled over the audience then as they waited for the Emperor and the Imperial Family to rise and depart—but instead a Senior Assistant to the Minister of the Left struck a small gong to gain everyone's attention. Moving with a grace surprising for his age the assistant took up a position in front of the dais, bowed twice, and removed a scroll from his sleeve. His voice was soft, yet it carried well to all of his audience.

"On behalf of the Minister of the Left, I have been charged to read these, the words of the most revered Son of Heaven.

"Today we have witnessed not only an ancient ceremony of lasting significance but also a metaphor which is descriptive of our own time. The northern border of Wa is again pressed by the barbarians and we have, as is our duty, turned our eyes there. Yet this is not the only place where the spirit of the primitive peoples has been manifested. Within the borders of our own provinces those who are barbarians in spirit make many of our roads and waterways unsafe and, to our lasting disappointment, the lords of the provinces have been unable to curtail this activity. It is our pledge that we will not allow barbarism to threaten our Empire, either from within or without.

"Therefore, it is the will of the Throne that this situation shall end. To accomplish this, forces of Imperial Guards and Functionaries of the judiciary shall be sent throughout the Empire for the purpose of making all our routes of travel and commerce safe for even the most humble citizen of our Empire.

"Due to recent circumstances on the Grand Canal we realize that this, the cord that binds our great Empire together, is in peril and therefore will be our first concern. To deal with this situation we have chosen to send the Commander of the Imperial Guard, General Jaku Katta, as representative of the Throne and Sole Arbiter on the Grand Canal. He will be charged with returning the waterway to its former state of peace and efficiency.

"Others will be sent out with the same orders to effect the same changes on all the arteries of our Empire.

"By order of Akantsu II, Emperor, and the Great Council of the Empire."

The bureaucrat bowed as he finished his reading and the assembled guests bowed in turn to the Emperor and his family. A sound went through the crowd, an indescribable sound that everyone recognized as the sound of mass approval. The Emperor smiled as he rose and stepped into his waiting sedan chair.

Among those bowing as the Emperor made his exit was one general in Imperial Guard uniform who did not share this sense of approval. Jaku Katta sat waiting for those of higher rank to leave, accepting congratulations and good wishes with what appeared to be a stoic nod but was, in fact, perfectly contained fury.

What had been done to Shonto at Jaku's urging had now been done to Jaku. The Black Tiger took long slow breaths and tried to calm his mind, but his anger seemed to dart everywhere, now aimed at the Son of Heaven, now aimed at Lord Shonto, now at the foolish courtiers who congratulated him while having no notion of what was happening. He was like a bow drawn near its breaking point with an arrow notched and ready—and he looked everywhere in his mind for the appropriate target.

The members of the First and Second Ranks had risen and made their way leisurely from the square. Jaku rose with the people remaining, those of the Third Rank, and began to make his way through the crowd. Around him people laughed and commented on the beauty of the ceremony and the perfection of the equestrians, but Jaku walked under a cloud as dark as his black uniform. It was all he could do not to push these fools out of his way, but he held himself in check—it was important to know when to release an arrow.

Coming finally to the edge of the square, he mounted a set of steps that few others would use and there he broke free of the crowds and the foolish prattle. On the top step he turned to survey the square out of habit; he was, after all, in charge of security in the palace. And there among the throng that passed the foot of his steps he saw his brother, Tadamoto, walking in the company of Osha, the Emperor's Sonsa—and they were laughing. Jaku could almost hear them. They laughed a shared laugh and their faces glowed as only lovers could.

My own blood, Jaku thought.

Twenty-eight

> *Whispers behind the sleeve,*
> *Words cooler than winter rain*
> *Touch me where I stand,*
> *Here, in the Governor's shadow.*
> *No one has named me a traitor*
> *To my province.*
>
> *It is gratifying to know that*
> *My sword retains its respect.*

Komawara Samyamu

THE AFTERNOON SUN broke through the storm clouds here and there, sending long shafts of light down to the earth; shafts that moved as the clouds moved, in swift, erratic formations.

The crests of waves tumbled into foam which was blown into white streaks across the dark waters. Crests mounted again, rushed on, and dashed themselves against the base of the stone wall.

Standing at the parapet, Lord Shonto looked down at the chaos below. Five days had passed since his arrival in Seh and Shonto had only that morning been able to free himself from the formal demands made upon a new governor. He had been frustrated by all the ceremony and was more than ready to begin the work that had brought him to Seh: the military work. He began with what was close at hand and launched an inspection of the capital's fortifications followed by an assessment of the state of the garrison.

The new governor walked along the wall with a stride that caused his companions to rush in a most undignified manner if they were not to be left behind. They weren't used to such exertions; governors were expected to travel by canal or sedan chair, perhaps, on rare occasion, by horseback. But this!—a walking tour was unheard of.

The men rushing along in the governor's wake were a disparate group, many in long formal robes which the wind attacked with a certain glee. They naturally arrayed themselves by rank: the Major Chancellor Lord Gitoyo, and his son, a Middle Captain of the Third Rank followed the governor; the Minister of War, Lord Akima, a very old man who kept pace without sign of discomfort; two Ministers of the Second Rank wearing their formal blue robes and sweating profusely; General Hojo and Lord Komawara were next and then a lieutenant colonel of the garrison. A dozen attendants of varying rank followed by an appropriate number of guards completed the retinue.

A certain General Toshaki's military rank placed him officially in the Third Rank, but as a member of one of Seh's most important Houses he walked beside Lord Shonto though deferring to him as was appropriate.

"As I said earlier, Lord Shonto," Toshaki said, not using the new governor's official title, "we do everything necessary to keep the city strong and the defenses in good repair." General Toshaki said this between deep gasps as he trotted along beside Shonto. It was the last set of stairs that had reduced him to this state and Shonto's pace was not allowing him to recover. The inspection had caught the men of Seh off guard though Shonto's own staff were not in the least surprised. They had learned the futility of trying to predict the action of their lord—it was better to keep abreast of all one's duties and let inspections come as they would.

Shonto said nothing in response to the general's statement which unsettled the soldier more than he would have expected. Stopping again, Shonto looked over the edge, down at the booming waves. The wall was indeed in good repair, that was clear even to his critical eye, but here and there at its base a dark shelf of rock extended out into the waves. Lack of rainfall that autumn had lowered the water level and exposed rock that was normally many feet under water. It caused Shonto concern. This shelf compromised the integrity of the defenses quite considerably, and worse than that, General Toshaki did not seem to realize it.

"Sire, you can see that Rhojo-ma is secure—her walls unbreachable. Perhaps we could . . ."

"There are no walls that cannot be breached, General," Shonto said as he stopped again and stared over the side.

"Of course you are right, Sire. On the land that is true, but here with a natural moat of three miles . . ."

"General Hojo." Shonto stopped and addressed his senior military advisor.

"Sire?"

Shonto nodded toward an exposed outcropping of smooth granite.

Hojo leaned out over the stone parapet. "I agree, Sire, this is a danger. A staging area is just what's needed to attempt these walls."

"Could you breach them, General?"

"From what I have seen I would say yes—if I could be sure of the element of surprise. The guards have too much confidence in the defenses and this is not good."

"General Toshaki?"

The tall soldier pulled himself even more erect. His words came out in a clipped mockery of politeness. "Sire; the general's observations are astute, but there are other factors to consider. A fleet large enough to attack Rhojo-ma could hardly be constructed in secret. There would always be some warning of such an attack. Any small scale excursion against the city, even if it was successful in passing beyond our first wall, would be isolated by our secondary walls. We would soon force them back into the waves, you can be sure. These rocks will be under water after only a few days of rain, and that rain will not be long in coming. The autumn storms are as reliable as the patience of Botahara, Sire."

Shonto and General Hojo glanced at each other but said nothing. Turning away from the parapet, Shonto continued on his tour.

It was a strange company of professional soldiers, bureaucrats, and peers of the realm who could be seen atop the outer walls, flapping in the wind like rag-guards in a peasant's garden. But it was not just the wind that controlled their movements: this new governor, this outsider, held sway over their futures in the hierarchy of Seh. It was a fact widely resented, and it showed.

But the situation was not that simple for the men of Seh; this new governor was no lackey of the Emperor's sent north to fulfill some political obligation. This was the Lord of the Shonto, a soldier of considerable fame, a man who was respected for more than just his ancient name. A name that history had woven into the very fabric of Seh. It was this complexity of situation that Shonto knew he must exploit if he was to succeed in the north.

The procession came to a large lookout station, a stone platform high in the fortifications. Here the new governor stopped, much to the relief of those following him. Stools were brought from a guard house for the persons of rank and they seated themselves in a semicircle around Shonto.

"Lord Akima," Shonto said, not waiting for anyone to catch his breath. "Tomorrow I will send members of my staff to outlying areas to begin inspections of our defenses. I am particularly interested in the border areas and our inner line of defense. Please detail senior officers from the garrison to accompany them. The details of this can be arranged with General Hojo.

"I will need to establish a primary base closer to the border and to the areas the barbarians have been threatening. This can be decided after I have assessed the present situation. Major Chancellor, I trust that if I leave the administration of Seh largely to you and your capable staff, you will not have cause for complaint?"

The Major Chancellor's surprise was quite well contained. He was a man selected by the former governor of Seh who had purged the remains of the corrupt administration that had typified Seh for the last hundred years. Shonto expected much from this man. All reports indicated that he was competent and just: even Komawara spoke highly of him.

"Lord Governor, I will do all within my power to see that the government of Seh is run efficiently and justly, as a bearer of the name Shonto would prefer it. I am honored by your trust."

Shonto nodded in return to the man's deep bow. The men surrounding the new governor were, in nature, typical northerners and Shonto couldn't help but like them despite their ill-concealed feelings of resentment toward him. They were a quiet, practical group showing little tendency toward extravagance. The hunting costume was their typical mode of dress and this was accepted at all but the most formal occasions: a marked contrast with the Imperial capital. The men who sat before Lord Shonto were tanned like men who worked the fields and they were not ashamed of it. From his other visits Shonto knew that a northern lord's saddle would be of good leather, worn by constant use, and that this wear was a mark of pride not of poverty—the horse was what mattered and the horses of Seh were the best in the Empire.

"General Toshaki, if you would take General Hojo on a tour of the barracks, I would be free to pursue other matters." Shonto rose to his feet suddenly and the others quickly followed suit. "I will request your presence when needed," Shonto said, addressing the entire company. "Lord Akima, Lord Komawara, if you would accompany me." Shonto turned and left the others scurrying to bow properly as he set off again along the wall. Guards preceding them discreetly cleared all nonmilitary and nonranking peoples off the walkway.

"Lord Akima," Shonto said, slowing his pace somewhat, "It appears that Rhojo-ma has benefited from careful attention, but I am told that the outlying fortifications have not received the same care."

The older man nodded, shaking his thick gray hair. "This is true, Lord Shonto. What allotments there have been for defense have largely been spent on the Governor's Palace and those areas immediately surrounding it. The Hanama Governors were, as you know, interested in filling their own coffers and extending the interest of their families. The governors appointed since the Hanama have been less opportunistic personally but instead have enriched the Emperor. There has been little concern for the security of Seh."

"An unfortunate situation and one over which I may have little control. The Son of Heaven demands his taxes. I understand you are of the opinion that the barbarians are no threat to your province?"

"Sire, the tribes are diminished, there is no doubt of this. There has been little rainfall in the desert these past years and it is said that the plague spread even across the sands. These raids . . . they are almost ineffectual. There have been virtually no losses from them. The barbarians have become timid, fearing to meet even our smallest armed parties. In this matter the Emperor has been poorly counseled, and I'm afraid, Lord Governor, that you will find your long journey futile. The barbarian threat exists only in the minds of a few Imperial Advisors whose knowledge of the situation is perhaps not as thorough as one would expect."

Shonto stopped at a major corner in the fortress and looked carefully along the two walls visible from that point. So, Shonto thought, in Seh the Emperor is not above criticism—how refreshing. "Do you not find the behavior of the barbarians strange—out of character for such renowned warriors?"

Lord Akima glanced at Komawara in obvious exasperation. "There are those who express this belief, Lord Governor, but I for one do not understand it. These raids are referred to as 'mysterious' by a small number of people, but the barbarians have been raiding throughout Seh for as long as we have recorded our history—what, then, is strange about that? The tribes have been drastically reduced in size and the warriors who remain are few in number and little able to afford losses. That is the explanation of the 'mystery,' nothing more."

"Huh. I appreciate your knowledge in this matter. Lord Komawara, do you share our companion's opinions?"

Komawara betrayed his anger as he had in the Emperor's garden, his face was flushed and his jaw tight, but his voice was controlled, even pleasant. "This is the common wisdom, Sire, and worth consideration but I believe there are reasons to look into the raids more closely, especially since it would cost so little to do so. Although it is often said that the tribes are reduced in number, it seems to me that it is merely a statement of hope. I can find no evidence for such a belief as no one ventures beyond our borders to make a proper assessment of the numbers of barbarians living in the wastes. The only thing we are certain of is a change in the behavior of the barbarians and though the explanation given by Lord Akima is perhaps true, it is only speculation and as such should not be given more weight than other explanations."

He learns quickly, Shonto thought, the argument was well presented, though perhaps not appreciated by Lord Akima.

"Excuse me for saying so, Lord Governor," Akima said, "but I have observed the barbarian tribes for many years and I cannot subscribe to this belief that the barbarians have suddenly begun to act in a mysterious manner. It can only appear sudden to one who has not been able to observe them over many decades. If it is not fear that causes the barbarians to run from the men of Seh, then perhaps Lord Komawara could tell me what it is?"

Shonto shifted his gaze to Komawara who shrugged and shook his head.

"I do not know, Lord Akima, that is what concerns me."

"And there is the weakness of the argument," the old aristocrat said with finality. "It explains nothing—if you will excuse me for saying so."

Surprising Lord Akima by turning behind a guard station and descending a little known set of stairs, Shonto let a silence accompany them to the foot of the steps where he stopped and addressed both of his companions. "Long ago, in conversation with one of the Shonto, Hakata observed that most people preferred an ill considered answer to an intelligent question. I have

come to Seh to seek truths, and in this endeavor I am prepared to ask difficult questions and then to live without immediate answers if that is what is
required. I hope all advisors to the Shonto are willing to do the same."

A hand signal to his guards set them off down a narrow street, the three
lords not far behind.

Let him not suggest again that age is synonymous with wisdom, Shonto
thought. "I will meet Lord Taiki after midday. I thank you for arranging this,
Lord Akima, it was most kind of you."

"It is an honor to serve, even in such small capacities," the older man said,
a coolness in his voice.

"Do you still feel the Lord Taiki will not support an increase in armed
effort?"

"I feel that Lord Taiki believes, as so many of us do, Sire, there is no real
threat and increased military actions drain resources which could better be
used elsewhere."

The seed of the resentment, Shonto thought; in paying for their own
defense the men of Seh pay for the defense of the Empire. And they are entirely right; this is not just.

"It is clear to the Shonto, if not to the Emperor's counselors, that the cost
of protecting Wa should be born by the Imperial Government. It is my intention to use what little influence I may have at court to see that this problem
receives the attention it deserves. It is unfortunate that the situation at court
is such that I cannot guarantee results. But I can tell you, Lord Akima, that
the matter will receive more careful consideration than it has had in the
past."

"You are to be honored for recognizing the justness of our cause, Lord
Governor, but I fear the Son of Heaven is more concerned with the health of
his treasury than with the health of the people of Seh. Of course he has sent
a warrior to govern us, but it is a case of the correct action in the wrong
circumstance, if you will excuse a candid observation. I must say, Lord
Shonto, that the Lords of Seh realize you have arrived with a significant force
of your own, well armed and trained. You are the first governor in memory
to have done so."

They came to the narrow canal that quartered the island city of Rhojo-ma
and mounted a high arching stone bridge. Stopping on its crest, Shonto stood
looking along the canal and its bordering walkways. Several bridges could
be seen in the distance arching delicately over the waterway like colorless

rainbows. The capital of Seh was a beautiful city, and though it had been built in the time of Seh's great power it was well maintained and, one might even say, loved by its inhabitants. Shonto was particularly fond of the roofs covered in tile of celestial blue. Faded as they were, he was sure they were more beautiful then when new.

A hand signal to a Shonto guard sent him scurrying off along the canal bank. "We will return to the palace by sampan," Shonto said, "we have walked enough for one day."

Little was said on the ride to the Governor's Palace, each occupied with his own thoughts. Shonto remembered Rhojo-ma from a previous visit and could see that the city itself was virtually unchanged—but for one thing. The throngs of people he remembered so clearly crowding the streets and waterways could no longer be seen. Rhojo-ma reminded him of a city on a day of spiritual rest—unnaturally quiet, avenues almost deserted or populated by such small numbers that the streets seemed broader than they really were. Announcing the hour of the crane, the ringing of a temple bell seemed to echo endlessly among the buildings as though searching everywhere for someone to appreciate its aural splendor.

Sadly, the healing Brothers came to Seh last, Shonto realized, and this is the result: the plague reaped its largest harvest here among the people of the north.

The sampan bearing the three lords rounded a curve in the canal and entered a gate in the high wall which surrounded the Imperial Governor's residence.

The palace of the governor of Seh was situated on the southern side of the city on a low hill. A simplified Mori period style had been adopted for the buildings, and with their sweeping blue tile roofs and high stone walls they gave the impression of solidness combined with a simple beauty. Enclosed within the compound were the official buildings of the government of Seh, and among them the Palace of Justice was noticeable for its classical beauty. The Governor's Palace itself was no larger than Shonto's ancestral home, but for Seh, where ostentation was traditionally disfavored, the palace verged on the extravagant. Shonto's staff found the surrounding gardens crude by the standards they were used to, and not just because the climate was harsher, but Lord Shonto found something about their lack of sophistication attractive and often walked in the governor's private garden.

Disembarking from their boat, Shonto bid Komawara and Akima farewell and retired to his own apartments. He planned to meet Lord Taiki Kiyorama later that day and wanted time to prepare himself mentally.

The province of Seh was dominated by three major Houses: the Taiki, the large Ranan family, and the very ancient House of Toshaki of which the Senior General of the provincial armies, Lord Toshaki Shinga was the head of a lesser branch. There were numerous Houses of the Second and Third Ranks, the Komawara among them, but it was the three major Houses that held sway in matters of import in the province and Shonto knew that it was among them that he must find allies.

Most of the minor Houses owed allegiance to one or other of the major families and followed their policies virtually without question. Only a few of the lesser Houses had managed to retain the degree of independence that the Komawara exhibited, and the Komawara's situation was a prime example of the cost of this independence—without the support of a major House they became poorer each year.

Of the three important lords, the head of the Toshaki seemed to feel there would be an advantage to aligning himself with the present dynasty while Lord Ranan was widely known to despise the Yamaku and resent the governors sent by the Imperial family. This was not surprising; the Ranan had been favored by the Hanama and for a century had acted as the family's right hand in the north, for which they had been richly rewarded.

Only the lord of the Taiki seemed unsure of his position. It was known that he had little love for the Ranan and little respect for the Toshaki. The rumors were that he believed the barbarian threat was imaginary, which would seem to place him with the majority of northerners. Despite this belief, he held the Emperor's new governor in high regard, which is to say that he had respect for the Shonto, and this Shonto in particular. Shonto was not sure how Lord Taiki felt about the new dynasty, and it worried him somewhat. This was the man Shonto hoped to win to his side, and he realized that things in the north would be much more difficult without Taiki support.

Traditional methods of forming alliances would not be applicable in a province that was so insular, especially when it was clear that Shonto's stay there would be brief. A marriage between the Shonto and the Taiki was not feasible, not only because of their difference in position, but Lord Taiki's only son and heir had just recently celebrated his fourth birthday. Of course, such an arrangement was not unheard of, but Shonto would never subject

Lady Nishima to such an indignity: he adored her far too much for the good of his family, he realized.

When Shonto took leave of Komawara and Lord Akima, the two men stood on the dock saying nothing, yet neither made a move to leave, as though there was something to be said but neither could grasp it.

Finally Lord Akima ended the silence. "Perhaps, Lord Komawara, if you stand close enough, you will one day be mistaken for a governor yourself." He bowed and walked down the quay to the place where his guards waited with his sampan.

Komawara felt like a man caught thieving: there was no denial possible— it *was* what he secretly hoped for, so secretly that he barely admitted it to himself. Yet old Akima had seen it easily. Seh, the young lord told himself, the welfare of my province is my true concern.

Akima, Komawara thought, is an old man, well past his prime, unable to see even the most obvious things: like the change in the pattern of barbarian raids. Yet was it not true that virtually all the lords of Seh agreed with Akima in this matter? Was the old man right? Was the lure of the Governor's Palace really what attracted him?

Komawara stepped into his sampan and seated himself without even a nod to his guard or boatmen, so lost in thought was he. The old lord's remark had stung him more than he would ever have expected.

"I find this an interesting habit, Lord Shonto, perhaps one that is native only to my own province." Lord Taiki said. "I cannot understand how anyone can take a position on an entire dynasty. Certainly I can weigh the accomplishments of a past dynasty and decide if, on balance, they were good or bad. But this desire to take a position on an Imperial Family that has existed only eight years and has placed only two Emperors upon the Throne— I can only judge one Emperor at a time, myself. The Yamaku may well produce a second Jenni the Serene, but I have no way of knowing."

Lord Shonto and Lord Taiki walked in the garden of the Governor's Palace. They were followed by General Hojo and Shuyun, while Lord Taiki's young son Jima ran around them in circles, imitating the motions of a man on a horse and occasionally charging Shuyun with a shout and then veering off after he had run the monk through with an imaginary sword.

A path of raked gravel led them through the trees of late autumn, almost bare of leaves; those few that were left were the most beautifully colored.

Wind cedars that had been shaped into living sculptures were placed where they would create the most striking effect, here among large gray rocks that suggested a cliff, and there beside a small carp pond. The palace walls blocked most of the wind, so the sunlight seemed to have more warmth than would have been expected.

"The present Emperor has allowed the thoroughfares of our Empire to fall into the hands of bandits. He has forced all trade beyond the Empire to take place through only one port, a port that is not close to Seh. This means that we must bring our ships into Yankura, instead of into our own province, pay exorbitant taxes and warehousing costs, then we must ship our goods a thousand rih on a canal that is infested with criminals." Lord Taiki gestured with his hands as if to say, "And you ask me my opinion of this dynasty?"

Shonto shook his head. He was sympathetic to the problem, and he would even state, in the right circumstances, that he felt this was unjust, but there was little he could do about it.

Lord Taiki had turned out to be an immensely likable man, not that "likability" was a quality that Shonto felt was terribly important, but all the same this northern lord radiated common sense and fairness and concern for others in a way that one almost never saw in the aristocrats of Wa.

"Lord Taiki, your logic is undeniable, and I must say that I wish others would cease this prejudging of entire Imperial lines—leave that to history and the historians—we need to be concerned with today. If the barbarians are truly diminished and represent no threat, I for one would be relieved. But these persistent raids have caused concern at court. If the barbarians are no threat, then why do we not stop the raids? That is the question continually asked."

"Certainly, Lord Shonto, you know the reason. A handful of barbarians in a large desert are very hard to find. We cannot fortify our entire border, it is not possible. And besides, these raids are little more than an annoyance; we of Seh are used to them. People often drown in the canals of the capital; you do not fill them all in with sand. It is true that occasionally the barbarians kill people of my province, but very few of them lately, and there is little we can do. You do not send an army to fight gnats; you learn to defend yourself and live with the occasional bite, that is all."

Shonto smiled. "I understand what you say, Lord Taiki, it is only that I would like more evidence that the barbarians are so small a threat. Because you have only seen one tiger in a forest, it may not be wise to assume that there is only one. I will not write to my Emperor that the tribes are diminished until I can clearly see that it is the truth. I agree that these few raids would seem to indicate that the tribes are small, but perhaps it indicates other things though I confess I do not know what. I would only stress that we do not truly know what the desert is hiding from us."

Lord Taiki stopped suddenly. "Jima-sum? What are you playing at?"

The young child knelt at the edge of the gravel, staring fixedly into the base of a wisteria vine that climbed the nearby wall.

"Jima-sum?" the lord said and started forward.

Shonto gripped his arm suddenly. "Do not move."

Hojo reached out and took the lord's other arm. "Lord Shonto is right. No one must move."

There, within reach of the child, the head of a sand-viper seemed to hover above the bush. It stood erect, ready to strike. The three men held their breath for an instant.

"Let me go," Lord Taiki said. "I must draw its anger to me."

"Lord Taiki, if you move, it will strike your son and then you. It is that fast." Shuyun said.

"Shuyun, can you save him?" Lord Shonto asked.

Shuyun did not speak for a second and when he did his voice seemed to come from farther away. "I cannot reach the boy before the viper, Lord Shonto." The monk paused and Shonto could hear his breathing change rhythm. "I may be able to save his life, though at a cost."

"What cost, Brother?" Taiki asked.

"He will suffer the fate of Kamu."

Lord Taiki let out a long, ragged breath. "Is there no other way, Brother?"

"I cannot stop it. You know what will happen when he is bitten."

The lord went silent and then Shonto felt the muscles relax somewhat in the arm he still held.

"Jima-sum, do not be afraid, my son. You must do everything Brother Shuyun tells you to do. Do you hear me? Everything."

Shuyun began to slowly shift his weight and turn his body.

"Lord Shonto, please take your hand, slowly, from your sword hilt. Very slowly.

"Jima-sum, you must close your eyes and then extend the hand closest to me toward the snake," Shuyun said quietly and Shonto felt the father's arm, which he still held, go tense again.

The child hesitated. He shifted as though he would bolt, and the snake swayed toward his face but stopped as the child froze.

"Jima-sum! You must do as Shuyun-sum has said. You must be brave. Close your eyes, now."

Tears welled out of closed eyes, but the boy raised a small clenched hand toward the snake—a hand that trembled.

The viper struck. Lord Shonto felt the sword leave his scabbard though Shuyun was as much of a blur as the snake. Everything then seemed to occur simultaneously: the snake seemed to disappear toward the child; Jima screamed and pulled back his hand, but his hand was no longer there. Shonto saw the snake's body writhing on the ground, the head, jaws twitching, beside it. Shuyun has swung the sword twice, Shonto found himself thinking: twice and Shonto had not been able to focus on either movement. Shonto's sword lay on the ground and he realized that Shuyun was holding an unconscious child and staunching the flow of blood from the stub of his wrist.

Lord Taiki was moving now toward his son.

"Does he live?"

"Yes, Lord, and I will not let him die. We must carry him into the palace. Lord Hojo, could you please find a servant to bring my trunk?"

Shonto sat reading by the light of a lamp. He read the letter twice and then refolded it carefully and placed it on his small writing table. It was from Lord Taiki.

Shonto touched his fingertips together at his chin as though he were praying, but those who knew him well would recognize this action as one of his several poses of thought.

The snake in the garden did not find its way there unaided, that was certain, and the snake's intended victim was not a small boy, who would now live his life without the benefit of two hands. Shonto shook his head. The letter had been infused, understandably, with an air of deep sadness. And Shonto found some passages quite unsettling.

> As you might expect it was all rather confusing for a small child: he does not realize that it was your Spiritual Advisor who took his hand, but believes instead that it was the viper.

His mother is understandably distraught and there is little that I can say that will comfort her. The snake was not meant to find a small boy playing in the garden, so it is possible that the loss of my son's hand has served to save another's life. Who can say?

It is certain, however, that Jima-sum would not be alive if not for the actions of your advisor, Brother Shuyun. Even for one who has made many hard decisions I can say that never have I been forced to make a choice more difficult than the one I made in your garden.

But my son lives, and for this I am forever in your debt.

I have considered the things we discussed and presented your arguments to my own staff. There is no denying what you say: the evidence we have does not prove conclusively that the barbarians are diminished. Perhaps there is a viper hiding in the desert—I do not know—but I believe we must find out.

Yes, Shonto thought, we must.

Twenty-nine

Having campaigned for seven years
And defeated the armies
Of the rebel general of Chou,
I was then spoken of at Court
As a threat to my Emperor.
Behind the sleeve I was said to be
Vain and ambitious
With my gaze fixed on the Throne.

So it is that I have come
To the house by the lake,
The House of Seven Willows,
And ask as a reward
For the years of my service
Only to rise each morning
To the sight of snow-covered Mount Jaika
Reflected in calm water.

> *The House of Seven Willows,*
> *by Lord Daigi Sanyamu*

IT WAS A three-decked Imperial barge ornately carved with dragons and cranes and painted crimson and gold. The Emperor's pennant was displayed high on the stern, and on carved staffs to either side of it the black pennant of the Commander of the Imperial Guard and the deep blue pennant bearing the Choka Hawk granted to the Jaku family waved in the gentle wind of the boat's passing.

Oarsmen pulled and the barge swept through the capital at first light, scattering all other craft before it. Along the quays people of all classes bowed low, wondering which Imperial Prince or Major Counselor hurried by to do the Emperor's bidding. Many of those watching offered a prayer to Botahara asking long life for the esteemed occupant of the barge, whoever it might be.

On the upper deck, inside the house, the two brothers Jaku—Tadamoto and Katta—sat on silk cushions and drank hot plum wine which the elder brother ladled from a heated cauldron. Servants set trays on stands beside the small table that sat between the two brothers. Once the trays were settled Jaku waved the servants out, for this was the traditional meal of farewell and the occasion required that there be no servants.

The meal itself consisted of the simplest foods, but each course represented the participant's hopes for the journey.

Tadamoto raised his wine bowl. "May you encounter the finest of companions on your journey, brother."

Jaku raised his bowl in return. "You honor me with your concern, Tadamoto-sum. May your companions be many and light of heart, as I'm sure they will be." They both drank, raised their glasses to each other again, and then set them back on the table.

"The Emperor does you great honor, brother, to send you off in one of the Imperial Family's own barges," Tadamoto said in his scholar's voice. As he spoke, he began to serve the first course, a broth soup made with a rare spicy mushroom.

Jaku nodded. "It is one of your many strengths, Tado-sum, this understanding of honor." Katta sipped his wine and tiny beads of the liquid clung to the ends of his luxurious mustache. "If our father were still alive, he would be proud to see what you've become. A respected scholar, a confidant of the Emperor, a man desired by the most beautiful women, and still one who honors his elders and retains an unusual loyalty to his family. He would be more than proud of you, my younger brother."

Tadamoto bowed slightly, as though modestly acknowledging praise. "I thank you for your words, brother, you are too generous, especially for one of your talents and position." He placed a bowl of soup before his brother. "May you carry the warmth of your family's home with you throughout your journey."

Jaku bowed slightly in acknowledgment. "And may the warmth of our home surround you in my absence."

Tadamoto bowed slightly in return and they fell silent for a moment as they ate. A fish hawker could be heard passing by, calling out the day's wares.

"I have not forgotten, Katta-sum, that it was your efforts that raised the Jaku from obscurity into the Emperor's favor." Tadamoto met his brother's gaze. "Just as it is your loyal service that has gained you your present appointment. Our Emperor is very wise and has long been aware of your labors. It is this wisdom that has allowed him to understand, as few others do, how well your efforts serve his purpose." Tadamoto glanced out the slightly open shoji as though suddenly taken by the passing scene.

"The common person who bows before you can little understand how tireless your efforts have been, Katta-sum. They do not understand what it means to reach above oneself, to exercise one's grasp." He began to raise the porcelain spoon to his lips, then stopped. "The common people are bound by superstition and fear and feel that it is the will of the gods that they occupy their place on this plane. These people do not even dream of moving up in the world, of knowing a life of refinement, or of courting a lady of high birth; but by and large they are not dissatisfied and thank the gods for what they have." Tadamoto raised a spoonful of the hot liquid to his mouth and drank it down slowly, taking time to savor its spices. "Not everyone constantly desires more, Katta-sum. Many feel they have been blessed to simply be alive—to be allowed to serve their Emperor would be a dream beyond imagining. And as the Emperor's boat passes, they bow readily and without resentment."

"It is a difference between you and me, Tadamoto-sum. Bowing is not an exercise I enjoy."

"That, brother, is obvious."

"But you see, unlike the common man, I do not fear the anger of the gods nor do I feel that my hands will not be strong enough. I simply reach out; it is my nature to do so and as a result the Jaku have risen with me." Jaku finished his soup and began to serve the next course, noodles covered with a pungent sauce made of marsh root.

"It is as you say, Katta-sum, you have brought the family honor. This cannot be denied. But now what will you bring us? Is it not enough to have become the Emperor's right hand? Is it not enough to have risen to the Third Rank and to have every reason to believe you will be raised to the Second, to one day perhaps be titled? I do not understand you, Katta-sum—how is it that the same blood flows in our veins?"

Jaku stopped in his preparations and placed his large hands on his thighs. He appeared to be completely calm as though he discussed the weather or the charms of the country in springtime. "It is a question I have often asked myself. I, for instance, would put loyalty to my House above desire for a woman, especially if desire for that woman were to endanger my House." He returned to his preparations and then set a bowl of noodles and steaming sauce before his brother.

Tadamoto did not seem to notice the food. "Ah. So this correspondence that you carry on so secretly does not endanger our House? I am glad to know this. You are aware of what the Emperor thinks of this matter?"

"This correspondence should do anything but endanger the Jaku. The lady in question is, after all, a woman free to make her own choices not bound to a husband . . . or lover. As for the Emperor's concern; I, for one, do not understand it. I cannot even imagine how such a trivial matter came to the attention of the Son of Heaven."

Tadamoto lit incense from the flame of a small lamp and placed it in a silver burner. "May Botahara bless your journey, brother," Tadamoto said quietly and they both raised their wine bowls again as they began their next course.

"I was also surprised," Tadamoto said, as though there had been no interruption, "when the Emperor mentioned this correspondence to me. Perhaps it was the unfortunate incident with the Lady Nishima on the canal that piqued the Emperor's curiosity. Who can say? No matter, I have assured the Emperor that, to the best of my knowledge, you do not continue to see the lady. I hope, as always, that I have spoken the truth."

"It concerns me little whether, in this matter, you told the truth, brother," Jaku said, leveling his gaze at his kinsman.

Tadamoto looked down at his wine. "It does concern the Emperor, however."

"Ah, yes, the Emperor. In your reading of history, brother, has it come to your attention that dynasties do not just rise, they have also been known to fall?"

Tadamoto shook his head as though overcome by great sadness. "It has not escaped my notice, General, nor has it escaped my notice that in all of our history there have been only six dynasties while the same period has seen the fall of ten thousand ambitious advisors. It is a point that I feel is worthy of careful consideration, just as I think you should consider the meaning of your present appointment. The Emperor does not need to act as a teacher to his advisors and would only do so when such an advisor was dear to him."

Jaku banged his fist on the table but then stopped the rush of anger and calmed himself. His face became almost serene. "I am not a child in need of instruction, brother. The Emperor owes much of his security to the Jaku and I have not forgotten this."

"Perhaps not, Katta-sum, but Denji Gorge has not been forgotten either."

Jaku now shook his head sadly, as though he had just heard a terrible lie from a favored son. "I am loyal to my family and their interests, brother. Has that been forgotten?"

"It is something we have in common, Katta-sum. I, too, am concerned with the interests of our family. I would not want to see the Jaku's position undermined by ill-considered ambition."

"Was it ill-considered ambition that secured us our present position, brother? Was it fear of our own shadows that brought the Jaku to the Emperor's attention? It is interesting to me that suddenly you have taken it upon yourself to arbitrate in this matter, deciding what is and what is not in the interests of our family. It must be a terrible burden to bear at your age. Of course, the Emperor must be delighted to see such a man making these decisions—a man with no personal ambition." Katta held his hand over his wine bowl as though warming himself—a hand that showed no sign of the tremor of anger. "I have forgotten to congratulate you, Colonel Jaku. I understand that you will act as Commander of the Imperial Guard while I am away from the capital. Your lack of ambition seems to have worked admirably for you."

Tadamoto stared down at his hands. "Perhaps this journey you undertake will allow you time to reflect on these matters we have discussed, Katta-sum. I believe that was the Emperor's true purpose in assigning you this task. Few rulers would overlook the implications of a situation such as Denji Gorge. You are being treated with great kindness, brother, though I know you do not see it. If I may give you some advice: don't underestimate our Emperor, Katta-sum. It is a grave and dangerous error; dangerous not just for yourself."

Katta said nothing but only stared at his younger brother with a look of undisguised contempt. The steady rhythm of the oarsmen stopped and the boat glided on smoothly.

"We have come to the edge of the city, brother," Jaku said coldly, "from here I go on alone."

Tadamoto nodded, but his gaze fell on the serving table where the final course of sweet rice cakes waited; the course that was offered for luck on the journey. He bowed deeply and rose to his feet, not meeting his brother's eyes. "It saddens me, Katta-sum, but perhaps you will reconsider in time. I am truly your loyal brother, more loyal than you realize. I would not see you . . ." Tadamoto stopped in mid-sentence as Katta rose and turned away, leaving the deckhouse by the rear shoji.

Jaku Tadamoto stood for a moment staring at the screen, struggling with an urge to go after his brother. This is not the companion of my childhood, Tadamoto reminded himself, nor is this one of the child's moods. This is a grown man who makes difficult decisions and lives by them. He will not listen to me. Only time can teach such a man . . . if he has that much time. Turning on his heel, Tadamoto left the cabin for the boat waiting to return him to the Island Palace.

From the upper deck Jaku Katta watched his brother go, watched his sampan disappear into the mist and the traffic on the canal. He gripped the railing that was wet with condensation and watched his breath come out in a fine mist. The cold of late autumn was in the air and a breeze from the far off ocean pulled at his uniform.

Jaku shook his head. The sight of his brother with the Emperor's Sonsa still haunted him. None of my lieutenants would have succumbed to such a ploy, he told himself. Jaku felt an unusual sadness come over him. My own brother, he thought, my own blood. He wiped his hand along the rail, sending a shower of water raining down onto the lower deck. Did not Hakata say that betrayal was the greatest unhappiness of honorable men? He dried his hand on his robe. Jaku Katta, the general thought, is not happy.

Turning from the rail, he returned to his cabin and, sitting down, ladled himself a bowl of hot wine. From the sleeve pocket of his outer jacket he took a sheet of pale green paper. It was the poem he had received a few days earlier from the lady in question, Lady Nishima Fanisan Shonto.

The wind whispers its secrets
To so many,
It is difficult to tell
From where the wind blows.

Perhaps it is loyalty we should speak of.

Jaku sipped his cha and read the poem again. He felt a thrill every time he looked at the elegant hand of the Lady Nishima. There was a part of him that would hardly believe such a woman could be his—yet he did not doubt that she was; or would have been if he had not been forced to leave the capital so suddenly. He had tried to see the lady before his departure, but she had been ill and unable to receive him. He cursed aloud. His plans were falling to pieces all around him and the Lady Nishima was central to his designs. Damn Tadamoto!

Jaku took another drink of his wine and calmed himself, breathing slowly. It was not over yet. The Black Tiger was still alive. There were still those at court who were indebted to him and there were even a few of his people, missed in the purge, who remained near the Emperor. It was far from over. That coward Tadamoto could do him little harm now, and Jaku's agents in the palace would be looking for a chance to undermine the younger brother's position with the Son of Heaven. The Emperor trusted no one, so it would not be difficult to arouse suspicions about the brilliant young colonel. Jaku smiled. It would be almost too easy.

Thirty

Our river boat
Pushes its bow into blue waters,
Dividing the rushing currents
Even as my spirit divides;
Half staying with you,
Half going north.

In the depths of the sky
The last geese are bound
For the hidden south.
I would send my spirit with them,
Stragglers all.

THE LADY NISHIMA swirled her brush in water, watching the black ink curl out from it in sweeping coils. I will call the series *Secret Journeys*, she thought as she read the poem again. Kitsura-sum and Lady Okara may see them after we arrive in Seh—a chronicle of our journey, and of my inner journey also. She set the brush carefully on a jade rest carved in the shape of a tiger, then rose from her cushion. Through the stern window she could just see the bow of the boat behind as it cut through the mist and the constant drizzle that seemed to travel with them.

The mist over the canal
and the sound of rain
on wooden decks,
Traveling companions.

Yes, Nishima thought, that will be part of *Secret Journeys* also.

She went back to her cushion and the charcoal fire that warmed her small cabin. Three days now they had been on the canal and she had not dared to show her face on deck. Lady Okara had gone out that morning and told Nishima that the mists would certainly hide her from the curious, but Nishima decided it would be better to wait. They were still too close to the capital for her to feel they had truly escaped. Kitsura shared this feeling, so the two young women spent their days below, often sharing meals and talking late into the night.

After lengthy discussion in the Omawara House, it had been decided that it would be best for Kitsura to travel north with Nishima before an official offer was made on behalf of the Emperor. No doubt Kitsura's flight would still be taken as an affront to the person of the Emperor, but it was believed the Omawara were prominent enough to survive such a thing. It was, after all, entirely the Emperor's fault for not conforming to the proper etiquette of the situation.

Of course it was uncommon for a family not to want their daughter to become an Empress, but Kitsura had confided to Nishima something her father had said: "This is a dangerous situation. If there is a new Empress there will be new heirs and that will raise the jealousy of the Princes and their supporters. If the Emperor were to fall or to pass on through illness, the new Empress and her children would be in grave danger."

So the Lady Kitsura Omawara set out secretly for the north in the company of her cousin and the famous painter, Lady Okara Haroshu.

A rumor was spread that a Lady Okara Tuamo traveled north with her two over-protected daughters. The name Tuamo was so common that a person bearing it could belong to any of a dozen families of moderate position. The few guards and servants who accompanied the women, though well enough appointed, wore no livery and could have been the staff of any well-to-do minor House. They would raise no suspicions.

Nishima rang a small gong and a servant appeared. "Please have my inkstone and brushes cleaned and ask my companions if they will join me for the evening meal." The servant took up the writing utensils, bowed, and left silently.

Is she afraid? Nishima wondered. Of course, no one on her staff knew all the reasons for this journey, but they understood that it was made in secret for they were, of necessity, party to the ruse. No doubt that had an effect on them. The Shonto have such loyal staff, Nishima thought, would I be like this if my karma had brought me into this world to a completely different station?

It was, she knew, idle speculation—duty was duty and the spirit that appeared in the world as Nishima Fanisan Shonto understood this concept only too well. It was duty that took her to Seh and duty that led her to carry the coins which she could feel lying against the soft skin of her waist. Despite her rather romantic view of this "Secret Journey" Nishima understood the danger she could be in. The coins she carried were like a terrible secret; one that she was sure had the potential to tear the Empire apart.

Rising again, she went to the small port which looked out the starboard side. Calypta trees lined the bank, standing in a litter of fallen leaves. Like tears, Nishima thought as she gazed at the scattered leaves, and the trees seemed bent under a weight of sadness. She felt this sense of melancholy herself as though it traveled through the medium of the mist.

The calypta gave way to a grassy shore and in the clearing stood a shrine to the plague-dead. She made a sign to Botahara. "May they attain perfection in their next lives," Nishima whispered.

Less than ten years since the plague had swept through Wa and already it seemed a distant memory, as though it had been a chapter of ancient history, yet it had taken a huge toll, including many people close to Nishima, even her true father. It is too terrible to remember, Nishima thought. We bury the memories so that they only surface in our most frightening dreams. A knock on the shoji brought her back to the present.

"Yes?"

"Lady Kitsura, my lady."

Nishima smiled, "Please show her in."

A rustle of silk and the scent of a fine perfume preceded the young aristocrat through the door.

"Ah, the artist has been at work." Kitsura said, glancing at the paper on Nishima's writing table.

"Notes to myself," Nishima said, the polite response when one did not wish to share one's writings with another.

Kitsura nodded; they had many understandings, and this was one—poetry was not shared until the author felt ready.

Lady Kitsura wore informal robes, though very beautifully dyed and embroidered, and matched in color by an artist's eye. Her long black hair hung down her back in a carefully tended cascade.

Nishima felt a flash of envy as she looked at her cousin. It is not surprising that even the Emperor desires her, Nishima thought. But there was something more there, a tightness around the eyes and the mouth. She worries, Nishima realized.

The two women drew cushions up to the heat, glad of each other's company.

"I am concerned about our companion, Kitsu-sum. Do you think the Lady Okara resents making this journey?"

Kitsura turned her lovely eyes to the fire and taking up the poker began to rearrange the coals efficiently. "She is troubled Nishi-sum. We have both seen this, though she tries to hide it. But I am not convinced that this is because she suddenly finds herself on the canal to Seh. It seems to me, though I am not sure why I think this, that it is something else that haunts the Lady Okara. My sense is that for Oka-sum, this is not a journey to Seh but a journey inward. . . . I believe she comes willingly though perhaps not happily."

"A secret journey," Nishima almost whispered.

A knock on the shoji was answered by Kitsura. "Cha," she said to her cousin and a servant entered bearing a cha service on a simple bamboo tray. "Look how completely we play the country peers," Kitsura laughed gesturing to the tray. "Am I overdressed for my part?"

"You are always overdressed for your part, cousin," Nishima said innocently.

Kitsura laughed. "Oh. A tongue as sharp as her brush."

"Now, Kitsu-sum, you know that I jest."

"Oh, yes, I do, and it is only fitting; I have always been jealous of your abundance of talent."

"You who have no need to be jealous of anyone's talent." Both women laughed. They had known each other all their lives and viewed even their differences with affection.

Kitsura ladled cha into a bowl and offered it to Nishima. "This first cup must be for you, cousin."

"Of course it must," Nishima said taking the cup that etiquette dictated she must first refuse.

Kitsura laughed her musical laughter. "So the mischievous Nishi-sum of my childhood seems to have returned."

"It is the pleasure of your company, cousin. How can I not be gay in your presence."

Tasting her cha, Kitsura smiled. "You know me too well, Nishi-sum. I am honored that you try to cheer me."

Nishima turned her cha bowl in her hands, suddenly serious. "You worry about your father, Kitsu-sum, but he has made his peace with Botahara. It is we who are in danger, we who are still trapped by the concerns of the flesh."

"What you say is wisdom, cousin."

"Easy wisdom, Kitsu-sum; it is not my father who is ill," Nishima said quietly.

The other woman nodded. "He often speaks of you—asks after you. I read him your poems and he praises them."

"The Lord Omawara is too kind, far too kind."

Kitsura nodded without thinking, her focus elsewhere. "Anyone else would have had his daughter marry the Emperor, though her life would have been a misery. Perhaps his . . . nearness to completion allows him to see this life differently."

"I believe that is true, Kitsu-sum. Perhaps we can discuss this with Brother Shuyun when we arrive in Seh."

"Ah, yes, Brother Shuyun." Kitsura said, obviously ready to change the subject. "Tell me about him, cousin. Is the rumor true that he shattered an iroko table with only a gesture?"

"Kitsura-sum!" Nishima said in mock disappointment. "You listen to rumors? It is not true. I was not present when this occurred, but I know he did not accomplish such a thing with a gesture. Tanaka told me he shattered the table by pressing on it with his hand, though he was sitting at the time."

"Ah. I did not really believe that he could have done such a thing without some direct force. Only Botahara could have done that. But still, that was quite an amazing act even so; wouldn't you agree?"

"Oh, yes. Tanaka said that if he had not seen it with his own eyes he would never have believed it."

"I look forward to meeting our Brother. Is he so forceful in appearance?"

Nishima shrugged. "He is not large, by any means, and he is very soft spoken, yet he does seem to possess some . . . power. I cannot describe it—a quiet power, like a tiger possesses. You will see."

"Like a black tiger?" Kitsura asked with a wicked smile.

"You have been listening to rumors haven't you?" Nishima said, though she was not as displeased as she sounded.

"I'm not sure, cousin. Are these rumors that I hear?"

Nishima sipped her cha, turning the cup in her hands the way Lord Shonto did when he was thinking. "I do not know what the rumors say, Kitsu-sum. The general in question has expressed his interest and I have not been as discouraging perhaps as one in my station should be."

Kitsura shrugged. "One cannot go on discouraging all those whom one meets simply because they are not suitable husbands. After all, one is not always looking for a husband," she gestured to herself, "as you can see." She smiled. "He is certainly the most handsome man in the Empire, or at least the most handsome I have seen. But can he be trusted, do you think?"

Setting her cha down, it was Nishima's turn to take up the poker and move the coals. "I don't know, Kitsura-sum. There was the incident in our garden. He is certainly very brave. I don't know." She thrust the poker into the fire and looked up. "I want to trust him. . . ."

"I understand, but he does seem too much the opportunist to me. I don't know how things stand, Nishi-sum, but I would be careful of how close I would allow such a man." She smiled engagingly. "I would allow him no closer than my own rooms on dark evenings . . . but not often."

Lady Nishima laughed softly. "He is, no doubt, the pawn of our Emperor, and our Emperor will be none too pleased with the Ladies Kitsura and Nishima when he finds that they have slipped away in the night like the heroines of an old romance." Nishima thrust the poker deep into the fire again. "How have our lives suddenly become so strange?"

Kitsura reached out her hand and touched her cousin's sleeve. "The word strange has no meaning in our lives. Our ancestors have lived in caves while they fought to regain their lands. Both of us have the blood of the old Emperors and know that Shatsima did not endure the wilds for seven years to ennoble her spirit but because she would never resign herself to the loss of her throne—and her uncle learned that it had been a mistake to allow the child to live, for a girl becomes a woman.

"What has history demanded of the Shonto? The sacrifice of a son in battle. A lifetime of exile. A hundred years of warfare.

"To flee to Seh in secret is nothing, it is child's play. And you, Nishima, are both Shonto and Fanisan. Who is this young upstart Jaku that he thinks to approach the heir of such history? If his intentions are what one would expect of an opportunist, it is Jaku I will be sorry for, not the Lady Nishima; he cannot know what he toys with.

"The Fanisan carved their fief out of the wilds, fighting both rival Houses and numberless barbarians. Have we forgotten this? Does Jaku Katta know that I carry a knife hidden in my robes and that I know how to use it? He is used to the ladies of the court, to the families that rise and fall at the whim of the Emperor. That is not the Omawara nor the Fanisan nor the Shonto. What we do now is not strange; what is strange is that we have not had to do such a thing until now."

Nishima sipped her cha. "I know what you say is more than true. Yet we do forget. Even Okara-sum's family has had its ordeals and the Shonto, of course, are the Shonto." The young woman straightened suddenly. "Excuse my weakness, Kitsu-sum, it is being shut up like this that begins to wear on me. Do you think that tomorrow we may dare to show ourselves?"

Glancing toward the stern windows, Kitsura nodded. "I don't think we need fear discovery in this fog, and it is possible that there is no one on any of these boats who would recognize us. We are already some distance from the capital. Fujima-sha was passed just after sunrise."

"We make excellent time," Nishima said. The conversation had lifted her spirits considerably. As the miles went by, she felt freer than she had in weeks. "I don't want to wait until tomorrow, I want to breathe fresh air now."

Clapping her hands together, Kitsura rose quickly to her feet. "I agree. I have been cloistered too long."

Sliding the shoji aside, the two young women mounted the steps to the deck, gathering their long robes about them, their sleeves swaying as they went.

Both sails and current moved the boats along and the Shonto guards who acted as rowers and crew lounged about the deck in small groups talking and laughing. The guards fell silent as the two women appeared so that the only sounds to be heard were the cries of the gulls and surge of the ship as it pushed north.

The mist moved among the trees on the shores, wafted among the groves by a light breeze. Many of the trees were barren of leaves while others appeared in fall hues muted by the fog.

"It is a scene for Okara-sum's brush," Nishima said quietly, as though the sound of her voice would break a spell and all of the beauty would disappear.

"It is a scene for the Lady Nishima's brush," Kitsura said equally softly.

"Perhaps. I like the swamp spears growing along the banks. They seem to have their own strongly developed sense of composition."

"Yes, that is true." Kitsura did not finish, for there was a creaking sound that carried to them and then a splash. They both froze. And then laughed at the other's reaction.

"We do not seem to exhibit quite the spirit of our indomitable ancestors," Kitsura said.

Nishima nodded, but she did not relax. "Should we go below, do you think?"

"Let's wait a moment. It is probably nothing. The canal is full of boats, we must remember, and there is nothing terribly suspicious about two ladies enjoying the scenery." Kitsura answered.

The creaking continued though it remained impossible to tell from which direction it came. Suddenly out of the mist the bow of a small boat appeared almost beside them. Nishima and Kitsura stepped back from the rail into the protection of the quarter deck.

"Guards!" Nishima whispered, and both ladies sank to their knees, afraid to cross the deck to the companionway.

"If they see us hiding, they will certainly be suspicious." Kitsura whispered in her cousin's ear.

"But it is us they look for. We must get below."

At a word from one "sailor," the nearest group of Shonto guards moved themselves to the rail, hiding the two women. Scrambling quickly, Nishima and Kitsura almost pushed each other down the steps. Hearing the clatter, Lady Okara emerged from her cabin and was confronted by the frightened faces of her companions.

"What is it?"

"Imperial Guardsmen, Okara-sum."

The painter stepped aside. "Come quickly," she whispered and followed them into her cabin. Voices could be heard alongside, but the words were unclear.

"What do they say?" Lady Okara asked as Nishima dared a few steps toward the half-open port.

"A fleet of Imperial Guards has attached itself to our own." She leaned closer. "I cannot hear . . . Imperial Edicts concerning canals. Something else . . ." she turned to face her companions. "Botahara save us! They enquire after the young women aboard."

The creaking of the oars began again and the voices faded. None of the women spoke for a few seconds.

"We do nothing illegal," Lady Okara said finally. "We may go where we choose. The Emperor would not dare interfere with us."

Footsteps on the stairs echoed in the silence. A knock on the shoji and then a maid's face appeared in the opening. "Pardon my intrusion. Captain Tenda of our guard wishes to speak with Lady Nishima."

"By all means, send him in," Nishima said.

The screen slid wide and a Shonto guard dressed like a common soldier knelt in the opening.

"Yes, Captain, please tell us what just occurred."

"Senior guard officers were passing up the line of our fleet, Lady Nishima. They questioned me as to the passengers of this craft. They saw Lady Kitsura and you, my lady, but I'm sure they did not recognize you. I explained that as you were dressed informally, you were embarrassed to be seen by officers of the Emperor's guard. Recent Imperial Edicts have been read and as a result Imperial Guards have been sent out across all the Empire with orders to make the roads and canals safe again. It seems that, at least temporarily, we will have the protection of Imperial forces. That is all I am able to report." He bowed and remained kneeling.

"Thank you, Captain. Your answer to their question was most clever. I will be sure to report this to my father. Thank you." The captain bowed again and was gone.

"What unusual timing," Kitsura said. "Though, of course, the canals have deserved this attention for too long. Yet is it not strange that the Son of Heaven would chose this moment when we are secretly on the canal?"

Sinking down near the charcoal burner, Lady Okara rubbed her hands over its warmth. "The world beyond my own island is something I know little about, but is it not possible that this is mere coincidence?"

"I think you are right Oka-sum," Nishima said. "We grow too suspicious. Perhaps it is due to being shut up with little knowledge of what goes on around us. We must send men ahead to gather some news. Sailors love to gossip, so we might learn something of value. We will see."

This was agreed upon and the Lady Okara and her two "daughters" sat down to their evening meal, followed by music and the reading of poetry.

It was long after darkness had fallen. The Lady Nishima was alone in her cabin, embroidering a sash by lamplight, when a maid knocked on the screen.

"Pardon my intrusion, my lady. Captain Tenda says he must speak with you despite the hour. He is most adamant."

"I will see him," Nishima said setting her work aside.

The captain knelt in the door frame; the cabin was so small that he dared come no closer without being disrespectful.

"Captain?"

"Lady Nishima, please excuse my presumption. I felt this was a matter too important to wait until morning."

"Of course. Go on."

"An Imperial Guard boat came alongside a moment ago and a guard handed me this letter." He produced a folded sheet of mulberry paper of gray-blue with a stalk of fall grain attached to it. "He said it was for Lady Nishima, and though I protested that he had made a mistake he had his men row off. Shall we lower a boat and try to return it, my lady?"

Nishima felt as though her thoughts had suddenly been disassociated from her body. It was as though the mind floated freely in the air some distance away watching the entire scene. She was surprised to hear herself speak.

"I see no point in that. Leave the letter with me. Thank you."

The guard looked shocked. "Excuse me, my lady, but is there not something we should do?"

"Do you follow the teaching of the Perfect Master?"

"Certainly, my lady, but . . ."

"Then you might pray. Thank you, Captain." The guard bowed and closed the shoji.

Nishima watched herself bend forward and retrieve the letter, yet she did not feel its texture and could not tell if it was warm or cool. We are discovered, she told herself. We thought the Emperor could be deceived, but we were the fools. What will he do?

She unfolded the paper slowly as though her sense of time no longer related to reality. Was this the state Brother Satake had spoken of? She opened the letter to the light and from her station, floating above her body, she read:

The wind from Chou-San
Bears us toward our destinations,
Yet it warms me to think
That I draw nearer to you.

   Your presence is known only to me.

"Katta-sum," Nishima whispered. The letter slipped from her fingers and fell to the cushion. She felt her senses return suddenly, joyously. She felt desire singing along all the nerves of her body and then just as suddenly she felt terrible, terrible fear. How could he have known? Every precaution possible had been taken. Botahara save her, she felt suddenly that he must know her very thoughts, her most secret desires.

Thirty-one

IT HAD BEEN months since Shonto had sat a horse and despite his awareness of what was being done to his unsuspecting muscles, he was glad to be riding again—glad to be beyond the long reach of the city and the court of Rhojo-ma.

The governor's party crested a small rise which afforded the briefest glimpse of a stone tower—gray blocks covered in lintel vine . . . then gone. Soon, Shonto thought, then I will see if the reports I receive are true.

The new Governor of Seh was on a tour of inspection within a day's ride of the city. The expressed object of his concern was the inner line of Seh's defense; a broadly spread chain of towers and, in some areas, sections of wall, built a hundred years before. Built in a time when the barbarians were truly strong.

The outer precincts of the province had fallen to the tribes then, and during a long, relentless war, the inner defenses had been built. The Imperial Armies had stopped the barbarians there, though driving them back to the borders of the Empire had taken three long years. In the end, the barbarians had been broken and the remains of their invading armies had been swept into the wastes of the northern steppe, and then into the deep desert—disappearing as they always did; without a trace.

Shonto's own grandfather had been a very young general in that war, perhaps the only time that the Empire had been truly threatened . . . from outside its own borders, that is. To say that one's grandfather or great-grandfather "fought the barbarians in the time of their great strength" was still a mark of pride in the families of the inner provinces. In Seh everyone's grandfathers and great-grandfathers had gone out to meet the barbarian armies, and too few had returned. It was a war remembered differently in Seh, and Shonto did not forget that.

Nor did the men of Seh forget that it was a Shonto who, with the young Emperor, had planned the desperate battles that finally halted the barbarian armies that had overrun their land. Shonto's famous ancestor had planted the banner of their House, the white shinta blossom, in the soil of Seh and it was a story still told by the north's proud warriors; that Shonto's name had also been Motoru.

"When I pass this place again, the barbarians will have hidden themselves in the deepest reaches of the desert; or my head will rest upon a barbarian pole. Shonto will retreat no further." So he had said, and though he had fallen in the final great battle, he had not retreated again. When he did pass the Shonto banner, he had been carried in state.

And the Emperor Jirri had fallen to his knees when told of Shonto's death.

> *The blood of our enemy*
> *Mixes here with the blood*
> *Of our brothers, generals,*
> *Foot soldiers.*
>
> *Motoru,*
> *An arrow, a flet of wood.*
>
> *To save an Empire*
> *And then to fall*
> *Among the nameless.*
>
> > *The Emperor, Jirri*

Shonto had known the poem since he was a child. As a boy it had been eerie to find his name linked to such deeds, to history. A man loved and mourned by an Emperor. Had that Motoru ridden this road? It was a disconcerting thought. Shonto shook his head and tried to force himself back to the present. But the link with the past would not let him go.

A guard carried the sword the Emperor had recently given Lord Shonto—

his ancestor's gift to another Emperor——awaiting his need of it. Even now, if he signaled and held out his hand, the hilt of that sword would be laid in his palm. Despite his certainty that the Emperor plotted his downfall, Shonto had to admit that the gift, the gesture, was worthy of an Emperor.

There were a few in Seh who saw the return of a Shonto General now as cause for concern, perhaps an omen. After all, there were rumors of the coming of the Golden Khan; coming yet again. To the superstitious, the return of Shonto at this time was too significant to be coincidence——and their sleep was troubled.

Shonto's party started into a small wood and there was a marked difference in the temperature once out of the sunlight. Here there were ferns that still bore traces of the morning's frost. A reminder of the true season, a season that the sun's heat was not yet admitting. The horses snorted and blew and their breath appeared like the breath of dragons in the calm air.

Shonto glanced over his shoulder and saw his Spiritual Advisor riding close at hand. They prepared him well, Shonto thought; I am a field commander and therefore I ride. Obviously my advisors must ride, though not one in five hundred monks have sat upon a horse.

Shuyun rode well. It crossed Shonto's mind to wonder where they had found someone to teach him——the Brothers would never trust instruction to anyone from outside, it was not their way. Shuyun also showed a rather unspiritual grasp of warfare: the Brothers had missed nothing nor had they let their spiritual beliefs stand in the way of their training of this young protégé. Even the followers of the Enlightened One had become creatures of expediency. Despite the obvious benefit he was receiving from this preparation, Shonto found it somewhat disturbing.

He shook his head and turned his mind back to matters at hand. They passed a party of soldiers, the second since coming into sight of the woods. Shonto spurred his horse forward in time to hear a junior officer report that the clearing beyond the wood had been swept by troops. It appeared that security measures were elaborate, which Shonto thought strange considering how often he was assured that the barbarians were no threat and brigands almost unheard of.

Shonto signaled to Lord Komawara and the young man came up beside him. "Sire?"

"Are outlaws so common in these woods that we need half the soldiers of Seh to protect us?"

Komawara cleared his throat. "I am as mystified as you, my lord. There seems to be no logic in this. I would ride to this place with three men. Truly, I feel I could come alone." Komawara contemplated for a moment. "Why. . . ? To impress a new governor? An officer overzealous in his duty?" Komawara paused for a second as the realization struck him. "Or perhaps something has occurred nearby to cause concern though I have of heard no such thing."

"Huh. I wondered the same."

They rode on in silence. "Who would know of such an occurrence?"

Komawara said nothing for a few seconds. He mentally listed all the ranking men in their party and realized that they would have reported any such activity . . . unless they hid such information from Lord Shonto.

"Almost anyone who lives within the area, Sire, I'm certain."

Shonto nodded. "Please find out what is known," Shonto said. "Don't let anyone beyond your own staff know your purpose."

Komawara looked around to see who might listen. "I will try to be at the tower before the hour of the horse, Sire."

Shonto spurred his horse on, looking up at the tower appearing through the trees—a crumbling tower.

The men of Seh were more than disconcerted. They did not know where their loyalties should lie. Shonto—Shonto Motoru had come to Seh to fight beside them. The feelings this engendered in them were difficult to understand. More than one man found himself looking at the lord, wondering how much of the spirit had been reborn, how much of the legend had returned to them.

Yet this Shonto was also the minion of a despised Emperor who would not contribute a handful of ril to the defense of Seh yet insulted them by sending a famous general now, when only the occasional barbarian incursion was dared. It was an insult almost beyond bearing.

And now the Emperor's governor had found one of the many run-down fortifications, left to decay for lack of Imperial funds, or lack of vigilance. And Shonto Motoru walked among the sorry ruin of stone, and the northerners felt they had somehow failed in the sight of the man who had given his life beside their own ancestors to preserve the borders of Seh. The war raging inside these men was written on their faces, and Shonto wondered at it.

The fort had been created around one of Seh's natural outcroppings of stone that thrust up here and there, breaking up the landscape with their stark, unnaturally angular forms. This one was almost a natural castle in its own right and had needed little help from the Imperial Engineers.

Shonto walked along the remains of a rampart, stepping up onto blocks of stone long dislodged from their places. Whole sections of the wall had been carted away and no doubt formed the foundations of some local land owner's buildings. The new governor had an impulse to have the stone hunted down and the party who had taken it executed for theft from the Province of Seh, theft affecting the security of the Empire, but he realized it would be likely that the thief was either dead or very old. He shook his head and the men of Seh looked at each other, questions in their eyes, for the lord had said nothing since his arrival at the tower.

"Is this tower typical of the fortifications I will find in Seh, General Toshaki?" Shonto spoke quietly.

The general assigned to Shonto by Lord Akima hesitated for a moment and then said with some difficulty, "There are others that are better, Sire— closer to the border—but the state of repair you see here would not be thought uncommon."

Shonto stared out at the view of the fields and forest, the road winding among the hills. "General Hojo, if this is the state of the province's defenses, how difficult do you think it would be for a barbarian army to push through Seh?"

Shifting uncomfortably from foot to foot, the Shonto general cast a glance at the northerners around him. "When your numbers are small and the area to be protected large, fortifications become more important, Sire." He paused again but then seemed to brace himself before speaking. "A committed commander with an army of reasonable size, perhaps fifty thousand, could push the warriors of Seh, for all their skill, back into the capital in a very short time, Sire."

General Toshaki turned to his supporters with a look that said, *have I not told you?—do you see what we must put up with from these southerners!* But when he spoke, his voice was full of respect. "General Hojo is a commander of great repute, Lord Shonto, there can be no doubt, and I cannot dispute what he has said. But where is this barbarian army? I have lived here all my life and I still have not seen it."

Shonto did not answer, but stared off as though Toshaki had not spoken. He raised his hand and pointed to the east. "Who are those horsemen, General?"

Toshaki moved to the wall. "I don't know, Sire." He turned and nodded to his second in command. "We will find out immediately."

Far off, a small party of riders rounded a stand of pine and plunged into a low mist that still hung in a small draw, half disappearing as though they forded a stream. Although they did not gallop, there was definitely haste in their bearing and their destination was obvious; they rode straight toward the tower.

Shonto stood watching as men from Toshaki's guard rode out to intercept the advancing horsemen. Squint as he might, Shonto was not able to make out even the color of their dress. Hojo looked over at his liege-lord and shook his head.

It could be seen, however, that one rider bore a standard with a figure on its crest, though what the figure was could not be guessed. Behind him Shonto heard men begin to whisper, but when he turned toward them they fell silent and did not meet his eye, which was unusual behavior for the men of Seh.

Toshaki's riders disappeared behind a rise and then appeared again, racing toward the party of eight whose numbers could be counted now. Twenty men of the capital's garrison wheeled up before the approaching riders who slowed, then stopped, then tried to push on and were stopped again.

"What is this?" Hojo muttered, but no one offered an explanation.

It was clear to Shonto that something was wrong. The men of the garrison reeled their horses back and forth and it appeared that threats were made. He could see arms gesturing, men standing up in their stirrups and pointing at the standard.

"Who commands our men?" Shonto asked.

General Hojo turned to Lord Toshaki.

"Lord Gitoyo Kinishi, Sire. The son of Lord Gitoyo . . ."

"Hojo!" Shonto barked. Suddenly, an all too familiar glint had appeared among the riders; swords were drawn! The Shonto general pushed past Lord Toshaki and the sound of men in armor, running, echoed among the stones.

Below, Shonto could see that no blades had crossed, but there was every indication that this would not last. What is it? Shonto wondered, and suddenly he felt truly the outsider. Truly the man cast into the unknown. And then Hojo and his men erupted out of the fallen gate, bent low over the necks of their mounts. The sound of their approach tipped the balance and the two groups separated, though no swords were sheathed.

*   *   *

"Well, General," Shonto said to Toshaki, "let us find out who has slipped through your net of guards."

Shonto turned and stepped off the stone onto the grass earthwork that backed the wall and descended toward the courtyard.

Horses jostled in the gate as Shonto found his way around yet more broken down stone. The men of the garrison pushed into the yard, their horses sweating from the run and agitated by the anger of their riders.

Outside the gate, Hojo sat his horse as though he marshaled the men inside. His face was set, cold as the broken stone that framed him.

Shonto felt his own anger rising but controlled it. *"To lose control because you do not feel in control is a most confused response, don't you think? I will certainly win now."* So Brother Satake had once teased him as they played gii. And, indeed, Shonto had lost the game—but he had learned the lesson.

The riders filed in behind the men of the garrison and Shonto recognized Komawara's livery, then Komawara himself appeared in the midst of his guard. Behind him rode the man bearing the standard. Shonto stopped without realizing it. It was the standard of no lord of Seh, for the man carried a pole *surmounted by a human head!*—the features slack, but twisted as though in rage or agony. The men in the courtyard cast their gaze down and none looked to their new governor.

Shonto continued to stare at the head of the barbarian warrior. Everyone waited.

"Lord Komawara," Shonto said quietly.

The young lord did not dismount nor, Shonto noted, did he take his hand from his sword hilt. "A holding nearby was raided two nights ago, Lord Shonto. One barbarian lost his horse when it broke its leg jumping a wall. He was surrounded and brought down." Komawara nodded toward the grisly pole. "We lost three men and four horses. No women or children were hurt."

Shonto noticed the "We . . ."—"We lost three men . . ."—men of Seh. It affected him somehow. Komawara obviously had no idea who the people were, they were simply northerners, people who fought the same battle.

Shonto looked around the circle of faces. Some looked away, others obviously fought to control their anger. Shonto thought of how recently he had sat in the Emperor's garden and watched the Sonsa dancers under a pale moon. But none of the men of Seh seemed particularly horrified by Komawara's prize.

I am far from the concerns of the courtiers, Shonto thought, very far.

The Imperial Governor looked from face to face. "Who knew nothing of this?" he asked.

Glances were cast from one man to the other. None spoke, as though the answers to all silent questions were known. Of this group, some turned to their governor and nodded.

"You may leave us," Shonto said.

Men, both on foot and on horse, turned and began to make their way toward the gate, leaving Shonto and his guard with half a dozen others. Komawara, too, had stayed, and Shonto noted that the young lord learned his role of Shonto ally quickly.

Looking at the men who remained in the courtyard, Shonto noted that there was little difference in demeanor between them and his own guard, though they stood accused of a crime approaching treason. They are northerners, the lord thought, and had to admire their calm.

"I trust no one has a satisfactory reason for keeping information that pertains to the security of Seh from the Imperial Governor?" Shonto let the question hang in the air. He looked from one man to the next, all met his gaze—he could detect no resentment.

"Let all senior officers step forward." Three men left their places, joined by another who dismounted his horse: Gitoyo Kinishi who had led the horsemen of Seh to intercept Lord Komawara.

Shonto stood before the four men. There was no question in his mind as to his course of action, though he wished it were otherwise. "You have your swords," Shonto said, his voice suddenly soft. "We will leave you to your preparations."

"May I speak on behalf of another, Lord Shonto?" A voice broke the silence. It was Komawara.

Shonto turned to his young ally and nodded.

"I do not think that Lord Gitoyo Kinishi understood what was taking place when he came out to intercept me, Sire."

Shonto stared at Komawara for a few seconds as if he needed to digest this information, then turned to the young man who stood his ground among the condemned. "It is not my habit to repeat myself, Lord Gitoyo. Did you know of the barbarian raid before meeting Lord Komawara?"

The young man opened his mouth to speak, but no words came. Finally he shook his head. "No, Sire," he managed, through a mouth without trace of moisture.

"Then why did you try to stop Lord Komawara?"

A soldier from Gitoyo's company stepped forward and gave his commander a draught from a water skin.

"I . . . I did not think it was necessary to bring the barbarian head into your presence, Sire." He hesitated again. "Obviously, some present must have known of the raid . . . bringing in the remains would be offensive to many. I was afraid such an act might influence your judgment, Lord Shonto."

Shonto eyed the young man for a moment as though he pondered what was said. "Yet you chose to stand among these others."

The young man nodded. "It was unlikely that I would be believed, after the altercation with Lord Komawara. I would have appeared a coward to claim ignorance, Sire."

Shonto shook his head and noticed two of the condemned officers did the same. He turned to his Spiritual Advisor who stood close by, watching as always. One of the Silent Ones, Shonto found himself thinking. "Shuyun-sum?"

"I believe he tells the truth, Sire."

Turning back to Gitoyo, Shonto said, "You risk being called a fool, young lord, but perhaps that concerns you less. Step away from these others. You are free to go."

Shonto turned away and walked back toward the lookout but then changed his mind and continued up the hill.

Shonto stood upon the hilltop and stared out toward the north. The position commanded a view in all directions. Fields and woods seemed to fold themselves to the rolling countryside. Even this far north a few autumn colors remained and in the fair sunlight they looked as though a painter of some skill had crossed the landscape, daubing his brush here and there in a brilliant design.

"Autumn refuses to let go, does it not?" Shonto said to Lord Komawara.

Komawara cleared his throat. "I remember only one year like this, Lord Shonto, in my youth."

Despite his mood, this brought a fleeting smile to Shonto's lips. He had watched another youth almost throw his life away only moments before, so the remark lost its humor immediately.

Shuyun came up the grass slope toward them. He had stayed in the courtyard to give the condemned the comfort of Botahara's blessing.

"I wonder how this will be seen in your province, Lord Komawara."

The young lord knew that Shonto did not refer to the weather. "It was certainly just, Sire; none can deny that. We live in a harsh world, here: pity is thought wasted on the foolish. These men knew who you were—they knew what would happen to them if they were found out. They did not show surprise at your sentence, Sire—only anger that they had underestimated you. Do not concern yourself with the reaction of the people of Seh. If anything, Lord Shonto, this act will increase people's respect for you."

"Huh."

Shuyun had come up and bowed, remaining silent when he heard what was being said. Now he cleared his throat.

"If I may speak, Lord Shonto . . . Lord Botahara sits in judgment, Sire, returning all those who are not yet ready to the wheel. Botahara has no mercy, yet He is all merciful. The Perfect Master will judge them, Sire, not you. And my Lord has not been harsh. There is no death as cruel as the lives some will be given. Yet it must be so if they are ever to attain Perfection. Mercy does not always appear merciful."

"Thank you, Brother." Shonto turned to the east, toward the sea. "And what of Lord Toshaki?"

Komawara did not hesitate. "He certainly knew, Sire. That is beyond question."

"To say this in public would mean a duel, yeh?"

Komawara laughed. "We would be well rid of him, Sire."

"Perhaps."

"I would be more willing to . . . speak my suspicions aloud, Lord Shonto . . ." Komawara said.

"We will keep Lord Toshaki near us, Lord Komawara. It is certain that he has been placed as close to me as anyone outside my own staff can be. We should appreciate such manipulations. Lord Toshaki shall have access to more and more of my most sensitive decisions.

"How long would it take to restore these fortifications, Lord Komawara?"

"Anything is possible, Sire, if the resources are limitless. Under most circumstances I would estimate eight months, perhaps nine. It could be done in five if need was great."

"And the rest of the inner defenses?"

"Much the same, Lord Shonto, though in places they are at least functional—a few places."

Shonto turned now to the great expanse of the northern horizon. He could not even begin to see the border from this spot, but he could feel it— an imaginary line drawn across a section of a continent and disputed for as long as history had been recorded. We drove the tribes into the desert, Shonto thought, it was their land once . . . once.

"We could do much by spring, if the Lords of Seh were committed to this."

"It would take until spring to gain enough support to even begin such a project, Sire," Komawara said with some bitterness.

"Huh. And we cannot prove that it is necessary, not even to ourselves." Shonto gestured to the clouds that swept low across the northern horizon. "It is all hidden from us, Lord Komawara. We know nothing. Yet something does not seem right. You have felt that. And I have questions that I cannot answer. We need a spy among the barbarians. Is there none that gold would buy us?"

Komawara seemed surprised by Shonto's words. "I had almost forgotten, Sire." The young lord reached into a pouch at his waist and what he removed jingled like the coins of Koan-sing, reminding Shonto again of his daughter. May Botahara protect her, he found himself thinking.

"These were found strung on a cord on the barbarian's sash." He held out his hand and indeed it did hold coins, but they were coins of *gold!*

Shonto's eyes betrayed his surprise. "He must have been a chief of some stature!"

"I agree, but there was nothing else about him that would indicate that this was so. His companions abandoned him without any attempt of rescue. Nor did he seem to lead the raid. Only this gold would indicate he was anything other than a typical barbarian warrior. Yet this is a great deal of gold— a fortune to a barbarian. I—I do not understand."

Shonto took a few coins from Komawara and examined them closely in the sunlight. "This is most curious. They are very finely minted. I have seen the 'coins' the barbarians use and they bear no resemblance to these. Huh. Look at this." The lord turned one coin over in his hand. It was like the others in that it was square and had a uniform hole in its center, but this one bore the design of a dragon. Not the Imperial Dragon with its five claws and its distinctive mane, but a strange, large-headed, long-tailed beast—though a dragon nonetheless.

He handed it to Shuyun.

The monk examined it carefully and then rubbed it slowly between his fingers. "This design was etched into the metal after the coin was struck. You can feel the edges of the lines: they are raised." He handed it to Komawara, who also rubbed it between his fingers.

"I cannot tell, Shuyun-sum, but I do not doubt you."

"These coins," Shonto went on, "would they be found in Seh?"

"They are certainly not Imperial coinage and if they were struck in Seh, or anywhere else for that matter, I cannot think they would be so finely made."

"And the barbarians have no history of working gold?"

"They have no gold to work, Sire."

"Most odd." Shonto turned back to the view north. "Another question without an answer. Did pirates break their vessel upon the northern coast? The coins could come from across the sea." The lord shaded his eyes and searched the horizon. "Somehow I cannot think that it is that simple. Everything is complex, hidden." His voice trailed off.

Komawara hesitated and then spoke. "I do not think we could buy a barbarian spy, but I believe there is a way that we may go into the desert—at least some distance. . . ."

Shonto turned away from his examination of the horizon and it was as though he returned to the present from some far off time. "I would hear this."

Komawara gathered his thoughts. "None may travel beyond our border without fear of capture. Although the wastes are vast, all have need of water and the barbarians control the springs. In the past, the men of Seh chased the tribes deep into the desert and, in doing so, charted all the springs between here and the deep desert. Of the people of Wa only those with the power to heal are welcome among the barbarians." Komawara rushed on, "I do not suggest a Brother should go as a spy but, with the assistance of Shuyun-sum, I could pass into the wastes as a Brother of the Faith." He turned to the monk. "I realize your faith may not allow you to assist in such an endeavor, Brother. Please excuse my presumption."

Shonto spoke before Shuyun could reply. "But how far into the wastes could you go? I understand that even the Brothers are only welcome to cross the border; they do not travel freely."

Komawara looked slightly embarrassed at having made this suggestion without consulting Shuyun first. It showed terrible manners and he knew it. "It is true, Sire. The monks do not penetrate deep into the tribal lands, but it is possible that a monk discovered far north of Seh's border would not be treated too harshly. Brothers have been lost in the wastes before and the barbarians have returned them to Seh's border. I would like to try, Sire, even if I may not have Shuyun-sum's help."

Shonto turned back to the north again. "It is an idea worthy of consideration." He faced his companions again. "Shuyun, what do you say to this?"

If he was offended by the idea of someone impersonating a Botahist monk, he did not allow it to show. "It is not possible," he said quietly, "it is the healing power that the barbarians respect. They have superstitions connected to the Brotherhood, it is true, but it is our ability to heal that makes us welcome among the tribes. They would not treat an imposter well; especially an imposter who came seeking to know their strength. It is a brave plan, but I fear, Lord Komawara, you would be throwing your life away for no gain, excuse me for saying so."

Shonto considered this for a moment. "I believe Shuyun-sum is correct, Lord Komawara. This is a brave plan, but it would be seen too quickly that you do not have the power to heal. You would fail, certainly. Our need to know what transpires beyond our border is great, but we are not so desperate that we will throw lives away needlessly."

Silence followed. Shonto saw General Hojo walking up the hill toward them. It is finished, Shonto thought, may Botahara have mercy on their souls.

Shuyun's quiet tones brought him back to the moment.

"I could go with Lord Komawara, Lord Governor. I can heal."

Shonto was stunned into silence for a second. "It is out of the question. You are a member of my personal staff. I would no more send you into the desert than I would send Lady Nishima. You have risked your life once already, for which I will always be grateful, but that was only at our greatest need; this can never happen again. I respect you for making such an offer, but it is not possible."

Shuyun and Komawara exchanged a look as Shonto turned back toward the north.

In the late afternoon light, the coins in Shonto's hands took on a richness of hue that did not seem real. He rubbed them between his fingers and felt the embossed dragon form.

"Power and mystery," he heard Nishima whisper.

Thirty-two

LORD AGATUA HAD never before been kept waiting in the Shonto house. Although he and Motoru-sum did not spend the hours together that they had years ago, there was still a lasting bond, a friendship strong enough that Shonto would choose him to deliver a message to Lady Nishima. He had no idea what the message contained or why it had to be delivered so circuitously, but Lord Agatua was the kind of friend who would never question those close to him: Motoru-sum felt the precautions were necessary so that must be true.

But he was kept waiting. Lady Nishima was ill, he had been informed, and when he had made a fuss the servants had rushed off to fine someone of authority. That had been some time ago. He was not a man who waited well.

A screen was pushed aside and Lady Kento whisked into the room. Agatua's face brightened perceptibly.

"Lady Kento, at last, a person of reason." He bowed and Lady Kento did the same.

"I apologize, Lord Agatua, it is unforgivable that you were kept waiting. Please, accept my apologies." She bowed again.

Lord Agatua shrugged. "These things occur, but it is past and forgotten. Please take me to Lady Nishima, I have a message of the utmost urgency."

Lady Kento bowed again quickly. "I will take it to her personally, Lord Agatua, be assured."

"Lady Kento, I have just finished explaining to a servant that I cannot allow that. The message is from Lord Shonto and he expressly instructed that

I should deliver it into the hands of Lady Nishima and no other. I will not break trust with your liege-lord by doing other than he has asked. We have no way of knowing how important this message is. I will do nothing but deliver it into the lady's hand, let me assure you."

The small woman stood her ground. "It is not possible, Lord Agatua. My lady is very ill, and her physician will not allow her to be disturbed. I'm very sorry, but there is nothing I can do."

Lord Agatua almost exploded with frustration, but when he spoke his voice was even and reasonable. "Lady Kento, Lady Nishima's own life may be in danger—we do not know. It would be the greatest folly to allow the instructions of a physician to overrule the orders of your liege-lord. Please, take me to your mistress at once."

Lady Kento did not move. She shook her head again. "I apologize again, but what you ask is impossible."

Lord Agatua stepped past Kento and headed for the door that led to the inner house.

"Guards have been ordered to detain you if you go further, Lord Agatua." Kento said quietly.

He turned toward her. "This is madness!" But he knew, somehow, that the woman was in earnest. "When will I be able to see Lady Nishima?"

Kento shrugged. "It is impossible to say—perhaps three days?"

Shaking his head Lord Agatua turned to leave, but as he reached the door he stopped. "You will have no opportunities to make such serious errors as a street sweeper." He left.

Kento stood staring at the door. It had been only a few days and already it was difficult to maintain the ruse that Nishima was in the house. First General Katta had tried to see her, though that had been not so difficult, and now this. Kento worried about the message from Lord Shonto. Certainly, it must be important, but there was no way to intercept Lady Nishima now, at least not without bringing a great deal of attention to her. She would be in Seh before a message, sent by any conventional means, would catch her. There was nothing to be done—except, perhaps, begin preparation for her new position. She believed the brooms were kept near the kitchen.

Thirty-three

LADY NISHIMA HAD never known a day so long. It had been only the previous evening that she had received the poem from Jaku Katta, and since then time had slowed as it never had when she practiced chi ten with Brother Satake.

Nothing—no word—and she could not bring herself to contact him: at least she retained that degree of dignity.

Watched from the deck of her river boat, the shore passed as it had throughout the first days of her journey, but now the eye of the poetess regarded it differently.

> *Calypta leaves drift toward winter,*
> *Borne on winds*
> *In the reflected surface*
> *Of the autumn sky.*
> *Trees line ancient canal banks,*
> *And weep for the passing procession*
> *Branches as barren as my heart.*
>
> *Why do you not speak my name?*

The Ladies Okara and Kitsura were resting and Nishima had come out on deck in the last light to be "alone with her thoughts." Alone with her desire, she admitted to herself.

Does he not want to see me as I wish to see him? It was the question that destroyed her tranquillity. I begin to feel like a fool, Nishima thought and resolved to return below to her cabin and her writing when a boat, sculled by two Imperial Guards, appeared under the bow. Nishima felt her pulse jump, but at the same time she felt more a fool to be standing at the rail as though awaiting word. It was too late to go below, so she turned her attention to the fading shoreline and feigned not to notice the boat and its occupants until it was before her.

"Excuse our presumption, Lady Nishima," the officer aboard said quietly, "we do not mean to disturb your contemplation," He seemed to have no doubt of whom he addressed. "If you will allow me, I bring you a letter from General Katta and will certainly return at your convenience if you wish to make a reply." He reached into his sleeve and removed a letter.

Nishima reached out automatically and took the letter. "I thank you," she said and walking a few feet toward the quarter deck, she leaned against the gunnel, took a deep calming breath, and opened the letter she had been awaiting for one interminable day.

Jaku's too large hand wandered down the page, but she found his failed attempt at elegance somewhat endearing.

> The wind, the wind, the wind
> I wish to hear no more of it.
> I am ruined for duty,
> A single brush of your lips
> Is all I can think of.
>
> > My heart will not leave me in peace
> > Until I speak to you.

Nishima found she was reaching out to steady herself on the rail. She realized that no matter what her head told her, she was going to ignore it in this matter. In fact, the decision was already made. She walked back to the gangway where the Imperial Guard boat waited.

"Where is General Katta?"

"The general is aboard an Imperial barge near the head of the fleet, my lady."

"Will you take me to him?" she asked, her voice much smaller than she expected.

The officer did not know how to respond. He had not been told to expect this. "I—I can, my lady, I can, if that is what you wish."

"It is." Nishima turned to the Shonto guard who stood watch at the gangway. "Tell my companions I will return shortly." She descended the ladder to the guards' boat. This is the worst foolishness, she found herself thinking, though she allowed herself to be assisted aboard.

The fleet was long. Nishima did not count the boats—more boats than hours in the day, she was certain of that. Anticipation built within her. The kiss she had allowed Jaku came back to her now and it seemed like no kiss she had ever known: tender and full of promise.

This excitement was balanced by a fear. Fear that Jaku would not feel as she did, despite his words. Fear that he would not even be aboard his boat, and her impetuous act would lead to nothing but embarrassment. She was going, unannounced and without invitation, to the dwelling of a man she knew hardly at all.

Finally they came to the Imperial barge that was Jaku's transportation to Seh. Nishima found the size and richness of this craft strangely reassuring, though she did not know why.

Waiting in the boat while her presence was announced, fear almost ate away her desire, but then Jaku arrived; his silhouette was unmistakable as he appeared at the rail—black uniform against the dark sky. He descended the stair with a surefootedness that was uncanny—catlike, as an entire Empire had noted. At least he did not merely have me brought to him, Nishima found herself thinking and was surprised that she felt gratitude.

"Lady Nishima," Jaku said in his rich tones. "I am honored beyond my poor command of words to describe." Jaku extended his hand to her. "Allow me to assist you."

Nishima ignored all the expected formalities of the situation and did not apologize for intruding; she merely extended her hand and felt the strong grasp and the heat of Jaku's hand as it enclosed her own.

The stern cabin of the Imperial barge was impressive: beams lacquered a deep red, large windows, now draped, looking out through the transom, celestial blue wall hangings, and cloud designs painted on the ceiling; all of this lit by hanging lanterns. The straw-matted floor had been covered with thick carpets from the land of the barbarians, a custom in Seh but only recently popular in the capital.

Jaku Katta and Lady Nishima sat facing each other on cushions spread upon the barbarian carpets. The rush of excitement at their meeting had given way to an awkward politeness.

"So often it seems futile," Jaku was saying. "I have long been counseling the Son of Heaven to make our roads and waterways safe. I don't know how often I have repeated this but there are so many counselors in the court, so many with the Emperor's ear. There is no end to the foolishness that passes for wisdom. But I have finally been heard: the lesson of history has won out. The Throne can only be secured by assuring peace in the Empire, and that must start with securing the roads and waterways."

Jaku paused for a second and caught the eye of Nishima. "And in doing this I will come to Seh . . . to a situation that is of . . ." he searched for the words, "military concern. If I may be of small service to Lord Shonto when I arrive, I would consider it an honor." Jaku lowered his voice and Nishima moved closer to hear. "I do not know what transpires in Seh, my lady, but I fear it is not the barbarians that will test your liege. Because of my duties on the canal, I cannot be there for several weeks, but I hurry. This situation is of great concern to me, Lady Nishima."

"But you have already done so much. If it weren't for you, I don't know what would have happened in our garden."

Jaku shrugged modestly. "Who can say?" He paused and then leaned toward her, his voice now barely a whisper. "I would not say this to anyone else, Nishima-sum, but I have begun to have doubts. I do not know what my Emperor intends nor how often I have been the instrument in the . . . Court's intrigues. I have been as loyal as a son and now I am uncertain of my loyalties. Not everyone is a man such as your father, renowned for constancy."

Nishima found herself whispering also, sharing secrets like a lover. "You have served more than the Emperor, Katta-sum, even as you serve the Empire and its citizens on the canal. You cannot bear responsibility for the actions of your liege: duty does not require that. Loyalty . . . is a matter of the heart."

Jaku reached out and caressed Nishima's cheek and a visible shudder of pleasure trilled through her. "Your words bring me comfort, Nishi-sum, they are Shonto-wise." Jaku leaned forward and kissed Nishima, a lingering kiss of great tenderness. Nishima found herself pushing into his arms and returning his kiss with a need that surprised her. Strong arms pulled her closer. Fingers brushed her breast through the folds of her robes.

Jaku whispered in her ear. "I do not know all of the details of what occurred in Denji Gorge. So many arrangements were made after I had initiated contact with the Hajiwara. If I had only known . . . thank the gods that Lord Shonto is the general he is and that no harm was done."

His mouth covered hers before she could respond. And suddenly Nishima was alarmed. What was he saying? What of Denji Gorge?

Jaku lowered her slowly to the cushions. His hands moved along her sash and Nishima felt the press of coins strung around her waist.

"No," Nishima managed weakly as Jaku began to pull at the knot. "No." More firmly this time, but Jaku did not seem to hear. She tried to push him away a little. "Katta-sum—what is this you. . . ?" He kissed her as though this would stop her questions.

Nishima felt panic grip her. What of my uncle? What is it that this man feels he must deny? Suddenly, Jaku's words seemed false to her.

Hands began to unwind her sash. She pushed against him, but he was so large he did not even seem aware. This must not happen. He is false. The coins—they were carried by Imperial Guards. How could their commander not know?

Grabbing the hand that unwound her sash, Nishima tried to hold it to her. She had allowed this to start. Had initiated it of her own volition. How was she to expect him to respond? But it could not be.

The trained strength of the kick boxer would not be denied, and Jaku began again to remove the length of brocade that held her robes and hid the silk ribbon around her waist. A hand touched the skin beneath her robes and Nishima felt a weakness wash through her. Warm fingers caressing her breast. He saved my uncle's life, Nishima found herself thinking, though why the thought surfaced amid the flood of pleasure she did not know.

Jaku's hand slid from her breast toward her waist, and Nishima's will returned in a rush.

"No!"

Jaku was flung back and found himself in an awkward heap at the base of a pillar.

Nishima stood before him, gathering her robes and sash into a semblance of order.

"Tell me what occurred at Denji Gorge," Nishima said evenly.

Jaku looked as confused as any cornered animal. "You are in league with the Brothers."

"I am in league with the Shonto, make no mistake. Has my uncle come to harm?"

"Lord Shonto . . ." He trailed off as though dazed. "Lord Shonto is, no doubt, in Seh, Nishima-sum, in Seh and unharmed. The Hajiwara tried to trap him in the gorge. I do not know what alliance planned this, though I would look to the court. I assure you Lady Nishima, I did nothing beyond establish contact with the Hajiwara, and that I did not do in person but left to my brother." Jaku moved to a more dignified position but did not rise.

"How is it you know the fighting skills of the Botahist monks?"

"I do not know what you mean, General," Nishima said. She had returned her clothing to order, but a flush remained on her face and neck. "If you have a boat that can return me to my own, I will impose upon you no further."

"Nishima-sum . . . I know you doubt me, but I am more of an ally than you realize. There is much I do not know that I may yet discover, to the benefit of the Shonto. I am a man of honor, and will only serve those who are the same."

Nishima crossed to the door of the cabin. "I must have time to think, Katta-sum," she said softly. "There is much going on below the surface, in the Empire and in my heart as well. I have treated you unfairly and for this I apologize; I cannot make decisions according to my desires. Lord Shonto saved my mother and myself—no, do not deny the Emperor's intentions, you know that it is true. I could be a threat to the Throne, if that were my desire. Your Emperor will never forgive that.

"I have many duties, too many duties. Please, Katta-sum, do not cause me more confusion." She slid the screen aside herself but paused before leaving. "Come to Seh. We will speak there—in Seh."

Thirty-four

THE PONIES WERE surefooted and strong, bred for hardiness and life on the northern steppe. As they picked their way down a narrow trail in failing light, hooves drumming up the long ravine, they inspired their riders with the utmost confidence.

Despite being wrapped in thick cloaks it was easily seen that these men wore the robes of Botahist monks—an Initiate and a Neophyte—out of place in this arid landscape.

The trail leveled and broadened somewhat as they found the bottom of the ravine. Scrub brush and the occasional stunted tree appeared here and there as though scattered down the draw by the relentless wind of the high steppe.

They rode on in silence until a large rock offered some shelter and here they dismounted. Komawara immediately began tending to the horses, the two mounts they rode and a third pony that acted as a pack animal carrying a burden that was largely water. Shuyun prepared a cold meal. It was a routine that they had fallen into in the six days they had been traveling north beyond the border of Seh and neither man seemed inclined to change it.

The northwest wind sounded like an endless breath from the lungs of a dying man, neither a moan nor a whistle but blending something of each. It was a voice that spoke of a long pain. The steppe was slowly being consumed by the desert, though no one knew why, but for a hundred years the men of Seh had been aware that the high steppe was disappearing. And the wind registered a desperate agony.

Whirling around their sheltering rock the wind picked up dust and spun it into the air, into the clothes, into the pores. Rubbing reddened eyes, Komawara came over to where Shuyun crouched.

"You must use the compress on your eyes again this night, Brother."

"I do not want to be blind in this place. It seems the worst possible course. We have no idea what may appear in the night."

"My teachers taught that in the darkness one uses one's hearing, one's sense of smell. Feel the vibration of movement—if you search the darkness with your eyes you will not focus on what is heard, what is sensed. We learned this lesson with cloth bound over our eyes. You can learn it with compresses over yours. You cannot continue with your eyes as they are. If we meet the tribal people, they will know. A Brother who is ill is not Botahist. I will prepare the compresses; let me worry about what hides in the darkness."

Komawara nodded and, as he did so, absently rubbed his recently tonsured scalp. A look from his companion and he withdrew his hand with an embarrassed smile. He was Shuyun's student in this endeavor: no longer a peer of the Empire of Wa but a Botahist Neophyte—not even that. Shuyun taught him some simple breathing exercises and meditations as well as the outward habits of the monks. To be truly believable, the monk felt Komawara should understand some of the basis of the Brothers' manner and had explained several principles of the training given to young monks.

At one point, as a demonstration of focus, Shuyun and Komawara had "pushed hands"—palm to palm trying to find resistance in Shuyun's movement, but whenever Komawara pushed, Shuyun's hands gave way though they never broke contact. It was, as Shuyun said, like pushing water or air, there was nothing to offer any purchase. Shuyun had twice put Komawara on his back and, the young lord realized, could have done it at any time but even so Komawara did not feel it was pride in his skill that led Shuyun to do this. The monk merely wanted Komawara to know what error he made by resisting.

After these sessions of pushing hands, Komawara had begun to question his martial training which was largely based on resistance. And so Komawara, a lord of the province of Seh, slowly and, at times, painfully, began to acquire some of the surface attributes, the mannerisms and posture, of a Botahist monk. He also began to develop a new respect for the Brothers and their level of skill and discipline. This respect was made even stronger by the knowledge that what Shuyun had revealed was not a thousandth part of his knowledge: there was that much the young Botahist was not revealing, and never would.

"I wish we could risk a fire," Komawara said.

Shuyun gave a small shrug. It was a gesture Komawara was getting used to: it meant that nothing could be of less importance to Shuyun, though he felt that it would be impolite to say so.

Komawara began to draw in the sand with his finger and a very rudimentary map appeared. He placed a small white stone on his cartography and said, "The spring should be only a few rih away." He tapped the earth. "We are here. This is believed to be an ancient river bed, though it is hard to imagine that water ever flowed here. If we follow it for another day, we should come to water—if the spring hasn't dried up. I don't know if we will meet barbarians there, but it is very likely. We must have water if it is at all possible."

Shuyun shrugged. "We can last many days on the water we have."

"*You* could last many days, Brother, but the horses and I have received poor training in survival without sustenance. We occasionally must eat food, also. Please excuse our weakness."

"For your weakness," Shuyun said, and passed the lord a flat bread stuffed with vegetables and a paste he did not recognize. The Neophyte monk, Brother Koma, looked at this offering with unconcealed disgust, making his teacher smile.

"You are a typically ungrateful student, Brother. You will not progress until you become thankful for your chance on the wheel. It is possible that even you will make some progress toward perfection in this lifetime. This food will help sustain you so you may do that. Therefore, you should be thankful for it: flavor is not important."

"I did not realize that striving toward perfection was so intimately entwined with continual discomfort, Brother. Tonight I will attempt to find a rockier place to lay my bed."

Shuyun lay still in the darkness. The wind moved over him and seemed to cause the stars to blur and waver in a cold sky.

I am assisting a man who is impersonating a Botahist Brother, he thought. I could be ousted from the Botahist Order forever.

He went over the argument in his head again. He had been given the task of serving Lord Shonto, a man of vast importance in the Empire of Wa. A man who supported the Botahist faith in a time when the Emperor did not favor this faith nor those who practiced it. This alone made Shonto vastly important to the Botahist Brotherhood. The lord was also responsible for the defense of Seh and, for all practical purposes, the Empire: an Empire that even under its present Emperor was still the one and only home of the Botahist faith. And despite the attitudes of the Son of Heaven, the true faith was practiced by most of Wa's population. The tribal people of the high steppe and the desert were not followers of the Perfect Master—if anything, they could be a threat to the practice of the Botahist faith. Shuyun went over the words of the Supreme Master at their last meeting.

"You must not always think of your own salvation. There may be times when your liege-lord will ask things of you that seem incompatible with the tenets of the Botahist faith. At such times you will have to make a decision that will favor the situation of the Brotherhood, for it is the Brotherhood and the Brotherhood alone that keeps the teachings of the Perfect Master alive."

So Shuyun had been told . . . and then he had met a young Botahist nun on the Grand Canal who cared for a respected Sister—a Sister who, it seemed, had lost her faith. A Sister who had seen the hand of Botahara and, miraculously had ceased to believe. A Sister who was convinced that what she had seen was false. The young monk no longer knew what to believe and what to disbelieve.

For the first time in his adult life Shuyun experienced unsettling dreams and awoke from his sleep with no feeling of renewal.

Komawara bent over the hoofprints, now touching them with his finger, then bending down till his face was almost in the sand and blowing into the depressions.

"A half-day ago, at most. Any longer and the wind would have hidden them completely. At least a dozen riders and perhaps eight animals of burden." He came back to his horse and took the reins from Shuyun. "There seems to be more and more evidence of barbarian . . . I do not know what else to call them but patrols." He shook his head. "Common wisdom says the barbarians move in their tribal groups: woman, children, animals, and all belongings. Groups of a hundred or more and never less than fifty or sixty. I am at a loss, Shuyun-sum. This is unexplainable."

Shuyun shaded his eyes and scanned the ridge of the dry river bed. "A young lord of Seh, Komawara, I believe, holds unpopular notions that the tribal people have changed their patterns in the last few years. You would do well to listen to his views if the opportunity ever presents itself. A senior member of my own faith believes there is something amiss in the historical pattern of attacks on the Empire—and the members of my Order hold historical evidence in very high regard. What do you suggest we do?"

Komawara mounted his pony. "We can do nothing but press on. As of yet we know nothing."

Shuyun gestured and Komawara again took the lead, picking his way among a maze of house-sized boulders.

The day was cool, made cooler by the wind and a high thin film of cloud which filtered the sun and muted all shadows so that things at a distance were harder to distinguish.

A hundred yards farther along, Komawara again dismounted and bent his knee.

"This seems to be turning into a trail again, Brother. There should be a spring not far off, if our maps are not too ancient. Who will be there, however, our map does not show."

They moved on again, single file until the trail became unmistakable. Here, Komawara led them up an incline of solid rock and into a grotto formed by massive boulders. He took some care to hide the marks of their passing and, when he was satisfied, returned to Shuyun who watered the horses.

"I don't think we should approach this spring without making an attempt to observe any who are there before they have an opportunity to observe us." Shuyun nodded his agreement. They each took a drink from a water skin— Shuyun's much smaller than his companion's—and made a light meal.

The ponies were hobbled and the two men proceeded on foot. Komawara took a staff with him, regretting again that he had no sword. The blade had been a matter of contention, but finally Shuyun had convinced him that there could be no explanation for a Botahist Neophyte to be carrying a sword, no explanation at all. Komawara had finally realized that Shuyun was right, but the sword was missed almost hourly.

They chose a path that seemed to run parallel to the trail they assumed led to the spring but soon were finding dead ends and forced corners that led them away from their goal. The trail appeared, unexpectedly, and they decided to cross it and try their luck on the other side.

After an hour of this maze they heard a noise that at first neither of them recognized, it was so unexpected.

"What is that?" Komawara asked.

"The wind. The wind blowing through leaves."

Komawara nodded. "It seems impossible but . . . I believe you're right."

They crawled up onto a shattered boulder and looked down into a long gully. The wind came down the gully and blew in their faces, a wind soft with moisture. Two stooped and aged trees bent down over a tiny pool of water as though they knelt to drink. The gully itself was a gradation of color from the stiff brown grasses of the high steppe to a deep green at the heart of the spring.

Shuyun reached out and touched his companion's sleeve and pointed. In the darkest part of the shadow at the base of the trees a man bent over the water filling a skin. He stood up so that his face came into the light, and if it had been Lord Shonto neither of the travelers would have been more surprised . . . the man was a Botahist monk.

Komawara turned to Shuyun. "What is this?" he hissed, and it was apparent that he believed he had been betrayed.

"I do not know, Lord Komawara, I have no explanation."

The Brother looked up at the two travelers and a smile spread across his face. He motioned to them to approach and gestured down at the spring.

"What do we do?" Komawara asked.

"He is a Brother of my faith, he will not lead us into danger, but I would suggest you say as little as possible, under the circumstances, Brother Koma."

Shuyun led the way, now, and they quickly picked up the trail and followed it into the grotto. Another surprise awaited them: tents and a rough corral containing ponies of the barbarians stood in the shade of the cliff.

The monk saw their reaction to this discovery and smiled and waved reassuringly. He did not speak until they were very close, as though he did not want others to hear. "It is indeed an honor to meet Brothers of the true path wandering here where so few travel." He made the double bow of his kind and Shuyun and Komawara did the same. "I am Brother Hitara," the monk added. "Welcome to Uhlat-la; the Spring of the Ancient Brothers." He gestured to the gnarled trees. "A fitting place for us to meet."

Shuyun bowed again. The monk who addressed him was young, perhaps only three years older than Shuyun, but his face was dark and creased from too much time in the sun and his body was thin and wiry from long ration-ing of water.

"The honor is indeed ours, Brother. I am Shuyun and this is Neophyte Koma, who has taken the vow of Barahama and apologizes for his inability to speak."

"There is no need to make apologies, Brother, the Way is difficult enough without need of making apologies for pursuing it." He gestured to the small pool. "The water is good, I have drunk it on several occasions."

Shuyun and Komawara went to the water where Brother Hitara offered them a half gourd for a cup. Shuyun drank sparingly and offered the cup to Komawara but then stopped the lord as he began to dip water from the pool. "Have care, Brother, too much water will destroy your focus and cause you other unpleasantness."

Komawara showed reasonable restraint, though not perhaps as much as Shuyun would have liked.

"It is a great honor and also a surprise to meet the Spiritual Advisor to the great Lord Shonto here in the wastes. I assume that you are no other?"

Shuyun was only slightly taken aback by the directness of the question. A Botahist monk wandering in the high steppe could perhaps be expected to have forgotten a few formalities. "You are well informed, Brother."

"Not at all, Brother Shuyun, you are merely unaware of your own reputa-tion. The youngest Spiritual Advisor to a Great House—in our history. Winner of the Emperor's kick boxing tournament at the age of twelve. I have even heard of your destruction of what I have been told was a finely wrought table. Even more is said about your level of accomplishment, but I do not wish to test your conquest of pride by saying more. I will confess to stand somewhat in awe of you, Brother."

Shuyun shrugged. "I am equally impressed to find a Brother of the Faith wandering here. How is it you have come to the high steppe alone, Brother Hitara?"

Hitara opened a saddlebag and began to remove the makings of a meal. "I minister to those of other faiths. It should never be repeated, Brother, but I have made more than one convert, though I have not spoken a word to bring this about. I heal the sick. If I am asked questions, I answer. I meditate in the ancient places. It is a small part that I play, Brother Shuyun, but it gives me ample opportunity to meditate upon the word of our Master. I do not need more.

"Would you join me in a meal, Brothers?" Hitara said and offered a stick of dried fruit to Komawara who reached for it readily. The fruit was drawn back, however, before Komawara touched it. "I had forgotten your vow, Brother. Please excuse me, I have been alone for too long. Please forgive my lapse."

A sound ended all conversation. A sound masked and distorted by the huge boulders and the high rock cliffs of the old river bed. It was some time before it was apparent that this was the echo of a horse's hooves.

"It is the man who guards this encampment. The others will be gone for several days," Hitara said offering food to Shuyun. "I once saved this man's son. He remains grateful."

They waited in silence for several minutes until finally a warrior of the tribes appeared, leading his pony. He looked up and caught sight of the monks and immediately cast his eyes down and turned back the way he had come.

Komawara was tensed like a man before battle and twice, while they waited, Shuyun had noticed him reach down to touch a sword hilt that was not there. If Hitara had seen, he said nothing.

"What is this camp, Brother, and where do they ride to from this place?"

It was Hitara's turn to shrug. "I find it is better not to ask." He began collecting up his belongings. "You should take water before Padama-ja returns. He cannot be expected to turn a blind eye always."

"You go so soon, Brother? I had hoped you would be able to speak with us longer. We have so many unanswered questions."

The monk strapped his few belongings onto a small brown pony and swung himself into the saddle. "I fear the questions you want answered I have found it wise not to know the answers to, Brother. I also fear that your purpose will endanger my own, for if you are found here, in the future all Brothers will be suspect. I do not mean to interfere, your karma is your own, but this is not a good place for you, Brother Shuyun. Return to Seh." He hesitated before he went on, speaking quietly now. "Tell your lord that his worst fears are true. Tell him to beware of those who worship the desert dragon." His horse began to shy suddenly and he fought to control it. "I do not know what transpires here, nor is it my concern . . . but war brings no soul to perfection—of this I am sure—so I do my small part to discourage its veneration. The tribes prepare for battle—I am certain of this. Gold has appeared among them and a new Khan commands the loyalty of all but a few. Look not to meet the few, for they are scattered and do not wish to be found. Return to Seh. Here you can do nothing."

Komawara stepped forward. "But we have seen nothing with our own eyes. Your word is all we have. Return with us. If there is a warning to give, then it is from you it must come."

"My place is here." He bowed from the waist, turned his horse then stopped and turned back to them. "If you must have proof, warriors gather not far to the north. I do not go there. Three days toward the spike mountain where the Two Sisters rise at sunset.

"Until the Udumbara blossoms." Hitara bowed again. "Brother Shuyun. Lord of Seh." He wheeled his horse and disappeared among the giant rocks of the ancient river bed.

Thirty-five

A S A PILGRIM and Seeker, Brother Sotura could afford only deck passage. As a Master of the Botahist Faith and chi quan instructor of Jinjoh Monastery there were other things he could not afford in his present situation: he could not afford to wear any sign of the position he held within his church, nor could he afford to use his name.

The fall winds continued to blow in from the sea and the river barge on which he took passage lumbered along the Grand Canal as the great waterway made its patient way toward the northern provinces. Some few days ahead of Sotura's own barge it was said that the Imperial Guard, led by General Jaku himself, was clearing the canal of pirates and those parasites who levied charges for safe conduct through sections of the waterway. There was a great deal of relief aboard the vessel, as far as Sotura could tell.

He sat leaning up against the side of a raised cargo hatch and watched the shore pass in the light mist and starlight. Although he was, according to the position he had attained in the Order, beyond the reach of earthly things such as beauty, Sotura found the Empire of Wa to be irresistible—even more so as he grew older. He was not sure why, but there seemed to be little he could do about it. At one point he even found himself sighing as they passed calypta trees with the stars caught in the net of their branches. He closed his eyes tightly and tried to focus on other things.

The disappearing Brothers, for instance. Except for the missing scrolls, there had been no greater mystery in the long annals of the Botahist Faith.

Sotura wondered again what, if anything, the connection might be and, as always, he could think of none.

He traveled now toward Seh because his Order felt that there was a focus there—events were about to occur that could shake the entire Empire. And somehow at the center of all this was a young monk and former student of the chi quan instructor—Brother Shuyun. Sotura pressed his fingers to his eyes as though he was in pain, but it was merely a reaction to his own confusion.

The confusion was caused by this news from Brother Hutto. . . . The Udumbara had blossomed! It was not true, how could it be? Sotura had once journeyed to Monarta and visited the grove where Botahara had attained Enlightenment. It was an experience he would never forget. And he found that place, too, unimaginably beautiful. The Perfect Master had said the Udumbara would blossom again to herald the coming of a Teacher.

But the trees had not blossomed in a thousand years, though they lived on, almost unchanged, through the rise and fall of dynasties and through the wars and famines of the centuries. How could there be a new Perfect Master and the Brotherhood not know? He could not believe it: it was simply not possible.

He opened his eyes as the barge passed the mouth of a small stream crossed by the arc of a stone bridge built in the northern style. Starlight reflected in the water and mist clung to the shore softening all the lines, blending them into the flowing river.

All streams lead to the river, Sotura thought, and sighed without knowing it.

Thirty-six

THEY RODE AFTER dark that evening, wanting to put as much distance between themselves and the spring as they could. They made their way east for several hours and then mixed their tracks with those on another trail. They rode over shelves of rock and doubled back down their own track. Always they set course by the constellation of the Two Sisters.

They passed more and more places where the dry grasses and scrub were broken by expanses of sand spreading like ulcers across the skin of the high steppe. Neither of them spoke of this, but it was apparent that the wandering tribes were losing their world to the encroaching desert and both Komawara and Shuyun knew what this meant for the province of Seh.

While it was still dark, they found shelter beneath a cliff and when morning came awoke to a view of the vast northern wastes. No grass—no sign of anything living. A few solitary rock sentinels thrust up from the growing dunes and in the near distance the sand gave way to a warren of eroded cliffs and toppled sentinels, all faded grays and reds that only a desert could produce.

The pack pony had gone lame in the night and Komawara cursed as no Botahist monk had ever done. He came and threw himself down on his saddle and Shuyun handed him a roll of flatbread filled with bean curd, vegetables cured to last, and cold rice. There was a sauce of delicate flavor over this that Komawara could not name. In light of his earlier reaction to such fare, he was not about to admit that he was developing a taste for the monk's food. Left to his own, Shuyun would not have bothered with even the time it took to prepare a meal such as this, but he made a concession for Komawara's sake. Obviously, the young lord had never produced a meal in his life.

"The gray is somewhat lame. It will be more than a day before she can bear weight again."

Shuyun shrugged. "We can carry more on our own mounts. We could even do with less."

"That is true, Brother, but we will not travel as quickly."

"Then we will travel slowly, it cannot be helped."

"Are you *never* impatient, Brother, do you . . ." Komawara caught himself.

"If impatience would help, Lord Komawara, I would become impatient."

"Excuse me, Shuyun-sum, I let my concern govern me."

"There is no need to apologize. We share a difficult venture, Lord Komawara." He smiled. "I will try to be a little impatient in the future."

The day was spent in camp. Shuyun meditated and neither ate nor drank. Komawara slept as he could and, when awake, paced. He tried all his skill with the lame mare and toward nightfall felt she could go some distance, providing she bore nothing. The other horses carried more of the burden and it slowed them noticeably.

In the night the wind carried voices to them, though Shuyun was more sure than Komawara that it was not the wind through the rock speaking in its own strange tongue. They hid themselves and were silent but were soon convinced the wind that brought the voices to them masked the sounds of their own passage.

They went on, more carefully now, and near sunrise they found a place to make camp that offered protection from the wind and afforded escape from more than one direction.

Komawara slept while Shuyun kept the first watch. The young monk had no strong desire to sleep: his dreams troubled him with questions he could not answer and feelings he did not recognize. Often he returned to his meeting with the young nun on the canal and the information he gained from her, information so momentous that he had trouble focusing his mind on its implications.

He realized also that he dreamed often of Lady Nishima and somehow the image of the Faceless Lovers carved into the wall of the gorge became confused with the images of his liege-lord's daughter. Often it was the face of Nishima he saw on the cliff, but the man she held close to her continually altered and changed. Sometimes her lover was unclear, as though viewed through water, and then Shuyun knew that it was he the lady embraced.

The monk was ashamed of the weakness of will that this indicated, but he also felt a quiet defiance which he did not recognize—the Botahist Initiate had begun to entertain the thought that he could have been lied to by his own Order and this thought began an erosion in his spirit much like the desert had begun in the high steppe.

They ate quickly and began to travel before sunset. The long ride of the previous night had done nothing to improve the condition of the gray, but the rest during the day had brought her back so that she could go on, though her pace was even slower.

"Does he not have a superior?" Komawara asked. They spoke of the monk they had met at the spring.

"All members of our Order have a superior, with the exception of the Supreme Master. I will enquire after Brother Hitara when we return. No brother could be here without permission of the Prefect of Seh, I'm certain."

Shuyun reined in his horse suddenly. "There is something on the wind."

Komawara reached for the sword hilt that was not there and looked about him with apprehension. "I hear nothing."

Shuyun turned his head from side to side, his eyes closed. "Men. Ahead of us."

They turned their horses immediately, and as they did so three barbarians slid down the steep walls of the gully in a cloud of dust and rocks. They had swords drawn but did not attack, as though it was sufficient to block the monks' line of retreat. Komawara wheeled his horse and found three others had appeared in that direction.

The men yelled to each other across the distance and began to advance slowly.

Komawara cursed his luck for not bringing a sword and pulled the staff from his saddle, letting the lead to the pack animal go.

"They are brigands," Shuyun said. "They intend to murder us for whatever we have. They do not imagine that we would know their language. These we face will rush us to allow those behind to cut us down." Saying so, he dismounted his horse.

Komawara started to protest and then remembered Shuyun in the fane and knew he had not been trained to fight from horseback. The young lord dismounted also.

"They are about to come, Brother," Shuyun said, and his voice sounded thick and far off. "When they do, drive our horses at those behind. That will provide the time we need to deal with these three."

A shout went up from the barbarians as they charged. It was easy for Komawara to turn the horses, who panicked at the charge. The lord turned in time to see Shuyun take stance before the first attacker. The barbarian risked little and aimed a long, downward cut at his opponent, intending to take him at the join of neck and shoulder. Shuyun's hand was a blur as it went up and matched the arc of the sword and then parried so that the blade passed harmlessly to one side. Even as he did so, he reached forward and took the brigand by his hair, pulling him forward, face first, into his driving knee. The man fell beside Shuyun who spun, and all in one endless motion, threw the man's sword, hilt first, to Komawara.

Although he jumped to the monk's assistance, the northerner was not quick enough. The next two attackers went down as quickly as the first, their joint attack turned against them and their sword strokes redirected so that they staggered to avoid disemboweling each other.

Komawara spun into guard position as the three robbers, who had been dodging fleeing horses, came out of the dust. The lord found himself blinking madly as the dust blew down on him, but his attackers seemed to be suffering at least as badly.

This time, one was not quicker or braver than the others and the three fell on the young lord together. This was not a haphazard attack, but a coordinated effort to bring him down. If it wasn't for the fact that they did not risk themselves, they might have taken him in their first rush. Fortunately the young lord had not gained his reputation as a swordsman without reason. He drew back and had them believing he was desperately retreating until one overreached, blocking another—this man fell to a lightning thrust of Komawara's point. And then the young lord returned to his retreat, pursued by two more careful opponents.

The larger of the two disengaged suddenly and his remaining companion fell to Komawara as he looked aside for a instant to see where his fellow went. The lord spun, prepared to give chase to a running man, but realized the other had turned aside, not out of cowardice, but to engage Shuyun.

Again the lord watched as the small monk deflected a sword stroke with his bare hand. This time Shuyun grabbed the blade in his hand and held it as though it bore no edge. Thrusting out with the flat of his free hand, he propelled the barbarian away from him with a force that Komawara did not believe possible. The brigand, who was larger than Shuyun by half, hit a rock and lay unmoving in the settling dust.

Surveying the field of battle and convinced that all opponents were, at least temporarily, not a threat, Komawara crossed to the monk and took the sword from his hand. And then forgetting his manners entirely, the lord lifted Shuyun's hand and examined it closely.

"How is it that you are unmarked?"

Shuyun did not answer immediately, and Komawara was surprised by the look in the monk's eyes. He achieves a meditative state in battle, the lord thought.

When Shuyun spoke, it appeared that he did so with difficulty. "You cannot let the edge press against the skin: I was scratched many times learning this. The hand must first match the speed and motion of the sword, but once the blade is grasped firmly along its sides it can be directed as you wish. It is a skill simple in principle, Brother."

Komawara stood stunned for a moment by the monk's words. It is a journey on which one constantly sees the impossible, he thought, and found himself looking at the monk's hands again as though he would discover the trick.

One of the tribesmen Shuyun had felled rolled over and moaned.

Komawara went to him immediately and bound the man with his own sash. The lord found that he was trembling with anger as he tied the man and it took all of his effort not to attack the helpless man. They raid my country, Komawara found himself thinking, they have killed people close to me, members of my family, they will never leave us in peace. He wrenched the knot tight and then glanced up and found Shuyun staring at him and mastered his anger.

A dagger, a skinning knife, and a pouch were found in the man's tunic. He bore no other possessions.

"We had best bind them all though I do not know what we shall do with them, Brother."

Shuyun went to the two men Komawara had dispatched and found them both dead and he wondered at the hatred he had just witnessed in the young lord. A brief entreaty for the tribesmen's souls and a prayer of forgiveness were all time would allow.

The first of the men Komawara had bound was conscious now, and looking from monk to lord with deep fear. Though the man's face was dark and lined from the sun, Shuyun realized that he was not old. A youth, the monk thought, no older than his two captors, perhaps younger.

"Look at this, Shuyun-sum," Komawara said and held out his hand. In the pouch the man carried, the lord had found gold coins identical to those that had been carried by the barbarian raiders in Seh—square, finely minted with the round hole in the center.

"They do not rob out of need, Brother," Komawara said, and there was disdain in his voice.

Shuyun nodded. "Their dialect is of the Haja-mal, the hunters of the western steppe. I do not know why, but they are far from their own lands."

"These are not the swords of hunters, Shuyun-sum. Nor do I see the spears or bows I would expect." He hefted the skinning knife. "Only this. I wonder what it is they hunt."

Shuyun turned to the tribesman and spoke to him gently in his own language. "Why do you attack us, tribesman?" the monk asked, "we meant you no harm."

The barbarian did not speak, but looked from one to the other until Komawara moved his sword to a position where it could be put to quick use. The man stared up at the lord's face and began to speak, though quietly, with neither anger nor resentment in his tone.

"He says that they follow the Gensi, their leader—one of the men who fell to your sword. The Gensi wished to attack us though they argued against this."

"Why?"

The monk repeated the question and listened patiently.

"He says he does not know, but it is clear that he does not tell the truth."

"What is his word for 'lie'?" Komawara asked.

"Malati."

The lord flicked the point of the barbarian sword against the tribesman's neck and repeated the word.

Again the man spoke, though this time his tone changed and he spoke quickly.

"He says the Gensi wanted our 'Botara denu'—I am not sure: perhaps 'gem of strength' is an approximation." Shuyun reached inside his robe and withdrew the jade pendant on its chain and showed it to the barbarian. The man's eyes went wide and he nodded as much as the sword pressed to his throat would allow. "He says they argued that this endeavor would bring them . . . *bad luck* is a poor translation, but there is no other.

"What would the Gensi do with this stone?" Shuyun asked and listened as the man spoke again.

"Make favor with the Khan, who desires the power of the gem," Shuyun translated. "These men are members of a tribe that does not support the Khan and he claims they hoped to be given gold for bringing the Khan the Botara denu. This seems to be a half-truth, lord."

Komawara lowered his sword. "Let him lie to us, Shuyun-sum. Lies will tell us the truth more quickly than he can be convinced of the value of honesty. Ask him where the coins came from."

Shuyun spoke again and the man answered readily. "He says the gold came from trade with the Khan's men for ponies, though this is another lie." Again Shuyun questioned him. "He says that he has never raided into Seh, and for once this appears to be a truth."

Without being questioned, the tribesman spoke again, and Komawara saw the man was uneasy.

"What does he say, Brother?"

"The raiders are also given gold; this is a reward for bravery and also to compensate them for taking no women, which the Khan has forbidden."

"How strange!"

"He assures us that the gold he carries was for honest trade and he bears no . . . grudge against the men of Seh."

Komawara snorted, causing the barbarian to flinch. His eye now flicked back and forth between Shuyun and the lord's sword blade.

"So. Where did he get the gold if not from this Khan?"

"I believe he is a brigand, Lord Komawara. From some luckless member of a rival tribe."

"Would you ask him who this Khan is and where he gets his gold?"

Shuyun spoke again and both men watched the transformation of the man as he spoke: the tone of his voice spoke of awe. "He believes the Khan is the son of a desert god and says that he is stronger than twenty men. He squeezes rocks with his hands to make gold for the worthy. The mighty fear him, even the Emperor of Wa pays him tribute and has offered him his daughters as wives. The Khan revealed the holy place where the bones of the dragon were buried. He calls this place 'Ama-Haji'—*the Soul of the Desert*. No one can stand against the Khan: all men are his servants, all woman his concubines."

"This man is obviously crazed," Komawara said.

"He does not appear to be crazed, Lord Komawara. He also believes everything he just told us. It is often the nature of faiths other than the True Path to affect men deeply, to draw them away from Botahara. Few will find the Way among so many false paths; the Way is difficult and offers no gold nor easy answers."

"Barbarians," Komawara said with some finality. "What will we do with these?" He gestured to the other tribesmen, who were showing signs of life.

Shuyun spoke to the tribesman again, and he answered earnestly and at great length. Shuyun listened and nodded, making no attempt to translate until the man was finished.

"This man says that the army of the Khan is camped not far from here, but he says that if we make him free he will not attempt to join the Khan but instead he will return to his tribe and give his word to do no harm to the men of Wa or any member of my faith. He says also that if we give him his life, he will be Tha-telor—in our debt or service. We may demand service or payment for his life. He offers us his gold. I believe he is telling the truth in this."

"Truth!" Komawara spat out. "They are entirely without honor, Brother. It is generous of him to offer us his gold when he is bound and helpless and the coins are already in my hand."

"It is the opinion of my Order, Lord Komawara, that the tribes have a code, though it is not as yours or mine, but it is a code nonetheless and they are as bound by it as you are by your own."

"My code does not let me easily take an unarmed man's life, but I do not doubt that this is what we should do, for our safety and the safety of Seh. I know you cannot be party to this, Brother, yet I am sure it is the wisest course."

"These men are all kin, Sire. If we take one with us, the others will not endanger his life. I believe we should take this man. There is no doubt that we need a guide."

"Brother Shuyun! These others will run to their Khan. This one has said that the Khan wants a pendant such as yours. If there is even a small force nearby, any number of men could be dispatched to track us. Once they know we are here, I have not enough skill to keep us from being found. Excuse me for saying so, but I cannot believe this is a wise course."

"These men are not in favor with the Khan, Lord Komawara. To go to this leader with nothing in hand but a story would be a dangerous undertaking. It is also true that they, too, would be Tha-telor. I believe that this binds them totally. If there is an army nearby, we must be sure of it and we must know its extent. I believe a guide would save us much valued time."

"Can you ask him how large this army is?"

Shuyun spoke again to the man who nodded eagerly. He knew they debated his future and was anxious to please them.

"He says the army is too large to count, but he has seen it with his own eyes and it is more than half a day's ride to encircle their encampment."

"He is a liar!—a crazed liar. There are not enough barbarians in a hundred deserts to make an army of half that number."

Shuyun questioned the man again.

"Though what he says is fantastic beyond belief, Lord Komawara, he tells the truth. He and his tribesmen observed the army at their encampment only five days ago."

"Botahara save us, Brother, I pray this is not so."

"Kalam," Komawara said, using what he believed to be the tribesman's name. In fact it was more of a title, though a title was perhaps too official: Kalam meant "sand fox." Most of the hunting tribes would have someone among them who bore this name, for it was traditionally given to a young hunter who ranged far and showed great cunning in his hunt. This was the one who guided the two men from the Empire of Wa, a young hunter who was Tha-telor, though neither Waian was aware of what that meant.

The tribesman reined in his horse and Komawara pointed at what appeared to be haze in the south. The barbarian nodded vigorously and then catching Shuyun's attention began to speak rapidly in his own tongue.

"He says that is the dust of the Khan's army. They travel now toward Seh, Lord Komawara." Shuyun could see the look of anxiety on the northern lord's face.

"Who would begin a campaign just as the winter is upon us? The rains will start. There will be snow and some weeks at least of bitter cold. Nothing he says makes sense to me."

"Perhaps not, lord, if we assume he is wrong about the size of the army.

If it is as the Kalam says, then an army of great size attacking a land that is poorly defended and unaware of the threat may expect a quick victory. Seh offers the fruits of a bountiful harvest. The winter rains will come, as you say, and the inner provinces will not send an army until late spring by which time the Khan will have had time to create defenses, if indeed it is his intention to take Seh and hold it."

Shaking his head, Komawara scanned the southern horizon again. "It could also be a dust storm, Brother, nothing more." He pointed to the western horizon where a faint haze was apparent. "There is also dust there. Is that an army?—and if so why do they travel away from Seh?" He scanned the entire horizon then, but found no more dust storms to support his argument. "How far to the encampment?"

Shuyun spoke again to Kalam.

"We will be there before sunset, Lord Komawara."

Shaking his head again, the young lord of Seh gestured for the tribesman to lead on.

Much had changed in the day since the barbarian ambush. With great reluctance, Komawara had agreed to take Kalam as their guide and had released the others. They had replaced their lame pack animal with one of the barbarian's own mounts and set off for the encampment of, what Komawara believed, was a mythical army.

They bound Kalam by night and stood watch turn about, but there was no sign of his kinsmen falling on them in the dark. They made good time now; with Kalam guiding, they took no false turns nor met with any dead ends. All in all, the tribesman was proving to be an excellent guide and he had even worn away a little of Komawara's suspicion that morning by killing a viper and providing the lord with meat for a meal.

Shuyun looked over at the young lord, riding silently, lost in a whirlwind of thought and concern. He carried a sword now and no longer bothered to keep up his tonsure and neither he nor Shuyun spoke of this. If they were captured by a leader who was about to make war on the Empire, it would not matter that they were healers . . . especially if it was true that the Khan desired a Botahist pendant for his own.

This thought made Shuyun worry about the safety of Brother Hitara, though there was something about this wandering monk that made Shuyun wonder if his concern would be better focused elsewhere.

Perhaps two hours before sunset Kalam brought them to the base of a cliff. "The way changes, Lord Komawara," Shuyun said as he dismounted. "From here we must leave our horses and proceed on foot." He stared up at the cliffs that rose above them, and Komawara's gaze followed.

"We climb again?"

"Yes."

Komawara rolled his eyes as he left his saddle.

They followed Kalam as he found his way upward among the shattered ledges and broken boulders of the cliff face. It was strenuous but not steep or difficult. Shuyun could see relief on Komawara's face—glad that he did not have to repeat their ascent of the face in Denji Gorge, for this, by comparison, was only a scramble.

Finally, Kalam motioned for them to stop and proceeded to a vantage where he hid, searching with his eyes for what Shuyun could not tell. Then, he motioned them forward and signed that they should be silent. Coming up to the rocks that hid the tribesman, the monk looked out and there, below them, stood a sentry in the shadow of the cliff—a sentry dressed entirely in a soft light gray from his boots to his turbaned head.

As out of place as a garden in the desert, Shuyun thought, for the man was richly dressed. The detail of his clothing was clear at a distance and they could easily see the gold worked into the hilt of his sword and onto the horn he wore slung about his shoulder. He leaned on a long spear and surveyed the view before him with some concentration.

"This is not a man asleep at his post," Komawara whispered.

The tribesman nodded and held a hand to his lips. He led them up again through a narrow cleft, doubly careful to kick no rock free. Twice more, they came to vantages where they could see the guard, but he gave no indication that he was aware of their passing.

Farther on, they skirted a second sentry dressed identically to the first and again were struck by the man's appearance. Shuyun found himself looking at their dust-covered guide and then at the guard again. These sentries do not seem to be of the desert, he thought.

They began to make their way down. A rim appeared before them and it was here Kalam finally stopped. Shuyun thought he heard chanting echoing up through the rock—low, eerie, haunting—but it may have simply been the wind.

Lying flat on his belly, the tribesman eased himself up to the edge and looked over. He signaled his companions forward and they did as the hunter did, sliding forward on their stomachs.

They peered over the edge of the rift and found a grotto into which a shaft of failing sunlight fell. Torches set into the rock mixed their red light with the rays from the setting sun and illuminated a sight that neither Shuyun nor Komawara expected.

"Ama-Haji," Shuyun whispered and Kalam nodded his eyes wide with wonder.

"Look, Shuyun-sum," Komawara said softly, and pointed to a part of the cliff face slightly hidden by an overhang of stone. Here, set into a bank of reddish clay, lay an enormous skeleton—large-jawed head, a snaking spine longer than ten men, the bones of small legs.

"A dragon," Shuyun intoned. "It is the skeleton of an actual dragon! Botahara be praised. A true wonder! The beast of antiquity . . ." And he sounded for the first time like the youth he was; entirely swept away by what he witnessed. And from Komawara he heard a sound like a weak laugh and the lord rubbed his eyes.

Men in long gray robes were preparing a pyre before the skeleton, a pyre of stunted, twisted wood and they chanted the low chant Shuyun had thought he heard.

"Kalam?" Shuyun whispered.

The tribesman spoke only one word.

"What does he say, Brother?"

"Ritual sacrifice. The goat you can see."

Kalam moved away from the edge, pushing past Shuyun, and he made a warding sign. Gesturing to the setting sun, he turned and made his way back as they had come; his companions from the great Empire followed him as silently as they could.

They sat in the darkness talking. Komawara could hear the sounds of the barbarian language from where he lay trying to rest. He wondered what had suddenly made the tribesman so talkative. But he did not wonder long, the memory of the dragon skeleton, the dragon that was etched onto the gold coins he had seen, returned to him over and over. It was as though the Five Princes had ridden down out of the clouds, lightning flashing from the hooves of their gray mounts. Impossible! Myth no grown man believed. A dragon! And he had seen it with his own eyes!

*   *   *

Morning saw a continuation of the eerie veil of high, thin cloud. The wind shrilled on unabated. The day was cooler. Only Komawara had dismounted, as though he needed to get closer to the ground to be sure his eyes were not deceiving him.

They had ridden to the center of an abandoned encampment—an encampment so enormous that the young lord's mind would not seem to accept it.

"No . . . no. This cannot be. This cannot . . ." He looked around him like a man returned to his fief to find it razed to the ground—sick to his heart yet the mind still refusing to accept what he saw.

"Lord Komawara . . . Sire? We must return to Seh as quickly as possible. We dare not linger here. Lord Komawara?"

"How do you know he'll return?" It was the first time Komawara had spoken since they had left the barbarian encampment the previous day.

"He is Tha-telor." Shuyun said. "And he is frightened of the Khan."

"Frightened of he who squeezes rocks into gold?—he who is as strong as twenty men?"

"The Kalam is in awe of the Khan, there is no doubt. But the Khan is cruel. The Kalam has heard stories."

"Cruel? He is a barbarian chieftain. I hardly think he can shock another of his kind."

"Perhaps, but a simple hunter from the steppe is another matter."

"A simple hunter who tried to remove your head, excuse me for reminding you."

"I pushed a man from the mouth of a cavern into the waters of Denji Gorge because he was the soldier of an enemy of my liege-lord. I do not think you would call me a barbarian. I pray that man will reach perfection in his next life, but his karma is his own, as is mine." Shuyun paused and scanned the horizon. "Our barbarian guide did not act so differently, Lord Komawara; we are not, after all, his traditional allies. The Khan frightens him, perhaps only because he upsets the accustomed order of their tribal life."

"Huh."

They fell silent again, riding on as quickly as they dared without exhausting the ponies. A rider on the horizon brought them up short, but it was soon apparent that it was Kalam returning to them. Behind him the dust cloud from the Khan's army rose into the sky and swept away on the north wind.

"They can be seen from the next rise." Shuyun translated as the tribesman began to talk, spouting words in his excitement as though he could not catch his breath. "Few outriders can be seen, they must not fear discovery. This is not the whole army, he says, and they have turned to the east, now."

Again Komawara returned to the state of shock he had experienced in the encampment. "We must see for ourselves," he said finally.

They did not hurry to the rise but kept their pace, perhaps even slowed it. There was no rush. Only their eyes lacked the evidence, but Shuyun and Komawara knew in their hearts what they would see.

Even so, the sight stunned them and they were silent for some time. Moving across the sand in the center of an enormous dust cloud was a mass of humanity.

"Fifty thousand?" the lord said finally.

"Not quite that," Shuyun said, his voice taking on that strange quality that Komawara had noticed before, "perhaps forty thousand."

"Forty thousand armed men," Komawara said slowly, "and look how many are on horse! There has never been a barbarian army this large. Not in the days of my grandfather, not in the time of the Mori—never. . . . This dust cloud must blow all the way to Seh and the people will think it is merely a storm in the desert."

Shuyun spoke to Kalam and listened carefully to their reply. "It seems you may have been right, Lord Komawara. These are warriors of the high steppe who have their lands to the east near to the sea. Kalam believes they return to their tribes to winter. If this is true, the campaign will not begin until the spring."

Komawara hardly seemed to hear this. "In Seh we might raise forty thousand if we also count old men and boys. The plague stripped us of our people, of our fighters."

Shuyun spoke quietly to Kalam, nodding thoughtfully to the tribesman's response. "The Kalam says the scattered tribes have sent their sons from the breadth of the steppe and the desert. No one knew that there were so many. No one knew how many clans there were. This is but half the number he saw at the encampment, and from seeing that place I believe he is not wrong."

"How do they feed them? You cannot grow food in the sand."

Shuyun spoke to Kalam and the answer seemed to shake him. "He says that they drain everything but enough to survive from the tribes, and also much food and many weapons come from pirates whom the Khan pays in gold."

"Gold he squeezes from rocks. . . ."

"It is a mystery. We must return to Seh, Lord Komawara. We have seen all that we need to see."

"You are right, Brother. And you were right in another matter." The lord nodded to the barbarian tribesman. "We should release him now. He has given us true service."

"I'm afraid, my lord, that it is not as simple as that."

Thirty-seven

THE DAY WAS chill, the light from the sun filtering through high cloud that covered the sky like a layer of sheer silk. Despite the temperature, Shonto sat on a small covered porch overlooking the gardens of the Governor's Palace. He progressed slowly through his daily correspondence, most of it official, routine, and of no great importance. A letter from Lord Taiki, however, required a second reading.

After describing how his son adapted to the loss of his hand, and praise for Shonto's steward Kamu, who had visited the child several times, the Lord went on to matters of greater interest:

> There is one thing that has come to my attention that seems most unusual, especially since our recent discussion. Coins such as those the barbarian raiders carried, have come to light in Seh. Only two days ago one of my nephews sold his prize stallion for a great deal of gold. The coinage was not Imperial nor was it stamped with a family symbol but was as you described: square, simply formed, with a round hole in the center. The purchaser was the youngest son of Lord Kintari, Lord Kintari Jabo. Lord Kintari's son is not known for his skills beyond the wine house, and it is surprising that he would have gold in such quantity to purchase one of the finest animals in Seh, if not all of Wa—for he paid dearly to become its master.
>
> This would be interesting enough as it stands, but more occurred: Lord Kintari Jabo's older brothers came to my nephew saying that a mistake had been

made and they asked most humbly if the horse could be returned and the gold refunded. My nephew, being a man of strict principle, felt that the transaction was fair and in all ways honorable and politely declined. This did not please the brothers who then explained that the gold was of importance to their father as an heirloom and that their brother had been in error to use it in this matter. Would my nephew consider exchanging the coins for Imperial currency?—of course, the Kintari would think it only correct to pay him a generous portion of the purchase price for his inconvenience and his consideration in this matter. This then was done, except for a few coins that my nephew had already used which could not then be found.

These few coins have since come into my possession and I will bring them to the palace when we next meet. I am quite certain that they are identical to those described to me when I last had the pleasure of the governor's company. This matter begins to concern me as greatly as it does my governor.

Your servant,

Shonto read the letter through a second time and then folded it and put it into his sleeve. He sat looking out over the garden for a moment. The obvious explanation for this was that the Kintari had been raided and the coins taken from them. If this was the case there was no mystery to the gold nor would it be difficult to discover if this was the truth.

Shonto clapped his hands and requested cha from the servant who appeared. Why, then, the lord wondered, were the sons of Lord Kintari so anxious to have these coins returned? If these were the same as the coins he had seen, then they would be new—hardly heirlooms.

Cha arrived and Shonto gladly accepted a cup, setting it on his writing table and turning it slowly, staring into the steam as though looking into the distance. Again he found himself wondering how Komawara and Shuyun fared, then shook his head. He should never have sent the monk to the desert . . . but what choice had there been? Shuyun was the only member of Shonto's staff who had any chance of surviving capture by the barbarians. The only one who could possibly return with the information they so desperately needed. Even so, the monk was too valuable an advisor to be used in this way.

What would the Brothers think if they knew that one of their own Order wandered in the wastes with a Lord of Seh disguised as a Botahist monk?

The Brotherhood were, Shonto was well sure, pragmatists to the center of their much vaunted spirits—they would swallow hard and then look away. As defenders of the faith of the Perfect Master, they had been involved in some questionable practices themselves.

There was noise in the hallway close by, and Shonto found himself very alert. He did not have his sword at hand, but he touched the hilt of a dagger in his robes. Two voices muted by the walls: a woman's and another that was certainly Kamu's. Shonto was on the verge of rising when the shoji slid aside and there stood his only daughter, Lady Nishima.

She knelt immediately, bowing deeply before entering the room. Kamu's face appeared in the opening and at a single gesture from his lord, disappeared. The shoji slid silently closed. Neither Shonto nor his daughter spoke for a few seconds.

"It seems, Uncle, that for once you have been caught without words."

"This is not true; I have so many words I do not know which to speak first."

They both laughed and then fell silent again.

"At this moment," Nishima said, "I wish I were seven years old."

"Oh?"

"For if I were that delightful age I could throw myself into your arms again."

"At your present age that would be a most unseemly thing to do."

Nishima nodded. "That is true."

"Brother Satake, however, had different beliefs about the nature of time . . ."

He did not finish. Nishima flung her arms about him and crushed him to her.

Shonto managed to emerge from the folds of her silk sleeves and said with difficulty, "As a seven-year-old you would never have missed my correspondence."

Without looking, Nishima reached back and tipped the contents of his table—cha, inkstone, and brushes—spreading them across the porch.

"Better," Shonto said and though Nishima laughed he felt a cold tear run down her cheek and onto his own.

At length, they parted and Shonto clapped his hands for a servant. "Cha."

The servant noticed the pile of correspondence and the lord saw the surprise register.

"Do not bother with it now."

The servant disappeared.

"Here only a moment and already creating disorder for the staff."

"They are fortunate my younger self is forever banished to the past." She gestured to the litter of ink and correspondence. "This, after all, is contained within a single room."

Cha arrived, which Nishima took charge of.

"Do you wish to hear the story now, or does your office require your attention?"

"Now would be convenient. I am most anxious to know how we will explain your presence here to our Emperor who expended great effort to ensure that you could not come to Seh without deeply insulting the throne."

"I would never dream of offending our Emperor, Uncle. The Son of Heaven generously arranged for me to study with an artist of great stature and I continue to do so. Lady Okara has accompanied me."

"I see," the lord said, and sounded annoyed. "That was my plan also . . . if I felt it was necessary for you to come to Seh."

Nishima looked down and sipped her cha. "I did not come without a good reason."

"I do not doubt you for an instant, Nishi-sum."

She smiled. "Kitsu-sum came also."

Shonto shook his head. "Naturally, one would hope she would not miss an outing to the country."

Nishima laughed. "She also has good reason."

Shonto nodded, half a bow of acknowledgment.

"But first my own. Only a few days after you had left, I received a letter from Tanaka. Your vassal-merchant had information that disturbed him and he acted accordingly. A former officer of the Shonto, now an old man, learned from his grandson, who is an Imperial Guard, that the guard was involved in the secret movement of very large quantities of gold. Gold coins being sent north by ship."

"Coins?"

Nishima nodded and reached into her sleeve. Removing a brocade purse, she emptied the contents into her hand and held them out to her uncle. "Shipped north secretly. The involvement of the Imperial Guard and the sheer quantity of gold. . . . It spoke only of Seh and our worst fears."

Shonto reached out and picked up one of the coins.

"I could trust this to no one else, Sire, nor did I feel I could remain in the capital with this knowledge. We have always known that he could not abide the Shonto strength and the name of my family."

"And who might that be?"

"Sire, only the Emperor, of course."

"And why not Jaku Katta?"

"It seems if Jaku plotted against you, he would hardly have saved your life so recently."

"True. If you believe that he saved my life."

"Father?"

Shonto rubbed the coin between his hands. "The Black Tiger saved his own life, I believe."

"The assassination was directed at Katta-sum?"

Shonto nodded and Nishima stared down at her hands.

"Have you heard of our delay in Denji Gorge?"

"Not in detail, Sire."

"There is every indication that Jaku plotted with the Hajiwara to end my journey there, though we escaped, thank Botahara. Now it is said that Jaku is in disfavor with his Emperor." Nishima looked up in surprise. "You had not heard? He comes north, apparently 'bringing order' to the canal that he kept in disorder for so long. It is rumored that this is an exile. I expect him to arrive in Seh at any time. No doubt he will have sensitive information with which to prove his break with the Son of Heaven. A perfect Shonto ally at a time when the Shonto need allies. Huh. He must believe I am a fool."

"No, Sire, I believe he reserves that judgment for me."

"Nishima-sum?"

She took a deep draught of her cha. "I have been in correspondence with the general recently and I met with him, briefly, on the canal as we came north."

Shonto said nothing.

"I was not informed of the truth of the incident in my lord's garden. I do not make excuses, but I labored under a mistaken impression that Jaku Katta had saved your life."

Neither of them spoke for several minutes. Finally Shonto broke the silence. "It is my habit to share information only where it is absolutely necessary." He looked for a moment at his daughter, who sat before him with her eyes cast down. "Discretion is not a characteristic of our race."

"The mistake, Sire, was mine entirely. Fortunately it has not proven too momentous. Have I come to Seh on the errand of a fool? Do you already know of the coins?"

Shonto shook his head. "You have acted wisely in this. It is true I know of the coins, but the information you have learned from Tanaka is new and valuable." Again he rubbed the coins between his hands. "The coins are put on a ship and what then?" He made as though he threw the coin off the balcony but palmed it instead, as though he did a magic trick for a child. "They next appear on the corpse of a barbarian raider; though one coin has been embossed with the design of a strange dragon. Remember your fortune telling?" Shonto smiled. "Most unusual. Today I discover that a major family in the province of Seh has coins that are very likely identical." He took the letter from his sleeve and read to Nishima.

"My assumption was," he said, returning the letter to his sleeve, "that the barbarian's coins had been stolen from the Kintari in a raid. We will see. Why is this great fortune in gold being secretly shipped north? Guardsmen, you say, ship this gold? Does that point to the Son of Heaven or the Commander of the Imperial Guard? And why does this gold appear in the hands of the least-favored son of a major family of the Province of Seh?" He gestured to the sky with his hands. "And how is it that a barbarian raider possesses what appear to be the same coins? Most unusual. Do you know my own staff tried to hide the evidence of raids from me?" he asked suddenly, outraged.

"Several men paid for this with their lives." Shonto shook his head somewhat sadly. The anger disappeared. "But you have acted wisely. The Emperor will be very angry when he learns that he has been outwitted. He trusted too much to Lady Okara's reputation. He did not know that her time with you would make her long for her youth again—long for adventure." Shonto laughed and smiled at his daughter.

"Certainly that cannot be the case. I'm sure I have had no such effect."

"Oh, I'm sure you have. It is a family trait; I have that effect on people all the time."

Nishima laughed.

"You laugh? Only moments ago you yourself wished to be seven years old—hardly younger than you are now but a year or two."

Nishima clapped her hands together and laughed. "The Emperor will be less pleased when he discovers that Lady Kitsura Omawara has also left the capital, and in my company at that."

Shonto raised his eyebrows.

"The Son of Heaven suddenly began to pay a great deal of attention to poor Kitsu-sum."

"Nishima-sum, are you saying the Son of Heaven paid court to your cousin?"

"I would not use the word 'court.' I have seldom seen such a display of bad manners. He acted as though she were . . ." Nishima searched for words and then said with disdain, "a Fujitsura, or a Nojimi. Not an Omawara. It was unconscionable. Lord Omawara acted correctly in this matter, though this has placed my lord in a less than comfortable position."

Shonto seemed to brighten; a look closely akin to a smirk threatened to appear. "I am far from the capital, Nishi-sum, and little aware of the goings on of the court. Lord Omawara asked if Lady Kitsura could accompany my daughter to Seh; after all, he is very ill and may wish to spare his daughter pain. Lord Omawara is a friend of many years. I agreed, of course. Do you have any other surprises for me?"

"Not that appear to mind immediately, my lord."

"Oka-sum is well?"

"She seems to be, though she is quite . . . thoughtful."

"Poor Okara-sum, torn from her retreat after so many years. And look where she has come? To the eye of the storm." Shonto produced the coin again, staring at it as though it might reveal its origin. "All because of these."

"I hope she will not find reason to regret this journey."

"That is my wish for us all."

"It was not possible for you to know." Kitsura said soothingly.

Nishima shook her head. "How is it that someone in Seh would know of Jaku's alleged fall from favor before I knew in the capital?"

"It seems that Jaku's fall occurred simultaneously with our departure from the city. You would be a fortune teller indeed if you had known." They walked along a high wall in the last light of the day.

"It was understandable. I would have been no less tempted than you." Kitsura flashed her perfect smile. "And may have shown less resistance at the end."

Nishima tried to smile and failed. They stopped a moment to admire the view of a garden.

"Does your heart ache, cousin?"

"My dignity is injured, only." They walked a few steps further. "A little, Kitsu-sum, a little."

They moved on until they came to a view of the Imperial park and its curving canal, the sun settling into the mountains beyond.

"Perhaps you should speak of this with your Spiritual Advisor."

Nishima shook her head. "I think not."

"You have said yourself that he is wise beyond his years."

"I—I couldn't. I don't wish to."

Nishima turned and walked on and her companion followed.

"At least we are here, beyond the reach of the Emperor."

"There are many things to be glad of, Kitsura-sum. I will try to be more cheerful. Please excuse my mood."

A guard in Shonto blue hurried toward them. When he came closer, the two women could see the flying horse of the Imperial Governor of Seh over the man's heart.

"Excuse my intrusion, Lady Nishima. Lord Shonto requests your presence."

"This moment?"

"Yes, lady."

Nishima turned to Kitsura.

"Of course, please, do not apologize."

Nishima set off, followed by the guard. It was a short distance to the palace proper and not much farther to the hall where Lord Shonto awaited.

The hallway and door were manned by an unusually high number of Shonto's elite bodyguard and Nishima noted this with some alarm. A screen was opened for her and as she knelt to enter she found herself across the room from what was certainly a barbarian warrior. Nishima stopped and then saw her father, Lord Komawara, General Hojo, Kamu, and Shuyun.

"Please. Enter. This palace is full of everyone's spies."

Nishima bowed quickly and moved into the room. A cushion was set for her and she took her place.

Shonto did not bother explaining why his daughter was present, though she had never attended important sessions of strategy or intelligence before. All present bowed to her.

"Nishima, this man is Kalam. He has come from the desert with Lord Komawara and Shuyun-sum."

Shuyun spoke to the man in his own language and the tribesman bowed as he had been shown. He hardly dared a glance at Lady Nishima but kept his eyes fixed to the mat in front of him. The man appeared suddenly disconcerted.

"Excuse us if we proceed. Certainly I will discuss this with you later."

Nishima gave a short bow of acknowledgment.

"How is it you agreed to these terms, Shuyun-sum."

"My understanding of the tribal dialect was at that time imperfect, Sire, I did not understand the full implications of Tha-telor. I believed that it meant he would buy his life and the lives of his kin with service of shorter duration. I did not realize that Tha-telor actually meant that we exchanged the lives and honor of his kin for his life and honor. He is bound to me for the length of his life. If I send him back into the desert, he will allow himself to die. The only honor that remains to him is in his service to me."

"Do you believe these claims, Brother?"

"Totally, Sire."

"Huh." Shonto shrugged. "I myself am less trusting."

"Excuse me for saying so, Lord Shonto," Komawara said, "but I believe Shuyun is correct in this matter. I did not trust Kalam myself but . . . I believe he would jump from the balcony if Shuyun ordered him to."

Shonto turned toward the balcony. "I wonder," he said. "It seems, Lord Komawara, that you once suggested to me that we should take a barbarian prisoner for the purpose of gaining information. Here is such a man."

"I thought we would have to resort to stronger means of persuasion, Sire. Kalam speaks readily, at least to his master."

"Most convenient. So you went on then with a guide toward this place of worship?"

Komawara took up the story. "Yes, to Ama-Haji. It is a grotto hidden at the base of the mountains . . . an ancient place, Lord Shonto, and difficult to describe. We slipped past several guards to the edge."

"These seem like very poor guards," Shonto offered.

"It seems that intruders are unexpected. Kalam's tribesmen seldom venture there and people from Seh, never."

"But for this Brother you have spoken of."

"Yes, Sire, and ourselves. Even so, they are little prepared for people venturing into their lands. In Ama-Haji we saw a sight that cannot be believed unless one sees it with one's own eyes." Komawara looked to Shuyun for an instant, who nodded imperceptibly.

"Embedded in a clay wall," Shuyun said softly, "we saw what is unquestionably the skeleton of a dragon."

There was silence in the room. Kamu was the first to speak. "How is it you are so certain? Did you see this at hand, Shuyun-sum? Did you touch it?"

"The skeleton was seen at a distance, Kamu-sum, yet I do not doubt what I saw. The situation was almost too natural to have been contrived. The position of the dragon was strange, somewhat twisted as one might lie having fallen in death, and there were parts of the skeleton missing, randomly as though from natural causes. It was also very large—larger than our ancient accounts would suggest. The proportion, too, was unusual; the head was not in proportion to the whole, and the body was thicker than one would have expected. These things convinced me that what I saw was real. If it had been contrived, I'm sure it would have been made more impressive, and more true to our idea of what a dragon should be. I believe that I have looked upon the remains of an actual dragon, as impossible as that seems."

Hojo shook his head. "I wish I had been with you, Lord Komawara, Brother. It is difficult for me to imagine such a thing."

"But such a thing," Nishima offered, "would be a powerful symbol to . . . those of less sophisticated culture. This is the same dragon embossed on the coins?"

"Undoubtedly," Komawara said. "It has strengthened the mystique of this Khan, I'm sure. Kalam is both awed and terrified by what we saw. I would imagine it affects others the same. I, too, was left with a feeling of awe. Ama-Haji is a place of power, regardless of one's sophistication."

"Perhaps we should hear the rest of the story and return to speculate upon this matter later," Lord Shonto said.

"Beyond Ama-Haji," Shuyun continued, "the Kalam took us down onto a plain where the army of the Khan had made their encampment. It was larger than we ever imagined. Large enough to have contained sixty to seventy thousand warriors. Perhaps more."

Hojo interrupted. "Encampments have been contrived to lie about the size of an army before, Shuyun-sum. We battle warriors, not encampments. How many warriors did you see?"

"We followed the tracks of a large force detached from that army—they seemed to be moving toward Seh, General Hojo. They altered their direction, though, and turned east toward the sea. This force contained forty thousand men, to my count, and we believe it was but a part of the larger whole."

Hojo cursed under his breath and Kamu clutched at the shoulder of his missing arm, his face contorted as though in sudden pain.

"This cannot be," the steward whispered, "cannot."

"If they have forces in such number," Shonto said, "and I do not doubt you, why do they hesitate? With such an army I could sweep through Seh in weeks. The north would be mine before the Empire awoke to the victory, and then the winter would guard me until spring. By that time I would be ready for armies from the south. Seh could be taken and held. This waiting makes no sense."

"They may not know the strength of Seh, Sire." Nishima offered. "The raiders who venture here see richness and concentrations of people beyond their experience. Perhaps they cannot tell how vulnerable we are. If they were to attack now and Seh were to hold for even a few short weeks, until the weather changes, then the element of surprise would be gone entirely. I am not a general, but it seems to me that the safe course would be to wait until spring. Surprise, they believe, will still be their ally, and if the campaign takes longer, the season will favor them."

General Hojo nodded, more than half a bow, to Lady Nishima, his face registering both surprise and an almost paternal pride.

Shonto eyed his military advisor. "General?"

"Lady Nishima's reasoning seems sound, Sire. Many battles have been lost that could have easily been won had the generals only known the exact moment to attack. We should also consider that there may be other reasons for the barbarians waiting—despite the importance of the information we have received from Shuyun-sum and Lord Komawara, there is still much we do not know."

Shonto nodded. "This is true. Shuyun-sum, can your servant cast a light on this matter?"

Shuyun spoke quietly to the Kalam who responded with what was obviously a question. Shuyun spoke again and then, nodding, the tribesman spoke at length. "The Kalam says the Dragon priests warned that an attack now would fail—that spring was the propitious time for certain victory—or so it is said. His Gensi, a term like hunt leader, believed that the Khan had heard that a great warrior chief came to Seh—this is not clear to me, Sire—the Kalam uses a word that has no meaning in our own language. Perhaps 'ancient reborn' would be an approximation. It was said that this chief came with a formidable army. The Gensi believed this was the real reason that plans were altered." Shuyun gave a half bow. "This great warrior chief is clearly you, Lord Shonto."

"Huh." Shonto shook his head. "This does not explain why they hesitate. I will be here in the spring." Shonto looked around the room but no one offered an explanation.

Reaching behind him, Shonto took his sword off its stand. He composed himself and all present waited without sign of impatience. "Though there is much we do not know, there can be no question, now, that war will come to Seh as winter ends. In four months we will face a barbarian army. We have that time to gain the support necessary and, even here where the blow will be struck, there are many who will not believe what has been seen in the desert.

"I must gain the support of the Throne, though how we will do this when gold, that in all likelihood comes from the Imperial mint, appears in the hands of our enemy, I do not know. This barbarian has said that the Emperor of Wa pays tribute to the Khan—but for what purpose? It is my fear that in an attempt to bring down the Shonto, the Emperor has been sending gold into the desert. Is this Khan a creature of our revered Emperor?" Shonto paused. "It does not take an army of sixty thousand to bring down one family. This has every indication of plan that has gone horribly awry. This Khan has designs of his own, do not doubt it."

Shonto fell silent for a moment but attention did not waver from him. "I do not believe that Jaku has fallen from grace with his Emperor. This is too convenient. If Jaku can be made to see the true danger, then I'm sure we will win the Emperor's support."

"I agree entirely, Sire," Kamu offered. "Jaku is the key to our Emperor, but I cannot see how we will accomplish Jaku's enlightenment."

Shonto looked down at the sword in his hands. "We will find a way," he said quietly.

"Seh is now on a war footing. In four months we will be prepared for the battles that will come if we have to strip this city of its furnishings and sell them to the Emperor himself." Shonto looked at his daughter for a moment and his face softened. Almost immediately he turned his attention back to the others. "There may be some unavoidable delays in the submission of Seh's taxes to the Emperor this year." Both Kamu and Hojo smiled.

"Four months to prepare, to win the support that we require. The fate of an entire province depends on how well we perform this task. We must not fail. We cannot." Shonto fell silent for a moment.

Shuyun cleared his throat. "Sire? There is another explanation for this delaying of battle. It is undoubtedly true, as my lord says, that an attack now would see the fall of Seh. But the fall of Seh would give the south warning and the entire winter to prepare." Shuyun looked up at those around him. "If one wishes to conquer Seh, one would attack now. If one has decided to conquer an Empire . . . one would wait."

Gatherer
of
Clouds

DEDICATION

To S.J.R. for grace and humor, always.

ACKNOWLEDGMENTS

Thanks to the many who have given support, encouragement, wisdom, and inspiration during the writing of these books: Don and Michael, Ian Dennis, John H., Ellen B., Jan, Jill and Walter, Margo, Kim E., Lady Murasaki, Bella Pomer, Stephan W., Betsy and Peter, Lang, Ted, Dave Duncan, Sei Shonagon, Erin, Sam, Shelley, Bob M., and David Hinton for his beautiful translations of Tu Fu.

Rain,
Chilled by endless winter,
Runs down blue tiles
To form a bead curtain
Between our room and the world beyond.
The courtyard a small lake now

With roads washing away like ink marks
News turns to a trickle of rumors.
In far off Oe they say
Rivers have forgotten their purpose
And wander across half a province,
A shallow sea dotted by island hills.
Farmers pole wagon board sampans
Eyes red from searching
They look everywhere for their lost lives

It is a sight to pain a traveler's heart
I'm told

When asked by the Emperor
What should be done,
The Minister of the Right answered
   A generation that has not known calamity
   Will never understand the cost of war.

It is harsh wisdom
But just, no doubt

The Court Lady's Lament
From "The Palace Book"
of Lady Nikko

One

THE WIND KNOWN as the Nagana blew in its season, turning the capital of the province of Seh into a city of whispers and sighs. The near empty avenues succumbed to the Nagana's invasion as it wound its way among the uninhabited residences, wrenching at shutters and filling the streets with the echoes of the city's former life—before the plague had swept the north. Rhojo-ma was a city half full of vibrant northerners and half full of the ghosts of the plague dead; only a decade gone, they walked in living memory still.

In the late afternoon the Nagana came out of the north to haunt the city with the voices of its past, and the people in the streets hurried on their way, attempting to ignore the sounds. No family had been untouched by the plague and the whispering of ghosts spoke to everyone.

By the curb of a lesser avenue, on the low wall of a bridge that arced over the canal, sat a Neophyte Botahist monk. Apparently oblivious to the life of the city, he chanted—a low, barely melodic sound that mingled with the wind echoing down an empty stone stairwell and off a nearby wall.

If he was unaware of the city around him, it could be said that the city, or at least those who walked its streets, were barely more aware of him. Their only acknowledgment, the reflex action of a sign to Botahara as they passed, but few turned their gaze to look for the source of the chant. A monk sitting by his alms cup was as common a sight as a river man at his oar.

A coin rattled dully into the monk's leather cup and he gave a quick double bow, not interrupting his chant or looking up to see who his benefactor might be.

Without warning the already cool air turned colder and the wind died to a calm. The whispering of ghosts fell to a hush. It seemed only the chanting of the young monk moved the air, and the pedestrians hesitated as though they'd suddenly forgotten the purpose of their outings.

There was a long moment of this eerie stillness, and then a deep roll of thunder shook the walls of Rhojo-ma, seeming for all the world to have originated in the depths of the earth, so substantial did it feel.

The air took on form and turned to white as hail pelted down in a sudden torrent. The staccato of ice stones drumming on tile drowned out all other sounds, but in moments it reduced its volume to a mere drizzle, then turned to rain.

At the first crash of thunder the residents of Rhojo-ma hurried to cover, leaving the monk alone on his wall, still chanting, apparently oblivious to the pelting hail despite the thinness of his robe.

The monk's recent benefactor stood under the bridge, hoping the downpour would not last and contemplating the timing of his offering with the bursting of the clouds. It was not the blessing he had hoped Botahara would bestow. He shook the hailstones from his robe, brushing the white pebbles off the shinta blossom and flying horse emblems embroidered over his heart.

Several of Seh's more humble residents shared the man's refuge, but they stood apart from him and had bowed deeply before stepping into the shelter, waiting for his invitation. Though still a very young man, Corporal Rohku was a member of Governor Shonto's personal guard and, as such, a person of some importance despite his lack of years and low rank.

The corporal's father was the Captain of Lord Shonto's personal guard and it was the young man's secret hope to bear this rank himself in his time. Even more, it was his dream that the Rohku name would be bound to that of the Shonto over generations of important service—as the Shigotu of old had attained fame for their service as elite guards to seven generations of Mori Emperors. For the time being he would have to accept a more humble position, for he was not sure that Lord Shonto even knew his name.

Beyond the shelter of the bridge, hailstones flowed down tiny rivers that ran between cobbles, disappearing before they made their circuitous way to the canal. Corporal Rohku found himself following their progress, trying to decide where the stones ceased to be ice and became part of the water. A second rumble of thunder shook the earth and, as though this were a signal, an ornate barge took form in the mist that hung over the canal. Before Rohku truly registered this, the barge faded again, reappeared, and then disappeared wholly into the clouds as though it had been only a specter of mist shaped by an errant eddy of wind.

Rain and hail forgotten, the Shonto guard mounted the stairs back to the avenue three at a time and ran out onto the bridge. So absorbed was he in trying to part the clouds with an act of will that he failed to notice the Neophyte monk was now standing at the bridge's far end staring into the fog with equal focus.

They did not have long to wait, for the barge appeared again, this time in more substantial form. It was intricately carved, painted crimson and gold, with banners hanging limp in the teeming rain.

One pennant did not need to stretch itself in the wind to be recognized for it was Imperial Crimson. A five-clawed Imperial Dragon would circle the sun within those folds of silk. The other pennants were unrecognizable.

Corporal Rohku waited with all the patience his young spirit could summon. A second barge, a typical river craft, appeared in the wake of the Imperial Barge, for that is no doubt what it was. Just when the young guard thought he could bear it no more, a hint of a breeze, a mere sigh, tugged at the pennants. Against a dark field, a Choka hawk spread its wings, appeared to take a single beat, and then collapsed as the fickle breeze died.

The guard was off at a run toward the Governor's Palace. As he crossed the bridge, a young Botahist monk hurried past in the opposite direction though the young soldier did not notice, let alone return, the monk's half bow. There was no time to be polite to strangers. Jaku Katta had arrived—and several days before he was expected.

Corporal Rohku pushed on, keeping up his pace until reaching his destination, whereupon he spent several moments regaining his breath before he could give his report with any show of dignity.

General Hojo Masakado, Lord Shonto Motoru's senior military advisor, knelt so that he was between his liege-lord and the two openings to the room—screens leading to an outer room and the balcony. It was an old habit, one which he had developed in service to Shonto's father during the Interim Wars. Having served two generations of Shonto was a source of great pride to Hojo and he often found himself comparing the two lords. Physically they were obviously father and son, the high, broad Shonto forehead seemed to miss few generations, and both lords were exactly the same height and weight—slightly more than average in both. Personalities differed, however. The father had been more reserved and formal, a biographer and historian of some note; his humor was dry and intellectual. Motoru was far less formal, more inclined to a social life, enjoying the company of those much older and noticeably younger than himself. He had the ability of great leaders to make everyone comfortable in his presence.

Lord Shonto sat before a low table across from Hojo and the Shonto family Spiritual Advisor, Initiate Brother Shuyun, each of whom bent over the table in turn and examined three small coins that lay on the fine-grained wood—square gold coins with round holes in their centers.

"There is no question, Sire," General Hojo said, "they are identical."

Shonto turned to the Botahist Brother, raising an eyebrow in characteristic fashion. Shuyun held the coin in the palm of his small hand, staring with the ageless eyes remarked upon by everyone who met him. Hojo reminded himself that this small monk, no larger, and barely older than Lady Nishima, had once defeated the most famed kick boxer in all of Wa. Despite his appearance and quiet manner, he was as formidable a warrior as General Hojo—perhaps more so.

"I agree entirely, Lord Shonto," Shuyun said. "They have even been struck by the same die. A small irregularity can be felt along the inner edge." He turned the coin over and ran the ball of his index finger around the central hole. Both Hojo and Shonto did the same, with some concentration. Shonto looked at his general and Hojo shook his head almost imperceptibly.

"I do not doubt that you are right, Shuyun-sum," Shonto said, "though it is beyond my senses to feel this." The lord turned the disk over in his hand and realized he held the coin that had been taken from the raiding barbarian warrior. The strange dragon etched into its lustrous surface seemed to look at him with some suspicion. "Lord Kintari's dissolute son, a barbarian warrior, and now the coins Lady Nishima brings from Tanaka: 'from a trunk the Imperial Guard spirited onto a ship,' Tanaka tells us. A ship bound north. That is all we know."

They fell silent and a sudden cloudburst unleashed a torrent of hail which battered the tile roof with a clatter that would not allow quiet conversation—private conversation. Shonto reached over and opened the screen a crack that they might watch the spectacle.

Hail turned to rain and Shuyun broke the silence. "It is one of the lessons of the Botahist trained that there are times when speculation serves little purpose, Lord Shonto, General Hojo, if you will excuse me for saying so. If we have considered all possibilities, then we must accept that we do not yet know enough. Coins come from Yankura and make their way into the desert: that is truly all we know. There are, however, other concerns which we can act upon. My teachers taught that we should begin where we may and practice patience where we must."

"Your teachers were wise, Shuyun-sum," Shonto said, surprising Hojo. He had never heard anyone but their former Spiritual Advisor, Brother Satake, come so close to criticizing his liege-lord. It was a measure of how much Lord Shonto had come to trust this monk in the short time he had been in the Shonto house. The lord turned the coin over in his hand one last time and then returned it to the table.

An almost imperceptible knock sounded on the inner screen and Hojo moved to open it a crack. He listened to a voice neither Shuyun nor Lord Shonto could hear, nodded, and pushed the shoji closed.

Lord Shonto raised an eyebrow, a gesture his staff did not need explained.

"Jaku Katta has arrived in Rhojo-ma, Sire."

Shonto reached unconsciously for the coins again but stopped himself. "Huh." He turned his gaze back to the opening in the shojis. "It would be interesting to know what the Emperor's Guard Commander could tell us of these coins."

Hojo nodded.

"Please arrange a meeting with General Jaku as soon as convenience allows. We shall see if it is true—in the dark tigers see more than men."

Even by Botahist standards the Prefect of Seh was a very old man and his age inhabited his body in manner uncommon among the Botahist trained. Monks typically remained lithe and youthful far past the age when the untrained had slipped into infirmity if they remained alive at all.

Brother Nyodo, Master of the Botahist faith and Prefect of Seh, moved so slowly that he seemed always to be progressing toward an early closure of the Form.

He set a tightly rolled scroll on his writing table and very slowly turned back to his guest, Senior Brother Sotura, the chi quan master of Jinjoh Monastery.

"There is no brother by that name in our registry; *Hitari,* yes but no *Hitara.* Was Brother Shuyun certain?"

"Prefect, I do not think it is possible for him to make such a mistake."

"You think highly of this young Initiate, Brother Sotura. I begin to wish to make his acquaintance."

"Perhaps that will become possible at some future time, Prefect. It is the Supreme Master's wish, for the time being, that we keep our meetings with Brother Shuyun infrequent. It is important that Lord Shonto feel that his Spiritual Advisor is truly his."

"I only hope this will not lead to . . ." the monk searched for a word, ". . . to the willfulness we experienced with Brother Satake."

"That is my hope also, Prefect."

"Hitara . . . ?" the Prefect said slowly. "It is not possible that he was an imposter." It did not seem to be a question, so Sotura did not respond. "Is there not a Hitara in the Book of Illusion, Sotura-sum? I seem to remember . . ." He trailed off, a look of confusion and then dismay at his failure of memory.

"In the description of the Divine Vale." Sotura picked up the thread. "I had forgotten. *Hitara*—he who died and was reborn. The servant who served the Perfect Master faithfully when all others left for fear of the Emperor. Hitara rose from the flames of his funeral pyre: *'It was as though he stepped from the mist, and though the smoke and flames threatened to consume him, Hitara was untouched by them. He was like one arising from a dreamless sleep. When told of the seven days he had lain dead while his family mourned, he fell to his knees and offered up his prayers. And his funeral became the celebration of his rebirth and the celebration of his birth became the celebration of his life to be, for no other man had known such a miracle.'"*

Both monks fell silent at this. Rain fell on the tiles in the courtyard, washing away the hail that had collected earlier. A knock rattled the inner shoji.

"Please enter," the Prefect said, surprised that his words came out in a near whisper.

The shoji slid aside, revealing an Initiate of the faith, head bowed to the mat.

"Initiate?" the old man said, regaining his voice somewhat.

The young monk moved forward and placed a small stand bearing a neatly folded letter within reach of his superior, then retreated and waited in silence.

"Please excuse me, Brother Sotura, I must attend to this." He unfolded the crisp paper and read quickly. The Prefect nodded as though acknowledging spoken words and turned back to the attending Initiate. "He must be observed whenever possible. I will receive daily reports."

The messenger nodded, bowed and retreated from the room, the screen closing behind him.

The Prefect turned to the chi quan master. "General Jaku Katta has entered Rhojo-ma. He comes in an Imperial Barge, making one wonder at Brother Hutto's recent news."

Sotura paused for a moment, reflecting. "The Son of Heaven has made no public gesture that would indicate that Katta does not stand in the light of the Throne. But I have found that one ignores Brother Hutto's information at great risk."

The older man nodded. "I agree, Brother. Appearances mean little in the world of the Emperor. He treats Lord Shonto as a great favorite, but only a fool would accept this as the truth."

"Jaku Katta in Seh . . . this is a cause for concern. I find this too much like the opening of a game of gii. There are too many pieces for one to see clearly. It is complicated even more with tales of alleged barbarian armies. It is as though another entire set of pieces waited to sweep onto the board at any second." Sotura met the Prefect's eyes. "We must inform the Supreme Master of these developments immediately."

"Oh, certainly, Brother Sotura. There is no question. I have only hesitated so that I may decide how much credence to give your young protégé's report."

"Brother Shuyun did not see the number of warriors that the encampment indicates, I agree, but I do not think this was a barbarian ruse. As Shuyun-sum has said, riders from Seh were unexpected there. I fear his information is horribly true, Prefect. I propose that we send word to Brother Hutto and to the Supreme Master immediately, and under both our signatures."

"I am not certain, Brother Sotura." The older man seemed to return to his former state of confusion. "It is so difficult to believe. An army of that size? How is that possible? Even the barbarians are not bred from the sand. We would appear to be alarmists at the very least if this army does not exist. I hesitate to sign my name to a report that is based on so little information."

"Excuse me, Prefect, but may I remind you that Lord Shonto does not question what Shuyun-sum reported."

The old man shook his head. "One can never know the true meaning of anything Lord Shonto says or does, Brother. He is engaged in a struggle for his life and the future of his House. If the Son of Heaven sent an army to Seh to save his Empire from the barbarians and Lord Shonto could control that army . . . consider—the balance in the Empire could be altered." The Prefect gestured slowly toward the walls as though they encompassed all of Wa.

"I do not profess to know the secrets of this Shonto's mind, Prefect, but I take nothing he does or says at its apparent value. We do have a Brother in the Shonto House, however—a trusted advisor to the lord himself."

The Prefect's motion suddenly lost its flow and became almost stiff. "We have had a trusted advisor in Shonto's House before, excuse me for reminding you, Brother, and he was more loyal to his lord than to his Order. We do not have verifiable evidence of the size of the army in the desert. I should tell you that this is not the first report of barbarian hordes I have heard."

Sotura considered this for some time. "If I send a warning to our superiors under my own signature, what will the Prefect do?"

"I will feel obliged to report that I am not convinced by Brother Shuyun's evidence."

"Conflicting reports will certainly ensure that no action is taken. If Shuyun's information is correct, there is little time for hesitation. Little time to seek more information."

"Excuse me for saying so, Brother Sotura, but Lord Shonto's Spiritual Advisor, for all his abilities, is a young man and new to the north. No experience from all my years in Seh would indicate that such an army could exist in the wastes. I do not feel I would be acting as my position requires to give credence to Shuyun-sum's report."

The old man seemed to slump a little as though this rebuttal had taken all the energy of his ancient spirit.

"I fear I have tired you, Prefect. Please excuse me if I have destroyed your harmony." The chi quan master bowed. He rocked slowly back on his heels, a look of concern registering on his face. I'm sorry, old man, Sotura thought, but I cannot allow your fears to stop what must be done. There is more at stake than your comfortable position. May Botahara forgive me.

Lady Nishima sat before a low table looking at the design for a robe which her servants would embroider. Only moments before, as was often the case, she had a melody in her mind, a folk tune that a talented court composer had borrowed to create a composition for the Imperial Sonsa troupe. But her visitor had disturbed her harmony and the music faded away as though the musicians in her mind traveled off into the distance.

"It is of no consequence to me, cousin," Lady Nishima said, trying to keep her voice even. "Jaku Katta could arrive at my door and I would not interrupt my painting."

The mere mention of Jaku's name brought back memories she would rather have left undisturbed. She feared she colored with embarrassment, perhaps even shame, at the thought of what had happened between her and Jaku when they last met. *I went to his rooms,* she whispered to herself.

Lady Kitsura Omawara nodded in response. "I did not mean to suggest that you would be . . . pleased by the news, cousin, I am merely the messenger." She smiled the smile that disarmed the coldest hearts.

"I did not mean to be abrupt, Kitsu-sum. Please excuse me. I am thankful for your consideration in this matter." She tried a smile in return. Kitsura had not intended to cause her discomfort, after all; Kitsura was entirely unaware of what had happened between Jaku and herself. Deciding it would be best to change the subject, Nishima observed, "You seem to be very well informed, Lady Kitsura. Does Lord Shonto have this information? Or does he rely upon you?"

"I'm quite certain your esteemed father has all the information that I possess, ten times over." She looked down at her hands folded in her lap and began to turn a delicate gold ring until the design had gone full circle. When Kitsura did not look Nishima in the eye, it was a sign that she had been engaging in certain activities that she believed her cousin disapproved of. "I simply wish to keep us both informed. I have befriended certain members of your father's staff and often act as a confidante to them. After all, whom could they talk to who would be more concerned for their lord's welfare, except perhaps the Lady Nishima?"

"I am not entirely convinced that their lord would view these breaches of security quite so benignly." Nishima said this with feigned disapproval while she fought the feelings of confusion that set her heart whirling. Despite all efforts, she was afraid that these feelings must show on her face. She tried to cover this with words. "However, it is important to know as much as we can."

"I agree entirely, cousin. So much is hidden and yet everything that is important to us is in danger of being lost." She moved to the next ring, turning it a little more urgently. "Do you think it's possible that Lord Shonto could be wrong? Could the Emperor's general really be in disfavor at court?"

Nishima took a last look at the design and began to clean her brush. This would not be a brief interruption. "I do not know Lord Shonto's source of information at court, Kitsu-sum, so I cannot judge. But my father has an uncanny ability to weigh information on the scale of truth. It is worth noting that he does not speak of Jaku's present situation in absolute terms."

"This is what worries me, cousin. If Lord Shonto is right, then Jaku Katta's fall from favor and banishment are but a ploy to place the Guard Commander within our circle of trust. But if Jaku has truly fallen, and one with so many ambitions could certainly do so, then Lord Shonto cannot hope to win the Emperor's support to battle the barbarians through Jaku. This situation is of great concern. It is as you have said; so much depends on so little knowledge."

"If Jaku Katta engineered the attempt on my father at Denji Gorge without the Emperor's approval, as Lord Shonto suspects, then it is possible that our handsome general is not in favor." Nishima pushed her table aside. "It is all very confusing. Being sent north to restore order to the canal is hardly a sign of disfavor."

"Being sent to Seh as its governor would not seem to indicate disfavor either, Nishi-sum." Kitsura held her ring up to the light, examining it carefully. "It is as Brother Shuyun says; at the gii board an opponent's design does not need to be strong if you are unable to see it."

"I did not realize you discussed gii with Brother Shuyun," Nishima said, her tone registering something close to disapproval.

"Shuyun-sum has been kind enough to instruct me in the intricacies of the board . . . and to discuss matters of the spirit, also."

The two women fell silent. A distant thunder rumbled, like a far-off dragon. Rain beat on the gravel border of the garden outside.

"Nishima-sum?" Kitsura said quietly. "We must be absolutely certain of Jaku Katta's situation at court."

Lady Nishima nodded. Yes, she thought, and I must know what this man expects of me. She remembered the last thing she had said to Jaku the night she had gone to his quarters—they would speak in Seh. Now she did not know what they would say.

"I think I know how this can be done," Kitsura said quietly, "though I fear you will not approve."

* * *

Sister Yasuko held the paper up and blew gently on the ink, careful not to spread it. The dampness of the evening invaded her rooms and she huddled close to the charcoal burner and her single lamp. She blew again, careful not to spoil the fine brush work.

"There," she whispered and held the paper up to the lamp. It was a letter to her superior, Prioress Saeja.

Honored Sister:

In this time of great doubt, I wish I had better news. Our dear Sister, Morima-sum, shows little sign of improvement since I last put brush to paper. She has times when her crises seems to be passing, but the scrolls of the Brothers haunt her dreams still. We do not give up hope, Sister. We do not give up hope.

The young Acolyte who accompanied Morima-sum has not fared well. It pains me to report that she left us three days ago. This was a tragedy, certainly, but nothing compared to the loss of a Sister of Morima's abilities. Our young Acolyte had her own faith shaken by the crises of Morima-sum and as she said to me, "If the way is too difficult for one such as Senior Sister Morima, how do I presume to walk such a path?" Perhaps she will return to us yet. I pray that this will be so.

The rumor that Lord Shonto's Spiritual Advisor went into the desert in the company of Lord Komawara seems, incredibly, to be true. Our friend in the Governor's Palace tells us that Shonto is convinced a large barbarian army will attack Seh in the spring. We can neither prove nor disprove the theory at this time, but if Governor Shonto and his staff believe this, it is my opinion that our Order should act as though there were no doubt.

When I think of the suffering that a war would bring and how it would affect our own efforts, my heart grows heavy. We always hope calamity will not overtake us in this lifetime, rather like children trying to avoid difficult lessons. But they must be learned: if not now, later.

Jaku Katta arrived today. It will be difficult to place someone close to him, but be assured our efforts will be tireless. We have a trusted friend close to the Lady Nishima, however, and will certainly know if she continues to correspond with the Emperor's guard commander.

At this time Lord Shonto's daughter seeks her companionship with the

Ladies Kitsura Omawara and Okara Haroshu, although the Shonto Spiritual
Advisor is also one of her regular visitors—occasionally staying in her rooms
later than could be considered strictly proper: I know no more at this time.

There have been no cases of plague reported in Seh for several months
now, for which we may thank the Botahist Brothers even if they have done
little else worthy of praise. Chiba has not been so fortunate, I am told. The
many followers of Tomso in that province have suffered terribly.

The rumor that the Udumbara blossomed (Botahara be praised, Sister!),
is not given credence in Seh—it is a rumor all have heard many times be-
fore—and, as you predicted, the Brotherhood have denied it. I find nothing
in all the Brotherhood's treacherous history as disconcerting as this denial.
If an Enlightened Master walks among us, why do they deny it? I am cold
with fear over this.

Work on the Priory goes well and at less expense than we dared hope:
Botahara watches over us. I would inquire of your well-being, Prioress, but I
know the polite response. I, too, am well enough to serve His Purpose.

> *May Botahara chant your name,*
> *Sister Yasuko*

Two

Distant hills rise up
Through an ocean of
Wind tattered cloud

Peaks become islands
In a chaos of pale crested seas

THE ERRATIC SPATTER of snow-melt on the undergrowth seemed to grow progressively louder. Lord Komawara tugged at the reins and moved his mare another twenty paces into the mist, stopped, and listened for the hundredth time.

Deep in the mist that had hung for days in the Jai Lung Hills it was impossible to determine the origin of sounds. They echoed and distorted and seemed to emanate from everywhere at once.

Komawara turned in a complete circle, a motion almost as slow as Brother Shuyun practicing his meditations of movement. Nothing . . . only the suggestion of mysterious forms: to his right a twisted, pointing limb perhaps belonging to an ancient pine; behind him, an outcropping of rock suggesting the face of a disapproving Mountain God.

Shifting the horse-bow to his right hand Komawara worked the fingers, cramped from holding a notched arrow for far too long. He returned the bow to the ready position and moved forward ten paces more, listening.

Years had passed since Komawara had last hunted the Jai Lung Hills—in company with his father then, when the old man still had strength to ride. Much had changed, more than he ever expected.

There were bandits in the hills now. Holdings had seen their gates battered down in the night and only armed parties would chance the roads.

The lord stopped again, listening as Shuyun had taught when they traveled in the desert. Armor bit into Komawara's shoulder blade where the leather shirt had worn through, his left hand cramped again, his boots oozed when he walked, and his horse favored her right forefoot. If that was not enough, he was also hopelessly separated from his companions and had only the vaguest notion of where he was. A soft drizzle fell, slowly soaking into the lacings of his light armor. He listened.

Snow, heavy with rain, slipped from a tree branch and fell in a sodden pile at the lord's feet, causing his horse to shy. That, Komawara realized, was a true indication of the turmoil of his spirit—his mare had sensed it, had caught it in fact. Every few seconds the same soft thudding could be heard somewhere out in the fog.

He moved forward, then paused, straining to hear. Was that the sound of a horse, far off? The creaking of a tree distorted by the distance, by the imagination?

Komawara tried to stretch the tension out of his back and shoulders. In a fog there could be more to fear than brigands: his own men he trusted, but the local men who had joined the hunt for bandits suffered in a silence of poorly hidden fear. Men quickly lost their inner calm in fog such as this. It was as Shuyun had said, robbed of sight, every sound became a threat—even a falling lump of snow would be in danger from an arrow quickly loosed. The arrow from an ally ended more lives in battle than men would speak of.

Ten paces forward. Stop. Listen.

And then, among all the thousand imagined sounds, unmistakably, the thud of hooves on stone. His own mount pricked up her ears. Komawara jigged at the bit and pulled her nose up to his cheek.

"Shh," he whispered as though she understood. Three paces put them among a stand of long-needled pines. The lord pulled the reins over the mare's head and made her lie down, saddle and bags still in place. Automatically testing his sword in its scabbard, he crouched down, intent on becoming part of his surroundings.

Horses moving, the scrape of loose rock shifting, the creaking of leather.

Komawara drew the arrow back by half. A horse stumbled and a man's voice could be heard making comforting sounds, but the words were not clear.

Where? Komawara turned his head from side to side, certain at first that the sound came from uphill, then equally sure its source was to his right.

He listened for a voice he might know. Be still, he told himself, let them pass, they would be easy to track in this snow. They'll make camp at dusk and it will be easy to find out who they are. But even as he gave himself this advice, he saw a movement in the mist not twenty paces away. A dark form in the blinding white. Moving toward him? Away? He tried to catch any hint of color, a familiar silhouette. A man on foot, walking slowly. Komawara almost stood for a better view, so surprised was he by the sight: dark beard on a face tanned to leather by relentless wind and sun, a vest of doeskin over light mail. *A barbarian!* A barbarian warrior leading a horse through the Jai Lung Hills.

Komawara sank lower as the man picked his way up the slope toward him. Behind the walker came others, their size amplified by the fog. Knowing that a man could look directly at him in this fog and see nothing, Komawara held himself utterly still. His mare shifted, he could almost feel her quiver. Do not move, he willed her, make no sound. Concentrating on stillness, he found himself controlling his breathing, forcing his muscles to relax.

The barbarians turned to Komawara's right and made their way across the slope, led by the man on foot who searched out the path between the trees and rock. Sixteen armed men and they did not have the look of the hunted.

Is it possible they do not know we pursue them? And then he felt reality waver for an instant. Cold awareness. No, there were no wounded, no riderless mounts. It was impossible that they could have escaped a meeting with Komawara's guard unscathed, of that he was certain.

The last man of the party disappeared into the fog less than a stone's throw away and Komawara let out a long held breath. Barbarians in the Jai Lung Hills! Bandits suddenly seemed an insignificant threat—a mere annoyance. *Barbarians* in the Jai Lung Hills!

The lord waited, listening as the creak of leather and the clatter of hooves faded. Looking around at the shadowless light he wondered how long it would be until darkness fell. He thought often of his companions, twenty of his guard and half as many local men, wandering somewhere in the mist.

They were well enough armed, as one would expect of men of Seh, but they were not fully armored.

Komawara had made a careful assessment of the men who had passed into the fog—they traveled light—little armor in evidence and only short bows and swords. They would carry skinning knives also, they always did. Weapons well chosen for fighting in the hills. He wished Shuyun was with him for there was no telling what his powers of observation might have added.

Komawara took up the reins and coaxed his mount to her feet. He began to follow. The footing in the melting snow was treacherous to leather soles, but the young lord chose to walk all the same. The mare would carry him, she had heart enough for that, but he preferred to give her a chance to recover—and walking allowed him to examine at first hand the barbarians' tracks in what appeared to be fading light.

The occasional distorted echo of horses passing came out of the fog and Komawara soon found the trail led out onto a narrow road that wound its way around the shoulder of the hill. Although this seemed vaguely familiar to him, Komawara was still not sure where he was.

Here and there hoofprints remained clear in the snow and a closer examination stopped Komawara abruptly. He'd watched the barbarians pass and not even marked that they rode *horses,* and fine ones, too. They rode horses like men of Seh—like bandits or barbarian chieftains! The horse was not adapted to life in the steppe and desert and was replaced there by the barbarian's hardy pony.

"Barbarians," Komawara whispered. And here he was, an advisor to the Imperial Governor, separated from his companions and lost in the hills. That would be a prize for a barbarian chieftain! If they had any idea that a man with intimate knowledge of the governor's plans wandered the hills alone, they would be searching the very clouds for him even now.

The Komawara who advised a governor knew that he acted rashly, but the young lord who was born and raised to the ways of the north could not ignore a threat to his province. It was opportunities like this that men of Seh prayed for—poems were made of such exploits, songs sung in the Governor's Palace and in the court of the Emperor.

The sound of falling water echoed out of the mist, how near, it was impossible to know. The barbarians' trail suddenly broke out of the trees and ran onto a wider path between the tall pines and cedars, their shapes barely suggested in the fog.

Walking in the clouds, Komawara thought, and then he found himself stepping onto a wooden bridge over a narrow stream. A small pool formed upstream and feeding that a twisting ribbon of white, falling water appeared like mist that had acquired density and weight.

A breeze stirred his horse's mane and began to move the surrounding fog in chaotic patterns. Out of the mist a granite wall formed above him and the smell of horses seemed to mingle with the odors of rotting vegetation and the indescribable smell of snow-melt.

The young lord brought his mount up sharp before her hooves drummed on the wooden planks. Would they make camp by the water? He backed her up five paces and dropped the reins to the ground. The faint breeze pushed holes in the mist—holes that opened like pupils for mere seconds and then swirled closed. It was like looking through a blowing curtain: a glimpse of something, then gone.

Komawara moved back to the bridge, straining to hear above the sound of falling water. The tracks of the barbarians became confused here and Komawara realized they had stopped to water horses at the pool. He crossed the bridge as silently as he could and discovered the trail leading on: there was no place to make camp.

Komawara followed the barbarians' lead and watered his mount, drinking himself and filling his water skin. It was growing noticeably darker now and despite the breeze moving through the mist, visibility would soon be left to one's imagination alone. There would no longer be a trail to follow. Komawara realized he would have to close the gap with his quarry or lose them in the darkness.

I have to give up this hope that my companions will overtake me, he told himself, it slows me and fosters indecision. He pressed on, leading his mount at a faster pace. The bow went back to the saddle and he kept his right hand free for his sword; at the pace he traveled now he would be upon someone in this mist before realizing it.

The young lord found himself wishing Brother Shuyun was with him, as he had been at Denji Gorge and in the desert. The Botahist monk did not seem to need his sight in the darkness and Komawara was sure this cloud would offer no greater challenge than the desert night. As well as possessing uncanny hearing, Komawara suspected that Shuyun could sense other living beings, could feel their presence. He senses chi, the young lord thought, whatever that might mean.

Despite his imminent danger Komawara found his focus slipping. He found himself wondering about the Lady Nishima and her cousin, Lady Kitsura Omawara. Since their arrival in Seh he had spoken with them only once, but he was left with a strong impression. Compared to the ladies of the capital, even the most sought after women of Seh seemed like the unaccomplished daughters of peasant farmers. Komawara feared that, having seen women of true culture and great beauty, he would have little hope of a happy life with the match he would likely make.

Another clump of falling snow brought him back to matters at hand. He could no longer see the barbarian tracks. Darkness had become complete. Bending close to the ground and feeling lightly with his hand, he discovered that the trail had not merely been hidden by darkness—it was gone.

An owl hooted somewhere in the mist. A dark-wing rattled its bill. They must have left the trail not far behind, he thought. By Botahara! the young lord found himself almost whispering, what if I have passed close to them in the mist? He whirled around and half drew his sword without intending to, convinced that barbarian warriors stalked him. Calming his heart with an effort, Komawara listened for what he feared most: the small sounds of armored men attempting to move in silence.

Waiting without the tiniest movement until his muscles ached, Komawara decided finally that the barbarians remained unaware of him. He began to retrace his steps, counting them consciously. Five paces, then stop; listen. He searched the ground as best he could, his hands beginning to ache from the cold of the wet snow and meltwater. Five paces more.

The tracks reappeared. Komawara could feel the depressions made by many hooves in the soft mud. Following them carefully, he found a path branching off down the slope into the black curling mist.

He searched about in the darkness until his hand encountered a sapling to which he tethered his horse, hoping she would not spook when he left her. As a precaution he took his saddlebags from her back and set them out of reach of her hooves, praying that he would be able to find them again. Opening one bag he found some bread that was not yet soaked and ate, crouched in the darkness and light rain. The barbarians would be forced to make a camp nearby, he thought, they are as blind as I in this darkness and fog.

He listened. The sounds of the Jai Lung Hills surrounded him: creaking trees, meltwater running into streams. An owl called again and the lord wondered if it truly was an owl. But nothing seemed amiss; there were no sounds that rang untrue to this place nor was there an unnatural silence. The tribesmen are part of their world, even here, he thought.

Finishing his bread Komawara set off to follow the track, now crouching, now on all fours—fighting an absurd fear that he would come upon a sleeping man in the darkness, discovering too late that he had blundered into the barbarian encampment. But this was not to be. The sounds of voices came to him and then, unmistakably, the smell of smoke.

Komawara stopped again. What would he do now? If the fog lifted in the morning, he could go looking for his guard, but the barbarians might well disappear while he searched. The lord was not confident that they could track the tribesmen, especially if they did not wish to be followed. Bandits, he thought, and snorted. Bandits indeed.

He moved toward the voices. I will watch them for now, he told himself, and make decisions when I know what they will do at sunrise.

The barbarians made their camp in an opening amidst the pines, a rock outcropping on one side giving protection from prevailing winds. Even before he could see the light, he could hear the hissing of wet wood as it steamed and smoked on the fire. Komawara felt his hunger waken as the smell of cooking came to him. They poach the Emperor's deer, he found himself thinking, and almost smiled at his reaction.

Hiding himself behind fractured rocks, the lord lowered himself to the wet ground, prepared for a long vigil but not sitting in a manner that would prevent him from rising quickly. He could see the barbarian encampment now. There were two fires burning, and men cooked at each. Crude shelters had been made of what appeared to be the roofs of the tents the wandering tribesmen called homes. Komawara knew this material—tough and, when treated with the boiled sap of the tekko root, virtually waterproof.

The men drank something which steamed in their bowls and though they were subdued, the lord realized they were all at least slightly intoxicated.

No one stood watch, not yet, not while the entire party was still awake. Later, no doubt, they would place sentries, but at this point it was clear that these were men who did not realize they were hunted.

The hunter looked on, unnoticed in the darkness; more than a little envious of the men who drank warm liquor and would soon be eating.

I must remain still, Komawara told himself, or I will quickly become the hunted. He made himself follow a simple breathing exercise that Brother

Shuyun had taught him, but his heart would not slow to a resting pace and he realized his muscles remained knotted.

A hard, cold point pushed into the back of his neck and a voice, heavy with the accent of the desert, whispered close to his ear; "Be very still, Lord. Be also quiet."

The scene before Komawara seemed to disappear and all that remained was a dark man-shape on the periphery of his vision. The fire flared briefly and Komawara felt sweat break out on his brow. They use fire to question their captives, Komawara thought, before letting them die.

Suddenly the pressure of the knife disappeared. "Brother Shuyun sends the Kalam with message. Friend," the voice whispered again. And then Brother Shuyun's servant, the tribesman who had become their guide in the desert, slipped down beside the astonished lord.

Komawara let out a long breath and then found himself almost immediately hot with anger. "Why . . . ?" He reached back, feeling for blood.

The tribesman shrugged. "You see desert man in darkness, how can you know it is the Kalam? You take your sword and I die and these," he gestured toward the men clustered around the fire, "hear and make hunt Lord Komawara." He shrugged, then turned his attention to the tribesmen and said nothing more for some time.

"How did you find me?"

"My guard are lost," he said, waving a hand at the darkness. Then, pointing at the barbarians, "I find them. Find you."

"Who?" Komawara whispered. "What do they do here?"

The Kalam seemed about to answer, but then he shook his head and Komawara could see him struggling with the language—missing his translator, Brother Shuyun.

"In desert . . . dragon bones. . . ." He shook his head again, showing frustration.

"Ama-Haji?" Komawara offered.

The tribesman nodded: he seemed surprised Komawara remembered, as though the separation caused by language somehow isolated their experiences as well. "Ama-Haji, yes. Men of the Dragon." He fell silent again, searching.

"The followers of the Khan," Komawara said.

The young barbarian shook his head in frustration. "No, no. The men of the dragon . . . these men," he said pointing. "They come to find . . . to look. The eyes of the dragon," he said and pointed again.

"Ah," Komawara heard himself say, though he was not sure he grasped what his companion meant.

They fell silent then, turning their attention back to the barbarians who had begun to eat and continued to drink. The conversation had not grown louder and though it was punctuated by occasional laughter, it was subdued laughter.

"The message," Komawara whispered, "from Shuyun-sum?"

The Kalam nodded. "Yes." He paused as if remembering. "A warrior . . . great warrior comes—Daku Kaita."

"Jaku Katta." Komawara corrected. "General Jaku Katta."

"Yes," the tribesman nodded. "General means great warrior?"

"Yes," Komawara agreed, "very great. Is he here now? In Seh now?"

An outburst of laughter brought their attention back to the men before them.

"In Seh," the Kalam said, "yes."

"Ah." Komawara whispered, but if he meant to say more it was lost.

There was a wild cry and armored men burst out of the trees, falling on the barbarians with drawn swords. Komawara jumped to his feet and drew his own blade but then stopped and grabbed his companion. "You must stay here!" He shouted into the Kalam's face. "My men will not know you!"

The young tribesman nodded, but Komawara saw him draw his sword all the same.

There was no more time. The battle before him was pitched and though they had the element of surprise it was quickly apparent that the men of Seh were few in number. Komawara dashed the ten steps to the struggle and cut down a barbarian who was about to finish a man who had fallen. Not waiting to see if the man would rise, he leapt at another. They crossed swords briefly and then this man also fell.

A soldier in full cavalry armor, green-laced, turned on Komawara and the lord had to parry a blow before his opponent realized he was not a barbarian.

But before Komawara could find another opponent, his head seemed to explode and he found himself on his knees, fumbling with his sword, slashing his hand on the blade. The green-laced warrior jumped past him and Komawara watched him engage a man swinging a staff. Komawara struggled to his feet in time to deflect a stroke from an enormous tribesman.

The lord found himself being driven back now, his famed reflexes and tactics dulled by the blow to his head. A second barbarian joined in, close on his right, forcing Komawara to parry. The larger of his opponents lunged at this opening and he tensed, waiting for the point to find him. But the pain did not come. Instead, the barbarian seemed to freeze and then his knees buckled as he was run through on the sword of another tribesman.

Komawara saw the Kalam pull his blade free, but that glance almost cost the lord his arm. The man he battled now sensed his present state and was intent on taking the weakened lord's life before he could recover.

Komawara found his vision blurring and kept shaking his head, hoping to clear it. The firelight did not seem to be helping. One second it would catch his opponent's blade, but as the sword moved and offered a different plane to the light it would appear and disappear, causing Komawara great confusion. "Watch his hands," Komawara said aloud, reminding himself of lessons he had received from his father. *In failing light watch the hands, they will tell you what the sword does.*

Digging deep into his experience, the young lord searched for something that would save him, for he could not last long as things were. The man would soon find a hole in his defense.

He overreaches, Komawara thought and changed the movement of his retreat so he stepped back first with his left leg. The man parried and lunged, point first at Komawara's chest. The lord swayed and turned away but not quickly enough, and he felt the point slip into his side through the gap in the armor under his left arm. But even as he felt the barbarian's steel, Komawara's own sword caught the man under the chin and it was over. The point wrenched free of the lord's side as the man collapsed at his feet.

Komawara was barely able to keep his feet, and his vision narrowed to a dark tunnel.

Only a few men stood, scattered about the encampment—but they were all men of Seh, green-laced like the one who had saved him. They seemed to be staring at him, but Komawara did not know why. Slowly Komawara became aware of a ringing of swords to his left and he turned that way in horror. The Kalam fought two men in green and a third was coming to their aid.

"No," Komawara said, but the shout came out as a whisper. He turned to intervene and almost fell. "No," he whispered again. Blood appeared on the Kalam's shoulder and quickly turned his arm red.

Komawara lifted his own sword and his vision blurred. With all his remaining strength he swung and took a sword out of one man's hands. Parrying now, he put himself between the men of Seh and his former guide.

"No," he said weakly, "he is mine."

The men before him hesitated, but none lowered their swords. They stared at him and Komawara could not read the questions in their eyes.

"And who are you that you claim this murderer as your own?"

Komawara looked at these warriors now and realized that the blow to his head had affected his judgment. These were not the locals who had joined his guard. They wore armor of good quality, well used, and laced in green. There was no family nearby that wore this color. The Kalam reached out and gripped his shoulder.

"I am Komawara Samyamu and this man is my servant."

Other men gathered before him and Komawara realized that there was no escape into the trees now. He was barely able to stand as it was.

The men in their green lacing looked from one to the other and there were protests and harsh words in low voices. Komawara heard someone curse.

"Lord Komawara, you keep unusual company," the man before him spoke. He pulled back his face mask and gave a half bow, removing his helmet. A man behind him stepped forward.

"Lieutenant, I saw a barbarian cut down one of his own kind—a barbarian who was attacking Lord Komawara. It surely was this man."

The one addressed as a lieutenant nodded his head. "Excuse my manners, Lord Komawara, I am Narihira Chisato, late of Lord Hajiwara Harita's cavalry."

By Botahara, Komawara thought, the green lacing—yes! The Hajiwara. The house I helped bring down at Denji Gorge. Against his will Komawara lowered his sword as he felt his arms were about to start shaking. Blood soaked his side now and a glance told him that the Kalam was faring no better than he.

Komawara returned the man's bow with a nod. "Lieutenant. I do not know your purpose, but my own men are nearby. We search these hills for brigands. Yet the hills, it seems, are full of surprises. I wish to thank you for your assistance in bringing down our enemy."

"Even as you assisted in the fall of our lord's house?" another man said bitterly. The lieutenant raised his hand and silence returned.

"Lord Komawara, as you might imagine, the fall of the Hajiwara House has left us feeling . . . some resentment to those who brought about our misfortune. And though Lord Shonto and . . . his allies were instrumental in this, we realize that it was a betrayal by others that led to our lord's fall. We honor his memory.

"It is the opinion of those with experience in such matters that our liege-lord did not make the wisest decision when he agreed to oppose Lord Shonto. Please realize that our anger in this matter is reserved for others. Lord Shonto could not have acted other than he did. Nor could you as his loyal ally. You are injured, Sire, and though we do not understand the service of this man it is obviously your prerogative." He bowed again, lower this time.

"We will put up our swords and see to our wounded. I would look to your own injuries myself, Lord Komawara. I have some skill in this."

Although there were dark looks among some of the Hajiwara men, swords were sheathed and men turned back to the fires. Komawara and the Kalam sheathed their own weapons and then supported each other over the few steps to the fireside. The lord collapsed close to the warmth, glad of it, for he found himself deeply cold. His ears still rang from the blow to his head and he was dizzy and weak.

Beside him he heard the tribesman dry heave. He has lost blood, Komawara thought, and he felt hands begin to remove his laced mail and then cut away the side of his leather shirt. He felt removed from his surroundings, as though everything he heard and felt came from far away. Vaguely he heard a report of two deaths and found himself hoping they were not his own guard.

Sleep. Komawara desperately wanted to sleep. He tried to shake his head, but his muscles did not seem to respond. Beside him the Kalam seemed so distant Komawara wondered how he had done that when, only a moment before, they had been within an arm's length. And then there was darkness.

When Komawara awoke, he did not know where he was or how long he'd been sleeping. The bed he lay in was soft and smelled of the forest. Pine boughs, he realized, and pulled the covering of deerskin closer about him. The fires still burned and men sat close to the warmth, faces out to the darkness, swords in hand.

Hajiwara, he remembered, Hajiwara's men. On the run now, without a House. Marked by the Butto and their feud. He shook his head. Probing his side, he found it wrapped in silk and damp from a small bloodstain. Not serious, he thought, but his head still rang and the men sitting at the fire kept blurring and doubling. Bandits, he thought, brigands in the Jai Lung Hills. He fell into a troubled sleep.

The mist was as thick when Komawara awoke as it had been when he followed the barbarians. Men stirred in the camp and Komawara smelled both cha and food. The ringing in his ears had largely disappeared to be replaced by a deep throbbing throughout one side of his head, extending down as far as his shoulder. He lay still for some time and then stirred himself to sit up. This caused his vision to tunnel but he braced himself and it passed. Someone crossed to him, bending to help him rise. The Kalam looked greatly relieved as he took Komawara's arm. The tribesman helped the lord with his soft riding boots and Komawara had to shake him off so he could walk the four paces to the fire himself.

"You are good, yeh? Good?" the Kalam kept asking and smiling.

Komawara nodded and lowered himself onto a rock set near the flames. Sitting alone with the Hajiwara men had obviously not been a comfortable situation and even now men cast unfriendly glances at the barbarian. The lieutenant bent over one of the wounded, but when he saw Komawara he rose and crossed the clearing toward him.

"Lord Komawara," the lieutenant bowed and offered a cup of cha which Komawara received gratefully. "We hope you are somewhat recovered. The wound in your side does not appear to be serious, but I am concerned about the blow you took to the side of your head. Is your vision clear? Do you feel unsteady or ill?" The man stared at the lord with a look of concern and Komawara noticed the man's glance stray up to Komawara's short hair—the mark of his time as Brother Shuyun's Botahist companion. Whatever questions the man had in his mind he kept to himself.

"I'm sure I will be well shortly, Lieutenant. Thank you for the care and for the attention you have shown to my guide." Bandits, Komawara thought again. Brigands.

The lieutenant waved at one of his men and food came the lord's way. He ate quietly and when he had finished and was sipping cha the lieutenant returned.

"We have been wondering, lord, what you might know of these barbarians—of their purpose."

Komawara nodded but said nothing. What goes on here, he asked himself.

What were these tribesmen doing in the Jai Lung Hills? *Eyes of the Dragon*, the Kalam had said. Eyes of the Dragon?

"These barbarians are of a sect, I believe, a sect that venerates the Dragon." Komawara offered no more, waiting, hoping the lieutenant would say something that would help him understand what transpired. But the Hajiwara man offered nothing.

Komawara tried again. "You will find on their persons a gold impression of the dragon embossed . . ." He stopped as the lieutenant held out a small gold figure on a chain.

"This?" the lieutenant asked.

The Kalam made a warding sign and drew away.

"Yes," Komawara said. He took the figure in his hand against the protests of his guide. It was not the embossed coin he had seen before but a tiny figure of ornate beauty. The same dragon to be sure, the dragon of Ama-Haji, but not the primitive depiction the barbarian raider had carried.

The Hajiwara lieutenant cleared his throat. "Lord Komawara, you must realize that we have come to Seh to escape the Butto. We have not done this from fear but because we have an oath to fulfill. Please do not ask its nature for I may not speak of it.

"There were eleven of us when we crossed the border . . . now we are nine." He looked around at his companions who began to draw nearer. "We have lived in these hills for some weeks now and, as you have no doubt guessed, our actions here have not always followed the most honorable course. Of this we are not proud." He paused then as if to gauge Komawara's reaction. The lord of Seh said nothing. The lieutenant went on.

"We happened upon the barbarians some days ago," he began, but a moan from one of the wounded drew his attention. A man rose immediately and went to see to this companion. "We happened upon them by accident and we have watched their camp since.

"We did not pursue the barbarians for any personal gain but only because they are the ancient enemy of our people and because there are rumors that they grow in strength again. Yet now we find ourselves in a most difficult position, Sire." He nodded to his men who had gathered around them and two stepped forward bearing a leather saddlebag between them. They set it down at Komawara's feet and pulled open the flap.

Coins glinted in the pale light as only gold could do. An entire saddlebag brimming with gold coins!

Komawara reached forward and took up one of the coins—square, finely minted with the round hole in its center.

"Here is more money than, together, we could have dreamed of seeing in a lifetime. It is most unfortunate, however, that we should find this now, for we are men who have lost our honor. Men who are hunted, not just by the family that murdered our lord . . ." He shrugged and shook his head, started to speak, then stopped again. He shook his head once more and went on.

"This gold can never profit us, Lord Komawara. There is nowhere we could go that this past we have made will not finally pursue us. Nor is there a way to escape our own knowledge of our recent errors. Karma . . ." He shrugged. "No, this gold will only tempt us from our chosen path.

"What we wish to ask you, Lord Komawara, is that you take this gold and compensate those we have wronged." He looked down at the saddlebag. "If that is not too much to ask."

Such a plain bag, Komawara found himself thinking.

"And you will do what?" Komawara asked, not taking his eye from the gold—more gold than his entire holdings were worth—many times more.

"As you slept, Sire, we spoke. It is clear that under any other circumstances what we did yesterday would have been considered a service to our Empire. I believe it is true to surmise that, considering this great treasure we have found, we would have been richly rewarded. But in our present situation this cannot be. There is a certain irony in this. Rather like the plight of Shubuta when he was tricked by the Goddess of Greed." He gave half a laugh.

"So all that is left to us is an oath that we swore when our House fell. It will guide us now."

Komawara thought for some time, staring into the fire.

"I do not know the exact nature of this oath, though it is obvious what it must be. Do you wish to revenge yourself upon my ally, Lord Shonto, or members of his staff?"

"No, Lord Komawara."

"Who would offer you service, lieutenant, if this oath would endanger their own House?"

"A House with the same enemies, Sire."

"Huh."

Komawara tossed the coins back into the bag. "It is not within my power to release those who have broken the laws of our Empire, but as you say, you have performed a service and it should not go unrewarded. Can you swear that carrying out this oath will not endanger the purpose of my House or my allies?"

The lieutenant looked around the group. "We are patient, Lord Komawara. We can wait until such a time as we would not endanger the Komawara House."

The lord nodded and returned his attention to the fire. His head throbbed. Forcing himself to sit, not slump, Komawara met the lieutenant's eye. "Then will you exchange your green for the colors of the Komawara house?"

There was a low murmur among the Hajiwara men and they gathered about the lord and their lieutenant.

"You would offer this knowing that we are hunted by the Butto and aware of our recent actions?"

"Lieutenant Narihira, I saw men fight the enemy of our Empire knowing that it would profit them not at all. You could have easily ridden by—what do you owe the Emperor? Men who would act so are men of honor, of this I have no doubt."

The lieutenant withdrew to confer with his men, leaving the Kalam and Lord Komawara to share food.

The Hajiwara men were not gone long.

"Lord Komawara," the lieutenant began, "we have weighed your words and we know that this offer is more than any of us had ever dared hope for. We were resigned to living without House or honor. Yet there is the matter of the Butto. They have sworn an oath to hunt down all of my lord's followers, sparing none. You would be standing between the Butto and ourselves and we cannot allow this."

Komawara smiled. "Lieutenant, the Butto believe they owe the Komawara a debt that they cannot repay in one hundred lifetimes. I think I can trade part of this debt for your lives . . . in return for your sworn service, of course."

"If this is as you say, Lord Komawara, then I may speak for all of us. We would be honored to wear the colors of the House of Komawara."

The Hajiwara men knelt before him and, one by one, laid their swords at his feet.

After this was done, Lord Komawara stood with difficulty. "It is good that you have proven that you can fight our enemies, for there is war awaiting us. Of this, have no doubt. In this war we must stand shoulder to shoulder with those we would consider enemies . . . or we will fall. And more than Seh will fall with us." Komawara looked at the men standing before him. Do they believe what I say? he wondered. It hardly mattered. They would believe soon enough.

"What has happened in this glade must never be spoken of. You have seen no barbarians in these hills. You must never say differently. I have rewarded you with service to the Komawara for dispatching the bandits who have threatened us, and also for saving my life. No one will question this. But the graves must be hidden so that no one can ever suspect otherwise. Likewise, you must say nothing of this gold. I do not claim it for my own but will give it to the Imperial Governor, for it was carried by these barbarians for purposes that I cannot speak of. When we arrive at my lands, you will be honored for vanquishing the bandits in these hills, and in a way this is the truth." He smiled.

"We must go down out of the hills now. There is much that we must do."

Three

THE SHIPS SET off in driving rain, heeled to a cold west wind, their sails reefed so small it seemed impossible that they would weather the headland. Yet they made way, if not quickly at least steadily.

Lord Shonto Shokan sat his horse on a high cliff and watched the ships pass. He raised his arm once, not at all sure he could be seen, and waved slowly. Turning his mount, he picked his way down the track that ran along the cliff edge. He didn't wish to keep Tanaka out on deck in this terrible weather, for the old man must stay at the rail until the son of his liege-lord was unquestionably lost to sight—anything less would be an unforgivable insult. After all, Shokan had ridden to the headland to see the older man on his way, paying him a great honor. Honor, Tanaka deserved—protracted suffering, he did not.

If Shokan had known, he would have been less anxious to leave, for Tanaka stood at the rail staring up at the distant rider and the streaks on his face were not all from the rain and salt spray. He looks much like his father did at that age, the merchant was thinking. And he is as dear to me.

Tanaka watched as the figure in Shonto blue waved and then turned back along the cliff, followed by three guards. So few, Tanaka thought, it's almost as if there were no danger.

The young Lord Shonto worked his way down to a stretch where the cliff path turned flat and broad and pressed his mount into a canter. He was delighted, as always, by the stallion's motion. He had brought the animal back with him from Seh, and it had survived the voyage, first by river and then by sea, without apparent harm to body or spirit.

Seh. . . . It was that province and his father's situation to which his thoughts constantly returned. Tanaka's visit had been most unsettling, adding fuel to the slow kindling of fear that had been smoldering since his father's most recent letter.

As he had feared all along, there was more hidden in the wastelands than the proud men of Seh would admit possible. And now this news from Tanaka.

He spurred his horse up a steeper rise, hooves throwing clods of soft turf as they went. Reining in, he turned back to the sea and took longer than he expected to catch sight of the small fleet disappearing into the sheets of rain that shrouded the entire Bay of Mists. There would be no more ships setting out across those waters now until spring returned; these were tempting the Storm Gods quite enough.

Late, late in the season for such folly. Shokan turned his mount toward the Shonto Palace. Folly, he thought, there has been entirely too much folly. Sensing his mood, his guard hung back as far as duty would allow, leaving their young lord alone with his thoughts.

Reaching down a heavily gloved hand, Shokan patted the stallion's shoulder as a sudden gust whipped its unplaited mane into a tangle. His father did not believe that Seh could be held. He shuddered though he was not cold.

Did the Emperor know that all that stood between his Imperial person and the loss of his Throne to a barbarian chieftain was Shonto Motoru? Shokan supposed that he did not.

If Shonto abandoned the north and fell back to the south, how long could he keep control of the army he was raising? Surely the Son of Heaven would order him to step down from his command in shame the moment he crossed the border of Seh. Shokan had not liked the tone of his father's last letter. Staying in control of the army long enough to defeat the invaders had seemed to be his father's only concern.

> *Wa is in danger as never before. We cannot be swayed by desires for revenge upon those who have allowed this to come about. It is not a question of losing our fief or Shonto honor—we are in danger of losing the entire Empire.*

So his father had written and Shokan did not doubt it for a moment.

There would be no support from the Emperor, and the men of Seh seemed equally blind to their plight and might well remain so until it was too late. My father needs an army, Shokan thought, he needs the largest force the Empire can raise, yet that is impossible. He fought off the bitterness and anger that had been growing since his visit from Tanaka.

He tried to replace this bitterness with the feelings of affection he felt for their vassal-merchant. Tanaka sailed into more danger than winter storms. If Lord Shonto was removed from command of his army, all of the Shonto House would fall with him. Tanaka, who controlled the family's vast trading interests, would be the third Shonto retainer the Imperial Guard would seek out, after Shokan and Lady Nishima.

Tanaka was convinced that the Emperor would invite the young Shonto heir to come to the capital for the winter social season and Shokan was certain he was right. He had been expecting the Imperial summons for days.

Of course he would stall as long as possible, but that would not be forever—the Emperor was not a patient man.

At least Lady Nishima was no longer within the Emperor's reach. This brought a smile to replace the anxious look on the young lord's face. He wondered how the Emperor would react to *that?* Nishima gone, and in the company of the woman the Emperor had himself appointed to be her instructor in the arts. Although he stood somewhat in awe of his adopted sister's charm, Shokan could not imagine how Nishi-sum had tempted the Lady Okara from her island sanctuary.

Shokan would like to see the Emperor's response to that news. The Yamaku Emperor was not patient nor did he like to appear a fool. The young lord laughed aloud. There were at least small victories to be enjoyed. Oh, Nishi-sum, how did you manage such a thing? He laughed again and spurred his horse in a wild gallop along the cliff top. Below him the sea battered the ancient cliff, endlessly: soft water against hard stone in an unequal contest.

Four

J AKU TADAMOTO TRIED to sit calmly, without betraying any sign of the fear he felt. It was a difficult exercise. The Emperor was known to fly into rages, but in Tadamoto's experience the sovereign could be at his deadliest when he was silent—trying to contain his infamous temper. The Emperor stood, apparently examining a figure in a three-panel painting of the battle of Kyo. He held his sword of office in its scabbard before him in both hands and Tadamoto could see the Emperor's right hand flexing like an involuntary seizure on the sword's grip.

Jaku Tadamoto's sense of tranquillity was further eroded by the knowledge that the object of the Emperor's rage was his own brother, Katta. He was not certain what caused him more apprehension: the thought that the Emperor's legendary distrust would now be focused on him because of his brother's latest betrayal, or whether he feared for Katta. Certainly Katta had gone off to the north, turning his back on Tadamoto, but even so, Katta was still his brother.

The Emperor turned suddenly and glared down at the kneeling guardsman.

"So, Shonto's daughter is in league with my former Guard Commander, damn his arrogance!" He gazed back at the figure in the painting again as though it calmed him. The figure, Tadamoto could not help but notice, was impaled upon a lance.

Very quietly, Tadamoto ventured to speak. "It is difficult to say, Sire, it is just as possible that their meeting was merely coincidence."

"I am not a believer in coincidence, not when your brother is concerned."

The Emperor paced back to his dais, paused to consider, then kicked a silk-covered pillow across the audience chamber. "And it was the Lady Okara? You are certain?"

Tadamoto looked at the floor directly in front of him. "It would appear so, Sire. Her staff report that she is ill and cannot receive visitors, the same explanation we are given at the Shonto House. The description I have received would seem to leave little doubt."

The Emperor dropped back to his cushions and stared at the mats as intently as did Tadamoto. "And you still do not believe he has secretly joined the Shonto?"

Tadamoto shook his head slowly. "It would be most uncharacteristic, Sire. My brother is ambitious, I will not deny it, but he believes that Shonto's famed loyalty is a sham. He thinks the great lord is loyal only to his own ambitions, all other alliances merely serve his purpose. I think Katta-sum's distrust of Lord Shonto is unwavering."

The Emperor shook his head. "He is your brother, Colonel, it is natural that you trust his motives more than others might." He looked up at the young officer in front of him. "You, however, must decide where your loyalties lie. You cannot serve two masters, Tadamoto-sum, be very clear on that."

Tadamoto bowed his head to the mat and returned slowly to his kneeling position. "My brother and I have had a parting of ways, Sire. Katta went north on the great canal, while I remained. . . . I am my Emperor's servant. It is my hope that my opinions regarding my brother are not dictated by family loyalties but come only from careful thought and concern for duty to my Emperor. If this is not the case, Sire, please dismiss me from my position and allow me to serve in some other way." He bowed again.

The Emperor stroked his chin, and though his eyes were fixed on the young Jaku, his focus was elsewhere. When he spoke again, his voice was quieter, softer. "No, Tadamoto-sum, I trust you. I am well aware that your brother's actions cause you great pain and that you still hope there is an explanation that will indicate his continued loyalty to the Throne. I hold the same hope, for Katta is dear to me." He paused. "But I cannot let my affection blind me entirely. If your brother does not soon act in a manner that proves our hopes are justified. . . ." The Emperor let the threat hang in the air. He began examining his scabbard.

After a moment he turned back to the young man who knelt before him. "Is there more to this report, Colonel, or is that all the bad news for the day?"

Tadamoto hesitated, offering a silent prayer to Botahara. "There is one other thing, Sire." He tried to work some moisture into a dry mouth. "It seems that Lady Nishima and Lady Okara have one other companion."

"Oh."

Tadamoto almost whispered. "It is possible they are accompanied by the Lady Kitsura Omawara, Sire."

The Emperor did not take his eyes from his sword.

"That will be all, Colonel."

"Yes, Emperor." Jaku Tadamoto touched his head to the floor and, without rising, backed from the room as quickly as concern for the Emperor's dignity would allow.

Akantsu II sat for a long time, staring at his sword of office. Insults such as this were not paid to Emperors. No doubt Lord Omawara believed his name and failing health would protect him. The Emperor pulled his sword halfway from its scabbard and then rammed it home savagely. Oh, there was nothing the Emperor could do openly—Omawara was correct in that assumption. But that would not protect the old man. Nor would it protect the rest of his House.

The Emperor thought suddenly of the Lady Kitsura, and her legendary beauty seemed an affront to him now. Such arrogance! The Emperor tightened his grip on the sword. The old families would never accept the Yamaku. This proved it beyond all doubt. There could be no other course of action if he was to preserve the Yamaku ascendancy. Once the Shonto were gone, the old families would realize their mistake . . . their many mistakes.

He turned and set his sword in its stand with exaggerated care, controlling his shaking hands with an act of will. He took a long deep breath and let it out slowly. The insult would not receive the slightest recognition, of course. In fact, he would send a letter inquiring after Lord Omawara's health that very day. He would also ask if Lady Kitsura's journey went well. A solicitous letter. Let the dying old man know what he had wrought upon his family. But the Emperor's mood was not so easily broken. Even the thought of what could be done to the Omawara brought him no comfort.

The Emperor took another long breath. He clapped his hands softly and a servant appeared.

"Send for Osha-sum," he said, "her Emperor desires her presence."

*   *   *

Destroying her lover's letters crossed Osha's mind when she received the summons to attend the Emperor. It will not matter, she thought. If he knows, the letters will not make a difference. Selecting robes to wear into the royal presence, an activity that could take many women several days, was comparatively easy. Calming her spirit, however, was not possible.

If the Emperor knew about her meetings with Tadamoto-sum, it would not matter that the Son of Heaven had lost interest in her . . . had not called for her in weeks. He would quickly forget that he had cast her aside without a word. That anyone would presume to pay her court would drive him to a fury, of that she was certain.

And they had been so careful! She sat down as a wave of fear weakened her limbs. What of Tadamoto-sum? Had the Emperor . . . ? She did not want to think of it. Hanging her head in her hands for a second, she tried to control herself.

No doubt this is not what I fear. It is more likely merely a good-bye—*your presence in the Imperial Palace is no longer necessary. Here is a gift from the Son of Heaven who is an admirer of your talents. It is said that Chou has need of dancers, and the air there is so healthful and pure.*

But would she be called into the presence of the Emperor for such a message? No, she thought, that is not likely. Perhaps, then, the Emperor would truly give her a gift! Perhaps he would allow her to continue to dance with the Imperial Sonsa troupe!

She thought warmly of Tadamoto. He had been so certain that he could sway the Emperor to allow her to stay in the capital. She smiled as she rose and examined her appearance in a bronze mirror. But as she left her apartments to walk to the Emperor's audience hall, her confidence seemed to waver a little with each step.

By the time Osha arrived at the guarded double doors, she was shaking and pale. Only her years of Sonsa training forced her knees to support her.

Osha barely noticed the two Imperial Guards who opened the doors. She knelt in the doorway, casting her gaze down, even when she had returned to a kneeling position. She sat thus, in the grip of more terror than she had ever known.

"Please, Osha-sum, enter," came the familiar voice. "Be at your ease."

She closed her eyes and bowed again. What could she read in that voice? He did not hide his anger well, but she had seen it done . . . had seen him toy with someone until they believed they were safe. Then he had exploded in one of his fits of anger. Osha rose and moved forward on her knees until she was a respectful distance from the dais. Folding her hands carefully in her lap, she tried to force herself into a calm but still did not meet his eyes.

"Your dancing goes well?"

"The Emperor is kind to inquire. My dancing goes most well."

"I am glad to hear this, though Colonel Jaku Tadamoto has said as much."

She closed her eyes and fought tears. Even without looking, she knew that the Emperor sat with his sword across his knees. An urge to prostrate herself and beg for forgiveness began to pull at the edges of her rising fears.

"I value the young Jaku brother's judgment," he said as though to someone else. "It pleases me that your dancing goes well. It is a demanding path that you pursue, I understand why you have so little time for mere social occasions. Demands are something an Emperor understands only too well. Though the demands made upon an Emperor do not give us the time we would wish to pursue the things that are close to our hearts. I do not think this is so with the Sonsa?"

Osha could hear the pounding of blood in her ears—a steady rhythm of fear.

"Please excuse me," she said with difficulty, "I am not sure what the Emperor means."

"Is it not dancing that is closest to a Sonsa's heart?"

"Ah." Osha smiled as if he had said something clever.

"I understand this passion that controls you, Osha-sum. I am sometimes jealous, but an Emperor must never give in to such things." He paused. "You must dance and I must spend my days listening to ministers and counselors, though it is not pursuing what is closest to my heart. Do you become jealous when the Empire takes so much of my time?"

"I . . . the Empire, Sire, cannot be compared to dance. Dance is but a trivial thing when set beside affairs of state."

"So many would say, though I am not sure I would agree. Let us say that we both are governed by things of importance. It does not matter." She knew he stared at her, and she tried to remain calm. "It warms my heart to see you, Osha-sum. You have grown even more beautiful these last months."

"I am honored that you would say so, Sire."

"We must learn to live with the demands of our lives, Osha-sum, and take pleasure in the moments that are truly our own."

His outstretched hand appeared before her.

Her heart sank entirely now. He did not know about Tadamoto! That was not why she had been summoned. He desired her! After ignoring her entirely and subjecting her to the greatest humiliation, he wanted her!

She closed her eyes and fought back tears. The Emperor wanted her again. Was she not pleased? She thought of Tadamoto and realized that she was completely terrified of arousing the Emperor's suspicions. She dared not refuse.

"Are these tears, Osha-sum?" the Emperor asked. "Is there something wrong?"

Shaking her head, she tried to smile. "Tears do not always indicate sadness, Sire."

With effort she reached out her hand and the Emperor grasped it. She had forgotten how strong he was. As she moved forward the Emperor pulled her, almost roughly, onto the dais so that her knee struck the frame, but he did not seem to notice.

A kiss that would have seemed passionate before felt coarse to her now. His hands touched her without concern for her pleasure, failing to arouse as they once had. The Emperor fumbled at her sash, for it was not a Lover's Knot and easily undone. She had to untie it for him, helping unwind the yards of brocade.

Pushing her down into the deep silk cushions, the Emperor opened her robes. There were no words of love, no whispers close to her ear. Osha felt nothing but revulsion. With all her heart she wanted to run. Until that moment she had not known what it was she felt for Tadamoto-sum. The Emperor lowered his weight onto her, his face close to hers, his breath coming in harsh gasps.

Five

THERE WERE FEW people as skilled at waiting as Brother Sotura. He could truthfully say that he had only known impatience twice, perhaps three times, in his life, and on each of those occasions he had mastered this emotion almost immediately. The chamber in which he practiced waiting contained a small shrine to Botahara on one wall and an austere, but very skillful arrangement of cedar boughs and autumn slip maple on a small stand against another. These two things in themselves would have provided the necessary focus for many days of meditation, even if Brother Sotura didn't have other things to consider. And he could barely remember a time when he did not have *other things* demanding his attention.

He was more than concerned that Lord Shonto had not allowed this second meeting with Brother Shuyun to take place in the Temple of the Pure Wind. The lord had insisted that the meeting should be held in the Governor's Palace so Shonto "would not be deprived of his Advisor's counsel at this crucial time." Of course, Brother Sotura had agreed immediately—one didn't argue with an Imperial Governor, especially one whose family name was Shonto—but still, he was concerned.

Lord Shonto was known to be a very convincing man and Sotura feared the lord's influence on his former student. Shuyun was too important to Botahist interests to go the way of Shonto's former Spiritual Advisor. The Brotherhood could not afford another renegade. He smiled at the term he'd chosen. Perhaps "renegade" was too strong, but Brother Satake had certainly pursued a course of independence. And independence was not something the Brotherhood either encouraged or admired.

Private discussion with Brother Shuyun was what the chi quan master required, and he was not convinced that it would be possible inside the Governor's Palace. Sotura turned his gaze to the paper-thin walls. Lord Shonto was certainly not above having the conversations of his Spiritual Advisor listened to; of that he was certain. Of course Sotura did not plan to make a request of Shuyun that the young monk could not fulfill in good conscience, so that was not the reason he was concerned with being overheard. It was what Shonto might learn of the Botahist Order that concerned Sotura. Knowledge of the schisms within the Brotherhood could prove most useful to some parties in the Empire.

So the conversation with Shuyun must be private, that was certain. The young monk had seen the evidence of armies in the desert with his own eyes, and that was a crucial factor. Sotura had to have Shuyun's support in what he was about to do, although Shuyun could be spared the details and reasons. The Initiate would undoubtedly be distressed to know that his information would be used to destroy the credibility of a senior member of their faith.

Brother Sotura turned his gaze back to the statue of Botahara in its shrine with its arrangement of leaves and branches. He felt a second of confusion as though the statue gazed back at him and the look was not entirely benign. Sotura shook himself out of this state immediately.

Footsteps could be heard approaching down one of the labyrinth of halls that wove through the fabric of the palace. *Shuyun.* The chi quan master recognized the sound of the footsteps as easily as he would the boy's signature or his style of chi quan. The older man smiled until the shoji was pushed aside and then the smile was replaced by the unreadable countenance of a Botahist Master.

Shuyun bowed low to the Senior Brother as he entered the room. There were few people he respected more, and though the Botahist Brothers neither showed nor felt much emotion, Shuyun felt something close to affection for his former instructor.

"My lord's House is honored by your presence, Brother Sotura."

"As I am honored by Lord Shonto's consideration."

The two monks knelt a few feet apart on thin cushions set on the straw-matted floor. There was a short silence while Shuyun, as the junior monk, waited for Brother Sotura to speak. His patience seemed every bit as developed as his former teacher's.

"I have many things to discuss with you, Brother Shuyun, but I have spent so much time indoors of late that I wonder—is it possible for us to speak outside without inconveniencing your lord should he have need of your counsel?"

Shuyun thought for a second. "I will send a message to Kamu-sum saying that we are to be found on the Sunrise Viewing Terrace. The terrace will be most pleasant at this time of day. Will that suit your needs, Brother?"

"Perfectly, Shuyun-sum. I thank you for your consideration."

A servant was sent running with the message and the two Botahist monks set out for the terrace. As they walked, the conversation stayed within the strict bounds of polite discourse between teacher and student. Sotura asked questions and Shuyun responded with short answers; they even laughed at a joke. To anyone listening, there would have been no hint of tension in their discourse.

The Sunrise Viewing Terrace was an excellent choice, for it was well situated to make the most of the sun while still offering some protection from the wind. The cold north wind typical of the season had relented that morning to be replaced by a sea wind that suggested spring more than the true season. The conversation, however, had a certain chill in it.

Lady Kitsura was followed by a maid and by the daughter of one of Seh's more senior military men— Kitsura could not remember the man's name or rank. His daughter was playing at the role of lady-in-waiting and though Lady Kitsura had been annoyed by this farce to begin with she admitted to herself now that the young girl had charmed her. There was something about the girl's naïveté that the woman from the Imperial Capital found very attractive, perhaps especially so during this time when everything seemed so complex, when there were so many suspected lies. The fact that the young woman admired Kitsura almost to the point of worship might have had some effect as well.

Now it seemed that the young woman was beside herself with excitement at the prospect of meeting Lady Nishima Fanisan Shonto. Much to her surprise, Kitsura found herself telling her companions that Lady Nishima was only human, after all. The tone of mild annoyance that accompanied these words was a bit of a surprise to the sophisticated lady from the capital.

Lady Kitsura walked as quickly as decorum would allow. She did not want to seem to be rushing, after all, but in her mind she ran. Her cousin, Lady Nishima, must be told the most recent news immediately.

The three women came to a doorway leading outside. Kitsura had insisted they venture out to appreciate this fine day and though this suggestion had met with some small resistance her companions had not wanted to disagree. The truth was that the route outside would save them several minutes. Stepping out into the bright sunlight Kitsura's two companions broke into smiles. Not only did the sun shine, but the day was almost warm. A gentle sea wind tugged at their elaborate robes and attempted to improve upon the studied arrangement of their hair.

Kitsura had to shepherd her companions along or they would have stopped to play the Cloud Game, looking for forms in the sky, perhaps hoping that the famous lady from the capital would compose a poem—excited, though somewhat apprehensive, that she might expect them to do the same.

For her part, the great lady from the capital felt a slight tugging of regret that she could not stop and play the Cloud Game or just walk in the sun and discuss nothing of importance. It was more than that though; it was a regret that, in some inexplicable way, these pleasures were no longer accessible to her. And this made her sad.

Bearing news to Nishima-sum was far too important to delay with such selfish concerns, so, to the disappointment of the two young women of Seh, Kitsura marshaled them along the covered portico.

All three of the women showed great surprise at finding two men deep in conversation on a terrace. If they had not been Brothers of the True Faith, the women would have been deeply embarrassed. How would such a situation be looked upon? Three young women meeting men alone outside on a winter day? Most unseemly!

It was rumored that the ladies of the capital did such things, but the women from Seh had certainly seen no evidence that either the Lady Nishima or the Lady Kitsura acted in such a manner. They hadn't actually believed the rumors anyway, they told each other, trying to cover their disappointment.

The monks gave their short double bow and the ladies bowed in return, except Lady Kitsura who favored the Brothers with an elegant, though modest, nod of her beautiful head.

The young lady of Seh found herself committing this gesture to memory and stopped herself as she began to imitate it.

A few polite inquiries were made before Lady Kitsura suggested that they continue on their errand, assuring the Brothers that their destination had not been the Sunrise Viewing Terrace and though they were very kind to offer, there was no need for the honored Brothers to leave. The ladies must be on their way.

And so they left, though the officer's daughter could not help but notice that Lady Kitsura looked back over her shoulder as she left and caught the young monk's eye in a manner that could only be described as flirtatious. The young woman looked away, trying not to notice. But she had noticed and she was more than a little disconcerted. She found it a bit difficult to catch her breath for a few seconds. Walking more quickly now, she hoped the blush on her cheeks would be attributed to the wind.

The apartments of Lady Nishima were not as elegant as those she was used to, but she laughingly told Kitsura that they were a great improvement over their cabins on the river barge. In truth, they were quite pleasant surroundings, though both Kitsura and Lady Nishima found all the rooms in the Governor's Palace somewhat colder than they were accustomed to. When her visitors arrived, Lady Nishima was practicing her harp so Kitsura and her two followers were treated to an ancient melody which wafted through the thin screens as though it echoed out of the past. The officer's daughter seemed close to tears, though whether this was due to the effect of the music or to finding herself in a social situation she had long dreamed of, Kitsura could not tell.

Informed that she had guests, Nishima put aside her instrument and rearranged her robe so that the pattern was arrayed to its best effect. The young women from Seh seemed almost to glow, for here they were in the company of two of the most celebrated women of their generation. Their friends would be envious beyond anyone's power to describe!

It was with some disappointment that they found themselves drinking cha, alone, while the ladies from the Imperial Capital retired to the balcony. They could just make out the two peers sitting on the wide railing engaged in a conversation that seemed much too serious for women who, it was said, were courted by every young man of worthy family in the entire Capital— including the sons of the Emperor! How could one be anything but constantly gay when one's life was perfection itself?

"We can hardly barge into an audience with the Imperial Governor, Kitsu-sum, we must think of something else," Lady Nishima was saying. She let her gaze wander out over the tiled roofs of the city.

"Considering what is at risk, cousin, I fear you may be paying too much heed to propriety. We will barge in on the Imperial Governor by *accident,*" Kitsura explained.

"I'm not utterly confident that this type of intrigue is your greatest area of skill, cousin. We must have some reason. I do not want my father to believe I am trying to see the Imperial Guardsmen. That would be unacceptable."

Kitsura turned away so her frustration would not be seen. Not to seem rude, she leaned over and made a show of checking her companions. The two women were trying not to appear too disappointed as they drank their cha and carried on a stilted conversation.

"I fear my *lady-in-waiting* is quite disappointed not to have been invited into our company."

Nishima shrugged. "It is the life of those who wait. Did she think it was otherwise?"

"Perhaps. You know all those terrible romances young girls read, the ones where the Princess' true friend is her youngest, least well-born, lady-in-waiting."

"Ah, like my Lady Kento," Nishima offered.

"Exactly!" Kitsura laughed. "Of course you would conform to the conventions of the romance, cousin, it is why you are so adored." Kitsura laughed again and squeezed her cousin's hand.

Nishima, however, did not catch her cousin's mood. She remained pensive, withdrawn. Her gaze kept straying over Kitsura's shoulder, and finally the young woman turned to see what it was that had caught the artist's eye. The view was lovely, there was no doubt—tile roofs of celestial blue, plumes of smoke lofting up from among the buildings, and beyond this, all of Seh stretching her green-blue hills off to the west. Beautiful, indeed, but Kitsura was looking for some unusual composition or play of light that stood out among all of the day-to-day beauty, something unique enough to keep demanding Nishima's attention. Kitsura was about to ask when she caught sight of the two monks still engaged in their conversation on the Sunrise Viewing Terrace. She turned back to Nishima who looked away, a faint blush blossoming on her neck and cheek.

"We should not disappoint them, Kitsu-sum, your young ladies-in-waiting. After all, when winter has worn on they may indeed become our truest friends." Lady Nishima tried to force a smile. "I will play my harp for them and you will charm them over plum wine with a scandalous tale from the capital."

"Which scandalous tale do you suggest?" Kitsura clapped her hands suddenly with joy. "How foolish I am! It is all too obvious! Tonight, over dinner, when Lord Shonto makes his customary offer to take me as a concubine, or maid, I shall tell him that I will prove I am worthy of consideration as a wife if for no other reason than my musical skills. You, of course, will have to accompany me. We will claim a need to rehearse, which will give our Governor several opportunities to comment on the questionable skills of musicians who, of all things, need to practice.

"Tomorrow we will arrive at the audience hall with our instruments. What gentleman could refuse two young ladies in such circumstances? Of course they will be honored that we have come to play. And Jaku Katta, I guarantee, will swoon." Kitsura broke into a smile, enormously pleased with herself. "Well?" she said when she received no response.

"It is not entirely impossible, though it will put you and me, not to mention my uncle, in a somewhat embarrassing situation."

"Embarrassment may have to be suffered to defeat the barbarian hordes, cousin."

Nishima laughed this time. "For the Empire of Wa I will dare to suffer it, then," Nishima said and then she thought for a second. "Perhaps there is a less obvious method of accomplishing the same end."

"Nonsense. My plan will work perfectly well. Come, cousin, if you play your harp for my young companions, I will overlook your suggestion that intrigue is not one of my many skills. No, no, come along."

One's ear for the truth, Shuyun knew, was not infallible, and after all, he was only a senior Initiate. The monk rubbed his head as though it had been mysteriously bruised.

It had been an innocent question, almost polite conversation, really. There was a widespread rumor in Seh that the Udumbara had blossomed, fulfilling a prophecy of the Perfect Master—the flowering trees of Monarta would not blossom again until a Teacher walked among men. Sotura had shrugged, saying it was a rumor that surfaced every decade. And though the senior Brother had been careful in his choice of words, Shuyun's sense for truth had wakened immediately—*he lies,* it whispered.

But even a senior Brother did not have an infallible ear for truth, so

Shuyun tried to push this incident aside though it resisted this treatment strongly.

Then there had been Brother Sotura's request for a written account of Shuyun's journey into the desert—and this, too, had seemed strange. Not the request, which was hardly out of the ordinary, but the senior monk's tone—he felt some guilt over this. Shuyun found the meeting with Sotura-sum most disconcerting.

A certain sadness had come over him as he walked. Sotura-sum had always been the man Shuyun admired most, the Brother he sought to emulate—Sotura of the *butterfly-punch*. And now he found himself doubting his former mentor—was, in fact, considering speaking to Lord Shonto about this meeting. This was also disturbing, Shuyun realized, as though a subtle shifting of his loyalties had taken place without him realizing. Had Brother Satake undergone this same change? It made Shuyun feel a pang of apprehension. Would he find himself following the path of his predecessor? Satake, it was said, had gone so far as to request his final ceremonies be carried out by the family he served—not by the Botahist Brothers! Such a thing was unheard of. I must keep my awareness of what transpires in my soul, Shuyun told himself.

He lies. The words came back to him like a whisper. Perhaps he should speak with Lord Shonto? The monk pushed this idea from his mind. But what was it about Shonto that made Shuyun consider going to him rather than to a senior of his own Order? He realized he did not know—not yet anyway.

The young monk mounted a set of wide stone stairs that led up from the gates. Slowing his pace only slightly, he admired the flying horse sculptures that flanked the first landing and then he was at the enormous main doors to the palace. The Palace guard bowed as he passed— solid men of Seh who would never think to question the Imperial Governor's Spiritual Advisor.

Shuyun's destination was his own apartment and his writing desk. The account Brother Sotura had requested was required almost immediately as the older monk planned to include it in documents he was sending to Brother Hutto in Yankura. But having written of his journey into the wastelands in detail for Lord Shonto, Shuyun felt this would take little time.

Several turns into the maze that was the Imperial Governor's Palace, Shuyun entered a narrow hallway that substantially shortened the route to his rooms. At a door that led into another corridor he stopped abruptly.

Voices from the other side confirmed what his chi sense had already told him—Lady Kitsura and two others had just arrived at the same door. He opened it for them, stepping aside to allow the women clear passage through the narrow opening.

"Ah, Brother," Kitsura said, "our karma keeps bringing us into your delightful company. Obviously this must be good karma." She smiled at her maid and lady-in-waiting who nodded agreement.

"My teachers told me always to turn a deaf ear to flattery, Lady Kitsura, but they did not warn me of its true power. I am, therefore, flattered." He bowed.

Kitsura motioned to her companions, who passed through the door ahead of her, and then she followed, tripping as she did so and falling lightly against Shuyun who reached out to steady her. She recovered almost immediately and before Shuyun could apologize she had passed on, her hand lingering on his own until the last second.

The monk stood holding the door open for no one and then realized how foolish he must look and moved on, missing the corridor to his rooms and stopping, for a second, lost. Shuyun had never had a woman so close to him, had never touched a woman who was not being treated for illness, and part of his shock was caused by his own reaction.

Flattery as a temptation, he realized, was hardly worthy of consideration compared to the softness of a woman's body. With great effort, he pushed the memory from his mind, but the thing that kept echoing back was the knowledge that this fall had not been an accident. There was no doubt of this.

Shuyun found this realization as disturbing as his meeting with his former teacher.

Six

THE SCULPTURE GARDEN in the Imperial Governor's Palace had not been created by an artist of great note, but it hardly mattered. The raw material was so superior in nature that it had almost worked itself.

Shuyun crossed the lotus pattern terrace at the garden's edge and then paused to admire the late afternoon light that slanted low into the garden. It created shadows that gave texture to even the most featureless surfaces. Already Shuyun could feel the stones releasing their warmth to the cooling air. The sea wind fell to a breath, then gusted, then fell again in a pattern that no man could determine. It would not be long before the clear northern night began to tug at the edge of the eastern sky.

Shuyun came to the garden to meditate on the sculptures and to purge himself of certain feelings. Stopping before the Mountain Dragon, he let his eye run over the fluted sandstone. He felt a certain awe at nature's work, thinking about the several lifetimes that the elements had scoured and carved this stone. Working patiently, waiting for the day when an artist would find it.

The artist, a lady-in-waiting of a retired Mori Empress, had set the three stones together in a fashion that, when seen from the north, suggested an animal poised to strike; when seen from the south, however, it appeared to be sleeping. The low light made the effect far more dramatic than at any other time of day and Shuyun found he was able to bask in the artist's skill as though seeing it for the first time.

The voice of the waterfall drew him and he wound down the narrow path and across the foot stones toward the sound. Shuyun had been in the garden many times and knew the illusion of the cataract twisting down a mountain-side was nearly perfect. The stone was cracked and sculpted in scale to an enormous cliff face and the effect was enhanced by carefully stunted trees, many the work of thirty years and more, let into ledges and cracks.

Shuyun stepped through the final copse before the waterfall and there he found the Lady Okara, paper stretched onto a drawing board on her lap, a brush held idly in one hand. She started as the monk appeared.

"Please excuse me, Lady Okara, I did not realize you were here. Please, I did not mean to interrupt your work." The painter was dressed in the plainest cotton robes and Shuyun was certain she must be deeply embarrassed to be seen so. He bowed quickly and turned to go.

"Brother Shuyun, do not apologize. I am hardly working at all. In truth, I have been sitting here weaving memories for some time." She smiled her warm smile. "Please join me, the light is changing color by the second. Have you seen?"

"Pardon me, Lady Okara—have I seen?"

"Ah, you haven't! Come, sit down, if you have the time. This will be worth the short wait."

Shuyun found a second sitting stone at Lady Okara's side and took his place dutifully. Lady Okara was not someone he knew well, but he liked her immeasurably. He often imagined that the ease he felt in her company was the way he would have felt with his own mother had he known her.

The evening sun lit the face of the miniature cliff, throwing every crevice into clear relief, the shadows stretching as the sun fell. The spray from the falls caught the light and a rainbow appeared.

"Watch the deep rose begin to change now," Lady Okara said.

Shuyun stretched his time sense in an attempt to see what the artist's eye would see. The waterfall slowed, each drop of spray catching the sun in a different way, with a different color. Indeed the rock was faintly rose hued; he had not realized this before.

"Rose to deep purple, but watch how many shades it passes through, Brother. It is a daily miracle, I should think."

"I had never seen this before, though I come here often."

Wind rustled the needles of the small pines and the light played among the greens and cast oddly elongated shadows.

"For many, the skills of brush and pigment are more easily learned than the skill of seeing, truly seeing. I came to Seh largely for this. Oh, not to see this garden, as lovely as it is, but to learn to see again."

"Lady Okara," Shuyun said, nodding toward her half-finished painting, "excuse me for saying so, but I find it difficult to believe that you have forgotten how to see."

"Ah, Brother Shuyun, it is kind of you to say so, but a good painter, an artist, does not see only with the eye. A skilled journeyman could learn to capture this scene, light and all. That, I have not lost. What an artist must seek and try to capture is the part of this setting that occurs within. What does this beauty evoke in my heart? In my spirit? A painter asks that question. The true skill, the skill that separates an artist from a journeyman, is the ability to find and express that—the part of this scene that exists within." She fell silent, as though she had begun to search within even as they spoke.

"You see, Brother, until Nishi-sum came to my home, I did not even know that I had lost that skill. Until I encountered her lovely, open spirit, I had thought the skill intact. But it was gone. I had lost it by forming habits of seeing and habits of feeling, as well. It is easily done. One can form habits in one's heart as easily as in one's day-to-day existence. Cha at dawn, a walk alone at sunset, meditation on the full moon . . . nostalgia, loss, bitterness, comfort. All of these habits shield us from the other parts of life. The journey to a new place, encountering people, considering new ideas, different landscapes, risks, excitement, joy . . . disappointment . . . grief.

"From the great palate that life offers I had chosen my colors—good colors, certainly, but few in number—and I had lived with them for many, many years. My spirit withered slowly in its habits. When Nishima-sum came to my house, I could see what this had done to my art.

"It is an odd choice to make, to dedicate one's life to a single pursuit, but if one has made that choice it would be terrible folly to limit what one can accomplish simply because of habit." She gestured with her brush. "Watch this rainbow fade. Isn't that wonderful? As though it had never been."

She reached down and for several seconds held the tip of her brush in the running water. "So I have come to Seh, hoping to find a way to open my heart and my spirit to the world again—hoping to revive my art. I do not know if this is possible: I am not the age of Lady Nishima, after all. But if there is a way, I must try to find it."

They fell silent again, watching the last light illuminate the miniature mountainside. Listening to the sound of the water as it fell into the pool and then ran among the stepping stones.

Lady Okara rose suddenly. "Please, Brother, you have come here for your own purpose. I grow cold easily and must go inside. But please, I insist. I can make my way indoors without an escort."

Despite her words, Shuyun rose and handed her across the stepping stones before giving way to her protests and allowing her to continue on her own, disappearing down the path, her plain robes in contrast to her great natural dignity.

Shuyun returned to the falls and seated himself where Lady Okara had been. It was almost dark now, the first stars appeared. He mulled over the painter's words. The touch of Lady Kitsura came back to him and hovered at the edge of Lady Okara's words as though speaking to him in some other language. He thought of Lady Nishima and how he dreamed of her in the desert, dreamed that he was in her embrace as the Perfect Master had been in the embrace of his bride on the cliff sculpture in Denji Gorge.

All of these spoke to him in their own way.

Words came back to him. *It is an odd choice to make, to dedicate one's life to a single pursuit, but if one has made that choice it would be terrible folly to limit what one can accomplish simply because of habit.*

The illusion of the mountain waterfall was hidden in darkness now, but the voice of the cataract still spoke, reminding him that Lady Okara had opened her spirit to this wonder.

She explores the nature of the illusion, Shuyun told himself, that is her purpose. Whereas it is my purpose to deny the illusion: yet what is the nature of this thing I deny? Lady Okara opens her spirit to the world, while I close mine. Who can say who will learn more in this process? Lord Botahara did not attain Enlightenment from denial but from exploration—as Lady Okara has said—both within and without.

This thought unsettled him and all of the voices in his head added to his confusion. He began a breathing exercise, chanting quietly, then sank himself into contemplation, driving out all the voices and focusing all of his mind on the words of his teachers.

It was the habit of a lifetime.

Seven

THE SERVANT HAD drowned in the canal the morning before and not been discovered for almost a day. The small sampan he'd borrowed was later found floating upside-down among the flotsam in a small eddy beneath a seldom used bridge. No one was sure how the accident had occurred, but it was well known that the boy couldn't swim.

General Jaku Katta, the servant's master, was surprised by the effect this death had upon him. The servant boy, one Inaga, had not held a special position in his master's house—a personal servant—a good one, yes, but no better than one would expect in the house of so powerful a man. And yet the death was felt throughout the household.

Jaku sat alone in his cabin on the Imperial Barge and considered his reaction to the loss. The river flowed quietly by, lapping at the barge, a reminder of every poem that had ever been written with a river as an image of life. The calls and shouts of the passing rivermen broke the calm and this seemed a great offense to the general's state of mourning. Of course he was not officially in mourning—one did not mourn servants—but in his soul Jaku Katta mourned and this unsettled him, for he was a soldier and not unused to death.

Inaga had been young, that alone explained some of Jaku's reaction, but this was more than the common response to the death of a child. Inaga had possessed qualities that were rare and, though Jaku hadn't known this, they were qualities he valued highly.

Attempting to alter his gray mood, the guardsman dipped a brush in ink and poised the tip over the report he was supposed to be writing, but no words flowed. He realized he had lost focus entirely when ink dripped onto the rice paper, spoiling it completely. Rinsing the brush, he set it on its rest to dry and gave up the pretense of work altogether.

Though he told himself he had no time for melancholy, Jaku could not force his thoughts elsewhere. Inaga had qualities that Jaku had seen too infrequently. It was not common to find someone who was entirely loyal and there was no doubt in Jaku's mind that the boy had been. There had never been any doubt, not from the very first day Inaga had come to service. That was another point about Inaga—he concealed nothing—was somehow incapable of hiding anything and it seemed everyone knew that instinctively.

Katta touched the paper on which he had been writing to a lamp, letting it burn, slowly turning it to avoid the flame. He waited until he dared hold it no longer and then dropped it onto his inkstone and let it burn itself out.

It was not the boy's death, Jaku realized, it was something more. The intrigue of the Imperial Palace and in the Empire was something he had always found exhilarating, like the kick boxing ring or a duel—one was truly tested—and failing the test meant more than losing a game of gii. Failing could mean loss of everything. But somehow the death of the servant had affected Jaku's love of the *game*. It had been such a senseless death, in aid of nothing.

Suddenly the game of court intrigue seemed as senseless as . . . Jaku was not sure what. And it was this game that had brought him here—to Seh where the Emperor plotted against the Shonto House.

Does the Emperor intend this as a lesson or is it his intention that I fall with Lord Shonto? Jaku asked himself again. Certainly the Son of Heaven knew that Shonto would not accept Jaku as an ally—and Jaku was not about to join forces with a man who was about to fall—not just fall from favor.

The last flame from the burning paper flickered and disappeared, leaving a pile of smoking ashes on the inkstone. The report would have been meaningless anyway, Jaku thought, just another arrangement of words on paper in a bureaucracy weighted down with words on paper.

In a few hours he would meet Lord Shonto. He could expect no honesty there either, and certainly no loyalty. Jaku touched his fingertips together as though he would meditate. There were so many lies now that even Jaku was beginning to lose his way among them.

He had spent hours searching among all the past lies, assuring himself that he knew his path so well that Shonto could never cause him to stumble. He thought of Lady Nishima, from whom he had not received word since his arrival in Rhojo-ma. She walked the path of lies also, though he felt somehow that she found herself there by accident, not by choice.

There was no one he could think of now whom he could rely on to be honest at all times. He thought of Tadamoto-sum and the usual anger he felt was replaced by a deep sadness.

A riverman called out to another and they both laughed. Jaku rose fluidly from his cushion and began to pace the cabin, six paces, side to side. A tap sounded on the screen and Jaku gave permission to enter.

"Your audience with Lord Shonto, General," a servant whispered.

Jaku nodded. He mustn't keep the Imperial Governor waiting. No. Every act of the farce must be carried out, without exception. An audience with a governor who would soon be a ghost seemed particularly appropriate to such a play. And Jaku had no doubt that a ghost was what Shonto would soon be. There would be no rest for the lord, nor for his retainers, nor for his son. Jaku was certain of that.

And now the architect of Shonto's downfall had arrived to participate in the lord's fate. The guardsman shook his head. It had been a beautiful stroke, Jaku had to admit. He had not thought the Emperor capable of such a pure act. He wondered if the Son of Heaven thought Jaku should feel honored to be in such esteemed company. An audience with a corpse. He must dress for the occasion.

His most finely made light duty armor, the suit with the Choka hawk worked into the black lacings along the shoulder covering. A purple border with tiny silver hawks. Jaku thought it quite possible that there had been no finer armor made in his generation. Certainly, Shonto had his garden, but Jaku was not a man without means as this work of the armorer's art would attest. And Shonto would recognize the work of an artist—Jaku was counting on that.

The Commander of the Imperial Guard took more time than usual with his preparations—almost as though he made ready for a duel. Shonto was undoubtedly an adversary deserving of such treatment. Perhaps it was this thought that made Jaku choose his *Mitsushito* from among the several swords he traveled with. He opened the rosewood case with great respect and examined the weapon most conscientiously before lacing it into his sash. It was very old, almost an artifact, yet the name of its maker alone would unnerve

most opponents. Jaku, of course, was too much of a pragmatist to rely on
another's reputation—the sword was a beautiful weapon, not an ornament.

So like a journey to a duel did this feel that Jaku had an urge to look over
at his Second as he took his place in the sampan. He even felt that strange
sense of unreality; "floating on the surface of illusion," his teachers had
called it.

The boatmen pushed off and began to scull rhythmically. Denji Gorge,
Jaku thought. Shonto had found a way out of Denji Gorge. Bribery was the
only possibility. Jaku felt himself begin to float higher and resisted with an
act of will. To have men so well placed in Hajiwara's army spoke of long
preparation. Unreality tugged at him again. Just how long, Jaku wondered,
had Shonto known that he would be sent to Seh?

Jaku rubbed the palms of his hands on the padded armrest. What did
Shonto know? Whose game was being played here? Perhaps it would not be
an audience with a ghost but the ghost that traveled to the audience. Jaku
looked down at his hands as though reassuring himself of their substance.

Even if Shonto was not aware of his situation, certainly he was aware of
Jaku's part in the debacle in Itsa Province. Using the control of the kick
boxer, Jaku forced a calm over himself. Shonto would not act openly, after
all, the lord was a gii master of some fame. No, this meeting might serve no
purpose other than to make Jaku aware that Shonto had no doubts about
who stood behind the attempt at Denji Gorge. That would be more worthy
of him.

The Imperial Guard Commander realized that the irony of the Emperor's
plan was quite complete. No doubt the Son of Heaven had divined Jaku's
plans for Lady Nishima, or perhaps it was truer to say that the art of divination had not been required . . . Tadamoto had seen to that. What was it the
Emperor feared? That Jaku Katta would join forces with the Shonto. And
now the Son of Heaven had sent Jaku into Shonto's palace knowing full well
that the Imperial Governor would never join forces with the man who had
arranged for him to be trapped in Denji Gorge.

Jaku realized that, for the first time in many years, he had very few op-
tions. He had become a traveler on a path without branches, a path that
narrowed with each step. So it was that he played out each act of the farce
as though it had meaning. What choice was there? He had even done exemplary work ridding the Grand Canal of its parasites. Jaku laughed softly. If
nothing else, he was still Wa's finest soldier.

*   *   *

"He is in disfavor or he has been sent north to oversee your fall, Lord Shonto. If he is in disfavor, our attempts to convince the Emperor of the true threat will not be successful. If General Jaku has been sent north to be sure there are no mistakes made and that my Governor is truly brought down, then there is a slim chance that he could be made to see the true danger . . . a very slim chance." General Hojo bowed.

Shonto nodded. He shifted his armrest unconsciously, considering what Hojo said. It was not that the general's words had not been said before, but Shonto believed that ideas, even bad ideas, in some mysterious way generated other ideas and one of those might be the truth or the beginning of wisdom. His former Spiritual Advisor had a saying that he used often: *search for the truth inside a lie.* So he searched, not that Hojo had lied, of course, but it was the same principle.

They sat in a plain room: General Hojo; Lord Komawara; Shonto's Steward, Kamu; Lord Taiki; and Brother Shuyun.

The wall paintings drew the governor's attention for a moment—on one side of the hall a scene of the great war with the barbarians in which his own ancestor had played a significant part—on the other a scene among the plum trees in spring in which Genjo, the great poet of Seh, chanted to a rapt audience. Shonto turned back to his advisors.

"We will proceed as we have discussed," Shonto said, finally. "Perhaps the guardsman will tell us more than he means to. Lord Komawara, you are prepared for your part?"

Komawara nodded, half a bow. His hair had still not grown back from his travels as an itinerant Botahist monk, and he welcomed the dressing on his head wound and wore it larger than necessary in an attempt to cover as much of his scalp as possible. His efforts to pretend this did not shame him were sometimes difficult to watch.

"Then we can do no more."

A guard opened the screen a crack, as though on cue, and a hand signal was given to Kamu.

"He is at our gate," the steward reported, and all present composed themselves to wait.

Jaku arrived with two of his black-clad Imperial Guards who stationed themselves, with Shonto's own guard, outside the entrance to the room. He knelt on a cushion that had been set for him and bowed deeply.

Shonto nodded and then smiled. "Does the chaku bush fare well, General Jaku?"

Jaku nodded. "I am convinced that my gardener never tended his own children so well. The chaku fares well and is without question the center-piece of my garden. I remain in the Governor's debt for such a gift."

"There is no debt between friends, or so Hakata said and I believe he spoke the truth.

"It is my honor to introduce you to my guests." Introductions were made and Shonto watched carefully the guardsman's reactions but even when introduced to Shuyun he gave no sign of what he might think or feel. Well played, Katta, Shonto thought, gracious even to the man who defeated you in the kick boxing ring.

"May we offer you refreshment, Katta-sum?"

Before the guardsman could answer, they were interrupted by screens sliding open to Shonto's right and then the rustle of silk and female voices. All eyes turned to find Lady Kitsura and Lady Nishima, followed by their ladies-in-waiting and servants who carried a harp and a flute.

The women bowed to Shonto and his guests. "Our apologies, Uncle," Nishima colored as she spoke, "It was not our intention to interrupt. Kitsura had promised a concert. . . . Please excuse us." She turned to go.

"Nishima-sum, please do not apologize." He smiled to reassure her. Certainly he would never think to embarrass his daughter and Lady Kitsura by sending them away. "I'm sure music would be welcomed by our guests. Especially music provided by players of such note. Please, join us." Shonto waved to the servants.

The ladies bowed and cushions were set for them before the dais. They were less formally dressed than the occasion demanded, as they were in the presence of guests, but even so their robes were of fine materials and matched to the layers of inner robes with the greatest care. Nishima's kimono was a pattern of snow-laden plum blossoms on a field of blue and Kitsura wore a robe of deep red bearing a flight of autumn cranes.

Although Nishima's hair was worn in a traditional arrangement, Kitsura's was most informal—worn in long cascades that flowed down her back. The ladies-in-waiting took a moment to arrange Kitsura's tresses for her hair all but reached the floor when she stood. It was not common for women to wear their hair this way except in the privacy of their own rooms or with members of their families or occasionally with trusted family friends. The effect this had on the gentlemen present was visible.

"You have met General Jaku, I believe?" Shonto asked. "Lady Kitsura Omawara, and my daughter, Lady Nishima." Servants arrived with wine and tables. The ladies' instruments were set nearby.

"Did your efforts on the canal go well, General Jaku?" Nishima asked. Shonto admired how quickly her poise returned.

"It is kind of you to ask, Lady Nishima. I believe the Grand Canal can now be traversed by unescorted women and children in complete safety."

A typically modest warrior, Shonto thought.

"That is welcome news indeed," Nishima said, her smile a bit forced. She turned immediately to Komawara who had been slowly sinking into himself since the women arrived. "And Lord Komawara, I understand that you also have been making the Empire safe from brigands?"

"A small altercation in the hills, Lady Nishima. Of little consequence." Shonto noted that Lord Komawara only met his daughter's eye for the briefest second.

"You are far too modest, Lord Komawara." She turned to Jaku. "Lord Komawara's men were twice outnumbered, and yet they did not hesitate. At some loss, and with many wounded, including our brave lord, they made the Jai Lung Hills safe for passage again." She rewarded Komawara with a smile that seemed to speak great admiration.

"Nishima-sum," Kitsura said, "shall we play and then allow Lord Shonto and his guests to return to their conversation?"

Nishima agreed and they took up their instruments. The melody they had chosen for the occasion was not in the modern style that they usually preferred but was of an ancient form known as "Poem Song." *Autumn on the Mountain of the Pure Spirit* was a melody that conjured up the sounds of the world and was thought to be one of the most evocative songs ever written. The flute led the harp through the first movement which captured the mood of the leaves beginning to fall.

It was not impolite to watch musicians as they played, which meant that the gathered gentlemen could regard the two women in a manner that would otherwise have been unacceptable. In the warm lamplight Kitsura and Nishima appeared to be two figures from the wall painting come back to a time where things were more real and mundane. With her eyes closed and her face covered in a blush from winding the flute, Kitsura seemed even more the ideal of feminine beauty. Shonto turned his gaze away with diffi-culty and found that both Jaku Katta and Lord Komawara appeared enrap-tured. At the same time Shuyun sat with his eyes closed as though he meditated—whether it was upon the music or something else Shonto could not know.

The melody followed the falling leaves down to a small waterfall that became a stream winding down the mountainside among the pines. The sound of temple bells echoed in the strings of the harp as the stream passed one of the many fanes among the mountain groves.

It was not a long piece, and when it was over everyone sat in silence for several moments. As though on cue, Kitsura and Lady Nishima rose and their servants collected up their instruments.

"Please excuse our interruption," Kitsura almost whispered. And before the men could protest, the women had retreated the way they had come.

The room seemed as empty as a bell after it has been rung. The men sat quietly, each lost in his own thoughts and the feelings the music and the presence of the women had stirred. Shonto finally broke the silence.

"All official business should have such interruptions. It provides the proper perspective from which to proceed." He looked at each member of the group in turn, holding each of their gazes for just an instant, and then he nodded. The audience began.

"General Jaku, may I begin by expressing the thanks of the government of Seh for what you have so recently accomplished on the Grand Canal. We are all in your debt and owe much to the Son of Heaven who sent you on such a worthy enterprise." He nodded to Jaku again.

"Do you plan to stay long in Seh, General? We could plan some fine hunt-ing and other entertainments, which your officers may also enjoy."

Jaku paused before answering. "I have completed my work on the canal sooner than anticipated, Lord Shonto. As I have no orders as of yet, I had hoped to offer some small service in your military efforts. It would be an honor to serve with such a renowned general."

"This is better news than I had expected, General. It would be an honor to have your counsel." Shonto smiled broadly. "If this is indeed your inten-tion, Katta-sum, then I would happily share what little I have learned of our situation here."

Jaku said nothing but composed himself to listen.

"Only this morning I have finished a long report to our Emperor detailing

the situation we have found in Seh. Although this is a report for the eyes of
our ruler I feel that, as you command the Emperor's Guard, I may speak to
you with complete confidence.

"As you no doubt are aware, there is a disagreement among the lords of
Seh regarding the barbarians and their intentions and also about their numbers. On both sides of this debate stand men with many years of experience
and proven wisdom. As you might imagine, this made deciding between the
two arguments difficult. I have always believed that the direct approach is
best whenever possible. We decided to send men into the desert to find out
what we could.

"The only people of the Empire who can travel north of the border of Seh
are the healing Brothers, so Brother Shuyun, accompanied by Lord Komawara disguised as a Botahist Brother, went into the desert." Shonto turned
to Komawara. "Perhaps, Lord Komawara, you should tell this tale."

The young lord nodded and, as agreed, told an abridged version of his
journey into the desert, saying nothing of the Kalam, or the cult of the
Dragon and its shrine. Shonto watched the Imperial Guard Commander's
face throughout, but Jaku betrayed nothing. When Komawara finished, he
bowed to Lord Shonto.

"Please, General," Shonto said, "I'm sure both Shuyun-sum and Lord Komawara would answer any questions you might have."

"I must have time to consider this information further, Lord Shonto.
Please, continue, it is a most intriguing tale."

Shonto took a long drink of his wine as though the talk of the desert had
caused him thirst. "As you see, General, I am much more concerned with
the situation in the north than I was when I set out on the Grand Canal." He
shook his head and then looked up and caught the guardsman's eye. "Do you
know anything of the barbarian Dragon Cult, General Jaku?"

It was a minute reaction, but Shonto was sure Jaku hesitated as though
surprised.

"I have not heard of it, though dragon worship is not uncommon even
within our Empire, Sire."

"Huh." Shonto looked thoughtful for a moment. "Perhaps that explains
it." He was silent for a moment. "I believe that we are about to encounter a
threat the likes of which we have not seen since the day of Emperor Jirri.
And this will not be a threat that confines itself to Seh, for though the men

of Seh are brave and skilled in the arts of war, they are few in number as the plague destroyed most of a generation here.

"The situation is complicated by other factors. It is my belief that barbarian raids on Seh fit into someone's design, someone within our Empire. Their purpose I leave to your imagination. For this reason the true threat will not be understood until it is perhaps too late."

Shonto stopped and looked at Jaku expectantly.

"Lord Shonto, I am not sure what you suggest, but certainly no one within the Empire would be foolish enough to betray us to the barbarian. Why would anyone do such a thing?"

"I was hoping, General, that you might tell me."

Jaku drew himself up to his full sitting height. "Lord Shonto," his voice showed signs of an effort toward control, "you come close to suggesting that I am party to a treason."

Careful, General, the lord thought, you speak to the lord of the Shonto. I will accuse whom I please. He nodded to Kamu who signaled an unseen attendant. A screen slid open and two of the Hajiwara men, now in Komawara livery, entered carrying a black, ironbound trunk on a pole. They set this on the mat before the dais and at a nod from Komawara they opened the lid and spilled the contents onto the floor before the Emperor's Guard Commander. A cascade of gold spread like a landslide across the floor and came to rest, glittering in the lamplight. An Emperor's ransom in gold coins!

The two Komawara guards retreated, and as they did so a third man entered. The Kalam, dressed in his barbarian clothing, came and sat between Lord Komawara and Shuyun.

When Jaku raised his eyes from the fortune that had been spread before him, his face seemed utterly changed. Perhaps it was the light reflected from the coins, but his skin had grown pale and appeared to be drawn taut over rigid muscles. The sight of the barbarian caused him to stop as he began to speak.

Lord Shonto caught the Tiger's eye again. Now you wonder what I truly know, Shonto thought. You even wonder if I know your part in our beloved Emperor's plot. "By the middle of the summer," Shonto said, his voice hard, "the Empire of Wa will have been overrun by an army the size of which has not been seen in a hundred years. Everything we strive toward will be destroyed utterly. Anything that gives meaning to the life of General Jaku Katta will have been rendered meaningless. . . . Everything you value— family, your command, lovers, estates—will all become the prerogative of a Khan who will sit upon the Throne of our Empire. And he will distribute what is left of your life among his lieutenants and chieftains." Shonto stopped to let his words have their effect.

"Akantsu," Shonto said, using no title or honorific, "does not understand what he has done. In his mad attempt to bring down the Shonto House, he will bring down his Empire and blacken the name of Yamaku for all of history.

"I am prepared to mount a force to take you into the desert, General Jaku, so you may see with your own eyes the things that Lord Komawara and Brother Shuyun have seen. I will spare no effort to convince you that the barbarian threat is real, for if we do not gain Imperial support before spring we cannot stand against the force that will come out of the desert. Without your influence at court, General Jaku, the Empire of Wa will fall."

Jaku reached out and took up a handful of coins, but he did this without sign of desire or awe, as though it was a fist full of sand he held. He let the coins run through his fingers, ringing as they fell back into the pile, the sound echoing in the silent room.

Picking up a single coin, Jaku turned it over, examining it as though the meaning of gold had just become clear to him, and its meaning did not bring him comfort.

He turned his gaze on the Governor's Spiritual Advisor. "Brother Shuyun, on the soul of Botahara, do you swear that this story of what was seen in the desert is true?"

Komawara almost rose from his cushion. "You cannot ask him to commit a blasphemy! It is against his . . ."

Shuyun reached out and grasped the young lord's arm and he stopped in mid-sentence.

"I cannot speak as you ask, General Jaku, but may my own soul be bound eternally to the wheel if what Lord Komawara has said is not truth. There is little doubt in my mind that the picture Lord Shonto has painted will come to be if the Empire does not rise to the defense of Seh. The army we saw in the desert was as real as the coins you see before you and the warriors more numerous."

Jaku gave a nodding bow to the monk and looked back to the coin in his hand, turning it slowly over and over. "I cannot guarantee that the Son of Heaven will heed my words, Lord Shonto. In certain endeavors our Emperor does not listen to the sound of reason. I will, however, do what I can. Certainly the Emperor will believe that this is only a ploy to gain control of a large force and that I have fallen victim to your cunning. Or the fact that I am convinced by your words may suggest treachery more than it will suggest an accurate military assessment." He placed the coin carefully back in the pile. "A way that we could strengthen our case would be to convince a certain lord in Seh of the danger to the Empire." He hesitated. "But I am concerned that revealing his name might bring about his own demise, and that would certainly put assistance from the Son of Heaven out of reach forever."

Shonto shifted his armrest again. "If I were to invite this lord to the palace and display the contents of this trunk to him, do you think you could assist us in convincing him of the true danger to Seh?"

Jaku nodded. "I believe I could help make the argument convincing. Again I stress that if I reveal his name, revenge must not be sought against him. This could damage our cause beyond any hope of repair."

"General Jaku," Shonto said, "the Empire has been brought into great danger through the rivalry of its Houses. If we are to save Wa, all such pettiness must be put aside." He turned to his steward. "Kamu-sum, invite Lord Kintari and his two oldest sons to come and hear the ladies of the capital play." He turned back to Jaku and raised an eyebrow. The Black Tiger nodded.

Each rhythmic sweep of the oarsmen sent the fine craft gliding along the silent canal. The speed of his boat often brought Jaku great pleasure; when he discovered an empty stretch of water he would exhort his boatmen to greater and greater speed for the pure joy of it. This evening, however, he seemed unaware of his crew's efforts.

Jaku Katta had absolutely no doubt that the Supreme Master of the Botahist Order could look him in the eye and lie as easily as he chanted the name of Botahara. He was equally convinced that Brother Shuyun was as incapable of this as his former servant had been.

Despite all that he felt about the Botahist Brotherhood and its meddling, he knew that this boy-monk had somehow remained pure, untouched by the hypocrisy of his Order. How else could one explain the feat that Jaku had witnessed in the kick boxing ring? The boy had deflected a blow without actual physical contact! Jaku had felt it.

Even though Jaku had long worn the humiliation of that defeat and the years of anger that it had caused, he knew that Initiate Brother Shuyun was not another Botahist hypocrite. . . . What the boy was Jaku could not be certain, but his suspicion caused him both awe and fear. Shuyun, he sometimes believed, was a child touched by Botahara himself.

Jaku considered what he had heard in his audience with the governor. The barbarians were no longer pawns in the Emperor's plot. The tribes had plans of their own, it seemed—were under no one's control except perhaps this Golden Khan. Should he tell Shonto what he knew about this one? Perhaps. He would see.

Jaku looked out at the thoroughfare that edged the canal. Like most of the streets of Rhojo-ma, it was almost without traffic. By the Gods, if he joined Shonto he would come to war with the Emperor. Akantsu would never be convinced that his barbarian chieftain had escaped his control. Never, never, never.

Jaku rubbed his temple. To join Shonto was probably a decision to commit suicide, there was no doubt of that. Yet only Shonto could save the Empire. That was also beyond doubt. And if the Empire was saved? What then?

Jaku thought of the Lady Nishima, sitting before her harp. Was it possible that there was another solution? What if he truly became worthy of Shonto's daughter? If Shonto won the coming war, the Yamaku would fall. Who would Shonto put on the Throne?

Perhaps, perhaps, perhaps. . . . Perhaps Shonto could escape the Emperor's trap. Shonto, Jaku was beginning to believe, was capable of anything. He thought of the trunk of gold and this brought him back to the question he had considered earlier. How long had Shonto known?

The canal slipped by and before Jaku realized it he had arrived at the Emperor's Barge. Absorbed in thought, the Commander of the Imperial Guard sat in his sampan. His boatmen waited without sign of impatience.

The path has grown too narrow, Jaku thought, I have no choices left. If Wa falls to a barbarian chieftain, it will be as Shonto says—the Jaku will lose everything. He shook his head. When there are no choices, one should not be frozen in indecision. The Empire must be defended. One cannot play gii without a gii board.

Jaku almost bounded onto the deck of the barge. Bowing guards fell back in surprise. Their commander laughed at their reaction. He mounted the steps to the upper deck as he tackled the question of how to raise an army. He considered any number of lies he could tell the Emperor, all of them far more plausible than the truth. But some part of him balked at this course, and he found this reaction somewhat strange as though it belonged to someone else and appeared in his personality entirely by accident.

Eight

OSHA KNELT BEFORE a low table and, in the soft light of a lamp, went through the ritual of choosing between two perfumes. As each bottle was unstopped, she would take great care not to breathe while a dab was placed on her forearm. This would be allowed to evaporate appropriately before the delicate fragrance was inhaled. Although the entire ritual was enacted with eyes closed in apparent concentration, in truth, it was a sham. Osha could not truly focus her attention on the scents and she let her arms fall to her sides with a sigh—an act of resignation or despair.

Before she had opened the perfume, Osha had sent all her maids away so that they would not distract her, but the truth was she wanted to be alone to tie her sash. She looked at the gold brocade but could not bring herself to take it up.

The women had left with some reluctance, running a last comb through her long hair, rearranging the hem of a third under-kimono so it would be properly displayed. Although Osha was very careful not to reveal her feelings to her servants, it still made her sad that they were so unaware of her situation. Osha shook her head sadly. They were excited to see the Emperor's renewed interest in their mistress, believing that this would make her happy.

Finally settling on a scent of ground conch shell, musk, and summer tulip, the Sonsa dancer carefully washed the other scent from her arm before dabbing tiny droplets behind her ears and on her wrists. Osha was circumspect in her use of perfume, unlike many of the women in the court. As a

Sonsa dancer she believed that beauty resided in movement—all else was unimportant.

The ritual completed, Osha took the long brocade sash that she had chosen to offset the pale green of her robes and laid it across her lap. Until this moment she had done so well, but suddenly her spirit sank like a stone through water. Taking deep breaths she mastered this moment of weakness. Sonsa dancers were trained to such control. Slowly winding the yards of fabric around her waist, Osha imagined that she bound her emotions inside with each turn.

A shoji slid aside somewhere down the hall and several sets of footsteps could be heard through the rice paper screens. The voices of Osha's maids were quiet but, all the same, projected a note of urgency. Osha stopped the winding of her sash and cocked her beautiful head to listen. It was not urgency that she heard, it was *protest* and the footsteps were those of a man or men.

Immediately the dancer imagined the worst. It was an enraged Emperor coming to confront her with her infidelity. The shoji to her chamber banged open and Osha started as though struck. Tadamoto stood in the opening, tall among the protesting servants.

Collecting her wits, Osha waved the servants out and Tadamoto entered, dropping to his knees a few feet before her. The resolve he had shown forcing his way to her rooms disappeared and he slumped, staring down at the floor. He raised his eyes to hers as though he would speak, but no words came and his gaze returned to the floor.

Nor could Osha find words for the turmoil that Tadamoto's arrival had sparked. They sat in silence for several minutes before Osha managed to form a few words.

"Tadamoto-sum," she whispered, "you must not, you . . . you place us in the gravest danger."

Tadamoto shook his head. The pain he felt was brushed in broad strokes across the features of his scholar's face. Yet he did not speak.

"Tado-sum," Osha whispered again, "I could not tell you." She reached out to take his fine-boned hands, but he pulled them away and left her, half reaching out to him. She covered her face then and silent tears glistened on delicate fingers. "I thought he was finished with me. It was my dream that, in time, he would . . . not care about us." She pushed small fists against her eyes. *"We have been so loyal!"*

Tadamoto reached out as though he would comfort her but stopped.

"I wanted to tell you, Tadamoto-sum, but there are no words to describe the confusion in my heart."

"How?" Tadamoto said at last. "How could you let this happen?"

Osha emerged from behind her hands now, tears still shining in her eyes. "Tado-sum," she said so quietly he almost did not hear. "What did you imagine? Did you imagine that I could make a choice? That we have a choice?"

The young officer said nothing and she reached out to take his hands again, and again he pulled away.

"You could have chosen to refuse," he said, his voice colder than he intended; it was almost a hiss.

When Osha answered, her voice sounded calm, with a touch of distance in it. "And what would have happened then?" When he did not answer she continued. "Could a member of the Jaku family visit me secretly in a monastery in Chou or Itsa Province? What would the Emperor say to that? I would have lost everything, Tadamoto-sum, my dance, my life here in the capital, and I would have lost you also. Do not deceive yourself. If I am sent to the outer provinces, it would be the end for us. There is no place where we could run, Tado-sum. You know this to be true."

She reached out and took his hands now and he did not resist. "What other choice is there?" She tugged his hands gently, but still he would not meet her eyes. "Speak to me."

"Osha, Osha-sum. You cannot. . . . You cannot." He was unable to finish.

"Our only choice is to never see each other again. Tado-sum my love, I cannot make that choice. Can you?" When he did not speak, she went on. "He will tire of me soon. There is no doubt of that. As soon as he has recovered from this slight by the Omawara girl, he will have no more need of me. If you want to truly help, find a girl of high birth who is ambitious for her family and a great beauty as well. I am nothing to him, truly." She paused. "And he is even less to me. Tado-sum?"

He looked up at her now.

"I know this is terrible, but. . . . Please, I would not do this thing if it were not for us."

Osha pressed herself into his arms and he responded, pulling her close against him. He could feel the struggle as she tried not to sob. Life was so unfair to her, this tiny girl trapped by talent and beauty, and yes, by ambition, too. Tadamoto buried his face in her hair. The delicate scent of her perfume was the greatest blow of all.

When he had gone, Osha sat staring at the lamp on her perfume table, watching the flame sway and dance to the will of imperceptible currents within the room. Taking the brocade in her hands she finished winding it and tied the Lover's Knot with barely a second's hesitation.

Later, in the chambers of the Emperor, Osha tried to focus on an image of Tadamoto. The Emperor was lost in his passion and held her tightly to him as he moved. To her horror, Osha felt her breath begin to come in short gasps. She heard a moan of pleasure, and the voice that uttered it was her own!

No, she thought, *Jenna, Jenna, please . . . let me be.* But the voice cried out again, uncaring in its own pleasure.

"No, Jenna," Osha whispered under her breath. "Oh, no. Oh . . ." But the protest was lost in a cry of passion that heeded no voice but its own.

Nine

Narrowing
High above Screaming Monkey Gorge
The footpath jags up
Into the Sacred Mountains

When one walks among clouds
The way becomes as insubstantial
As a strand of moonlight

"Verses From a Pilgrimage"
Initiate Brother Shinsha

SHUYUN CAME EASILY to the Fifth Closure and altered his pattern. He had been practicing this same exercise now for several weeks though he had yet to achieve the results he desired. Jaku had tried to strike him thus: Shuyun moved through the complex pattern of punches and deflections as though the Black Tiger had returned to fight their bout again. Shuyun closed his eyes and concentrated on his memory, trying to find the same reaction in himself, trying to achieve the identical state.

Again he felt close, but yet it eluded him. Without hesitation he began the Fifth Closure and continued, practicing the broadening of his focus that would eventually include his entire musculature, the flow and precision of his movements, breath, and his meditative state. Far off, a rapping entered his realm of consciousness. A pause and then it came again. Three punctures of his meditative state that echoed endlessly through his altered time sense.

He interrupted his exercise and stood calmly for a moment, adjusting his sense of time. The tapping came again, though they seemed short quiet raps now.

"Please enter."

The shoji slid open to reveal a Shonto guard kneeling in the opening.

"Corporal?" Shuyun crossed toward the open screen so that any interchange would be as quiet as possible. The Governor's Palace had too many ears by far.

"Excuse this interruption, Brother but you left instructions for this situation and Kamu-sum confirmed them."

Shuyun waved this aside. "Please, Corporal, do not apologize."

The guard gave a nodding bow. "On the Grand Canal you were visited by a young Botahist nun—Sister Tesseko?"

Shuyun nodded.

"A young woman is at our gate claiming to be this woman, though she is not dressed in the robes of her Order. She has requested a meeting with you, Brother Shuyun. Kamu-sum confirmed that you had left orders to interrupt you were this young woman to come again. She is waiting in the Spring Audience Hall. I hope we have acted correctly, Brother."

Shuyun hid his surprise. "You have, thank you, Corporal. Please inform Sister Tesseko that I will join her in moments."

There was not enough time to bathe, so Shuyun settled for washing in cold water and changing his robes. Acolyte Tesseko . . . He remembered her well—young, tall, the bearer of unsettling news. He had often wondered what had become of her charge, Sister Morima. Had she survived her crisis of the spirit? There was more than concern for the nun's spiritual well-being at issue here; there was self-interest also and Shuyun knew it.

He finished dressing and left his chambers, passing down the halls quickly though somehow without seeming to hurry. The Spring Audience Hall was a small, simple room with a low dais, painted screens depicting spring in the mountains, and a simple shrine to Botahara set into a tiny alcove in the wall. The shrine was no doubt what had led the guard, or perhaps Kamu, to choose this hall for their meeting—that and the fact that the room was so seldom used.

Guards knelt on either side of the double wooden doors to the chamber.

They bowed as Shuyun approached, and with a quiet knock of warning they pushed open the doors.

Sister Tesseko looked up as Shuyun entered and her face seemed to register terrible grief. If not for a lifetime of training, the strength and immediacy of the woman's pain would have drawn all of his attention, but as a follower of Botahara he was more affected by the fact that she sat with her *back* to the Shrine of the Perfect Master.

Shuyun stopped and gave the short double bow of the Botahist-trained. "Acolyte Tesseko, your visit honors me, as it does the House of my Lord." He knelt a polite distance away.

The nun bowed. "I am no longer called Sister Tesseko, Brother. I am Shimeko, now." She bowed again. "I thank you for your kind words, though I realize that, in truth, I have broken all convention and exhibit the worst possible manners coming here unannounced."

"Shimeko-sum, I am honored that you would trust me enough to come without sending word, as I asked you to do when we traveled together on the Grand Canal. Please, be at your ease." Shuyun paused to gauge her reaction, but she did not meet his eyes. "May I ask, how fares our Sister, Morima-sum?"

The young woman shrugged. "She has shown some improvement, Brother, though not as much as the Sisters had hoped." She shrugged again.

There was a silence then, and Shuyun had an opportunity to study Shimeko while she stared down at the grass mats. She was dressed in the plainest cotton robes, like the wife of a poor merchant, and she covered her head with a rough woolen shawl. Her face was careworn and Shuyun thought she looked older than she had when they last met. There were other signs of great strain, for she was thin and her skin was mottled and lifeless as though her diet had been very poor for some time. Shuyun was concerned.

"Are you well, Sister?" he asked quietly.

She seemed to consider this for a second, a sad smile almost coming to her lips. "I am no longer a *Sister,* Brother Shuyun. I . . . I find I must keep reminding myself of this." She fell silent again, then looked up and held his eyes for an instant. "The Way," she said, returning her gaze to the floor, "is difficult. I-I had not the strength."

Shuyun nodded slowly. "Ahh," he said almost under his breath. "Is there some way that I may serve you, Shimeko-sum? Please do not hesitate to ask."

The conversation was punctuated by a long silence then. "Brother . . .

Brother Shuyun, I have come to beg that I may be allowed to take service with you." She put her hand to her mouth as though she would stop it from causing her more embarrassment.

Shuyun put the tips of his fingers together as in meditation. "Shimeko-sum, what you ask is not possible, I am sorry. This is not my decision to make. And certainly it would not be proper for a young woman to serve me. It is out of the question." Shuyun watched her as he spoke but could not be sure of her reaction, for her face was partly hidden by her shawl. "Shimeko-sum? Why do you ask this?"

She shrugged, tugging with one hand at a strand of grass from the floor mat. "I believe, Brother Shuyun, that you are a pure spirit, untainted by the . . . present state of the Botahist Orders."

"You believe the Sisterhood is tainted, Shimeko-sum?"

She stopped playing with the strand of straw, covering it with her palm as though this would somehow repair the damage. Her voice dropped to a near whisper. "I believe both of our Orders are corrupt, Brother Shuyun. Excuse me for saying so."

"I see. Is this belief related to Sister Morima's crisis, Shimeko-sum?"

Lifting her hands she found that magic had not occurred. The straw remained as it had been. She nodded. "Yes, Brother. That and other things."

"I do not wish to pry, Shimeko-sum, but, in truth, I wonder what has occurred that caused you to turn your back on Botahara."

She shrugged. "I . . . I have not truly turned my back, Brother." She seemed to struggle for words. "I am no longer sure how to serve the Perfect Master. I feel that those things which I learned from my teachers have been . . . tainted, debased in some way. To worship the Perfect Master in such a way . . ." She shivered visibly. "This must be wrong, Brother," she said, her voice suddenly gaining clarity. "It must be."

"You make strong statements, Shimeko-sum. Did Sister Morima speak of her concerns specifically? Again, I hesitate to pry."

"As you know, Brother, Morima-sum suffered a crisis of the spirit. She is convinced that the scrolls she saw at the Ceremony of Divine Renewal were not the scrolls of Botahara. I am not sure what evidence convinced her of this, but Morima-sum is a scholar of great repute, Brother. I do not doubt her assessment." She folded her hands in her lap now and closed her eyes as if searching her memory.

"Because of Sister Morima's crisis, she has spoken to me of things that I should otherwise never have heard. She did not seem to care, Brother. It is my understanding that the Sisters have methods of collecting information, even from within your own Order. They seem to believe that the Sacred Scrolls have disappeared. That the Brotherhood searches for them secretly." She opened her eyes and met Shuyun's own. "Though Sister Morima believes the scrolls have not been in their possession for a long time, perhaps hundreds of years."

"I see," Shuyun whispered. "The Scrolls of Botahara are guarded night and day by the Sacred Guard of Jinjoh Monastery. It is inconceivable that they could be stolen, Sister."

"*Shimeko*, Brother, *Shimeko*. The Sisters seem to agree, Brother Shuyun. Some do not believe they were removed by men. They believe it was divine intervention."

"Shimeko-sum. This can hardly be the belief of the Senior Sisters."

She shrugged. "It appears to be, Brother, Morima-sum reported this to me as though it were commonplace. And there is more." She began to worry the loose straw again. "No doubt you have heard the rumor that the Udumbara has blossomed?" The straw broke free of the mat and she began to weave it through her fingers. "It is not a mere rumor, Brother Shuyun. Sisters witnessed the blossoming before your Order closed the grounds of Monarta. It is beyond all doubt, Brother, the Teacher who was spoken of is among us."

"I have discussed this rumor with a senior member of my own Order," Shuyun said quietly. "He assures me that this is not the case, Shimeko-sum. Why would he lie to me? Why would my own Order deny the rumor?"

"The Sisters ask this same question, Brother. It is an issue of grave concern to them. It is thought that the Teacher is as yet unknown to the Brotherhood, and they cannot proclaim him. If they admit the Udumbara has blossomed, as the prophecy was written, and they cannot bring forth the Teacher. . . . As you see, Brother Shuyun, the activities of the Botahist Orders seem to reflect a self-interest that I find repugnant. I apologize for the insult that is implied, but I cannot help but speak the truth, Brother, please excuse me."

"I value the truth, Shimeko-sum, but it is not always easy to discern or to accept." Shuyun fell into a long silence and was finally brought back to awareness when Shimeko cleared her throat.

"Please excuse me, your words have given me much to consider." He tried to smile. "I come back to the question of how I may serve you, Shimeko-sum."

"But it is I who have come to serve you, Brother Shuyun." Suddenly she prostrated herself before him. "I ask this most humbly, Brother."

"Please, Shimeko-sum, sit as you were. Do not do this." He looked around in acute embarrassment as though afraid someone would come in and see them. "This is most unseemly. Why are you doing this?"

Shimeko spoke from her position, prostrate on the mats. "Brother Shuyun, there are some in the Sisterhood who believe that you may be the Teacher who was spoken of. I wish to serve you."

Shuyun rocked back on his heels. What could possibly make the Sisters believe such a thing? "Shimeko-sum, I assure you, if I were the Teacher I would not keep such a thing secret."

"Awareness is often preceded by accomplishment, Brother."

"In truth, Shimeko-sum, my own faith is not unassailable *by* questions and doubts. Shimeko-sum, rise up," he ordered and the young woman complied. She rose to a kneeling position, the texture of the straw mat marking an intricate relief on her forehead.

She obeys her Teacher, Shuyun realized, and this unsettled him more than her words. *You stopped a blow without it touching you.* It was like a whisper in his mind. *Brother Sotura was not even aware that such a thing was possible. Senior Brother Sotura!* It cannot be true, he told himself, my faith is so easily shaken, doubts grow in me like weeds. I cannot be the Teacher—I may never be a senior Brother if I continue as I am now.

"Brother," Shimeko said flatly, bringing him back to the world. "I have nothing, no coins, no roof, no walls, no skills, no family. If you send me away, I shall live in the street, and though I have no compunctions about begging, I have no experience of this life. I will live outside your gates, Brother, until I am given some task or until I am driven away. I do not know what else I can do."

Shuyun sighed. He believed she would do exactly as she said. Botahara have mercy on her; a lost one. "Your calligraphy is presentable?"

"I am told it is sufficient. Brother. I acted as Morima-sum's secretary often."

"Would you object to serving a highborn lady in the same capacity?"

"If she is within your household, Brother, I would accept gratefully."

"I serve within *her* household, Shimeko-sum." He paused, thinking. "I can promise nothing, Shimeko-sum, but I will inquire." He shook his head. "And please, we can have no more displays of . . . this kind. I am not the Teacher, I assure you."

"If that is your wish, Brother Shuyun."

"Come, I will find a maid who will take you to the kitchens for now. You have not eaten in some time?"

"Three days only, Brother." She tried to favor him with a smile. "I—I thank you, Brother Shuyun."

"Yes, but no more of this. You must promise."

She started to bow but turned it into a nod.

Ten

LORD SHONTO'S STEWARD, Kamu, wove his way unsteadily down the hallway. He held a lantern ahead of him in his only hand and occasionally used his elbow against a post to regain his balance. Guards bowed smartly as the old man passed. Despite his appearance—gray hair in a tangle, robes obviously thrown on and belted in the most haphazard manner—Kamu had once been a famed swordsman and the young men among Shonto's guard treated him like a legend who had descended from some Great Beyond to walk briefly among them.

The old steward careened down the hallway like a ship with a broken rudder, bow lantern swinging. Four of Shonto's personal guard watched the doors to their lord's chambers—solid doors, not screens. The four bowed as Kamu approached and hands went to sword hilts.

After speaking the password, Kamu was forced to set the lantern down to give the accompanying hand signal. The force with which the lantern made contact with the floor indicated the steward's level of annoyance.

The senior guard tapped on the door and a viewport slid open. Quiet words were exchanged and the night guard, one of the few allowed into the lord's chamber while he slept, slid the port closed.

Kamu left the lantern on the floor as he waited. The viewport slid aside again and the senior guard nodded, stepping aside as the door opened.

Passing through the small entrance hall that acted as a guard room, Kamu entered an inner chamber. A lamp flickered on a small table, casting a weak light in the almost empty room. Kamu had barely knelt when Shonto entered the room, looking only slightly less disheveled than his steward.

The lord nodded in return to his retainer's bow but did not take the second cushion. Instead he placed his back against one of the deep lacquered posts and crossed his arms, waiting.

"Excuse this . . ."

Shonto held up his hand and the steward stopped in mid-sentence. "Despite our apparent youth, Kamu-sum, I believe we are too old for such formalities, under the circumstances. Please, speak directly."

Without a hint of a smile, Kamu began. "The Kintari, Sire. . . . They have fled."

"Huh." Shonto rubbed his chin.

"I have taken the liberty to awaken and inform your advisors, Sire. I've tripled the guard around the palace."

Shonto started to speak, but the night guard appeared in the doorway.

"General Hojo and Lord Komawara, Sire."

Shonto gestured to allow them entrance.

The sounds of doors and rustling clothing. By their dress, both Hojo and Komawara had also been caught unaware. They bowed to Kamu and their liege-lord.

Shonto said, "The Kintari have refused our hospitality, General Hojo."

Hojo nodded.

"Most unfortunate. All of them, I suppose?"

"It appears so, Sire," Kamu answered. "We will know in a few hours."

"We should take precautions, but I don't believe this means the Emperor is about to move against us." Shonto pulled his robe closer. "His plan is more subtle than that."

Kamu waved his arm in a sweeping gesture that seemed to take in all of Seh. "I believe, Sire, that the Kintari are less important than what this incident tells us. They were warned, there can be no doubt."

Shonto paced across to the opposite post, then back again. He looked up at Hojo.

"I agree, Sire. They must have had knowledge from within the Governor's Palace. Unless it was a sudden loss of nerve, and I consider that unlikely. Even the Emperor does not choose the fainthearted to carry out his treachery."

"I have also had word from those who watch our new ally. A messenger came to Jaku's barge about the same time as we received word of the Kintari. Apparently this caused quite a stir aboard the Guard Commander's barge. Jaku is on his way to the palace as we speak."

Shonto nodded. "Lord Komawara, if you were Lord Kintari, where would you go?"

Komawara pressed the bridge of his long, thin nose. "The quickest escape would be down the river, but once the sea is reached they will find few ships willing to risk the winter storms: it seems unlikely that they would make such a choice unless utterly desperate. The Grand Canal is the most easily searched, despite the numbers of craft that would be involved." He looked around the room, meeting each set of eyes in a manner he would never have done a few months before. "If everything we believe about Lord Kintari is true, I would seek them in the desert, Sire."

"Ah." Shonto gave half a laugh. "How far ahead of us do we think they are?"

Kamu and Hojo exchanged glances. "We are not yet certain, Lord Shonto," Kamu said. "Their servants may have been keeping up a pretense for several days, though no more than three or, perhaps, four."

"Excuse me, Sire," Hojo said quietly, "we should also consider what this may say about our friend in the Imperial Guard. Jaku was well aware of our intentions; he received a message just as we did. Could he be the ear in our midst?"

"Jaku's loyalty will always be in question. It is only comforting to remind oneself that the Emperor must be haunted by the same question." Shonto stretched his arms high. "Morning is too near for a return to sleep. Please, join me for my meal." Shonto clapped and a servant appeared. He gave quick orders and then began to pace again, an activity his retainers had seldom seen him indulge in.

Before servants arrived with the meal, the night guard again interrupted, whispering to Kamu.

"Brother Shuyun and General Jaku have both arrived, Sire."

"Ah," Shonto said to those around him. "As in all good tales: mention the spirit by name and he appears." Shonto crossed to the small dais upon which his sword sat in its stand and took up a place on the cushion, pulling an armrest closer in a familiar gesture.

Shuyun appeared, his tonsured scalp and simple manner of dress allowing him to arrive looking as he always did. Oddly, Jaku, who had the farthest to travel, was impeccable in his black uniform.

The monk and the general bowed as their stations required.

"I set out as soon as the news reached me, Lord Shonto." Jaku seemed very calm, Shonto thought, despite the fact that he certainly knew he would be under suspicion—someone warned the Kintari.

Shonto looked around the group. "I trust, General Jaku, that you learned of this independently?"

Jaku nodded. "I do not, however, know where the Kintari have fled or when they first disappeared. It would seem, Lord Shonto, that the Kintari must have learned of this from someone within the palace or within my guard. I have very tight security among my own officers, Sire."

"I do not doubt it, General. More blows through the walls of this ancient maze than winter winds. Such things are inevitable in this situation."

Servants brought a light meal and tables were arranged for Shonto and his guests. As though no matters of greater weight had been discussed, polite conversation flowed seamlessly until the servants had left and Shonto gave his guard orders to secure the chamber. The discussion went from the best time of year to hunt various game birds back to the issues at hand without a sentence of transition.

Shonto sipped his cha, then set the cup back on his table, turning it slowly. "It appears that the palace is not about to be stormed by forces loyal to our enemies. The suggestion that the Kintari were warned is no doubt true. Perhaps our hopes that the Kintari would become allies in our attempt to gain the Emperor's support were vain."

Shuyun gave a half bow before speaking. "If the Kintari could have been convinced of our intentions, they may well have become the support we hoped. We will not likely know this now. We must find support without them. The men of Seh and the Emperor both need to be convinced of the truth of our discoveries in the desert. It is a pity that we did not return with evidence other than words."

"As Brother Shuyun says," Jaku added, "I have been convinced by words and the belief of the witnesses. Not everyone will think as I do. I have composed my letters to the Emperor and certain of his counselors. As you are aware, the court functions according to an elaborate, unwritten system of debt and payment—the coinage is favor. If one understands the workings of the court and has given credit to many, one can collect accordingly. In the palace they say: it is improper to ask the Great Council of the Empire to add a wing to your home, but it is quite possible to have the Great Council offer to build such a wing.

"I am not a great lord nor do I hold high position, but I will call in what credit I may have given. We shall see." Jaku tugged at the corner of his mustache. "If there is no support forthcoming from the Emperor or the men of Seh—what will we do?"

Hojo nodded. "It is the very thing we have debated these past months, General Jaku."

A gong sounded and somewhere in the darkness the guard changed. The night guard appeared in the doorway and signaled Kamu. All was well.

"It has been our hope to convince others of the true threat, General Jaku," Shonto began, "but as you have said—this may not be possible. When the barbarians cross our border in the spring, the men of Seh will rally to our support . . . too late, unfortunately." The lord rearranged several objects on his table as he gathered his thoughts. "We will make these final attempts to gain the support of the men of Seh and the Emperor, but we cannot plan as if these attempts will succeed. It must also be realized that to gain the support of the Emperor but not the men of Seh, or the reverse, will not be adequate. Our needs are great.

"If we have not gained the support we need, our concern will no longer be the defense of Seh but the defense of Wa. We will attempt to raise an army as we move south. It will become a question of how many men of Seh will be willing to follow, for they will form the heart of our army."

"Sire!" Komawara blurted out, "you will abandon Seh. . . ." Suddenly aware of the naïveté of this statement, Komawara reddened noticeably, adding to his embarrassment.

Shonto's tone remained calm as he answered. "I do not wish to abandon Seh, Lord Komawara, but to throw a tiny force at a vast barbarian army will accomplish nothing. If our tactics are prudent and our courage does not falter, we may slow the barbarian advance long enough to allow an army to be raised in the south. I am the Governor of Seh, Lord Komawara, and would not consider such a course if it were not for the grave danger to our entire Empire. If the men of Seh and the Emperor will not act to secure the borders or to protect the Empire, then we must act in their place.

"I believe, Lord Komawara, that the people of Seh will be largely safe from the barbarian threat due to our retreat. This Khan cannot have an army large enough to hold Seh and pursue us south to the inner provinces. If Botahara smiles upon us, the barbarian army will pass through Seh like a wind, pulling only a few leaves from their branches."

In the long silence that followed, no one met the young lord's eye. "Excuse my outburst," Komawara said evenly. "I bring shame to the Komawara House. Please excuse me." He shifted his sword in his sash. "There is one other question that I must ask at risk of again appearing naive. What will happen if the barbarians wish only to conquer the province of Seh, and we allow them to take it without a fight?"

Shonto nodded. "It is as we have often asked, Lord Komawara. This would probably fit the designs of some. Then Shonto and all who support him will be brought down. We still believe that if the barbarians only desired Seh they would have taken it in the autumn when surprise was assured. We all will gamble our lives on this assumption . . . be certain you believe it."

Komawara nodded. "I will risk my life to save Wa, though I would rather it were Seh I hoped to save. Still, for me there can be no choice."

"Truly, Lord Komawara," General Hojo offered, "there can be no choice for any of us."

"Kamu-sum," Shonto said, "we must begin to gather the craft needed to take us south and make preparations to destroy all others. Leave no boats for the barbarians. Begin an inventory of river boats at once."

The steward nodded.

"We must consider ways to raise an army as we pass south. Who can be won to our side? Once we cross the border of Seh, the Son of Heaven will try to remove me from command of the army. Who will be sent to do this? General Jaku, perhaps your knowledge and contacts at court could answer this?"

Jaku nodded.

"Much to do. We will make our last attempt to win over the lords of Seh at the Celebration of the First Moon. Lord Komawara, I will have to prevail upon you to describe your journey into the barbarian lands again."

The cool, first light of a northern morning glowed through the unshuttered paper screen and cast the shadow of Jaku Katta's large hand across the paper.

The brush hovered in the air, as it had often in the last hours. The soft bristles seemed to contain only ink and no words.

Again he dipped his brush.

My dear brother:

It is with some difficulty that I write to you, not only because of the nature of our parting, which I regret deeply, but I have arrived in Seh to discover things that neither of us had ever expected. I do not know how to convince you that the words I write are true but I must find a way, Tadamoto-sum. On the souls of our father and mother I swear that every word is true. The fate of Wa depends on your ability to recognize the truth—seldom has so much depended on the heart of one man.

Eleven

IT WAS A small entertainment arranged for the high-ranking residents of the Governor's Palace and for those who frequented Seh's court—perhaps seventy people in all.

The evening's entertainment was provided by a wrinkled, elderly man who moved with the stooped carriage of someone who'd spent his life toiling in a rice paddy. His threadbare robes, sewn in the country style, did nothing to deny this impression, though in truth this man had once been a respected scholar, holding appointments at the Hanama court where he was renowned for the quality of his verse. Long ago he had retired to seclusion in the far north and only the promise of a concert by the Ladies Nishima and Kitsura had lured him out this night—that and a suggestion that Lord Shonto might provide him with a cask of a certain rare wine.

The old man, one Suzuku, sat on a raised platform built to resemble a balcony and behind this a silk hanging bore a sunset and far off, a V of geese winging south among crimson clouds. Skillful arrangements of dried leaves and cedar boughs symbolized the autumn, just as the flying geese were the common symbol for letters or messages.

The old man's voice had no doubt lost much of its power and timbre to the years, but his great refinement of speech and the beauty and richness of the language he used more than made up for it.

He would speak softly, the meter of the verse as subtle as the rhythms of rain, and then he would break into a chant, strong cadences driving the images like drumming drove dance.

Earlier in the evening Lady Kitsura had played without the accompaniment of her cousin, who was not in attendance, but if this had initially been a disappointment it was soon forgotten. Kitsura Omawara could hold the attention of the most critical audience without assistance. She had taken her place among those listening, now, and seemed hardly less the center of attention there. In contrast, the gathered peers of Seh, guard officers, ladies-in-waiting, and members of the administration seemed like a gathering of the dull and the gray. It was not just the refinement of her dress and manner that set Lady Kitsura apart, it was as though life flowed more strongly in her veins and gave her the ability to find pleasure and delight where it escaped others. She easily stole the hearts of all men present and gained the grudging admiration of the women.

Among those in attendance, General Jaku Katta had the most difficulty concentrating on the verse. He hoped to speak with a certain lady, and carried a poem in his sleeve that he thought might melt some of the coolness of her manner. Although he realized it was absurd, he felt like a suitor scorned to find that Lady Nishima was not present. He tried to turn his thoughts elsewhere and redoubled his efforts to focus as Suzuku began a new poem.

Autumn in Tu's brocade hills
Leaves find a death of such beauty
A man's sad end pales

Poems seek out the unsteady hand
Words dropping from the brush
Like leaves.
Still awake at first light
Eyes red as the sunrise
Letting no leaf escape

Ink falls, drop by drop
Yellow of weeping birch
Crimson of blood-leaf.
I send poems south with passing geese
But who is left to receive them?
So many leaves adrift
On this chill wind

Up here it is better to forget early days
It is enough to ache from damp mornings
To ache from memories too
Is more than a man can bear

Outside my open room
A small cloud
Tangles in the ginkyo's branches
So white against the endless blue.
Searching among a lifetime's clutter
I find my worn inkstone

What words will come now?
What wisdom will I speak
To frightened trees?

The evening's last poem read, the gathering broke into small, informal groups and plum wine flowed as smoothly as gossip. Jaku found himself in the company of several of Seh's most well-born young ladies.

"It is a shame," said the youngest of the women, "that Lady Nishima was not present also. I had so looked forward to hearing her harp and had hoped she might trade a poem-sequence with Suzuku-sum."

Jaku could not have agreed more, though he said nothing.

"General Jaku," said another, "you must have heard Lady Nishima play at court?" She tried to hold the general's gaze as he answered and was disappointed that he looked away so quickly.

"Oh, many times. Not four days ago I heard Lady Nishima and Lady Kitsura play here in the palace. They complement each other perfectly, as you might imagine." He was immediately embarrassed—a short time in the north and he was already playing the fool's game of trying to impress the provincials.

As he spoke, Jaku's eye was drawn by Kitsura as she broke away from a disappointed group of young men and made her way across the hall. There is no doubt, Jaku thought, the rumor that she spurned the Emperor had made her even more desirable. Despite the fact that he had come hoping to meet another, Jaku could not help but feel excitement at Kitsura's presence.

Lady Kitsura stopped briefly to speak to Lord Komawara and Jaku shook his head. Komawara, he remembered, had made a fool of himself in Shonto's chambers the morning before. It was bad enough he had not realized that Shonto might be forced to abandon Seh but to reveal his ignorance so blatantly exhibited the poorest judgment. Jaku was surprised that Shonto allowed the boy into his councils. Strange.

Jaku's attention was drawn back into the conversation as he was asked to comment on the most current fashions in the capital. He was forced to disappoint them, explaining that Lady Kitsura dressed in a more timeless style and was not a follower of the latest fad. The conversation then drifted into a discussion of the relative merits of silks from Oe and Nitashi. Lady Kitsura again caught the general's eye. She had finished her conversation with Lord Komawara, and as Jaku looked up she motioned to him with her fan.

Waiting for an appropriate break in the conversation, Jaku excused himself, inflicting a second disappointment upon the young women from Seh. Lady Kitsura had retreated to a quieter corner and stood fanning herself slowly, though the room was not overly warm.

The guardsman bowed as he approached and she nodded from behind a ginkyo leaf shaped fan, jade and silver combs catching the light as her head bobbed.

"I hope you have come away inspired by Suzuku-sum's verse, General. Were his poems not exquisite?"

"Certainly, Lady Kitsura, but not less so than your playing. I feel doubly inspired."

She nodded at his flattery, and lowered her fan enough that he caught a glimpse of her famous smile. "I am sorry Nishi-sum could not be present. My poor description will not do justice to the evening."

"Lady Nishima is well, I trust?" Jaku said as matter-of-factly as he could.

"I am certain we need not be overly concerned, it is kind of you to inquire."

She did not offer to convey his concern to the lady herself, as Jaku had hoped she would.

A gong marked the hour of the heron and the crowd seemed to thin noticeably in response.

"The evening has flown, I must make my good nights. If it is not too much to ask, General," she reached a small hand out from behind her fan and he found a tiny fold of paper in his palm, "would you read this before leaving? I would be in your debt." Her eyes seemed to plead with him over the edge of her ginkyo leaf.

"I am your servant, Lady Kitsura."

"You are so kind, General." A brief touch of her hand on his wrist and she was gone, leaving the guardsman to catch his breath.

It was several minutes before Jaku could find a moment alone. He opened the intricately folded letter with great anticipation—she had not been able to erase him from her mind after all! The disastrous meeting on the Grand Canal came back to him and caused him a second's discomfort, but he made his fingers continue. Why would Lady Nishima put her fine hand to paper if she was not still intrigued?

He read:

My Dear General Jaku:

> *I find myself in the awkward position of having to ask a favor. Is it too much to ask that you meet me this evening? My servant will await you until the hour of the owl at the door to the Great Hall. If this is not possible, please, no explanation is preferred.*

Lady Kitsura Omawara

Lady Kitsura! Jaku pushed hard against the post that hid him. The depth of his disappointment shocked him. He had so expected to find a poem from Nishima-sum. Lady Kitsura? He could not imagine what favor the Omawara daughter could need of him. No doubt he would soon find out. At the very least, he could now easily ask that Kitsura deliver his own letter. She could hardly refuse.

Jaku said his polite good nights as soon as he could.

As Kitsura had written, a servant awaited him at the Great Hall—an older woman whose accent, even in the few words she uttered, was noticeably from the Imperial Capital. Jaku knew—it was an accent he's spent some time acquiring. The servant took a route through seldom used halls until they came to a door like many others.

A soft knock was answered by a woman's voice and for a brief second Jaku found himself hoping this had all been an elaborate ruse arranged by Lady Nishima so that they might meet secretly.

It was not to be so. The opened door revealed Lady Kitsura sitting in the light of a single lamp, its golden light heightening her complexion.

"General, I am honored that you would come." She smiled, no fan now to hide her beautiful face.

"Lady Kitsura, it is I who am honored." He knelt upon the second cushion that had been set, closer to hers than he expected.

"May I pour you plum wine, General?"

"Thank you, Lady Kitsura. If I am not being too presumptuous, please call me Katta-sum."

Kitsura held back her long sleeve as she poured wine into the small cups. "I would be honored." She passed him his wine cup. "Please, call me Kitsura-sum, whenever the situation allows."

Jaku gave a half bow. Polite conversation followed. Discussion of the night's poetry, the customs and manners of the people of Seh, and even a little gossip. More than once they found cause for laughter. Such formalities completed, Jaku broached the true subject of their meeting, hoping to save the lady embarrassment.

"If you will excuse my boldness, Lady Kitsura, is there some service I might perform for you? I would deem it an honor to do so."

Kitsura took a small sip of wine. "You are kind to inquire, Katta-sum." She set her wine cup back onto the small table and turned it as though examining the quality of porcelain.

"As you are no doubt aware, I left a most awkward situation in the capital. Unlike many families, my own would not argue my decision. . . ." She looked up at him, her face suddenly troubled. "Yet now I fear the repercussions of that decision—not for myself, General—but I fear for my family. My own decision was perhaps too selfish."

"You acted according to the dictates of your heart, Kitsura-sum, a woman of integrity could do nothing less. Is there some task I could perform that would relieve some of this apprehension you feel?"

"Truly, you are kind," she said warmly, a sense of relief apparent in her tone. "I am concerned that my family could be in a delicate position. I am not sure . . ." Her voice became so small that words ceased to come.

"Perhaps I could draw upon my friends in the capital, particularly in the court, to find out if there is reason for worry, Kitsura-sum. Would this be of service to you?"

"Oh, yes, Katta-sum, very much so!" She reached out and squeezed his large hand. "But please, enough risk has been taken for me. Do nothing that would jeopardize your position. I could not bear it. Will you promise me this?"

"Lady Kitsura, it would be an honor to take any risk on your behalf but, truly, what you ask is no cause for concern, let me assure you."

"You are kind, but you must be careful. I would not forgive myself if anything untoward should result."

"Your spirit is burdened with enough concerns, Kitsura-sum," he laid his fingers gently on her arm, "do not add this to what you carry." He removed his hand and took a sip of his wine. "Is there anything more I may do?"

She hesitated for a time before looking up, a slight blush apparent on her beautiful face. "I wish to send a message to my family, but I fear that it might be intercepted. I'm certain Lord Shonto would do this, but . . ."

"Lady Kitsura, say nothing more. I can send a message to your family in complete secrecy. Tomorrow, if you wish it."

"Katta-sum," she said, a tiny tremor of emotion in her voice. "I am in your debt for this kindness. I don't know how I can repay you."

"There can be no debt in such matters. Please do not concern yourself with such things."

"Katta-sum," she took his hand in both of hers now, "there is debt and I will not forget it. Is there nothing that I might do in return?"

He felt a soft tug on his hand, so soft he wondered if his imagination toyed with him. And she did not release his hand.

"If I may ask such a favor, Kitsura-sum," Jaku said, with obvious difficulty, "would you convey a letter to your cousin, Lady Nishima?"

As though all of her features had frozen, Kitsura paused but then, almost immediately, she recovered. Sitting up, she reached for her wine cup though she did not drink from it but only held it with both hands as though she suddenly did not know what else to do with them. "Certainly . . . General, though it seems a small thing indeed."

"It may seem so, but it is I who am in your debt now." Jaku produced the letter from his sleeve, slightly misshapen from the hours of neglect.

Slipping it into her sleeve Kitsura reached again to pour wine.

"Please, Kitsura-sum, I have duty awaiting me."

"Excuse me, General, I did not mean to detain you."

With a bow and a promise to send a trusted guard for her letter, Jaku Katta slipped away as quietly as the cat he was named for.

Kitsura sat for some time without moving. Never had she been so thoroughly rebuffed. She had expected him to fail this test, had wanted him to. And he had asked her to convey a letter to her cousin!

"Uncouth, common soldier!" Kitsura whispered.

For a second she felt anger toward her cousin but then realized how absurd this was. By Botahara, she thought, Jaku must be truly smitten with Nishi-sum. What a disaster that could mean.

* * *

Canal's end,
We have traversed uncertainty

A maid interrupted as Lady Nishima contemplated the poem's next line.

"Excuse me, Lady Nishima, Brother Shuyun inquires of your well-being."

"Ah, how thoughtful," Nishima dipped her brush in water. "Please offer him cha."

Pushing aside her table Nishima quickly straightened her robes.

The maid appeared again. "Brother Shuyun, Lady Nishima. Cha will be served immediately."

The servant bowed as Shuyun entered and in turn he bowed, Botahist style, to the daughter of his liege-lord. Though she knew full well that Shuyun was small of stature, hardly taller than she was herself, Nishima was always surprised when she saw him. In her mind his presence was larger.

"Brother Shuyun, please be at your ease. It is a pleasure to have your company." Nishima smiled.

"I came to inquire after your well-being, Lady Nishima, not to interrupt." He nodded to her work table.

"Notes to myself. I was filling time, Brother, nothing more."

Shuyun knelt on the cushion set for him. For a second he met Nishima's eyes and she wondered, as she often did, if it was great wisdom or great naïveté that dwelt in those large, dark eyes. She often wondered if it was this ambiguity that touched her.

"You are well, Lady Nishima?" Shuyun said in his soft voice. A voice that always seemed to suggest intimacy to her. "I grew concerned when the poetess did not attend Suzuku-sum's reading."

"I am well. Despite Suzuku-sum's reputation, one does not always feel the desire for the company of many." In truth she thought Suzuku's reputation was somewhat greater than his talent.

Shuyun nodded. Servants arrived with a cha service and laid out the utensils with some care. Their mistress was very conscious of detail and they did not like to disappoint her.

"And how fares the Shonto Spiritual Advisor?" Nishima asked and smiled.

"He fares well enough, my lady. In my Order we say, *well enough to serve His purpose*. The Botahist-trained do not ask for more than that."

Nishima nodded and checked the heat of the charcoal burner that warmed the cha cauldron. "Perhaps we should all learn to ask less for ourselves and more for others, Brother. In my *Order* we say, I fare well, thank you—meaning, *I am well enough to enjoy all of the pursuits that I hold dear, whatever they may be.*" She kept her eyes cast down, fussing with the cha preparations.

Shuyun seemed to consider this for a moment. "Excuse me for saying so, Lady Nishima, but there is a dedication to duty among many of your *Order* that is worthy of recognition and praise. The Shonto are renowned for this."

Nishima nodded. "It is true among fewer than one would hope, Brother, though certainly in reference to my uncle it cannot be denied."

With great care she ladled cha into bowls and offered the first to her guest.

"This bowl must be for you, Brother," she said, as etiquette demanded.

"I could not, Lady Nishima. Please, this bowl must be yours."

Though this was the proper response, the sincerity of his words stopped Nishima and she found herself staring into his eyes again, trying to read what lay behind the words. The monk looked away and she collected her wits.

"Your presence honors me. Please, Brother Shuyun." She held out the bowl and he took it from her hand with surprising gentleness.

As though there had been a lapse, a moment of too much familiarity, Shuyun's tone became formal. "A matter has recently arisen, Lady Nishima, about which I require advice." He sipped his cha, looking away.

"Brother, if it is possible to repay some of the debt I feel to our Spiritual Advisor, I would not hesitate to do so. Please, what is this matter?"

Nishima watched him take a calming breath before speaking. "While I traveled with Lord Shonto on the Grand Canal, a young Botahist nun approached me for advice. A Sister with whom she traveled was unwell and there were no others of her Order to refer to. I shared what knowledge I could and told her she might ask for me at any time. I have often wondered since if the Sister recovered but have had no way of knowing. Earlier today this same young Acolyte came to our gate, asking to speak with me. As I had given orders to allow this woman access, and Kamu-sum remembered this, she was not sent away."

He paused to sip his cha.

"This all seems most irregular, Shuyun-sum. Please go on."

"This young woman has left the Order of the Botahist Sisters—it seems she has suffered a confusion regarding her faith. It is my hope that she will return to the Sisters but until such time needs some way to live. She is Botahist educated, Lady Nishima, and has been a secretary to a senior member of that Order. It occurred to me that there might be a place for her in the Shonto household. Even more specifically, I wondered if you or Lady Kitsura, or perhaps Lady Okara might have use for someone of such talents?"

Nishima stopped to ladle more cha, obviously considering this.

"It is difficult for me to say, Shuyun-sum. There is no question that our flight to Seh has left us with a very small staff, and no secretary. This girl, is she intelligent?"

"I would say yes, Lady Nishima."

"Huh. Is it not unusual that she would seek you out, Brother? What explanation could there be for this?"

"Perhaps what she considered to be an act of generosity—my assistance to her on the canal—stayed in her memory, Lady Nishima. It seems entirely likely that, outside of the Botahist Sisters, she knows no one else."

"The Sisters take an interest in the events of our Empire, Shuyun-sum, do they not?"

"They do, my lady."

"Is it not possible that this young woman has been sent to us to that end, Brother? The Shonto are often the objects of such scrutiny."

"I believe, in this case, Lady Nishima, that this girl is truly what she claims."

Nishima sipped her cha and regarded Shuyun, who sat looking down, as politeness dictated. "You have an ear for truth, Brother Shuyun?"

"So my teachers believed, Lady Nishima. Though it should be remembered that this ability is never infallible."

"How unfortunate." Nishima swirled her cha leaves as though she would change the message written there. "I would be pleased to assist a seeker who has lost her way, if I can. Please have her sent to me and I will see what she seems suited for."

"I thank you, Lady Nishima. I do not think she will disappoint you."

Nishima smiled. There was an awkward silence. Shuyun finished his cha, but before he could excuse himself Lady Nishima spoke again.

"How do you recognize truth, Shuyun-sum, what is it that informs you? More cha?" As she said this, she poured cha into his bowl.

"Well, perha . . . certainly. Thank you." He took up the full vessel and sipped.

"I am unable to explain, Lady Nishima, I apologize. I simply know."

"It is a feeling, then?"

"Perhaps. It cannot be described but only named."

"It is most intriguing, Brother. But do those who are raised to the Botahist Way know feelings, Shuyun-sum? Are feelings not part of the Illusion?" Nishima found a small crease in her robe that she smoothed.

Shuyun considered for a few seconds. "Botahara taught that feelings were illusory, yes. It is written that our desires trap us in the world of Illusion."

"Then you are not troubled by feelings, Brother Shuyun?"

"I am not so enlightened, Lady Nishima." He gave a small, almost embarrassed, smile. "Even the Botahist-trained have feelings—one does not allow them to rule one's actions, however."

Before he could protest, Nishima ladled more cha into his bowl.

"You resist them, then?"

"I'm not certain that *resist* is the proper description, Lady Nishima."

"You do not resist them?"

"Followers of the Way order their lives according to the principal virtues, not according to their desires."

"But Brother, when a follower of the Way feels desire, or any other emotion, do they resist it? Did not Botahara teach that resistance was folly? I find this concept difficult."

Shuyun set his cup on the table and placed his palms together, touching his fingers to his chin in thought. "When one has traveled far enough down the Sevenfold Path, one does not feel desire, Lady Nishima. Until such time we practice meditation, we chant, and we learn focus. Certainly duty and desire are not always compatible, Lady Nishima, but, as you have said, the Shonto choose duty."

Nishima nodded slowly. "Though I often wonder at what cost, Shuyun-sum," she said softly.

Shuyun looked away as though some detail in the room begged his attention and what Nishima said had not been heard. "I have not seen Lady Okara for several days," Shuyun said evenly. "Does she fare well?"

Nishima smiled at the sudden change of subject. "Well enough to serve art's purpose, Brother. I often wish I could say the same."

"I have heard Lady Okara speak of your art in the most flattering terms, Lady Nishima," he said, his voice losing its edge of formality. "She speaks also of your artist's soul. It is my impression that she is somewhat envious."

"Oh, certainly she is not!" Nishima felt her face flush with pleasure at Shuyun's words—even a fan would not hide this.

"Recently she spoke of her quest to learn to see again. It seems Lady Okara believes that over the years she has developed habits of being and feeling that act as a wall to the world and prevent her from seeing. But she does not seem to mean seeing the world, she means seeing within. 'The part of the scene that exists within,' were the words she used.

"It is Okara-sum's belief that you have the open spirit of the true artist, Lady Nishima, and she traveled to Seh with you in an attempt to recapture this. Perhaps you are her teacher, Lady Nishima."

"Lady Okara is my teacher, Shuyun-sum, make no mistake. I have been blessed with brilliant teachers."

"It is said that a child learns wisdom from the parent, but the truly wise parent learns joy from the child. Do not be confused by appearances; a wise teacher learns from the student, always."

"And what have the esteemed Brothers learned from Initiate Brother Shuyun?" Nishima asked suddenly and watched his reaction closely.

Shuyun shrugged. "I do not know, Nishima-sum, I do not know." He opened his hands in a gesture that seemed to indicate emptiness.

"We know only those things which we allow ourselves to know," Nishima said.

A troubled smile appeared on the monk's face. "That is Botahist teaching, Nishima-sum."

Nishima gestured with her hand as though she encompassed her entire life, and her long sleeve swept gracefully through the air. "I have been blessed with brilliant teachers."

"Brother Satake?"

Nishima nodded. There was an awkward silence while Lady Nishima prodded the coals in the burner, causing them to spark to life.

"My Order guards its teachings with a certain jealousy, Nishima-sum," Shuyun said at last.

She nodded again, poking distractedly at the coals. "Give me your hand, Shuyun-sum," she said suddenly, and she reached out and took his hand and placed it palm out against her own. Regulating her breathing with some skill, she pushed. Shuyun resisted for the merest fraction of a second and then pulled away slightly. When he pushed against her own hand there was almost no resistance. Shuyun could feel the chi flow. Chi in an uninitiated woman—a peer of the Empire of Wa!

Lady Nishima took his hand in her own. "As impossible as it may seem, there is much in common in our experiences, in our lives, Shuyun-sum."

"Brother Satake broke his sacred oath," Shuyun said. He felt his focus wander as he said this. Even though he had suspected Brother Satake had broken his oath, the shock of proof was great.

"He lived by his own oath, Shuyun-sum. His teachers could have learned much from Brother Satake, but they were mired in their own ways, their own habits."

Gently Shuyun removed his hand from her own. "Please . . . excuse me . . . I must go." Without further ceremony Shuyun rose and walked out like a man in a daze.

For a long time Nishima sat staring at the door where Shuyun had disappeared. Then she shook her head as if to clear it. Reaching for her writing table, she prepared her brush with exaggerated care. She read the lines she had already committed to paper and then continued.

Canal's end,
We have traversed uncertainty
To arrive here,
Purity and desire
Tangled

She could find no words to complete her thought.

Shimeko sat with her eyes cast down while Lady Nishima examined her brush work in the dim morning light that filtered through the screens of her chambers. The former Botahist nun sat without movement as she had been trained to do and nothing in her appearance betrayed the confusion she felt. Was she truly going from serving a respected senior Sister to the service of this pampered aristocrat, barely older than she was herself?

"It is a fine hand, Shimeko-sum, strong without being plain." Nishima nodded toward her, half a bow. Setting the paper aside, she smiled warmly at the young woman who sat before her. Shimeko sat with her shawl pulled tightly around her face, hiding her cropped hair.

"You will excuse my curiosity, Shimeko-sum, I can't help but wonder why you would seek service with the Shonto. I do not wish to pry into your reasons for leaving the Sisterhood, but life in the Shonto House will be very different."

Shimeko spoke without raising her head. "Do you wish to hear the truth, my lady?"

"Always," Nishima said, the word coming out clipped and controlled.

"I did not come to your gate to seek service with the Shonto. I came to offer my service to Brother Shuyun." She sat looking down, her expression unchanging, her tone even.

"I see. May I ask why?"

"I believe Brother Shuyun is a pure spirit, Lady Nishima, untainted by the machinations of his Order."

"Huh. Then you take service with me against your will?"

"No, my lady, I will gladly serve the household that Brother Shuyun serves."

"I see. Will you be able to make the adjustments necessary, Shimeko-sum? You do not have to treat me with this level of deference, I am not a senior Sister who demands utter humility from others."

"Please excuse me, Lady Nishima." She raised her eyes and met Nishima's for the briefest second. An attempted smile showed some potential. "If someone will instruct me, I'm certain I will learn."

"We could find you a teacher, Shimeko-sum." Nishima glanced at the page of brush work again. "You are a scholar?"

"I was only an Acolyte, my lady. An Acolyte cannot call herself a proper scholar. My accomplishments were modest compared to the Sisters I served."

"I see. Could you go to the Palace Archives and find information for me?"

"If the information is there and somewhat ordered, I am confident I could, Lady Nishima."

"Good. This is what I want to know. On the canal did you see the fane of the vanquished Brothers? The one called the Lovers?"

"My lady, it endangers the spirit to look at such things," the young woman said, casting her gaze down again.

"You did not look, then?"

The former nun struggled for a moment and then she shrugged, her cheeks coloring a little.

"Well, it is not necessary to look. I want to know what the scholars have written about the sect that inhabited that fane. Scholars, mind you, not members of any Botahist Order. Certainly the Imperial historians could not have allowed such a thing to pass without comment. Are you able to do this without compromising your beliefs?"

"My beliefs, Lady Nishima?" She traced a circle on the floor. "Yes, I think so."

"Excellent. I would like this information as soon as possible, thank you."

Shimeko sat, her posture and expression unchanged.

"You may go, Shimeko," Nishima said.

"Thank you, my lady." She bowed in the Botahist manner and backed toward the door without rising.

"Shimeko?"

"Yes, my lady?"

"You know that servants are seldom addressed as sum?"

The former Sister paused in her retreat. "Brother Shuyun calls me Shimeko-sum, my lady," she said simply.

Nishima considered this. "Then I will call you Shimeko-sum also."

Twelve

SISTER SUTSO HURRIED down what seemed an endless hallway until she found the door she had been looking for. Pulling her robe closed at the throat, she pushed open the door that led out into an unlit courtyard. A cold wind swirled about her, pulling wildly at her robes and whistling among the pillars. An occasional drop of rain was smeared across her forehead, though due to the wind they did not seem to fall from the sky. Almost running, the secretary to the Prioress found the door she was looking for, despite the complete darkness, and pushed into a second hall.

Pulling up the hem of her robe, she ran up several flights of stairs, surprising a group of Acolytes who had never seen such undignified behavior in a senior Sister.

Another long hallway, then a shortcut through the Archives of Divine Inspiration, another hall and then the great stairway. There, one flight down, went the Prioress, Sister Saeja, her sedan chair carried by four Acolytes.

Sutso descended the stairs and only slowed her pace as she came up beside the chair. She controlled her breathing with great discipline so that it seemed she had not hurried at all, perhaps had come upon the Prioress by accident.

"Prioress," Sutso said, bowing as low as the situation would allow.

The old woman's eyes seemed to appear out of the wrinkled folds that were her eyelids. She nodded and closed her eyes again as though conserving her strength.

"Is there anything I can do, Prioress?" Sutso asked, pitching her voice in tones the old woman could still hear.

"There will be no change of plan," came a soft whisper. "Continue with our preparations. There is so little time."

"Do you have commitments I am unaware of?" Sutso asked.

"No, child," the ancient head moved from side to side, "but this is not unexpected. Since Morima-sum's time of testing, they have been gathering like the carrion eaters they have become. I remain this still only to draw their attention from things of importance." Her face creased in a smile and her eyes flickered open, eyes full of humor.

"Why do they call a council now?"

"They hope to tire me, child, that is their true purpose." She smiled again. "Sister Yasuko's letter. They have learned that there are events outside of their narrow world that could adversely affect their dearest ambitions. Seh is on everyone's lips suddenly, replacing talk of Monarta."

The chair wobbled slightly and then the bearers recovered. The Prioress held out a thin hand. "Give me your hand, child. I do not want to slide down the grand stairway alone."

Sutso took the frail hand in her own. Botahara protect her, she prayed silently. So much is dependent on this woman, so much.

At last they came to the bottom of the stairs, to the relief of Sister Sutso, and then to the Chambers of Council. A gong was rung as the Prioress approached and the large doors swung open, the Door Wardens carved into their panels seeming to gesture entrance. A last squeeze of the Prioress' hand and Sutso stopped short of the Chambers. The bearers returned almost immediately and the doors were closed, no one to enter until the Council was over. She stood a moment, staring at the doors, and then hurried off. There was so much to be done.

Lamps suspended by gold chains hung from the lacquered beams and flamed impressively, casting shadows into the deepest corners of the room and the highest reaches of the ceiling. The floor of polished woods reflected the light like a bronze mirror and the twelve senior Sisters who knelt there seemed almost like some mysterious part of the structure, positioned in two straight lines as they were.

The Prioress sat, propped on pillows in her sedan chair, facing her Council. The lines were not drawn clearly in this arrangement: of the twelve Sisters four, including their leader, were of the Sister Gatsa faction; five, including the Sister who sat in Morima's place, supported the Prioress; and the remaining three were called, when they were not present, the *Wind Chimes*—those who swayed this way and that, making sounds according to the direction of the wind. As one would expect, the Wind Chimes were both courted and despised.

The Sisters bowed their heads to the floor and rose, waiting impassively.

"Who called this Council?" The Prioress asked the ritual question.

Sister Gatsa spoke in her refined aristocratic voice. "This Council was called by the collective will of the Twelve, Prioress."

"Then let the will of our Lord, Botahara, be done through word and deed."

Signs to Botahara were made and silence reigned as each woman present prayed to the Perfect Master for guidance. A gong sounded softly and the Council began.

"Who will speak for the Twelve?" the Prioress whispered.

"Sister Gatsa," the women answered together.

The Prioress nodded to Sister Gatsa, conceding the floor.

Sister Gatsa drew herself up to her considerable sitting height before beginning. "Prioress, honored Sisters, there is news from the Province of Seh that is of grave concern to our Order. There are reports that a large barbarian army makes ready to assault the Empire's northern borders. Does our Order have information about this situation?"

A silence ensued. The Prioress sat looking at her Council who, as was proper, did not meet her gaze. Only Gatsa would dare to do that. It occurred to the Prioress to wonder who in the Priory in Seh had managed to find a copy of Sister Yasuko's letter. Most annoying.

"I have received information from Seh that would indicate this is true, Sister Gatsa," the Prioress said at last.

There was a minute shifting of position as though in discomfort among some of the Council.

"Excuse my presumption, Prioress, but should not the Council have been informed of this?"

"In time of war," the Prioress said so quietly that she forced the others to lean forward to hear, "the Prioress has authority to act without the Council. It has always been so."

Gatsa nodded, her face not quite masking her pleasure. She had sprung her trap. "In time of war, Prioress, this is true. But war has not yet come and there is much that should be done in case a calamity should befall us. There is much that we all should do."

"A fine point, Sister," the Prioress said. "Shall we put it to a vote?"

Sister Gatsa hesitated noticeably. She had expected to request this herself. "If the Council so desires, Prioress."

The Prioress smiled her beatific smile, unsettling Senior Sister Gatsa even further. Of course, the Prioress knew she would lose—she could read her Council that well. But after the Wind Chimes had gone against their Prioress once, they would be less willing to do so on each subsequent issue, especially when the true nature of the situation was made clear to them. Today they would ring to the words of Prioress Saeja, the old woman was certain of that.

"Let the proceedings begin," the Prioress whispered. Yes, let them begin. In three hours she would have approval of everything she had already begun. Let the vultures gnaw on that. She smiled again and closed her eyes to wait.

Thirteen

THE GREAT AUDIENCE Hall of the Empire of Wa was the largest chamber in the known world and considered to be a marvel of both art and engineering. The rows of pillars that lined the central hall were each carved from a single iroko tree and lacquered to a deep sheen. Rafters soared in elongated curves up into the tiered roof structures and light filtered down from on high without an identifiable source. So polished was the marble floor that it reflected images and light as faithfully as clear, still water.

At the farthest end of the hall the dais seemed to float on this unrippled surface. Three steps of the finest jade led up onto the dais, the blocks joined so seamlessly that the steps appeared to have been carved of a single, massive block of green-blue stone. Behind the dais, seven painted panels showed the Great Dragon in flight among stylized clouds above a landscape of rugged beauty—ancient Cho-Wa of the Seven Princes. The Princes themselves sat their gray steeds at the foot of the Mountain of the Pure Spirit about to create the Seven Kingdoms that would one day become the Empire of Wa.

Below the center panel sat the Dragon Throne of Wa carved from a single block of flawless green jade.

Upon the Dragon Throne sat Akantsu II, Emperor of Wa. His voluminous ceremonial robes flowed over the carved stone, reaching almost to the floor, where a small cushioned stool protected his feet from contact with the earth. His sword of office stood in a silver stand to one side, and it was apparent to any who knew him that he missed its feel and hardly knew what to do with his hands without it.

The Ministers of the Left and Right sat in their appropriate places, before the dais to either side, while down the length of the Audience Hall the Great Council of State was arrayed: Reminders, Major and Minor Counselors, and the senior Officials of various ministries. They sat in rigidly defined rows, dressed in their state robes that created a most pleasing pattern of color and form, each man a tiny island on the unbroken, liquid surface.

Behind the senior officials sat functionaries of high rank, scribes, and bureaucrats, and behind them stood the ceremonial guards—generally younger sons of favored peers—dressed in ornate armor.

On the first step of the dais knelt the Major Chancellor who governed all proceedings, listening carefully to the whispered comments of the Son of Heaven and proclaiming these to the Great Council.

At the moment all sat listening to a senior Counselor who spoke in glowing terms of the recent efforts to rid the canals and roads of brigands. Several minor decrees, that had been issued almost after the fact, were singled out as showing great foresight and the senior Counselor bowed in the direction of the officials responsible for these—members of his own faction, as everyone present knew.

While the great statesmen of the Empire involved themselves in this activity, the man who had convinced the Emperor to embark on this program sat quietly in the ranks of the minor functionaries. It would be out of the question that Colonel Jaku Tadamoto would ever speak on such an occasion or to such an august assembly, yet in his sleeve rested a summons to the Emperor's private chambers. He would meet alone with the Son of Heaven later that same day—something many of the senior officials present had never done.

The Council carried on, largely ceremony, for, in truth, real government took place elsewhere, in less impressive chambers with far fewer involved. Jaku Tadamoto waited patiently, trying to keep his mind focused on the conversation, not for the content but for what it told him of the shifting alliances within the Council. Even so his gaze shifted and he found himself contemplating the Dragon Throne, remembering the history, or perhaps myth of the ancient seat of power. He turned away before the Emperor might notice his gaze, but the image stayed in Tadamoto's mind.

It was said the artist Fujimi had cleansed his soul through fasting and prayer for seven days before locking himself in his studio with the untouched stone.

Fujimi's apprentices gathered outside the doors while the Master toiled. The sounds of stone being worked would go far into the night and whenever they stopped the apprentices could hear the Master chanting in a language none had heard before. In the early morning of the twelfth day all noise ceased—no sound of stone being polished, no chanting . . . stillness. By midday the apprentices' concerns were such that they appointed their most senior member to knock on the door and call out the Master's name. Three times this was done, but there was no answer and still no sounds came from within. They waited.

By sunset it was decided to break down the doors to the studio. With some effort this was done. The shattered doors swung open and the setting sun illuminated the throne shining as though it had its own light within. A dragon flowed around the seat and back of the throne, a dragon so real, so alive it seemed to have turned to stone in mid-flight.

The apprentices stood in awe until the light of sunset faded and then, remembering their purpose, lit lanterns and began searching the building. The Master could not be found. All the doors were securely locked from within, yet Fujimi was gone, never to be heard of again.

Taken to dwell among the gods, some said. Murdered by the Great Dragon for stealing her soul and encasing it in stone, said others.

When the final ceremonies were completed and the Emperor and senior officials had left, Tadamoto rose and returned to his chambers without retinue or fanfare. In the privacy of his own rooms he removed a letter from a locked box and held it a moment as though the thought of opening it caused him pain. With some care he unfolded the paper on which he had written a deciphered version—the letter in his own hand noticeably more elegant than his brother's original.

Moving to a nearby screen, Tadamoto opened it a crack to catch the gray winter sunlight that a covering of cloud did its best to obscure.

My dear brother:

It is with some difficulty that I write to you, not only because of the nature of our parting, which I regret deeply, but I have arrived in Seh to discover things that neither of us had ever expected. I do not know how to convince you that what I have learned is true, but I must find a way. Tadamoto-sum, on the souls of our father and mother I swear that every word I write is true. The fate of Wa depends on your ability to recognize the truth—seldom has so much depended on the heart of one man.

There is no doubt that beyond the border of Seh a barbarian army of unprecedented size waits to invade in the spring. I realize that this defies the common wisdom that says the tribes are diminished, but the common wisdom is false, have no doubt. Seh is not prepared for such an attack and will fall within days.

The chieftain who has gathered the tribes and will lead them across our border is a formidable man, familiar with the situation in Seh and not unaware of the plots within our own court. You realize, I am sure, that the Emperor will not send troops to support Shonto. The barbarian chieftain knows this also, I am convinced.

The barbarians will not stop once they have swallowed Seh. They have a force that will allow them to push into Wa. If we begin to gather an army now, it is possible that the barbarian advance could be stopped in Itsa Province or perhaps Chiba. If the Son of Heaven cannot be convinced of this, the Emperor will lose his Throne to a barbarian chieftain, and this will be one of the lesser evils of such a defeat.

It is difficult to be here in the north knowing my own part in all of this. If the men of Seh realized what destruction this feud will bring, I would certainly not be allowed to live. Yet the men of Seh do not even realize that the enemy sits on their border and such is their arrogance that they will not listen to Lord Shonto Motoru. You would think that the Shonto House had not once made great sacrifice to rescue Seh from the barbarians.

I realize the Emperor will think I have sided with the Shonto, but a way must be found to convince him. Above all, you must not lose your place close to the Son of Heaven or there will be no voice of reason in the entire court.

Tadamoto-sum, it is a task of enormous weight I charge you with, and I confess I do not know how it can be accomplished, but the future of our Empire depends on you now. All we can hope to do in the north is slow the invasion—there are not enough men in all of Seh to do more.

I remain your Servant,
Katta

Tadamoto let the letter fall to the mat where he knelt. It was so impossible! If what Katta said was true, and he had trouble convincing himself that it was so, then the Empire was almost certainly lost. Tadamoto knew Akantsu II as well as any man and he did not believe for a second that the Emperor could be convinced that Katta had done anything but joined the Shonto. That Fanisan daughter and Katta's interference with her . . . that was the seal on his fate. It was all so impossible.

Tadamoto reached for the letter, read a few lines, then let it drop again. He shook his head. Katta, he thought, knew what words to use, it had always been one of his gifts. Tadamoto had never heard his brother swear by the memory of their parents, no matter how desperate, he had never done that. Somehow Katta had known that this was the one thing he could do that would shake his brother's certainty. Could he be telling the truth?

He slumped against the frame of the opening and looked out into a fine curling mist, letting the cold air wash across his face. Wasn't it just like Katta to get himself into an impossible situation and then expect Tadamoto to get him out of it! Botahara save him—save us all. He was an impossible man. But was it true? If it was and he refused to believe, then Tadamoto would bear some responsibility for the calamity that would ensue— because he could not believe in his own brother. He rolled his head against the cool wood of the frame. Katta, Katta, Katta. Why do you always demand so much of me? How can I be loyal to you and loyal to my sworn duties?

A gong sounded the changing of guards. He must make himself ready for his audience with the Emperor. As Tadamoto began his preparations, his mind went back to Osha. Osha in the Emperor's embrace. Both of their lives were terribly at risk now, Osha was correct in this. Still the question echoed over and over again: what kind of man was he that he could continue to advise this Emperor? Advise him, *comfort him,* knowing that he allowed the woman he loved to act as a common street harlot with this same man? What kind of man was he?

Tadamoto never wore armor into the presence of the Emperor, not even his lightest duty armor. He felt it was a ridiculous affectation and the fact that Katta had done it often had always bothered him—embarrassed him, perhaps, would be closer to the truth. Tadamoto wore his black uniform with its dragon insignia and the marks of his rank but no more. Even this was less ornate than it easily could have been.

It was the courtiers' obsession with signs of rank and favor that drove the young Jaku wild. What pettiness! *Could functionaries of the third rank wear a gold sash? Could officials in the Ministry of Ceremony wear the peaked cap?* It was obvious to Tadamoto that the honorable officials who governed the Empire of Wa were far more concerned with the hierarchy in the palace and signs of rank than with the governing of the land.

Realizing how angry he had become, Tadamoto tried to calm himself. It was this situation with Osha and the Emperor that was affecting him so. He was an advisor to the Emperor—it was important that he put emotion aside.

As acting Commander of the Imperial Guard he was whisked through to see the Emperor with less formality than even the most senior officials. After his morning in the Great Council, he took some satisfaction from this. He knelt before the entrance to the Emperor's chamber and waited to be announced.

Bowing his head to the mat, Tadamoto waited until the Emperor deigned to acknowledge him.

"Colonel Jaku," the Emperor said, "be at your ease."

Jaku rose to a kneeling position and moved forward to within a respectful distance of the low dais.

"Thank you, Sire."

The Emperor nodded. He was studying a scroll and seemed barely aware of Tadamoto. "You have received a letter from your brother, Colonel?"

"I have, Emperor."

"But not from Lord Shonto?"

"No, Sire."

The Emperor looked up from his scroll and picked up a letter from a small table. He set this before the dais, nodded at it, and went back to his reading.

Stretching as far as he was able, Tadamoto got two fingers on the letter and retrieved it. So, he thought as he began to read, this is the hand of the famed lord. It was a strong hand of the older style.

Sire:

As I have recently written, the transition of governments in Seh is complete and I have been able to devote myself to the problem of the barbarian raids. This situation has been found more complex than one could ever have suspected.

As there seemed to be no agreement among the Lords of Seh regarding the extent of this problem and due to the consistent rumors that a new Khan had risen to power among the tribal peoples, it seemed the best course to gather my own information directly. To this end I sent highly reliable men into the wastes, secretly. After journeying as far as the desert they came upon a recently abandoned encampment that had contained seventy thousand warriors. The men sent into the desert were experienced in such matters and I do not doubt their estimate is true. This army had since decamped, but one branch of it was observed and consisted of forty thousand armed men, many on horseback.

It is clear that there will be an invasion as soon as the spring rains have ended. I believe that more than Seh is in danger from this attack. At this time I am sure that in all of Seh there are not twenty thousand men of fighting age and only half of these are trained in the arts of war. It is possible that all of Wa could be under threat.

I believe, Sire, that the Empire has not faced such a threat since the time of Emperor Jirri. If we do not raise an army by spring, Seh will fall and a barbarian army will come down the path of the great canal.

I have spoken to General Jaku Katta concerning this issue and I believe he concurs with my assessment. I cannot stress enough the peril the Empire is in.

> *I remain your servant,*
> *Shonto Motoru*

Tadamoto looked up at his Emperor who continued to read.

"What is your response to this, Colonel?" the Emperor asked, still not looking up.

"It is similar to the letter I received from Katta-sum, Sire, though a less emotional appeal." Tadamoto weighted his words carefully. "It is difficult to know from this distance precisely what is occurring at the other end of the Empire. For that reason I hesitate to dismiss this information entirely."

The Emperor looked up from his scroll. "What would you advise, Colonel?"

"It seems most prudent that we seek outside corroboration of this information. We should send someone whose loyalty is beyond question to Seh, Sire."

"I had such people in Seh, Colonel Jaku."

"Excuse me, Sire?"

"They disappeared at almost the same time your brother arrived in the north. Gone."

Tadamoto swallowed hard.

"Coincidence seems to follow your brother, Colonel, it does not fill me with confidence."

Tadamoto said nothing. The Emperor stared at him for some seconds and though he did not wish to do it, Tadamoto looked away.

"Write to your brother. Tell him that we will make him the Interim Governor in Seh when Shonto falls. But if he sides with Shonto . . . he cannot be saved. Tell Katta-sum that my anger has passed, he may return once the task is complete. But above all find out what truly transpires in the north—your brother certainly will know." The Emperor set his scroll aside and shifted to face Tadamoto. "We will answer Governor Shonto's request for support. I will send my son, Prince Wakaro, north to Seh before the spring in company with a force of Imperial Guards—an honor guard only, but that need not be stated. We will charge him with assisting Lord Shonto in his task."

The Emperor played with a stack of Imperial reports. "It causes me grief to do this, Colonel, my own son but . . . he is not fit to rule." The Emperor shook his head, a slow gesture. He glanced up at Tadamoto for the briefest second and left the younger man to wonder if it was truly anguish he had seen written there. "He is not fit . . . so few are." The Emperor's head sank down and he stayed like that, face hidden for many minutes. "It is a difficult role that I play, Tadamoto-sum, sometimes . . . very difficult."

Tadamoto nodded. "Hakata said that Emperors are always alone, Sire. When difficult decisions are made, it is sadly true."

The Emperor nodded. "Yes," he almost whispered. "That will be all, Colonel, thank you."

Tadamoto bowed and began to back away, but as he reached the door the Emperor spoke again.

"Tadamoto-sum?"

"Sire?"

"Please, have Osha sent to me. Thank you."

Jaku nodded and backed out. Once outside he rose and walked with great calm down the hallway.

Why do I feel nothing? his thoughts echoed. Why nothing? He seemed to walk suspended in a place where the emotions did not dwell, a place of pure intellect where all thought was cold, disinterested. It would have been frightening, if he could have felt fear.

There is no hope for my brother—*governor* indeed. If he returned to the capital while Akantsu lived, Katta would die. And Osha. . . . The Emperor was destroying everything they felt for each other as surely as he would see Katta dead. And Jaku Tadamoto was his most loyal advisor. He heard himself laugh, high-pitched, half strangled. He could not feel fear at that either.

Fourteen

THE ARCHIVIST WHO bore responsibility for administering the records of the Province of Seh was surprised to find a young woman requesting access to his domain—a secretary to the governor's daughter, no less. He was even more surprised to find that this young woman, Shimeko-sum, was not only educated but a great admirer of the order he maintained in Seh's archives. He had seldom felt so appreciated and found himself wondering why his own daughters did not have such inquiring minds.

Shimeko applied herself to her task with practiced discipline, determined to make a good impression on her new mistress but also because it was work she was familiar with, and in such alien surroundings there was some comfort in that. It was fortunate, for she found little comfort in the history of the Sect of the Eightfold Path.

The story told by the Imperial Historians was very different from what she had been taught in her own studies. As objective as she tried to remain, still, she had found it distressing. And now this well-bred young lady wanted Shimeko to relate all that she had learned to her. How was she to do that?

Carefully gathering her scrolls and papers together, Shimeko set out for Lady Nishima's chambers. The halls of the Imperial Palace were an astonishing maze, but to Shimeko's Botahist-trained memory they were barely a challenge. Several of the Priories in which she had lived were at least as complicated.

As she made her way toward Lady Nishima's apartment, she was aware that people often turned and watched her pass. She supposed that failed

Botahist Sisters seldom took service with Great Houses though she really did not know and, in truth, it seemed unimportant to her.

To gain admittance to the wing that contained Lady Nishima's rooms Shimeko had to give a password and a hand sign, which reminded her that she had once memorized a Shonto hand signal on the Grand Canal. It seemed so long ago.

A servant went off to announce Shimeko to her mistress, and she worked to control her nerves as she waited.

Lady Nishima was still haunted by her conversation with Kitsura. Jaku Katta had readily agreed to use his sources within the Imperial court to find out if Kitsura's family were in danger. To Nishima's surprise he had even agreed to have a letter delivered secretly to the Omawara family—both acts that the Emperor would find deeply suspicious if he were to know of them, and there was every chance that the Emperor would know.

Did this mean that Jaku had truly fallen out of favor at court? If so, then her uncle's belief that Jaku could help secure the support of the Emperor was entirely wrong and most dangerous.

All of this she found disturbing news. She touched the folded letter Kitsura had delivered from Jaku and tried to control her anger. Such presumption! To have made advances to Kitsura and then to ask her to deliver a letter to Nishima! One expected more, even of an Imperial Guardsman. She shuddered. How close she had come to making a fool of herself. How very close.

There was no doubt that Jaku Katta was an opportunist of the worst order. And now there was a great possibility that he was no longer in the Emperor's favor. All that remained was to hear from Kitsura's family to see if indeed Jaku had risked delivering the message. Did he really believe that Kitsura Omawara had no way of sending letters secretly to her own family?

He expects so little of us, Nishima thought, not for the first time. With some effort she pushed Jaku from her thoughts.

It had been three days since Nishima had asked the former Botahist nun, Shimeko, to research the cult that had dwelt in Denji Gorge, and she had been consumed with curiosity the entire time. Shimeko was on her way with the results of her efforts even now. Nishima found it difficult to maintain her tranquillity.

Fortunately, she did not have to wait long. A servant tapped on her door and announced Shimeko.

"Ah, yes. Please, bring her to me."

The young woman was shown in and knelt, bowing, Nishima noted, in the plain fashion rather than in the style of her Order.

"Shimeko-sum, I trust you have been given quarters and some instruction as I requested?"

"I have, Lady Nishima, thank you."

"Is it more difficult than you imagined? Life beyond the priory?"

Shimeko shrugged. "It is not as different as one would expect, my lady. It is a small world contained within its own walls, seldom encountering the world beyond. In this way it is much the same. In other ways," she shrugged again, "it is not so similar."

Nishima nodded. "How went your search of our archive?"

"It is a small archive, Lady Nishima, as one would expect of an outer province. References to the Sect of the Eightfold Path were, therefore, few." She began to arrange her documents on the mats in front of her.

"Most of the written works of the Sect of the Eightfold Path were destroyed during what the historians refer to as the Inter-temple Wars. Much of what is now believed is undoubtedly conjecture. As you suggested, the Imperial Historians of the time—the reign of Emperor Chonso-sa—made their dutiful records.

"The fanes beside the Lake of the Seven Masters were built after the time of our Lord, Botahara. References in the travel journals of Lord Bashu indicate that followers of Botahara had made their dwellings there as early as one hundred and sixty years after the Passing. It may be true that originally the sculptures were not meant to be dwellings but were only adapted to this function when the Botahist Sects began to war. Excuse me, Lady Nishima, do I speak only of things already known to you?"

"I confess to a poor memory for history, Shimeko-sum. Please, continue."

Shimeko looked back at her papers. "After the Passing, several different branches of Botahist teaching developed and these flourished according to the support of different Houses or even the Emperor. Large grants of land were often made to the temples and these, it is said, became the source of considerable wealth. This wealth was coveted by different Houses and by rival branches of Botahist doctrine—by the Emperor himself in some cases. This led to the Botahist fascination with the arts of war. They defended their possessions ruthlessly."

"At this time Botahist monks went about armed and some of the temples supported large armies. They rivaled the Emperor for power and often were able to make demands of the Great Council of State that the government dared not refuse. But the temples warred among themselves, and during this period many Botahist sects were destroyed, including the Sect of the Eightfold Path."

She looked up. "This differs from my own teaching, Lady Nishima. I was taught that the sects were destroyed by overzealous followers of the rival temples and also by the Emperor." Having said this, she returned to her papers.

"According to the histories, the Botahist temples weakened themselves during the Inter-temple Wars and finally the Emperor Chonso-sa, recognizing the opportunity, crushed the remaining sects. He limited the size of the Botahist estates and forbade the Botahist monks to carry arms."

Pausing for a moment, she pointed to three rolled scrolls. "These histories are written here, Lady Nishima, if you would care to read them yourself."

"I may look at them later, Shimeko-sum. I am curious, what did these Brothers believe? What was their doctrine?"

The former nun looked back down at her papers.

From what Nishima knew of the Sisters' training, this reference to written material was entirely unnecessary— the Acolyte's memory should have been close to flawless. Most curious.

"They believed in the Seven Paths to enlightenment, Lady Nishima." She hesitated. "They believed also that the act of physical love was the Eighth Path . . . you call them Brothers, Lady Nishima, but it seems there were Sisters also."

"How very strange. Do we know the nature of their beliefs, Shimeko-sum?" Nishima said with studied casualness.

"The scholars do not agree on this, Lady Nishima. It seems likely that the sect's doctrine was akin to the ancient Shodo Hermits' belief that the path through the Illusion lay in overcoming the senses. Unlike the Sect of the Eightfold Path, however, the Shodo Hermits did this through the experience of pain." Shimeko took a long, involuntary breath. "It is said they achieved levels of focus through meditation while undergoing what could only be described as torture. They would never cry out or show the slightest signs of pain no matter what was done to them. Indeed, it is believed that the Shodo Masters could turn the agony into any feeling they desired, and it would be of equal intensity. The followers of the Eightfold Path may have believed something similar, though they substituted pleasure for pain."

Lady Nishima suppressed a shudder.

"It is all written here, my lady," Shimeko said, looking down at her gathered scrolls.

"Yes. You said the scholars did not agree?"

Shimeko nodded. "There are other thoughts. One school believes there is evidence that the sect believed the soul was divided into halves that could only be united through the act of physical love. Another thought the Sect of the Eightfold Path believed that denial of the Illusion was futile, one found one's way through it like a person groping through fog. They wrote that the followers believed one must experience the falseness of the Illusion to see beyond it and desire is the essence of Illusion. There are other scholars with other thoughts, but these represent the main schools of belief, Lady Nishima."

"I see." Lady Nishima sat, lost in thought and then she met her secretary's gaze. "And what were you taught in the priory, Shimeko-sum?"

Shimeko looked down. "Only that the Eightfold Path was a heresy, my lady. Acolytes needed to know nothing more than that."

Nishima nodded. No doubt this was true.

"Will that be all, Lady Nishima?" Shimeko asked flatly.

Nishima smiled. "I thank you for your efforts, Shimeko-sum." She straightened a fold in her robe. "There is something else. . . . Before I left the capital, it came to my attention that a senior Sister of your Order . . . your former Order, had taken an interest in one of my maids. Before this was known, the Sister had managed to learn some few things about myself and my House. Why would they have this interest in me, Shimeko-sum?"

Shimeko opened her hands. "You are Shonto, Lady Nishima."

"That would be all?"

"I do not know, Lady Nishima, but it is certainly enough."

"You know nothing of the Sisterhood's effort to spy on the Shonto?"

Shimeko sat in silence for several seconds. "I know, my lady, that senior Sister Morima, with whom I traveled to Seh, had come to observe your Spiritual Advisor."

"Brother Shuyun." Nishima said unnecessarily.

"Yes, my lady."

"Why?"

Shimeko sat staring at the floor for some time. "Within the Sisterhood it is the belief of some," she said in a whisper, "that Brother Shuyun is the Teacher who was spoken of. The Udumbara has blossomed in Monarta. I know it is said to be a rumor but it is not. Sisters have seen it."

"I see," Nishima said, surprised by the flatness of her voice. She looked at the young woman who sat before her, staring at the floor, almost huddled into herself, unable even to look up. She is in the grip of some terrible inner battle, Nishima realized. "Do you believe Shuyun is the Teacher, Shimeko-sum?"

The woman seemed to draw into herself even more. "Brother Shuyun says he is not, Lady Nishima." She shrugged, tried to speak, then her shoulders moved again like a weak convulsion. "Perhaps . . . perhaps he is not. I do not know."

The two women sat for some time, the distance between them a vast gulf of experience, belief, and desire.

"That will be all, Shimeko-sum," Nishima said at last, "I thank you."

Fifteen

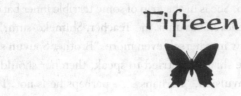

SNOW FELL ON the night of the Celebration of the First Moon—the substance of clouds floating to earth, layering Seh with white, like the Plum Blossom Winds of spring. Snows were neither frequent nor extreme in the Province of Seh and for that reason were greeted as pleasant novelties, relief from the winter rains. The First Moon Festival proceeded without pause for the weather.

The people of Seh gathered in the villages and the Manor Houses of their liege-lords where the rites and festivities took place. By far the most elaborate, if not the largest, gathering was held in the center courtyard of the Imperial Governor's Palace. Many of the peers of the northern province had accepted invitations and the fact that several of these lords represented the military power of Seh was not incidental.

The governor watched the celebrations from the top of the covered stairs that led from the Great Hall down into the courtyard. Shifting about occasionally in his unfamiliar state robes, Lord Shonto sat in the place of honor and managed to appear captivated by the scene. Below him on the stairs sat the Ladies Nishima and Kitsura, senior officials of the Council of Seh, several lords of high rank, and various guests of note, Lady Okara among them. Those who did not sit with Lord Shonto in comparative comfort, stood under parasols in throngs about the courtyard. Above them, strings of lanterns cast a pleasing light on the long silk robes and illuminated the slowly falling snow.

Dressed in costumes of fox and bear and owl, children performed a dance to the music of flute and drum. It was a more complex dance than one would have expected of their age, very stylized and rigid in its movements, yet it was not marred by a single misstep. The performers approached their roles with the utmost gravity, apparently unaware that this was certainly the least serious part of the ceremony.

Earlier in the evening Botahist monks had performed ancient rites in observance of the First Moon and to ensure a bountiful and harmonious year—burning incense to the four winds and chanting the prayer for spring rains. Once that had been done, however, the celebration took on a more festive air. Many-colored silk banners stirred in response to the occasional breath of wind as did the fine robes of the men and women present. Perfume mingled with the scent of burning oils and the pungent odor of charcoal, stirring themselves together as though the courtyard were a giant perfumer's bowl.

The children's dance ended and Lord Shonto, in his official capacity, congratulated the performers as though they were the finest Sonsa in all of Wa. Gifts were distributed, and the dancers bowed their thanks in great style.

Servants hurried about with cauldrons of steaming rice wine, for no one could be without rice wine for the first glimpse of the moon. Anxious eyes kept looking skyward, hoping that one of the breaks that appeared occasionally in the clouds would position itself propitiously, but their attention could not remain there.

A sudden burst of flame signaled the entrance of the dragon, as one of Seh's finest dancers appeared in the elaborate costume. Lady Okara had taken a hand in the design and her efforts, coupled with the skills of the dancer, created a stunning effect. Long of tail, the blue-scaled monster slithered most convincingly from shadow to shadow to the delight of man, woman, and child. After several attempts the dragon captured the moon, a silvered disk illuminated by lantern light. Attendants snuffed many of the lights then, casting the courtyard into partial shadow.

Far off, a conch sounded a long, lonely note muted by the falling snow. The dragon slithered on, gloating over its prize. Again the note, closer this time. The dragon pricked up its ears but then went back to its exploration of the courtyard, darting suddenly at a group of children who fled, screaming.

A long, sustained note came from over a nearby wall. The dragon stopped in its tracks, turning dramatically. Fire licked from a strategically placed pot as though it were the breath of the dragon.

Backlit under a great arch, Yoshinaga, the Seventh Prince, appeared, leading his gray war horse. The dragon began to thrash its tail and sway back and forth.

Leaving his mount behind, the second dancer drew his sword and entered the courtyard. Battle ensued—dragon cunning and claw against courage and steel. The dance itself was ancient of form though visitors from the capital were surprised to see that, in Seh, some liberties were taken.

Wooden drums beat out an ominous time. The climax of the battle took place as Yoshinaga, wrapped in the dragon's tail, drove his sword into the dragon's soft breast. The dragon fell upon him and with his last strength the Prince tossed the disk of the moon out into the darkness.

Everyone turned now, for if all had been timed correctly the crescent moon should rise over the wall in that instant. A soft glow in the cloud began to grow and then, through a small tear, the moon appeared to sighs of relief and raised cups of rice wine. Eyes returned to earth in time to see the spirit of Yoshinaga, now clad in a flowing white robe, mount his gray steed and ride off into the night. The dragon was gone.

The performance at an end, the gathering began to move inside except for those few who remained on vigil hoping to sight a falling star—said to be Yoshinaga riding across the heavens—a sign of good fortune for those who witnessed it.

The celebration broke into many groups and spread through three halls. Music and dance and poetry and endless talk were the evening's fare and there was no one to complain of too rich a diet.

Lady Nishima planned all her activities so that she might avoid contact with General Jaku Katta, and so practiced at this skill was she that the General was beginning to realize that, as a tactician, the lady showed more subtlety than he had ever aspired to. Once, when he had been close to speaking to her, Nishima had drawn him into a discussion with several of Seh's least interesting conversationalists and then abandoned him there, without the skills to make a polite escape as she had done.

With her practiced eye, Lady Nishima noticed that a number of prominent lords had disappeared, as had most of Lord Shonto's senior advisors. She turned toward the governor's dais and found her father slipping out through an open screen followed by personal guards and Initiate Brother Shuyun. She offered a silent prayer to Botahara.

There were perhaps a dozen and a half men gathered in the room, dressed in their finest robes and seated on silk cushions. Shonto sat before them on a low dais and to his right and left knelt the Major Chancellor, Lord Gitoyo, and the aging Lord Akima, Minister of War. Kamu, General Hojo, and Brother Shuyun, as the lord's senior advisors, sat nearby, while General Jaku and Lord Komawara were barely farther away.

Facing the dais were the lords of Seh's most important Houses, each sitting with the kinsmen and senior members of their staff. Prominent among them was the Lord of the Toshaki House accompanied by his eldest son and Toshaki Shinga, general of Seh's standing garrison. Shonto knew of Lord Toshaki by reputation only and was surprised by the man's apparent youth. Toshaki had seen at least seventy First Moon Festivals in his time, yet he seemed like a man whose gray hair and beard had turned long before their time. Lord Toshaki was aware of his status in Seh, and though there was no greater distance between him and the others, he sat apart all the same. If Shonto was any judge of such things, Lord Toshaki would allow his kinsman, Toshaki Shinga, to speak for him.

Of the province's other major Houses, Lord Taiki Kiyorama came accompanied only by his senior officer and he bowed lower than required to Shuyun and Kamu in recognition of their service to his son who had come near to losing his life in the palace garden.

Lord Ranan was another matter. The Ranan House had been the right hand of the Hanama Emperors in Seh for two hundred years and had enriched themselves accordingly. To say they were resented in the north would be an understatement of considerable proportion. Nonetheless, they were wealthy and still held power in the province, if not the favor of the Emperor that had nominally passed to the Toshaki.

It was this group that Shonto needed to win to his cause if he were to raise an army. Lord Taiki was already preparing his forces, but the rivalry between the Toshaki and the Ranan did not bode well for an alliance.

Shonto nodded to Kamu who turned and bowed to the gathered lords and officials.

"Lord Shonto Motoru, Imperial Governor of the Province of Seh."

All present bowed as their rank required and returned to the sitting position.

Shonto nodded in response and sat quietly for a moment, surveying the gathering. "The Shonto House is honored by your presence, Lords of Seh. The ancestor for whom I was named rode into battle with your grandsires and great grandsires." Shonto reached back and took a sword from its stand. "This is the sword my grandfather presented to the Emperor Jirri—legends now—yet this sword rode into battle in an Emperor's hands, and Seh retained its borders." He paused and looked around the group again.

"My Emperor has charged me to end the barbarian raids across the border into Seh and to this end I have focused my efforts. It became apparent that we needed to inform ourselves of the situation in the wastelands. To accomplish this we chose the most direct course—we sent men into the desert to look with their own eyes."

A small shifting of men in the room, eyes meeting for an instant, then all attention returned to Shonto.

"What we have learned will be related to you and no doubt you will find it as disturbing as I have. We enter a time of great decisions where our actions will affect the course of the history of our Empire. Let it be said by future generations that at this time we were filled with the wisdom of Hakata and the spirit of Emperor Jirri.

"We must speak openly, my lords, for the guarded spirit and the hidden intentions will bring us down as surely as a barbarian sword. I would know your thoughts, Lords of Seh, if you will honor me with them." Shonto fell silent for a moment, but before he could proceed a cousin of the Ranan Lord bowed to Shonto and spoke.

"In this spirit, Lord Governor, I would ask of rumors that whisper throughout Seh." He was an older man, obviously chosen for his habits of speech, for he sounded like an old scholar though he looked as hardy as an old peasant. "The people ask, where are the Kintari? And it is said there is a barbarian in your service."

They were bold questions put in a manner more direct than should have been used with an Imperial Governor, not to mention a lord of such note, yet Shonto could see the approval of the men of Seh.

"Lord Ranan," Shonto's voice was low, "I should like to ask the same question of the Kintari. . . ." He laid his sword across his knees. "As to the barbarian, we shall speak of him now, if you will consent to hear of the journey into the desert?"

The lords nodded and Shonto continued.

"As it is difficult for men of Seh to travel in the barbarian lands, it was with some risk that we did so. The only men of our Empire who can travel into the desert with any hope of living should they encounter tribesmen are the healing Brothers. For this reason my Advisor, Brother Shuyun, traveled across our border. He was accompanied by Lord Komawara, also dressed as a Botahist monk."

Turning to Komawara, Shonto nodded and the lord bowed. His wound no longer required binding and all of it but a small purple mark on his temple was hidden by newly grown hair.

"Brother Shuyun and I traveled into the steppe at the time of the Field Burning Festival," Komawara began, his voice stilted but strong. "Although we saw increasing signs of barbarian patrols the farther into the wastes we traveled, we met no tribesmen for many days. At the spring of the Brothers we found signs that barbarian tribesmen used it as a camp, though they were not there at the time. One can only surmise where they might have been.

"We traveled farther into the steppe, indeed we approached the edge of the desert itself. As we did so, we were trapped in a draw by a band of tribesmen but, due to the skills of Brother Shuyun, we were able to overcome these brigands. We questioned one—Brother Shuyun speaks their tongue—and found that they were of a tribe that hid from the Khan, refusing to join the chieftain's armies.

"As we were convinced these men did not raid across our border, it was agreed that one of their number would guide us in return for the lives of the others."

Again the lords exchanged glances but said nothing.

"This is the tribesman you have heard rumors of, Lord Ranan. Our understanding of the tribes' customs was imperfect and we did not realize that this one barbarian had traded his life and honor for the lives of his kinsmen. That is why he is with us still. He is honor bound to serve Brother Shuyun and cannot be released from that now."

"Barbarian honor?" General Toshaki smirked. "A spy in your midst seems more likely, Lord Komawara."

"I have placed my life in this barbarian's hands on more than one occasion, General. I am still alive. He is more than honor bound, as the barbarians understand it. He is truly frightened by the chieftain called the Golden Khan, believing this man will bring destruction down upon the tribes and their way of life."

"He shows wisdom in this, at least," General Toshaki said to half-smiles from the other lords.

Komawara continued his tale, saying nothing of the dragon shrine or the gold coins. The lords of Seh listened with apparent politeness until Komawara described the encampment of the army they had found in the desert.

"Excuse me, Lord Shonto, Lord Komawara," Akima interrupted. "But it is difficult to imagine a barbarian army that has more men than the total population of barbarians has ever been. How can you explain this?"

"As I am unaware of the last Imperial census of the barbarian tribes," Komawara said acidly, "I cannot answer you, Lord Akima. When were these figures compiled?"

"My lords," Kamu interrupted, "before we begin to discuss what is and is not possible, it may be best to hear what Lord Komawara and Brother Shuyun have seen with their own eyes."

Both Akima and Komawara gave half bows toward the dais.

"We left the encampment following the trail of the force that made its way toward our border. We were a day catching them. From a rise we were able to see a barbarian force of no less than forty thousand men. It was clear daylight—there could have been no mistake. This army turned east, it is believed to winter with the tribes of the steppe. Having seen this, we returned to Seh as quickly as our mounts would travel." Komawara bowed to Lord Shonto and the gathered lords and then sat rigidly silent.

"I thank you, Lord Komawara. I honor you and Brother Shuyun for this journey undertaken in our time of need." Shonto turned to the gathered lords. "As you see, the situation is one that requires decisive action. Now is the time for questions and discussion, my lords."

No one spoke. Shonto wondered who would be chosen as the voice of this group and watched the silent selection with interest. Finally, General Toshaki Shinga bowed to his governor. So, Shonto thought, the Toshaki will lead here.

"This is a delicate situation, Governor Shonto. We have been asked to speak our thoughts, but I for one do not wish to offend anyone present by arguing their beliefs . . . or calling their judgment into question."

"General Toshaki, in Shonto councils we speak our minds openly—to do otherwise could bring us to the greatest disaster. I have asked you all to share your years of experience and wisdom. If this requires that you disagree with me or any of my staff, so be it. Please, speak as you would in your own council."

Toshaki bowed. "The estimate of the size of this barbarian army seems beyond possibility, though I would hesitate to question what Lord Komawara and Brother Shuyun have seen with their own eyes," he added quickly. "Is it possible the barbarians war among themselves?"

Shonto turned to Shuyun who gave his double bow.

His voice was a surprise in this company, soft and quiet as though he felt no need to force his opinions on anyone. "It is the opinion of the tribesman Lord Komawara has spoken of that the Khan has every intention of invading Seh in the spring. The tribes that oppose him are small in number, Lord Toshaki, and scattered. They are no threat to this Khan. I can conceive of no other reason to gather an army of such size except to war upon our Empire."

"Excuse me, Brother, if I have difficulty believing one can hear truth from a barbarian," General Toshaki said evenly.

Shuyun's face did not change, though the hue of Komawara's skin seemed to darken.

The kinsman of Lord Ranan bowed now and Kamu acknowledged him.

"Sire," the younger man said with a note of respect, "there is yet another question that we would ask." Reaching into his sleeve, he removed a small leather pouch which he opened with some care. Retrieving something from its interior, he passed it to a Ranan officer who in turn moved forward to give this to Kamu.

The Shonto steward placed the small object on the dais before Lord Shonto who barely looked down.

"Yes, Lord Ranan?" Shonto said. Many eyes strained to catch a glimpse of what lay glinting on the dais.

"Coins such as this were taken from a raiding barbarian in my lord's western fief. You will see a strange dragon form on its face. What do these signify, my lord wonders? To our knowledge there has never been gold found among the barbarians before."

Shonto reached out and pushed the coin with the tip of his sword. "Let the others see this," Shonto said quietly and Kamu retrieved the coin, handing it to Lord Akima.

"What you see, Lords of Seh, is a talisman of the cult that is linked to this Khan who has risen among the tribes."

"You have seen these coins before, Lord Shonto?"

Shonto nodded. "Other raiders have carried them."

"There seems to be a great depth to your knowledge, Lord Shonto," the senior Ranan lord said. His voice was deep and rich and carried weight among the voices heard so far. "Do the barbarians mine gold, then? Or shall we assume it has been stolen from some source we are not aware of? Some lord's secret treasure?"

Shonto contemplated this for some seconds. "The gold comes from Yankura, Lord Ranan, that is all we know. How it makes its way into the desert is unclear. What purpose it serves is also a mystery."

One could almost hear the snow falling in the courtyard. The senior Ranan Lord looked at his palm as though he would read his next words there. A lamp sputtered, a drop of condensation finding the flame.

"Do you suggest that someone in our Empire pays some form of tribute to the barbarians, Lord Governor?" the Ranan Lord said, his voice suddenly quiet.

"It is a likely explanation," Shonto answered calmly, as though what he said was not an accusation of high treason. Whom the accusation was aimed at no one needed to ask.

Ranan nodded. The coin had reached General Toshaki now.

"The purpose of this cult," General Toshaki said, "is it known?"

"It seems to give legitimacy to the Khan, General."

"How is it that we have learned this, Lord Shonto?" Toshaki asked.

Shonto nodded to Komawara.

Komawara bowed rigidly. "The Kalam, the tribesman who serves Shuyun-sum, he has spoken of the dragon cult. Also, when we traveled in the desert, we saw the shrine of the dragon."

General Toshaki looked at the senior member of his House who gave the smallest gesture with his hand.

"Lord Komawara," the general said, taking his cue. "There is another rumor that has been whispered in Seh." The edges of his mouth curled in the slightest smile. "It is said that you saw the remains of a dragon on your recent journey. Can such a thing be true?"

Hojo interrupted, ignoring the general and looking directly at his Toshaki master. "Rumors, Sire, are often smoke without flame." And he smiled also.

The senior Toshaki lord held Hojo's gaze for a few seconds, then he visibly dismissed him, turning to Komawara. "Lord Komawara, on the honor of your family, do you believe you saw the remains of a dragon in the desert?"

Komawara hesitated, darting a glance at Shonto. "I saw the skeleton of a large beast, Lord Toshaki."

"A large beast, Lord Komawara?" he asked, as though addressing a child. "What nature of beast?"

"A beast that resembled the dragon embossed on the coin, Lord Toshaki." Komawara kept his voice even.

General Toshaki shook his head, looking down as though he hid a smile. Then he spoke suddenly. "One dragon, Lord Komawara, or forty thousand?"

Stifled laughter was heard around the room.

"One beast, Lord Toshaki. One only," Komawara said too quietly.

Toshaki nodded toward the young lord, almost a mock bow.

The senior Toshaki Lord gestured his kinsman to silence.

"This situation we have heard described is of consequence to the entire Empire. General Jaku, does the Son of Heaven prepare an army as we speak?"

"That is our hope, Lord Toshaki, though we do not yet know," Jaku said fixing the older man with his cold gaze.

"Ahh," the lord said, looking away. "Lord Shonto, this is a grave matter. I wish to take council with my kinsmen and advisors." He bowed to Lord Shonto.

Lord Taiki spoke without warning. "Lord Toshaki, Lords of Seh. I tell you in all truthfulness that if we do not begin to prepare an army now, we make a decision to surrender Seh to our ancient enemy. It is not the epitaph I would choose for my tomb."

There was a short silence.

"My lord wishes to consult his advisors, also, Lord Shonto," the junior Ranan lord spoke into the silence.

The council was at an end. With great dignity Shonto nodded to those around him, rose and left, carrying his own sword.

Shortly after the Lords of Seh had gone, Shonto returned to speak to his staff. Jaku and Lord Akima were not present. Komawara, Lord Taiki, and the Major Chancellor, Gitoyo, were the only outsiders. Shonto seated himself on the dais and regarded the men around him. *"Blind are the sighted and deaf the hearing . . . only those who look within will find truth."*

Shuyun made a sign to Botahara at this quotation.

Shonto shook his head slowly. "General Hojo?"

"It would appear that the Lords of Seh believe you are to be the victim of a hired barbarian army, an army paid in gold by our revered Emperor. No doubt the Lords of Seh believe that you try to raise an army in your defense. They cannot believe the Emperor would endanger part of his Empire to bring down the Shonto. There will be no support coming from these men. Lord Toshaki, I think, will do nothing that has not been ordered by the Emperor. And Lord Ranan, though he hates the Yamaku, will take no unnecessary risks to thwart their Imperial ambitions. The minor Houses, even if they could be convinced, would make little difference."

Shonto nodded. He gestured to the others and each man in turn nodded agreement. Shonto clapped his hands loudly.

"And the Emperor's support? Truthfully?"

"It is entirely dependent on Jaku Katta. But in all honesty, I think it is unlikely. After Denji Gorge, it seems the Emperor has reason to distrust his Guard Commander—it takes very little to earn the Emperor's distrust. The rumors that Jaku has fallen from favor may have truth in them. Katta-sum may not even be sure of his own situation."

Shonto looked at Kamu.

"I agree, Sire. We may hope for the Emperor's support, but we should begin to take the actions we would take if it were not forthcoming. We dare not wait."

Shonto sat contemplating this like a man considering a move at gii—and like a gii master he showed no sign of being affected by his situation. It gave his retainers hope.

"Lord Komawara," Shonto said warmly, "you could do nothing but tell the truth. It could not be helped. I regret this deeply, but tomorrow we meet to plan our retreat from Seh." He pulled the sword that was the Emperor's gift partly from its scabbard. "Kamu-sum, starting now we will have no one but those present in councils unless I order otherwise. We give up this pretense—the government of Seh seems to be made up of informers. No guards but our own around our chambers." Shonto slid the blade in and out of its scabbard.

"We have one other move that we can make in this game before retreat and cover. Kamu-sum, prepare a tract that says the Government of the Province of Seh is paying gold for the service of armed men. They will not come in time, perhaps, but they will come as we move south."

The Major Chancellor, Lord Gitoyo, bobbed quickly. "Sire, Lord Governor . . . the Emperor demands his taxes. We dare not delay longer. There is certainly not enough gold to raise an army."

"Huh." Shonto examined the flawless metal blade. "We must not keep the Emperor waiting for his taxes. That would be unthinkable." He smiled at those around him. "Entirely unthinkable."

Komawara gave a deep bow. "There is one other action we could consider, Lord Shonto."

Shonto nodded.

"The springs closest to our border in the steppe—they could be poisoned as winter ends."

Komawara returned to the festivities, though his heart wanted to be gone. An urge to race a horse with a great heart across the hills took hold of him, as though he could leave what he felt behind. *His own countrymen, northerners, were surrendering Seh to the barbarians!* When the Khan swept across the border with his army, *then* these men would be ready to fight—when the only sensible course of action would be to retreat as Lord Shonto planned. They would all die so it could be said that they did not abandon Seh, despite the odds. The bravery of fools. . . .

Pulling his thoughts away from this problem, he searched the gathering for a glimpse of Lady Nishima. She had spoken to him earlier and he had alternately felt delight and despair ever since. Her robe of rich blue with its pattern of snow falling on the Mountain of the Pure Spirit was nowhere to be seen. Despair.

Lord Toshaki's eldest son, Toshaki Yoshihira, surrounded by a group of laughing kinsmen, rose from a low table. He spotted Komawara as he gained his feet and stopped. Breaking into a grin, he made a sudden extravagant bow and then rose, his face flushed from drink.

"Lord Komawara," he enunciated with the care of a man who had drunk his limit, "it is my hope that in future First Moon Festivals that Prince Yoshinaga slaying the dragon will be replaced by Lord Komawara *meeting* the dragon."

Toshaki's cousins showed some concern at this insult and their laughter

was subdued. Komawara had a reputation as a swordsman that was respected.

"Perhaps it could be replaced by Lord Toshaki discovering foolhardiness
in a wine cup," Komawara said evenly.

Suddenly Shuyun and Lord Gitoyo's son were beside him. "There are
more important fights than this, Lord Komawara," Captain Gitoyo said quietly.

"Listen to your friend, Lord Komawara," Toshaki slurred. "You must save
your courage for the barbarian hordes."

Komawara felt restraining hands on either of his arms. "I would not have
the blood of a fool on my sword," Gitoyo whispered. "Come away from this.
You of all people do not need to prove bravery."

Komawara gave way to the pressure on his arm and began to turn away.

Toshaki bent over the nearby table and retrieved a lacquered chopstick.
He brandished this like a sword and stepped into the guard position. "Lord
Komawara, you need a proper weapon to slay dragons and barbarian hordes.
I would be honored if you would take mine."

Komawara broke free of his companions and spun back toward the
Toshaki lord but, impossibly, Shuyun stood facing Toshaki, his back blocking
Komawara.

"My lord," Shuyun said quietly, "that is a dangerous weapon to wield in
the governor's hall."

Toshaki stood with his chopstick before him like a sword, suddenly looking unsure of himself. Botahist monks did not confront peers.

The implement disappeared from Toshaki's hand as the monk's arm became a blur of motion. Toshaki stepped back into his kinsman.

"Such a weapon should never be drawn in polite company."

Again Shuyun moved with a speed that was impossible to follow. There
was a crack of wood hitting wood, not loud but strangely piercing. Shuyun
bowed low before Toshaki who stared down at the chopstick Shuyun had
driven into the table.

"May your journey bring you wisdom, Sire," Shuyun almost whispered.

Toshaki stood staring at Shuyun for several seconds, his face contorted
and unreadable. Then, realizing that his supporters retreated, he turned
away and disappeared among the crowd.

Shuyun stood watching the young lord's retreat, then he faced his companions.

Komawara's gaze was fixed on the point where Lord Toshaki had disappeared. He looked at Shuyun suddenly and he shook his head. "You should not, Brother," he whispered. "Such things are beneath you."

With a nod to Gitoyo, he turned and went off in the opposite direction Toshaki had taken. The people present became a blur of colored silk and the sounds a low roar in which nothing could be distinguished. Komawara trembled with anger.

I have become the object of ridicule among my own countrymen, the lord thought. *And despite all that I have done, my province will be put to the sword and the torch.*

He stumbled out beyond the row of pillars toward the doors. And there he saw Lady Nishima in serious conversation with General Jaku Katta, of the Imperial Guard. She faced toward Komawara as she spoke, but she did not see him, that was clear.

He stood for a moment looking at this scene and then passed through the great doors into the courtyard. Like Yoshihira, he disappeared into the night.

It had not been easy for Lady Nishima to slip away; she was, after all, the governor's daughter, but she was becoming experienced in such matters. The sounds of music and conversation from the hall were barely muted by the pillar she stood behind yet it would be difficult to leave the hall entirely without passing out into a cold night.

She tapped a closed fan into the palm of her hand in what looked like impatience but was really a disguise for anxiety. After she had successfully avoided Jaku Katta all evening, he had sent her a poem that he knew she could not ignore.

She had struggled to read in the poor light:

Season of cold hearts
No warmth from the white robe,
Snow upon the shinta leaves.
Who knows how deep the frost shall reach?

> *There is something you must hear*

Nishima's heart raced. Some part of her hoped that Jaku would prove to be honorable and this hope unsettled her. Surely it was the worst foolishness.

Look how he had acted so recently with Kitsu-sum! She was about to return to the gathering when a dark form appeared down the row of columns. Though it required some effort, Nishima waited with what she hoped would be an appearance of calm.

Jaku walked toward her, his strong, graceful form appearing and disappearing as he went from light into shadow into light again. Finally he stepped into the same shadow that Nishima occupied. Gray eyes almost seemed to glow in the pale light. Jaku bowed deeply.

Nishima nodded. "General. . . ." She was about to pursue a polite course of conversation but caught herself. "What is this matter you have written of, General Jaku?"

If Jaku felt this was an insult, he did not show it.

"It is something that should be spoken of in more private surroundings," Jaku said, his voice low.

"Perhaps it should be spoken of in the presence of my uncle," Nishima said curtly.

"This is information for your ears, Lady Nishima. It is to show that my intentions are honorable, though I fear that they will be misunderstood as they have been in the past."

"You wrong me, General—I was not aware that your intentions had been misunderstood." Nishima waved her fan open. "What is this information you speak of? The night grows cold, General Jaku."

Jaku nodded, looking over his shoulder quickly. "I am concerned, Nishima-sum," he met her eyes for a second, but when she did not react to him dropping her title he went on quickly. "I fear the Emperor will not respond to my plea for troops: the intrigues of the court are beyond imagining and difficult to untangle, even while living in the palace. The webs spun in the Emperor's court are such that I risked much to have written as I did, for myself and my family."

"Do you suggest, General, that the Emperor will not respond to your letters as you hope?"

Jaku hesitated. "It is a possibility, Lady Nishima."

"Huh." She waited.

After it was apparent she would say no more, Jaku went on. "The Emperor's support is desperately needed, I know, but if it cannot be obtained, Lady Nishima, I will not return quietly to the capital." Again he searched her eyes. "I will warn my family and remain in Seh to do what I can. Though it is said by some that Jaku Katta takes only the course of greatest opportunity, I will fight beside the Shonto though I will gain the enmity of the Son of Heaven."

Nishima looked away. A man stepped out from behind a pillar not far off, hesitated, and then passed through the doors leading to the courtyard.

"Tell me, Katta-sum," Nishima almost whispered, "will the Emperor send troops to us? Is there no hope?"

She watched the guardsman as he considered her question.

"I am not without influence at court, Nishima-sum, but others may hold sway—while I am here. It is . . . it is possible that my voice will not carry, it pains me to say."

Nishima nodded sadly as she looked down at the floor. "And this mad design to bring down my father, you took no part in it?"

"Once I had learned of it," Jaku stepped closer and lowered his voice, "I took some time to speak, it is true. My loyalties were tested . . . until I spoke to you at the Celebration of the Emperor's Ascension. My shame that I did not speak sooner."

Nishima's fan stopped in the middle of its sweep. A warm hand touched her cheek and she pulled away. Looking up she met Jaku's gray eyes, as impenetrable as cloud. Turning away she walked back into the bright hall.

Sixteen

NISHIMA UNFOLDED THE letter for the second time and read the single poem.

Season of cold hearts
No warmth from the white robe,
Snow upon the shinta leaves.
Who knows how deep the frost shall reach?

There is something you must hear

Nishima's thoughts whirled as though the Nagana blew through her mind, swirling everything into a tangle. Jaku had lied to her. She was more sure of this than she was of her own name, and far more sure than she was of her feelings. Although she would not have evidence until letters arrived from Kitsura's family, there was no doubt. Jaku Katta was no longer in favor at court. It was all a pose. She wondered again if her father truly relied on the guardsman to gain the Emperor's support—for in reality, Jaku's efforts would almost certainly insure the Emperor's refusal.

And Jaku had been involved in the plot to bring down her House. No doubt he hoped to raise the other Great Houses against the Emperor who had brought down the Shonto, or perhaps it would just be a quiet murder in the Imperial Apartments, and then place Nishima Fanisan Shonto on the Dragon Throne . . . destroying her life in every way.

And yet, and yet. Nishima had pulled away at Jaku's touch . . . not because this brought her no pleasure. A single touch of his hand caused her body to betray her entirely. She found herself wanting to believe him, or worse yet, knowing what Jaku was and not caring. No, she could never allow him close to her again. He was worse than an opportunist, he was without honor. To bring down those she loved and pose as her savior! She pulled his letter from her sleeve and tore it deliberately into shreds. Childish but satisfying.

A bell sounded far off, muffled by the few inches of snow that covered Rhojo-ma. It was almost morning and she had not slept, still wore formal robes under the lined over-robe she had donned against the cold. She plunged a poker into the charcoal burner and rearranged the coals to let the air flow through. A wave of warmth reached out and Nishima pulled the fine silks of her robes close, pushing her hands into the sleeves.

Nishima lay down on the cushions and closed her eyes, but sleep was not near. She examined the room she had been given. A pleasant place, almost bare but for her writing table, a small stand bearing an arrangement of winter flora, and a three-section painted screen displaying scenes of a spring party under the plum blossoms. A thick rug made by the tribes was set squarely in the middle of the straw-matted floor and on this her cushions were arranged. Three lamps washed the room in warm light, reflecting off the lacquered beams and posts.

A simple place, without the clutter some people preferred. When very young Nishima's true father had once taken her to the home of the Shonto vassal-merchant, Tanaka. A lifetime of trading had burdened him with the most unbelievable collection of furnishings. Cabinets and trunks, chests with drawers, and, most surprising to her, Tanaka owned *chairs*. She had never sat in a chair before. Nishima had a clear memory of climbing up into one of these elaborate oddities to perch, swinging her feet, pretending she was a princess. The idea of being a princess had not seemed frightening then.

Nishima closed her eyes again. Her thoughts became lost in other images; Jaku Katta's animal eyes, a dark wooden box of tiny drawers each containing a child's treasure, the view from Lady Okara's terrace, the sound of spring rain on tile, the touch of a man's hand on her breast. Nothing that could be remembered when she awoke to early morning light.

She was *cold*! The charcoal had long since given up its heat. She sat up awkwardly, not allowing her hands out into the frigid air. A servant peered in through a crack in the screens.

"There is a warm bath waiting, Lady Nishima."

"May Botahara chant your name," Nishima said and her servant bowed.

She felt like ice as she slipped into the steaming water and expected to bob to the surface as she had once seen a block of ice do as it slipped from the shore into the moving river.

I will never be warm again, she thought, or at least not until spring.

Nishima came back to the question that she had asked herself most of the night: should she tell her father about Jaku's situation at court? And if so, how would she present this information so that it would not seem she doubted his abilities. It was a delicate situation. Her uncle indulged her terribly, she knew, but his knowledge of the intrigues of the Empire was vast and his ability to gather and sift information was legendary. Nishima wondered at her own temerity venturing to advise the gii master.

He has so much to consider, she told herself, and Jaku has an interest in me that I have been able to use to my father's advantage. I wish only to help. I am only another source of information and what I have to say he can weigh as he does every other report he receives. Presented as information only I'm sure he will not take offense.

By the time feeling had began to come back into her body, Nishima had decided to wait a few more days and hope that Kitsura would receive a message from her family. It was slim evidence, but it would strengthen her argument at least somewhat. She could also fall back on a ploy of her youth: go see her father and test his mood before proceeding.

Shuyun waited with his usual ease. It was early morning, just barely light, but it often seemed to the monk that Lord Shonto slept as little as the Botahist trained. He had been summoned to his lord's chambers by a half-awake servant—the First Moon Festival of the previous night had taken its toll on the palace staff.

Despite the calm that he displayed, Shuyun was anxious to complete his meeting with his liege-lord so that he would be free to attend to another matter: Lord Komawara had not been seen since the incident with the young Toshaki lord the night before.

A guard entered the room and bowed to Shuyun. Lord Shonto would speak with him.

The Imperial Governor of the Province of Seh sat upon a cushion this morning, not a dais, and he seemed absorbed in peeling a piece of fruit. He nodded in return to Shuyun's bow and bobbed his head toward a second cushion.

To Shonto's left a second table stood, a lacquered chopstick embedded vertically in the top.

"I begin to wonder if this is an odd dislike of tables, Brother Shuyun," Shonto said as he worked at his fruit. The lord turned his head to regard his Spiritual Advisor and raised an eyebrow before returning to his task.

Shuyun gave a half bow. "I was concerned that Lord Komawara would injure or perhaps kill the son of a man you would hope for an ally, Lord Shonto."

"Huh." Shonto nodded. "Lord Komawara should not need to be restrained in such circumstances. Toshaki was very insulting?"

"According to my understanding of the ways of Seh he could hardly have offered more offense, Sire."

Shonto finished peeling and began to break the fruit into pieces. "It is not likely that Yoshihira would have behaved so if he had thought his father was planning to come to us." He popped a piece into his mouth and chewed with some concentration, eyes closed. "It is hard to know which of the two was more foolish." He opened his eyes and smiled. "Ah, well, youth will find foolishness in the house of wisdom. Perhaps, in the future, it might be possible to find some less conspicuous way to deal with such a situation?"

Shuyun bowed. "I apologize for acting in this manner."

Shonto waved his hand. "I regret not witnessing it more than I am concerned for the effects on young Toshaki's reputation."

"I could demonstrate this as we speak, Sire, if you wish."

Shonto held up his hands. "We will let the furnishings live in peace for while, Shuyun-sum, I thank you."

The monk nodded.

"Lord Komawara has not been seen this morning, I understand?" Shonto began eating a second piece of fruit.

"I was told the same thing, Sire."

Shonto did not answer immediately. "I will have him found if he does not appear by midday. We need his knowledge of the desert. As Lord Komawara suggested, I will send parties into the wastes to poison the nearest springs. This is an arrow that will have to be aimed perfectly. We must send out men before the Khan's army moves but not too soon or the springs will run themselves clean before the barbarian army comes to use them.

"Tactics of delay," Shonto said popping another section of fruit into his mouth. "Not to be mistaken for tactics of desperation."

Seventeen

LORD KOMAWARA SAMYAMU turned his horse off the road into a narrow path through snow-covered trees. The day was gray, windless, cast over with snowclouds that stretched from horizon to horizon with monotonous uniformity.

So still was the day that the horse's breath appeared in the cold air and floated there as unmoving as the clouds overhead. Cries of birds and the creaking of trees penetrated by frost were muted by the snow so that they seemed to come from far off. It was early morning: the first day of First Moon.

Hunched down over his saddle, Komawara was glad he had not been so foolish as to ride out without dressing for the season. He had slipped out of Rhojo-ma in the darkness, eluding his own guards who still would not forgive themselves for becoming separated from their lord in the Jai Lung Hills. They would not be pleased.

Breaking out of the cover of the trees, Komawara pulled his mount up. His destination: the crest of a low hill north of Seh's Capital which afforded a view of the city and surrounding countryside.

In the middle of a lake skimmed with ice and snow, Rhojo-ma clung to its island—a complex geometry of white walls and sloping roofs stacked into a structure of labyrinthine beauty. Tears appeared in the covering of white where the snow could not retain its hold, and here tile of celestial blue showed through. The single bridge to the shore spanned the distance in a series of delicate arches, too fine, it almost seemed, to win a struggle against gravity.

Beyond the city, the countryside of Seh rolled away to the south where it disappeared into the clouds. Komawara's vantage was not high enough to give him the view he would have preferred, but even so the land was beautiful under its cover of snow. Stands of trees huddled along ridges and hilltops, forming patches of gray in a landscape of white. In a distant draw he could see the signs of a village, feathers of smoke pulled up toward the cloud.

Komawara dismounted and dropped his reins to the ground. Walking further up the crest, he stopped and steadied himself against the bole of a tree. The wound in his side made itself felt at this motion, but he ignored it.

So soon, so soon . . . it will all be ruins, the lord thought. My home, my people. And I will be retreating down the Grand Canal, trying to defend other provinces and the throne of a traitor and criminal.

The sun tried to break through a weakness in the cloud, throwing part of the countryside into sudden relief as shadows appeared. A few snowflakes drifted down from the branches above, and Komawara was reminded of the robe Nishima had worn at the celebration—snow falling on the Mountain of the Pure Spirit. But more than that he remembered her tall, perfect form as she stood in the shadow of a column whispering to Jaku Katta. There was no doubt, she had looked directly at Komawara and did not even realize who he was. I am not worthy of her notice, he thought bitterly. Her attentions to me indicate good manners, nothing more.

He looked down at his snow-covered boots. In Seh they were the proper thing to wear: unadorned and well worn. They seemed shabby to him now, the footwear of a country lord.

"It is what I am," he said aloud. "I can be nothing else." He looked out across the familiar vista. "A country lord—and not even that, for soon I will lose everything." He hit the tree twice with the heel of his gloved hand as though testing for soundness, and the sound echoed through the still woods.

His encounter with Toshaki Yoshihira the previous evening came back to him. It would have been somewhat satisfying, he realized, to take a sword to that one. It would be the last thing Komawara would lose—his ability with a sword. Perhaps all he could hope for now was an opportunity to prove his worth in battle. It might not impress a lady from the capital, but it was within his grasp.

Komawara began to search under the snow with his feet. He would make a fire and sit a while before returning to Rhojo-ma. He could not bear to give up Seh just yet.

Eighteen

THE SNOW THAT had fallen during the First Moon Festival was only a memory by the time Second Moon appeared. Winds had blown in from the sea, bringing comparative warmth and what seemed like endless rain. The frigid cold had been replaced by a pervasive dampness, and though the nights were hardly warm they had not the same raw edge evidenced a few weeks before.

Spring came early to Wa, even in the north. By Third Moon the rains would moderate and by Forth Moon the Plum Blossom Winds would sweep in like a sigh.

Nishima sat alone in her rooms, trying to concentrate on the poetry of Lady Nikko. Though she turned the scroll and her eyes passed from one character to the next, it seemed they did not penetrate beyond her eyes.

There had been no response from Lady Kitsura's family, and this weighed on her more with each day that passed. Unable to proceed as she had planned, Nishima found the decision to put off discussing her suspicions about Jaku Katta with her father was turning into a decision not to discuss her suspicions at all. She had been so certain the night she had talked to Jaku, but that certainty seemed to be fading with each day that passed. What would she tell her father, that she had suddenly developed truth sense? If a letter came from Kitsura's family, indicating that Jaku had sent Kitsura's message, perhaps this would strengthen her resolve.

But what if Jaku had not had the letter delivered as he promised? It was most confusing. Of course there was always the chance that the letter had been intercepted. If that were the case, and the letter had fallen into the hands of the Emperor, then Jaku would certainly be out of favor now, whether he had been previously or not.

I will wait, she told herself, Satake-sum invariably said that impatience would be my undoing and though I often thought he teased me, I begin to believe he did not say this entirely in jest. I will wait.

But she did not wait well and was aware of it. "Tranquillity of purpose is as far from my nature as Enlightenment is to the toads," she said to herself.

Nishima began to reread the poem she had just finished, for not a word of it had registered. The lamp wick needed trimming, but she didn't want to disturb the servants . . . nor be disturbed by them. The rain fell with such force that it seemed like gravel clattering ceaselessly on the tile roof, but rather than find this constant rain oppressive she welcomed it—as though it somehow insulated her from the outside world. It was a comfort.

A tap on the screen that led to her room was hardly welcomed, yet Lady Nishima made some effort to speak in a pleasant tone. "Please, enter."

The face of a maid appeared in the opening. "Brother Shuyun returns a book of poetry, Lady Nishima. Do you wish to speak with him?"

"Oh, indeed," Nishima's tone was suddenly no longer forced. "Please, invite him in."

Shuyun entered a moment later, the grace of his Botahist-trained movements delighting her as much as any dancer's. There was not the slightest self-consciousness in his motions, yet she knew there was total awareness. He knelt on an offered cushion and gave the Botahist double bow.

"Brother Shuyun," Nishima favored him with her most disarming smile, "I hope you have found the works I have given you enlightening or at least diverting."

Shuyun nodded. "The poetry of Lady Nikko is enlightening for me, certainly. My education has consisted largely of Botahist texts, Lady Nishima. Lady Nikko's poetry tells me much of the world I now live in."

Nishima gestured to the scroll she had been trying to read. "She wrote so much and all of it equally illuminating, I'm sure."

They fell into a second's awkward silence.

He has not come to return scrolls, Nishima thought, and that realization shattered her natural command of social situations. Looking up at his ancient, childlike eyes, she searched for an answer to her confusion, for a reaction to what she felt. But when he met her eyes, Nishima looked away, afraid of what her own gaze would reveal.

"Shuyun-sum, I. . . ." She swallowed involuntarily. "I did not understand what I did when Satake-sum taught me. I was only a girl. . . . It was not my intention to give offense to the Botahist Order. When Satake-sum told me they were secret teachings, I thought they were secret between Satake-sum and me." She paused. "I can apologize, Brother, but it is not possible to forget what I have learned."

"Lady Nishima, my reaction was not shock at what you had done. I pass no judgment on your actions. It was Brother Satake's oath breaking that affected me so strongly. I am the one to apologize if it seemed that I blamed you."

Nishima glanced up again but his eyes appeared as always—filled with impenetrable calm. She tried to smile. "Satake-sum was a man of great curiosity, Shuyun-sum. To find out what a woman could learn . . . though I began at too advanced an age to ever achieve the mastery that you display, Brother."

Another awkward moment. The rain continued, like a frame around the silence in the room.

"Curiosity, Satake-sum told me, was not encouraged within your Order," Nishima said tentatively, as though afraid she breached a sensitive subject.

But Shuyun only nodded.

Nishima pulled her robe closer. Gathering her nerve, she pressed on. "I understand, Shuyun-sum, that there have been differing Botahist teachings in the past? Those who dwelt in the fane on the Lake of the Seven Masters, for instance."

"It is so, though the one true Way still guides us, while the others have disappeared."

"I wonder—did the sect that dwelt in Denji Gorge not believe they followed the teachings of the Perfect Master? Were their beliefs not interpretations of the words of Botahara?"

Shuyun shrugged. "Their beliefs were heretical, Lady Nishima."

"Ahh," Nishima looked down at her hands. "It seems difficult to judge their beliefs when no one is sure what those beliefs were."

Shuyun took a long breath and let it out slowly. "Others have judged the doctrine of the Eightfold Path, Lady Nishima. It does not need to be done every generation."

Nishima nodded though it hardly seemed like a nod of agreement. "Do you ever wonder, Brother? Are you entirely sure of your path? I question my own—often."

Shuyun touched his fingertips together as though he would meditate. "My teachers warned that the world beyond the monastery would test my faith, Lady Nishima." He paused, deep in thought. Then, softly, "I did not realize how hard this testing would be."

Nishima nodded but did not answer immediately. The rain on the tile seemed to respond to the sadness she felt in the room. Perhaps all ways were difficult.

A tap on the shoji interrupted Nishima's thoughts. A kneeling maid opened the screen a hand's breadth. "Lady Kitsura calls, my lady."

Nishima hid her annoyance with enormous care, well aware of how sensitive a Botahist Initiate was to tone of voice.

"How kind of her to call. Please, ask Lady Kitsura to join us."

Nishima smiled as her cousin entered, but Kitsura's air of excitement quickly gave way to embarrassment. She was dressed in an unpatterned silk robe in a shade of peach that was matched with only a single under-kimono. Her sash was a silk scarf quickly knotted and her hair was worn long. It was clear she had not expected to find male company in Nishima's apartments.

"Excuse me, cousin, Brother Shuyun. I did not realize you were here, Brother. I apologize."

"Kitsura-sum," Nishima smiled, "please do not apologize. Our discussion of the spirit will only be more interesting with your participation. Please sit with us." She gestured to other pillows and Kitsura took her place though she did not seem at all sure this was the proper thing for her to do.

"Brother Shuyun and I had just been discussing the development of Botahist doctrine." Nishima looked over at her cousin and realized that with so few robes the shape of Kitsura's breast was hardly hidden. Glancing at Shuyun, she wondered if he noticed this himself. If desire was the nature of Illusion, how was he so unaffected by it? Nishima looked back at her cousin. Men were usually all but overcome with desire when in Kitsura's presence— Nishima had seen it many times. She was aware of being somewhat jealous of her cousin's affect on the men of the Empire.

"Ah, Lady Nikko," Kitsura said, bending over to retrieve the scroll. As she did so her poorly belted robes opened, and Nishima was sure she had seen Shuyun's eyes drawn in that direction for an instant.

Shuyun bowed suddenly. "Lady Nishima, Lady Kitsura, please excuse me.

I have other duties that call me." He bowed again, responding politely to the women's expressions of regret. The screen closed gently behind him.

Nishima smiled at her cousin, a rather sheepish smile. "Plum wine?" she asked.

"Now that I have ruined your evening," Kitsura said, "coming to your rooms dressed like a street woman." She pulled her robes closed at the neck.

Nishima laughed. "You did have a most surprised look on your face when you saw Brother Shuyun." She laughed again.

"Well, I was hardly expecting you to be entertaining a gentleman. Your maid admitted me so readily. Had she said that Brother Shuyun was here, I would never have come in—dressed like this. Really, you should speak with that girl."

"Kitsu-sum, you would be beautiful dressed as a street sweeper."

"Well . . ." Kitsura looked embarrassed, "that hardly means one is allowed to appear socially, half-dressed!"

Nishima laughed again. She seemed rather pleased with Kitsura's discomfiture.

"But I have not told you! I have just received letters from my family. Jaku Katta did have the message delivered!" Kitsura's eyes shone with excitement. "It is information your father must have. Certainly the handsome Guard Commander is no longer in favor at court. He would never have dared send a message to my family otherwise—especially as he did not know what my letter contained. There can be no doubt."

Nishima nodded her head. "No doubt at all," she said quietly. "You are quite right."

Nineteen

WORD REACHED THE acting Commander of the Imperial Guard within minutes of the discovery. Jaku Tadamoto hurried down a hall and turned into the grand corridor that connected the palace proper with the Palace of Administration. Like much of the Island Palace this had been built on a scale barely approachable by mere humans—broad and high-ceilinged with a polished stone floor that shone in the soft winter light.

In the distance he could see a party of officials moving at a pace inappropriate to their station. Peaked red caps denoted at least two Senior Ministers and the robes of the others indicated officials of high rank. In the midst of this group a sedan chair was being hurried along, but it appeared to have no occupant. Tadamoto increased his pace. An Emperor too impatient to ride as his station required was never a good sign.

Tadamoto attached himself to the rear of this silent party and matched its pace without a word. The Minister of the Left, puffing to keep up, gave him a barely perceptible nod. The silence of the party hung in the air, poised like a sharp blade.

Guards and officials and courtiers knelt with their foreheads to the floor as the Emperor passed. The palace would be alive with rumors within minutes—try to control the flow of gossip when the Emperor behaved like this!

They entered the Palace of Administration and turned into another hall. The shuffle of feet on stone, the breathing of the rushing officials, robes of silk and brocade sweeping along the floor, conversations dying abruptly as the Emperor came into view.

Another hall, smaller now, some confusion about a door, and then a large room in the core of the ministry. Tense, chalky faces turned toward the entering party and then foreheads were pressed to the floor. A small, iron-bound chest stood in the center of the room and, with the bowing officials surrounding it, Tadamoto had the fleeting impression that it was an object of veneration. He pushed past the sedan chair bearers and nodded to guards to close the doors.

The Emperor paused, holding his sword in both hands. "This is the chest?"

Nods from several quarters. Stepping forward, the Emperor lifted the lid of the chest with the tip of his scabbard so that it slid off and fell to the floor with an ominous clatter. He leaned forward to look in and stepped back as though the contents offended him. Glancing over his shoulder, the Son of Heaven saw Tadamoto and nodded.

"Colonel," the Emperor waved his sword at the chest.

Tadamoto stepped past the frightened officials, staying a respectful distance from the Emperor. He rounded the chest and peered in, closed his eyes for a second, then reached down and removed a small brocade bag—the single object the chest contained. Untying the cord with trembling fingers Tadamoto emptied the contents into his palm. A dozen gold coins, square, with round holes in their centers.

The Emperor spun around looking at the gathered officials, most of whom stepped back in obvious fright.

"And there was nothing taken from this chest? It came exactly thus from Seh?"

Heads bobbed. "Exactly as you see it," a senior official offered, "though with seals unbroken." He was an old man whose voice quavered terribly. "The theft must have taken place on the canal, though the Imperial Governor's own troops were the guards."

The Emperor tapped the edge of the chest with his sword, raised the scabbard suddenly as if he would strike the edge, then stopped himself. "Find them," the Emperor said to no one and, turning, scattered the officials before him.

Tadamoto stood for a moment, looking down into the empty chest. His gaze drifted back to the coins. He pushed one with his finger to uncover another—it bore the mark of a strange dragon.

"Colonel," the Minister of the Left said, his voice jarring in the silent room, "these guards were best found quickly."

Tadamoto thrust the bag and coins into the old man's hands and stormed out. In the hall beyond he broke into an undignified trot. There was no doubt in his mind that there had been no theft. The chest and its contents were a message from Shonto—a declaration of war. Tadamoto had not received confirmation yet, but it was rumored that Shonto had published a tract offering gold for the service of armed men.

Civil war was all but inevitable. And what of this barbarian army? If Jaku told the truth, it would be more than civil war; it would be the war that ended the Empire. He went from a trot to a run.

The Great Audience Hall of the Empire was lit by only a half dozen lamps, spaced around its great perimeter, and the small light they provided appeared to be drawn into the hall's vast darkness. It gave the chamber an eerie feel and distorted one's sense of the space and distance. Tadamoto stood just inside a door to one side of the dais, waiting for his eyes to adjust. He could hear the sound of footsteps. They seemed to come toward him, then stop, then retreat again. Someone muttered—words he could not understand.

Staring into the gloom, Tadamoto was finally able to make out the silhouette of a man moving before the dais. He was unsure of what to do. After waiting in the dark for some minutes longer Tadamoto knelt down where he stood and waited until the footsteps approached and then stopped again.

"Emperor?" he said quietly.

The unmistakable sound of a sword being drawn from its scabbard.

"Sire? I have come with my report as you wished. It is Colonel Jaku."

"Tadamoto-sum?"

"Yes, Sire. Please excuse my intrusion."

"You are alone?" The voice came out of the dark.

"Yes, Sire."

"Get up," the Emperor commanded.

Jaku bowed to the darkness and rose to his feet.

"Come along," the voice said.

Tadamoto walked toward the sound. The Emperor's form materialized in the poor light. Tadamoto could see him returning his sword to its scabbard.

"Walk with us, Colonel." At this the Emperor turned and started down the hall, his pace deliberate if not hurried. Halfway down the length of the great chamber the Emperor broke the silence.

"The Shonto guards are not to be found?"

"This is so, Emperor. It seems very likely that Shonto's most senior retainers have slipped away also, though appearances are being kept up faithfully at their residences. I have failed. . . ."

"The gods take them!" the Emperor interrupted. "I did not truly believe they could be found. They did not steal Seh's taxes—their lord did."

Tadamoto nodded. They came abreast of a lamp and he could see the Emperor's face, strangely distorted by the half light. The eyes hidden in dark holes and the forehead standing out like a deformity. The young guardsman looked away.

This man touches the woman I love.

"I had hoped to avoid civil war," the Emperor said softly. "I had so hoped to avoid it.

"Of course, Shonto will drive the Empire into this war. I should have realized." His voice was sad as though he spoke of an errant child.

She spends her nights in his arms.

"We will have to raise an army now. If Shonto tries to split the Empire and establish himself in Seh, we will be forced to go north to fight. If the lord chooses to come south, we will let him come to us. Either way the Empire will pay a great price."

They strode on until they came to the massive entrance doors where the Emperor changed course abruptly and started back toward the dais.

I have let this occur, frozen into inaction.

"Are preparations complete for sending the Prince north?"

Tadamoto fought the rage that swelled inside him. "They have been complete for some days, Sire," he said tightly.

"Then he shall drag his feet no longer. Send him off even if you must use force."

Tadamoto nodded again.

"And the Omawara. We watch them with great care?"

"Both by day and by night, Emperor."

"Do not let them slip away, Colonel. I will have plans for them yet."

They walked in silence to the foot of the Dragon Throne and then turned back. Half the length of the hall passed beneath their feet with nothing but the sounds of their footsteps and the hiss of the Emperor's brocade robe along the stone. Occasionally the jeweled scabbard the Son of Heaven carried would catch the dim light, and it seemed he almost brandished it as though at an enemy.

"Sire . . . ?" Jaku struggled to collect his thoughts.

"Speak your mind, Colonel," the Emperor said with some impatience.

"Excuse me for saying so, Sire, but perhaps we play this game too openly." He took a deep breath. "If we locate Shonto's retainers and they are taken by Imperial Guards, no matter how carefully disguised, the Empire will soon know. We risk dividing the Great Houses." Tadamoto glanced at the Emperor, but it was impossible to read his face in the low light. "There are other courses. We could announce that we raise an army to send north—the situation in Seh is not critical, but it is not what we originally thought. Of course, we will keep this army here under our control until we see what Shonto does. It will be a message for Shonto's allies."

Tadamoto could see the Emperor nodding. "But what of this gold we have received from Shonto?" The Emperor turned toward him in the dark. "You understand its significance, Tadamoto-sum?"

"I do, Sire." They walked a few paces more. "We could send a message to Shonto saying we are confused by this. Certainly the Imperial Treasury should contribute to the efforts against the barbarians, but this action of Shonto's staff is foolish in the extreme. Could not the governor look into this matter and tell us his province's needs?"

The Emperor considered this. "Ah, Tadamoto, this is wisdom. Why do my other counselors not advise me so?" The Emperor slapped his palm with his scabbard. "We will do as you suggest, though Shonto's retainers should be found if it is at all possible. I'm certain Tanaka could provide a wealth of information, and not just about his lord."

They had walked the hall's length and returned now to the foot of the throne.

"What of your brother? Has he written in return to your letter?"

"It may yet be too soon, Sire."

"Ah." The Emperor paced across the foot of the dais and then stopped.

"Begin to raise the army. My son will leave for the north immediately . . . to assist Shonto until our entire force can be made ready." The Emperor mounted the steps and disappeared into the total darkness surrounding the Dragon Throne. Tadamoto heard him settle into the cushions.

"Prepare a letter for our governor," said the voice in the darkness. "Tell him that we are confused by the action of his staff. Say we prepare an army as quickly as we can. Let him wonder what we plan, let him lie awake and wonder.

"Colonel," there was real warmth in the Emperor's voice now, "I shall reward you for this, reward you richly. Tell us your desire, Tadamoto-sum."

Tadamoto knelt and bowed, his spirit sinking as he did so. "To serve my Emperor," he forced himself to say, "that is my desire."

This man. . . .

"You are a man of honor, Tadamoto-sum, but I'm sure something can be found that will be worthy of you. We shall see."

Tadamoto sat on the lowest step of the dais, brooding in the darkness. The Emperor had gone, leaving the young officer in a turmoil.

Osha, Osha, he thought. He had not seen the dancer for several days, had been unable to face her, though he could not say why. It was one thing for him to be avoiding Osha, but now he began to believe that she was avoiding him as well.

We have come to this, he thought, two people who felt and thought as one. Damn him! May all evil take his soul!

Tadamoto stood and walked along the step a few paces, then sat again. If nothing else, an army would be raised. If Katta had written anything near to the truth, then Tadamoto would feel he had done what he could. The Empire would not be entirely unprepared. And if Katta joined the Shonto in an attempt to overthrow the Yamaku . . . ? Tadamoto put his face in his hands.

"Osha-sum," he whispered, and the sound disappeared into the dark hall without an echo.

Twenty

THE IMPERIAL GOVERNOR'S Palace was a riot of preparations and though most of the people involved, beyond Shonto's own staff, thought the governor was mad, they were not allowed to let this feeling be reflected in their work. Shonto's retainers made sure of that.

Shuyun found himself with little to do, for he had no specific responsibilities other than to advise his lord when required. Lord Shonto's staff were masters at logistics, so advice from an Initiate Brother, who owned almost nothing and had moved only twice in his short life, was highly unnecessary.

The day was comparatively mild, but a strong wind blew out of the west, whipping up and pushing at Shuyun where he moved along the top of the palace wall. He had walked the perimeter of the Imperial Palace atop its various sections of wall and through its towers for no other reason than to be out in the air after all the hours spent in the palace during the winter. Though it seemed to indicate lack of Enlightenment, Shuyun could feel his spirit lift with each step.

The palace sat atop a low rise on the city's eastern edge, the highest point on the natural island that formed the anchor of Rhojo-ma. Much of the rest of the city sat upon manmade islands built on a rock shelf that lay just under the lake's surface. The palace's position hardly offered a high vantage, but it afforded some views that were worth contemplating and Shuyun had stopped at each of these.

Below, Shuyun saw two guards in Shonto blue who looked up and pointed in his direction, then one of them began to make his way at a trot toward nearby stairs. Lord Shonto must have sent for his Spiritual Advisor, the monk thought, and increased his pace.

"Brother . . . Shuyun." The guard puffed to the top of the stairs, holding his sword hilt as he ran. "There has been a missive left for you." He bowed. "My corporal was not sure of its urgency, so he sent me immediately."

Shuyun gestured down the stairs. "Please, I will follow."

They did not have far to go, for the guard led the way to a nearby gate that opened into the streets beyond the palace—quiet streets. Guards bowed as the governor's Advisor approached and the few pedestrians who passed by stepped aside. Inside the gate house the corporal the guard had spoken of bowed low to Shuyun.

"Excuse me for interrupting your contemplation, Brother, but I thought this might be of importance."

The corporal's name was Rohku; Shuyun had met his father during his brief time in the capital. He took from a table what appeared to be a scroll wrapped in plain gray paper and handed it to the monk.

Shuyun nodded his thanks. It was not a missive, certainly, for there was no stamp of his Order upon it.

Corporal Rohku bobbed in a second bow—the story of Shuyun's confrontation with the young Lord Toshaki had made its way down through Shonto's guard, and it brought even greater respect to the monk. "It was delivered by a Botahist Brother."

Shuyun turned it over and found a wax seal with a name-character impressed in it.

Hitara.

Shuyun felt his time sense stretch as though he practiced chi ten, yet he did not.

"How long ago?" Shuyun asked, his mouth suddenly dry.

"Moments, Brother Shuyun, only moments."

"Did you see the direction he set out in?"

"Toward the market streets. . . ."

Shuyun placed the scroll in his hands. "Guard this," he ordered and then was out the door at a run before the corporal could protest.

"Follow him," Rohku snapped. "He is not to leave the palace without an escort."

The young guard set out at a run but was soon outdistanced by the small monk. By the time he reached the market streets, Shuyun was lost from sight.

Shuyun ran.

"A Botahist Brother? Did he pass?" he yelled at a peasant leading a mule. The man nodded and pointed down a narrow side street. Shuyun ran on, increasing his pace.

At the next meeting of streets he asked again and was directed left. Then right. Then up a flight of stairs and across a bridge. Coming to a small square, he was stopped by the many streets and stairs and alleys.

An old man sat on a step, working at a strap on an ancient sandal. "A Brother," Shuyun panted, "did he pass?"

The old man tugged away at the strap, looking off into the distance as he did so. After several seconds of contemplation he nodded.

"Which way?"

Without taking his eyes from the point in the distance or deigning to look at his inquisitor, he answered. "I am only a poor old man, Brother, do not ask me to point the Way."

"I have no coins, old man, but I will see you receive coins aplenty if you answer my question."

The old man smiled. "The Way, Brother is not so easily found." He paused to concentrate on his task for a second. "And I am not a teacher."

Shuyun went to speak again but realized what he should have seen immediately—the man was blind. Looking around at the many alleys and stairs, Shuyun shook his head. There was no one else to ask.

"Who shall I ask if not you, old sage?" Shuyun leaned against the wall to catch his breath.

"That is the worst of it, Brother. Until the Teacher comes, there is no one." He managed to free the broken strap suddenly and explored the damage with twisted fingers. He did not like what he felt. "Tell me your name, Brother."

"Shuyun."

The thin smile appeared again. "He who bears. What is it you carry, Brother Shuyun?"

Shuyun sat staring for a moment—he had once been a scholar, this shriveled old shadow of a man. Only a scholar would know the origin of his name. He looked down at the man's feet. His other sandal was as much a ruin as the one he held in his hands.

Shuyun slipped quickly out of his own footwear and put these in the man's hands. "To aid you in your search for the Way, old sage."

The man ran his fingers over the soft leather, his smile returning. Shuyun turned back the way he had come, bare feet over cold cobbles. He had not gone three paces before the old man spoke again.

"If you do not know what it is you bear, Brother, you risk taking the wrong path."

Shuyun looked over his shoulder. The old man sat, gaze still fixed on a distant point, stroking his gift.

"I bare my feet, old sage, and pray to Botahara to guide them."

The old man smiled now, rocking back and forth like a child. He laughed gently.

As he walked back to the palace, Shuyun was met by an anxious young guard whose great relief at finding his lord's Spiritual Advisor unharmed was visible. When the guard realized that the monk walked barefoot, he immediately tried to give him his sandals and was somewhat disconcerted when Shuyun refused.

Returning to the palace gate, Shuyun retrieved his scroll from Corporal Rohku and retired from the bustle to his own rooms. After an insistent servant had bathed his feet, Shuyun was able to be alone. He retreated to his balcony with the package, broke the seal with great care, and unwrapped the scroll, holding his breath as he did so, much to his surprise.

The scroll was new, doing away with Shuyun's most irrational expectation—Shimeko's words had affected him more than he realized. The paper was plain, common in fact, a dull shade of yellowish-brown, and the brush work, though perfectly executed, was unremarkable. He read.

Brother Shuyun:

I regret that we will be unable to speak, but it is my hope that everything you might ask will be answered here. I have come recently out of the desert and do not know when I shall be able to return.

The army that you searched for in the north is, even now, approaching the border of Seh. The brave men of Seh who rode into the desert to patrol beyond your borders have been returned to the wheel, may Botahara protect their souls. Although the Khan's army is near, it will take ten days to reach

your border, such is its size. Over one hundred thousand follow behind this
Khan, Brother, and they are well armed.

Once across your border the barbarian forces will take another six days to
reach Rhojo-ma. It appears they will enter Seh north of Kyo. There is so
little time, Brother.

Lord Botahara took out his sword and shattered it upon a great stone.
His armor he sank into the rushing river and his war horse was set free
to run across the hills.

"In the struggle that comes," He said, "such weapons will be as the toys
of children." Saying this, the Lord left his army and walked down from
the mountain. And so began the struggle for the souls of men.

> May Botahara smile upon you, Brother,
> *Hitara*

Shuyun sat for a long moment, looking out over the roofs of the palace.
The wind still blew, pulling the clouds into long ragged banners. He unrolled the scroll further, hoping there would be more and something soft fell
onto his knees. Looking down, Shuyun closed his eyes and began to pray. As
he did so, tears ran onto his cheeks though he did not feel them. He chanted
the long prayer for forgiveness and then the prayer for thanksgiving. Yet he
still dared not open his eyes.

When finally he looked upon this gift, he thought his soul would swell
until it spread across the sky. His fingers trembled when he reached out and
took Hitara's gift into his hands. A simple white blossom, five elongated petals tinged with purple, as soft and supple as if it had just been plucked.

"Botahara be praised," Shuyun whispered. "The flower of the Udumbara."

Twenty-one

SHONTO ROLLED THE scroll with great care as though it were very old and rare. He sat near a screen partially opened to the cool day and, like the others present, Shonto still wore outdoor garb. Preparations for the move south were in motion and Shonto had walked the quay to see some of this firsthand. It was the lord's way to have his presence known in times of difficulty.

Shonto seemed more grave than usual though one could hardly detect any effects of the burdens he bore or the work he had been doing. It was part of the lord's persona—his apparent youthfulness was due less to his appearance than to his manner, his exuberance. But today the exuberance was muffled under a layer of seriousness.

"It is beyond question, Shuyun, you have no doubt?"

The monk nodded. "Though this man is a mystery to my Order, there is no doubt that he is a true follower of Botahara. I am convinced that what Hitara has written is true."

Shonto looked to General Hojo Masakado.

The general did not hesitate. "If this information is not true, I am at a loss to know what purpose such lies would serve. It is my counsel, Sire, that we should act as though Brother Hitara's information is beyond doubt."

Shonto nodded, then turned to Kamu.

"I agree, Lord Shonto, though I would feel more at ease if we knew more of this Brother from the desert." Kamu threw up his hand in resignation. Of all Shonto's senior staff, Kamu was affected most by the preparations that they engaged in. His age was beginning to tell. Yet he went about his work with customary efficiency and though he seemed to be aging daily, there was never a complaint.

Shonto turned to Komawara next.

"I do not claim to have a truth sense, Sire, but I met Brother Hitara in the desert and I do not believe for a moment that he would lie to us. The guard's description fit Brother Hitara perfectly and, like General Hojo, I can't imagine that giving us such information, were it wrong, would benefit anyone. Even the barbarians would rather we stayed in Seh where they could easily defeat us. We have only a few days, Sire, I think we should act immediately." Komawara bowed.

Shonto looked over at Nishima.

"Certainly we should act, Sire, but I don't think we can leave Seh before the barbarians have crossed the border. I do not mean to tell you your duties as governor, but we cannot abandon the people of Seh entirely."

Shonto considered this. "We can begin our move down the canal, though some may stay behind until the true situation is realized in Seh. A small group can still easily outdistance a large army." Shonto bowed to Nishima, then turned to the Imperial Guardsman. "General Jaku?"

The presence of Jaku Katta at this council was a mystery to everyone but Shonto who had invited him. It was doubly a mystery, for Jaku had not been told of Brother Hitara in the original story of the journey into the desert. Perhaps it was not such a surprise to Jaku that he had not been told everything—he had lived in the Emperor's palace after all. The Guard Commander bowed formally.

"Lord Shonto, I agree with Lady Nishima. We cannot begin to move our forces south until the barbarian threat is realized by the people of Seh. I am forced to admit that this is a matter of pride as well as prudence. If we leave now, we will be seen as either mad or cowardly. If we leave after the barbarian army has been seen for what it is, our actions will be viewed differently by the lords of this province. As I say, it is a matter of pride—I am a soldier, please excuse me."

Other men in the room nodded. Pride was at issue here with all but Shuyun and perhaps Lady Nishima, though none had spoken of it.

Shonto nodded thoughtfully. "Lord Komawara, what do you think your countrymen will do when they see the scale of the barbarian army?"

The young lord considered for a moment; he had embarrassed himself in

Shonto's council in the past and was taking some care not to repeat this. "I fear that fewer men than we would hope will follow us south, Lord Shonto. The Taiki prepare as we speak but, as General Jaku has said, pride will dictate the actions of many. Some will stay to fight, though they will understand the futility."

Shonto pulled his armrest closer. "Kamu-sum, the tract that you distributed—when can we expect to see some response to that?"

Kamu did a mental count of days. "Soon, I would expect, Sire. The lure of gold is great. Armed men from Itsa and Chiba provinces should be making their way toward us as we speak."

"Send recruiting officers and staff down the canal," Shonto said, "as soon as you can—tomorrow if it is possible. Have them begin work in a station south of Seh's border. Then have them move in seven days. We will keep them ahead of us. Put a responsible man in charge of this, we do not want a stream of soldiers joining our flotilla and slowing us as we move. Camps must be created in strategic places for these men. It will mean thinning our ranks, but we'll have to assign officers to the recruits—we need to have them ready and useful. General Hojo, it will mean promotions for many junior officers—see to it."

Kamu and Hojo bowed.

Shonto stared out the open shoji for a moment.

"There is other news." Shonto reached out and moved Hitara's scroll as though its angle to the light was not quite correct. "I have received word from the Emperor," Shonto said quietly. He looked up at the others. "The Son of Heaven writes that an army is being raised for the defense of Seh."

Shonto seemed to enjoy the response of the people present or perhaps he made some secret assessment of those present by observing how they responded to the unexpected.

Lady Nishima stared openly and with some degree of contempt at Jaku Katta, thinking to herself that he had again proven himself incapable of telling the truth.

Kamu was not the first to recover, but he spoke first. "Si-Sire, did the Emperor not receive his empty tax box?"

"The Son of Heaven has asked that I look into this matter. The governor's staff, the Son of Heaven suggested, have acted in a most foolish manner. Certainly Seh must retain some of her revenue for defense, but. . . ." Shonto shrugged. "We are asked to prepare a document describing our exact needs.

Our failure to remit our taxes has been overlooked. So, as requested, we will prepare a report for the Emperor explaining our military needs."

"What will we tell him?" Hojo asked.

"The truth." Shonto smiled. "Does that shock you, General?"

Everyone, including Hojo, laughed.

"General Jaku, perhaps you can explain the significance of the Emperor's decision."

Jaku bowed. "I had begun to lose hope myself, Sire. My friends at court could not prevail in the council to have an army raised to defend Seh. You can imagine why. This army the Emperor writes of is intended to defend the capital from the army that Lord Shonto raises—the tract offering to pay gold to armed men must have caused a great deal of discussion. The Son of Heaven fears other Houses joining with us.

"The Imperial force is not being prepared to fight the Khan, but it is an army nonetheless: who will control this army once the true threat is apparent, that is the issue."

Shonto's staff bowed toward Jaku.

"It is some sign of hope, General Jaku. At least the Empire will not be entirely unprepared. How large a force does the Emperor gather?"

Jaku opened his hands. "This is not yet clear. I hope to know soon."

Shuyun bowed to his liege-lord. "Undoubtedly the Emperor's force will be large enough to counter Lord Shonto's army—that is the threat the Throne perceives. If it is to our advantage that the Emperor raise a large force, we could assist our cause by exaggerating the number of our own soldiers."

Komawara almost grinned. "Brother Shuyun, you surprise me. Is this what one learns from the writings of Botahara?"

Shuyun responded as though no one present smiled. "I have recently tried to broaden my education, Lord Komawara. I have heard it said that the lie no one doubts is spoken by an honorable man. We may tell a great lie and be believed."

"We will begin to move our people south the day the barbarian army crosses the border," Shonto said. "We are a laughing stock for gathering so many river craft . . . but that will change soon enough. Boats will transport what forces we have faster than the barbarians will ever ride. And rafts handled by men who have lived their lives on the desert will be slow—especially when they find the canal locks impassable. Plans must be complete to burn all other craft in Seh and also to keep the canal open ahead of us. Once the news of the barbarian army passes us on the way south, we will be dealing with thousands fleeing toward the inner provinces. We cannot have our progress impeded."

Jaku Katta bowed quickly and not as low as he had previously. "I have left garrisons of Imperial Guard along the canal, Lord Shonto. We can use them to open the waterway before us."

Shonto nodded. "Good." He considered for a moment. "The Emperor sends his useless son north with what will no doubt be a small guard. The Prince will be a nuisance, I'm sure, but we will treat him with proper respect. Who knows what part he may yet play."

"Certainly he will never make a hostage," Hojo offered. "The Prince is not dear to his Imperial father. The Emperor may be hoping we will send him to his end fighting barbarians." The general considered this. "And perhaps we should."

Shonto nodded. "Too many will find such an end, Masakado-sum, and I will wish it on no one."

Twenty-two

Beacon fires flare
From hill to tower
To hill
Like sparks escaping the brazier
In a tinder dry house

LORD KOMAWARA STOOD at the window in the top of West Tower, watching. At intervals around the horizon he could see beacon fires blazing with a distant urgency. By morning the news would have spread to the remotest corner of the province.

It was a cold evening with a harsh wind, but the lord did not seem to notice. He had been standing in the same place for more than an hour, and though he felt numb to the center of his soul it was not from the night.

They come, he thought, *they come.*

His mind seemed to have no focus, starting down one path to veer suddenly into another. Thoughts of his retainers making their way up into a stronghold in the mountains were lost to images of riders, relaying from the northern border, racing to Rhojo-ma with news of the barbarian army. Could it be as large as Brother Hitara wrote?

A fire blazed to life on an eastern hill, and then, far off, another.

Lord Toshaki sat upon his horse outside a small inn. In the background a narrow river flowed and the light from the almost full moon wavered on its surface—liquid moonlight rushing off into the night. Toshaki's son, Yoshi-hira, sat nearby on the stump of a pine tree, his horse cropping some poor, winter grass beside him. Neither man spoke. Their guards sat upon horses or stood at intervals around the clearing without sign of either impatience or intent. Warm light from the inn reflected off lacquered armor here, a helmet there. A cold wind jostled among the pines, making them sway and creak.

The moon drifted west. The innkeeper came out with cups and a cauldron of steaming rice wine, but his suggestions that the lords would find the night less forbidding inside were politely rebuffed. The horsemen waiting in the dark felt that the wildness of the night gave their vigil a certain purity.

The sound of horses at the gallop. A guard stationed up the narrow road came into sight and whistled. Toshaki's son vaulted into the saddle and joined his father.

Men burst out of the inn and disappeared toward the stable. These were men Toshaki had spoken with earlier—retainers of Lord Taiki Kiyorama, though they bore the flying horse emblem of the Governor of Seh on their surcoats. They reappeared almost immediately with three saddled horses and spent a moment checking girths and bridles in the light from the inn.

Three men on horseback broke out of the trees and pulled their mounts up before the inn, horses in a lather, driven to their limits. A crowd appeared on the porch, talking among themselves. The riders were off their exhausted mounts, taking a moment only for drink before setting off on fresh horses.

Lord Toshaki and his men rode up then, half surrounding the messengers.

"What news?" Lord Toshaki's son called. "How large is this army?"

The three riders looked up to see who questioned them, and at a whisper from one of the Taiki handlers the men went back to their drinks, handing bowls to servants to be filled a second and third time.

Young Toshaki rode closer now, blocking their path. "The Lord of the Toshaki asks the size of the barbarian army," he said with some anger.

One rider, a young captain, swung into the saddle, his horse stepping sideways, catching the excitement of the men. "Does your lord wish to measure the size of the force he has spent the winter raising against the size of the barbarian army?" he asked with little show of respect. "Go back to your gii board, young Sire, we do the governor's bidding."

Toshaki spoke now, riding up beside his son, the wind whipping his long hair out of its ring. "We will all fight together now, despite the past. We are men of Seh, tell us what it is we face."

The captain rode forward, working to control his mount as it tossed its head, ready to run. His voice was pitched low and taut with anger. "You will bow at Lord Komawara's feet and ask for forgiveness, lord," he said to Toshaki's son. "That is the size of the barbarian army."

The messengers spurred their horses then and pushed through Toshaki's guards. The riders disappeared into the darkness where the trees tossed like confused seas driven before a great storm.

The morning after beacon fires appeared, the first riders bearing the reports from the frontier officers arrived in Rhojo-ma. By first light a great human stream was flowing into the provincial capital from the nearby countryside and villages. It was inconceivable to these people that Rhojo-ma could fall, and so they came, bearing everything they could load into carts or carry on their backs or drag.

It was late winter and still cool, but the skies were a clear northern blue during the days and filled with stars at night. Those who had experience with the movement of troops prayed for the rains that would be common at this time of year. Rains would slow the invasion, could even bring it to a halt for some time. The horizon was studied with an intensity that was unprecedented, but there was no sign of cloud.

The reports from the frontier officers came to Governor Shonto and he shut himself up with his staff for most of a day. They waited for the major lords of Seh who would arrive late that evening. For the first time in two generations a Council of War had been called by the Governor of Seh.

The fisherman stood with his family on the muddy edge of the River Chousa and watched the flames change his life forever. Smoke and steam from wet planking plumed up in great clouds, racing toward the heavens, an offense to the purity of the sky. Tugging at the flaming hull, the river lapped the shore and passed on, bearing a slick of oily soot. The fisherman's wife sobbed and shed bitter tears, holding their two small children close, but the fisherman stood looking on without a sound, a deep sadness in his eyes.

Downstream, toward the bend in the river, he could see another boat pulled up on the bank and put to the torch. The governor's soldiers rowed on. The fisherman could see them searching the mouth of a tributary overhung with willows, a guard standing up in the boat parting the curtain of branches with his sword.

The fisherman's burning boat heaved now, as though some part of it was alive and in agony. This drew his attention and for a second he looked as though he would join his wife in tears. But this passed and the sadness returned. The flaming pole of a mast toppled slowly to the bank, hissing where it touched the wet mud. More ribs buckled and the boat settled even farther onto its side.

Turning away, the fisherman went to the pile of goods tossed up on the bank and half covered by a patched sail—everything he now owned in this world. He pulled aside the sail and dragged a net out from under a chest. There were wooden floats somewhere. War or no war, people would need to eat.

Shonto sat in his own apartments, writing by the light of two lamps. His brushwork was deliberate, though not slow. The silk and brocade robes of the Imperial Governor were a bother to him, especially now when his armor laced in Shonto blue had been readied. He dipped his brush in ink and wrote:

Shokan-sum:

I pray this reaches you. I will send men down the river and along the coast, hoping they will find a boat to carry them through the straits. With all of Seh running before barbarian armies, it will be a miracle if they find a way.

The barbarians have crossed the border and will arrive at Rhojo-ma within six days. I will retreat down the Grand Canal, hoping to slow the barbarian advance long enough that Akantsu can raise an army. Of course the Emperor will remove me from my command if he can. Look to yourself. I will control the army as long as I am able, but there is no way to know what will occur—the Yamaku will have time to consider their course of action with some care.

Look to yourself. If this war is lost, our lands will mean nothing. Do not waste time or men defending them.

Nishi-sum stays with me and is a great comfort and help. Often she speaks of her concern for you.

I have sent word to the capital and to Yankura. It would be best if Tanaka were with you, but if this is not possible do not be concerned——our merchant is ever resourceful.

May Botahara protect you.

Shonto signed this, folded it carefully, and sealed the letter with his stamp. It was very late, the middle of the night had passed. He rose and walked to the door. The Council of War awaited him.

The Great Hall of the Governor's Palace held perhaps a hundred men in all and though they were men used to the uncertainties of life in the north most of them showed some signs of the deep shock they felt. Shonto had seen the look before in swordsmen——the split second when they realized they had made a mistake from which there was no recovery, and so waited for the inevitable touch of steel.

Shonto watched with great detachment as the gathered lords bowed. For each man present the governor knew there was a number and that number represented how many armed men they could raise. For some of the lords the number would be less than fifty. Komawara's forces consisted of three hundred and fifty men, and he had mortgaged his future to raise that number. The major lords might raise a thousand men, perhaps two thousand for Toshaki and Lord Ranan.

Fifteen thousand men in all was the estimate of Hojo and Komawara. Add to this the thirty-five hundred men that Shonto had brought with him to Seh. To face a barbarian force of almost one hundred thousand.

Shonto nodded to the assembled lords. The lamps flickered around the hall and the scent of burning oil almost covered the odor of riders——so many had arrived barely in time for the council. It was readily apparent that this was not the Imperial Capital where such an assembly would be dressed in clothes of unequaled finery. Many of the lords of Seh wore hunting costume——practical for riding and ease of movement——clothing one never saw anywhere inside the Imperial Palace grounds.

Without prearrangement, the men present arrayed themselves according to their earlier beliefs: Shonto's advisors and allies aligned themselves to the governor's right, apart from the others who sat in rows facing the governor's dais. Shonto looked over at Komawara who knelt stiffly among his allies. It is a moment of vindication, Shonto thought, no one has suffered as Komawara has. Yet Komawara hid anything he felt behind a mask of earnest concern.

Off to the left the governor noticed the Toshaki Lords sitting near the Ranan—hardly a natural alliance—their only bond the fact that they had all recently been utterly wrong. Yes, Shonto thought, there will be few moments in Komawara's life as gratifying as this.

Shonto nodded to Seh's Major Chancellor, Lord Gitoyo, who bowed and gave a signal to someone unseen. Outside the hall an enormous drum boomed, twelve even beats, echoing across the city and the lake long after the drumming had stopped.

Lord Gitoyo bowed again and pulled himself up to his full sitting height so that his voice would reach the back of the hall. "The Council of War of the Province of Seh has been called. The Imperial Governor, Lord Shonto Motoru, has summoned you. Are there any who would dispute the Imperial Governor's right to lead us in time of war?"

Some few shook their heads, but most indicated their answer with silence.

"Until the state of war is declared past, the commands of the Imperial Governor, Lord Shonto Motoru, will be the law of Seh above all but the word of our Emperor."

The gathered lords bowed.

The Chancellor fell silent, waiting. Shonto nodded and the Chancellor again drew himself up. "The reports of the frontier officers have been received and what they have written shall be made known to you, Lord Akima. . . ."

The old man who had for so long tormented Komawara about his "foolish" opinions, unlike the rest of the men present, did not look like he was about to taste steel for his own foolishness—he looked like the blade had slid home as Gitoyo spoke.

Akima gathered himself together to speak, but his voice emerged small and old. "The reports from . . . from our northern border are grave indeed. A barbarian force crossed into Seh west of Kyo before sunset yesterday. This force consists of cavalry, soldiers, bowmen, and train. The combined force . . . the combined force approaches one hundred thousand fighting men." He could not go on then for some seconds, but it was hardly noticed. Some of those who had believed this number to be rumor were as shaken as Akima.

With a visible act of will Akima continued, forcing some strength into his voice. "I am assured by Governor Shonto's staff that this barbarian force will take six days to reach Rhojo-ma—its apparent destination. This force is well armed and horsed, with a supply train large enough to support an extended siege." Akima finished reading and let his hands fall back onto his knees. He met no one's eyes but seemed to stare out to Seh's distant border. "And I would not listen to reason," he said with what sounded like disbelief.

"Lord Akima," the Major Chancellor whispered almost sharply.

Akima seemed to come out of a daze, and he bowed toward the dais. He returned to a kneeling position, but his face could not hold the rigid impassivity of the other lords despite his efforts.

Shonto looked out at the men before him. They did not seem like men of great pride in that moment, but he knew this was deceptive. How many could he convince to follow him down the Grand Canal? That was the question. Proud northerners, none afraid to die. Let their names be sung in the ballad of a great battle, that would be reward enough for them—especially now. Seh was about to fall because they had known too much to listen to others and now they were proved wrong.

Shonto reached over and took his sword off its stand, laying the scabbard across his knees. Seh would have been lost if they had listened to him the first day he had arrived: Shonto knew this to be true. The barbarian army was overwhelming. How to convince them to abandon Seh to save the Empire? That was the true task.

Shonto took a long breath and began. "Lords of Seh, we have often debated the extent of the barbarian threat . . . that debate has come to an end. Those who argued that the barbarians were not a threat believe that their lack of foresight has brought us to this situation, but they are wrong. If we had begun to prepare for this war the day I became your governor, we would still not be able to meet the army that rides toward our capital. One hundred thousand barbarian warriors." He let the number hang in the still air of the Great Hall.

"Without the support of the Emperor and all of Wa, we cannot mount a force large enough to counter the barbarian threat. Rhojo-ma is a strong city, but force of numbers will tell even in a siege. One hundred thousand attackers and only fifteen thousand defenders. Despite the bravery of the men of Seh, it would not be a battle long enough to allow the rest of Wa time to raise an army. And that is what we must do . . . slow the barbarian advance long enough that an army can be raised.

"This Khan who has gathered the uncounted tribes of the desert—he could easily have taken an unprepared Province of Seh in the autumn. But that would have given the Empire a winter to raise an army. Seh is not the prize the Khan desires. With an army of one hundred thousand he seeks the Throne of Wa." Shonto looked out over the hall, trying to gauge the reactions of the northern lords, but he could not read their faces. It was too much for them to take in all at once—too much for them to lose at one time. "Yet I am certain that we can save the Province of Seh." Shonto paused to let his words have their effect. "The Khan must reach the inner provinces before a force can be raised to stop him. If there is no army to fight in Seh, the Khan will not linger here but will push south. He has no choice. To move a force of that size the length of the Empire will take many weeks—and that army must be fed. We can slow his march south, there are ways. There are places that will allow the few to battle the many. If the barbarians can be defeated in Chiba Province or Dentou, Seh will bear the marks of the barbarians' passing less than other parts of Wa."

Yes, Shonto thought, he could see that he was being heard, by some at least. "I will take my forces, and those who will follow me, and set out south. All other craft in Seh will be put to the torch. It is my intention to slow the barbarian march south and to destroy everything that an army could use for sustenance. When the barbarians have gone far into Wa, they will be very hungry indeed."

Shonto glanced over at Hojo who gave an almost imperceptible nod.

"I cannot command that you follow me. The course of honor will not be the same for every man. By sunrise I wish to know your choices." Shonto rose and left the hall as the attending lords bowed.

The Kalam appeared after a quiet tap on the screen leading to Shuyun's rooms. The tribesman dressed in Shonto livery was a sight Shuyun had trouble adjusting to, though not as much trouble as many others. It had been decided that the Kalam should be dressed like this for his own safety—the times dictated it. Emotions ran high among the men of Seh and it was not for them to make a distinction between a member of a hunting tribe and a follower of the Khan.

The tribesman executed a bow that was a credit to his blue livery. Shuyun did not need to be told the reason for the interruption—there was only one thing that could make the Kalam blush: Lady Nishima must be calling.

"Yes?" Shuyun said.

"Lady Nishima," the tribesman said, mangling the "sh" even more than usual.

Since he had first seen Lady Nishima, the Kalam had believed that she was a great princess and he still seemed to think that the distinction "lady" was a foolish technicality.

It was very late for a visit from Lady Nishima, but no doubt few had slept in the hour since the Council of War.

"Please tell them to enter."

A moment later Nishima appeared in the opening and stopped as though unsure of herself. Shuyun knew by the sounds of her footsteps that she came unaccompanied by servants or ladies-in-waiting and he was surprised.

In the light from the lamp Lady Nishima seemed so slight standing in the door. This evening she did not display the imperious air that so impressed Shuyun's barbarian servant. Instead she seemed fragile, vulnerable. Large dark eyes looked out at him and Shuyun was not sure what it was they asked, for certainly there was a question there.

"No one sleeps, Shuyun-sum," she said softly. No apology for the interruption and indeed, Shuyun felt it unnecessary.

He gestured to the cushions, "Please, Lady Nishima, like everyone else I have been sitting wondering. . . ."

Nishima retained her customary grace, despite all, and lowered herself to the cushions as lightly as a dancer. She pulled her robes close at the throat and looked around the room. "You have no charcoal burner?"

Shuyun shrugged. "But I am not cold," he said rising to his feet and disappearing from the room through another screen. Returning almost immediately, he brought a thick quilt and gave it to Lady Nishima. She smiled her thanks and wrapped herself in Shuyun's offering.

They did not speak for some time. More than once Shuyun thought Nishima would break the silence, but something stopped her. It almost seemed that what was occurring in the Empire was too momentous—defying the power of words to describe. Shuyun felt that everyone was in such turmoil that they could not find a place to begin discussing what they thought and felt.

Nishima looked up at Shuyun almost shyly. "What is everyone else doing, I wonder?"

"This," Shuyun said quietly. "Sitting in rooms alone or with others, saying very little."

Nishima nodded, it seemed true somehow. Rearranging the cushions, Nishima curled up and propped herself on one elbow. A hanging lamp went out and began to smoke, but neither seemed to care. Reaching for the remaining lamp, Nishima said, "May I?" Shuyun nodded and she turned the lamp low. She lay down, folding her arm under her head, but her eyes remained open.

"If the Yamaku fall . . ." Nishima began, her voice small, almost childlike. "If they fall, someone must ascend the Throne." But it was not a question, and the lady did not look to Shuyun for an answer. She stared at the flame of the single lamp for a long time, drawing Shuyun's attention there. When Shuyun looked back at his guest, her eyes were closed. Not wishing to wake her, but feeling it was improper to be in the same room while she slept, Shuyun started to rise.

Nishima stirred then, coming half awake. Reaching out, she took his hand in both of hers and settled back, her forehead against his wrist. She slept.

I must leave, Shuyun told himself, but even so he did not move. Nishima's soft hand in his own held him more strongly than any oath and he struggled with feelings he barely recognized.

Eventually Shuyun stretched out on his cushions, resigned to the fact that Nishima would not let go of his hand. He lay so that they were head to head and willed himself to sleep so that he would be rested for his duties in the morning.

A bell sounded the hour of the owl and Shuyun heard Nishima moving. Her hand slipped from his and he felt the air stir and the warmth of the quilt descended on him. Footsteps crossed to the screen but there was no sound of the screen opening. A few seconds passed and then the footsteps returned. Shuyun felt Nishima squirm in under the cover, pressing softly up against his back. Her arm encircled him and she searched until she found his hand, pressing it. Breath like a caress on his neck.

Shuyun could feel Lady Nishima struggling to control her breathing, but this passed. They lay close like this, neither of them sleeping for some time. Nishima finally gave in to sleep, exhausted from worry, no doubt, and Shuyun lay awake, feeling her soft breathing, the warmth of her hand in his and something more that he could not name.

Botahist training told Shuyun that Lady Nishima had reached out to draw him into the Illusion and he felt as though he did not resist as he should, felt himself stepping into a cloud of desire and tenderness and emotion that no Botahist monk should know. The path upon which he should walk was becoming lost in the same cloud.

Rohku Tadamori, formerly Corporal Rohku, now Captain, looked down at the camp of the barbarian army in the first light of day. It was at least five rih off, but from his vantage atop a cliff he had a clear view and it chilled him to the center of his heart. He had been sent to assess the possibility of raiding the barbarian train—a large army on the march was an unwieldy thing and often easily harried.

Rohku handed the reins of his horse to one of his men and bent over the cliff edge to look at the corner they had seen from below. It was almost a chimney, stone shattered into uneven blocks. Sixty feet below there was a ledge with a good sized bush growing on it. From Rohku's vantage it looked possible.

He turned away from the cliff and began to strip off his armor, handing each piece to a Shonto guard. He pulled warmer robes on then and a surcoat and then strapped his sword to his back. When he was done, he nodded to his guards and turned back to the cliff.

Two of Seh's best trackers assisted him over the edge so he would not disturb the sod that clung to the cliff top. Reminding himself of Shuyun and Lord Komawara's feat in Denji Gorge, he began to climb down, stilling his fear of the height. Concentrating on each step. Above him he heard the sound of the trackers hiding the signs of his party.

The Khan's army would pass directly below him here. Only a few hundred feet would separate him from the barbarians. It would be the closest look they would have at this force.

Though much of the rock was loose, he reached his destination without mishap. The ledge was half sheltered from above by overhanging rock which formed a natural cave behind the bushes. He settled himself to wait. It would be at least two days until the entire barbarian force would pass—and then he would be in barbarian lands.

Daylight ceased to be a welcome sight in the province of Seh, for it meant the Khan's army was on the move again, drawing closer to Rhojo-ma. Shonto's senior staff were so aware of this that when the conversation paused they seemed to be listening for the sounds of an army drawing near. The lords of

Seh had made their decisions and Shonto met with his staff to decide what would be done now.

General Hojo held the tally scroll in his hands. "Ten thousand armed men, most on horse. Combined with our own men we will field thirteen thousand, five hundred men in all."

Against one hundred thousand, was left unsaid.

Shonto nodded to Hojo to continue.

"We do not yet know how possible it will be to attack the barbarian train, but it seems unlikely given the size of their force. Lord Toshaki Hirikawa and Lord Ranan have chosen to remain in Seh, though they have commanded their sons to join the governor's forces. The lords who stay are determined to stay in Rhojo-ma, hoping to slow the barbarian advance by several days. If the Khan can be convinced that Rhojo-ma is well manned, he will be forced to waste time preparing a siege and making rafts—an activity barbarian raiders may not be masters of. Death in battle, Sire, it is the penance for their error."

Shonto shook his head. "Huh." He tapped his thumb on his armrest. "It is unfortunate that they put their pride before the safety of the Empire. A glorious death—their glorious deaths—is preferred to a retreat. A rearguard action that does nothing but provide others time to raise an army and perhaps perform the great deeds." Shonto banged his hand on the armrest, but his face displayed no anger. "It cannot be helped. There is little time to mount an assault on the enemy train before it reaches Rhojo-ma. Our own assessment of the barbarian force?"

"Will take two more days, Sire, if all goes as planned," Hojo said.

Shonto turned to Kamu. The old steward knelt as rigidly as a bronze figure, yet Shonto could detect a tremor in the man's frame, a sign of the effort being expended. "Kamu-sum, are preparations for our departure complete?"

The steward bowed stiffly. "Our first boats are on the canal now, Lord Shonto, clearing the way. I have seen to my lord's craft personally."

Shonto nodded. "I will wait until we have our own assessment of the barbarian force. General Hojo, speak with Lord Toshaki and Lord Ranan—if they will sell their lives, be sure they are sold dearly."

Twenty-three

A FAINT RAINBOW APPEARED above the western mountains, forming a high, pure arc across a tumultuous sky—ragged clouds trailed dark ribbons of distant rain.

There was no sign of rain where the newly appointed captain, Rohku, lay—concealed on a ledge high above the broad valley. In fact the sun shone on what seemed to be a pleasant, early spring day. Unfortunately, Rohku's cave looked north and no sun came to warm his hiding place. Although the rock was both hard and cold, he would not chance movement for many hours to come. It was early morning, the second day of his vigil.

The perimeter of the barbarian camp lay not far to his right and stretched back up the valley in the direction of the border. Rohku's initial shock at the size of the Khan's forces had been replaced by a growing sense of despair. *One hundred thousand men.* Since the plague had swept through the north, the entire population of Seh numbered barely more than that. Once Rhojo-ma alone had contained one hundred and forty thousand people, but now it boasted only half that number.

How can they be so many? the guard asked himself again. It was a question without answers: the question that had led the lords of Seh to ignore all warnings about barbarian invasions.

Rohku wasn't sure which was more disturbing—the barbarian army by day or by night. The fires in the barbarian camp had been beyond counting. The fires in their camp! How could they be so many?

Patrols had left the encampment before dawn. Rohku had not been able to see them, but he had heard them pass. The Khan sent out both large and small parties. Perhaps thirty men to a small patrol and more than two hundred to a larger group. It was a conservative strategy; the small groups would travel farther afield but would be able to retreat back to the larger patrols should they encounter Seh's warriors in any number. And Rohku found this, too, unsettling: such a vast army willing to risk so little. It was not the bravado he had been led to expect from barbarian warriors.

The army of the desert had come awake like a dragon, a slow ripple passing from head to distant tail. The head aware and moving before the extremities had even quivered. The dragon was on the hunt, now, snaking slowly across the landscape like a great worm.

The van passed below Rohku, riders on fine horses, well armored in the style of the Empire and carrying swords and short lances. Rohku could see bronze helmet ornaments flashing in the sunlight, but he could not distinguish their shapes.

Banners waved their colors in the breeze, displaying characters and symbols that Rohku did not recognize. Banners bearing the shapes of animals; a running horse, a winged tiger, the blue desert hawk, a coiled viper. Prominent among them were standards of gold silk bearing the shape of a strangely twisted dragon.

Behind these warriors came a vast cavalry mounted on the ponies of the steppe though among these men rode captains or chieftains on horses.

This sight forced Rohku to control his anger: where did the barbarians find horses except among the men of Seh and he knew that the raids could hardly have brought the tribes so many fine animals.

The cavalry were not outfitted with the consistency of the vanguard. They had not the well matched armor and elaborate helmets, but that hardly mattered. Their arms were more than adequate and appeared to have seen use. By the time the Khan's cavalry had passed, the sun was at its zenith.

The faces of the tribesmen were far enough off that they were hard to distinguish, but Rohku could see that this army was made up of men of all ages—from boy-men to seasoned fighters of the age of Lord Shonto and older. None looked frail; life in the wastes saw to that. It was a hard testing ground, and the tribes had their own rites of passage. The weak, no matter what age, found no place at the fireside.

After the passing of the cavalry came bowmen and foot soldiers, marching so close they ceased to appear human, as though a nest of ants had spewed its contents onto the valley floor. A great moving mass bristling with pikes and spears—and even these men were armored and wore helmets.

A sea of banners followed the foot soldiers and behind these rode turbaned men dressed in gray. There were rumors of these men in gray—it was said Lord Komawara and Brother Shuyun had seen them on their journey to the desert and that they guarded the skeleton of an ancient dragon. The Shonto guard caught himself straining forward for a better view and pulled back. The gray men were few in number and passed quickly, followed by what looked like an honor guard wearing armor laced in black with crimson and gold. Rohku could see the backs of these riders now. Imperial Crimson, he realized suddenly— *they wore the colors of the Emperor of Wa.*

A chieftain rode among them, a man upon a great bay horse—a horse that would have been the envy of a lord of Seh. His armor was crafted in the style of the Empire but worn with the high boots favored among the tribes. Even from a distance, Rohku's practiced eye told him that an artist of the armorer's art had created this suit—armor worthy of an Emperor. Rohku shook his head as he watched the man pass, armor laced in Imperial Crimson with trim and sash of gold. This barbarian chieftain wore a helmet crested with high plumes of deep red which bobbed and swayed as he rode. Rohku leaned forward again, a sudden realization shaking him: the Golden Khan rode before him dressed as an Emperor of Wa. Rohku pressed his eyes closed for a second. The men of Seh believe they are about to fight for control of their province, yet Seh is the smallest of this barbarian's concerns, he thought.

Inside the circle of the Khan's guard, Rohku saw other chieftains riding and though none wore the crimson, they were finely outfitted in laced and lacquered armor with surcoats of wolf and tiger skins. These men talked among themselves and laughed as though they were on a hunt or riding for pleasure. Down the length of the great column riders passed and reported occasionally to a chieftain near the Khan.

A pebble bounced on the ledge before the Shonto guard, and he pulled back against the cold stone. He stopped breathing. A trickle of dirt scattered across the moss. Something or someone, was on the cliff above. *Had he just been muttering to himself?*

Voices came down to Rohku now. Despite being raised in the south it was a tongue the guard recognized—he had heard Shuyun speak it to his barbarian servant several times. Horses now and more men. May Botahara protect me. Rohku tried to push himself into the rock, hoping no part of him could be seen. With great care but little expertise the captain had studied his ledge—hiding a footprint in the moss, being sure he snapped none of the bush's branches. He hoped that a barbarian tracker would not be able to see signs of his passing from so high above, but he was not convinced this would be the case.

The reputation of the barbarian trackers was legend among the men Rohku had met in Seh, and this made the young captain slowly unsheathe his dagger. The ledge would be too small for a sword. The Shonto guard's left leg was asleep and he knew that it would not respond if needed quickly. He offered a prayer to Botahara.

Another pebble bounced on the ledge and more talk drifted down to him. If only, he had taken the time to learn some of this language from Kalam!

The sound of hoofs seemed to echo through the stone and then grew fainter. There were no more voices. Rohku lay without daring to move for some time, realizing that he would do exactly this if he wanted to take a man hidden on a ledge: ride away and let the man believe he was safe, taking him when he was unprepared.

Something in the long line of barbarians drew the guard's attention. Within another circle of the Khan's guard Rohku was amazed to see women. They rode like the men of the desert, though Rohku could see hints of fine silk being worn under robes of rougher material. There were perhaps a hundred women, their heads wrapped in bright scarves that covered all but their eyes and foreheads.

And thus they go to war, Rohku thought, how amazing.

Late afternoon came, the clouds scattered across the sky grouped for an assault on the expanse of blue and the day turned gray. Rohku began to shiver. He ate some food and drank water from his skin, but not having room to move was making him very cold. It would be at least another day before he could leave his ledge and he began to wonder if he would be able to manage the climb up.

Following another group of armed riders came the supply train. The barbarians did not seem to have carts or wagons, so everything came on the backs of ponies and mules. Darkness came before the train had passed and the man of Wa spent the first part of the night listening to the sound of the barbarian flutes wafting up from innumerable campfires.

A soft rain fell, but Rohku's prayers for a downpour were not answered.

*   *   *

Shonto sat on the railing of the balcony outside the governor's personal apartments. The day was fine, hinting at warmth to come. Billowing white clouds scattered themselves against the great expanse of spring blue sky. It would be a day to lift the heart—if the heart were not burdened with other matters.

Shonto could see the long line of people being forced to leave the city, so many of them only newly arrived. There were no boats to carry the population of Rhojo-ma and animals of burden were being taken for the war, so the refugees were forced to flee on foot. They crossed the long bridge to the shore and then made their way up a low hill to the crest where the road divided. About half the people chose to go south toward the inner provinces while the rest turned east toward the sea. One could almost see them hesitating at the top—suddenly unsure of their decision.

It is a gamble either way, Shonto thought. His own course was already set—to leave as he'd come, along the Grand Canal. And that was a gamble, too.

Shonto read Lord Toshaki's letter for the second time.

> *Lord Shonto,*
> *Imperial Governor of the Province of Seh:*
>
> *It was your own ancestor who said; "The way a man dies is as important as the way he lives." I honor his memory.*
>
> *Having realized how poorly I have lived, I will take more care with my death. When this is delivered to you I will have returned to the wheel. I have chosen this course to erase my shame and because I am not worthy enough to die beside my comrades fighting the barbarians.*
>
> *You see, Lord Governor, I have conspired with my Emperor to end the life of one Shonto Motoru. No doubt the design is known to you, though perhaps my part is not clear. Send Lord Shonto north with express instructions to end the barbarian raids—an impossibility of course—especially when the barbarians are being paid to raid across the border by the Emperor. You would have failed, Sire, it was inevitable. I would even surmise that the situation could have become worse.*
>
> *You would be removed from your appointment and ordered back to the capital—or so it would be said. In truth I was to remove you from your*

*position by force. The Emperor would claim that you had refused to return
to the capital to face the consequences of your failure. In your desperation
you tried to establish yourself in Seh. The Emperors loyal subject, Lord
Toshaki, however, would not allow this—saving the Empire from civil war.
Among other rewards I would become the Governor of Seh, as would my son
after me.*

*I have betrayed Seh, the people of Wa, and neither of these I intended. I
admit to my part in the plot against the Shonto House: I did not intend to
assist the barbarians in their invasion. Like the rest of the lords of Seh I did
not imagine the barbarians could mount such a force—can still hardly believe it. Even as you struggled to save my province, I worked against you.*

*I give my oath that my son, Yoshihira, knew nothing of this, and so I have
commanded him south with your army so that our House might continue or
that he might find an honorable end. It is my hope that you will allow this.
My countrymen will believe that I have chosen this course to pay for my errors: I would not allow an army to be raised in Seh nor would I listen to
reason. It is my hope that you will let them continue to believe this. In return
I will give you information. The man who devised and guided this plot
against you is in your midst: Jaku Katta planned every detail of your fall,
Lord Shonto. Why he is here now I am not sure—you have heard the same
rumors as I.*

*At the gii board
It is not possible to sacrifice
Honor for position.
I take my place on the battlements.
The plunge as cold as steel
As soft as ashes.*

Lord Toshaki Hirikawa

Shonto looked off at the long straggling line of humanity that wandered
up the side of the hill. So sad.

Was it true that Toshaki's fool of a son was innocent? Perhaps. Certainly
Toshaki Shinga was party to this plot—there could be little doubt of that.
But Toshaki Shinga had chosen to stay in Rhojo-ma—where he commanded
the garrison. That was a life put to better use than his lord's! The fool should
have stayed alive long enough to die slowing the barbarians' advance.

Shonto rose from his position and returned inside. He had shed the official robes of the Governor of Seh that morning and was dressed more comfortably now—ready to travel. Prodding the coals of a charcoal burner to life, the lord went to toss Toshaki's letter in but stopped himself. No, he would save this—it might be of interest one day—historically at least.

The last inhabitants of Rhojo-ma trickled out of the gate and set out across the bridge. Bells rang from many towers throughout the empty city—the gates were about to be shut for the last time. Shonto stood on a quay that would soon be on the lake bottom—such was it designed. Far off he could see men beginning to work on the single bridge that spanned the distance to shore. It, too, would be under water within the hour.

Toward the north end of the quay, Shonto could see Lord Toshaki's son surrounded by his retainers. Word had spread about the old Toshaki's suicide—a plunge off the battlement into the depths of the lake. The lord had worn full armor. It was an odd suicide—one that indicated great shame. Nonetheless, Lord Toshaki had been a man respected in Seh and there was obvious concern for his son among those present, though, as northerners, they were equally concerned with his pride. All expressions of concern were therefore kept within bounds strictly defined by an unwritten code which said: *young Toshaki is a warrior and lord of Seh, therefore he is strong. All expressions of regret will be offered formally—the Toshaki do not require comfort. This is a matter of respect only.*

Shonto's senior staff continued to work nearby, attending to the thousand details that would allow an army of thirteen thousand, plus a few thousand others, to move south at speed. The barbarian army could travel five rih in a day, but the canal would carry Shonto much faster than that.

Men cut away the branches of an ancient lintel vine that clung to the stone around the city's gate. This seemed like a sign of things to come to Shonto, and he looked away.

A delegation appeared at the gate. Guards pushed through, heavily armed and bearing banners. The lords of Seh had arrived—the lords who would remain behind. Most of the older generation had chosen to pay their penance by defending Rhojo-ma—an endeavor whose outcome was as certain as the night following day. Five thousand warriors stayed with these men, chosen for this great honor: to die with their lords in a battle that could not be won.

A crier preceded the fated warriors.

"Make way! Make way! Make way for the lords of Seh. Make way!"

The fools of Seh, Shonto thought, brave fools.

As the senior member of the most important House, Lord Ranan led the delegation. He bowed as he approached Lord Shonto and the lord returned this with a deep bow of respect rather than the nod his position allowed.

"Our preparations go as planned, Lord Shonto," Ranan said with an air of importance. "We will be ready before the Khan's outriders appear."

Fool, Shonto thought, *arrogant fool!*

"You are to be honored, Lord Ranan, as are all who prepare for Rhojo-ma's . . . defense."

Ranan bowed again. "It is our intention to slow the barbarian force by as many days as our strength will allow. May those days be well used, Sire."

Everyone on the quay bowed to those who would remain.

Shonto was about to step back toward his boat when a tunnel opened up in the crowd and the young lord of the Toshaki stepped forward. Bowing quickly to Shonto and Lord Ranan, the young lord turned to Komawara whom Shonto had not seen arrive. Members of Komawara's guard stepped closer to their lord—the Hajiwara men, Shonto realized. Though they wore the Komawara colors, deep blue and black trimmed in gold, the former residents of Itsa retained a length of shoulder trim in Hajiwara green. "Lord Komawara," Toshaki began with great formality, as though he repeated a speech carefully rehearsed, "I once suggested that you would need a proper weapon to fight barbarian hordes." He reached his hand back to a retainer who laid a sword in a scabbard across the lord's palm. Bringing this around, he held it in both hands as though it were a treasure. "This blade belonged to my father, Toshaki Hirikawa. It was made by Toyotomi the Younger and gained great renown in the Ona War. This blade has been in the Toshaki family for seven generations and has proven its worth in many battles against the barbarians. It is my hope that you will accept this as a mark of my respect. Among the lords of Seh you were the first to realize our position though so many of us argued against you." He offered the sword now with a slight bow.

Komawara seemed frozen in place and for a second Shonto thought he would refuse it. But then Komawara bowed and reached out, taking the blade from Toshaki in a gesture almost equally reverent.

When he spoke, Lord Komawara's voice was tight as though he choked back emotion with difficulty. "This is a great honor, Lord Toshaki. I hope that the hands of the Komawara will wield this with even half the skill of your ancestors. If so, it shall be a blade of great fame indeed."

Toshaki bowed again, and at a gesture from Shonto his senior staff began retreating to their appointed boats. We are at war, Shonto thought, there is no time to sit and drink wine and fabricate lies about the great esteem our ancestors felt for each other.

As the boats pushed away, Shonto walked back to the quarterdeck. Sails were raised, luffing and snapping, until the helmsmen fell off the wind and the sails were sheeted home. Shonto saw Nishima wave from a nearby boat as did Lady Okara and Lady Kitsura. A sailor pointed, and Shonto looked up in time to see the Shinta blossom at Rhojo-ma's high tower quiver and then come down. Seconds later it was replaced by the Flying Horse of Seh.

A line of boats tacked into the breeze, heading toward the mouth of the Grand Canal and the first set of locks. Shonto's boat found a place near the end of this line, for in the campaign to come the command would need to be in close contact with the retreating rear. A strange thought.

Lady Nishima leaned against the rail, glad of its support, for she felt a weakness in her will that was disturbing. Despite all of her prayers, war had come. As they cleared the end of the city, she looked off toward the north. Barbarian armies would appear there in only a few days. All of her other concerns seemed petty and trivial now. People would die—and not just from battle.

She thought about the people of Seh setting out south and toward the sea. Not all of them would escape, nor would they understand their danger. They would try to hide themselves, hoping the storm would pass by without harming them. Her father had left a small force behind, hidden somewhere in Seh's hills for this very reason. Its only purpose was to be sure nothing would be grown where the barbarians could find it. They would raid upon and quite possibly be forced to kill their own people. *Leave nothing for the enemy,* her father had ordered. Which meant nothing for the peasants.

A report like strange thunder echoed across the lake and Nishima turned in time to see the first span of the bridge collapse into a cascade of white. For the briefest instant a rainbow appeared in the spray, but then the waters rushed back together like a healing wound. Rhojo-ma's tie to the land was gone.

Around the south end of the city a funeral barge appeared, covered in the white flower of the snow lily. The light breeze picked up the petals, strewing them like a wake on the calm water. Lord Toshaki, Nishima realized. The barge set off with purpose toward the lake's southwestern end as though its destination had never been in doubt. Nishima raised her hands to cover her face but realized what she did and stopped herself. Instead she made a sign to Botahara and offered a silent prayer.

The boat suddenly began pitching in the waves created by the falling bridge. Nishima clutched the rail until the water was calm again and then made her way quickly below. In the privacy of her small cabin Nishima took out her writing implements and prepared ink in what was almost a ritual.

> *Our boat of gumwood and dark locust*
> *Her paint scaling like serpent's skin*
> *Sets forth into the throng of craft*
> *On the Grand Canal.*
> *Uncounted travelers,*
> *Uncounted desires*
> *Borne over blue water.*
> *Only the funeral barge*
> *Covered in white petals*
> *Appears to know its destination.*

Twenty-four

AN ABANDONED STABLE, recently refurbished for the presentation of plays, had been commandeered by Shonto's recruiting officers. The thatch leaked in places when rain and the west wind joined forces and there was still an unrecognizable odor in one corner, but otherwise it suited well.

Two officers sat behind a large, low desk upon what had been the stage. On three sides men knelt in more or less straight rows. In the light from hanging lamps they seemed to be of one type, but upon closer inspection it became apparent that they were of all ages, sizes, accents, experience, and temperament.

Despite this, they had one thing in common. They were warriors without Houses and though some had actually been raised to the way of the sword, many were the sons of merchants or farmers who had broken with their families to take up this life. The men who gathered in the hall had all passed a test of skill with both sword and bow. Those who failed had been sent elsewhere—all men would find a place in the war to come.

Of the hundred or so who had passed the test of arms, most seemed to be without serious criminal records. The senior recruiting officer, a Shonto sergeant, looked at his list and pointed to a name which his assistant called out. A man of perhaps forty years rose and crossed the room to kneel before him. Like most of the men in the hall, his clothes were rough, though, unlike many, his were clean and bore the marks of expert mending. He was a large man, well formed, his face hidden by a dark beard. What wasn't hidden had been darkened by time in the sun and lined with deep creases, especially across the forehead and in the corners of the eyes.

"Shinga Kyoshi?"

The man nodded, a half bow.

"Your weapons are in order?" the sergeant asked.

The man nodded again. "Complete armor and sword. I-I have no bow." A deep voice.

The sergeant nodded. There was a note by this man's name—he was very good with a sword, apparently. "Your sword," the sergeant said holding out his hand.

The kneeling man hesitated for a second, as though not sure of the request, but then drew his blade and handed it to the officer, pommel first.

It was a fine weapon, beautifully balanced and honed to a perfect edge. The sword guard was a small work of art—a lacquered scroll of sea shells over polished bronze. The maker's name on the blade was *Kentoka,* undoubtedly a forgery, but it was a well crafted weapon nonetheless—not what you would expect from a wandering soldier. The sergeant fixed the man with his gaze—a gaze that melted strong young men. "It says here that you are from Nitashi."

The man nodded.

"I'm from Nitashi," the sergeant said. "You don't have the Nitashi way of speaking."

"It has been many years, Sergeant."

The officer continued to stare. He would wager that if he looked in the man's armor chest he would find new lacing in some neutral color.

He returned the man's sword. Stared for a few seconds more, then looked back to his lists. He pushed a scroll across the table and held out a brush. "See the quartermaster," the sergeant said. The man signed his name, bowing low and hurrying off.

Looking at the man's signature, the recruiting officer hid his reaction. That was the third man the sergeant had seen in the last two days who he believed had served the Hajiwara—and this one had been an officer! He shook his head. If there were too many more, he would have to consider turning some away. There were the Butto to consider.

"Ujima Nyatomi!" the officer's assistant called.

Another bearded man hurried up and knelt before the sergeant who leaned over his reports.

"Ujima Nyatomi?"

The soldier nodded. If the sergeant had looked up, he would have noticed that this one was older than the last, and less powerfully built.

"Your weapons are in order?"

The man nodded again.

"Your sword."

The man placed the pommel in the officer's hand. The sergeant looked up from his list, eyes widening. This was a sword indeed! It came into the hand like a dream. The handle was covered in the skin of the giant ray, then wrapped in blue silk cord, and the sword guard, the sergeant suddenly realized, was formed in the shape of a shinta blossom!

The sergeant looked up at the man kneeling before him. Before he could begin to react the man spoke. "My armor is of similar quality, Sergeant, and I have bow, lance, and horse as well." He shook his head almost imperceptibly.

The sergeant returned the man's sword then and searched his lists. Pushing the paper and brush across the table he said, "See the quartermaster."

The man signed, bowed quickly, and hurried off. Another name was called, but the sergeant did not register it. He had just enrolled Rohku Saicha, the Captain of Shonto's guard, into the lists of the army of Seh. He wondered how many others had escaped the capital. He smiled in spite of himself.

The flotilla had entered the Grand Canal and immediately slowed to what seemed like a walk. Kamu knew that progress south would not compare with the speed they achieved passing north—there were too many refugees on the canal and the number of boats used by the retreating army was greater. Still, an army of one hundred thousand could hardly make better than seven or eight rih a day over level ground.

It would take the barbarians over three lunar months to reach the Imperial Capital by land. With fair winds the river craft could often traverse the distance between Seh and the capital in less than thirty days—half that time if they had crew enough to travel both day and night.

At our present speed, Kamu reminded himself, we'll travel twice as far in a day as do the barbarians. Shonto's fleet had left at least two days, probably three, before the barbarians would reach Rhojo-ma. It was a significant lead.

Kamu's cabin was a riot of paper, scrolls stacked in holders like firewood, sheets of paper and letters in carefully laid out piles, none without a paperweight. Folders of paper, rolls of paper, notes written on scraps, rice paper, mulberry paper. There seemed to be no end of this valuable commodity. And every piece of paper bore information Kamu could not lose. He found himself occasionally daydreaming about a small thatch house beside a river in some quiet range of hills.

A knock on the door was followed by Kamu's assistant, Toko, entering bearing a folder that seemed to contain more paper. In the months since the attempted assassination in Shonto's garden this young man had proven to be an invaluable assistant. Oh, he had much to learn, there was no doubt of that, but he learned well and seldom made mistakes twice.

Kamu raised one eyebrow at his assistant in an unwitting imitation of Lord Shonto.

"Requests for passage or to join the flotilla, Steward Kamu," Toko said quietly. He had not lost the ways of those who served. The boy was still almost entirely unobtrusive—silent of movement, and quiet of voice.

Kamu nodded. He pointed with a brush. "There will do."

Toko placed the folder on the appointed pile and then stood quietly. Kamu realized the young man was waiting to be noticed, which almost made the old warrior smile.

"Toko?"

"Steward Kamu," the young man started, his tone revealing a lack of certainty, "several of these requests are from members of the Botahist faith. I was not sure if I should let them wait."

"Huh." Kamu considered the column of numbers in the report he read. "How many, precisely?"

"Two Sisters and five Botahist monks—one claims to have been a teacher of Brother Shuyun."

"Ah, yes—Soto . . ." Kamu trailed off.

"Brother Sotura, I believe, Steward."

Kamu squinted to make out a figure. "Yes, I have met him. Give them quarters somewhere well out of harm's way. This is an army at war—not an Imperial Progress."

Toko nodded. He quickly opened another ledger, made entries, and then was gone.

Kamu shook his head. It isn't an Imperial Progress, the old steward thought, may Botahara protect us.

* * *

Dusk and rain. Young Captain Rohku was stiff with cold and lack of movement. He stopped climbing and tried to control a persistent tremor in his left leg. If one of his men had not thought to bring a rope, he realized, he would never have been able to climb up on his own. Five more feet, then stop. Water ran down the corner he climbed, making the rock as slippery as ice.

He moved again and his feet came off their hold—he fell. For the third time the rope held him. Flailing until he felt the rock under his feet and hands again, Rohku leaned his cheek against the cold stone. Perhaps fifteen feet remain, he told himself. It would be shameful if he had to be pulled up by his men. This thought gave him some strength and propelled him upward.

There were barbarian patrols close by, so silence met Rohku when he clambered over the cliff edge. He sat on a stone and ate a little cold food. Something warm to drink was what he wanted, but a fire could not be risked even if they could find enough dry wood. Finally, nodding to one of his men, Rohku rose stiffly and went to his horse. It took every bit of strength he could find, but he mounted without assistance. There were men of Seh present, it was important that he keep their respect.

A long ride awaited them. First a report to Rhojo-ma, then onto the canal. They would catch up with Lord Shonto's fleet within three days. Rohku had a great deal to tell. A great deal indeed.

Tadamoto found the Emperor walking near the Dragon Pond. A flower viewing had been arranged, for the blossoms of late winter and early spring were pushing up toward a sun that showed signs of warming. Although the Emperor was ostensibly in the company of members of the court, he walked off by himself and none dared interrupt his sullen mood.

Tadamoto looked over the gathered courtiers and noted with some satisfaction that there were a number of young women of great beauty who had recently come to court. May one of them catch his fancy, Tadamoto thought—it was almost a prayer.

But then among the pure young faces and elaborate robes Tadamoto saw Osha. She was watching him with a look of such sadness that he almost wept at the sight. *Osha, Osha. . . .* To Tadamoto's eye there was a great depth of spirit reflected in her face, while the faces of the young women around her seemed almost like masks painted with only a single, vague expression.

Tadamoto's step almost faltered. Tearing his gaze away before anyone should notice, he continued on toward the Emperor. It was a familiar exercise now, closing off his emotions. Tadamoto often thought of himself as some spiritual hermit who had developed this control through meditation. He could make himself feel nothing almost at will. When he knelt before the Emperor, he was as devoid of feelings as a stone.

The Emperor nodded and then beckoned to Tadamoto to rise and walk with him. The colonel hesitated, casting a glance toward the gathered courtiers who pretended not to watch. A lowly colonel being invited to walk with the Son of Heaven—that might raise an eyebrow or two.

They moved slowly away from the others, the Emperor pausing to look at a spray of snow lilies that clung to the shade of a chaku bush. A few more days of sun and they would be gone.

It was a warm day for the time of year. A breeze so gentle it barely rippled the surface of the Dragon Pond felt as sensuous and delightful as a lover's secret touch. A sky, bright as a ringing bell, bore a smattering of clouds like echoes and overtones in the midst of clarity.

"You have something to report, Colonel." The Emperor continued to look at the snow lilies. Let the courtiers wonder what they discussed, there would be no clue from the Emperor.

"I do, Emperor. We have finally managed to get officials into Ika Cho Province. Lord Shonto Shokan has disappeared with a force of significant size, perhaps four thousand men."

"It is a difficult trick to perform—to disappear with so many. We don't know how this was done?"

"It seems that the Shonto son may have taken his force into High Wind Pass, Sire."

The Emperor nodded. "It is early in the year to attempt the pass. Is it possible that he could win through?" The sound of women's laughter pealed across the water.

"It is thought unlikely, Emperor. The snows in the mountains were substantial this winter." Tadamoto almost turned his gaze back to the courtiers but caught himself. "I find it strange that he did not go north to Seh by ship. Certainly the storms would be no greater risk than attempting the mountains."

The Emperor plucked a snow lily and examined it closely. "The High Wind Pass would bring Shokan to northern Chiba, yeh?"

Tadamoto nodded.

"Huh." The Emperor handed the blossom to Tadamoto. "For your honored wife from the Emperor, Tadamoto-sum." The Emperor gave him a distracted smile. "Set men to watch the western end of the pass. If he were not Shonto, I would say a prayer for his soul but. . . ." The Emperor shrugged and walked on, leaving Tadamoto scrambling to bow, clutching his snow lily.

The voices of several hundred women raised in a melodic chant seemed to emanate from the floor and the walls. The Prioress reclined in her litter, eyes closed. It was impossible to tell if she slept or simply lay listening in a state of total concentration, for there was only the merest movement of her breathing. Sister Sutso hesitated to approach her.

From the nave below, the singing soared up into the rafters where a balcony perched like a well hidden nest. The room that opened onto the balcony was one of the Prioress' favorite retreats and her staff preferred not to disturb her there.

Sutso decided it would be better to wait and took a step toward the balcony. The Prioress did not move, but her voice sounded almost inaudibly over the chanting.

"Sutso-sum?"

"Yes, Prioress."

The old woman did not open her eyes or move in any way at all. "I believe our singers become more inspired with each year," she said in a voice that seemed dry and withered.

The Prioress' secretary came and knelt at the side of the litter. "I agree, Prioress. I feel closer to Botahara even now."

"It is the height, child," the Prioress said and a beatific smile spread across her wrinkled face. Sutso did not laugh, she dared not, even though she was quite sure the Prioress intended humor. No, this ancient woman was as close to perfection as anyone Sutso had ever met. In the presence of the Prioress one did not act in any way that could be interpreted as disrespectful.

"You have something weighing on your mind, Sutso-sum." It was not a question.

Sutso nodded though her superior's eyes remained closed. "I wrote to Morima-sum, as you instructed, but I am concerned. There has been no response."

Still, the Prioress could lay so utterly still. "Morima-sum will not fail us, Sutso-sum, do not concern yourself. Much goes on in Seh. Writing a letter may not seem as important to her as it does to us. Wait a little yet."

Sutso nodded again. She bowed and started to rise when the Prioress spoke again.

"You are concerned about the coming war."

Sutso sank back to her knees. "Everyone is concerned, Prioress. It is not like the Interim War where all concerned were followers of the Way. The barbarians will not treat us with respect. Our Sisters will be in danger."

The Prioress' large dark eyes sprang open and she studied her secretary for a moment. The eyes closed again. "If the men who fought the Interim War had truly been followers of Botahara, there would have been no war, Sutso-sum." She fell silent for a second. The chanting suddenly became slow and gentle. "The Empire is vast. This war will be like others—parts of Wa will suffer terribly while other regions will be entirely unaffected. It saddens me. . . . Until the Way is truly followed, there will always be wars. We have made every preparation we can. Let wars be the concern of others. Our concern is the Teachings of Botahara." She smiled again.

"But think, child, the *Teacher*—in our own lifetime! It is a miracle beyond imagining. We can spare no effort, even if the Empire collapses around us. It has been one thousand years, child—forty generations! The Teacher . . . we must find the Teacher. It is the reason for our being."

The collective voice began to grow, it reached up like hands in prayer. It touched Sutso with its beauty and a tear appeared at the corner of one eye. She reached out and touched the sleeve of the Prioress' robe so softly it seemed she caressed a sleeping child.

Twenty-five

Spring's first swallows
Glide down from winter's sky
They soar across rivers,
Finding joy in every turn.

Twilight lingers like a lover
Unable to leave,
Unable to say what is in the heart

From "The Palace Book"
Lady Nikko

THE CHAMBERS OF the Empress Jenna. Jaku Tadamoto sat on the ancient bed of the Empress herself and wondered if Osha would come— it had been so long. Perhaps she had been unable to leave her rooms without being seen or had been intercepted by some agents of the Emperor's. Or, worst of all, she had been summoned by the Son of Heaven. Because this disturbed him the most, Tadamoto's mind filled with images of Osha in the Emperor's embrace.

Did she respond to his touch? The image in his mind showed Osha driven to heights of passion she had never known with Tadamoto. He began to feel like a fool for waiting.

The lantern Tadamoto had used to guide him sat on the floor casting a faint circle of light out into the large room. They had spent their first night together here. It was Tadamoto's hope that returning to this place might allow them to recapture things felt in the past.

Running his long fingers across the sheet covering the bed, he had a clear recollection of touching Osha's breast for the first time, here, on a warm autumn night.

For some weeks now they had been avoiding each other, but seeing Osha among the courtiers by the Dragon Pond that afternoon had affected him in a way that he could not explain. Suddenly he was desperate to see her—would not eat or sleep until he spoke with her.

So he sat wondering if he was making a fool of himself—wondering if Osha was lost in pleasure in the Emperor's arms even as Tadamoto sat pining for her. And yet he could not make himself leave.

An impulse to do something took hold of the young colonel and he went to the screens opening onto the balcony and pulled them aside. He was not concerned with being seen this high up in an unfrequented section of the palace, for even if someone did notice him the reputation of the Hanama chambers being inhabited by ghosts would be all the explanation anyone would require.

Tadamoto stood looking out over the impossibly complex curves and planes of the palace's roofs lit by a waning crescent moon. It seemed so tranquil. It was difficult to imagine that Wa was about to be shaken by war, for Tadamoto was certain that was about to happen. A civil war with the Shonto against the Yamaku or the barbarian war Shonto and Katta warned of: but war either way. Less than a decade since the Yamaku ascendancy and already war seemed to be flickering to life, like a fire that had only disappeared temporarily into the earth.

Pacing the perimeter of the room made Tadamoto realize how little control he felt and he forced himself to sit and be calm.

The screen leading to the room slid aside a few inches and Tadamoto started. Osha! He could not really see her in the dark, but he was so familiar with her size he knew this could be no one else. She slipped in through the crack and pushed the screen closed behind her. Leaning against the wall she stood regarding him. In the darkness Tadamoto could not see her eyes and this unsettled him. He felt he needed to look into her eyes to know what whispered in her heart.

Osha favored him with a nod and then crossed to the open screens, her movements slow and deliberate as though her life force had been reduced to a flicker.

She does not glide, Tadamoto found himself thinking.

Silhouetted against the night Osha seemed very beautiful to him—perfect, in fact. Small and extraordinarily delicate. He could almost feel the warmth and softness of her skin. Beyond Osha the sky was not black but the deepest possible blue. Banners of cloud so distant they seemed to be in the heavens reflected a hint of moonlight. And the stars lacked definition, as though seen as reflections in dark water.

Osha turned and leaned her back against the frame of the opening, her hands clasped behind her. "This room . . ." she began, her voice flat, "it brings me deep sadness to come here."

Tadamoto sat, suddenly awkward, his hands on his thighs. "Yes," he said, "I thought it would be different."

Osha took a deep breath as if she would speak but then let it out slowly. She turned and looked out at the night, not seeming to care that the air was cool. "My heart . . ." she began, "my heart is in ruins, Tado-sum, and I do not know if anything can survive the wreckage." She almost seemed to fall back into her former position.

There was a long silence and then Tadamoto braved the question that tormented him. "Do you love the Emperor, then?"

Osha looked down at her feet, shaking her head slowly. When she raised her face Tadamoto could see her cheeks shining with tears in the starlight. "I do not love him."

Tadamoto nodded; it was a gentle motion, heavy with resignation. He seemed so weighed down with sadness that it stopped him from moving— and so he sat on the bed, slumped as though something inside him had col- lapsed. The sound of Osha crying pained him even more, but he could not rise to go to her. Even when she sank to her knees and buried her face in her hands, he did not move.

twenty-six

The canal runs thick with rumor
Overflowing its banks
Spreading to the four directions.
Intrigues and betrayals
Flood into the countryside
Banishing truth to the rooftops

Lady Okara Haroshu

A YOUNG OFFICER GAVE the orders which were carried out by stone-faced soldiers and dismayed peasants. Everything that had been planted in the early spring was destroyed. Winter's remaining hay was piled in the yard and set to the torch, going up in a blast of heat. The blaze was fed stores of seed and grains and the farmers' carefully nurtured seedlings. The soldiers were determined to leave nothing for the barbarians. And nothing for the villagers and peasants either.

Shimeko could see it written in each peasant's face: *but we will starve. Is it better to be murdered by your own people?* The sight of this had been more than she could bear, so she had set off, avoiding the road used by the fleeing peasants. I am a servant of the family that turns them from their homes, she had said to herself, and it was not a thought that brought her comfort.

Shimeko had been forced to walk some distance up the canal to find a place where she could be alone and not be an unwilling witness to the destruction. Part of the fleet had stopped in this valley to "create the desert" as she had heard one soldier say, and Lady Nishima's boat had been unable to pass.

Under the branches of a willow that hung over the canal, Shimeko set out a grass mat and made herself comfortable. The fine curtain of willow branches was covered with delicate green buds and would be in leaf in mere days. Boats from the flotilla had been moored against the opposite shore, and she could see them busily taking aboard cargo from the surrounding farms. *Leave nothing for the barbarians.*

A family sailed past in a small river boat, the sail filled by a soft breeze from the east—the Plum Blossom Wind it was called, and it was eagerly awaited by the people of Wa. And though it invariably meant warmer days and planting and the blossoming of cherry and plum and apple, this year it was not being celebrated. At least not in the wake of Shonto's army.

Shimeko could see the looks of anxiety on the faces of the man and woman in the river boat. He looked up at the sail and then off to the east. Her years in the monastery told her that he was praying for the wind to hold. All boats had been ordered to pass ahead of the flotilla or be destroyed.

A kingfisher dived into the boat's wake and came out of the water in a flash of iridescent green. It darted off with its prize, disappearing into the branches of a willow.

In the privacy of the bower she tried to meditate, but after several minutes she gave this up. It seemed even that comfort was lost to her. Taking a comb from her sleeve, she ran it through her still very short hair. Lady Nishima had told her that in little more than a year she would be able to put her hair up in such a manner that it would be impossible to tell how long it was. This is foolish vanity, she told herself, but continued to comb as though the action would hurry the course of nature.

Shimeko found herself wondering again about Lady Nishima. It was difficult to dislike her, Shimeko found, though she had been prepared to. And certainly the rest of Lady Nishima's staff adored her. Even so, it seemed odd to Shimeko. Lady Nishima was so young and had not spent the years of discipline and denial senior Sisters had—and yet she was renowned throughout the Empire for her accomplishments.

Shimeko shook her head. Certainly Lady Nishima was a harp player of great skill and her hand was one of the finest she had ever seen. No doubt her social discourse was charming and witty, but they were only social conversations. Shimeko tossed a pebble out into the water. In her former world, Lady Nishima would have been a senior Acolyte, no matter what her accomplishments, and many years away from becoming a senior Sister. Yet in the world of Wa, Nishima was something of a sensation though barely more than a girl.

Shimeko tossed a second pebble after the first, gaining the brief interest of a kingfisher that hovered over the rings where the pebble had disappeared.

This interest that the Lady Nishima showed in Brother Shuyun . . . Shimeko was beginning to wonder if it was entirely proper. The former nun was aware that she had little experience of the world, but even so—the way Lady Nishima brightened when Brother Shuyun appeared, it was difficult to mistake. If Brother Shuyun is the Teacher who was foretold, then this situation with the Shonto daughter was most unseemly.

Shimeko remembered searching the archives for Lady Nishima and this brought to mind the sculpture of the Two Lovers—an image she found most disturbing. Though, if truth were told, it was an image she had had difficulty taking her eyes from when they had waited in Denji Gorge. She had found herself drawn to it more than she would ever admit.

Is Brother Shuyun the Teacher who was spoken of? she asked herself again. If there was only some test she could perform . . . but she knew of no such thing.

The day wore on until she felt it must be time to return. She had been given leave only to stretch her legs, not to disappear for an extended period.

Rising, she rolled the mat and found her way through the curtain of willow wands. A few steps brought her back to the path which ran along the top of the raised bank. Plum trees were planted here and she could see that only a few days would bring them into bloom—an event awaited with great anticipation by everyone in Wa. An image of lines of refugees passing through the plum tree orchards came like a sharp pain.

Some distance off, coming toward her, Shimeko could see a large peasant woman wrapped in cotton robes and shawls. And she had so hoped to avoid the refugees who had been turned from their homes. But then her head snapped up again. It could not be! That walk, Shimeko was sure she could not mistake it.

The woman came closer and raised her covered head. "Sister Morima?" Shimeko said.

The senior nun nodded, her face contorting in a brief, forced smile.

Before she realized what she did Shimeko bowed as Acolyte to senior Sister. But then she rose slowly and forced herself to look the older woman in the eye.

"This is a pleasant surprise, Sister," Shimeko said.

Morima nodded again. She waved her hand to the side of the track and they turned and took a few steps among the plum trees. "Do not be surprised, Tesseko-sum, the Sisterhood releases few entirely."

Realizing that Morima labored as though from great exercise, Shimeko laid her mat on the grass and helped the nun sit. She knelt on the mat facing her, fighting an impulse to take on the posture of humility.

"Thank you," Morima wheezed. "A moment." She sat regaining her breath and then she tried another smile—marginally more successful.

"The Sisters will not release even me, and I have lost the Way almost entirely." She stared at Shimeko who finally had to look away.

"Is the path you follow easier, child?" she said in a voice full of concern.

Shimeko shrugged. "I do not yet know, Sister."

Morima nodded as though she understood. "You appear well enough." A genuine smile this time. "And you will have a proper head of hair very soon."

Shimeko colored at the mention of this. "I must be getting back, Sister Morima, I have duties."

"Do you, indeed?" Morima said. "May I speak briefly, Tesseko-sum?"

The younger woman nodded. "I am Shimeko now, Sister—Shimeko."

Morima tried to smile again but failed. "The Sisterhood has sent me to speak with you. They advised me to come dressed as a peasant and to claim that I had left the Order also. They want information about Lord Shonto's Spiritual Advisor and anything they can learn about the barbarian war and the intrigues within the Empire."

The senior Sister looked up at her former charge and shrugged, apparently embarrassed. "It is the worst foolishness. You might think they would become tired of lies and intrigues, but that does not seem to be so." She reached down and tightened her sandals. "I must be getting back myself, now that I have fulfilled my duty." She rose with some effort and stood looking down at Shimeko.

Shimeko could not hide her look of confusion. "That is all you have to say, Sister?"

"Yes, child." The older woman wiped her forehead with the tail of her shawl.

Shimeko nodded though she was not sure why. They remained as they were for a moment—an echo of their former lives: the younger woman kneeling, the elder standing.

"Morima-sum?" Shimeko said suddenly. "You have met Brother Shuyun. Do you think it is possible that he is the Teacher?"

Morima thought for a moment. "I cannot say, child."

Shimeko pulled up a blade of new grass and twirled it slowly. "Brother Shuyun claims he is not. Is it possible he could be the Teacher and not be aware of it?"

Morima shook her head. "I don't know, Shimeko-sum. When did Lord Botahara know that he would become the Perfect Master? It seems possible that Brother Shuyun may not know."

Shimeko nodded. "I am concerned . . ."

Morima cut her off with a gesture. "Take care in what you say, Shimeko-sum, I do not know what I may yet repeat to my Sisters."

The young woman nodded slowly. She rolled the mat with exaggerated care.

"Go," Morima said, "I will wait a while." She met the former Acolyte's gaze. "And may Botahara walk beside you."

On impulse Shimeko reached out and the two women squeezed hands. Shimeko turned and hurried back to the path.

The river craft that Shimeko traveled on with the ladies from the capital lay where it had been despite her worst fear that it had gone off without her. She nodded to the guards as she came aboard. A maid passed her as she scrambled down the steps to the cabin.

"Lady Nishima has gone ashore, walking with the other ladies, Shimeko-sum."

The young woman sat down on the bottom step, deep in thought. She felt vaguely uncomfortable for having talked to Sister Morima. I should not have done this, she said to herself, I cannot serve two masters nor do I wish to. She thought a while longer, then rose and retraced her steps.

She had noticed Shuyun's barbarian servant on the boat moored just down the bank, a place he would not have been without his master. Approaching the guards of this craft, she gave a password and the appropriate hand signal.

"Is Brother Shuyun aboard?" she asked.

The guard nodded.

"Will you ask if I may speak with him? I am Shimeko, Lady Nishima's secretary."

The more senior guard nodded and his companion hurried off. Shimeko nodded to the tribesman who served Brother Shuyun. He paced the deck, looking off toward the destruction taking place in the fields, then down at his feet as he resumed pacing.

The guard returned in moments. "Shimeko-sum, please," he gestured toward the boat ramp. "Brother Shuyun will be only seconds."

Shimeko went aboard and saw the barbarian crossing toward her. They had met once or twice in the palace in Seh and she had been struck by his devotion to Brother Shuyun. The sight of him dressed in Shonto livery she found quite incongruous.

The Kalam waved at the fields as he approached her. "Bad, yeh? A bad thing." He shook his head vigorously in case she did not understand his use of the language.

Shimeko nodded. "It is a very bad thing. Very sad."

The tribesman nodded agreement, obviously happy that he had been understood.

Shuyun appeared from a hatch behind the barbarian and the Kalam bowed low. Shuyun gave the Botahist bow in return, to both the Kalam and Shimeko.

"We speak," the Kalam said with some pride, nodding toward Shimeko.

Shuyun smiled and said something in another tongue. The Kalam bowed to both Shuyun and Shimeko and returned to his pacing.

"Shimeko-sum, it is a pleasure to see you. How do you fare in your new position?" They walked across the deck and stood by the rail where their voices would not carry to others on deck or on the bank.

"Well, Brother. I thank you again for your efforts on my behalf."

"Lady Nishima has said that you are becoming an invaluable member of her staff. Consider this as a compliment of high order."

Shimeko gave a half bow.

Polite conversation continued for some minutes. Cha was offered and refused. The weather was commented on. The nearness of the plum blossom season was noted and the lengthening of the day came under some scrutiny. Finally it was appropriate to go on to other matters.

"Is there some way that I may serve you, Shimeko-sum?"

Shimeko shook her head slowly and Shuyun nodded, waiting for her to speak.

"Brother Shuyun . . ." she began. "Brother, I was approached today by Sister Morima, the nun I served on my journey to Seh. She came dressed not as a Sister but in lay clothing. Sister Morima freely admitted that she had been sent by the Sisterhood." Shimeko paused, overcome by a sudden need to swallow. "She had been sent to ask me for information or to persuade me to become an informant—it was not clear which. All of this she admitted. Her Order wanted to know anything I could tell about the barbarian invasion, the intrigues of the Empire, and you, Brother." She hesitated. "I thought you should be told of this."

Shuyun nodded. If he found this news disturbing in any way, he did not show it. "Do you know what specific information she was looking for, Shimeko-sum?"

The woman gestured with opened hands. "I did not inquire further, Brother, nor did Morima-sum pursue the matter. It almost seemed that she was performing a duty so that it could be reported done. I do not think it was a true attempt to enlist my assistance."

"Huh. This interest in me I find most strange, and the interest in the Shonto House . . . What did you say to her?"

"She did not try to impose on me, Brother, so I did not need to argue or even refuse. We spoke briefly. When Morima-sum thought, erroneously, that I was about to speak of the matters she mentioned, she cautioned me that my words might be repeated to her Sisters."

"Might be repeated?"

"That is what she said, Brother."

"Most strange." He gazed down into the waters of the canal. "Is there more I should hear?"

She shook her head.

"I thank you for speaking of this, Shimeko-sum. I am not sure what I shall do, but it is possible Steward Kamu may wish to speak with you also."

She gave a tight nod.

"Most strange," Shuyun said again.

Twenty-seven

The Plum Blossom Winds
Spread leaves and flowers among the hills
Laughter and song echo from
The Hill of the North Wind,
Harp and flute from
West Wind Hill.

THE VALLEY BETWEEN the Hills of the North and West Winds became the center of focus for a disturbing meditation by the men of Seh. Barbarian patrols had appeared there the evening before and again that morning. Now everyone watched, waiting without talk for the barbarian army to show itself.

General Toshaki Shinga stood at a narrow opening in the north tower and looked toward the point in the landscape that had become the morbid fascination of everyone in the city. The rhythmic sounds of sword polishers working drifted up to him.

It is too fine a day, the general thought. He leaned out and looked down the wall to the water lapping at its base. It is a strong city, Toshaki told himself, but it was not built to be defended by so few.

Silence had invaded the city more completely than any army could. Toshaki could almost feel men waiting. The gap between the hills drew his attention again.

A small barbarian patrol could be seen among the budding trees at the base of the Hill of the North Wind. They had not moved from that place since first light.

Two boats swung to anchors off the lake's northern shore, waiting for the last scouts returning to Rhojo-ma. Toshaki wondered what choice he would make if he were out on patrol. Would he return to the doomed city or would he strike out, hoping to catch Lord Shonto's fleet? He pushed on the edges of the opening, rocking back and forth on his heels. It was the waiting that was the worst.

The men remaining in Rhojo-ma had received a detailed description of the barbarian army from a Shonto captain. Toshaki shook his head. That had been the strangest intelligence he had ever received for, rather than assist them with their strategy, the report had destroyed all hope. The sheer numbers in the barbarian army reduced their defense of Rhojo-ma to absurdity. The sole purpose of the men in Seh's capital now was to convince the Khan that the army remaining in Rhojo-ma was too large to leave at his back. If the barbarians spent several days mounting an attack across water, Shonto would have a few more days to raise his army. *A few days,* Toshaki thought, we sell our lives for so little! At least it would be an honorable death.

Watches were changed on the city's walls as the men of Seh began to create the appearance of a large force. *The Scarecrow Army,* someone had named it, winning a forced laugh.

Toshaki was making an inspection of defenses when the vanguard of the barbarian army appeared between the hills. Banners as numerous as the blades of grass came down the valley, fluttering in the spring breeze. Slowly but inexorably the riders spread across the plain north of the lake. Only when they had established a perimeter of two rih did the leading edge of the army stop but, behind this, the barbarians continued to spill out onto the plain. Tents began to appear almost immediately and horses were staked out to graze. There was little to indicate that this army feared attack. With the colored banners waving and the tents beginning to appear, the scene almost looked festive.

Barbarians on foot and on horseback came out to the edge of their camp and stood staring at Rhojo-ma, then they would return to their camp to be replaced by others who would then be replaced by others again.

When the sun set, the barbarian army was still arriving. Just as the dusk descended, the first tree was felled and dragged to the shore of the lake.

Twenty-eight

THE DINNER CONVERSATION had faltered badly and each attempt to fan it back to life had ended in silence and embarrassed smiles. The news that the Golden Khan's army was poised to strike Rhojo-ma destroyed everyone's tranquillity and purpose.

Attempting to collect their wandering thoughts in music, Ladies Nishima and Kitsura played the harp and flute for Lady Okara. Though famed for her gracious manners, Lady Okara found it difficult to concentrate on the music of her young companions and it showed in her face. In truth, the players kept losing their focus, resulting in a less than inspired performance. Lady Nishima, especially, seemed to be elsewhere.

A clatter from the deck of the river barge was enough to destroy their focus altogether and the music lost its rhythm and failed. A dull thudding of footsteps passed over their cabin and then back again. Traveling in the dark often led to emergency maneuvers and even these did not always prevent groundings.

"It is nothing, I'm sure," Lady Okara said, and gave them an encouraging smile.

Neither Nishima nor Kitsura showed any indication of continuing and, after a moment's hesitation, set their instruments aside with apologies.

"Even though we have known what was occurring for many months, I still find it difficult to believe that war has begun," Kitsura said.

"Yes," Nishima said quietly. "So many men in Rhojo-ma. It is a foolish waste for the few days we will gain." She rubbed her hand down the frame of her harp. "I'm glad that our Lord Komawara is not among them."

Kitsura nodded and then she smiled. "I've grown quite fond of him. It seems a very long time since we met at the Emperor's celebration."

Lady Okara shifted her pillows and reached for her wine. "He seemed so young then." She shook her head sadly. "It is difficult to believe this Lord Komawara is the same young man. He has become very grim."

The conversation faltered again and finally Kitsura and Nishima bade their good nights and left Lady Okara in her cabin. The barge they traveled on now was markedly different from the one that had carried them north. This one was larger and far more elegant—not a cargo-carrier with a few cabins aft but a boat designed for passengers from Wa's wealthier class.

At the door to Nishima's cabin they hesitated to say goodnight and when neither of them seemed ready to sleep, Kitsura was invited in. Nishima's cabin was lit by a single hanging lamp which cast a warm glow on the rich woods of the walls and beams. Being in the stern the cabin had actual windows rather than ports, though these were all shuttered but one. Spread over the straw mats were two thick wool carpets made by the tribes. Nishima always tried to bear in mind something the Kalam had said about the tribal people—they did not all support the Khan. In her mind her rugs were made by those tribes that hid themselves from this new chieftain.

"Oh, Nishi-sum," Kitsura said to an offer of wine. "I have had enough for one evening."

They sank onto cushions and back into silence. The coolness of the night was just starting to find its way into the cabin, so Nishima called a maid and asked for a charcoal burner.

Kitsura held her hands close to the heat when it came. "It is a sign of spring, Nishi-sum. The heat from this burner is not immediately stolen by the darkness. It may even warm the cabin." She flashed her incomparable smile.

Nishima nodded. Kitsura was not one to remain sad, no matter what the circumstances, and she could never bear to see her cousin anything but cheerful. But Nishima could not pretend happiness; any smile she summoned would be entirely artificial. Kitsura fell silent for a few seconds before she spoke again.

"Do you wonder what part Jaku played in the sudden decision to raise an

Imperial Army? He claims it was the influence of his friends at court, but . . ."

Nishima opened her fan and looked at the pattern of plum trees in blossom. "I think our test told the truth, Kitsu-sum: he is no longer in favor at court. I do not think Jaku would align himself so closely with my father if he were at all concerned with the Emperor and what he might think. No, he is ever the opportunist—when the Emperor decided to raise an army to protect himself from any designs the Shonto might have, General Jaku stepped to the fore and claimed credit. I do not trust him, Kitsu-sum. I do not trust him at all."

Kitsura shrugged. "Still, he is a handsome man. . . ."

"You are impossible," Nishima said, and though her tone was meant to be mock dismay she did not quite carry it off. "Jaku Katta is so embroiled in plots that it is a wonder he knows who to tell what lies to."

Kitsura smiled tightly. "We all plot, cousin. For some reason those of us from older families think we have a right to plot, while those who have only recently risen step beyond social conventions when they do the same." She shrugged.

Nishima did not know what to answer. "I made the mistake of allowing myself to be drawn by his appearance, Kitsu-sum, but I was acting in a very foolish manner."

Kitsura regarded her cousin, who stared at the pattern on the charcoal burner. "You have not developed another interest, have you, cousin?"

Nishima glanced up, then went back to her examination of the burner. "No, of course not. I simply feel that I was foolish in my regard for Jaku Katta."

"Huh." Kitsura produced a brush and began to comb out her long hair. "We will pass the fane of the Lovers again—in a few days if we do not pause. A fascinating thing, don't you think? It would be interesting to know more. I regret that I did not look into the archives while we were in Seh."

Nishima carefully smoothed a crease in her robe. "Yes, it would have been intriguing, I'm sure."

The silence returned. The sounds of water lapping and bubbling past the hull. A tap sounded on the door, making them both start.

"Please, enter," Nishima said.

Shimeko's face appeared as the door opened. She bowed quickly. "Brother Shuyun calls, Lady Nishima."

Nishima was not quite able to hide her pleasure at this news. "Ahh. Please, ask him to join us."

Kitsura nodded to her companion and started to rise. "I must be going, cousin."

"Kitsu-sum, I'm sure Brother Shuyun would welcome your presence."

As she said this, the door swung open and Shuyun stepped past a bowing Shimeko. Kneeling, Shuyun bowed and as he did so Nishima noticed Shimeko perform a sign to Botahara as she pulled the door closed.

Kitsura and Nishima nodded to the monk.

"It is kind of you to visit, Brother. I am having difficulty convincing Kitsura-sum to stay. . . ."

Kitsura favored them both with her most disarming smile. "Please, cousin, Brother Shuyun, I have other matters calling me. I regret missing your company," she said to Shuyun, then nodded again. "If your duties allow you time for gii, Brother, I would be delighted to have your company." She nodded to Nishima. "Cousin." Kitsura slipped out, opening the door herself and giving a final smile as she left.

The sounds of the river craft's progress seemed to fill the cabin.

"I received a message from Lady Okara," Shuyun said quietly. "She was concerned that the news from Seh had affected both you and Lady Kitsura most adversely. I came to inquire of your well-being."

"You are kind, Shuyun-sum, and Lady Okara is most considerate." She gestured to the windows. "It is difficult to remain tranquil when war has returned to Wa. So many men remained in Rhojo-ma. It is a tragedy, certainly. To provide us with a handful of days . . ." She shook her head. "It is like the coming of the plague. You look around you and ask 'who will live and who will die?' I'm certain it haunts everyone equally." She looked up and tried to smile. "Do not be overly concerned, Brother, the shock of it beginning—becoming real, will soon wear off."

Shuyun nodded. "It is a sad truth, Lady Nishima. The shock of war wears off. Perhaps if it did not, fewer wars would be undertaken."

A look of pain flickered across Nishima's face, but she recovered her poise immediately.

"And you Shuyun-sum, how do you fare, now that war is with us?"

Shuyun thought for a moment. "When I traveled in the desert, the monk I met there . . . he said that war brings no soul to perfection. The suffering to come—it is difficult to imagine that it is the karma of so many to suffer this way." He fell silent, looking toward the stern windows.

"I am a follower of Botahara, yet my Order has instructed me to support Lord Shonto in all of his endeavors—for the good of the Brotherhood which preserves the teaching of Botahara. So I go to war also." He looked up and met Nishima's eyes. "It is not the place of a Spiritual Advisor to burden his charges with his own conflicts. I apologize." He bowed low.

Nishima reached out and caught his sleeve as he bowed. "Shuyun-sum, please, do not apologize. Outside of this room I must be Lady Nishima Fanisan Shonto—I have great obligations to my uncle and our House. I confess that I find this role taxes me to my limit at times. If I did not have some place and someone with whom I could speak openly. . . ." She shrugged. "Your role is as difficult, I'm sure. It seems to be true that our lives are fraught with contradictions and I am honored that you would speak of these to me." She gestured with a sweep of her sleeve. "This room feels like a haven in which I do not have to play out my role of Lady of a Great House. In truth, Shuyun-sum, I feel less need for a Spiritual Advisor and more need for a friend."

She took his hand. "What happens in this room is between us and no one else. I would not speak of it even to my liege-lord. Be at your ease, Shuyun-sum. It is my hope that here the Lady and the Advisor may be only Nishi-sum and Shuyun-sum. Nothing else." She tugged at his hand as if she would draw him closer and he seemed to become stiff and awkward.

"It is difficult, Lady Nishima," he said formally, "to forget that I am a Brother."

Nishima stared into his eyes until he looked away. "It is not easy to forget that I am the daughter of two Great Houses. I have been trained to always be thus." She bowed formally, returning to a kneeling position, her posture relaxed but erect. The look on her face spoke of lack of involvement with the world around her—the pose of the sophisticated aristocrat. Then she broke into a smile.

"And you, my friend, are always so." She performed a perfect imitation of a Botahist double bow and then returned to the kneeling position, hands on her thighs, her face an impenetrable mask of serenity. She let out a long controlled breath as though she would enter a meditative state.

So perfect was her imitation that Shuyun was at first shocked and then he broke into a grin.

"There!" Nishima said in triumph. She moved quickly to his side, still facing him. "I have just seen the true Shuyun-sum." She took his hands and his smile was gone as quickly as it had come. "Please, do not disappear again," she said in a small voice.

Shuyun's face almost seemed to flicker like a candle, wavering between the mask of a Botahist Brother and the expressive face of the young man that Nishima had just caught a glimpse of.

"This discomfort you feel in the presence of women, Shuyun-sum, it simply has to be overcome."

He started to protest, but before words formed she reached out and pushed him, almost toppling him over.

"Ahh, a point of resistance! Your teachers would be most disappointed." She slipped into his arms and buried her face in his neck. "This is the comfort I need. The comfort of a friend," she whispered. "And you, Shuyun-sum, must learn comfort in the company of women. I will be your teacher in this."

They stayed thus for a moment and then Nishima spoke again. "Breathe as I do," and they went through a breathing exercise designed to relax the muscles.

"The night we spent together—I could feel your resistance, as I can feel it now." She pushed against him with her body and again there was a second of resistance. Pulling away, she stood quickly and blew out the hanging lamp. She took his hands then in the dark, a hint of light coming in the stern windows. "Promise me you will not leave?"

Shuyun hesitated and she squeezed his hands until he nodded. She disappeared into another part of the cabin and returned almost immediately. In the dim light she rearranged the cushions and spread a thick quilt over them. She turned to Shuyun who sat like a stone.

"Lady Nishima, I . . . ."

She took both his hands again. "There is no Lady Nishima present and all Spiritual Advisors are henceforth banned from my chambers. You, Shuyun-sum, are welcomed."

He followed as she gently pulled until he was in the hastily made bed. She joined him, pulling the quilt over them both. Taking his hands between her own she said, "The object of tonight's lesson is to attain a state of tranquillity in the presence of a woman." She reached out and squeezed the muscle in his shoulder which was a knot of tension. "You must begin by relaxation of the muscles. You do know how to do this?"

He nodded.

"Begin," she instructed and felt him control his breathing, sinking into a meditative state. After a few moments she pushed herself into his arms again. She was wearing only a single robe of the thinnest silk and when Nishima came close to him she felt the tension return. "Do not let my presence destroy your tranquillity, Shuyun-sum," she whispered in his ear. "I intend to let your presence enhance my tranquillity." She took a long deep breath and released it like a shudder. "Your arms are around me, but your hands float in the air. You cannot possibly be relaxed like this . . . That is better."

They lay close in the dark for a long time, neither speaking nor moving. Then Shuyun felt soft lips kiss his neck and Nishima whispered in his ear, her words as soft as a sigh.

"We come soon to the Faceless Lovers."

He nodded.

"Lord Botahara knew women?"

He nodded again, more slowly.

"And yet he attained perfection. . . . Meditate upon that if you will not sleep." She kissed his neck again, then he felt her breathe herself to sleep.

Shuyun lay awake for some time thinking of the image carved into the wall of Denji Gorge and then he, too, forced himself into sleep.

Later Nishima awoke, feeling Shuyun's warmth close to her. They were of a size in height, but the years of training had given his muscles a tone that could not be equaled and yet he did not have the massive physique of the kick boxers she had seen. She turned carefully, trying not to wake him but was unsuccessful. Gently pushing her back into his chest, she felt him stir.

"Shh, sleep," she whispered. She took his hand in the dark and kissed it softly. Holding it for a moment as though making a decision, she guided his hand through her open robe to her breast then held it there firmly. Stifling a small moan, she began a breathing exercise. That is enough for this lesson, she thought, I will certainly frighten him away. Thinking this she pressed his hand tighter. The burbling of the boat passing through calm water was like the music of delight itself, joyous, irrepressible.

When the watch changed, Nishima awoke again, warm, languid. Shuyun's hand still caressed her breast and she felt her entire body flash with heat, her breathing became urgent. She started to control this but then felt Shuyun wake in response to her own state. His hand moved on her breast and she turned toward him, shrugging her arm out of the sleeve of her robe.

Pushing as close to him as was humanly possible, she began kissing his neck, then his cheeks and the corners of his eyes. He reacted by pulling her closer, so close that she could not move.

"Nishi-sum . . . I cannot. . . ." He started to pull away, but she would not release him.

"No, Shuyun-sum, please . . . stay a while. I will feel I have acted terribly if you go. I will never forgive myself."

He stopped trying to pull away and they lay rocking each other gently until both found their breath again. Nishima made no attempt to replace her robe but lay in the circle of Shuyun's warmth.

He ran his fingers slowly up her spine and she found herself focusing on this touch as if nothing else in the world mattered. Heat seemed to radiate from his hand. Slowly his fingers went down her back and she willed him not to stop. Pushing his palm flat against the base of her spine, she felt the chi flow, like a glowing warmth, like a tiny branch of lightning.

And then the chi flowed out from his hand and Nishima felt it touch the center of her desire. She could not catch her breath. She smothered a moan, fighting not to let him know what she was feeling. As though it had a will of its own, she felt her body push closer to Shuyun's. The lightning branched from his hand.

Burying her face in Shuyun's chest Nishima moaned uncontrollably. She began to convulse, his hand almost unbearably hot on her back. Shuddering for what seemed like moments on end Nishima finally lay, unmoving, in Shuyun's arms.

Botahara save me, she thought, did he feel nothing? Could I have felt the skies open while he felt nothing?

Before the darkness disappeared, Shuyun slipped out onto the deck, finding himself a place to sit among the cargo. He had left Nishima sleeping, using his Botahist training to move silently. And now the cold air and infinite night were an almost painful contrast to the warmth of Nishima's cabin, the warmth of her presence.

Shuyun began a silent prayer for forgiveness but lost the thread of it almost immediately. What is to become of me? he wondered. For what I have done I should be stripped of my sash and pendant and turned out of my Order. He brought a lifetime of training to bear on the chaos he felt within, but the turmoil resisted the attempt to impose order.

Shuyun sat as though in meditation, but in fact his mind was filled with an image of the Lovers in Denji Gorge—features beginning to appear on the two faces. This was mixed with a strong memory of Nishima in his arms, lost in a pleasure so overwhelming that it was like a moment of great discovery.

Twenty-nine

IN THE MIDST of the vast sprawl of the barbarian encampment a single plum tree had blossomed, appearing like a lone act of defiance, a statement poetic in its purity. The cloud of white blossoms floated just above the tents and teaming thousands as though the land itself had unfurled its standard.

It was early morning on the second day of the siege of Rhojo-ma, though not an arrow had been loosed nor a sword drawn other than to test its edge. A fast boat sailed along the lake's northern shore out of range of barbarian bows. Toshaki Shinga wished he were in that boat himself. He desperately wanted to look into the faces of his enemy, see them for what they were, though he could not explain this impulse.

The barbarian rafts lined the shore and the men of Seh waited. The wind was not terribly strong, but it would gather its reserves intermittently and send a great gust down the lake and this might be what was stopping the expected attack. *They wait for the Plum Blossom Winds,* was the phrase Toshaki heard again and again; it was said with a note of scorn.

The men who sailed along the shore had reported that there were pirates in number among the barbarian warriors. It was an indication that the barbarians were capable of better preparation than the men of Seh had wanted to believe—the second time the barbarians had been underestimated. Toshaki wondered about this Khan—where did he come from and how had he gathered so many?

A young man recently given an officer's rank appeared at the top of the stairs to the tower from which Toshaki observed the plain. He bowed quickly.

"Lord Ranan reports that the fleet is in readiness, Sire."

Toshaki nodded. "We must be patient. The barbarians gather their nerve slowly." Looking back out at the enemy's army, Toshaki said, "The signals are understood."

"They are, General."

"Good." He nodded a dismissal, and the officer returned the way he had come.

Horsemen came and went from the barbarian camp, usually in patrols of some size. No doubt they had realized by now that the army of Seh had retreated south. And how many do they think remain in Rhojo-ma? Toshaki asked himself. The men in the city had been entirely true to their Scarecrow Army ruse and perhaps that explained some of the hesitation the barbarians were showing.

A boat set out from the shore toward the city. Toshaki had to look twice: a boat! They had found a boat that Shonto's men had missed. A flag of truce flew from a staff at the bow and, as it approached, the general could see that it was manned by experienced oarsmen. Pirates were among the barbarians, indeed. Toshaki could see their brightly colored turbans. The enemies of Wa had formed an alliance of the unholy—not a follower of the Perfect Master among them.

The city's own boat changed its course to stand within arrow's shot of the pirate's craft, holding that position until they approached the walls.

Toshaki turned and yelled for an aid. A young soldier appeared immediately at the stairhead.

"Go to the signalmen," the general snapped, "have them signal our patrol boat. If this strange craft attempts to round the city, they must take it at all costs."

By the gods, Toshaki thought, we can't have them seeing everything we prepare.

But the boat made no attempt to round Rhojo-ma, continuing toward the tower Toshaki had made his command position. Realizing what they did, the lord made his way down the flights of stairs to the top of the wall.

As the boat pulled closer, Toshaki could see a single man sitting in the bow not handling an oar. The lord squinted.

"That man in the bow," Toshaki said to a young bowman standing at hand, "can you see him?"

The bowman focused for a second. "I can, Sire."

"Is he a barbarian?"

The younger man shook his head. "He is not, Sire, nor is he a pirate. He is dressed as a man of Seh might dress."

Toshaki took hold of the stone wall, leaning out over the water. A gust of wind pushed the bow of the boat off, and the steersman fought to put them back on course. Five strokes closer, then ten. A muttering began down the wall and progressed from man to man. Toshaki turned to his aid.

"Some say this is Lord Kintari, General."

Toshaki turned back to the scene before him. By Botahara, it could be. The general thought Shonto had done away with the Kintari clan.

Lord Ranan appeared at his elbow followed by several other senior lords. "Lord Kintari," Ranan said, "reincarnated as himself. May Botahara be praised." Even Toshaki smiled at this.

"Reincarnated as a traitor, I think, Sire," said another and there was a quiet nodding of heads.

The boat came close enough for shouted speech. The steersman turned its head to wind and the oarsmen held that position. The man in the bow stood, and if there were any still unsure of his identity the doubt was buried now.

"Lords of Seh, I come with a message from the Great Khan of the tribes." Kintari paused as if time were needed for his words to be fully understood. His voice sounded small against the noise of the wind and the waves lapping the stone wall. Kintari was so close that Toshaki could see the man's robe ripple in the breeze, could make out a strand of hair in a streak across Kintari's forehead.

"He is without sword," Ranan said quietly and Toshaki nodded.

"Your numbers are known to the Great Khan, my lords. You cannot hope to stand against the force of the tribes. What will you gain by this futile defense? Did your Yamaku Emperor send an army to protect Seh? You give up your lives for an Empire that will not even notice you have done so." He paused again.

"The Yamaku care only for their own ascendancy. They are not Emperors of Wa—they do not govern, they divide the Empire against itself and rob from all. You will give up your lives for blood-suckers?" His voice rose on the last word, and it echoed from the buildings.

"I know you, lords of Seh. You are brave men—all of you—but your sense of duty is misplaced. The Khan has come to bring down the Yamaku, not to destroy Wa. The Khan is a man of greatness, lords—greatness the like of which we have not seen since Emperor Jirri rode upon this very plain.

"You are invited to feast with the Khan, lords. You may know for yourselves. The Yamaku have bled Seh for ten years. The Khan will bring us peace and wealth as we have never known. Those who ride with him will be great men in the Empire to be. Consider this army." He pointed to the encampment. "Among one hundred thousand only the Khan and a handful of others are men of culture. When the Yamaku are brought down, the Khan will need men of skill and knowledge to govern the new Empire. If you are those men, how can it not be an Empire of justice and culture?

"A feast, lords, not a trap—for you have already trapped yourselves. What word shall I take back to the Great Khan?"

There was a second's hesitation as men looked from one to another, questions in their eyes.

"Bowman," Toshaki Shinga said quietly.

"Sire?"

"Silence that traitor."

An arrow flashed, appearing in Kintari's heart as though it had sprung from there. The lord did not move to clutch his pain but slowly toppled over the side like a falling tree. The pirates set to their oars in a frenzy, pulling to get beyond bow range, but no arrows fell among them.

Lord Kintari was left bobbing, facedown, in the small waves that broke the surface of the lake. The pirates' craft, under its flag of truce, raced to the far shore where the oarsmen ran it up on the bank as though arrows were aimed at their hearts.

Toshaki looked down at the floating lord. There was silence on the wall.

"It was a better death than he deserved," Lord Ranan said so that all might hear, "but it was the best that could be managed." He bowed to Toshaki and nodded to the bowman, then turned and started back to his duties.

A shout echoed across the lake, as powerful as distant thunder, and Toshaki looked up to see rafts being pushed out onto the waters.

"Give the signals," Toshaki said calmly to his aide. "It begins."

Along the wall he saw men make signs to Botahara and then, in a warrior's ritual, they tightened their helmet cords.

Toshaki loosened his sword in its scabbard and mounted the stairs to his tower, pulling his helmet tight as he did so. There would soon be little he could do, but he would try to give some direction to the defense while it was still possible.

There must not have been enough pirates to man all the rafts, for many were paddled by barbarians under the tutelage of screaming, gesturing pirates. On at least one raft Toshaki saw a fight underway, swords flashing.

Fools, the lord thought, come a little further.

The vast flotilla moved slowly toward Rhojo-ma, the cumbersome rafts colliding and hampering each other. Against all efforts the crosswind blew them off to the west and soon they were strung out, paddling into the wind and trying to make their way crabwise toward the walls.

Toshaki almost laughed. In an attempt to send the greatest number of men against the city, the barbarian chieftains had built too many rafts and now they became their own enemy. At least one raft had broken up, leaving terrified tribesmen clinging to the logs, armor trying to drag them under.

Boats appeared beyond the east wall of the city, towing makeshift rafts piled with shattered furniture and straw floor mats. The men of Seh were not strangers to the water and their operation was executed with a precision that would have made a naval officer proud. Positioning their craft quickly upwind of the enemy, the men of Seh fired the rafts and cut them free.

Toshaki hit the stone with his fist. The barbarians on the windward rafts saw what bore down on them and stopped paddling, which sent their craft into the rafts behind.

A gust of wind fanned the fires into hot blazes and pressed the fire rafts down on their victims. The barbarian flotilla lost all way then as men on the windward craft jumped to the rafts behind. The fire touched the first barbarian raft and flaming straw started to blow free.

Toshaki saw men in flaming clothes and men falling into the waters to slip beneath the surface with barely a struggle. The fleet blew east now, all chance of making the walls of Rhojo-ma gone.

Someone pounded up the steps behind him and an out of breath Lord Ranan appeared at his side.

"Ah, Admiral Ranan. Your squadron has done well."

"Who thought it would become a naval battle, General?" Ranan said with obvious satisfaction. "And the men of the desert make poor sailors." A bitter laugh forced its way out from behind his face-mask.

The remains of the barbarian flotilla ended up on the west shore of the lake. Most of the logs were new cut and too full of spring sap to burn, so the fire rafts did less damage than one might have hoped.

"We have given Lord Shonto the gift of another day at least," Lord Ranan said. "May his army swell by a thousand men."

Toshaki turned to his aide. "Order our patrol out again. I want to know everything the barbarians do."

Ranan leaned his back to the wall and opened his face-mask. "I wonder what they will do? Is it possible they might dare this again?"

Toshaki shrugged. "We will soon have the measure of this Great Khan. If he cannot take an almost undefended city in a few days, he will be no match for Shonto Motoru. The great lord is a gii player of some fame. He will never let this upstart catch him where mere force of numbers can win the day."

He turned back to the north. In the midst of the barbarian army the plum tree swayed and released a flurry of petals to the wind.

Thirty

THE FLOTILLA CARRYING Lord Shonto's army south sailed by night, trailing a wake of terrible destruction. Word had spread quickly down the canal and the people of Wa fled before Shonto's fleet as though it were the barbarian army itself. In places the canal choked with the boats of refugees and when this slowed the progress of the flotilla, soldiers were sent ahead to clear the way. Everyone in the flotilla had seen the results of this earlier in the evening. They had passed the still smoldering hulks of half a hundred craft, stranded on the canal banks.

I feel as though we follow on the heels of war, not precede it, Brother Sotura thought. He stood at the aft rail watching the following-wave pull a ribbon of moonlight along their wake. Just at dusk he had heard the sound of a flight of cranes passing over and it had saddened him in a way he could not control.

It was a night of great beauty. The Plum Blossom Wind pushed the river craft along the waterway like a gentle, guiding hand, and the scent of budding trees and opening flowers perfumed the air. In so steady a wind and a section of canal free of hidden bars, the sailors on watch had little to do. A charcoal fire smoldered amidships and the sailors cooked and brewed cha and lounged about the deck talking quietly, awaiting their turn as lookout or at the steering oar.

A sailor approached Sotura, offering the senior Brother a bowl of cha which he accepted with a nod. He sipped cha and watched the night landscape slip by. The constellation of the Two-Headed Dragon appeared above the calypta trees lining the bank, and the breeze murmured in the branches. It was night rich in beauty.

Steps approached, not the barefoot slap of a sailor, but a studied gait. Sotura turned and saw a woman walking toward him. She seemed at first bent and tired, but the Botahist Master could see that this was not a statement of truth: she was neither. The moonlight outlined the familiar shape of a square jaw.

"Sister Morima," Sotura said quietly. He bowed. "I am honored to find myself traveling in your company."

She was dressed in the yellow robe and purple sash of her Order though over that she wore shapeless robes of gray and brown, her head wrapped in a shawl. She nodded in return and leaned against the rail as though she had just expended great effort.

Sotura thought she was thinner than when he had last seen her—at Jinjoh Monastery where she had come for the opening of the scrolls. To an untrained eye, her clothing would have hidden this change.

"You keep close watch on your protégé, Brother Sotura, one would think his judgment was in question."

It was an insulting statement and doubly so, for the nun had shown the worst manners, refusing to respond to his polite greeting.

"Shuyun-sum seems to be watched by many, Sister, which is the true question."

"Huh," Sister Morima blew the syllable out like a sharp exhalation. "True questions," she mused. "Tell me, Brother, do you not have true questions now that the Teacher has arrived and is not among your senior Brethren?"

Sotura turned and looked back at the boat's wake. "You listen to rumors, Sister. I am surprised."

"The blossoms were seen, Brother," Morima hissed in a low whisper, "touched by my own Sisters. Touched! Do not play the fool with me, Senior Brother Sotura."

He shrugged. "Believe as you will, Sister."

"That is the conclusion I'm coming to, Brother." She fell silent then, and only the wash of boat slipping through water was heard.

Sotura looked over at the steersman, but the man was too far off to hear and too well mannered to notice.

"Do you wonder, Brother, who Shuyun-sum was in his past incarnation?

A child of such accomplishment was not a merchant or a lord. It is not possible."

Sotura shrugged. "As you are aware, we cannot always know."

"With the unaccomplished, perhaps," Morima answered but carried the thought no further. She turned also, leaning over the rail and joining her hands. "It must be difficult for you, Sotura-sum; the blossoming of the Udumbara, Sacred Scrolls that are missing or worse, the coming of the Teacher you cannot find, and a young protégé with an ear for the truth." She paused looking down into the dark water. "Lies cannot come easily, even to the seniors of your Order. What will you say when Shuyun-sum asks of these things?"

Sotura stood away from the rail so that he looked down at the woman. "It is rumored, Sister," he said icily, "that you have had a crisis of faith. I will pray to Botahara to guide you." A stiff bow and he was gone, leaving Morima at the rail.

The monk made his way to the bow where he sat in the lee of the gunnel. It was as far forward as he could go and yet he still felt the lies that pursued him close behind.

Thirty-one

THE ENTIRE LINE had come to a halt for perhaps the hundredth time that day. Lord Shonto Shokan looked down the draw at the horsemen strung out behind him. Like their lord, they had long since dismounted to lead their horses. Shokan stepped to the right for a better view and plunged through the softening crust up to mid-thigh. He cursed.

They were completely surrounded by mountains now, above the snow line and into an area that, each afternoon, became truly frightening. The guides had signaled a stop and gone ahead to assess the danger. They had lost thirty men to avalanches already and Shokan wanted to lose no more. Of course, this was quickly becoming a moot point. Could they go ahead at all? That was the question they asked now.

Willing himself lighter, Shokan tried to pull his leg free and step back onto the crust. His other leg broke through and he sat down, sinking to his waist. He cursed again and then laughed.

The night before they had debated leaving the horses, hoping men could win through where horses couldn't. With care, men could travel in the mornings when the surface of the snow was still frozen from the bitter cold of the mountain nights.

A boy ran lightly up the line of men, earning Shokan's envy. When we have no more food, perhaps we will all run as lightly as this one, Shokan thought. The child dropped to his knees on the crust before his lord and bowed. Shokan nodded for him to speak.

"Sire, Lord Jima's men have reached the end of our line, but the snows caught seven and swept them into the gorge."

Shokan made a sign to Botahara. "Can they go on?"

The boy hesitated. "Lord Jima says they are prepared to proceed, Sire."

Shokan nodded. This might be as far as they went this day though it was barely midday. With some effort he stood and looked up the draw. There were perhaps twenty men above him and then the track of the guides disappearing over the curve of the endless snows. Movement caught his eye and he turned quickly. Yes! he was certain this time.

"I saw it, also, Sire," the boy said, his tone tentative. He had just spoken to the great lord without being requested to do so.

Shokan did not seem to notice. He pointed up at a ridge line above them to the south. "There?"

"Yes, Lord Shonto."

"Huh." They had started appearing on and off two days before. It was considered good luck to see one of the Mountain People, so men had begun keeping a lookout. Down the line he saw others pointing.

Turning back, he looked up the slope. Certainly it is not possible, he thought, we will have to leave armor and all the horses behind. He looked at his stallion, the horse he had brought from Seh, and shook his head sadly. They would butcher the horses for all the meat they could carry; there was no other choice. He smiled at the child.

"Tell Lord Jima that I await word from the guides. We will not move until then."

The boy bowed low, rose, and jogged off. Thirty paces away, he plunged through the snows up to his chest and had to be rescued by a wallowing rider.

Thirty-two

The ruin of a treed hillside
Wounds the heart.
Plum Blossom Winds
Whisper across still water.
Spring's gentle arrival
Lifts the eternal spirit

Lord Akima

LORD RANAN AND Lord Akima stood at the wall on the city's eastern extremity and watched the building of a floating bridge. The barbarian army had spent a day skidding logs from the western end of the lake, where they had been blown after the first failed attack. The arrival of the Plum Blossom Winds had precipitated this tactic, and the men of Rhojo-ma looked on with something approaching approval: it is what they would have done in the barbarians' place. With the breeze at the barbarian army's back, it would be impossible for the men of Seh to position fire rafts upwind.

The floating bridge grew by the hour, reaching out toward the walls of Rhojo-ma. The last sections of the bridge were being readied near shore. When done, these final sections would be easily floated into place, connecting the shore to the wall of Rhojo-ma with a causeway wide enough to allow fifty men abreast. It was only a question of when this would be done.

"There are too many sections, look." Lord Akima pointed to the north and south of the floating bridge where work was going on at an astonishing pace.

Lord Ranan watched the activity briefly and then nodded. Teams of horses kept arriving with planks torn, no doubt, from nearby barns and houses. These were being used to tie the bridge together and provide a relatively even footing for the attackers. "They must plan to make the bridge wider at this end. I would do the same." It was the ultimate approval of anything the barbarians did: *I would do the same.*

Akima looked over his shoulder at the position of the sun. "They might finish while there is still light."

"But they will not attack until dawn—when we will have the sun in our eyes. That would be my choice."

Akima nodded.

Most of the men who remained in Rhojo-ma were concentrated on the defense of the city's eastern end now, drawing them away from the more easily defended Governor's Palace and inner city. Lines of retreat to the western end had been prepared through the city—bridges destroyed, streets blocked. Only a man who knew the route could move quickly from east to west and that route was the most easily defended. Even so, the men of Seh were preparing to hold the city's eastern end for as long as possible.

Lord Ranan bowed suddenly. "Please excuse me, Lord Akima, I have matters that must be attended to."

Akima bowed and watched the man go. "How the great have fallen," Akima said to himself. Ten years earlier the Ranan had been the virtual rulers of Seh—Imperial Governors generation after generation. And now here was the senior lord of that House—a general at the fall of Seh's capital.

How we pay for our mistakes, the old man thought and turned back to the eastern shore for a final look before attending to his own duties.

The sound of the barbarian flute-pipes echoed across the water in the night. It was a melancholy air played in the strange scale of the desert tribes and it did nothing to raise the spirits of the men in the city. A night attack was unlikely but not impossible, so large numbers of men stood watch and others stayed in the recently abandoned buildings nearby.

Boats had been sent out from the city to patrol the lake to be sure the barbarians did not move their bridge in the dark. An attack at first light on some other quarter of the city would be a disaster. The men of Seh were too few to be spread around Rhojo-ma.

Other boats were readied after the moon set, but they had their own purpose. Men, armed and armored, went aboard these boats in number. In complete silence they pushed off, setting course by stars and the barbarian fires on the shore. The light evening breeze bore them along, barely rippling the sails as they tacked. It was a difficult exercise, for the boats could risk no lamps, so there was a very real danger of being separated or colliding.

Fires set in sand burned at intervals along the floating bridge, and they illuminated the span from one end to the other.

A torch on the wall of the city was extinguished, and the boats turned toward the agreed upon fire on the bridge. There was not enough wind to give them speed, so the helmsmen aimed the boats directly at the floating span and ran their bows up on it, snapping anchor lines in the process.

A shout went up immediately from the barbarian guards, and the sound of swords shattered the peaceful evening and stilled the playing of flutes. Torches came to life among the attackers in an attempt to fire the bridge planking.

Lord Ranan reached the top of the wall and found Akima and Toshaki there ahead of him.

"It does not burn," Ranan said.

The noise was fierce now and men appeared at all the stairways, believing the siege had begun. In the light of the fires, barbarians could be seen pouring out along the floating causeway. Torches were kicked into the water though here and there the planking burned feebly.

Out beyond the point where the attack had been aimed, a watch fire burst apart and men could be seen spreading the burning wood across the float. Suddenly there was a tearing sound and the outer watch fires began to drift toward the walls of Rhojo-ma.

"They have broken it!" Akima said. "Look!"

A cheer went up from the walls of the city, but the sound of swords continued. Bowmen strung their weapons then, ready for a section of the bridge to come covered in barbarians and hard-pressed warriors of Seh. So slowly did the section of bridge move that men's arms began to grow tired holding arrows at the ready.

The sound of clashing swords stopped abruptly and the shouting of the barbarians fell silent also. On the section of bridge that had been broken free, flames began to spread as the dry planking caught. It drifted on like that toward the wall of the city, a long torch illuminating the area for more than a rih. Barbarians standing on the end of the now truncated bridge could be seen clearly in the orange light. A small boat under sail passed by the burning raft—a patrol boat, no doubt looking for survivors.

The men of Seh watched as the burning hulk began to break up as it drifted near the city. Signs were made to Botahara. The first defenders had died, and the attack slowed by half a day.

Morning came, a clear spring day. Another tree had blossomed on the hillside north of Rhojo-ma. General Toshaki stood at the wall, looking at the scene. He tried not to think of the funeral barge that had born his lord across the lake only a few days earlier, for it had been white with blossoms also.

The sound of the barbarian army preparing their siege echoed across the lake, ruining the perfect stillness. It would be only a few hours now. Toshaki loosed his sword in its scabbard for the hundredth time. The men on the wall around him were silent. There was no need to discuss plans and strategy—their intent was not that complicated.

Captain Rohku stood on a hill south of Seh, hidden by brush and trees that had not been taken by the barbarians for their great floating bridge. He wondered how he had been chosen for the function he now performed. Perhaps being the first to report the arrival of Jaku Katta had started it. Rohku knew that events of even less significance had set men off on a life's endeavor. Whatever it was, the young captain had become the watcher—the witness.

It had been Rohku who had hidden on the ledge and watched the army of the desert pass. Having reported all he had learned from that to Rhojo-ma and sent reports on to Lord Shonto, he had been given sealed orders. And now he and a few of his company were to be witnesses to the fall of Seh's capital. No doubt what he saw would tell Shonto and his staff much about the barbarian army and its leaders, but Rohku did not relish the duty. As foolish as he thought the lords of Seh were, he did not want to watch them die.

Much had happened in the dark the previous night though it had been difficult to know what. The men of Seh had obviously staged an attack on the bridge and cut a section of it free, setting it to the torch. Rohku had watched the flaming raft as it spun slowly, breaking up before it reached the wall of the city. It was impossible to tell what had happened to the men of Seh. They had seen only barbarian warriors in the light from the burning bridge section which had led to much speculation. His companions had finally agreed that most or all of the men from Rhojo-ma had escaped in boats, but Rohku was sure they didn't really believe this. The attackers from the city, the captain thought, lay on the bottom of the spring cold lake, weighted there by their armor for all time—may Botahara protect their souls.

The last section of the span that would connect the barbarian army with the walls of the island city had been warped out to the bridge's far end where preparations were being made to move it into its final position. The Shonto guard looked around to make sure his men watched the woods behind and not the drama that unfolded on the lake.

A guard appeared at Rohku's side just as he turned back to his duty.

"Another barbarian patrol passes to the west. They should appear below us." He waved off to their left.

Rohku nodded. Barbarians were exploring the surrounding countryside with great determination and this resolve was showing occasional results. More than one patrol returned with some hapless resident of Wa in their midst. Not everyone had left quickly enough. By now the Khan would know where Shonto's army had gone.

The barbarian patrol appeared as had been predicted—this one without captives. Watching them ride past, Rohku had to admit that they were fine horsemen. If they handled the sword and bow as well, they could make a formidable army.

"Captain," one of Rohku's men pointed.

The final section of bridge was beginning to move. Using ropes and poles, the pirates and barbarians began maneuvering the makeshift structure into place. With the Plum Blossom Wind still wafting in from the sea, there was nothing to struggle against but the inherent momentum of the raft itself, and they had enough men a thousand times over to deal with that. Slowly it moved, so slowly there was not a ripple in its wake.

Barbarians holding shields over their heads began to make their way out to the section's far end, guarding against a foray by the men of Seh. Arrows arced out toward the bridge as it came within range of the strongest archers, but the barbarians knelt down and shields gave protection.

Looking quickly toward the shore, Rohku saw the banners of the Khan close to the shore where the bridge began. Warriors in red were stationed there on horseback, and the Shonto captain assumed the barbarian chieftain was there, inspiring his warriors to perform great deeds.

When the bridge was almost under the city walls, a shadow appeared on the waters like a passing cloud, but it was a cloud of arrows. Realizing that he held his breath, Rohku tore his eyes away to be sure his guard watched behind, for he would need to give his full attention to the battle now so that he could give as complete an account as possible to Lord Shonto.

As the bridge bumped against the wall, Rohku saw the men of Seh swarm down the wall on ladders and ropes at the same time as the vanguard of the barbarian army started across the last section. The barbarians who guarded the bridge's end were pushed back almost immediately, much to Captain Rohku's satisfaction. Those will be their strongest fighters, he thought, and yet they could not stand against the men of Seh.

The barbarian army and the men swarming out of the city met in the center of the bridge, and a great shout went up from both sides. The sound of steel ringing on steel echoed across the valley like the sound of an enormous bell.

Toshaki turned command of the city over to Lord Akima and grasped a rope, lowering himself quickly down the wall. The floating bridge heaved as his feet struck, swaying and jerking like the deck of a ship. Men dropped to the bridge around him; they were the third wave of men from the city and would replace those falling where the opposing sides met.

Despite the number of barbarians, the Khan could not bring his great force to bear, for the causeway to the city would only support fifty men abreast. The second wave of men from the city had won another hundred feet, not pushing the great column of tribesmen back but driving them into the lake and cutting them down where they stood.

Toshaki turned and made his way among the fallen, the deck slick with water and blood. He drew his blade as he went, not looking at the faces of the dead and wounded. He did not want to know who had fallen. As he came up behind the wall of men fighting, he saw men of Seh poised, ready to cut as much of the bridge away as they could if the barbarians began to push them back. It was their intention to drive the barbarians as close to the shore as could be done and then cut the bridge away, forcing them to build again.

We are five thousand strong and we will lose five hundred in this very hour, Toshaki thought, how long can we carry on such a defense?

Thinking this, he threw himself into the fray, cutting down a barbarian in a single stroke. After that it was as if he had lost consciousness—a lifetime of training took hold and he fought on without his mind grasping what truly occurred.

A barbarian tripped and Toshaki felt his boot take the man in the ribs, knocking him into the cold waters. He felt a blow to his shoulder and registered vaguely that he might be wounded. He slipped and fell hard and found himself jerked to his feet by a young giant he did not recognize. He fought again.

He fell back to rest, and others took his place. Forcing himself up before truly rested, Toshaki returned to the battle. Arrows whistled overhead and suddenly the men of Seh began to win ground again. He tripped over a barbarian, dead from an arrow in the throat. The smell of smoke. A huge warrior knocked him down with a shield, but a man of Seh stepped in and took the blow while yet another felled the giant. Those men wore Toshaki colors, the lord realized afterward.

The sound of fire crackling and hissing. Again Toshaki fell to the rear to rest. The men of Seh were being driven back now. Toshaki turned to look for his reinforcements and saw the bridge behind him in flames, beyond the fire men of Seh had severed the span and maneuvered their section away.

We are cut off, some part of Toshaki's mind informed him. He looked back at the battle raging and realized that they were all exhausted and falling. Forcing himself to rise, the lord moved to the platform's edge. He would not chance capture; the waters could take him but never the barbarians.

A lifetime
To discover a single truth.
A solitary white petal
Drifting on the wind
Comes to rest on my breastplate
More beautiful
Than all the works of man.

Lord Toshaki Shinga

Thirty-three

Brave heart
Contemplating the plum trees blossoming
Against the infinite blue

From "Poems Written in Old Age"
Lady Nikko

ALONG THE BANKS of the Grand Canal willows and calypta trees began to unfurl tiny, embryonic leaves adding yet another scent to the complex perfume of spring. Rushes appeared, straight and green, in the growing shade of the trees, and the banks were newly grassed and awash in spring flowers.

Shonto sat on a low platform placed on a high point of the bank. A silk awning in the blue of the Shonto banner protected the platform and a fence of silk hangings bearing the shinta blossom created an enclosure, giving the lord privacy in all directions but east, toward the canal. Boats of armed guards patrolled the water before the enclosure, forcing all traffic to the opposite side. Other guards were posted around the enclosure and beyond them another ring of armed men both on foot and on horseback.

Nishima watched her father as her sampan approached. In the midst of war he has set himself in a place where he can truly appreciate the changing season. Her boat hissed to a stop in the mud, its bow barely on shore, and guards hurried down to pull it up far enough that disembarking would not be difficult.

Nishima looked up again and saw that her father was deep in conversation with a senior military aide. She nodded to the guard who had assisted her and walked a few paces along the grassy bank looking at the spring flowers. The last of the snow lilies were spread there in the shade of a great calypta, but a few days of such warmth and they would be gone until the next season.

She picked a tiny purple flower not recognized, reminding herself to ask Lady Okara what it might be. An aide of Kamu's hurried down the bank toward her, and she looked up to see Shonto smiling at her as though they had not met in a long time.

On the platform a cushion had been arranged for her and Nishima slipped out of her sandals. She bowed to her father and he surprised her by bowing low in return, a large grin appearing.

"Lady Nishima," he said in mock formal tones, "your presence honors me."

"The honor, Lord Governor, is mine entirely," she answered.

Shonto waved to a servant. "Governor is no longer a title I claim. When our esteemed Emperor learns that I have abandoned Seh and travel south with an army, I will have achieved a new office—that of Rebel General."

Nishima's smile disappeared. "It is a frightening thought, Uncle."

Shonto continued in the same tone, not showing any of the signs of distress that his daughter displayed. "Not at all, Nishi-sum. Think of all the great men of history who have borne this same title: Yokashima, Tiari, even our beloved Emperor's own father. My only concern is that my accomplishments will pale in such esteemed company." He reached out and touched her arm. "Do not be of barren heart, Nishi-sum, the Shonto are in the best of company."

A servant brought cups and wine, placing them on a small table. Waving him away before the wine was served, Shonto proceeded to pour the wine himself, surprising his daughter for the second time.

"You are in a bright mood today, Uncle. I wish I could feel as light of heart in our present circumstances." Nishima started to refuse the offered wine, as was polite, but Shonto took her hand and curled the fingers around the cup, squeezing her hand gently. She laughed.

"Hakata wrote that, as he grew older, spring became more beautiful and more painful each year. I, personally, have reached the age where spring is more beautiful but has not yet begun to cause me too much pain. Perhaps in a few years you will be able to appreciate the spring as I do. War cannot be helped now, but there will be beauty in spite of it. The truly brave soul will find time for beauty in the midst of the most terrible destruction."

"Lady Nikko," Nishima said. "Though I believe she meant that the truly brave hearts would see beauty at the hour of their death."

"Poets . . . why must they all be so dramatic?" Shonto gestured toward a branch of the plum that grew down to eye level, not an arm's length away. "See these blossoms? I have been watching them all morning. They prepare to open. They gather their resolve as we speak. Their opening will be an act of singular beauty, more lovely than the blossoms themselves. In the midst of all that occurs, we will sit here and observe. It will be a test of the bravery of your heart."

Nishima nodded and they both shifted their cushions to face the emerging flowers. They stayed like that for more than an hour, side by side: a tall, willowy young woman and the strongly built older man. Despite this contrast in their appearance, there was little doubt that they both focused on the same thing.

The plum blossoms unfolded in the sun. "As slowly as the timid heart," Lord Shonto whispered at one point. A quote from another poem and the only words either of them spoke until a flower had spread its petals like fragile wings. A bee came then and thrust its head into the flower, emerging covered in pollen.

The two renegade aristocrats turned away then, Nishima holding back her sleeve as she poured more wine into their cups.

"There is one other matter, Nishi-sum, that I hesitate to speak of."

Nishima nodded, recognizing seriousness in her father's tone.

"The river people have a saying: 'A whisper aboard ship is a shout upon the land.' Keeping secrets aboard a boat is a difficult thing." Shonto looked down into his cup, turning it slowly, then up at the plum blossom again.

Nishima nodded, sipping wine into a suddenly dry mouth.

"Brother Shuyun is a magnetic young man, but he is a monk who has taken a sacred oath. A heart can be broken against more malleable things, Nishi-sum, I have seen it."

Nishima gathered her nerve, not quite certain whether she heard disapproval or concern in her father's voice. "Satake-sum had taken this same sacred oath, Uncle, yet he did not live according to its letter, as we both know."

Shonto nodded. "He remained a monk despite his independent spirit. Shuyun-sum—what will become of him?"

"Do you fear to lose your Spiritual Advisor, then?"

Shonto considered this. "Shuyun-sum would always be invaluable, there is no question of that. I feel little need of a guide to the words of Botahara—I can read them myself. That is not my concern.

"You are a lady of a Great House, Nishi-sum, and though I have often spared you the responsibility that comes with your position I may not be able to continue to do so in the future. This war will require sacrifices of everyone—perhaps even of you. You may not be able to choose your own course, Nishi-sum, any more than I chose the path followed now."

Nishima nodded stiffly. She looked out over the canal at the trees blowing in the soft breeze, wafting their spring greens like new robes. A guard stood up in one of the patrolling boats, looked off to the far bank. Years ago Nishima had trained herself to remove such things as guards and walls and strong gates out of any scene she viewed, but she knew this was only an act of the imagination—they had not gone away.

She swallowed with difficulty. "Your words are wise, as always, Uncle. I thank you."

Shonto nodded, half a shrug.

"Uncle, there is something I have not spoken of. Kitsura-sum asked Jaku Katta if he would have a letter conveyed to her family, which he agreed to do. Kitsu-sum received word from her family that this letter arrived. This would seem to indicate. . . ."

Shonto held up his hand. "Kitsura-sum has already informed me of this. It raises another question of the Guard Commander's claims."

Nishima suppressed her annoyance at her cousin's interference. "I believe Jaku Katta is no longer in favor in the Emperor's court, Sire."

"Huh." Shonto looked down at his cup. "I agree, daughter, but I am not sure who this young Jaku supports—Tadamoto—is he loyal to his brother and family or is he loyal to his Emperor? It appears to have been Jaku Tadamoto who convinced the Emperor to raise the army. Does the younger Jaku intend that army to fight barbarians or to fight Shonto, and perhaps even his own brother? It is a curious puzzle. For the time being, at least, Jaku Katta has little choice but to side with the Shonto and hope the Yamaku do not stand. He plays out the charade quite admirably, I think."

Nishima picked up her cup but did not drink. "I confess that I no longer find much to admire in the guardsman," Nishima said softly.

Horses were heard coming to a halt outside the compound and General Hojo appeared at the opening.

"I must excuse myself, Uncle. Please give my regards to General Hojo."

Shonto nodded. "I thank you for viewing the plum blossoms with me. It added another facet to the beauty entirely." Shonto bowed again to his daughter as he had when she arrived. She bowed as her position required, slipped into her sandals, and made her way down the bank.

The boatmen pushed out into the slow moving current and began to scull toward Nishima's barge.

But Uncle, she thought, I have discovered the rarest beauty in the midst of terrible destruction. If my heart is truly brave, can I turn away?

Guards cleared a way through the long line of refugees strung out along the south road. It seemed a last indignity for these people. They had been turned from their homes, crops torn from the fields, livestock taken, feed stores set to the torch, and any food they could not carry confiscated to feed the growing army. And now they were being forced to stand aside for the lord who had failed to stop this alleged barbarian army in Seh where such things should be done.

Yet when Shonto and his company rode past, the refugees bowed low, displaying nothing of what they felt. They were fatalists in a manner that a person of action like Lord Shonto would never understand. Karma dictated that they would occasionally be the victims in the machinations of the Empire. It had always been so and would never change—unless one progressed, perhaps becoming a monk or a sister of a Botanist Order.

Passing on horseback, Shonto was saddened by the endless procession of villagers and peasants, some leading ox-drawn wagons, others carrying everything left to them on the backs of mules or on poles slung across their own shoulders. It affected him, but he knew what he had said to Nishima was true—everyone would make sacrifices in this war. There would be few exceptions.

They crossed a stubble field, damp from the spring rains but firm enough for horses. Another group of riders waited on a low rise and Shonto could see the banner of the Komawara House—the mist-lily against a night blue background. Komawara bowed from his horse as Lord Shonto approached while his men dismounted and bowed properly. Shonto noticed the trim of green lacing on two of these men—the Hajiwara Komawara had found in the Jai Lung Hills.

"This is the place?" Shonto asked.

Komawara nodded.

Spurring his horse, Shonto gained a few feet in elevation and then turned to look west toward the hills, trying to gauge the height of the undulating land.

"This entire plain has been under flood many times," Komawara said, coming up beside Shonto. "Six years ago there was a sea here sixty rih wide. We can dam the canal and defend the dam. This defense could last many days. Once the dam is burst the land will still be impassible for days until it dries."

Shonto nodded as he looked both east and west again. "What of the canal? It will have no source of water, yeh?"

Hojo pointed off to the south. "Ten rih away the river Tensi joins the canal. There will be no difficulties once the fleet has passed that point. The section of the canal from here to there may be shallower than usual, but . . ." He shrugged.

"And the roads through the hills are narrow and perfect for ambushes," Komawara added with satisfaction. "We can hold the barbarians here for many days, I think." The young lord rubbed his sword hilt and Shonto realized this was not the weapon Komawara usually carried. The Toshaki gift, the lord realized.

"General Hojo, Lord Komawara, begin planning the tactics to be used in the hills. Lord Taiki will take responsibility for seeing the dam built and defended. We will move the fleet south immediately." Shonto gestured to the line of refugees. "These people must be clear of the area by this time tomorrow." He looked around again as though weighing the plan one last time. "We will see what this Khan can do when he meets the unexpected."

Thirty-four

THE FIRST SWALLOWS had returned to the north that day, and the wood vibrated with the excitement of birds calling and courting. Rohku Tadamori held his horse by its bridle and watched the city of Rhojo-ma. The Flying Horse Banner of the Province of Seh had come down from the high tower of the Governor's Palace and the gold banner of the Khan with its strangely twisted dragon had appeared in its place. The dissonant sounds of horns and clashing of metal had echoed across the water then. Rohku's horse nudged his shoulder, pulling at the lacing of his armor.

Seh had fallen. For the first time in the history of the Empire the province had been taken by the barbarians. And Rohku served the man who had allowed that to happen. Though not a man of Seh, the captain felt the loss all the same.

Smoke curled up from the eastern end of the city, but there were no signs that the rest of Rhojo-ma was being put to the torch. If anything, the smoke was diminishing.

Five thousand men, Rohku thought, may Botahara rest their souls. It was impossible to say how many barbarians had fallen. More than five thousand, Rohku thought, many more. He looked out at the floating causeway that connected the shore and the eastern edge of the city. Beneath the waters lay uncounted warriors of both armies. The fighting had been hard.

The barbarians had not shown themselves to be brilliant tacticians, but they had not exhibited any lack of resolve either. The Khan had thrown wave after wave of men against the walls of Rhojo-ma, spending as though he had endless resources, and in the end this had won the day.

Rohku made a sign to Botahara and mounted his horse. He looked back at the city again.

Now we play gii, he thought, struck by how cold this seemed to him— but it was true. Who would learn the most from this first encounter? Who would come to the board next time armed with greater wisdom? He prayed that he could provide his lord with all the information they would need. The good name of his family depended on such things.

Thirty-five

SOLDIERS WERE NEITHER numerous enough, nor skilled in the work, and in the end, peasants were pressed into the effort as well. Poles with baskets hanging from their ends proved more effective than oxen and carts when loading and unloading were considered. Shonto's advisors in this matter soon realized that stopping the flow of the canal would not be enough—the dam needed to stretch from higher ground further back from each bank to create the depth of water required. The volume of water flowing into the new sea was simply not great enough to backup sufficiently due to a mere constriction. Near the forming dam, workers dug away the bank to allow the blocked waters quicker access to the lowlands beyond.

Imperial messenger boats had been confiscated for the war effort and they plied back and forth to the north bringing news and moving observers. The word had passed to most now——Rhojo-ma had fallen and this news cast a shadow of desperation over the men who built the dam. Suddenly the war seemed real and the odds truly impossible.

There was as yet no news of the barbarian army moving south and, predictably, there were some that speculated the Khan had already achieved his goal. The victory in Seh would be consolidated and all this dam building would prove a fool's work.

Rhojo-ma had stood for five days. Five thousand against one hundred thousand. Though no one would ever truly know what had happened inside the city's walls, poets and writers of songs would not hesitate to fill in the missing details.

Ten days had passed since Shonto's fleet had left the northern city and in that time they had not traveled far. Creating the desert in their wake took time.

Captain Rohku Tadamori stood on top of a section of the new dike and watched the teeming workers. His report would have reached Lord Shonto by now, but his presence would still be requested. There would be questions not answered by his report.

Riders came up the rise toward him, wearing night blue and black. Lord Komawara Samyamu himself pulled his horse up before the young guard.

"Captain Rohku?"

Rohku bowed. "Captain Rohku Tadamori of Lord Shonto's guard, Lord Komawara."

"Lord Shonto would have you join him." A horse was led forward and the young captain mounted.

"It is a ride of several rih, Captain. I have not eaten today, would you share a meal with us?"

"The honor, Lord Komawara, would be mine entirely."

Motioning for Rohku to ride at his side, Komawara turned his horse and set off.

Passing the lines of workers, both men and women, coming from the stone and gravel pits, Rohku was astonished by the numbers who toiled. They passed an old man who sat on the ground in the grip of a fit of coughing. A young girl bent over him, obviously frightened. A soldier rode down the line toward this pair. Seeing the rider, the girl reluctantly tore herself away from the old man, tears appearing as she went. Rohku turned away.

"We have little time," Komawara said softly. "The rains this spring have not been great, so it will take many days for the waters to gather." He said nothing for a moment but then spoke again. "It has been said that we have created a desert in our wake, but now we will create a sea. I am told, Captain, that the barbarians proved to be poor sailors so perhaps seas will serve our purpose better than deserts."

Rohku kicked his foot free of a stirrup and shortened it as they went. "The lake surrounding Rhojo-ma proved an excellent defense. If it had not been for the pirates, the siege would undoubtedly have taken days longer."

"Pirates!" Komawara exclaimed, proving again that he was from the outer provinces. "I had not heard there were pirates." Komawara looked at his companion in amazement. "Brother Shuyun and I saw no pirates among the barbarians."

Rohku found his now properly adjusted stirrup. "I am sure that is true, Sire, but there are pirates in the Khan's army now."

"This Khan, he has built an army out of impossibilities." Komawara could not get over his surprise. "Pirates!"

"It would indicate that my lord was correct, Sire. The Khan has enlisted pirates so his army can follow the great canal south to the inner provinces. It seems the barbarian has considered the possibilities with some care before embarking on this endeavor."

Komawara nodded. "I agree, though I suspect it never occurred to the Khan that the army of Seh would not stand and fight. Once the army of Seh had been defeated, the canal would take him easily and quickly to the undefended center of Wa. Lord Shonto has done the unexpected," Komawara said with satisfaction. "The canal will prove a difficult road indeed."

Komawara raised a hand to stop. "This seems a likely place for a meal, Captain, would you agree?"

Rohku nodded. They were on a low hill, the first of the range that lay to the west of the canal. Below them a large plain stretched north toward Seh, black soil ready for planting—though it would bear a crop of weeds this season.

They dismounted and a bamboo mat was rolled out for the lord and the man he treated as a guest.

"As you say, Lord Komawara, I am sure Lord Shonto will slow the barbarian advance to a crawl. If only the Emperor will raise the army we need."

Komawara smiled. "Yes. It is the one instance where we may pray the Emperor's spies are alert. Once they have seen the barbarian army, one would hope the Son of Heaven will respond accordingly. Though we may be in Itsa before that happens," Komawara said with a show of frustration.

A small fire was lit and food was laid out for the two men. Rohku was unused to the company of lords—even minor ones from outer provinces—but Komawara was so natural and likable he soon found himself put at ease. War, the captain thought, may break down more walls than one would expect.

"You have served the Shonto long?" Komawara asked, trying to carry on the polite conversation he believed Rohku would expect. Rohku was obviously too young to have served anyone long.

"Not long, Lord Komawara. My father is the captain of Lord Shonto's personal guard," he said, trying not to show any sign of pride.

"How is it that I have not met him?"

"He stays in the capital performing duties for our lord."

"Ah. And you are also a captain."

"Recently promoted." He waved to the north. "This war has already seen many a junior officer receive ranks that would otherwise be years away."

"You are modest, Captain. Lord Shonto would not have sent you to watch the barbarians and witness the battle of Seh if he did not hold great respect for you."

Rohku shrugged, coloring almost imperceptibly. "You are too kind, Lord Komawara. I myself wonder if any number of lieutenants will not find themselves generals before many months have passed—such is our need."

"Lord Shonto is off in the hills somewhere?" What Shonto did and where he was at any given time was not considered a topic for general discussion, especially now that war had come, but there was no one within hearing and Komawara seemed at ease with Rohku—he might drop a hint at least.

The lord waved to the west. "We make plans for defending the hills. Perhaps Lord Shonto will explain."

Rohku nodded. Pressing the point was out of the question. He looked off to the west. The barbarians might try to skirt the new lake, and then there might be opportunities for ambush.

"Perhaps," Rohku said, "I will take a more active roll in the near future."

Komawara nodded as he ate. When he spoke again, he seemed quite serious. "What you have just done, Captain Rohku—witnessing the battle of Rhojo-ma—I would have found this a most difficult duty." He gave a nodding bow. "You are to be commended for this."

Rohku did not look up as he spoke. "At the battle of Rhojo-ma I watched, Lord Komawara. I did not lay down my life."

"Exactly," Komawara said softly.

The conversation failed then and they ate in silence. Finishing the meal, they set out into the hills, the conversation stilted until Captain Rohku commented on the quality of Seh's horses and then it flowed like a steep river.

They found a road among the hills and followed that, riding out of the direct sunlight into the trees robing themselves in new leaves. Shonto guards blocked the way until Komawara gave the password and they continued on, encountering more and more riders in blue as they went. Finally, Lord

Shonto stood before them in a clearing surrounded by guards and officers. Conspicuous among them was an ill-dressed soldier, unarmored like the senior military men, though armed. He carried a sword in Shonto's presence.

Komawara and Rohku waited beside their horses until General Hojo waved them forward. The ragged man turned and then a smile flickered across his face. It was Rohku Saicha, the young captain's father.

The two monks sat on mats that had been placed in the bow of the river boat. The fair wind of the season moved them south, if not at great speed, with a consistency that saw the rih pass in surprising numbers. A rain shower had blown over earlier, but the sun soon dried the decks and only the occasional droplet from steaming sails indicated that there had been rain at all. Plum and cherry trees flowered on the banks and where there would normally be gay parties out under the boughs to observe the blossoming, frightened refugees streamed south instead.

Brother Sotura was glad that he could speak to his former student in privacy—only the tribesman in Shonto livery stood nearby and he was not close enough to overhear. The sailors had little to do and, as they followed a boat with deeper draft, there was no lookout in the bow nor did anyone sound the bottom, but out of respect for the Botahist monks they confined their idling to midships.

"These events are unsettling, Shuyun-sum," the senior Brother was saying. "So many people torn from their homes. Already they are hungry and, with such numbers on the roads and canal, disease is appearing. I spend time as I can now with the sick, but there are more every day." He shook his head. "I have written to Brother Hutto in Yankura, but it will be some time before our Order can respond to a situation that grows worse as we speak."

Shuyun touched his hands together, rocking back and forth slightly as though nodding agreement. "I have asked Lord Shonto if I could assist you, Brother, but he will not spare me, though often I have little to do. Every precaution is taken to isolate the sick from the army and Lord Shonto's staff. Even our meeting was difficult to arrange. I regret this."

"It cannot be helped, Shuyun-sum. Your part is to advise Lord Shonto so that the interests of our Order are represented among the powerful of Wa. Now that the situation gathers momentum by the hour, your role is even more crucial."

At this Shuyun stopped rocking.

"We do our best to prepare for this calamity, Shuyun-sum, but it is difficult. The future is uncertain." Sotura caught the eye of his student. "If we knew more of Lord Shonto's intent, we could act to assist him and to preserve our Order so that Botahara's word would not be lost."

Shuyun examined his palm, rubbing it slowly. "My lord hopes to slow the barbarian advance so that an army may be raised to defend the Empire."

Sotura paused for a second as though he had suffered a small insult and was unsure how to respond. When he spoke, he had lowered his voice. "No doubt, Brother Shuyun, this is true but the Yamaku still sit upon the Dragon Throne and we could do much if we knew what Lord Shonto . . . thought about this situation."

Shuyun shrugged. "In truth, Brother Sotura, I do not know."

"Perhaps it would be useful to find out."

"My lord gives me the information he feels I need in my capacity, Brother. I do not presume to ask for more."

"As his loyal Advisor it might be to your lord's benefit if you spent time informing yourself of the situation in the Empire and of your lord's intent."

Shuyun blinked.

"Jaku Katta is another question, Shuyun-sum. Does he truly have Lord Shonto's confidence?"

Shuyun watched a sampan drift past, carrying men in Shonto blue. "Did not Botahara say, 'Do not trust truth to a liar.'"

Sotura nodded. "The guardsman is an opportunist of the worst sort. Trusting him would be an error indeed. Does he still seek the company of Lady Nishima?"

"Perhaps. I do not know," Shuyun said slowly.

"Maybe she has seen him for what he is and has another interest?"

Shuyun shrugged. "The personal lives of my lord's family . . ." Shuyun threw up his hands.

Sotura nodded.

"It is a crucial time, Brother Shuyun. Much could be lost in the coming struggle. We must be vigilant. The True Path must be protected and we are its chosen protectors."

Shuyun stared at the chi quan instructor until the master became uncomfortable.

"Brother Shuyun?"

Motioning to the Kalam suddenly, Shuyun leaned toward the tribes-man and spoke in the man's tongue. The Kalam gave a proper bow and hurried off.

"There is something you should know, Brother," Shuyun said quietly. "It will make many things clear to you. We must wait for my servant."

The Kalam appeared a moment later, bearing a brocade bag containing something small and angular. Giving it to Shuyun, he retreated to his former station by the rail and stood silently.

With great care Shuyun slid a plain lacquered box out of the bag. He set the box carefully on his knees and unlatched it. "There is a matter we have discussed before, Brother Sotura. Let me show you what I have found." Saying this he opened the box gently.

On the lining of green silk lay the blossom of the Udumbara. The breeze touched it and the petals moved as though still fresh from the branch.

It was not possible to tell from Sotura's face if the older monk was over-come with joy or deep sadness. He did not move for some time and then, almost tenderly, he reached out, but as he did so Shuyun withdrew the box, closing it sharply. The young Brother's face was very cold.

"I will not trust it to you, Brother," Shuyun said firmly.

***

I fear that our young protégé is following the path of Brother Satake—I regret to say that Shuyun is not inclined to provide the information we seek about his liege-lord. The change in him is remarkable considering the short time he has served the Shonto House, but there are circumstances we could not have foreseen. Shuyun has in his possession a blossom from a tree at Monarta. I do not know where this has come from, but if it was Lord Shonto's desire to undermine the Initiate's loyalty to our Order he could hardly have chosen a more effective ploy. This situation will be difficult to retrieve now, especially as Lord Shonto controls my meetings with Shuyun and allows far fewer than I request. How Shonto came by a blossom from the Udumbara is a mystery—one can never underestimate this man. Although Shonto's situ-ation in the Empire does not appear to be secure, I hesitate to say more. The Emperor may yet discover that circumstances are not what he believed.

As to Shuyun I am not yet certain what should be done—he was always a perfect student in the past. Some action must be taken soon or he will have turned so far from the light that he will find it difficult to return.

Sotura stopped writing suddenly. He wondered what the Supreme Master and Brother Hutto would decide about Shuyun. *We have been caught in a lie by one who believed what he was taught about lies. The deeper reasons for our decision cannot be seen by a young Initiate, no matter how talented—all he will see is our hypocrisy. The Teacher has come and we deny it. How can Shuyun but think we act from motives that are less than pure ? He has not stepped off the True Path—we have pushed him. May Botahara forgive us.*

Sotura picked up the letter, read through the first few lines by the light of his lamp, and then very slowly crumpled the paper into a ball. He was not certain that any action his superiors took with the willful Initiate would not drive this young man further away. *Even I have begun to distrust my superior's judgment,* Sotura realized, and he made a sign to Botahara.

The monk remembered the interview with his former student. *Even sitting as far as I was,* Sotura thought, *I could feel the strength of his chi. I have never known its like.*

Thirty-six

THE HUNTING PARTY followed a winding road down the hillside, riding slowly in the spring sunshine. It had not been a successful day as the tiger the villagers claimed to have seen could not be found. The Emperor was disappointed. They had shot some game birds, certainly, but when one has set out after tiger, pheasant is a poor substitute. Still, it was a beautiful day and Akantsu II, Emperor of Wa, was coming out of his sullen mood.

Many varieties of cherry and plum flowered along the roadside and scattered their petals like a snowfall across the soft ground of spring. It would not be long now until the Plum Blossom Wind would perform the feat it was named for, stripping the trees of their petals and carrying them aloft until the wind seemed laden with blowing snow.

The rivers, too, would be covered in fallen blossoms, for the people of Wa loved to plant their flowering trees along the waterways—the sight of the perfect blossoms borne toward the sea was symbolic of Botahist thought. Over the centuries so many poems had been written about the Plum Blossom Winds that it was said nothing new could ever be written about them—though that stopped no one.

The Emperor rode a gray mare of the same line as the animals used in the Ceremony of Gray Horses. Unlike the Hanama who seldom hunted, the Yamaku men rode and rode well. Perhaps a family that had won its way to the Throne only a decade before was not yet willing to give up the skills that had brought them their victory, so sword and bow and lance and horse were thought of as essential disciplines in the Imperial family. Akantsu was a fine horseman and skilled with a sword, though his sons, under the influence of the Empress, had never achieved the mastery of their father.

The Emperor's hunting garb was plain by the standards of the lords of the inner provinces, though it bore trim in Imperial Crimson which more than made up for its lack of style. As he had hoped to meet a tiger that day, the Emperor's garb incorporated a certain amount of lacquered and laced armor, although light and incomplete by battle standards. A dragon-crested helmet swung from the saddle, and the Son of Heaven carried his own sword in his sash—not the ancient sword of office but a blade that had seen many battles and duels.

It was well known among the courtiers that when Akantsu wanted to show displeasure to one of the many officials who attended him he would sometimes invite them on a hunt. It was invariably quite unpleasant, for few of the higher officials rode, having spent their entire lives caught up in the functions of the government and court—and, of course, in the capital, as in much of Wa, one usually traveled by boat. The Emperor reserved this treatment for officials who had done something mildly annoying. To cross the Emperor seriously would mean postings in the outer provinces or far worse.

Today there were no victims in the party. A distant cousin from Chou rode near the Emperor though they spoke little. The Son of Heaven's earlier mood had quickly curtailed attempts at conversation.

A dark feathered hawk floated across the road, disappearing into the cloud of white blossoms and when the Emperor turned his eyes back to the road he saw a column of Imperial Guards appear around a bend, led by Jaku Tadamoto. The Emperor's men made way for their acting commander, who dismounted quickly and bowed before his ruler.

"Colonel." The Emperor smiled, much to the relief of his party. "Your arrival was foretold. Only seconds ago a hawk I believe was a Choka passed before us." He turned to his cousin. "Almost an apparition, wouldn't you agree?"

His cousin, Lord Yamaku, a small man perhaps a dozen years older than the Emperor, most definitely agreed. He nodded his head vigorously. More than anything else, Lord Yamaku resembled a successful merchant. He had that wealthy, ill-bred manner and dress that bad taste damned many with in the Imperial Court. Not that the man's taste was glaringly awful, but among people whose standards were strict and whose imagination was limited he stood out like a farmer in a Sonsa troupe.

"The Choka hawk has proven to be well chosen, then," Tadamoto said. The Emperor had given the Jaku House the symbol, raising their status considerably among the new Houses.

The Emperor smiled again. "It is kind of you to ride out to meet us, Colonel. I intend to stop at the shrine for the view. Would you accompany us?"

"I would be more than honored. May I ask, Sire, how went the hunt?"

A cloud drifted across the Emperor's face, but then a wan smile replaced it. "I believe the tiger we hunted today was mythical. Or a master of subterfuge. We had beaters out for several rih and managed to move nothing. And Lord Yamaku had so wanted to use his new bow."

"I am sorry to learn this, Sire. Tigers make poor subjects, sometimes— ignoring their duties, leaving without being dismissed, and eating perfectly dutiful subjects. I don't know what can be done about them."

The Emperor laughed. "Yes, this one is said to have eaten a loyal woodsman. A beastly thing to do when I have any number of courtiers and officials I could willingly spare. Most inconsiderate." He laughed again and the others nearby, deeming the Emperor's mood changed, laughed as well.

Turning off the road they followed a trail out onto a rounded promontory where a small shrine to the plague-dead stood. Knowing the Emperor's opinions on the matter, no one made signs to Botahara. They passed on to the lookout point where the Emperor and his party dismounted.

"String your new bow, cousin," the Emperor said pleasantly. "Tadamoto-sum is an appreciator of fine weapons."

An archery contest was quickly organized among the officers of the guard using Lord Yamaku's bow. Much laughter accompanied the Emperor's suggestion that an officer donate his very stylish hat for a target. This was fixed to a nearby tree and the Emperor took up a seat on a rock, flanked by Tadamoto and his cousin as judges.

Lord Yamaku did not join the contest as it would have been very impolite for anyone to best a member of the Imperial family and Tadamoto was the guard Commander, so a similar etiquette applied.

Each contestant shot three arrows and though not every one found its mark, the hat was soon well ventilated indeed. The archers could not be said to be remarkable in their skill, but they were well matched so the contest was close and therefore more enjoyable for all concerned.

Once the contest had drawn everyone's attention, the Emperor turned to Tadamoto. "I trust you did not ride all this way to view the blossoms, Colonel?" he said quietly.

Tadamoto nodded. "I have received a report from the north." He searched for the right words. "It is a disturbing report, Emperor."

The Emperor nodded. He watched a young officer make a shot and applauded the result. Leaning over, he spoke quietly to his cousin who bowed quickly. The Emperor nodded to Tadamoto and the two men rose. All present dropped to their knees until the Emperor was several paces away.

Walking to the lookout, the Emperor leaned against the railing that protected the foolish from the steep drop. Behind him the land stretched off to the Imperial Capital and the Lake of the Lost Dragon. The river wound its way toward the sea and as far as Tadamoto could see the landscape was decorated with flowering trees. Even the distant Mountain of the Pure Spirit seemed to be covered in a haze of white.

"Colonel." The Emperor nodded for Tadamoto to continue.

"I have a report that Lord Shonto has left Seh and proceeds south on the canal accompanied by an army."

The Emperor nodded calmly as though he had not just heard an announcement of civil war—civil war *with the* Shonto.

"A missive has arrived bearing the seal of the Governor of Seh. I broke all protocol and brought it with me, Sire."

The Emperor nodded again. "There is more?"

Tadamoto nodded. "Reports have been received that a large barbarian army has crossed the border of Seh. I do not consider these substantiated at this time, however. "

"The missive?"

Tadamoto signaled one of his guards, and a small box was brought forward. Opening this, Tadamoto removed the official letter and, to the guardsman's surprise, the Emperor reached out and took it directly from the Colonel's hand. Looking at the seal, the Emperor broke it and opened the letter with no show of haste. He read.

Tadamoto pretended to admire the view. It was impolite to look directly at the Emperor for more than a few seconds and, under the circumstances, Tadamoto thought even a few seconds might not be advisable.

The Emperor lowered the scroll. He looked off at some unseen distance for a moment and then handed the paper to Tadamoto. "Read this," he said, his tone mild.

Sire:

A barbarian army has crossed the northern border of Seh, an army of one hundred thousand armed men. Their immediate objective appears to be Rhojo-ma, but I do not believe this army plans to finish its campaign in the provincial capital. As the entire force available in the Province of Seh is less than a quarter the number in the invading army, I do not feel we can stop the barbarians from advancing into Itsa Province and then further south.

Our decision, therefore, has been to leave Seh and move our army down the canal, resisting the invaders as we go. If all goes well, I believe this will give the Empire until midsummer to raise the force necessary to combat the barbarian army.

Five thousand men of Seh stayed to defend the city of Rhojo-ma, hoping to give the main force time to cross the border and begin the recruitment. This we will do.

I regret to say that I do not think this barbarian force can be countered successfully without assistance from the Imperial Government. I do not expect to be able to raise enough men to meet the threat to the Empire even by the time we reach Chiba Province.

We can say little yet of the skills of this barbarian army and its command- ers and will report as soon as more is known. Certainly, the tribes are led by the Golden Khan who flies a banner of gold bearing a dragon of crimson. I believe, Sire, that this chieftain has designs upon the Throne of Wa.

Those who have followed me in this move south are brave and industrious men and I have faith that we can slow the invaders' advance, but an army must be raised to meet this threat, preferably in Chiba Province. We destroy all crops as we go, but once the barbarians have reached Chiba, this will become more difficult and if they cross the border into Dentou it will be impossible. They will also be within striking distance of the Imperial Cap- ital.

I remain your Majesty's servant,
Shonto Motoru

The Emperor had no compunctions about watching Tadamoto's face as he read and the young man found as he finished the letter that he was being stared at.

"He makes no mention that it was his sworn duty to protect the borders of the Province of Seh."

Tadamoto nodded, not needing to ask who "he" referred to.

The Emperor turned and looked out at the view, his hands resting lightly on the rail. For some moments he stood like that in silence and when he spoke he did not turn his head.

"We did not think he would be able to find the support for a civil war— not in Seh. He fails to mention how large a force accompanies him south?"

"That is true, Emperor."

"A significant oversight in the former governor's report. It is not possible that Motoru has raised the force he needs in Seh." This did not seem to be a question, so Tadamoto said nothing. The "thunk" of arrows striking wood punctuated the silence. "How goes the raising of our army, Colonel?"

"Well, Sire, but I will redouble our efforts now."

The Emperor nodded. "We will do more. We must prepare a plan to meet Shonto's army—somewhere beyond the capital. There is no telling who will flock to his banner once he enters Dentou Province." The Emperor fell silent again. "Where on the canal is my useless son?"

"He has not yet crossed the border into Chiba Province, Sire." Tadamoto brushed white petals from the small dragons embroidered over the breast on his uniform.

The Emperor's shoulders went stiff. "Not yet in Chiba?"

"Yes, Sire."

The Emperor snorted. "I will send a letter to the Prince in my own hand: an Imperial directive to proceed north with all haste and relieve Shonto of the command of the army. He is then to stop any barbarian invasion he is able to find and send Shonto to the capital under guard. How do you think the former governor will react to that?"

"To do anything but obey the son of the Emperor, Sire . . . would be a foolish mistake."

"Yes, but it would do away with this pose of protector of the Empire. He will be a rebel and called one."

Tadamoto nodded even though the Emperor looked out toward the capital.

"Have you heard from your brother, Colonel?"

"I have not, Emperor."

The Emperor rubbed his hands slowly along the railing. "We might hope that he stayed in Seh to *defend Rhojo-ma*. All who accompany Shonto support a rebel."

"He shames the Jaku House, Sire. We will turn our back to him."

The Emperor nodded slowly. "I believe this matter should be discussed immediately in the Great Council. We will have the Empire know that Shonto has abandoned his duties in the north and comes south with an armed force. It is not this ragged Khan who has designs on the Throne. If we had only kept that Fanisan daughter in the capital!" It was the closest thing to an expression of anger the Emperor had made, but when he spoke again his voice was calm. "She will not sit upon my throne, Colonel, nor will Motoru stand behind it." He turned now and looked directly at Tadamoto. "So we must raise a great army, Colonel. My father fought the Shonto and won—I intend to do the same. But I will not be so generous after my victory."

Thirty-seven

SHOKAN LAY STILL in the darkness wondering what one felt when overcome by the cold. Did a person simply sleep and not wake? Or was it painful or frightening? If one still felt the cold, was that a sign that one was closer to life than death? Cold was what the young lord felt: deep, pervasive cold. The bones of his legs ached with cold and in his feet there was no feeling at all.

With some effort the lord pulled his mind away from this avenue of thought and tried to consider the coming day. He had held a brief council with his staff that night, huddled in a circle in the dark, no fire to offer warmth or even cheer. Hard choices had been discussed and decisions made. Destroying the horses had weighed heavily on everyone; unfortunately, no one had offered an alternative that would allow the group to continue. It had been a fool's hope that the snows would not be deep in the pass so early in the season, but then there had been few paths open to them. Bringing the horses was a risk perhaps not everyone had understood.

Shonto Shokan had made the decision to destroy his stallion himself, though certainly it was not a task a lord of a Great House should even consider. Still, he felt this situation was of his own making and could not ask another to perform the duties his poor decision had made necessary. This kind of thinking was a trait of the young lord's that drove his father mad. The senior Shonto even went so far as to blame their former Spiritual Advisor, Brother Satake, for encouraging this trait, saying it was good education for children but the worst foolishness for the lord of a major House. Shokan almost laughed aloud at the memory. It was his impression that Brother Satake had quietly defied everyone; may Botahara protect him.

There had been no wood for fires that night and the sky had remained perfectly clear, allowing the bitter cold of the mountains free rein. The eastern sky was barely gray behind the white peaks that loomed above, but that was enough to have men up and moving, trying to restore circulation, praying the sun would not tarry and the sea wind would bring them warmth. It was a great irony that by night they huddled together in teeth-chattering cold while by day the sun burned their faces and had them stripped down to their lightest robes.

Shokan pushed his cover aside and turned onto his back. He had been rolling over at regular intervals all night trying not to expose one side for too long to the bitter chill that seeped up from the snow—not a restful night. He was hungry and worried about their food supplies. Horse meat would take them some distance, no doubt, but they were still many days away from the western end of the pass. In a purely foolish act they had, to a man, fed some of their precious grain to the horses the night before—a last meal—but the lack of fires to melt snow had meant no water. There was no doubt that the horses would soon be dead without any assistance from their reluctant riders.

Forcing himself to sit up, Shokan felt the chill wind that still swept down from the peaks. He stayed sitting for a moment, beating his hands on his arms and shoulders. The snow would be frozen into a steel-hard crust now, a surface that would support a man's weight with ease, but it was also steep, treacherous ice and had led to the loss of many of their party.

From up the gulley Shokan heard the measured rhythm of footsteps as the guides moved higher. The previous day they had made a stairway while the snow was soft and now they climbed up to its top where they would continue by cutting more steps in the hard snow. It was a slow, laborious process.

Shokan thought again of their limited food supplies, wondering if he led his retainers to a futile end in some frozen pass. My father needs every armed man he can find, he reminded himself. Every risk is acceptable.

Looking up at the mountains, Shokan thought of the vast valley that lay on their opposite side down which ran the delicate ribbon of the Grand Canal. It seemed very far away, almost unreachable.

A single peak above caught the light of the rising sun and the young lord felt a great relief. Around him he could make out the shapes of men and horses. Shades of gray began to take on color and shapes definition.

"Sire?" a voice whispered.

Shokan turned to his guard who pointed up the slope. Not far away, half a dozen bearded men crouched down on their heels and watched, their faces impassive. Mountain people. . . .

Shokan turned to his guard who stared openly, unaware that his lord regarded him. Moving with great care, Shokan found the small platform he had stamped out before the snow froze and got unsteadily to his unfeeling feet.

Though he half expected them to start like deer and bound off, the crouching men made no move. It was the worst manners, but Shokan found himself staring like his guard. Mountain people! He could not hide his surprise.

The men crouching before him were dressed so completely in furs and skins that nothing showed but weathered faces. At their belts they carried long knives, almost swords, and, on their backs, bows of an almost pure white wood. As he had read, these men had deep blue eyes, like one sometimes saw among the southern barbarians.

Slowly, Shokan extended his hands, palms out, all the while searching his memory for words he had heard Brother Satake speak in the mountain tongue—but none came. His father had said that Shuyun spoke their language, and Shokan wondered if this was not uncommon for a Botahist scholar.

Turning to his guard Shokan said, "The Botahist monks often know the mountain tongue—pass the word down the line to anyone educated by the Brothers."

The mountain people looked on as Shokan extended his hands, but there was no reaction visible—it might have been his private morning ritual for all the response it received. He tried gesturing to the snow nearby and smiling in invitation, but the men crouching in the snow did not move. Both parties were soon reduced to staring at each other in silence.

After this had gone on for some time, Shokan noticed a movement higher up on the guides' stairway. Another group made its way down toward the snowbound lowlanders.

As this second party arrived, the first group turned and bowed stiffly. The object of this show of respect seemed to be an old, leather-faced man in a worn hooded robe gathered at the waist by a silk sash of faded purple. What animal had contributed its coat to this old man's warmth Shokan could not say, for the fur was unknown to him— deep gray with tips of silver.

The old man continued right past the bowing mountain people and stopped about three paces beyond Lord Shonto's guard who had been unable to move quickly enough on the treacherous footing to stop him. Shokan gave them a signal to stand ready but do nothing for now.

The old man stood, arms crossed, hands buried in the sleeves of his robe. His face was as impassive as his companions' though his eyes were the color of a sky washed with a high mist. The mountain race seemed to be smaller than the people of Wa though Shokan suspected they were broad of shoulder under their layers of fur.

The old man pointed at the Shonto lord. "Name," he said, not inflecting the word like a question, though Shokan assumed it was meant to be one.

"Lord Shonto Shokan. And you?"

The old man did not respond, but among his companions there was a whispering. Shokan was certain he heard the name of his father's Spiritual Advisor spoken more than once, as impossible as it seemed.

"Brother Shuyun," Shokan said. "Do you speak of Brother Shuyun?"

After a moment the old man nodded his ancient head once, his expression never altering. It was such an odd movement, Shokan was not sure the man's head had not simply fallen forward and then been returned to its upright position. It hardly seemed an expression of agreement.

With a quick motion the old man pointed up the slope. "Fight," he said with some animation.

Shokan was not sure what this meant but obviously some response was desired.

"Shu-yung fight!" the man said with more urgency.

"This is hopeless," Shokan whispered to his guard. "What does he mean?"

"Tribes . . . fight, shu-yung," the man said, and pointed up into the mountains again.

Tribes; the word struck the lord like cold wind. He nodded slowly, still far from certain. He was not even sure that nodding meant agreement to these people. Shu-yung, the old man was saying, a word so close to Shuyun in their odd pronunciation that to Shokan's ear it was barely different—a slight ring in the last syllable, that was all.

The old man's face split in a smile then and he broke into his own tongue, speaking so fast that the men listening could have easily been convinced it was all a single long word. He smiled again. "Fight tribes, shu-yung," he said with some finality. Turning to his companions he spoke again, and Shokan was almost certain he heard the word *Yankura*.

A man detached himself from the others and ran easily up the slope, causing the men of Wa much envy.

"Yankura?" Shokan said. "Yankura?"

"Yan-khuro," the old man enunciated slowly, as though he corrected a child.

"Yan-khura. Yul-khuro, yan yul. Shu-yung," he said, and then, as if for good measure, "fight."

Shokan nodded and smiled. Am I agreeing? he wondered, and if so, to what?

Pointing at Shokan's horse with that same quick motion, the old man spoke in his tongue again, then shook his head. Holding his hands together as though he held a bowl, he made a drinking motion and then pointed at the horse, his face suddenly sad.

"Sire," Shokan's guard said quietly, "above us."

A small army of fur-clad mountain dwellers descended the slope, many down the stairway but as many walking directly down the steel hard snow without losing their footing. Shokan realized he stared openmouthed, but then it was a wonder indeed.

"What will happen now?" Shokan heard someone say. He gave a short laugh.

"I don't know." Despite a lifetime's training in suspicion, the lord somehow knew these people meant them no harm. "I don't know," he said again.

The mountain people passed by Shokan with barely a nod and a half smile, but the horses were another matter. These were objects of great admiration. Shokan was afraid the numbers of people milling around would spook the animals, but it quickly became obvious that the mountain dwellers were well versed in the handling of animals and undoubtedly horses, too.

The old man came a few paces closer to be heard above the noise of his people. He spoke a few words in his own tongue and then pointed at Shokan's horse. "No fight," he said quietly. Then pointing at Shokan's saddle bags and assorted gear. "Shuyunal." He gestured to his people. "Shuyun." Then he pointed up the pass and gave his odd single nod.

Shokan copied the gesture, then turned to his guard. "Find the boy. Have him tell everyone to offer no resistance to these people. We will leave them the horses and they will assist us over the pass . . . I think."

Shokan turned back to the old man, but he had turned and was trudging slowly up the stairway.

"Shuyun," a voice said beside him. Shokan turned to look at a beardless, smiling child. Tapping his chest, the child smiled again. "Shuyun," he said.

"Ah," the lord said. This is Shuyun? But then he realized the same word was being repeated up and down the line. Two others were fitting the pole to Shokan's armor box and lifting it easily to their shoulders although the lord knew it contained suits of both heavy and light armor as well as other arms and assorted pieces of gear for repairs.

The smiling child beside him began to collect the lord's belongings, and a guard quickly moved to intervene.

"No," the young lord said. "I will allow it." He began to roll his own bedding, though rather clumsily.

"Shuyun," he heard someone say down the line, and then again and again as though it were a chant.

To Shokan's surprise the mountain people led his party back down the gulley, making steps for the lowlanders as they went. He feared that there was a great misunderstanding and the mountain people were returning the lowlanders to the valley they had escaped, but he decided to wait a bit and see what would happen.

As the party came out from the shade of the great stone peak, the sun hit them and Shonto saw signs being made to Botahara by his men. They smile now, the lord thought, but in only a few hours the snow will soften and then the dread will return. They had seen what happened as the softening snow began to lose its hold, seen it come thundering down in great, white waves.

Looking over his shoulder, Shokan could still see the horses—surrounded by admirers. He hoped they were not to suffer the same fate at the hands of these people that they were about to at the hands of their owners. His foot slipped, but he recovered quickly. This was no place to be looking about or admiring the scenery. The footing was treacherous and would be until the sun had done its work.

The great coastal plain appeared around a corner, stretching off to the sea lost in a mist. The lowlands seemed green and warm and welcoming from this height and Shokan felt an urge to return. But there was no returning. Imperial Guards would be waiting below and had no doubt taken possession of the Shonto fief. There was only the mountains and whatever lay on the other side, if he were fortunate enough to see the western slopes.

Unlike his retainers Shokan carried no weight but his sword, and even so he did not go as lightly as the mountain people who bore the heaviest burdens. The lord had watched with fascination as the mountain people made up their loads, rigging these to be carried by a single strap across the forehead. The smallest mountain dweller bore twice what the largest lowlanders could carry, and with ease. Altitude was said to rob a man of his breath and Shokan did not doubt it now.

Before the sun was high they had come down around the peak to the south and here they dug down through the snow bank of the trench that formed on either side of the gulley, leaving a wide gap between the snow and the rock. Water ran in the bottom of the trench now and water skins were filled. A brief but slippery scramble took them up to a ledge as wide as a man was tall. The sun had melted whatever snow had lain here and the rock was dry and almost warm to the touch.

There was no talk. The mountain people seemed little inclined to chat as they went, and the lowlanders needed every bit of breath just to keep the pace. The height may have had something to do with this silence, for though the ledge only sloped up slightly the floor of the gulley widened and sloped away so that they were higher with each step. The lowlanders crowded the rock wall and tried to keep their gaze fixed ahead, which meant all but a few missed an astonishing vista.

The ledge narrowed here and there, enough to make the passage of certain sections a test of nerve. Shokan knew that Shonto guards would go into battle, no matter what the odds, without hesitation, but heights were a different matter. Slipping off a ledge was hardly an honorable end. Of course, none wished to be seen as cowardly before their fellows or the son of their liege-lord, so much effort went into disguising fears. Still, Shokan was sure that he had seen men famed for their prowess on the battlefield traverse the more difficult sections with far less confidence than some of their younger and less fearsome companions. It almost made him smile.

Where the ledge narrowed to nothing, wooden walkways appeared to bridge the gaps and these were constructed in so flimsy a manner that all the lowlanders said a prayer for the protection of their souls before crossing.

Shokan wondered how they bore the weight of snow or if they were recon-structed each spring. So poorly engineered did these walkways appear, the fact that they had no railings went almost unnoticed. To everyone's surprise they did not collapse.

By late afternoon the long snake of humanity had wound its way around to the south, and the ledge ended in a saddle between two peaks. They began to descend again, at first on soft snow and then, as they came into the shadow of the southern peak, on hardened crust.

Steps were cut again and the party slowed accordingly. The valley wid-ened and the west-moving sun found its way down to them again, making the snow heavy. In compensation, trees began to appear with greater and greater frequency, raising hopes for fires that evening.

A stream appeared out of nowhere and wound its way down the valley. Looking into the running water, Shokan could see rocks and earth and real-ized the depth of snow was much less than he had expected.

Suddenly the mountain people came to a halt on a small bench and with smiles and nods and gestures made it clear that this was as far as they would go that day. As camp was made, Shokan tried to estimate numbers. His retainers numbered thirty-three hundred, remarkable when one considered the losses they had suffered to the snow slides. There were easily that num-ber of mountain people, whom his own men had begun to call "dwellers" or even "the Shuyuns" which they thought funny. Close to eight thousand people.

Shokan hoped he would be able to describe this to his father one day. Eight thousand people over the most impossible terrain and they had covered at least twelve rih, maybe more. It was astonishing—it was more than as-tonishing; it was impossible!

The dwellers surprised the lowlanders again by starting the tiniest twig fires to brew cha and do some meager cooking. These they fed constantly with dried grasses and moss and dead needles from trees. They had reacted with horror when the Shonto men had begun to cut down trees for proper fires and Shokan had quickly ordered this stopped.

The lord had to admit that despite the fact that a terrible war was perhaps already under way across the mountains he found his own situation fascinat-ing. Almost nothing was known about these people, and here they were, chatting away cheerfully beside him.

There was so little room in the encampment that everyone was in the closest proximity. Shonto's men had, naturally, kept a suitable distance from their lord so that he might have a semblance of privacy, and this area had quickly been filled with the dwellers, who did not seem to have much concern for rank unless one were a wizened old man in rather bedraggled furs.

Shokan's guards were not terribly comfortable with this, but the lord reasoned that they were entirely at the mercy of these people who could easily have murdered him before now if that was their intention. The lord resolved not to worry though it was obvious that his guard could not reach the same resolution, for they watched the dwellers near their lord and exchanged the darkest looks.

Using his hands and an art for pantomime that would have given Lady Nishima cause for pride, Shokan tried to discover the words for common things—fire, trail, food, drink. It was more difficult than he might have expected and caused much laughter.

The greatest reaction came when the lord tried to learn the words for man and woman. He was so obviously surprised at discovering the boy who carried his belongings was in fact a young woman that he thought the laughter would never stop. And the poor woman, it seemed, would be teased forever, but she took it well enough and didn't seem to hold him responsible for his own ignorance.

Darkness came with a suddenness that was almost startling. Despite attempts to stay awake and pry as many words as possible from his fireside companions, Shokan fell asleep. The last thing he heard was the dwellers singing softly in high, thin voices—a sound both eerie and oddly comforting.

It was much later, in the middle of the night, that Shokan awoke with a start. He took a moment to sort out his memory of the evening from his dream and then convinced himself what had startled him to consciousness had been part of a dream, nothing more. Laying back down, the lord tried to banish the feeling he was left with, but with little success. In his dream the dwellers' song had been a Botahist chant, translated into the mountain tongue and modified to suit the dwellers' ideas of music. It was strangely disturbing to him and he lay awake for some time, unable to shake the emotions the dream had evoked—unable to shiver away the feeling of cold.

Morning arrived long before the light. They were on the west side of a mountain now and the sun would not find them until past midday. Shokan had begun to believe that the dwellers were people of infinite patience, but as preparations were made to set out this was proven wrong. "Ketah," he learned, was the word for *hurry*. If *Shuyun* had been the refrain of the previous day, *ketah* had taken its place. The highly trained fighters of the Shonto guard were bullied and badgered and hurried until Shokan feared there would be an incident, but frayed tempers were kept in check and in remarkable time the company was on the move again.

Shokan took his place behind Quinta-la, the woman he had caused so much embarrassment the night before. A small scene with his guards had ensued when Shokan insisted on carrying some of his own belongings, but he had prevailed and now carried a load, dweller style, which he was certain would soon disconnect his neck from his shoulders. Before him walked a much smaller woman carrying three times his own load; her step was light and sure. It made him smile.

If Nishi-sum had been able to bear three times as much as he, there would have been nothing to do but throw himself on his sword—a warrior had a certain pride. But the fact that this child could carry more than he could ever hope to bear caused him nothing but amusement and delight.

I have been transported to a strange world, he thought, like the stories read to me as a child.

The work of carrying a load and matching the pace of his guides soon warmed Shokan and hunger replaced the feeling of cold, for they had started out having taken neither drink nor food. There was no indication that the dwellers planned to stop for a morning meal and inns seemed sadly few.

The lord wondered idly if his retainers suffered the soreness of leg that he felt. It was obvious that Quinta-la knew no such discomfort. And this made him smile also.

There was perhaps one thing that saved the lowlanders that morning—they were taller than the mountain people, so the steps that were cut in the hard snow seemed quite close together to them. Even this small step down soon had thighs burning from the effort for every step down meant taking the extra weight of the carried load. Fatigue caused a few slips, but none of these became disasters.

By noon the leaders of the party had reached the snow line and soon only the deepest shadows still sheltered patches of white—the oddest effect; white shadows. The ground, however, was wet from days of snow-melt and this offered its own hazards to footing. Sometime after midday the sun worked its way down among the peaks, warming the walkers and illuminating the view. Shokan was impressed with the size of the valley—broad and long and green. Still-frozen lakes like pieces of jade strung together on a bubbling stream lay in the valley bottom. As the party made its way down, the trees grew larger and less twisted. The scent of pine on the breeze was strong.

The way became a road of rock suddenly, wide slabs of stone set as though they had once been a perfect avenue but shifted by frost and time and neglect. Shokan pointed at this and made the gesture that he believed meant a question, but all he received in reply was a string of unknown sounds and a smile. He looked at his guard captain who had come up beside him.

The captain shrugged. "It is either a giant's road or a natural formation, Sire, and I must admit I prefer neither explanation over the other."

And this delighted the lord also—he realized he preferred it to be a mystery. They walked on with ease along this broad avenue.

What the lord had believed was mist ahead he was becoming convinced was actually smoke. Gaining the attention of Quinta-la, he pointed ahead. She spoke one of the dozen words Shokan knew—the one he believed meant fire.

"Well, yes," he said, "but does that fire signify anything? Food, perhaps?"

The young woman broke into her childlike smile and rattled on in her own tongue, gesturing off at the distance as she did so.

"Ah, I suspected as much," Shokan said, as though he had understood every word. "Will there be baths at this inn as well as fine meals?"

Quinta-la answered without a second's hesitation.

They carried on this preposterous conversation for some time, talking in turn, as though there were perfect communication. Both laughing and gesturing like children.

Shokan did not see the faces of his men nearby, or he chose to ignore them, but they kept glancing at him as though he had taken leave of his senses. Only the guard captain found the exchange amusing, and he was careful not to show he was listening.

The inn turned out to be a small village, though anyone from the Empire would have had a different image in mind if given the word village as a description. It sat upon what amounted to a hill on the north side of the valley and was almost one rambling building made of a gray-white stone and roofed with a simple dark tile. Stone walkways and walls connected all the various wings and alleys, and courtyards filled in the spaces that were left.

Shokan could not guess how many people lived in this place, but shutters opened and smiling faces appeared at windows to watch the arrival of the lowlanders. It was almost as if it happened all the time.

Thirty-eight

When faced with an overwhelming force there is only one possible response: limit your opponent's ability to bring such power to bear. Make them place pieces that will hamper their own attack and you will have enlisted their pieces in your own defense. Position becomes the essence of survival, the only hope for winning.

Writings of the
Gii Master Soto

SHUYUN RODE ALONG the rise in the late afternoon. The shadows of the plum trees stretched across the ground, twisted into impossibly elongated shapes. The blossoms had not yet begun to fall, but there was a dusting of white on the ground—a sign of what was to come.

To the monk's right lay the sea that had been created by Lord Taiki's dam; its surface rippled like the scales of a dragon. It was impressive in its size. Shuyun stood in his stirrups for a better view. To the east he could not see the shore that lay somewhere beyond the old canal banks, but then there had been extensive areas of marsh there—lands that resisted draining.

If not for the odd tree growing out of its surface and the top of a meandering stone wall, it would have appeared a natural lake—one that had known these shores for a thousand years, not mere days. Too new for dragons to have taken up residence, Shuyun thought. But even so it seemed a likely dragon pond. Crows screamed over the bloated form of a dead horse lying half submerged in the middle of the sea—a result of the Khan's attempt to march his army through the waters.

In many places, the water would only be inches deep, but the soil underneath was so soft it would turn to impassible mud with the least agitation. Extricating horses and men had taken an afternoon, and more animals than the one Shuyun could see had broken legs.

So the Khan had done as was expected, skirted the sea to the west through the hills. As Shuyun topped a slight rise he could see, in the distance, the van of the barbarian army making its camp for the night. The gold banners of the great Khan himself fluttered in the Plum Blossom Wind. Shuyun often wondered about this mysterious barbarian, wondered what Hitara could have told him of this man if Shuyun had ever caught up with the monk in the streets of Rhojo-ma. Shuyun shook his head—Brother Hitara was himself a great mystery.

The men the monk could see were only the tip of the army of the desert. The largest part of the Khan's force would be spending the night on the road that wound through the hills. It would not be a comfortable night despite clear skies and the promise of warm breezes. Lord Shonto's archers controlled much of the forest that bordered the road and even in the dark an army of one hundred thousand would be an easy target. There would be no fires for the barbarian warriors that night nor much rest either.

Shuyun's guard whispered among themselves, and the monk realized they thought he came too close to the army of the desert. He stopped for a last look at the scene, offering a prayer to Botahara to protect the souls of the men who would soon be lost here.

A soft zephyr brought the scent of plum blossoms to the monk and the sigh of wind in the trees. The sounds and the perfume reminded him of Lady Nishima, and he felt his memory stir. With an effort he forced his mind back to the present.

Much of Lord Shonto's plan had resulted from an observation Shuyun had made over cha—a quote from the gii master Soto—and Shuyun felt the weight of that.

A council had been called to decide how best to take advantage of the change in geography they had initiated. The argument had gone thus: the barbarian force was virtually limitless; to pass the sea that had been created by the new dam the army would have to march to the west through forested hills; the way through the hills was narrow and winding; if barbarian patrols discovered an ambush in the hills the Khan could muster unlimited numbers of men to destroy it; if the barbarian patrols simply disappeared in the hills, the Khan's response would again be to send in large forces; a serious defense of the road through the hills was possible but the result inevitable, and the cost in lives would be great. Therefore, what was the purpose of the exercise?

The resulting decisions were largely dependent on timing for their success, timing and several tenets of the gii board. Once a player is certain he perceives his opponent's plan, does he continue to search for other threats?

Shuyun turned his horse around. The sun would make its daily plunge into the mountains soon, and he had several rih to ride to the boat Shonto was using as his command position. The plan was set, the forces had been committed days ago. There was nothing to do but wait.

A single encounter with a barbarian patrol in the darkness would put the entire exercise at risk. Fortunately, the softness of the ground allowed horses to pass in relative silence and barbarian patrols were either few or concentrated elsewhere.

Jaku worried that they would not arrive at the canal with enough men to perform the task entrusted to them— it would be easy to lose half the company in such darkness. Even recent breaks in the cloud cover which had begun to provide some starlight did nothing to relieve the Guard Commander's growing pessimism. To his right Jaku could make out Lord Komawara riding easily, setting the pace. Perhaps it was this that soured the general's mood—command of the company had been given to Komawara Samyamu, not Jaku Katta.

Even in this low light Jaku could see they were skirting the northern edge of the small sea that had been created—putting them uncomfortably in barbarian controlled lands. The Khan's army was camped on the road through the hills where they awaited morning. When the sun rose, the barbarian army would hurl their massive numbers against the makeshift defenses around the newly built dam. It was the prayer of the men of Wa that the Khan believed he knew his enemy's intentions and saw no traps nor surprises.

The plan, as it had developed, was simple. A false ambush had been set on the road through the hills and this had been discovered by a barbarian patrol. A significant skirmish ensued, resulting in the ambush failing, though at some loss to both sides. A spirited defense of the road through the hills had then been staged by Shonto's forces, led by General Hojo. Two days it had taken the barbarian army to force its way through to within striking distance of the dam. And now almost the entire barbarian army was stretched along the single narrow road, unable to move quickly either forward or back.

The supply train for that army, however, was borne by rafts moored against the canal bank to the north of the sea, waiting for the army to open the canal. Of course, the barbarian chieftains had not been foolish enough to leave the supply train untended—five thousand barbarian warriors stood guard—but it was perhaps the smallest guard such a valuable objective would ever have.

Shonto had gambled, leaving Komawara and Jaku hidden north of the lake with a force of eighteen hundred men, hoping they would not be discovered, hoping the barbarians would do exactly what they had done with their supply train.

Komawara's force had waited in utter silence for several days until a single rider had come from General Hojo bearing the orders to attack. The general had fought a wily battle on the road through the hills, offering enough resistance to convince the barbarian it was a true defense but keeping losses to a minimum. And now the barbarian army was strung out along a twelve rih road with their command virtually isolated at the southern end. A small force under the command of Rohku Saicha would fall upon the northern end of the barbarian force at dawn, their objective to cut off all assistance to the supply rafts.

Jaku admired the plan and had made some suggestions himself though it had been Shonto who had outlined the original idea to his staff. No one could say that the Shonto were timid! It was a bold plan in conception and required execution in the same manner. So why put this bumbling child in charge of the most crucial element? Jaku worked to control the anger caused by this slight. The coming fight would require absolute focus.

They skirted the perimeter of a wood now, staying on the edge of the shadow, giving the company as much camouflage as possible while providing enough light to find the way. Earlier a soft rain had fallen and found its way under Jaku's armor—just enough water to make him cold and uncomfortable—and the light breeze was not helping matters. The general kept working his left arm as he rode, keeping it limber and warm, knowing that being wet coupled with a cool breeze could slow his muscles considerably. He was surprised others did not do the same.

Lord Komawara pulled up his mount to be sure the entire company was collected and then sent two riders ahead. An open meadow about half a rih across stretched out before them. Low walls of stone divided the area with a pattern of erratic dark lines, creating a hundred fields, irregular in both shape and size.

The two riders crossed the open area, losing shape as they went until they became a single, black shadow moving over the starlit field. No one spoke while waiting, but the sounds of horses shifting and rolling bits broke the stillness. One of Jaku's guards dismounted to tighten his girth—the thud of a knee against a belly and a sharp exhalation of breath.

The black shape of the two riders appeared again, returning, moving over the dark landscape that played tricks on the eyes. The black shape divided and became two riders who approached Komawara and spoke so quietly that Jaku could not hear the words.

The young lord nodded and then turned to Jaku. "We move, General," Komawara whispered. "Please signal your guards."

Beyond the field lay the last hill before the canal. A stand of ginkyo coming into leaf whispered with the sound of wind among the branches. The plan was already agreed to, though men would be sent out to survey the barbarian position to be sure it had not substantially altered. They came into the shadow of the hill and Komawara dismounted, crouching down on his heels without word or signal. His own men followed this example and after hesitating, Jaku did the same, his guards copying their commander.

In name they were Imperial Guards, but it was to Jaku Katta they owed their allegiance. Rumors that Jaku defied the Emperor to be on the canal with Shonto or that their commander was no longer in favor at court meant little to them. Without question, they would follow Jaku into battle and lay down their lives for him. Jaku Katta was the great warrior of his time and to fight at his side meant more to these men than the favor of a thousand Emperors. None of them doubted that after tonight Lord Komawara would defer command of any future raids to General Jaku. He would see the Black Tiger in his true element.

Komawara signaled and eight men rode off into the night.

As the sound of horses moving over soft ground died, the company fell silent. The voice of the breeze in the ginkyo sounded like a complex form of music, varying its tempo, falling to whispers, then rising to crescendos, the pitch and timbre altering with a subtlety no instrument would ever duplicate. One could listen for hours and never hear the same pattern repeated.

Having made himself aware of what constellations rose and set closest to sunrise, Jaku watched the stars against the horizon. The rotation of the heavens seemed to have slowed that evening, for the stars appeared to hang utterly still with only the blowing clouds giving an illusion of motion.

The riders began to reappear in pairs, whispering with Komawara as soon as they arrived. Jaku desperately wanted to know what was being said and felt that as a general of some reputation he should be kept informed, but he was certainly too proud to ask.

The star Jaku had picked as the signal to move touched the earth at a distant point, and the general stopped himself as he started to rise and signal his men. Komawara made no indication of being ready to move. The last riders arrived just as Jaku was losing patience. Komawara rose to talk with these men, nodding and asking the occasional question.

He turned and signaled to Jaku who did not respond well to being treated like a retainer whether this country boy was a peer of the Empire or not. As a professional soldier Jaku knew that a battle was no place to discuss such things, so he crossed to where Komawara stood, holding his face-mask open.

"The barbarian defenses are unchanged, General Jaku." Komawara said, his voice far calmer than the guardsman expected. "There is movement in the barbarian camp, but I am prepared to follow the plan as we discussed it: surprise appears to still ride in our company." Komawara smiled. "The novelty of limitless supplies of firewood does not seem to have worn off—there are more than enough fires for our needs. Is your company ready, General?"

Jaku nodded.

Komawara clamped his face-mask closed and tightened the cord on his helmet. Riders mounted horses and the company split into two: Jaku leading his guards north and Komawara turning south. A hint of gray appeared over the ginkyo wood as the men of Wa rode off.

Komawara kept his horse at a canter, fighting a strong desire to race ahead—Shuyun would be pleased to learn that he was gaining patience. Eighteen hundred men attacking five thousand was not much to the lord's liking, but he knew that there were several factors in their favor. The men guarding the supply rafts were cut off from the body of the barbarian army and in unfamiliar lands, which must weigh upon them to some degree. The hope was that a surprise raid at dawn would disguise the number of attackers and perhaps send the barbarians into a panic. Even if they recovered from this fairly quickly, much damage would already be done.

They skirted the wood, keeping in its shadow. Komawara glanced up at the sky with concern. Darkness would begin to draw back soon—not too soon he hoped or the impact of their attack would be lost. They began to round the southern end of the hill then, and the lord increased his pace slightly without meaning to. In a moment they would be in sight of the barbarian position. Komawara loosened his sword in its sheath.

Another tenth of a rih. There was gray in the sky now, and Komawara could make out objects at some distance if not in detail. As they passed a large willow, the fires of the barbarian encampment appeared suddenly. Drawing his sword with some care for its edge, Komawara spurred his horse into a canter.

It was only a matter of time now. Sentries would certainly hear them even if they had been staring at a fire and ruined their night sight.

Even as this thought passed through the lord's mind, a shout sounded in the camp and was quickly taken up by others. Komawara heard his voice screaming, as bloodcurdling as any dream he'd had of barbarians attacking, and his company joined in the cry, trying to make nine hundred sound like thousands.

Aiming for the southern end of the barbarian position, the lord could see men milling around, though what they did was not discernible. Few will be armored, he found himself thinking. His company began to split as the bowmen who would stay outside the camp and send their arrows into the enemy ahead of Komawara's attack moved left. A third group would try to fire or otherwise destroy the supply rafts.

Although there was some attempt at a low wall of logs and dirt on the perimeter of the barbarian position, it was sparsely manned and Lord Komawara's mount cleared this as though not carrying a rider in full armor.

His personal guard had come abreast of him now, determined not to let their lord be the first to throw himself against the barbarian defense. The light was growing rapidly, and Komawara could see barbarian warriors struggling to push rafts away from the bank while others prepared to defend them. Almost none had made it to horse and those that had were without saddles.

Picking a swordsman on foot, Komawara spurred his horse to ride the man down. The barbarian stood his ground and raised his sword and just as Komawara was about to turn aside to spare his mount and engage the man, the barbarian's nerve broke and he turned and ran. A single stroke brought the man down and Komawara rode on.

It was the lord's intention to push into the barbarian camp until resistance stopped them, creating as much panic as possible among the greatest numbers. If the gods smiled on them, the separate attacks on the encampment would roll the ends of the barbarian position up before them until they met in the middle, sending the panicked tribesmen running toward the cover of the ginkyo wood.

An arrow lodged in the lacing of Komawara's shoulder piece and he found himself hoping it was not from his own men. Although some stood and fought, the raid was having its desired effect—many more were running, abandoning the rafts as they headed away from the river, nonswimmers to a man.

Whistling-arrows were falling among the barbarians ahead of Komawara now, adding their eerie screams to the din. A half-dressed rider made for the lord suddenly, sword and helmet glinting in the dim light. The darkness on the man's hand and arm turned to red as he came closer.

They clashed with an impact that shocked the lord, but his larger horse sent the other staggering. The barbarian's blade had severed Komawara's reins, but he had been born in Seh and his horse responded to pressure from his knees as quickly as to its bit. Before the other could collect his horse under him, Komawara struck, aiming at the man's wrist and then watching the horror on the barbarian's face as he realized this was a feint. The sword Toshaki had given him cut true to its reputation and severed the man's leg above the knee, the point cutting into the horse's side. The man's mount jumped sideways and threw him half off, so that he clung to the mane. It was an ugly stroke, aimed only to maim, for Komawara would not risk ruining his edge on the man's helmet. The barbarian fell under the hooves of his own horse and the lord of Seh passed by toward another, a foot-soldier with a lance. One of the Hajiwara men took this man before Komawara had time to raise his sword.

Fighting went on everywhere around him, but the lord found himself, for the moment, unopposed. He stood up in his stirrups, surveying the scene. Rafts burned behind him and on others he could see the supplies going into the water. It was a rout of some proportion, he realized with satisfaction.

Clouds of smoke billowed up to the north and he thought he could see black-armored riders in the melee ahead.

Quickly collecting the riders around him, Komawara threw himself against the barbarians again. Daylight was full when he realized that beyond the knot of barbarian warriors before them Imperial Guards did their work.

Behind his face-mask, Jaku Katta was grinning broadly when Lord Komawara appeared before him, the stump of an arrow in his shoulder piece. The two commanders pulled up their mounts in the midst of chaos. A riderless horse galloped between them and disappeared into the melee. Resistance had been broken.

Komawara waved his sword toward the base of the hill behind which they had hidden that morning. "They will collect their forces there," he shouted over the noise. "The barbarians will soon realize how few we are. Gather every man you can and we'll carry the fight to them once more." He gestured now to the rafts that his men swarmed over. The barbarians had managed to cut loose more rafts than he had hoped and these floated slowly in the current. Others had simply been abandoned at their moorings and not yet dealt with by his men. "We need more time to complete this."

A shout went up then and Komawara realized it came from the barbarians gathering under the ginkyos.

"There, Sire." One of Komawara's guard pointed to the south. A host of mounted barbarians were rounding the base of the hill, banners waving.

Komawara looked back at the work progressing on the rafts.

"It is a patrol only," Jaku said quickly, "no more than a hundred men." He pointed his sword toward the barbarians at the hill's base. "They hope it is reinforcements."

"Sound the call," Komawara shouted to his guard. He looked back at Jaku. "What have your losses been?"

Jaku waited as three long notes from a conch echoed across the field. "I cannot say, Lord Komawara."

The lord looked around the field, strewn with both barbarians and men of Wa. "Nor can I, General."

Men began to ride to Komawara's banner, and the lord wheeled his horse to face them. "Corporal, your company will join General Jaku in an assault on the forces gathering there." He pointed toward the men at the base of the hill.

"General Jaku . . ."A shout from the barbarian horse patrol, echoed by the men who were forming ranks, cut off the lord's words. The sound of galloping horses came to them. Komawara shouted as he turned his horse. "General Jaku, engage the barbarians who are reforming their ranks. My company will prevent these horsemen from joining them."

Komawara spurred his horse and waved his men to a gallop, aiming to intercept the horsemen before they reached the others. Banners waved and pipes shrilled. The shout from the men of Wa caused a visible hesitation on the part of the barbarians struggling to prepare an assault of their own. Most were without horse and armor, though they outnumbered the riders of Wa almost three times.

Jaku Katta quickly marshaled his own men and the company given him by Komawara and sounded the charge. It was his intention to drive directly through the center of the enemy, thwarting any attempts to fight in an organized fashion. If the barbarian formed solid ranks, the advantage of being on horseback would be seriously reduced.

The initial charge broke the front of the barbarian warriors, but in the ensuing fighting the tribesmen showed greater resolve and their superior numbers began to tell.

A sword blow to a foreleg brought Jaku's horse down and the kick boxer jumped clear. On his feet immediately, Jaku found himself surrounded by barbarians. He jumped over a stroke aimed at his leg by the same man who had taken down his horse and dispatched the man as he spun toward the attackers at his back. This display of skill caused a second of hesitation and Jaku used this to cut down two near-boys and jump clear of the circle.

Without men on all sides the fight would be different though Jaku was not sure how long he could maintain this situation. He parried a blow and kicked the man under the chin, engaging another as he did so, but each time a barbarian fell another took his place. An Imperial Guard on horseback was desperately cutting his way toward his commander, but just when Jaku was convinced he would win through, an arrow took the guard through the face-mask. He slumped over the neck of his mount which bolted into the fray.

It is an honorable end, Jaku told himself, deserving of a song. Pressed on all sides again, Jaku knew he was fighting to stay alive from minute to minute. A rider in darkest blue drove his horse into the barbarian warriors at Jaku's back sending them sprawling, and before the barbarian could recover the Guard Commander vaulted onto the rider's horse. The two men fought their way toward a group of Imperial Guards on horseback, hard pressed on all sides.

Komawara spotted an officer and gestured to him as he continued to fight. A moment later the clear note of a conch lifted over the battle. It was the men of Wa who would retreat now.

Joining the Imperial Guards, Jaku grabbed the reins of a riderless horse and managed to calm it enough that he could mount, barely touching the ground as he moved from one horse to the other. The men of Wa began to fight their way free of the battle, one knot of riders joining another, then another until they gathered enough force to push toward clear ground.

Once free of the fighting, Komawara turned his mount to assess the situation. Most of the barbarians still fought on foot. In their midst a few riders swung their last sword strokes. An urge to attempt a rescue was swallowed down quickly—Komawara had an entire company to consider.

The men of Wa who destroyed the supply rafts had been caught by the barbarian assault and boarded rafts, pushing out into the canal where they tried to protect themselves from arrows while poling the rafts toward the dam. There is nothing to be done for them, Komawara realized. Their situation is probably better than ours.

Jaku stopped beside him. Komawara opened his face-mask and let it hang, conserving the energy it took to hold it. "We ride north and west, General. If we can make the hills, we may be able to rejoin the main army. Our work is done here." He pointed with his sword. Perhaps a third of the barbarian supply rafts had been fired or their cargo turned into the canal.

Jaku looked at Komawara, his gray eyes striking behind the black lacquered face-mask. It appeared he was about to speak, but Komawara nodded to him. "Gather your company, General. We must be far ahead when these barbarians recapture their horses."

Calling over an officer, Komawara turned and spoke to him. The conch sounded again and the banner of the Komawara House was raised aloft on a lance where it fluttered in the breeze.

"We must ride, General. Any wounded who cannot keep the pace are to be left behind without horse." The young lord wheeled his mount and set off at a slow canter. To the west the ginkyo wood was already alive with crows and blackbirds.

Thirty-nine

COLONEL JAKU TADAMOTO considered the idea of *fortune* as his sampan swept through the Imperial Capital. Fortune, both *good* and *ill*, seemed to be holding sway in his life just when he thought he had taken control of it. Were he a more devout Botahist, Tadamoto would never view his life in such terms. Rather than *fortune* he would believe in *karma*, and would think the sense that one was in control of one's life was merely part of the illusion. But he had not been a devout follower of the Perfect Master since his childhood, so he was beginning to believe in fortune, both good and ill.

The young guard officer pulled aside the curtain and contemplated the world beyond. The city lay silent in the darkness, almost peaceful—although, as acting Commander of the Imperial Guard, he knew that was without question an illusion.

He let the curtain fall back into place. It would be foolish to risk being seen; for all he knew Lady Fortune might not be smiling on him at that moment and some informer of the Emperor's, returning home after an evening of drink, might chance to see him. That would be ill fortune indeed.

One could never be sure of the favor of Lady Fortune. She was more fickle than any woman, more volatile than the Emperor. Tadamoto believed it unwise to rely on her.

Fortune had certainly favored Tadamoto that evening but, at the same time, it had been the worst possible fortune for the man he journeyed to meet. No, perhaps that was untrue. The guards who found the man could have reported their discovery through official channels and the Son of Heaven would have been informed. That would have been much worse.

As a retainer of Lord Shonto, this man was the object of an Imperial search—Shonto himself had defied Imperial orders and betrayed his duty as Governor of Seh. He was a declared rebel now, a general in charge of a growing and illegal army. All of the rebel lord's senior retainers had disappeared like phantoms before the Emperor's guard could reach them. Only one had been apprehended, and that was due to fortune only: misfortune. This unfortunate man had his river junk go aground on a shifting sand bar outside the capital. A boat bearing Imperial Guards had stopped to offer assistance and the response of the crew had raised suspicions. A subsequent search led to the man's discovery. Good fortune for Tadamoto, ill for Shonto's retainer.

Some important questions plagued the colonel; *did what appeared to be fortune have significance? Were there powers beyond that moved the pieces on the board to some end Tadamoto could not discern? If so, what was the meaning of this "discovery?" and what was Tadamoto's part to play?*

He pulled the curtain back and watched the city slipping past. If all was controlled by some unseen power, did it matter what choices he made? Did he, in fact, choose any of his actions?

"I waste my time," he whispered to the night. Who can know the truth of this? Perhaps there is no such thing as fortune but only coincidence. Either way I must blunder along not knowing, doing what my instincts tell me is correct, for now that the Empire is thrown into chaos the intellect is giving way to instinct.

Instinct had brought him here. Fortune or coincidence would dictate the results.

The sampan glided to a silent halt beside stone steps and boatmen stepped ashore to hold the craft in place. A man appeared at the top of the stair and whispered. One of Tadamoto's guards leaned close to the curtain. "The way is clear, Colonel."

Tadamoto moved quickly, coming ashore with a grace that would have seemed more appropriate to his famous brother. Light duty armor had been chosen by the colonel for this meeting, not because there was any foreseeable danger, but the helmet visor shaded his eyes well. Tadamoto's green eyes made him immediately recognizable and there were times when that was not desirable. Even on a night this dark he was not willing to take chances.

He crossed the stone quay to a small guard house. The doors opened immediately and Tadamoto found himself facing a bowing officer of the Imperial Guard.

"Captain." Tadamoto nodded. "You have spoken with him?"

"Only in an attempt to establish his identity beyond doubt, Colonel." He paused, then almost smiled. "He asked for a chair. We have treated him according to your orders."

"How many men know of our guest?"

Doing a quick mental tally, the captain, a man twenty years older than his acting commander, answered formally. "Nine, Colonel Jaku. We have kept him well hidden."

"None of these men can leave this compound. Keep them to themselves until I order otherwise. I will speak with him."

They climbed a set of stone stairs and walked down a dimly lit hallway. Outside a heavy wooden door stood two guards. They bowed when the officers approached and at a signal from the captain one unbolted the door.

As he stepped into the room, Tadamoto held up a hand to the captain. "I will speak with him alone, Captain, thank you."

A single lamp set on a low table illuminated the tiny room. The floor was covered with grass mats and in one corner bedding had been neatly folded. An expensive hat sitting on the table cast a shadow like a boat under sail. On a wooden arm chair sat a large man, well dressed, calmly regarding his visitor and making no effort to rise.

Tadamoto nodded. "Tanaka."

The man shrugged and opened his hands as if to say, *I would deny it, but what good would that do me!*

Tadamoto continued to regard the man. He realized that if he sat he would be staring up at his prisoner, as though he sat at the foot of a throne. Sly old fox, he thought. Stepping back, he leaned against the door frame. The older man did not seem to be made at all uncomfortable by this examination; he sat calmly returning the colonel's gaze. The younger man reached up and removed his helmet, tucking it under his arm.

"You are a merchant," Tadamoto said suddenly, "so I have come to offer an exchange."

The man nodded. "You have captured my attention, Colonel Jaku."

The green eyes, Tadamoto thought. The guardsman nodded. "I wish to be told everything you know about the barbarians; this Khan and his army."

"You spoke of an exchange, Colonel?" Tanaka said dryly.

"The Emperor does not know you have been found. I will not hide you from the Son of Heaven, for it would mean my life if your capture became known. When I report your capture, the Son of Heaven will want to know everything about your lord's intentions and his holdings. You will be required to divulge these things. In return I will protect you—the Emperor, as you know, is neither patient nor refined in his methods. If you fall into the Emperor's hands, I think you will answer all these questions even if you don't wish to, and the process will be far less pleasant than the one I propose."

Tanaka nodded sadly. "You ask me to betray my liege-lord and his House with an impressive casualness, Colonel."

Tadamoto walked across the bare room, looking down at the floor. When he returned to the door, he put his back against the jamb again. "Let us be open, Tanaka." He paused, choosing his words. "Civil war has all but been declared. If the Yamaku win this war, your lord's holdings will mean nothing—there will be no Shonto to inherit them. If Lord Shonto wins, all of his holdings will be returned to him. Either way your betrayal will hardly matter. If I can give this information to my Emperor, he will be satisfied, at least for a while, and it is unlikely he will want to question you himself." Tadamoto kicked at the floor. "For myself, I need to know what transpires in the north. This Khan, does he truly pursue Lord Shonto down the great canal?"

Tanaka regarded the young man for a moment. "And if you are told that he does and that the Empire is threatened and you also learn, if you don't already know, that the Emperor has played a part in bringing this about, what will you do with this knowledge, Colonel Tadamoto?"

Tadamoto stopped kicking at the mat and looked up. The merchant was obviously less afraid than Tadamoto had anticipated. He is used to trading and knowing the value of what he offers, the guardsman thought. And then Tadamoto realized the truth. Tanaka believed Tadamoto kept him hidden so that he could acquire the Shonto wealth for himself. "I am not certain. Be assured, however, that my loyalty is to my Emperor."

"That is why you have me hidden from his view and why you have offered me this exchange?"

Tadamoto looked away for a moment. "If this Khan comes to take the Throne, I must convince the Emperor to prepare for that war and forget this feud with the Shonto. But I must have proof."

"You have your own sources, I am sure. What do they tell you?"

"I ask this question of you, merchant, in fair exchange." And then he added, "I tell you in truth that I do not share my Emperor's hatred of your lord's House."

"Perhaps, Colonel, I should be the one offering the exchange." Tanaka leaned forward in his chair, putting his palms together. "My liege-lord cannot hope to defeat the barbarian without an army. You raise an army to defend the Yamaku against the Shonto, but the threat comes from beyond our borders. The man who controls the Imperial Army will decide if Wa stands or falls." Tanaka looked up at the younger man; it was an appeal. "As you are the man raising this force and the acting commander of the Emperor's Guard, you are the man most able to seize control of the forming army. Would you not rather have the histories say that Jaku Tadamoto saved the Empire than Jaku Tadamoto followed his Emperor, loyally, in Wa's destruction."

"Treason, in either act or word," Tadamoto said coolly, "is a serious crime in our Empire and I view it as such. You are aware of the penalty."

"Treason . . ." Tanaka said, ignoring the threat. "It was treason to pay gold to the barbarians to raid into our Empire, Colonel Jaku."

Tadamoto turned slowly, trying not to show any response to this last remark. Raising his hand to knock on the door, he said, "All of the Shonto holdings. I will have paper and brush brought to you. And I must know Shonto's intentions."

"I am only a vassal-merchant, Colonel, do you really believe I am party to the plans of Lord Shonto Motoru?"

"You have known him longer than anyone. He calls you sum—I know this."

Tanaka seemed to struggle for a moment before speaking. "You have a reputation as a historian, Colonel, so you are aware that the Throne of Wa has been within reach of the Shonto many times . . . yet they have always refused it. Imperial dynasties come and go, the Shonto have seen many. If one wishes, without doubt, to eliminate one's House, ascend the Dragon Throne. Every Imperial Family falls within a few generations."

Tadamoto raised his hand to knock again. "All of his holdings, to start with."

"I will need a table and another lamp."

Tadamoto nodded toward the table at Tanaka's feet.

Holding his hand up the older man said, "This high, and a second lamp."

Tadamoto rapped on the door which was immediately opened by the guard. The colonel stopped as he was about to step out. "If you will not assist me, merchant, I cannot help you."

Forty

DESPITE THE SEASON and weather, the entire situation seemed very familiar. Lord Komawara walked his horse through the forest in the hills west of the man-made sea. Unlike his time in the Jai Lung Hills, the day was warm and filled with the sounds and scents of spring.

War seemed of no concern to the animals of the hills. Birds sang their mating songs and hawks and falcons hunted without regard for the long line of warriors that snaked through the trees.

Thirteen hundred men had survived the attack on the barbarian supply rafts and the several skirmishes that followed. Rohku Saicha must have performed his task admirably, bottling up the enemy army on the road, for no barbarians came to the rescue, allowing Komawara and his force to escape. Pursuit by barbarian warriors from the supply rafts had been tentative at best; they were not willing to risk the rest of their supply train by leaving it undefended. Jaku and Komawara had easily beaten back these attempts and then had led their men into the hills.

Lord Shonto's archers had controlled the hills since the barbarian army had started down the road, and though many of the bowman were gone now the barbarians were still quite reluctant to venture far from their road.

From out of the foliage ahead one of Komawara's several guides appeared, trotting at the pace they never seemed to vary. The lord was sure these men could run like that all day without signs of strain. The man stopped, leaning on his bow, waiting for Komawara to approach. A huntsman by trade, he was typical of his type, tall, lean, and sinewy. There was an air of the forest creature about this man. Even now the lord realized that the guide had stopped where anyone but Komawara would find him hard to see among trees and bushes.

Bowing quickly the man almost whispered, "There is a glade with a stream and new spring grass less than a rih distant. It will be a good place to refresh the horses." Looking around with the air of a wary animal he went on. "There are signs of barbarian patrols coming into the forest ahead. They are small in number, however. If we see them, we will make them believe Lord Shonto's bowmen are still here in force." A smile flashed and was gone. "Tomorrow we will be through the hills, but the danger will be greater then, for a time. The barbarians control the lands immediately beyond the hills, now. We will need to have rested horses to travel quickly. If Botahara smiles upon us, we will be back with Lord Shonto's fleet in three days." The smile flashed again.

"What of Captain Rohku?" Komawara asked. "Is there no sign of him?"

The man looked down as he shook his head. "None yet, Sire, though there is no reason we should cross the captain's track. The hills," he waved at the trees, "spread over many rih and it is no doubt Captain Rohku's intention to avoid detection."

Komawara nodded. "Lead us to the glade, then. Our horses are in need."

They pressed on. Komawara called a retainer forward and sent him to check on the wounded—so many had been victims of their injuries since the retreat. A second man he sent down the column to inform Jaku Katta of their pending rest. The Guard Commander stayed close to his men and showed great concern for the injured. It gained him much respect and loyalty.

Despite the losses Komawara did not think they had spent lives unwisely in their raid on the supply rafts. It had been impossible to destroy the entire train with such a small force, for there had been many more rafts than Komawara had believed possible. Still, they had acquitted themselves well. Even Jaku Katta had paid him a compliment when the attack was over, not something Komawara had expected.

After Komawara's force had reached the relative security of the hills, he had listened with some surprise to the reports of the men who had destroyed rafts. Much that the rafts carried was not grown in the desert: grains, rice, corrapepper, dried fish. Many of these foods could have originated only on the islands of the southern barbarians, which unsettled Komawara. Despite the common pejorative, these two races had nothing in common. Komawara would have guessed them barely aware of each other's existence—two non-seafaring peoples separated by a wide ocean. Impressive what gold and the ships of pirates could obtain—if, indeed, it had been pirates. He remembered Lord Kintari.

The sound of running water mixed with the sound of the Plum Blossom Wind, wafting through the trees. The forest was more than half pine here, mixed with plane trees and slip maple. The scent of the trees was strong. Unfolding leaves waved in the soft breeze, dappling the sunlight where it touched the forest floor. The paper white of birch trees appeared and beyond them Komawara could see the sun green of spring grass. It was a bigger pasture than Komawara expected and spoke of itinerant herdsmen; there was likely a hut concealed nearby.

The huntsman stopped at the edge of the glade until he received a signal that the lord never heard. "It is secure here, Lord Komawara. There is grass like this on either side of the brook, both up and down stream. It will mean spreading your company out but there is pasture enough for each horse."

"The woods are free of barbarians, you are certain?"

The huntsman nodded.

"Then we will do as you suggest. The animals need to graze or they will never manage this last sprint you speak of." He turned and gave the command.

One of the Hajiwara men who had taken service with Komawara took his lord's horse and led it off to drink and feed. Komawara walked across soft grass to the stream and bent stiffly to drink and fill his water skin before the creek was muddied by horses. He jumped heavily to the other bank, feeling the weight of his armor as he landed.

Finding a fallen tree on the far side of the glade, Komawara sat and pulled his helmet off. He ran a hand through his hair, much of which had grown back since Shuyun's ministrations in the desert. Sweat and the weight of his helmet plastered it tightly to his brow and the lord suddenly longed for a bath.

The coolness of the air and the warmth of the sun were like the differing flavors of a complex wine, opposing but complementary. Slipping down to the ground, Komawara leaned back against the log, closing his eyes against the brightness of the sky.

He was not sure how long he rested like that, nor if he even slept for a second, but suddenly he was aware that the sun no longer warmed him. A cloud, Komawara thought, but then the sound of a man clearing his throat reached him. His eyes flicked open almost involuntarily.

"General Jaku."

The guardsman bowed. "Excuse me for interrupting you, Lord Komawara."

"Do not apologize, General." Komawara struggled into a more upright position. "I managed to fill my water skin before the hordes, General Jaku, please." He proffered the water to the guard.

Jaku nodded and accepted the water. Returning the skin to Komawara, the guardsman sat down on the log and followed the lord's example, pulling off his helmet. "Three days, I have been informed? Do you think Lord Shonto will have moved his fleet again?"

The lord pulled a burr off the lacing of his armor and rolled the spines gently between his forefinger and thumb. "It seems most likely, General. The barbarians move slowly, but Lord Shonto will not risk his army. It may be the Empire's only hope."

"It is sadly true," Jaku observed dryly. "Though the Emperor raises an army, it is impossible to predict what he will do with it—and I know the Emperor." Jaku produced a square of cotton and wiped his face and neck with it.

The same huntsman Komawara had spoken to earlier appeared out of the trees twenty paces off, looked around and then spotted the lord. Trotting over, he dropped to his knees and bowed so as not to stand above the seated peer. When he spoke, the man's voice quavered slightly.

"Sire, we have discovered . . . something of great concern." He gestured to the forest behind him, words failing him. "Close by."

Komawara glanced at Jaku, questions unspoken. Signaling to his guard, the lord waved the huntsman on and he and Jaku fell in behind. Walking through the spring woods filled with the sounds of birds Komawara felt suddenly cold. He did not know what had been found, but the huntsman's reaction was not reassuring.

As the tracker had said, it was not far. The perfume of the spring forest was replaced by a sudden stench and flies buzzed up, agitated by the presence of people. The huntsman stopped, saying nothing. At his feet lay a corpse, belly down, stripped naked, its head severed. Stubs of three broken arrows protruded from the throat and shoulder.

"There are more," the huntsman said, making a sign to Botahara.

"Who?" Komawara whispered.

Shrugging the huntsman stepped away, covering his mouth and nose. "Not barbarians, certainly."

Twenty feet away lay two men who had been felled and mutilated also. The grass and bushes nearby had been well trampled, perhaps by a struggle. A horse without saddle or bridle was found, its head twisted at an improbable angle.

Several of the huntsman's company could be seen searching the bush, stopping now and then as they discovered another corpse.

"Captain Rohku's company," Jaku said quietly to Komawara, "or some of it."

Komawara nodded. "No doubt you are correct. This man wore armor often." The lord pointed to familiar marks on the man's shoulders. He waved the huntsman over. "Hide men behind us. Be certain we are not pursued."

The huntsman nodded. "What shall we do for these?" He waved at the ground around him.

Komawara turned in a slow circle, examining the area. "Leave them to the forest."

"Sire," the man started to protest but was silenced by a cold stare.

"There will be many more like these before this war is over, and we will not be able to perform ceremonies for one in a thousand." He looked down. "May Botahara have mercy on their souls."

Forty-one

THOUGH HE WAITED to speak with the Emperor of all of Wa, Jaku Tadamoto had not yet decided what he would say to the Son of Heaven. Perhaps the glimpse he had caught of a woman leaving the wing of the Emperor's apartments had unsettled Tadamoto more than he realized, though he was not at all sure it had been Osha. The woman had appeared briefly down a long hall, her hair in an elaborate style, ornate robes of canary yellow—a color Osha despised and the Emperor loved. But she had moved with such ease. . . .

Tadamoto felt like he was drowning in deep sadness, unable to focus his will sufficiently to stroke to the surface. Things of the greatest import hardly drew his attention. What would be said and left unsaid in this audience with the Emperor was crucial, he knew, yet that knowledge did not seem to galvanize his energies. Despondency was what Tadamoto felt, and his famed intellect did not seem able to exert control over his other faculties.

Through the screens Tadamoto could hear the Emperor's voice as he spoke to some official. From where Tadamoto waited, he heard brief silences in which, presumably, the official spoke and this made Tadamoto wonder if he was equally quiet when addressing the Emperor. It was a strange thing to listen to, as though half of the dialogue was silence.

Tadamoto turned a scroll he carried, examining it carefully as though he would suddenly be able to assess its impact in the meeting to come. Would the Son of Heaven respond as the young officer hoped? If the Emperor's greed was caught by the information in the scroll, he might forget to ask when the Imperial Guard had found Lord Shonto's vassal-merchant—if the answer was not already known. Why have I played this foolish game with this merchant? Tadamoto asked himself.

The Emperor's voice had not responded to the silence now for several minutes, and Tadamoto made a last attempt to focus his will. A secretary appeared and bowed to the guard officer, saying nothing. Rising, Tadamoto followed the old man through a bare anteroom. Double screens opened onto a terrace tiled with small stones and shards of porcelain forming a lotus blossom pattern. Beyond was the view north across the Dragon Pond toward the Mountain of the Pure Spirit.

Kneeling before the screens, Tadamoto waited to be announced. It was done so quietly that the officer did not hear. The Emperor's mood must be dark.

At a signal, Tadamoto moved forward on his knees across grass mats that had been laid over the stones. On a small dais at one end of the terrace the Emperor sat under a silk awning. To his left the view stretched out toward the far mountains and to his right stood a small ornamental cherry, ancient despite its size and famous for the perfection of its shape. The Emperor tapped the tip of his sword on the edge of the dais, staring at neither view nor blossom—he scowled openly and his eyes were not focused on anything another could see.

Tadamoto touched his forehead to the mat.

"Be at your ease, Colonel," the Emperor said, irritation lodged in his tone like a thorn.

Tadamoto returned to a kneeling position feeling anything but at ease.

"I am told the raising of our army proceeds apace, Colonel." The Emperor gave a slight nod.

Tadamoto bowed in return. "The reports of Lord Shonto's force would indicate he has fewer than twenty-five thousand men, Sire. Our force will equal that very soon."

The Emperor nodded. He still tapped the dais with his sword. "Once Motoru reaches the inner provinces it is impossible to say who will join him. We must be prepared to face all manner of treachery, Colonel, or we will not even have the luxury of time to regret our mistakes."

"Recruitment continues, Emperor. I'm confident we will raise an army of adequate numbers."

"And no experience!" the Emperor shot back.

Tadamoto froze for a second. "We are training now, Sire," he said quietly. "At least our army will be no less battle ready than Shonto's."

Tadamoto pressed his eyes closed for an instant, then glanced out over the Dragon Pond and back to the mats in front of him.

The Emperor fixed the young scholar with a hard stare. "You have a scroll for me, I see."

Tadamoto nodded.

"Not more news of pending disaster, I trust?"

Tadamoto lifted the scroll with both hands. "A complete, detailed list of all of the Shonto House holdings and properties."

The Emperor stopped tapping the dais.

"We have taken the Shonto vassal-merchant into our custody," Tadamoto said evenly.

"Tanaka?" the Emperor said with more than a trace of disbelief.

Tadamoto gave a half bow, keeping his eyes cast down. Leaning forward he set the scroll on the edge of the dais though the Emperor almost snatched it from his hands.

Breaking the seal with a thumbnail, the Emperor unrolled the paper and held it up to the light so that it hid his reaction. When he appeared again, his face was creased with delight. "This rebel general was once a very wealthy lord." He waved a finger at the scroll. "Astonishing that his merchant could hide so much wealth!" He let the itemization fall back into his lap. "You are to be complimented, Tadamoto-sum. I will see that you are given," he paused to think, "a fortieth of the Shonto wealth as a reward. But what else has this merchant said? What of Shonto's plans?"

Tadamoto nodded, as though acknowledging the question though he was trying desperately to gather his thoughts. "I—I am honored by your generosity, Emperor." He bowed low. "It is difficult to be sure what Tanaka knows about his lord's intentions, Sire. I have spoken with him now on several occasions and I am not convinced Shonto has been as open with Tanaka as we had believed."

The Emperor set the scroll aside and reached for his sword. "Perhaps a less gentle method of inquiry would produce the results we require, Colonel."

"I . . . I hesitate to do so, Sire. I would rather gain his confidence and convince him with arguments." An idea. "After the war is over, Tanaka will have no liege-lord. He would make a valuable addition to your staff, Sire."

Tadamoto gestured toward the scroll. "Imagine what such a man could do to increase the Imperial fortunes."

The Emperor raised an eyebrow at this. "Is this possible? A Shonto retainer?"

"This list is an example, Sire—which, by the way, was done entirely from memory. Tanaka agreed to create this itemization after I had convinced him that such an act would not affect Lord Shonto, no matter what the outcome of the civil war. He is not a warrior, Sire. One can appeal to his intellect and see some result. It is also well known that he enjoys the trappings of wealth himself. Many a lord would be happy to live in this vassal-merchant's home. When there is no Shonto House," Tadamoto shrugged, "where will Tanaka's loyalty lie?"

The Emperor looked out toward the Mountain of Divine Inspiration, lost in thought. "If you can win his willing service, Tadamoto-sum, I will double your reward, and more. But we cannot let him hide behind this." The Emperor gestured to the scroll. "We desperately need to know what Motoru plans. Be certain this merchant is hiding nothing."

Tadamoto bowed. Wealth . . . Tadamoto thought, enormous wealth . . . on the eve of civil war. The irony threatened to make him laugh. "I will spare no effort, Sire, be assured."

The Emperor favored him with a controlled smile. "Is there more that I should hear, Tadamoto-sum, or will we stop now, while the gods smile upon us?"

Tadamoto hesitated for a second and saw the Emperor's face darken as he did so. "I have had reports from the north, Sire. Lord Shonto dammed the canal and flooded a large plain north of Fuimo. A barbarian force was certainly following close behind the men of Seh at that time."

The Emperor stared hard at Tadamoto for a moment and then rose suddenly, causing the younger man to flinch visibly. Crossing the terrace, the Emperor descended a set of stairs. When all but his head had descended out of sight, the Emperor turned and nodded toward Tadamoto to rise and follow.

Waiting on another terrace, a level below, the Emperor stared off to the north and when Tadamoto caught him he set off again, Tadamoto in his wake. They descended another flight of stairs which put them on the lawn that ran down to the edge of the Dragon Pond. The Emperor walked toward the eastern wall of the palace where a complex hedge-maze stood, planted generations past and renewed and altered over the centuries.

The Emperor stopped before the entrance to the maze, waving Tadamoto ahead with his sword. "Colonel."

Tadamoto stepped into the maze, not sure what was required of him, his mouth drying quickly. He walked down the path, the fall of the Emperor's step close behind. The maze branched both left and right almost immediately and the guardsman continued straight, not knowing if he should have chosen one of the other paths.

"Have you been through the puzzle before, Colonel?"

Tadamoto shook his head, but before he could speak the Emperor went on.

"It is a most ingenious maze. Unlike others of the type it does not give up its secret easily. In fact, few find their way to the center. To unexpectedly arrive back at the beginning is the common experience or at one of the several gates which lead out. Turn right, Colonel."

Tadamoto obeyed, walking slowly and fighting the urge to look back at the Emperor.

"From whom did you receive this information about the barbarian army, Colonel?"

"Spies working in the north, Sire."

"Ah. Stop where you are and look carefully around you."

Tadamoto did as he was told. The stone pathway was somewhat wider than a man was tall, bounded on both sides by high, dense foliage. There was a blind-end visible ahead and a branch-left perhaps six paces away. Turning further, Tadamoto found the Emperor watching him, all traces of his earlier lightness of spirit gone. Reaching right with his sword the Emperor thrust the tip of the scabbard into the hedge.

Looking at the spot the Emperor indicated, the guard realized that there was something out of place there and a more careful inspection revealed a low, impossibly narrow passage, well camouflaged.

"A gardener's secret," the Emperor said quietly. "You will have to push your way in."

Tadamoto parted the branches with care and bent low to enter. It was surprisingly dark in the passageway, the density of the growth admitting little light. Sounds of the Emperor parting the branches behind kept Tadamoto moving despite the tightness of the tunnel. Sunlight appeared ahead and the officer pushed through into another stone pathway running between the hedges.

"Turn left," the Emperor said before he had emerged from the passage.

Tadamoto set out again at the same pace and again the Emperor's footsteps followed. Another gardener's tunnel, and then left, then right and again right. They were at the center of the maze. The hedges formed a circle a dozen paces across and in the center of this lay a round, jade pool, flashes of gold and crimson sunfish like visions of flame in the depths of a mirror.

The Emperor sat on a stone bench carved with Imperial Dragons, his sword across his knees. Tadamoto hastened to kneel, the stones digging into his knees.

The Emperor stared into the green water of the quiet pool. "You see, Colonel Jaku, uncounted people have tried to unravel this puzzle but, in truth, only a few have ever managed to stand where you are now and look into the Jade Mirror. Ministers, princes, court ladies, great lords, famed generals . . . so many have failed. Yet the humble gardeners of the palace all have been here, often. They know how to go directly to the heart of the puzzle." The Emperor pointed the tip of his scabbard at the young officer. "It is the secret of all great men, Tadamoto-sum.

"If there is a barbarian army, I believe it is in league with Shonto or is of little consequence and Shonto draws it along behind him as an excuse to invade the inner provinces. This half-breed Khan cannot threaten the Empire of Wa with a ragtag army of hunters and herdboys. You have had your confidence in this matter shaken by your brother. This impairs your effectiveness as a counselor to the Emperor.

"Cut through to the heart of the matter, Colonel, so you can set it aside. We have war in sight—it gathers on the northern horizon like a winter storm. Your entire focus will be called for." The Emperor stood and walked to the opening in the hedge. "The place where you sit, Colonel is so difficult to reach most believe it impossible. Wander without focus for even a short time and you will find yourself on the outside. May the gods guide you, Colonel Jaku."

Forty-two

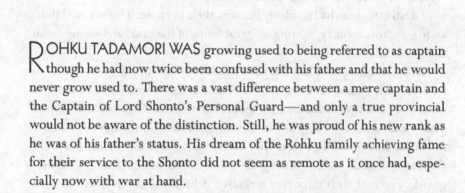

ROHKU TADAMORI WAS growing used to being referred to as captain though he had now twice been confused with his father and that he would never grow used to. There was a vast difference between a mere captain and the Captain of Lord Shonto's Personal Guard—and only a true provincial would not be aware of the distinction. Still, he was proud of his new rank as he was of his father's status. His dream of the Rohku family achieving fame for their service to the Shonto did not seem as remote as it once had, especially now with war at hand.

The young officer rode along the canal bank through a grove of flowering plum trees. The spring winds were just now starting to coax the petals of the plum blossoms free, carrying them aloft and scattering them across the green countryside. The wakes of the passing river boats disturbed the petals as they landed on the canal and the Plum Blossom Winds turned them into sails, stranding them on the western bank.

Behind Rohku Tadamori rode a small company and the young captain realized that he had achieved a certain level of recognition since he suddenly warranted a guard. He shook his head. Perhaps now that war was upon them, he would have a chance to prove himself in battle as his father had. A few days earlier Rohku Saicha had led an attack on the barbarians in the hills. Despite his recent recognition Tadamori was not senior enough to know any details of his father's duty—that would come with time. Worrying was something that Tadamori had been taught not to indulge in, but his father's company had not returned and those who knew had begun to whisper. He focused his thoughts elsewhere.

Functioning in the capacity that had somehow become his own, Rohku Tadamori had been sent south down the canal as a lookout. The boats had grown so numerous that it was becoming impossible to pass to the front of the fleet by sampan in any reasonable time, so he had chosen to ride. Perhaps the fact that it was a perfect spring day and he preferred horses to boats had entered into the decision also.

Although the Grand Canal ran virtually straight throughout most of its sections, the area it passed through now was strewn with outcroppings of gray stone, making a straight line impossible. So the ancient engineers had routed the waterway among them as though providing travelers with the most aesthetic views had suddenly become their purpose. This allowed Rohku to go across country, cutting off great loops of the canal and saving much time and distance.

Rohku and his guard had not passed half the ships in the great flotilla so far and yet they had been on horseback half a day. A small stream met the canal and Tadamori dismounted to let his horse drink. Others did the same. There was no sense of urgency in this assignment, and though his men did not know what his orders were they had soon realized that he did not rush. Conversation had started among the riders, uncommon among Shonto's guard, who took their duty very seriously. A beautiful day such as this even lightened the spirits of the warriors.

"There is a mess for you," one of the guards said, pointing down the canal.

Around one of the giant rock towers came an ornate river boat, fighting not only the current of the canal but also the current of events. Barges from the south-going flotilla pulled up to the bank to let the river boat pass. Rohku could not distinguish the crests on the banners, but the color was impossible to mistake—Imperial Crimson. Prince Wakaro had arrived, not appearing out of the mists as had Jaku Katta, but in the full light of a fine spring day, forcing his way north against a torrent of refugees swept before the coming war.

Even at this distance Rohku could see the people on the bank and on barges bowing as the Prince's boat passed. Rohku ran up to the top of the bank and watched for a moment, then trotted back down and mounted his horse. There was nothing more he needed to see.

Turning quickly, Rohku spurred up the bank followed by his guard. At the top he paused to get his bearings in the strange countryside and then set off across the country at a canter. Lord Shonto would want to know this immediately.

Although official greetings had been sent and the Prince had made it known that he wished to have Lord Shonto attend him immediately, still nothing of significance had occurred. The Prince's flotilla carrying personal staff, his small court, and an honor guard of black uniformed Imperial Guards sat moored to the east bank of the canal while Shonto's own vast flotilla passed by on its way toward the inner provinces.

On the bank opposite the Prince's retinue, a silk pavilion had been erected surrounded by a fence of banners laced to bamboo frames. The Emperor's banner, the five-clawed dragon on crimson, wafted from a staff before the enclosure and beside it Prince Wakaro's own banner of dragon and crane, also on crimson, though bordered in gold. Shonto's blue banner waved there, also, as did the Flying Horse of the Province of Seh. Armored men in Shonto blue stood guard and there was a ring of several hundred yards which only specific Shonto retainers were allowed to enter.

On the bank before the pavilion a dock had been built so that people of rank might disembark from boats with some semblance of dignity. A sampan of the most common variety wobbled down the canal to the stroke of its single oar. Aboard this craft were three guards in armor with blue lacing and an old man, formally dressed, sitting with one hand in his lap while the other sleeve of his robe creased and rippled in the breeze.

The sampan made a careful line to the elaborate barge that bore the Imperial Prince. Steward Kamu was left waiting on the boarding platform for some minutes, but eventually an Imperial Guard officer came to the head of the stairs and bowed.

"The Prince will speak with you now, Steward Kamu," the officer said.

They still bow, they continue to use my title, they are not as confident as they pretend, Kamu thought. With some care he ascended the stairs to the main deck and then a second stairway to an upper level. There, on the stern, protected by a yellow awning, sat the Imperial Prince, Yamaku Wakaro, listening to a lovely young woman who played the melody of a spring dance on the harp.

Kneeling immediately, Kamu waited, listening. The woman was not the equal of Lady Nishima, in either beauty or in the skill of her playing, but she was certainly more than competent and the composition was well matched to the day.

The Prince did not seem to notice the presence of Lord Shonto's representative but concentrated his attentions on the young musician. Sitting on cushions around the stern of the boat sat several richly dressed men and women of similar age to the Prince. None were immediately recognizable to Kamu, but he was well informed of who fluttered about the flame of the Imperial Prince and though they were not individuals entirely without virtue, there was not one among them who it could be said was marked for great things. Another Imperial dynasty that had achieved mediocrity in three generations.

A second song was called for and plum wine was served. Kamu knelt unmoving on the hard deck controlling his not insignificant temper. Occasionally he glanced up at the Prince. He decided His Imperial Highness favored his mother in appearance, round of feature, yet fair. Large, wide-set eyes with long lashes drew the attention and would, no doubt, be the talk of the young women at court. The Prince kept teasing the corner of a long, spindly mustache. Like his mother, the Prince had a shock of white hair on his left temple, distorting the symmetry of his face.

Finally, after the second song and some idle conversation and laughter, Kamu was summoned forward. Bored with their charade, the old man thought.

Bowing, the steward waited with every indication of infinite patience.

"Steward Kamu," Prince Wakaro said, his voice slightly nasal. "I trust you have come to arrange the surrender of Lord Shonto and to pass the control of this upstart army over to my Guard Captain."

Kamu gave a half bow as though of compliance. "The edicts you bear from the Son of Heaven would certainly not be ignored, Sire. As we are at war, however, Lord Shonto is anxious to give a full report of the military situation before the Prince takes command of the army." Kamu bowed again.

"Tell your lord that the military situation is no longer his concern. I am more interested in his compliance with direct orders from the Emperor."

Kamu nodded to the pavilion on the opposite bank. "Lord Shonto is a general of great skill, Sire. Given your experience in these areas, it might be prudent to speak with him, Prince."

Wakaro raised an eyebrow, a flash of anger was replaced by a smirk. His followers became very quiet. "Your insolence has earned you a particularly small, dark cell for the brief period remaining to you, Steward."

Kamu's deferential manner did not change. "Certainly, Sire, this will be as you wish, but this must wait until after your meeting with my lord."

"There will be no meeting with your lord, you old fool!" the Prince exploded, slamming his armrest.

Kamu nodded. *He shares his father's temper if little else.* "Perhaps, Sire, I might suggest that you look behind you," Kamu said softly.

Wakaro's eyes widened at this and his flash of temper seemed to burn down to coals. Others of his party glanced aft and Kamu heard them curse under their breath. Hearing this the Prince turned. On the deck of the boat behind, formerly awash in the black-laced armor of Imperial Guards, stood men in armor of blue. As the Imperial Prince turned, they bowed and then returned to position as if they were his own guard.

Wakaro turned and regarded Kamu. Before he could respond to what he had seen, the old steward spoke quietly.

"As we are at war, my lord is concerned with the Prince's safety. He has provided you with his own personal guard. I trust the hour of the dog will not be an inconvenient time for this meeting?"

"To threaten the son of the Emperor of Wa is a crime that will not be forgiven," the Prince said, his voice not sure enough to bear the weight of the threat.

Kamu could not help himself. He shrugged. "There is no threat, Sire. Only concern that you are fully aware of the situation you inherit." Without waiting to be dismissed, Kamu bowed low, rose in the Prince's presence, and walked with great dignity to the stairs and then down to his waiting boat.

The sampan carrying Prince Wakaro crossed to the small dock where it was met by Shonto's steward, who bowed low, greeting the Prince with proper formality. Accompanying the Emperor's son was the senior officer of his guard and another young man of similar age to his royal highness. They ascended the bank to the enclosure between rows of bowing, blue-armored guards. Under the awning of the pavilion sat Lord Shonto and his senior military advisor, General Hojo Masakado.

All bowed accordingly as the Prince approached. A small dais had been provided for Wakaro and cushions set for his counselors. Taking his place, the son of the Emperor sat and glared at Shonto with undisguised anger.

"Do not wait for me to speak," the Prince said quickly. "Despite this dais and the formal homage, there is no question of who controls this situation. Enjoy it while you may," he added, the Yamaku temper flaring briefly.

Shonto favored the Prince with a smile of great warmth. "I apologize most humbly, Sire. If we were not at war, I would never have presumed to use such measures."

"I am not aware of any declaration of war, and I receive news from the Island Palace daily. Refusal to comply with the Imperial Edicts will be considered an act of treason, *Governor.*" He spat the word out. "It does not show great wisdom to erode your already tenuous situation."

Shonto spoke quietly. "Refusal to learn what is known of the enemy you will face when you take control of the army could not be considered great wisdom either, Sire." Shonto smiled again. "As the Empire is under great threat, I did not feel such a mistake could be allowed."

The Prince eyed Shonto. "What will you have me do?"

Shonto favored the Prince with the look a tolerant parent gives an unreasonable child—amusement and affection mixed with sadness brought about by the knowledge that children will insist on learning difficult lessons for themselves, though their conclusions will hardly be startling. "The barbarian force is not far behind, not as far as we would like it to be, at least. If you can be ready at sunrise tomorrow, General Hojo will accompany you personally so that you might view this force and make your own assessment and plans." He nodded to Kamu who reached behind him for a scroll. He laid this within reach of the Prince's guard.

"This is an accurate assessment of the barbarian force. General Hojo will certainly be able to answer any questions you might have as he is familiar with every aspect of our efforts and has recently engaged the vanguard of the barbarian army in a significant skirmish."

Silence followed. The Prince finally nodded, moving his head as though he suffered from great exhaustion. "As I have little choice, I will go view this great barbarian army. May I assume my guard captain will be allowed to accompany me?"

"Of course, Sire," Shonto answered. "Take the advisors deemed necessary, by all means. I personally will be interested in the opinions of the Prince and his staff when they return."

Shonto nodded to Kamu who gave unseen signals and wine appeared. "Excuse me for not asking, Prince," Shonto said, lifting his cup. "The Emperor is well?"

Forty-three

Upon first awakening, for the briefest of moments, one believes in the dream.

Brother Hutto
Seventieth Primate of Wa

PRINCE WAKARO WORE the black-laced armor of an Imperial Guard officer, though under a surcoat bearing twin silver dragons and a trim of crimson. A dark bay stallion was the Prince's favored horse, and though it was a powerful animal General Hojo suspected that it had been chosen to complement the Prince's attire.

And the silver-trimmed black saddle and bridle . . . ! These earned many a glance from the other riders who favored tack that showed signs of use. Such a saddle and bridle would be a prize to attract a barbarian's attention!

Hojo turned back to the scene that stretched out before them. It had taken some time to find an appropriate place from which to view the passing barbarian army. Lord Shonto had insisted that the Prince should never be at risk—not an easy requirement to fullfil in such times— but this hill was as secure as could be found. Unfortunately, what it gained in security it lost in proximity.

Far off to the west the Grand Canal wound across the landscape, shining like a bronze ribbon in the late afternoon light. Rafts were being pulled along this ribbon of molten metal, their dark shapes distorted by their own shadows. Along either bank moved the army of the desert, like an enormous herd of unknown animals wandering in search of new feeding grounds.

Prince Wakaro said nothing though he repeatedly glanced over at the captain of his guard as if he tried to read the officer's response. It was a small, but telling, gesture.

"It is possible to go some short distance closer, Prince, if this would help in the estimation of the army's size," Hojo offered calmly. He was not seeing the barbarian army for the first time. He had fought them, in fact. To the general they were only men, not some ominous, unknown entity. They fought and made mistakes, felt fear, and even bled, just like any other men he had known.

The Prince looked over to his captain who shook his head. "We have seen all we require, General." He looked over at the western horizon. "It will be dark soon enough. Perhaps we should return."

General Hojo nodded, signaled his guard, and turned back the way they had come. That will take some of the arrogance out of the whelp, the old fighter thought—and to think this boy's father began all of this; paid gold to this Khan to help bring down the Shonto House. Has this young Prince wondered why he was sent to Seh? Let him ponder that, Hojo told himself. If nothing else can shake his imperial confidence, that should.

It was a curious aspect of the natural world and Lord Shonto had often wondered about it. The willow trees that lined the canal bank had branches that hung down close to the water, like green robes swaying in the breeze. Yet, from even a short distance, it appeared that all of these branches stopped the same distance short of the water, as though a gardener had trimmed them with great care. Surely it is only an illusion, the lord thought, but it appears to be so. Tree after tree all with their long, flowing wands grown to the same length.

The canal bank slipped past, the spring winds still hurrying the river boats south. A haze of petals floated on the waters among the reflections of passing clouds, and other petals took to the wind like a flight of butterflies. Spring in Wa was disappointing no one, at least as far as weather was concerned. Shonto sat on the upper deck of his barge, watching the scene pass.

Unlike his Spiritual Advisor the lord did not wait well, but one did not hurry an Imperial Prince nor demand that they arrive at an appointed hour—by definition, the appointed hour was the precise time the Imperial party made its appearance.

It was surprising enough that Wakaro came to Shonto, for a Prince need never wait upon another. There was little doubt that this act was a message—the sight of the barbarian army was a convincing argument—but what the Prince would be willing to do in the coming war remained a question.

"Sire," Kamu appeared at the stairway, "the Prince comes."

Shonto nodded. It had been decided that the lord would meet the Prince as an equal, not kneeling at the stairhead as the Prince came aboard—and this, too, was a message. The Yamaku prepared for war against the Shonto, had tried to do away with the Shonto House altogether; there were certain truths that each House would have to live with now. One was that the Shonto would no longer recognize the Yamaku claim to the Dragon Throne. This did not mean that Shonto would treat the son of his enemy with disrespect, but he would not credit him the full regard reserved for the son of a legitimate sovereign.

An elegant white boat shot past, controlled by skilled oarsmen. It turned easily and brought up beside the platform at the bottom of the boarding stairs. They were not within Shonto's sight, but he could hear voices and footsteps on the stairs.

Two attendants and two Imperial Guards preceded the Prince onto the upper deck and knelt to either side while their master ascended the stairs. Everyone on the deck, with the exception of Lord Shonto, bowed low.

The Prince wore a robe the color of the summer sky embroidered with a pattern of plum trees in blossom. In his sash he carried a sword in a black leather scabbard adorned with the dragon and crane. Crossing the open deck, Wakaro nodded to Shonto and took the cushion to the lord's left. Shonto returned the nod and gestured for a cushion to be set for the Prince's Guard Captain. Kamu and General Hojo approached and took places on their lord's right.

"Have you traveled the canal before, Prince Wakaro?" Shonto asked, not waiting for the Prince to open the conversation.

"Not so far north, Lord Shonto," he waved a hand toward the shore. "It passes through some of the most beautiful scenes in the Empire, I am certain."

Shonto nodded, looking out over the landscape. "I agree. Years ago I traveled south from Seh. It has changed little." Shonto looked down in slight discomfort. "Though we will not say that after the barbarians have passed." The lord looked up at the young man before him, his question unspoken: *Now that you have seen the truth of the world, young Sire, what have you to say?*

Wakaro could not meet the lord's gaze for more than a second. "I now realize, Lord Shonto, why you so . . . strongly advised that I increase my understanding of the military situation. Let us say no more about it." The Prince rubbed his palms together in a slow circular motion. "I have read your report, as has my Guard Captain. Though I have not received thorough training in the arts of war, I realize that this Khan and his followers are a great threat to the Empire and to our Emperor. My Guard Captain concurs with your staff's estimate of the army's size. There is no doubt that the resources of the entire Empire must be utilized to combat this threat." He looked up now, regarding Shonto with the look of one who has resolved to tell another the hard truth.

"I am not certain that the Emperor can be convinced of this threat, Lord Shonto." He looked out over the canal, brushing back a wisp of white hair. "The Emperor believes that you proceed south with the intention of overthrowing the Yamaku House." The Prince shrugged. "I cannot say what your intentions are, Lord Shonto, but certainly the choice you have made to retreat south with so small a force and allow the Empire time to raise an army of defense was the wise choice. Though I am certain it was a difficult decision."

The Prince shifted on his cushion. "It is my shame to admit that my assessment of what happens here will hold little sway over the actions of the Emperor." He paused for a second and Shonto wondered if this was pain the young man felt, but the Prince's face showed little sign of emotion. "It is likely," Wakaro said at last, "that any report I send will be disregarded. Many an Imperial Prince has plotted to overthrow his father. The Emperor will believe that I have joined you, Lord Shonto, unaware that I am loyal to him, despite all." The Prince paused again, looking down at his hands. "I am unsure how to proceed. . . ."

Shonto nodded. "It is a difficult situation, Prince Wakaro. My own staff have discussed it endlessly. Allow me to say that the Shonto interest is the safety of Wa, nothing more. As you can see I have already sacrificed everything to that end. *Rebel General* I am named, yet the subject of every Shonto council is: how can the Empire be preserved?

"The Emperor must raise an army. It is the only answer. I have gathered as many men as we will likely see, yet the total of our forces is not a third of the barbarian army. As we speak, an army is being raised in the capital, though it is not an army for the defense of Wa. What will happen when we reach the inner provinces and the scale of the barbarian invasion is seen?" Shonto regarded his young companion. "I fear it will be too late, Prince Wakaro. We must have a plan—now—a plan and an army large enough to meet this threat from the desert."

The Prince nodded slowly, looking down at the wooden deck. "I can send a message to my father describing what I have seen and urge him to send officers he trusts to assess the situation for themselves. I can also travel south by fast boat and speak to the Emperor, though I may find retirement to a well-guarded estate as my reward. But even so, I would do this. As you have. Lord Shonto, so would I risk all to preserve the Empire."

"I think a message to the Emperor is appropriate," Shonto said quietly. "Even if it does not change the Emperor's mind, it must cast some doubt on the counsel he has received. As you say, it may be unwise to travel to the capital yourself, especially as you have orders to take control of my army and send me south under guard." Shonto looked over at General Hojo as though remembering an earlier discussion. "General Hojo's report could be sent along with your letter though I think it may be wise to say nothing of the size of our own army. Let the Emperor wonder how many men we have gathered— perhaps he will raise a larger army if he is unsure."

A silence fell for a moment. Along the shore refugees appeared again and after a morning of seeing very few it was a doubly sad sight. The Prince brushed back the strand of white hair again, without thinking. "Then, for now, I will accompany your flotilla and offer what assistance I can. If you will allow it, I will fly my banner beside your own, Lord Shonto. When we reach the inner provinces, perhaps I will be the bridge between the Shonto and the Emperor."

Shonto bowed to the young Prince who rose suddenly. "Please excuse me, I will write to the Emperor immediately. Will you see that this letter goes to the palace?"

"Certainly, Prince Wakaro. I thank you for your counsel. Perhaps there is hope yet, if the Yamaku and the Shonto can join to defend Wa. . . ."

The Prince gave a half bow and, followed by his retinue, descended the stairs to the lower deck.

As the white boat passed, the Prince nodded toward Shonto and then the oarsmen dug in and sent their craft shooting ahead leaving a whirl of white petals spinning in their wake.

Kamu bowed to his lord, his face drawn and serious. "I have received word from Brother Shuyun, Sire. He has spoken to the Brothers at the nearby monastery and there is no doubt—plague has broken out among the refugees. The numbers are small and it is hoped the Brothers isolated them quickly enough to stop the disease from spreading. I have given permission to use one barge to transport the victims. The Botahist monks will man it and tend the sick." Kamu made a sign to Botahara—uncharacteristic for him. "May Botahara protect us all. We need do nothing more for now, but if the disease spreads among the population moving south we will have a calamity, for the Brothers may not be able to deal with the thousands who would become ill. Brother Shuyun has suggested that senior Brother Sotura could be asked to oversee this problem."

Shonto nodded, thinking for a moment. "Brother Shuyun has taken no risk of infection himself?"

"I spoke to Shuyun-sum of your concern in this matter, Sire, and he assured me that he would employ all necessary precautions."

Shonto sat turning his cup slowly and looking out at the people moving along the canal bank. "We cannot afford to assign many river craft to transporting the sick." He shook his head. "Have Brother Sotura take charge of this matter. If the plague finds its way out among these people," he waved a hand at the canal bank, "thousands may die before the Botanist monks are able to control the disease. We would have been better to leave them in their homes, barbarian army or no."

Shonto turned back to Kamu. "Once this becomes known among the refugees, there will be a panic that will itself cost lives. We have no more men to police the travelers." He looked down into his cup. "Let us see what happens. If the diseased are isolated, the problem may grow no worse."

A silence fell over the men on the deck for a moment. Memories of the plague years were still strong among the people of Wa. No family had been untouched by the wave of death that swept through Wa. And then the Imperial family had become ill and the war began. It was all too familiar.

"Excuse me for asking, Lord Shonto," General Hojo said, interrupting everyone's thoughts. "I do not understand why my lord did not allow the young Prince to speak directly to the Emperor? The fact that the Prince would take such a risk would light his story with a flame of truth. Men often will take great risks when they believe they are the bearers of an important truth, as though the purity of their knowledge will somehow shield them from the malice and ignorance of others. The Emperor may have been given pause to think."

Shonto nodded. "It is possible, one can never know what will impress the Son of Heaven. But if the Emperor did not believe his son . . . ?" Shonto signaled a servant for wine. "If the son stays with us, what will Akantsu think? That I have offered the Prince the hand of my daughter and the Throne of Wa—two things of inestimable value, neither of which the Emperor will ever offer. If the Emperor loses a civil war, a Prince who is wed to a daughter of the Shonto, a bearer of the Fanisan blood, would be the most likely to ascend the Dragon Throne. There is more to overthrowing an Emperor than winning a war. One must have a suitable claimant or even the winning side can faction." Shonto smiled. "The more threatened the Emperor feels, the larger will his army become."

The lord shrugged. "And who can say, perhaps the Prince's letter will make the Emperor wonder. If the Son of Heaven sends officers north to assess the barbarian army, they will see what the Prince has seen."

"The board," Hojo said, dryly, "has become too complex."

Lifting the wine cup that was set before him, Shonto raised an eyebrow. "For the time being, General." He drank, then set the cup on a small table. "The exchange of pieces begins soon."

Returning to the flotilla had become more difficult than Komawara had expected. They had met a barbarian patrol as they emerged from the hills and somehow one of the tribesmen had escaped. After that they had been hunted by barbarian companies and forced to fight more than one running battle. Of the eighteen hundred men that had attacked the supply rafts only a thousand remained. There had been no further signs of the company led by Rohku Saicha and Komawara was not sure if this was propitious or cause for sadness.

"Sire," a guard interrupted Komawara's train of thought. The lord sat with his back against a tree, looking out over a field surrounded by tree-clad hills. Grazing horses were guarded here, and Komawara thought how lucky the animals were—his company had not eaten since morning the previous day and his stomach occasionally complained loudly.

"Sire, the guides have found the flotilla. We may reach it by late afternoon."

Komawara nodded, it was all the reaction he felt he had energy for at the moment. "The scouting parties?"

"They report that the barbarian patrols keep their distance from Lord Shonto's fleet, Sire, we have not seen sign of them all this morning." The man paused and then said with some pride, "The patrols the men of Seh ride keep the tribesmen wary."

Komawara nodded. "Tell General Jaku that we must ride again. Has our position been reported to Lord Shonto?"

The guard shook his head.

"Send someone ahead to inform Kamu-sum of our position." Komawara heaved himself up with some effort.

"The patrols have one other thing to report, Lord Komawara."

The lord had begun to turn away but stopped.

"It appears that a large party is separating from the main body of the barbarian army."

"How large?"

"Perhaps twenty-five thousand men."

Komawara nodded, looking down at the ground for a moment. "Six men will carry this news directly to Lord Shonto. Give them our strongest horses and remounts also. Tell them to ride their horses to death if need be. Lord Shonto must know of this immediately."

Komawara signaled for his horse. *The barbarians cannot let Lord Shonto continue to deprive their army of food—not after what my party has done. This smaller force will set out to catch our own army and engage it or drive us south at such speed that we cannot continue to empty the lands before us. This Khan has finally awakened.*

Forty-four

FOURTH MOON FLOATED free of the tree, sloughing off a robe of copper and wrapping itself in pure silver-white. Ladies Nishima, Kitsura, and Okara sat on cushions laid out on a carpet spread over the quarterdeck. So bright was the moonlight that the pink of the cherry blossoms and the white of the plum could be distinguished as the trees slipped past, their blossom laden shapes hanging like clouds over the dark canal bank.

At the request of Lady Okara, Nishima had played her harp, a subtle melody known as "The Lovers' Parting," though in the southern provinces it went by the name "Traveling the Spring River."

This done they had begun a poem-series, each composing a verse in turn. Nishima had been given the honor of both the first and last verses in recognition of her poetic skills.

> *"Fourth moon,*
> *Ten thousand broken hearts*
> *Line the banks of the spring canal*
> *Strewn among the plum petals."*

And then Lady Okara had taken the wine cup that went to the composer of the next verse.

> *"Blossoms as white as lintel vine*
> *Drift south against flowing waters.*

How do we return to houses
Their gateways crumbled?"

The cup passed to Kitsura.

"Last autumn's leaves
And spring flowers
Are whirled up into clouds
On the backs of cool winds
Like the lifting of one's heart."

The cup returned to Nishima who took the required sip and then sat holding the cool porcelain in her lap, thinking.

"A flight of cranes
Passes in silence
Along the river among the clouds.
Ten thousand hearts rise up,
Taking flight toward an unseen lake
At the foot of an unnamed mountain."

When the poem was finished, the three women sat in silence contemplating the moon and the passing scene. After a suitable time had passed, Kitsura raised her flute and played a soft air that spoke to the mood like a well-chosen quotation. When she was finished, a bamboo flute answered from the canal bank, the unseen player offering a melody none had heard before but which matched the music of Kitsura perfectly.

"That was a spirit speaking to us, I am certain," Lady Okara whispered, and the other women nodded.

Conversation ceased for some time and then Lady Nishima rose, her smile failing even as it formed. "It pains me to leave your delightful company," she said, "but I must sleep or I will be of no use to my uncle. It has been a perfect evening, Oka-sum, cousin." A half bow and she retreated toward the companionway.

Kitsura started another song but could not keep her focus and stopped. "I fear this war has affected my cousin in ways that are difficult to understand. Her artist's spirit is too open and in times such as these. . . ." She did not finish.

Lady Okara nodded. "May she never learn to wall her spirit off from the world—though it causes her heart to break a thousand times."

The fires of a refugee camp appeared on the bank for the next half a rih and then there was only the landscape lit by moonlight, the calyptas and willows, in full leaf now, silhouetted against the stars. Intent on not disturbing the women who sat contemplating the moon, the watch changed in near silence.

"I have heard no word of the company sent to raid the barbarians' supply train," Kitsura said suddenly, and though it was entirely out of place to discuss such things at a viewing of the moon, such breaches of etiquette were becoming more and more common.

"Yes, and I am concerned," Okara answered, not seeming to notice or perhaps care that it was not a suitable topic for the occasion.

"Lord Komawara has grown very grim, don't you think? Far more than even the senior members of Lord Shonto's staff—though of course they have seen war before. Still. . . ."

Lady Okara sat quietly for a second. "There is much that has happened to our young lord of Seh. It gives me sorrow to see him change in this manner, but I would expect little else. He has lost the estates the Komawara have held for generations, Seh is occupied by barbarians who no doubt burned the beautiful city of Rhojo-ma. And though Lord Komawara has regained the respect of the men of his own province, the months of ridicule have not been forgotten, and . . . there are other things as well."

"Other things, Oka-sum?" Kitsura asked.

Shrugging, the artist pulled her over-robe closer. "Please, say nothing of this, but I believe Samyamu-sum has been spurned, Kitsu-sum, and after all that has befallen him Lord Komawara feels there is nothing left to him. Such a feeling can lead to terrible recklessness, I fear."

"Spurned," Kitsura said in a whisper, her interest obvious. "Who do you think?"

Okara shrugged, not meeting the other woman's gaze. "I thought it might be the Lady Kitsura. . . ."

Kitsura gave a small laugh. "Certainly not. There were, however, several lovely young women who frequented the Governor's Palace in Seh. There is no shortage of possibilities. Do you think it was because Lord Komawara's views were thought to be so peculiar?"

Okara shrugged again. "Perhaps."

"Huh," Kitsura touched her fingers to her chin in contemplation that looked almost like prayer. "All the other men I am aware of are smitten with Nishi-sum. . . ." The young woman sat up. "You don't think it was Nishima-sum, do you? She certainly said nothing to me."

"I do not know, Kitsu-sum. I only mention it as a possibility. I know nothing for certain."

Kitsura rubbed her hands together, imitating a character in a play. "I must find some way to have Nishi-sum tell me," Kitsura said, obviously already plotting. "Poor Lord Komawara. My lovely cousin will break ten thousand hearts before she settles."

"I must say," Lady Okara spoke sharply, "this rivalry between yourself and Lady Nishima is something you will both regret."

Kitsura stared dumbly. She had never heard Lady Okara say anything that was not entirely pleasant. What rivalry? she thought. With my dearest cousin?

Nishima lay in her cabin awash in the moonlight filtering through the open window. She had changed out of the elaborate robes she had worn against the cool evening and a maid had laid out her bedding. Although Nishima had been able to participate in the viewing with some focus, this had suddenly disappeared and she had excused herself before the others guessed the turmoil that possessed her.

It had been several days since Nishima had spoken to Shuyun, had not even seen him except once at a distance. The monk was avoiding her, there was no doubt, and this caused her great anxiety.

In a sense Nishima felt she was engaged in a struggle for this young man's spirit—a lifetime of Botahist training and doctrine on one side and whatever charms Lady Nishima had to offer on the other. And the longer he was away from her the more likely it became that training and comfortable habit would be victorious. Even now she was certain the monks had won their pupil back, even if they did not know that they were in danger of losing him.

Nishima was surprised at how little guilt she felt from playing the temptress—drawing the devoted away from the path of the spirit. It made her question her own goodness. Certainly nothing could be more improper than this affair she was engaged in, yet her heart did not care and it was her heart that had taken control.

The pain she felt at this thought was almost physical, so deep inside that she could not find its center. For some time she lay in this state and then forced herself to follow one of the several exercises that Brother Satake had taught to force her spirit away from such turmoil. And this finally brought a fitful sleep.

A stair creaking brought the young woman awake as surely as the sound of someone entering one's room. After the noise of the telltale stair tread Nishima heard nothing at all and knew that the only person who could move that silently was Shuyun. She sat up, wrapping the quilt around her, every sense alert, but there was no other sound and her door did not ease open as she hoped.

For several minutes the young woman sat, struggling with her fears and desires. Then the need to know what transpired in the heart of this young monk won out and she almost jumped up, throwing a robe over her thin sleeping garment, forgetting a sash.

She opened her door a crack and watched the corridor and the stairs that led to the deck, dimly lit by a shaded, bronze lamp: nothing stirred. Though she did not have the skill of Shuyun, Nishima did have Brother Satake's training and her motions exhibited the harmony of movement and balance that allowed the Botahist trained to move with almost no sound.

At Shuyun's door she paused to listen, but when she heard nothing she pushed it open and stepped quickly out of the light of the corridor. Shuyun sat up in the bedding spread over the straw mats, the moon lighting the planes of his cheek and brow.

"Lady Nishima?"

His voice was a whisper, but even so it carried tones of formality and distance. Nishima felt her heart sink. A pace from the bed she knelt and found she could not speak.

"Lady Nishima, is something wrong?" Shuyun asked.

Distance, words as cool as the spring river. I cannot win him with weakness, she thought, I must be strong. I must find the aspects of myself that drew him before.

Despite her resolve her voice was small and shook slightly. "I had not seen you in some time, Shuyun-sum. . . ." Words ceased there and finally she could only shrug and fight tears. It was as she had feared—habit and training and doctrine had argued in her absence. What could she do now?

Shuyun stared at her and though it may have been merely a trick of the light, his face, normally devoid of emotion, seemed to mirror her own confusion and sadness.

"I do not understand the ways of the heart, Lady Nishima," he said quietly, his voice utterly calm.

Shaking her head, Nishima heard herself whisper, "No one does." A second of silence and then with difficulty, "I only know that my heart is breaking."

Shuyun's lack of experience would no longer stop him from offering comfort to a woman whose heart was breaking. Nishima felt his arms encircle her and she pulled him close, burying her face in his bare shoulder. Neither moved for some time, as though afraid motion or words would somehow signal acceptance of the changes they both sensed coming.

"I have a memory from my childhood," Nishima whispered, "perhaps my earliest memory. I was crying, I can't remember why, and my mother held me as you do now."

"My first memory is singing a child's chant with my fellow neophytes. I have no memory of my family."

"Were you that young, then, when you came to the Brothers?"

Shuyun shook his head. "When you are very young, the teachers have you perform exercises where you imagine your mother's face changing—from round to sharp, or long to round. Soon you can no longer remember her true appearance. It is the first lesson that we live in the illusion."

"It seems a terrible thing to do to a child," Nishima whispered.

"Perhaps." Shuyun put his mouth close to her ear. "There is something you must know." Pulling away slowly, he held up a hand. "Place your palm against mine."

Nishima did so.

"Push."

Beginning slowly Nishima applied pressure, controlling her breathing, feeling the slight tingle of "inner force" through her hand. Shuyun stared at her with great earnestness all the while. Suddenly Nishima found her hand being forced back, not quickly but steadily. Only when this steady pressure had stopped pushing her back did Nishima realize that there was moonlight falling between Shuyun's hand and her own. She faltered and withdrew her hand, staring openly.

"Brother Satake did not tell me of this," Nishima whispered. "I . . . would not have thought it possible."

Shuyun shook his head. "There is no record of such a thing being done before," Shuyun said, his voice so filled with awe that Nishima found herself moving away as though the monk was suddenly something to be wary of.

"Are you the Teacher, then?" she whispered.

Shuyun shook his head, almost a tremor, and shrugged, looking down at his hands. "I do not know. Certainly this confusion I feel is not the Enlightenment the Brothers describe." He met Nishima's gaze and she felt he asked her, silently, to reach out to him, and despite her discomfort and questions about the nature of this man she could not refuse.

Gently, Nishima pulled the quilt aside and slipped into the bed beside Shuyun. They lay in the moonlight, close, in each other's arms—too much to be said, neither able to find words to begin.

The sounds of the boat swaying and rocking through the waters were all around them and the moonlight arced slowly across the cabin. The entire effect was one of strangeness—a room that moved and hissed and burbled, cool pure light illuminating the cabin, bright enough to cast shadows. It was as though they had been transported to some other realm where the laws and forces of nature were unknown.

Nishima felt Shuyun's finger trace the shape of her ear, his touch so light. Down the curve of her neck and she realized she was holding her breath. Out along her shoulder, pulling her robe back. She felt the soft silk slide across her breast and then the soft warmth of Shuyun's skin against her own.

Brave heart, Nishima thought, *what beauty we have found.*

Lord Shonto Shokan awoke in a small gray room, a thin line of daylight finding its way through a crack in the window shutter. Early, he thought, it must be very early. The furs he slept under kept him warm, but the stone walls drew all the heat out of the air and the lord's breath was visible. He rolled over again and was startled by pain in his back and neck. Carrying a load, dweller style, had asked much of him.

A night's sleep uninterrupted by the cold: Shokan had to admit that he was not meant to live high in the mountains. He could not bear the cold.

Unwilling to face the air in the room and unable to think of a pressing reason to rise, Shokan lay in his furs wondering about the people who had found him—rescued him was perhaps more accurate.

In some ways they were not unlike the people of Wa, the lowlanders. The mountain dwellers' dress and habits differed, there was no question, but there was a familiar focus of duty among these people which reminded Shokan of the retainers on the Shonto fief.

There appeared to be no aristocracy here, though the elders were accorded a level of respect that was impressive. But even their lives did not compare with that of a pampered member of Wa's peerage—his life, for instance.

If Shokan were to characterize the greatest difference between the mountain dwellers and his own people, it was in the dwellers' seemingly consistent ability to find delight in virtually everything. More than innocence, this was a quality of joy and spontaneity that was seldom seen in the Empire of Wa—a world smothered with rigidly structured etiquette, formality, and ceremony. Even his stepsister, Nishima, who flouted the rules of her station almost without regard—and with impressive impunity!—did not share the spirit he witnessed in the dwellers. He realized he was somewhat jealous.

The door opened a crack and Shokan was not sure whose face appeared in the dark hall beyond. The door was pushed open by a foot and Quinta-la appeared. In her hands she bore a covered wooden tray and the smell of food permeated the cold air. She set this on what appeared to be a low, round stool and went directly to the window, speaking as she went. There was no way to be certain, but Shokan had the distinct impression that this young woman was scolding him. Unfastening the latches she flung the shutters open and sunshine flooded the room, warm sunshine, and the young lord was not sure that the outside air was not warmer also.

Quinta-la squatted down on her heels and gestured to the food and smiled.

Shokan said the word he hoped meant "eat" and received a delighted smile and a torrent of dweller language, not a single word of which he recognized.

When he had eaten, every bite watched with apparent interest, Quinta-la rose and gestured to the door, speaking as she did so.

"I would love to stroll in the sunshine in your lovely company, Quinta-la," Shokan responded, "but it is improper for you to be here and certainly very improper that I should dress in your presence, so. . . ." He waved her out, smiling so that she would not take offense, and when this did not work he rose, wrapped in a fur, and guided her out the door which caused much laughter, but then many things he did made her laugh.

Dressing quickly the lord went out into the hall where Quinta-la crouched down against the wall.

"Ketah," she said and jumped up, waving down the corridor. She walked beside him, her pace forcing Shokan to hurry, yet, except for the speed at which she walked, she showed little sign of being rushed. She smiled at Shokan when he looked at her and seemed to be walking quickly out of excitement or perhaps sheer pleasure, but not because there was pressure to be somewhere.

They left the building by a very substantial wooden door and crossed a stone courtyard to ascend a set of narrow stairs. In the shade between the building and the high wall the air was frigid and occasional patches of ice appeared on the stone treads.

As they reached the top of the stairs, and another of what seemed to be an endless number of courtyards and terraces, a shout went up and in seconds a swarm of children appeared, converging from all directions. Round faced, with perfect, white smiles they were a contrast to the quiet, decorous children Shokan was used to encountering. They ran in circles around the stranger and his tiny guide or pranced along beside Quinta-la tagging on to her hands and clothing, laughing and jabbering and letting go the occasional shriek, apparently for sheer joy.

They crossed yet another stone terrace toward a wide set of steps, just high enough that Shokan could not see what lay at the next level. As they came closer to the stairs, the children became more subdued and then fell completely silent. A few at a time they began to drop behind so that the adults reached the foot of the stairs alone. There Quinta-la stopped also, her face uncommonly serious.

Shokan looked back and the children stood watching him, big eyes unreadable to his outsider perception, their smiles gone. Quinta-la nodded, the strange gesture of the head falling forward then jerking up. Waving her hand at the steps, she tried a reassuring smile though it was so forced it did anything but reassure.

I have no sword, Shokan thought. He had left it in his chambers out of respect and trust for the people who had saved him, for they did not carry swords in their own village. It is a groundless fear, he told himself, a thought without honor. The dwellers are not treacherous.

As there seemed to be little choice, he bowed and turned up the stairs, watched intently by his strangely mute audience.

Though he was not certain what he had been expecting, what greeted him at the top of the stairs did not fulfill those expectations. A round terrace surrounded by a waist-high stone wall. In its center a stunted tree lifted twisted branches against the background of white mountains and the broad valley.

The scene was so dramatic that Shokan almost did not notice the tiny figure sitting on a stone bench, looking out across the valley. A woman dressed in long robes of dark colors belted with a faded purple sash. She turned as Shokan stood regarding her, unsure what to do. A gesture, not unfriendly, to join her.

If this woman was not the sister of the old man Shokan had met when the mountain dwellers first approached him, then the lord would feel his powers of observation had deserted him entirely. Tiny and wrinkled, her face looked out from the folds of a rough woolen scarf of faded blue.

"You," she said in a thin but surprisingly deep voice, "are Lord Shonto?"

Shokan hid his surprise, for she was the first dweller he had encountered who spoke his language, and almost without accent it seemed. "I am." He bowed.

She motioned for him to sit and he took the other end of the bench to the one she occupied, her knees drawn up in a posture much like a young girl's. "I expected you to be older," she said.

"I am Lord Shonto Shokan. Perhaps you mistake me for my father, Lord Shonto Motoru?"

"You are the son?" she said. "I expected you to be younger."

The lord smiled. "I was not told your name or title; excuse me, I do not know how to address you."

"Alinka-sa," she offered. "I am," she paused. "I do not know your word . . . an old-one."

"Elder," Shokan offered.

She gave the dwellers' peculiar nod. "Elder. I am, perhaps, *the* elder. I am the voice of my people."

"You speak my language very well."

She shrugged, offering no explanation. "May I ask what led you to be in the pass before the snows had melted?"

"We were attempting to make our way to Chiba, the province on the western side of the mountains."

Alinka-sa did not hide her look of displeasure at this answer. A few seconds of silence followed and then Shokan went on.

"There are events in the Empire that led us to attempt this crossing of the mountains too early. There is a war beginning or perhaps it has already begun. It will take place beyond the mountains." He nodded west.

Silence followed while this was considered. Unlike the rest of her people, there was no sense of lightness in Alinka-sa. Hers seemed a personality devoid of humor or joy.

"Why does the Emperor allow the army of the Alatan, the desert tribes, to move south on the canal?"

"It is a long story, Alinka-sa."

She looked at him sharply. "Perhaps there are things even a lord of Wa does not understand. The Shonto name is ancient and honored, but my people saved you and all of your company: your debt is great, Shokan-li. How it will be paid is yet to be decided. What part you play in the events of the world will become part of the decision."

"You will not allow us to continue through the mountains?" Shokan did not hide his shock as well as he hoped.

"What will become of you, Shokan-li, has not been decided. The world beyond our valley is large. Some play parts larger than others. Perhaps you should pass through the mountains to the battle beyond. But it is also possible that you should stay with us, preserving the Shonto House through a time of great turmoil. This cannot be decided easily."

Shokan nodded. "You are a Seer, then?" It might explain why Quinta-la and the children were afraid of her.

"I do not understand this word," she said bluntly.

Questioning an elder, the lord was beginning to suspect, was not acceptable. "The situation in the Empire, Alinka-sa, is difficult to explain and much that I would tell you is conjecture only." He took a long breath. "It began this summer past when my father was appointed Imperial Governor of the province of Seh. . . ."

There seemed to be nothing else to do, so Shokan began the tale. Slowly at first, and then the words began to flow more easily. He told her of the Emperor's plot and what he thought it meant, the coins Tanaka had found, his own time in Seh. The sun had traveled a good distance across the sky before he was done. During the entire telling, Alinka-sa did not ask a single question. Occasionally her eyebrows would rise or she would give the dwellers' nod of the head, but she never interrupted Shokan's story.

Even when he finally finished, the old woman did not speak but stared off across the green valley floor.

"The tree with the fan-leaf, what is it called?" she asked suddenly.

"Ginkyo?"

She nodded. "Alinka means ginkyo in my tongue. This tree does not grow in the mountains and is something of a legend among my people. They believe that the leaves are quite large and that the ladies of Wa simply pluck a leaf from the tree whenever they need a fan. Though I often told my people the truth of this, after some discussion they decided that, in this matter, I was not well informed." She gave the tiniest smile. "My mother was like you—she became lost in the mountains and was saved by the people of this village. When my father died, my mother went back to Itsa and we lived for some time in Wa before returning here."

She looked over at Shokan, meeting his gaze. "For this reason I know your language and something of your ways, strange as they are to us. Some of your story was known to me, though much was new. Great tragedy is about to shake Wa and this saddens me." Alinka-sa looked away again.

"Tell me of this monk who serves your father," she said, not looking at Shokan.

The lord hesitated before speaking. "The people who brought us here used his name often—Shuyun. Why was that."

Obviously controlling her annoyance Alinka-sa answered. "Shu-yung, it is a word in our language: it means bearer, those who carry. To the ear of an outsider the word meaning to bear would be indistinguishable from the word meaning bearer. Tell me of him."

"I have never met Brother Shuyun, in truth. It is said that he is very advanced in the skills of the Botahist monks. Both my father and my sister have written of him in very flattering terms. That is all I know."

She nodded. "My people will guide you through the mountains. You will leave at sunrise." Alinka-sa rose to her feet with an ease that one would not expect in one so aged. Standing, she was eye to eye with the young lord.

"But why have you decided this? I am grateful, certainly but what has made your decision?"

Very gently she reached out and touched his cheek. "Quinta-la will accompany you to the lowlands. May Botahara go with you." She turned and crossed the terrace, disappearing down the steps.

Forty-five

T HE SKY WAS as confused as a lover's heart. Clouds torn and buffeted by conflicting winds rolled overhead, moving against a background of higher clouds, striated like sand revealed by the tide.

It had rained earlier that day and threatened to do so again. The wind was steady from the east though it had blown from every point of the compass that morning, making the rivermen curse under their breaths.

Shuyun knelt before his liege-lord, waiting. They sat on the deck of Lord Shonto's barge which was moving south at its best speed. Dipping his brush in ink, Lord Shonto added three characters to the letter and then waved for his secretary who had servants remove the writing table and all of its contents. Turning to his Spiritual Advisor, the lord smiled.

"You have heard the news of Lord Komawara, Shuyun-sum?"

"I have, Sire. Botahara protects us."

Shonto nodded. "It is good that He does. Perhaps you do not know that Rohku Saicha has returned to us also, though his losses were even more severe than those of Lord Komawara and General Jaku." Shonto hesitated and his face showed a trace of the strain he no doubt felt.

"The Khan has done the correct thing. Driving us south will give him the possibility of food by summer. If he is wise enough to put the peasants he captures to work rather than to the sword, his army will not starve." Shonto pulled an armrest closer. "This smaller barbarian army will soon be beyond assistance from the larger army. . . . If our own force were not so small, it would be an opportunity." He fell silent, lost in the great game of gii that he played.

Shuyun sat quietly waiting. The monk was aware that he felt a growing sense of disquiet as he sat before his liege-lord—the father of the woman with whom he had so recently spent the night. Not that Nishima was not of an age to make her own decisions in such matters, but Shuyun could not believe that Lord Shonto would be pleased by such an alliance.

I am torn in every direction, the monk thought. There was a part of him that felt closer to Shonto and the lord's purposes as he moved further from the faith of his own Order. As though the concerns of the world became more real as the ways of the spirit became more confusing. Yet he was a Botahist monk still and he had spent the night in the embrace of his liege-lord's daughter—certainly an act that would shock anyone who lived in the Empire of Wa. Although Shonto did not pry into Lady Nishima's affairs unduly, was it possible that the lord was unaware of what was taking place? Shuyun thought it unlikely and thus the discomfort.

Shonto focused on his Spiritual Advisor suddenly. "You have a report for me, Shuyun-sum?"

The monk nodded, pushing his feelings into one corner of his being. "It appears that we have isolated the plague for now, Sire, though I think we will see other cases yet. The refugees are frightened, but this has resulted in them moving south more quickly—a good thing. We have placed the barge for the sick at the front of the fleet and it flies a plague banner. All the Imperial Guards in the Empire could not clear the canal more quickly than the sight of that terrible flag. There has been only one more death, may Botahara protect her soul." The monk made a sign. "I pray that the situation does not grow worse, Sire. Brother Sotura is a man of great skill—he has the present situation well in hand."

Shonto nodded. "I wish to be kept informed of this matter. If plague finds root in our army, it will not matter if the Khan is followed by one man or one hundred thousand—our army will be reduced to ghosts." Shonto waved at the mouth of a small creek hung with willows. "Master Myochin will no doubt hear of our approach. He will not be pleased at the prospect of leaving his home." Shonto shook his head. "We all hope for peace in our old age. . . . It will be some time before we see peace again, Shuyun-sum. Even if this Khan can defeat the armies of Wa, holding the Empire will be another matter entirely. Children born today may find their way into this war before it is over, though I pray it will not be so."

Forty-six

T HE STONE SHIP appeared to float in its own reflection in the middle
of the Lake of the Autumn Crane on the western edge of the Imperial
Palace. It was largely carved of marble though jade had also been employed
by the ancient artisans—uncommon materials for a ship. In truth, it was no
boat at all but a small island of stone blocks carved to form an elaborate,
somewhat fantastic ship though to a small scale.

Over the centuries the Stone Ship had been the favorite retreat of many
an Emperor or Empress and had only fallen into disfavor with the recent
dynasty. It remained, however, an ideal place to find peace and to carry on
conversations that one did not want overheard. Perhaps it was this that had
brought the Emperor out to the Stone Ship.

An awning of spring green had been spread for the Son of Heaven and he
sat on silk cushions attended by only a single secretary who stood on the
bow, signaling the shore for anything Akantsu requested, occasionally scurrying back to the stern at a nod from the Emperor. So that the Son of Heaven
could spend a few hours in this blessed isolation an entire retinue of officials
and servants and secretaries waited on the shore, kneeling patiently—only
the most senior members involved in conversation. To maintain this company a kitchen had been constructed behind a screen of willow trees, and
runners stood ready to hurry to the palace to retrieve anything or anyone
the Emperor might request.

Swallows and kingfishers crossed the lake, weaving intricate patterns,
and ducks cut vees into its calm surface. Jaku Tadamoto watched three swal-

lows chasing a downy white feather, one picking it out of the air and rushing off, then dropping it for the others to dive at. This may have been a struggle for possession of nest material, but it looked for all the world like a game, and the acrobatics of the players were impressive.

Tadamoto was being sculled across the Lake of the Autumn Crane's calm waters in one of the elegant craft used by officials of the Island Palace. As was often the case, the young colonel came to his audience with the Emperor carrying written reports and scrolls, not all of which bore good news.

As well as official writings Tadamoto also carried, hidden in his sleeve, a letter from Osha. It was a conciliatory letter, full of apologies for offenses she had not committed, washed in sadness, her pain tearing at his heart. They must not give up, she had written, their love would survive if only they believed it would. So he tried to believe.

Tadamoto also tried to push this letter out of his mind as it would undoubtedly affect his ability to serve his Emperor—something that could not be allowed now that civil war was all but upon them.

The sampan came alongside a stone dock built in the shape of the platform one found at the foot of a ship's ladder. Tadamoto mounted the steps to the "deck" where the secretary greeted him with a low bow. Crossing to the quarterdeck on his knees, Tadamoto bowed at the foot of the stairs and waited to be acknowledged.

The Emperor pored over a long scroll, completely absorbed. The ruler's robe of yellow embroidered with a flight of cranes among clouds created a disturbing contrast. Although his garb was perfectly appropriate for the season—light of spirit—the Emperor's face was drawn and pale like that of a man who had not known a night of peace in many, many days. Tadamoto kept his eyes cast down, concentrating on the wood-grain that had been carved into the planks of the stone deck.

Letting his arms drop, the Emperor laid the scroll across his legs. "Colonel."

Tadamoto bowed again.

"Let us begin with your news. My patience has worn away to nothing and pleasantries have become most unpleasant. What do we know today?"

Tadamoto unrolled a small scroll—notes for this audience. "Shonto's flotilla is three days north of Denji Gorge, Sire, and has increased its speed considerably in the last few days. The first refugees have crossed the border of our own province and they will begin to arrive in the capital in numbers within a few days. I have detailed officials and guards to deal with this influx.

"Our own army has reached twenty-five thousand in number, Sire, and will be thirty thousand before the next moon." Tadamoto lowered the scroll. "I have reports here, Emperor, if you wish to read them." He tapped the pile of rolled paper. "I estimate that Lord Shonto could be within the border of Dentou within fourteen days if he continues to travel at his present speed. There has been a report that Shonto's fleet is preceded by a barge flying the plague banner. This report has not been substantiated and even if it proves true it would appear to be a ruse to keep the canal open before Shonto's fleet. Nonetheless the rumor precedes the flotilla like a bow wave."

The Emperor shook his head. "Shonto would think of such a thing. It is entirely without honor but effective, no doubt." The Emperor lifted the scroll he had been reading. "I have received my own reports. Prince Wakaro has sent this, a complete report of the military situation prepared by Shonto's staff. My son claims to have seen a barbarian army of one hundred thousand and it is accompanied by a letter written by the captain of the Prince's guard—a man we selected together, Colonel. He, too, claims to have seen this army." The Emperor set the scroll aside. "My son is not a warrior and easily duped, but from the captain of his guard I expected more. It is most curious."

Tadamoto nodded. "Excuse me, Sire. . . ."

"Speak, Colonel, this is no time to be shy."

"At your suggestion, I sent the most reliable men I have north to assess this situation. According to their count—they saw the barbarian army with their own eyes—the force pursuing Shonto is no more than thirty thousand and perhaps less. Shonto's own army appears to number between twenty and twenty-five thousand, a significant number of these being Imperial Guards. Alongside the shinta blossom fly the banners of both Prince Wakaro and my brother Katta. It grieves me to bring you this news, Emperor."

The Emperor looked toward the white walls of the Island Palace as though he meditated upon their form. But his breathing did not exhibit the controlled rhythm of meditation and his hands would not lie still on his knees. "Betrayed," the Emperor almost whispered, "betrayed by my own son and by the man I treated as a son." Picking up his sword, he laid it gently across his knees. "Is this army in league with Motoru, do you think?"

"My own men believe there have been real battles with the barbarians though reports that Lord Shonto scorched the earth as he passed south appear to be unfounded. They saw no evidence of this. So it seems unlikely. There truly is a barbarian invasion but not the hordes some would like us to believe."

"Two invading armies, one on the heels of the other." The Emperor toyed with his sword. "Betrayed by my own son," he said again, his voice filled with disbelief and pain.

The son you sent north to share in the fate of Lord Shonto, Tadamoto thought.

Forty-seven

THE BARGES ALMOST never stopped now and though it meant the countryside was left untouched by the devastation formerly wrought upon it, it also meant that Shimeko could not get off the boat to walk on the bank. This made it very easy to avoid Sister Morima and all of the influences from her former life. But she was shut up on the ship among people who were very different from her—the three ladies from the capital and their attendants. It was difficult for her.

The Plum Blossom Winds filled the air with clouds of petals from the plum groves planted along the canal. When a gust came, standing on the deck of the boat was like being in a warm snowstorm, so thick were the petals in the air. The canal was almost a white waterway and the decks of the ships were constantly needing to be swept clear, for a rain shower would render a petal-covered deck dangerously slick.

Shimeko had given up brushing the petals from her robe despite the fact that on the deep blue they were very apparent. The robe had been a gift from Lady Nishima, one of the lady's own, no doubt, and though it was a cast-off it had obviously been worn infrequently for the silk was as new as the day it had come from the loom. Having seen the size of Lady Nishima's wardrobe, Shimeko was not surprised that signs of wear would not be found on the lady's clothing—and Lady Nishima often complained that she had left the capital with hardly anything to wear!

Shimeko smiled. Such a statement would have offended the former nun only a few weeks before, but now it only made her shake her head and laugh.

The Lady Nishima Fanisan Shonto was difficult to dislike and, despite having been raised in the greatest luxury, could not be said to have been spoiled by it. She was a Lady of a Great House, there was no doubt, but Lady Nishima was a person of substance and accomplishment and depth. Shimeko could not dislike her.

Shimeko turned away from the rail, leaning there with the breeze at her back. Pulling her shawl down onto her shoulders, she enjoyed the feeling of the wind blowing through her hair; though it was still short by the standards of lay-women, it was longer than Shimeko had ever known it.

The decision Shimeko made was a difficult one. Although she had found Lady Nishima admirable in many ways, there was this other matter which the former nun found very disturbing. Shimeko was almost certain that Lady Nishima had more than once spent the entire night alone with Brother Shuyun.

The young woman looked off at the white-capped mountains rising along the western horizon. Having little experience of the world, she did not know how such news would be received by the population at large. What would Lord Shonto think of such a thing? Sister Morima always claimed that the Brothers were entirely corrupt, but Shimeko never suspected she had meant corrupt in ways such as this. And Brother Shuyun! To think that many of the Sisters hoped he was the Teacher who was spoken of.

A vision of the Faceless Lovers carved into the cliff of Denji Gorge came to her. This was the subject of Lady Nishima's curiosity. Shimeko brushed petals from her robe unconsciously. Was it possible that this sculpture was not a heresy? Was Lady Nishima aware of things that Shimeko was not?

Sister Morima had also claimed there were things written in the Sacred Scrolls of the Perfect Master that were not included in any copies of these texts——things the Brotherhood wished to keep hidden. Botahara had taken a bride, everyone knew that, but when had he attained Enlightenment? That was the question that had once caused a war. The bride was not spoken of in the writings of Botahara and his disciples only mentioned her in passing. Shimeko shook her head. Despite having left the Sisterhood and rejected its doctrine, she still found Lady Nishima's relations with Shuyun disturbing and a part of her feared this might be jealousy.

There had been a night when Shimeko had heard Lady Nishima cry out and though the former nun would admit she knew little of such things, a cry of ecstasy was difficult to mistake. Her own body had responded to this sound in a manner that was surprising and her imagination had . . . well, it had not been under her control.

A servant appeared at the head of the companionway and, seeing Shimeko at the rail, crossed to her.

"Lady Nishima awaits you, Shimeko-sum," the woman said.

The young woman replaced her shawl, nodded her thanks, and proceeded to the stairs, controlling her nervousness with care.

Bowing at the door to Lady Nishima's cabin, she entered at a smile from her mistress.

"Shimeko-sum, it is a pleasure to see you." Nishima gestured to a cushion. "You are well, I trust."

"I am well, Lady Nishima. It is kind of you to ask."

"Are the petals on the wind not a most impressive sight today?"

Shimeko nodded. "I have just come from the deck." And then she realized that not only were her robes covered in petals, but it appeared a small snowstorm had focused its efforts around her. "Please excuse me, Lady Nishima." She was obviously dismayed. "And all over your gift to me."

Laughing with great delight, Nishima reached out and touched Shimeko's hand. "These blossoms complement the robe beautifully. As for this," she waved her hand at the petals on the mat, "I would like nothing better than to have my chambers covered in plum blossoms, like the floor of a grove. Would that not be charming?" She laughed again.

Shimeko smiled, not quite reassured.

"I was told, Shimeko-sum, that there was some matter you wished to speak of?"

Nodding, the former nun gathered her courage. "It is not my intention to appear ungrateful for your favor, Lady Nishima; serving the Shonto House has been a great honor. There appears to be a matter that has arisen which is more suited to my particular skills. I have come to ask if I may be released from your service so that I might tend to the sick aboard the plague ship." She bowed when she finished and kept her eyes fixed on the floor.

For a moment Nishima did not respond but only looked at the woman who had come to be a trusted secretary. "I regret to hear that you wish to leave, Shimeko-sum, for your skills are far beyond those of anyone who has served me in the same capacity. Will the Brothers allow you to assist them? Is there not a certain antagonism to the Sisterhood, not to mention great secrecy about the ways of healing?"

"As you say, Lady Nishima, the two Botahist Orders are not allies, but I am no longer a Sister and Brother Shuyun has said that the Brothers' need is great. I may assist and learn little or nothing of their secrets, I am sure."

"And you would be in no danger from this illness?"

"Certainly not, Lady Nishima. I am no longer a Sister, but I have not forgotten all that I learned. It is also true that the Brothers could cure me if I were to become ill—though I assure you this is next to impossible." She paused and then said quietly. "Your concern touches me."

Nishima arranged the hem of her robes. "When you first came to me, you spoke of a desire to serve the Shonto Spiritual Advisor, Brother Shuyun. If you go to care for the sick, you will be more removed from Brother Shuyun than you are presently. Does this not concern you?"

Shimeko nodded reflexively. "I do not know, Lady Nishima, I. . . . There are sick who I may offer help to. In a time such as this, it seems that I must do what I am able." She shrugged.

"I see. Have the Brothers agreed to accept your assistance, Shimeko-sum?"

The young woman shook her head.

"If they agree to allow you to assist them, I will release you upon one condition—you will send messages to assure me that you are well."

Shimeko bowed. "Certainly, my lady."

Nishima forced a smile. "You are no doubt anxious to proceed with this matter. Please inform me of the Brothers' decision. Certainly you are welcome to stay with me if this plan is untenable."

"I thank you, my lady." She met Nishima's eye for the briefest second. "It has been an honor to serve you."

With that she bowed and retreated to the door, receiving a last reassuring smile from the young aristocrat as she went. Shimeko was surprised at the feeling of emptiness this decision left. She had almost embarrassed herself in conversation with Lady Nishima, so touched was she by the woman's concern.

My life will become quite simple again, she thought. I will tend the sick, I will eat and I will sleep. There will not be the turmoil and confusion of my present position. No Sisters will come to me with demands that I can not fulfill and I will not have my heart torn by growing loyalties and attachments that I am not suited to.

Forty-eight

FOR THOSE THAT had journeyed north in Lord Shonto's fleet, Denji Gorge was remembered not for its unique beauty but for the days when no one had been certain what would befall those traveling with Seh's Imperial Governor.

The country surrounding the gorge itself had changed so much in the intervening months that it was like returning to another time. Over the Imperial Guard Keep at the gorge's northern end flew the Emperor's banner, and the locks were administered by Imperial Functionaries and guarded by black-clad Imperial Guards. Nowhere could one find signs of the Hajiwara presence. The armor with green lacing had disappeared—unless one looked very carefully at the men who formed Lord Komawara's guard. There, among the armor of night blue, one could find a trim of green on the occasional shoulder piece or sleeve.

All of the earthworks and fortifications constructed over the years had been dismantled and several of the larger manor houses that had been protected by moats were in the process of converting these to decorative ponds or filling them in altogether.

Arrayed along the stone quay of the northern locks were several rows of kneeling guards in purple-laced armor, hands on their thighs, faces and posture rigid. As Lord Shonto's boat bumped up against the quay, the warriors bowed low. Out from among this group emerged a youth of such small stature that it brought a smile to the lips of all who had not previously encountered the Lord Butto Joda.

"I greet you, Lord Butto," Shonto said from the deck. "It is a great honor to be met by such an esteemed company."

Lord Butto gave a half bow. "The honor is mine entirely, Lord Shonto. I bring greetings from my father who asks that you forgive him for not meeting you himself."

"Lord Butto does me great honor. I trust that he is well."

Butto Joda gave a half nod and a smile, acknowledging the question but giving no specific answer—the senior lord of the Butto had not been well for many years.

Steps were set out and Shonto and several of his advisors disembarked.

"Certainly you remember Lord Komawara, General Hojo, and Steward Kamu?"

"I could not forget those who fought so valiantly beside the Butto. I am forever in your debt," he said bowing. "And Brother Shuyun, he travels with you also?"

"Brother Shuyun monitors the progress of the ship bearing the sick through the locks. We are taking care that there is no transfer of disease."

The young lord nodded. "I am less concerned knowing this."

Jaku Katta was delivered to the quay at that moment, his sampan coming alongside the stone wall. The Imperial Guards on the quay bowed low in unison.

"General Jaku," Lord Butto greeted him with a great smile. "I see that my concerns regarding who would control the locks were groundless." He looked around. "There seems to be no delegation from the Imperial Governor of Itsa. New to his position, perhaps the worthy governor has not yet learned proper protocol for such occasions."

The smiles were polite. The Governor of Itsa was no doubt under orders to detain Shonto but had not the troops to do so. Ignoring the flotilla's passing was the only choice left to the poor man, and his situation was made worse by the fact that Imperial Guard on the canal were loyal to Jaku Katta. An appeal to the larger Houses of Itsa for assistance would have been futile as the most powerful family in the province was the Butto—sworn ally of Lord Shonto.

The group walked slowly along the quay in the direction of the gorge, the line of Butto guards bowing in turn as the party passed. On a lookout that had recently been a Hajiwara military position, mats and cushions had been spread. Calypta and willow trees coming newly into leaf shaded the lookout from the early afternoon sun so that no awning or pavilion was necessary.

The great gorge stretched out to the south, the surface broken by the breeze and sparkling in the spring sunlight. Off the gravel bar below the fane of the lost Brothers, river craft of every type and size swung to anchors, so close together that fouling of rodes and lines must have been constant.

Along the eastern cliff more boats huddled, mooring to unseen irregularities in the rock face and countless more sailed back and forth or drifted free, unable to find anchorage or moorings. Smoke rose from many of the craft and a ragged camp had been erected on the gravel bar itself, shelters of all shapes and colors arranged in random patterns.

In contrast to this chaos of refugee craft, a line of ships in formation passed down the middle of the gorge, the foremost boats almost at the southern locks—Lord Shonto's flotilla continuing south.

A meal was served by Butto attendants and plum wine, a gift from Lord Shonto, was poured for the young lord and his guests.

"It is unfortunate that Prince Wakaro was unable to join us," Shonto said to Lord Butto.

Setting his wine cup down, the young lord nodded. "Most unfortunate. I had the honor of entertaining the Prince on his journey north. He was most kind."

Lifting his cup to Komawara and Jaku in turn, Butto Joda said, "I have heard tales of your recent exploits, Lord Komawara, General. It was a bold stroke—a frontal attack on the barbarians' supply train." He gave a half bow. "Your reputations have become great. I consider it an honor to join you in your struggle." He bowed also to Hojo.

"This barbarian force," the young lord continued, "has divided, I am told, and a part of it is now in close pursuit?"

Shonto nodded at Hojo.

General Hojo bowed. "There is a force of about twenty-five thousand not far behind and they come slightly closer each day—the number of refugee craft fleeing south is slowing our progress." Hojo stroked the gray hair of his beard, staring out over the gorge. "This is becoming a cause of some concern."

Butto Joda nodded. "I have considered this situation myself. I have taken the liberty of allowing no boats to pass through the southern locks for six days past. River craft accumulate in the gorge at an alarming rate, but the canal south is now open for many rih. In a letter, Lord Shonto suggested that we prepare this set of locks so that, once your fleet has passed, it would take engineers of great skill to restore them to use. These measures, General Hojo, should improve the speed at which you travel and, at the same time, impede the progress of your pursuers." He held up his cup. "This is excellent wine. Does it come from Seh?"

Shimeko had slept three nights on the deck to be away from the endless coughing and the odors of the sick. Although she had often treated the sick before, she had been too young to minister to those stricken by the plague during the previous outbreak. It was a frightening disease, so she spent as much time out in the fresh air as her duties would allow.

Upwind, and not far off, a small boat sailed a parallel course and aboard it, standing at the rail as she did herself, Shimeko could see Initiate Brother Shuyun. The distance was such that, had they attempted to speak, they could not have heard each other over the wind and boat sounds nor could the other's expression be seen. To the former nun this distance seemed great— as great as the distance between her present life and her days as a Botahist nun. Did she still hope he was the Teacher and would help her find tranquillity of purpose again?

She looked off to the south where the locks awaited them. She was a healer now and though it was a simple life, as she had hoped, the confusion she had felt in Lady Nishima's service had not disappeared.

Earlier the plague ship had passed the fane of the Brothers of the Eightfold Path—the Faceless Lovers. It had been difficult to view the figures, for she did not want to be seen looking at something so unseemly. Even so, she had managed a glance or two. Thoughts of Lady Nishima with Brother Shuyun would not leave her in peace.

The wind moved the pine branches in slow circles, constantly spoiling Rohku Tadamori's view of the advancing army. The young guard officer had abandoned his blue-laced armor in favor of the brown and green garb of the huntsmen and this clothing helped to camouflage him where he lay. The forest floor was cooled by occasional rain and the consistent wind out of the east, and Tadamori found that his muscles were growing stiff.

The *small army*, as it was becoming known, traveled at a pace that was impressive. Even those born of the desert could learn the handling of rafts, and the crude sails the pirates had fabricated from bamboo cloth were surprisingly efficient with such a fair wind. Horsemen still rode along the bank but they led strings of the barbarian ponies which were able to cover much more ground without riders. Constant changing of mounts for the riders was required, but this was not difficult.

There was no doubt in Tadamori's mind that the small army was gaining on Lord Shonto's flotilla. Occasional refugees were being overtaken by the barbarians now, and the Shonto guard did not like to contemplate what might happen to them—especially the women.

The huntsman who was Tadamori's companion touched his arm and cocked his head toward the passing army. Among the hundreds of rafts one came into view bearing banners, some gold and crimson. Tadamori and his companion had hidden themselves atop a hill overlooking the canal from the west, but they were still half a rih from the bank—close enough to assess the army but not able to see who its leaders might be.

The question in the minds of the two men of Wa was: does the Khan lead this expeditionary force? If the great chieftain had taken it upon himself to pursue the retreating army, then Lord Shonto might consider a battle. It was believed likely that the Khan was the only force that held the various tribes together. Brother Shuyun's barbarian servant was utterly convinced that without the Khan the natural rivalry between the tribes would soon lead to the dissolution of the great army if not an outright war between the factions.

Rohku reached up and stopped the branch from blocking his view. It was difficult to say. Almost certainly that was the Khan's banner, but then the Emperor's banner was seen over all of Wa, above Imperial Keeps and palaces of government. This might be the banner of the desert chieftain, but the Khan himself might be here only in spirit. It would be the worst foolishness for the men of Wa to destroy their army fighting this force and find the Khan was not present. Foolish indeed.

It had been seven years since the Supreme Master had set foot on the land of Wa. Normally his arrival was heralded by celebration and ceremony and pilgrims would come from across the Empire just to kneel outside the temple grounds in which he resided. On this journey, however, the Supreme Master came quietly, if not quite secretly. His ship arrived in Yankura without gaining any notice, and the head of the Botahist Brotherhood boarded a smaller boat that bore him swiftly to the Jade Temple.

Peering out a slit between the curtains the Supreme Master watched the activity of the Floating City. The canals and docks and quays teemed with people in motion, for Yankura was the center of shipping and commerce in the Empire of Wa and it appeared never to rest. Such lack of tranquillity, the monk thought, how can they live such lives? Even more to the point, how did Brother Hutto live in the midst of this? It was not conducive to the contemplation of Botahara's words, there was no doubt of that.

Botahara's words were more on the Supreme Master's mind recently— His true words. The blossoming of the Udumbara, the missing scrolls— these matters disturbed even his sleep. And now news of this barbarian invasion. He had returned to Wa as soon as word had arrived on the first ship of spring.

There was about to be war with an army that did not even know the words of the Perfect Master, a dynasty might fall, civil war was almost certain, and the Shonto House seemed likely to finally suffer the fate that overtook all other Houses—extinction.

Small river craft of all description lay alongside the quay, loading cargo from the great stone warehouses. In the midst of this a ragged child wriggled out of an open port and was spotted by a river man who sent up a shout. Jumping to the next boat, the child was barely able to grab the rail. Shouts echoed the alarm as the child pulled himself up onto the deck. Scrambling over stacked boxes, he leaped an open hatch and dodged a burly sailor. Holding something in his robe, he made another impossible jump to the quay where it seemed certain he would disappear into the clutter and the uncaring crowd.

The Supreme Master watched in fascination. Suddenly a man appeared from behind a pile of sacks and the child ran into him head-on, allowing one of his pursuers to grab him by the hair. A wild struggle ensued until the much larger man landed a blow that drove the child to his knees, and a series of punches and kicks left the child an unmoving pile of rags on the stones.

The scene was lost to view then and the Supreme Master slumped back against the cushions, fixed in his mind was the image of triumph on the man's face as he beat the child to the ground. *And this is what I have come to,* the old monk thought, *a brutal, violent land.*

The Lake of the Seven Masters was not large enough to develop much swell except in storm winds; still it was not as calm as a canal, and Lady Nishima steadied herself by clutching the frame of the port. The fane of the Brothers of the Eightfold Path was quickly falling astern. Nishima could see the cliff that appeared almost to have been carved with shadows and light—carved into the form of a man and woman in the act of love.

She moved away from the port and returned to kneeling on the carpet. After a moment, she lay down and cradled her head on her arm, pressing her eyes closed, the image returning as she did so. The boat rocked her as she lay there, making her feel like a child, though she knew the ache she felt was not the ache of a child.

Forty-nine

JAKU TADAMOTO, FOLLOWED by officers and engineers, strode along the top of the earthworks. Stopping suddenly, he let his eye follow the line of the newly built defenses which ran between two steep hills broken only in its center by the Grand Canal. The earthworks swept up at each end following the curve of the hills and provided a surprising degree of symmetry to the entire composition.

Only a day north and west of the Imperial Capital, the position had been chosen after long deliberation. Tadamoto's eye examined the plain that stretched out for several rih north of the hills. It was there that the battle would take place—the fortifications were only built to ensure that.

Despite all the discussion that had led to this decision Tadamoto was not entirely convinced this was the best course. The Emperor wanted to be certain that Shonto could not reach the capital where there was every possibility that the population would rise up to support him. It was also true that the Imperial Capital would be a difficult, if not impossible, position to defend. After all, the capital was not a fortified city but an enormous sprawl without continuous walls or towers and festooned with gates and canals.

And so Tadamoto had been sent north of the city to create these defenses. But who would the battle be with? That was the question in the young colonel's mind. There were two armies hurrying south on the canal—one appearing to pursue the other. Once they encountered the Imperial Army, what would occur? The situation was so confused and unclear that anything the Emperor did was undoubtedly a gamble.

What if Shonto had agreements with this Khan the Emperor had thought was his own toy? Would the rebel army suddenly join the army of the desert, creating a force double the size of the army Tadamoto had raised?

Recent reports indicated that Shonto was rushing down the canal as fast as an army could be moved. This, despite the fact that his own letters claimed he did everything to slow the barbarians' advance so that the Emperor could raise an army. What was Shonto thinking?

Turning south, Jaku looked out over the encampment that was slowly filling with the newly recruited troops. Beyond that lay the commandeered mansion that would be the residence of the Son of Heaven. As he trusted no one and felt everyone to be less capable than himself, the Emperor had made it known that he would assume command of the Imperial Army himself. There was no doubt that the Yamaku would survive or fall according to the decisions made on this field, and the Emperor did not intend to let another take control of his fate.

Tadamoto continued toward the canal. A continuous flow of refugees passed by, both day and night, swelling the population of the capital and straining the ability of the city to support such an influx. Crime was growing at alarming rates and the Imperial Guard were hard pressed to deal with this, preparing for war as they were.

A messenger approached Tadamoto's guard and was allowed through. He bowed and knelt before his commander. Tadamoto nodded for the man to speak.

"We have brought the merchant, Colonel Jaku, as you requested. He is under guard in your quarters."

Somehow the capture of Shonto's vassal-merchant had been kept a secret and even now Tanaka's name was never used. *Merchants* were as common as street women and a reference to one meant nothing. Tadamoto was not sure what part Tanaka might play in events, if any, but it seemed prudent to have the old man present. He was someone Shonto respected and there were few of whom that could be said.

A hundred paces more brought Tadamoto to the canal bank. Although most of the flowers had been swept from the trees this far south, farther north the Plum Blossom Wind was still blowing, for the boats of refugees were decorated with white and the canal still bore petals south toward the sea.

Turning in a slow circle, Tadamoto surveyed the scene one last time.

When his gaze fell on the mansion where the Emperor would dwell, the question that had bothered him all morning flared up: who from the Imperial Court would accompany the Son of Heaven? He whispered a silent prayer. Let the gods spare Osha that indignity—that she be brought along like a common camp woman.

Fifty

> *Here, above the clouds*
> *Mountain paths*
> *Lead always to the unexpected.*
> *Rush ahead*
> *And see it with the eyes of a child*
>
> *Lord Shonto Shokan*

THEY HAD ASCENDED and descended so often that Shokan no longer knew how high in the mountains they were. The type of vegetation that grew seemed to be an indicator but was affected by too many other factors to be relied upon entirely.

The lord lay in the darkness, looking up at the stars. The world he traveled in was so strange that he was surprised to see constellations he recognized floating overhead—the Two Sisters were peeking over the shoulder of a mountain now.

It was not as cold as usual, which might be a sign that they were at a lower elevation. Whatever the reason he was thankful for it.

A few feet away Quinta-la slept, wrapped in a fur. Since they had left the village in the valley she had refused to teach him new words in her language but insisted he teach her words in his own tongue. He was not sure what had led to her decision to learn the tongue of the lowlanders, but she approached this task with an earnestness that Shokan could not help but find charming—

almost comic. Even so, Quinta-la was learning at a pace that surprised the men from the Empire.

Closing his eyes, Shokan felt sleep hovering close by. Earlier in the evening he had bathed in a hot spring—an experience almost worth the days of walking. It had been a large pool, one of several etched out into the rock by ten thousand years of moving water. The dwellers had a different sense of propriety—the women bathed with the men and no one seemed to care.

Quinta-la had slipped into the pool beside him and continued her language inquiry without being self-conscious about the naturalness of their state. Shokan smiled. He had fallen into the strange world of a story; at least for now.

The litter was lifted carefully over the river boat's rail and set gently on the deck where it was secured against movement. Sister Sutso stood by, her hand to her mouth. Stepping forward, she opened the curtain a hand's width and was surprised to find the Prioress awake, her lively eyes turned to a half-open curtain on the litter's opposite side.

"Excuse me, Prioress," Sutso said pulling the curtain closed. "I did not mean to intrude. Excuse me."

The dry voice filtered through the curtain. "How far to the river, child?"

"Perhaps seven rih, Prioress," the senior nun's secretary answered. "This creek is quite narrow and not straight. We will be some time,"

"It is a day to be enjoyed, Sister Sutso. A shame the trees have lost their blossoms, but the new leaves are beautiful, are they not?" Before Sutso could agree, the Prioress went on. "Have you heard the most recent news?"

Sutso shook her head. The Prioress took delight in surprising her and usually succeeded. "I have not, Prioress."

"He arrived in Yankura, three days ago; the Brotherhood's Supreme Master. We cannot tarry. Are Sister Gatsa and her companions content with our pilgrimage?"

"They speak of little else, Prioress." The faction lead by Sister Gatsa had been told that the Prioress was on a pilgrimage to Monarta. The fact that the Prioress had sent a message to the Brotherhood demanding that they open the grounds to the Sisters had caused a hum of discussion—so much so in fact that no one had yet thought to wonder if Monarta was their true destination.

The Prioress did not speak for a moment, but Sutso was used to this and waited. One could never be sure when the Prioress slept and when she was awake.

"War could sweep away the prize for which we have lived all these lives. That fool of an Emperor has gone off with his toy army?"

"He has, Prioress."

"May the hand of Botahara guide us. Pray for fair winds, Sutso-sum, the currents are against us."

The officer was awakened in the night and found he was dizzy and disoriented when he sat up. Imperial Guards, he seemed to remember gambling and Imperial Guards . . . and rice wine. His men—the men Lord Butto had left at the northern end of Denji Gorge to be certain the locks were filled—were billeted in the Imperial Guard Keep. Not perhaps the best idea.

"Captain?" The voice came from outside the door to his tiny room.

"What is it?" he said, unable to sound civil.

"Barbarians, Captain. Many barbarians—they are only two rih off."

The officer was on his feet. "Botahara save us! Alert the Imperial Guards."

"The Guards will muster immediately, Captain. Your armor is being readied. I have a lamp."

The Captain opened his door a crack and a lamp was passed in. He began pulling on the clothing that would go under his armor. "What hour?"

"The owl, Captain."

"Huh. And we hoped these barbarians did not even know of Denji Gorge."

A clatter in the hall announced the arrival of his armor, and he threw open the door to his attendants. He could hear men shouting now, the sound of men running.

It could not be a large barbarian force, or Lord Shonto's patrols would have known of it, he reasoned. They would not allow functioning locks to fall into barbarian hands, of that he was certain.

Shimeko had taken up chanting again, not because she had found her faith but because the chant was like a curtain between one's heart and the world. The smell of smoldering maji was thick in the converted hold of the ship. Maji cleansed the air and inhibited the spread of disease, but it stung the eyes despite its health-giving properties. She lifted the head of a young man and fed him his drug cake a small piece at a time. He was the only soldier on board, a cavalry man in Lord Shonto's army.

"You must make the effort to chew, Inara-sum," Shimeko chided him. "Come, just a little."

The young man made a tiny nod and moved his jaw in a feeble effort. He was racked by the cough that marked the disease then, and Shimeko had to wait some time for him to recover enough to take a sip of water and then she fed him another piece of drug cake—the Brothers' great secret.

"That is better, Inara-sum. You will be well before you know it if you make an effort."

He shook his head a little. "You would be less concerned, honored Sister," he whispered hoarsely, "if you had seen the army that pursues us."

"I do not want to hear this talk. All of your focus must be given to becoming well. Let Lord Shonto and his able staff worry about barbarian armies. You fight your own battle."

The young man nodded weakly.

Most of the sick were slowly recovering, but this boy-man was getting weaker and this concerned the former nun greatly. Of all the patients on the ship this man was without doubt the most devout follower of Botahara and he was the only one who did not seem to respond to the Brother's ministrations. It was as if he was resisting the treatment in some way.

Shimeko was chilled by the conversations she had overheard between this young man and the Brothers—talk of completion and rebirth. This obsession with the size of the barbarian army also unsettled her. It had obviously had a great impact on his young mind. *He is choosing to die,* Shimeko thought. Her recent crisis of faith made this realization extremely disturbing.

Completing her rounds, Shimeko bowed to Brother Sotura and made her way up to the deck. It was a dark night, thin clouds covering the stars. She took many lungfuls of the clear air and walked to the rail, leaning over it and staring down into the black water. They were back in the canal now, south of Denji Gorge. The fleet proceeded at a faster pace, for the canal was almost free of the boats of the refugees which had been detained in Denji Gorge until Shonto's fleet passed.

The evening was warm, full of the scents of spring, the sounds. Had she heard a nightingale earlier?

"Do you fare well, Shimeko-sum?" a whisper came to her out of the dark. A woman's voice.

The quiet swirl of an oar in the water. There in the dark, the shape of a boat and someone sitting to paired oars.

"Morima-sum?"

"Yes. I have come to be sure these fool monks have not let you become ill."

Shimeko had to stay absolutely still to hear—even the noise of her robe moving would mask the words. "I remain well, but you should not come so close, Sister. It is unwise."

Shimeko was not sure if she heard a chuckle or if it was merely the bubble of oars in the water. "You have left your Teacher to come serve the sick, Shimeko-sum, or perhaps it was his bidding?"

The younger woman felt herself relax a little in resignation. It was as Morima said, they would never let her be.

"What is it you wish to know, Morima-sum?"

The sound of oars, unmistakable this time.

"I wish to know what is truth and what is merely a fabric of lies, Aco . . . Shimeko-sum. But the Sisters have other concerns. They wish to know if this young monk is the one so many await. Recently rumors have been whispered—Lady Nishima . . . she is an attractive woman." A pause. "You were her secretary, Shimeko-sum."

The former nun resisted the urge to hang her head in her hands. She shook her head in the darkness. *A woman's cry of ecstasy. . . .*

"Shimeko-sum?"

She said nothing. The swirl of oars holding a boat in position. Again. And yet again.

"May you find tranquillity of purpose, my young seeker," the voice whispered and the dark form disappeared into the shadow of the canal bank.

Fifty-one

THE RIVER BOATS of Shonto's fleet passed slowly by on the constant east wind and on almost every craft warriors lined the rail, bowing low to their liege-lord. Shonto sat on a wooden dock under a blue silk awning and though his retainers bowed as they passed, the lord was hidden from sight behind screens of bamboo and Shonto banners.

Aboard the passing ships there was an uncommon silence, almost funereal in its pervasiveness and emotional weight. News had spread very quickly.

Kneeling before Shonto were the lord's senior advisors, several ranking officers, and sundry allies. Dressed in robes of blue over which he wore a surcoat in the same color bearing only the shinta blossom in a circle, Shonto was an imposing figure. A powerful man in more than just position.

As was the lord's custom, he allowed the silence to last longer than one would expect, like a Botahist Master who gave his students time to attain the proper state of tranquillity so that they would be better prepared to learn. The lord's retainers were used to this and all others present remained respectfully quiet and still.

"General Hojo," Shonto said at last, "could you explain the situation."

The senior general bowed and composed himself before addressing the council. "It was artfully done, Sire. Our own patrols monitored the progress of the small barbarian army which made its way down the canal and the western bank, but the companies that took the locks at Denji Gorge were from the main barbarian force and made their way secretly through the country east of the canal."

Hojo paused to collect his thoughts. "The locks were to be filled in with stone by workers from Lord Butto's fief and this task was to be watched over by Imperial Guards and Butto House Guards. The attacking barbarian forces were large and unexpected. We do not know details, but the locks and positions of defense at either end of the gorge are in barbarian hands; losses are unknown. This gives the Khan access to large numbers of river craft, for many of the refugees had not yet locked out of the gorge. We expect the small barbarian army to increase its speed as a result."

The banners fluttered in a small gust and conversation waited until this noise stopped. Both Jaku Katta and Lord Butto sat calmly, showing no sign that it had been their troops guarding the locks. Shonto sat quietly for a moment, watching a hawk soar high over the canal.

"It appears that we have few courses left open to us. If we turn and fight the small army pursuing us, even were we to win, our own force would be reduced substantially. Yet if we continue south, we must meet the Imperial Army. Commanded by whom?" Obviously the lord was thinking aloud and no one attempted to answer.

Shonto put his fingertips together, staring at nothing. "No matter who commands the Emperor's forces, I would prefer to meet them with an army at my back rather than as a ragtag company of survivors." He turned to Jaku Katta. "General Jaku, who do you imagine will command the Emperor's army?"

Jaku bowed and returned to a sitting position, hands on his thighs. "There are several generals who served the Yamaku in the Interim Wars who could be called from retirement, Lord Shonto. At least three are worthy commanders and still young enough to wage such a campaign, but none of these are favored by the Emperor. My own brother, Tadamoto-sum, is the acting commander of the Guard, but he has no experience in warfare. I have given this much thought, Sire, and I believe that the Emperor will act as his own commander of forces. The Son of Heaven trusts few and of the few he trusts he doubts their abilities." Jaku bowed again.

Shonto nodded. "Huh. I have allowed myself to hope that the commander of the Imperial Army might be convinced to betray his Emperor. . . . Difficult, yeh?" Shonto shrugged. "I believe we must go on. Somehow the armies must be joined or the barbarians cannot be defeated. The armies cannot stand alone, no matter what the cost." Looking around the gathering, Shonto said, "I will hear other opinions of this matter."

Lord Komawara bowed. "If the barbarians are to be defeated, I agree, Sire. Our army must be kept whole until we meet the Emperor's force. The Son of Heaven must realize what we face. He will certainly fall without our support. All possibilities will be open for discussion then."

Shonto nodded to the young lord. The fact that Komawara had actually spoken first was not lost on the others.

"It is impossible to know what will happen when we meet the Emperor, if indeed it is the Emperor, Sire," Kamu said. "I would prefer not to leave a matter of such import so open to the whims of fate and situation. Can we not approach the Emperor now? If he realizes he will lose his throne without our support, as Lord Komawara has said, the Emperor should welcome discussion."

"I agree with Steward Kamu, Lord Shonto," Lord Butto said. "We should not wait to begin discussions with the Son of Heaven. We are in a position of power— the Emperor cannot continue to sit on his throne without our help."

Jaku Katta shook his head. "Excuse me for saying so, but I have had quiet contact with the palace. The Emperor believes the entire barbarian army is represented by the mere fraction—the small army—that pursues us. The Son of Heaven will not be willing to listen until he realizes the true peril. To approach the palace now would be to no avail."

General Hojo stroked his beard as he did when lost in thought. His bow was barely perfunctory, though no one appeared to notice. "The suggestion that Prince Wakaro approach his father comes to mind again. Perhaps the Prince could be an envoy in his father's court."

Shonto frowned. "I suspect that having received no response from the Emperor to his letters has led the Prince to reconsider his offer. Even a son of the Emperor can lose favor at court. Certainly we could send the Prince to the capital, but I believe it would be a course of futility. The Prince may serve a purpose among us yet. We should keep him close.

"It is only a matter of days until we arrive in the capital. If we are to have another course, we must decide now. Consider this. Our enemy is showing himself more resourceful than we had previously thought possible. After the clumsy attack on Rhojo-ma I did not consider him a general of note. But now. . . . This barbarian chieftain has stopped our destruction of crops which will allow him to feed his army, and he has seized the locks at Denji

Gorge from formidable warriors. As Soto wrote: we cannot rely on this Khan to make a mistake. If we do not raise a force of sufficient size to challenge this desert army, then retreat may be our only recourse. It is not beyond question that we would allow this Khan to take the Imperial Capital—and then he will sit upon the throne he so desires."

Fifty-two

THE BOAT THAT bore the Emperor to war had sails of crimson silk, a hull ornate with carvings and gilt, a dragon's head on its prow, and sixty men to man the oars should the Son of Heaven lose the favor of the Wind Goddess. On the decks beautiful women played music while other women of equal beauty danced, their long sleeves swaying with the intricate movements of their hands. The Emperor did not go to war as did other men.

Tadamoto waited at the dock that had been prepared for the Emperor's arrival. Banners rustled in the wind, and guards knelt in curving rows forming the shape of a dragon fan. The petals of fresh flowers had been strewn across new mats laid out on the dock, and a guard stood at the end of this fragrant path holding a gray stallion of famous lineage.

An Emperor who rode a horse rather than a sedan chair, who led his own army, turned his back on the religion of Botahara, and in whose hand a sword was more than a sign of office. Tadamoto shook his head—he served an Emperor who would go down in history as defying the pattern, there was no doubt.

Shonto's army was only days away, certainly less than seven, moving by both day and night and reportedly burning any craft that hindered its progress. With the rebel lord's army came Tadamoto's elder brother and this must lead to a reckoning that the young colonel could not think about with ease. Tadamoto had begun to sleep poorly and felt the effects of this more each day.

A sudden strengthening of the wind caused the Emperor's boat to heel slightly and pick up speed, a white wave appearing at the bow as though the dragon on the prow rode forward on a cloud. Willow trees billowed in the breeze, hissing like angry old women waving their arms at truant children.

Straining to overcome the distance, Tadamoto searched the deck of the Emperor's boat for a familiar form—seeking among the flowing silk robes of the dancers, among those who watched. He could not find her there and he was both disappointed and relieved. If Osha was in the Emperor's retinue, then there would be a chance for her and Tadamoto to speak—with the first battle just over the horizon he would welcome such an opportunity—but he neither wanted her in danger nor in the Emperor's company.

With sails dropping and sailors swarming to smother them, the boat fetched the dock just as she lost all way, as perfectly executed as one could imagine. Like everyone within sight, Tadamoto bowed his head to the ground. The Emperor showed no sign of disembarking, however, at least not until the melody and dance was complete. All waited.

At last the performance ended and the Emperor rose and made his way among the bowing retainers to the stairs. As he stepped onto the dock, the Emperor spoke Tadamoto's name and gestured for the colonel to walk with him.

"Shonto's army has reached Chin-ja?"

Tadamoto nodded. "It has, Emperor. They progress at speed."

"And this rumor is unquestionably true, then?"

Tadamoto lowered his voice. "The Prince's banner flies beside the shinta blossom." Saying this he cast the briefest glance over his shoulder at the women on the Emperor's boat.

"We both have known betrayal, Tadamoto-sum. It is a great sadness." They walked a few steps further, the Emperor lost in thought. "You will be the new Commander of my Guard, Colonel Jaku," the Emperor said suddenly. "May you erase the shame your brother has brought to your name."

Tadamoto bowed. "I shall strive to be worthy of this honor, Sire."

"See that you do." They approached the guard holding the Emperor's horse. "Ride with me, Colonel, I wish to inspect our defenses."

Fifty-three

AFTER DAYS OF haste Lord Shonto's flotilla lay against the bank, only the current moving the hulls, causing them to tug lightly on their lines. The lengthening day had worn on to dusk, the sun setting behind the western mountains—the colors of an autumn hillside washed into the sky.

Shonto and Nishima walked along the bank, followed at a discreet distance by guards. In the near distance other men in Shonto blue had established a perimeter, keeping the refugees and the curious at bay.

"Are you concerned about the safety of Master Myochin, Uncle?" Nishima asked. Lord Shonto seemed withdrawn, quieter than usual. He had sent a party to the home of his former gii master, who lived nearby, and they had returned without the old man. Myochin Ekun the legendary master of the board, blind from birth yet six times champion of Wa.

Shonto waved to the small creek mouth that opened across the canal. "I have left guards and archers in the woods. Eku-sum's home is difficult to find. There is no path to lead one there and the barbarians keep most of their force on the canal's opposite side. If there is trouble, my guards will hide Master Myochin in the hills." Shonto shook his head. "He would not leave his home, saying he has nothing even the poorest barbarian would desire. He is getting very old. In a note Eku-sum had a servant write, he suggested that I would soon have an opportunity to perform a move no gii player could ever choose—I could sacrifice an Emperor." Shonto smiled. "He will never cease to offer me lessons."

They walked a little farther along the bank, saying little.

"Do you not find this strange that they would suddenly give up the chase?"

Nishima asked. It was the subject on everyone's mind. The small army had ceased to pursue Shonto's flotilla.

"Perhaps, but they are not really such a large force and we draw near the capital. If a large Imperial Army suddenly appeared, the small army would be at risk. Twenty-five thousand is almost a third of the Khan's army. He is wise not to risk them. It is also true that they have accomplished their main purpose: in the wake of the small army crops are growing which will allow the Khan to feed his entire army very soon."

Nishima nodded. "So we have stopped to rest our forces."

Shonto nodded. "That, and for other reasons. The Emperor has moved north of the capital with his army. If we were to meet that force before the Emperor has seen the true size of the desert army, the Son of Heaven may be led to foolish actions. We cannot allow a battle between ourselves and the Emperor. As it stands, our combined force is likely less than the Khan's. I will risk no more men."

They came to a stand of plum trees, the canal bank almost white with decaying petals. The leaves were quickly reaching their mature size, opening like blossoms. Long shadows stretched out onto the surface of the canal and in the warm light the water took on the color of burnished copper. The thinnest sliver of a crescent moon floated overhead.

Coming to a tree trunk that curved out almost horizontally over the water, Shonto stopped and leaned against it. Nishima circled its base and leaned against the opposite side beside her uncle. They stayed like that, side by side facing opposite directions, without speaking for some minutes.

Shonto reached down and plucked a new strand of grass and twirled it distractedly. "We will be forced south again within days. The large barbarian army moves more quickly now that they have true river craft and river men to sail them. Once we meet the Emperor's force, I cannot predict what will happen. Any agreement we make with the Emperor at that time will be illusory, only respected as long as there is the common threat of this Khan and his army. If we defeat the Khan, Akantsu will turn on us if he is able." Shonto wound the blade of grass around his finger like a ring. "The Emperor is not a man whose actions can easily be foreseen. He may retreat once he sees the barbarian army in its true strength; it is impossible to say. I must tell you now that the safety of the Empire will take precedence over the interests of the Shonto House." The lord fell silent for a moment. A soft breeze rustled the leaves of the plum grove.

"If the worst befalls us, it is my plan to retreat into the mountains. You should know this—one cannot predict who will survive a battle."

Nishima took a long breath. "If we must run, why to the mountains? Ika Cho would seem to offer better possibilities for raising an army? The mountains are not hospitable to those not born there."

"The Emperor holds Ika Cho and Shokan-sum has fled. I have reason to believe we would find friends in the mountains."

Nishima looked up at her uncle's face. He would always surprise her—friends in the mountains? She wanted to ask but knew that if he had wanted her to know more he would have continued.

"I had thought you bore the news of Shokan-sum's retreat into the pass with great poise. Is there hope for him, then?"

Shonto nodded. "I know nothing for certain, but his situation is certainly no worse than our own." The lord tossed the blade of grass like a dart and it was swept away on the breeze. "In the coming battle the forces of Wa will lose if there are factions holding back, hoping to save their troops to win a civil war after the barbarians are vanquished. The army of the desert is too large. We can only hope to meet it with total commitment and intelligent selection of the battle ground. If you are forced to go into the mountains, do not become separated from Shuyun-sum. He will be as valuable as a thousand guards. Do not forget. The Shonto have fled the Empire before and lived in the wilds. If Botahara smiles upon us, Shokan-sum will not find his way through the mountains before this war is decided. Let the Yamaku know that the Shonto are beyond their reach, waiting."

Nishima laid her hand on Shonto's arm. "Uncle, I do not doubt your wisdom, but neither do I doubt the wisdom of the people of Wa. They will not allow the Yamaku to call themselves Emperors after this war, no matter what the outcome."

Placing his hand over his daughter's, Shonto squeezed. "I hope you are correct, Nishi-sum. May the people of Wa not disappoint you."

The last trace of sunset disappeared before Shimeko's eyes, but the sky retained a hint of the darkest blue among the myriad stars and the crescent moon. The young woman leaned against the rigging of the plague ship, forcing an appearance of calm over herself. Although Botahist monks were notoriously observant, she hoped they would not notice her despair. The fact that, commonly, she was almost entirely ignored by them would no doubt work in her favor.

A short distance down the bank the last embers of a funeral pyre were glowing like the molten colors of the sunset. Inara-sum, the young Shonto soldier, had attained completion. Death, the former nun realized, should hardly shake her as it did. As a devout follower of the Way, the young man could only look forward to returning a step closer to Perfection. Yet. . . . Shimeko did not feel the conviction necessary to keep grief at bay.

The growing belief that Inara's funeral had been seen as a celebration by the Brothers caused a constriction inside her. The young man's death was somehow regarded as a triumph. The Brothers' attitude was frightening to her, seemed almost monstrous. *They had celebrated his death because he believed with such conviction,* she realized. And this war would bring death to thousands of Botahara's followers. Would the Brothers celebrate that?

News was traveling quickly now—news of the atrocities committed by the invaders. She had been watching the faces of the refugees as they passed, frightened, unable to believe what was occurring. The faces had begun to haunt her dreams.

With an effort Shimeko forced a calm over her mind and focused on her situation.

The plague ship was moored to trees and held close to the canal bank. No other ships lay within a half rih of it and the long lines of refugees gave the ship flying the plague banner a wide berth. Turning as casually as she was able, Shimeko surveyed the deck. Other than the single man guarding the gangway, only sleeping river men could be seen.

In one graceful motion Shimeko slipped over the side, lowering herself easily into the water which rose to mid-thigh. Two quiet steps brought her to the bank and several more put her among the trees. She stopped then to be sure there was no sudden movement on board ship, no sign that she had been observed, but there was nothing.

I will not be missed now until morning, she thought, and by then I will be far to the north—and on my way from all the things that cause my turmoil. May Botahara forgive me.

Fifty-four

THE PLUM BLOSSOM Winds gave way to the fitful breezes of late spring and the nights and mornings saw the occasional fog from cold air descending the mountainsides into the lowlands after the sun set. Although this mist slowed the flotilla that bore Lord Shonto south, the barbarian army suffered the same, putting off the inevitable day of battle—though only briefly.

A day's march north of the Imperial Army's position, Shonto landed his force and spent several days engaged in the final preparations for battle. Reconnaissance parties were sent both north and south to gather information about both hostile armies and a constant stream of riders came and went bearing reports and orders.

The main body of the army of the desert had rejoined the smaller force and they continued their push into the inner provinces. Skirmishes between barbarian patrols and the companies Shonto sent north became more and more frequent as the armies vied to control the lands that lay between them.

Accompanied by General Hojo, Lord Taiki, and Prince Wakaro, Shonto rode among the troops, speaking to the various company commanders, making his presence known. An army caught between two enemy forces needed the reassurance of a confident commander and, in this capacity, Lord Shonto lifted spirits wherever he passed.

The army itself was a patchwork affair made up of the well-armed and trained retainers of various lords, Imperial Guards, and the recruits who had arrived with every variety of weapon and armor—many of them looking like patchwork themselves.

Horses were being exercised and fed on green pasture, many a man squared off against another with swords, and archers loosed their arrows on makeshift targets. More than one wager had been laid on these various contests and officers were alert to see that no disputes erupted into real violence—with men from all regions of the Empire such things were not unknown. Despite the activity in the encampment there was also an air of something being amiss—laughter that was too loud, many a young man deliberately alone with his thoughts, men looking suddenly embarrassed when Shonto approached as though the lord might read what was in their minds by the looks on their faces.

Prince Wakaro turned to Lord Shonto as they rode. "I can't help but wonder about these men, Lord Shonto." He tugged at a braid in his horse's mane. "Are they afraid? I myself cannot find words to describe what I feel. I don't even know if it is fear."

Shonto stroked the neck of his mount with a leather gloved hand. "Anticipation of a battle wears away at men, Prince, until they reach a point where they want a decision to be made: either they will live or die, but they will stand no more of this existence, suspended somewhere between life and death. At a certain point battle comes as a relief."

The Prince looked up at Lord Shonto who surveyed the army with an experienced eye. He was coming to respect this man whom his father considered the Yamaku's greatest enemy, and this he found unsettling.

Shonto waved his hand to encompass the entire encampment. "Your opinion, Lord Taiki."

Taiki brought his horse up and looked slowly around. "It is an army, Lord Shonto. There have been better and there have been far worse. Battle experience is lacking among the young, and I do not know that we will have more than one battle in which to gain this. The other armies, I'm sure, suffer from this same weakness," he hurried to add. "The barbarians, however, fight in a land that is so different from their own that I cannot believe this does not unsettle them. Retreat must also look daunting, should they fail in their purpose. Such factors must be weighed in a battle."

"I agree, Lord Taiki. Numbers are not the only measure of an army."

Three riders in blue came at a gallop through the encampment. As they approached, Shonto recognized Rohku Saicha followed by Shonto House guards. They pulled up before Lord Shonto and dismounted to bow low before the Imperial Prince and their liege-lord.

"Captain Rohku?" Shonto said, nodding to his retainer.

"There is a party from the Emperor approaching, Sire, under a flag of truce." He pointed south. "They come by fast boat."

"Send for General Hojo, Kamu, and Brother Shuyun. We will ride to meet them. Prince, Lord Taiki, will you meet the Emperor's emissary with me?"

The two men nodded though Shonto thought the Prince showed a tightening around the jaw that had not appeared even during discussions of the coming battle.

The three set off at a canter, followed by their guards. Men in the encampment bowed low as the Prince and Lord Shonto passed and stared after them as they went. Rumor went quickly through the encampment. *The Emperor has sent his minions to bargain with Lord Shonto.* Did this mean there was hope of an alliance?

Just south of the encampment a decked boat that boasted thirty oarsmen swung to an anchor in the middle of the canal. Off its stern the Emperor's banner fluttered in the breeze as did the banner of a senior official and the green flag of truce. Beneath a plum tree, mats had been spread, and it appeared that men had chosen this spot to drink wine and perhaps compose a poem-sequence, for there was no armor worn but by the guards standing at a distance. Those who knelt upon the mats drank from wine bowls and laughed cheerfully.

"Lord Shinzei," Prince Wakaro said quietly to Shonto. "The Emperor's favorite talking bird."

Shonto pulled his horse up and dismounted. Several more Shonto guards had joined them and others had taken up positions close by and stood with hands on their swords.

Rohku Saicha rode up in haste. "Lord Shonto, General Hojo comes now. Kamu is across the canal and Brother Shuyun has been called to the plague ship."

Shonto nodded. "We will do without them, then." Shonto turned and saw men riding toward him at a gallop. "General Hojo is here." Then turning to the Emperor's son, "Prince Wakaro, does this talking bird have power to speak for the Emperor?"

"I would be shocked if that were so. No, this will be an offer from the

Emperor. Shinzei will have no power to negotiate. He is but the first move of the game and, as is common, the most expendable piece. Though I doubt he will realize this."

Hojo rode up and dismounted bowing quickly.

"General Hojo," Shonto said, "please approach the Emperor's emissaries and ask them the purpose of their embassy. Or perhaps they have come merely to enjoy the fine day and the view?"

Hojo bowed quickly and set off toward Lord Shinzei and his party.

A moment later he returned. "They will speak to Lord Shonto only, Sire. They do not have concerns about who accompanies you."

Shonto nodded. "And they expect the Prince and me to attend them?" Shonto cast a glance over his shoulder. What happened here would be known by everyone in his army within the hour. What fools did the Emperor send that they would allow such a situation to develop?

Shonto looked back at the Emperor's men and shook his head. "Take them prisoner, bind them, and bring them to my boat." He mounted his horse abruptly, leaving the Prince and Lord Taiki hurrying to follow. They rode off at a canter toward the boats that carried Shonto's family and senior advisors. Much of the activity of the camp had come to a halt and men tried not to be seen watching.

Shonto's own boat was protected by a bamboo fence forming a large open space on the canal's eastern bank. Riding past the sentries, Shonto dismounted and left his horse to a guard. He stormed up the gangway of his boat, throwing gloves and surcoat at a servant. Mounting the stairs to the upper deck, he took up a position under the awning on the stern.

Kamu appeared suddenly. "Sire, excuse me, my attentions were drawn elsewhere . . ."

Shonto waved a hand to cut the old man off. "That guard who is a kick boxer—is he still in our service?"

"He is, Lord Shonto."

"Bring him to me." Shonto turned to Lord Taiki and Prince Wakaro as they came up onto the deck looking unsure if they should have followed. "Please, join me," Shonto said pleasantly. He gestured to cushions. The two men took the offered positions and an awkward silence ensued.

They did not have long to wait, for Hojo appeared with his charges moments later. A boat ran up on the canal bank and the bound men were assisted onto the land with some degree of concern for their dignity.

Kamu appeared with a young guard and Shonto nodded to have the man brought forward, speaking to him privately and demonstrating several hand signals. "Turn Lord Shinzei over to this guard," Shonto said to Kamu.

The Emperor's emissaries padded up the stairs then and guards requested that they kneel. Shonto sat regarding them for a moment.

"We come under a flag of truce—emissaries of the Son of Heaven. Be certain that this will not be forgotten, Lord Shonto." Shinzei spoke Shonto's name with as much disdain as he could muster.

Shonto gave a hand signal to the young guard who spun quickly and kicked Shinzei in the diaphragm, doubling him over on the deck.

When the lord's struggle to breathe had begun to subside, Shonto nodded and the man was pulled roughly back to a kneeling position. His voice perfectly calm and pleasant, Shonto addressed Lord Shinzei. "Perhaps you can relate the purpose of your visit, Lord Shinzei. Or was this merely an outing to drink wine and enjoy the fine spring weather?"

Shinzei visibly collected himself, trying to gain control of his breathing. "The Emperor of Wa has sent me to demand the immediate surrender of Prince Wakaro, Jaku Katta, Lord Shonto, and all senior advisors and officers of the same."

Shonto waited for a moment and then signaled the young guard who again doubled the kneeling aristocrat over on the deck. His recovery this time was lengthy, the others in his party staring down at the deck, afraid to move. At last, the emissary was set back on his knees, managing not to collapse.

"My liege-lord," Kamu explained quietly, "is addressed as Lord Shonto or Sire, Lord Shinzei."

Shinzei nodded, unable to hide the pain he felt or to maintain his dignity in such a situation. As a favorite of the Emperor he encountered nothing but deference in all of his dealings.

"Lord Shinzei," Shonto began again, his voice remaining calm. "I am well informed on the size and state of the Emperor's army. It is no larger, and certainly less experienced, than my own. You cannot afford arrogance. Not two days north on the canal a barbarian army that, despite our efforts, numbers eighty-five thousand men is moving toward the Imperial Capital. In my estimate, their chieftain is four, perhaps five days away from the throne he seeks—your lord's throne, Lord Shinzei. Already it grows late for the alliance that we require."

Shonto looked at the man kneeling before him and shook his head. "Take this message to your Emperor. If he will provide written pardons for myself, my family, and all who support me, I will consent to join forces with him to face the barbarian threat. If the Emperor will not agree to this, I will allow him to face the barbarian army alone. It is a simple choice—to retain his throne or to be overthrown, perhaps it is a choice between life and death. Be very clear when you explain this point to Akantsu, Lord Shinzei—it is important that he understands his position."

Shonto nodded to Hojo who signaled the guards to take the Emperor's men away. "General," Shonto said to Hojo as the captives were led down the stairs, "put them on horses with their hands bound behind them and trot them through the camp on the return to their boat. Then throw them on the ground before their fine ship and leave them to be unbound by their own guard. Show them not a single sign of respect."

Hojo bowed and hurried off.

Shonto signaled for cha and once it arrived, his spirits lifted noticeably.

"Excuse me for saying so, Lord Shonto," Prince Wakaro said in a soothing voice, "but this will infuriate the Emperor."

Shonto smiled. "But it will lift the morale of our own army to the very skies. We would only dare treat the Emperor's advisors this way if there was no doubt of the outcome of the battle. It will give your father cause to think also, Prince. The next battle we fight will not require swords—it will be a battle of wills and I have answered his opening with a message which says the Shonto have nothing to lose, while the Emperor has everything."

The army of Shonto Motoru moved south as soon as the fog lifted the morning after Lord Shinzei had paid his visit. The bulk of the army went by land though some ships were still in use and these paced the army as it went. Open fields bordered the canal in this area and stretched east to foothills and west toward distant mountains, jagged against the horizon.

Many of the "rebel army" rode horses, though companies of foot soldiers marched among the mounted troops. Despite the patchwork nature of this force, Shonto's officers and the officers of his allies had marshaled it into a tight formation, better to impress the watching patrols of the Emperor.

Shuyun stood beside his liege-lord at the rail of a river craft. Before his arrival in Wa, he had never seen an army and he found the sight both impressive and very sad. In the next few days many of the men before him would die. The words of Brother Hitara came back to him: *"War brings no soul to perfection.*" My Order has bound me to serve this man and now I am at war also—a follower of Botahara, Shuyun thought, a poor follower.

Something the monk had never anticipated was the sound of men going to war. There was silence in the ranks, but the sounds of men and beasts tramping over the land was ominous, disturbing, like the pulse of a dying man—the strength of its rhythm came from fear. Unspoken fear.

"There are no reports of a new outbreak of the disease?" Shonto asked Shuyun.

The two men stood at the rail of Shonto's ship watching the army as it moved.

Shuyun shook his head. "I have sent men out among the refugees and to the villages. The plague seems to be under control. We have had only one report of a woman of Shimeko-sum's description, but this was not certain and whoever it was made an effort to avoid contact with others."

"Huh." Shonto tried to turn the hemp shroud, the muscles in his forearm bunching into knots. "Nishima-sum told me this young woman was a person of education and intelligence but caught in a crisis of the spirit."

Shuyun nodded. "I believe Lady Nishima was correct, Sire."

"Perhaps she seeks a monastery or wishes to live the life of a hermit."

"Perhaps." Shuyun seemed lost in thought. The dull pounding of the army on the land kept calling his attention. "She seeks escape, I believe, Sire."

Shonto let go of the shroud and shaded his eyes against the sun, staring off toward the south. The Emperor's position would not become visible until the next day at the earliest, but it was common to see people standing with their gaze focused on the horizon as though meditating upon a distant point.

"It is a fine balance we must achieve, Brother," Shonto said suddenly. "If we meet the Emperor's force before the barbarian army is seen for its true size, then we risk the Emperor making a foolish mistake. If we do not arrive at the Imperial Army's position soon, we will not have time to join the two armies into an effective force. Once we have committed a piece, we cannot retrieve it. There can be no mistakes."

"May Botahara guide us, Lord Shonto." Shuyun had watched his lord carefully since he had come into his service and though it could be said that Shonto always kept much to himself, Shuyun was noticing a change. The lord often shared information that was not truly necessary for others to know, yet at the same time the monk was convinced there was some knowledge that Shonto was keeping entirely to himself. If asked, Shuyun could not have explained why he felt this.

"Once we reach the Emperor's position, I will move the members of my household to the northeast of the probable battlefield. When battle has been engaged, you will join Lady Nishima. Be prepared to run toward the mountains, Shuyun-sum. Leave everyone else behind if they cannot keep your pace." Shonto turned to regard his Spiritual Advisor. "If the Shonto army falls and I cannot escape, Lady Nishima must be protected at all costs. I charge you with this, Brother Shuyun. Do not fail."

Shuyun gave a half bow in response. "Perhaps Lady Nishima should be closer to the mountains now?"

Shonto shook his head. "There is danger whichever course we choose, Shuyun-sum." The lord shrugged. "Perhaps it is the selfish path, but I wish to keep Nishima-sum close for now."

The river men dropped the sail behind Shonto and Shuyun as the breeze had come up and was moving the ship ahead of the marching army.

Shonto waved a hand out toward the patch of dark blue uniforms among the men on horseback. Shuyun could see Shonto pull his focus away from the knowledge he was hiding. "I am concerned about Lord Butto and these Hajiwara men in Lord Komawara's guard. Lord Butto has not spoken of it, but certainly it must weigh upon him."

Shuyun leaned out over the rail looking down into the water. "I have considered this matter also. Lord Komawara believes that their sworn oath binds these Hajiwara men and that all of my lord's allies are safe from any plans for vengeance. Perhaps that is true, but men have been known to word their oaths in ways that are understood to mean different things to different people. I would keep the Butto and the Komawara companies separate on any battlefield."

"Huh." Shonto shook his head. "Within our own ranks to have such concerns. . . ." He left the thought unfinished.

Fifty-five

FOG PERSISTED IN the morning so it was not until the sun was high that Lord Shonto was able to move his army south again. Even after the fog had cleared, the sky was covered with a high, thin mist that filtered a weakened sunlight down to the earth.

Several of Shonto's advisors had voiced the concern that the Emperor might move his army north under cover of darkness and surprise Shonto's force in the morning when the fog lifted, but this turned out to be a groundless fear. Patrols reported that the Emperor kept his army behind earthworks that had been dug into the side of hills on either side of the canal.

Shonto sat under an awning on the stern of his ship, giving no sign that he was only hours away from meeting his enemy. He pored over a scroll with great focus of attention; a secretary knelt in attendance and Kamu also waited at hand. Sitting only a few paces off, a servant played a quiet melody on the harp. Occasionally the lord would look up and give his attention to a passage of the tune and then, with a nod to the musician, return to his reading.

Finally Shonto rolled the scroll and set it aside. Reaching for a cup of cha, he sipped and found it cold and returned the cup to the table.

"It is an interesting position, don't you think?" Shonto said to his steward. With some care he unrolled a map and placed four jade paperweights, carved in the shape of the shinta blossom, on the corners. He waved a hand at the map and Kamu moved closer to look on.

"The Emperor has split his position to either side of the canal." The lord tapped the spot with his finger. "What is your opinion of that?"

Despite his age and apparent frailty Kamu had once been both a swords-man of great reputation and a senior officer in the Shonto armies. Stewards of Great Houses seldom had such a depth of knowledge in military matters and Lord Shonto did not let this expertise go to waste.

"The Emperor must believe it is his function to stop an army from de-scending on the capital, therefore he blocks the canal. In truth, I believe he could position his army anywhere and the Khan would not pass it by. This division of his forces . . ." Kamu shook his head. "The Emperor makes a foolish mistake. The bridge that connects them across the canal . . . it is too vulnerable to fire rafts."

Shonto nodded. "I suspect our Emperor has not blocked the canal to stop the barbarian advance but to stop our army from passing. No doubt the Son of Heaven would like to keep the Shonto between his own army and that of the Khan."

Shonto ran his finger up the line of the canal. "And I certainly do not wish to spoil the Emperor's view of the barbarian army." Moving his finger to a hill east and slightly north of the Emperor's position, the lord said. "We will concentrate our troops on this slope. The Khan will array his forces here—there is no other choice." Shonto traced an arc east from the canal north of the Emperor's position.

"That will form a triangle." Shonto said, tracing the three sides with each army being a point. "If the Khan is an intelligent man, he will not wait but will attack both positions at once—the barbarian army is large enough to do this. If the Khan waits, there is a possibility that Akantsu and I can reach an understanding. Once the Emperor sees the army of the desert with his own eyes it is my hope that he will be more willing to listen to our arguments. We shall see."

Shonto stared at the map for a moment more without speaking. "If the Emperor will join forces with us, Kamu-sum, we will have two choices. Fight the barbarian army with a force perhaps two-thirds its size, or retreat to the southeast. If we choose to retreat, we will see if you are correct. Will the lure of an undefended Capital be more than the Khan can resist? If so, there is a chance that we can raise an army large enough to be sure of defeat-ing the barbarians. A battle now is a difficult decision. Such a fight is likely to be inconclusive and, at worst, could result in the annihilation of the armies of Wa. It is a great risk, Kamu-sum, a great risk indeed."

A guard approached, bowing and waiting to be acknowledged. Kamu gestured and the man came forward to speak quietly to the steward. The old man nodded.

"Sire," he said turning back to his liege-lord, "our forward scouts can see the Emperor's position."

Shonto nodded. "I will take a fast boat. Have a horse ready at our forward position. And I will speak with General Hojo and our senior commanders." The lord rose suddenly. "Well, steward Kamu, the endgame is always the most interesting, is it not?"

Late in the day Shonto's army came upon the plain that lay before the Emperor's army. Patrols reported the barbarians only half a day behind now and the rear of the Shonto columns were under constant observation from barbarian patrols. Due to sheer numbers, the barbarians had taken control of the shifting lands between the two armies and they tracked the Shonto army as silently and relentlessly as a predatory animal.

Shonto was still not in armor as he rode before his army though he wore a sword in his sash—the sword the Emperor had given to him. A group of concerned Shonto guards stayed close by, eyes turned to the earthworks that sheltered the Imperial Army.

"The Emperor will wait," Shonto said to his senior advisors. "He will not undertake to accomplish with swords what he hopes can be done by words. It is good to remember that he hates the Shonto because he fears us."

Shonto stood up in his stirrups, looked around the horizon, and then shook his head. "Excuse me for saying so, Prince Wakaro, but the Emperor is not the general your grandfather was. His position is untenable."

Wakaro gave an almost imperceptible shrug. He was the only man in Shonto's party who wore full battle armor and he was no doubt suffering some embarrassment at not demonstrating the acceptable bravado in the face of the enemy. Having tied his helmet to his saddle, the Prince's streak of white hair was at the mercy of the breeze and waved like an ominous flag. The Prince was struggling to maintain his Imperial dignity and this was made more difficult by his lack of skill with horses—appearing far worse than it was by proximity to the men of Seh; riders of the first order.

Shonto nodded to the hill upon which he proposed to establish his own army. "What is our assessment of that position?"

Lord Komawara spurred his horse forward three paces and bowed from the saddle. "Lord Toshaki and I have ridden and walked every section of the hill, Lord Shonto. It is not defendable from all directions due to the small size of our force, but it is a reasonable position in which to weather an attack from the west and north. It is certainly more defensible than the Emperor's earthworks," Komawara said with disdain. "The slope is steep at the base and rolls off to a series of benches halfway up the flank. The crest is thickly wooded. Considering this is not a battleground of our choosing, we could do much worse."

Shonto looked over at Hojo, who nodded agreement.

"We will secure that position and move our forces there in the dark," Shonto said. "Light fires to guide the way. Tomorrow we will witness the arrival of the barbarian army, and our Emperor shall have the same pleasure."

Shonto turned his horse to face his advisors. Lord Taiki and Butto Joda had become friends over the past days and sat on horses side by side. Jaku Katta, General Hojo, Lord Komawara, young Toshaki, and Shuyun formed a loose group. Only the Prince and his captain rode apart—outsiders, Yamaku; of questionable loyalty.

"We will move our forces to the hill and then set a pavilion on the plain between the Emperor's position and our own. I will attempt to establish contact with the Emperor at the earliest possible moment." Shonto looked into the faces of the men before him. "In the history of Wa no foreign enemy has ever penetrated the inner provinces. It is impossible to separate the clouds that cover the future, but it is beyond doubt that a loss to the army of the desert would mean the loss of the capital, if not the Empire. If the Khan is an intelligent general, he would pursue our army to the southern borders, for our army is the basis of all our hopes for the future. We do not know which action in the days to come will be a deciding action. We must never forget that anything we do could be the single act that changes the course of history. Do not lose courage, not for an instant. History will turn on the events of these next days and it will be shaped by each of us. Do not lose courage."

Nishima lay awake long into the night. She had crossed the small plain that men were referring to as the "battlefield" in the dark and found the experience disturbing in the extreme. The fires illuminated rows of armed men who marked the way in the dark and fog—an eerie spectacle of yellow-red light reflecting off armor and weapons and faces distorted by the light and darkness.

As Lady Okara had insisted that she did not want a sedan chair, Nishima and Kitsura had gone on foot when Nishima would rather have ridden. Her experience with horses was limited, for ladies of breeding were not supposed to ride, but in the unsettled years after the Interim Wars Lord Shonto had thought it prudent that she master the basics of riding.

A large pavilion had been pitched on a ledge dug into the hillside, just inside the sheltering edge of the wood, and this had been divided with hangings into three rooms for the ladies from the capital. Mats and rugs made it comfortable and lamps and a few other furnishings created an impression of order and security—all seeming a great sham to Nishima.

In an attempt to gain some sense of tranquillity, Nishima had turned to the poetry of Lady Nikko.

Sky
Torn to rags and tatters.
Earth
A ruin of storm shattered trees.
The riches of summer have been scattered
To the four directions.
The first days of Autumn arrive
Like invading armies
Wisdom is more fragile
Than a young girl's love,
Lost between one generation and the next.
These boys drop stones into the village well
To break each morning's ice
Never asking, "How long until the well is filled?"

In Itsa peasants work the family fields
Season after season without rest
Until the soil bears nothing
But thistle and scrub

The moon drifts toward winter
Each night colder than the last,

Soon women will sell winter clothing
For a few sticks of firewood

From A Journey to Itsa
by Lady Nikko

Not precisely the reassurance Nishima was looking for. She set the scroll down.

Earlier it had been decided that Lady Okara would be taken south toward the capital by Shonto guards who would shed their blue livery. Skirting the Emperor's army would be difficult, for he sent patrols out into the countryside, but there was no doubt in anyone's mind that Lady Okara's reputation would protect her from all but the barbarians. She was anxious to see her island home again and Lord Shonto was equally anxious to have the great painter out of harm's way.

Nishima knew the parting in the morning would be difficult. Oka-sum had risked so much for her, for so little return, Nishima felt. Poor Oka-sum, the young aristocrat thought, I tore her from her solitude and cast her into the center of a war that may see the fall of our Empire. May Botahara protect her.

The thin fabric of the tent seemed impossibly fragile to a woman who had spent most of her life surrounded by substantial walls, and the reality that pressed against this material was not the wild beauty of the world but the coarse brutality of men. She longed to have Shuyun come and lie beside her. It was not entirely a desire to be protected by someone stronger, for Nishima knew that wars could bring down even the mightiest, but a desire to comfort and be comforted in the face of the utter uncertainty of the world.

It was close to dawn before she managed to fall into a fitful sleep.

Fifty-six

SHONTO WALKED ALONG the path that had been dug into the side of the hill, followed by his guards. The gray light of early morning had become the gray light of a foggy day. Reports from outriders indicated that this propensity for morning fog diminished only a few rih south, indicating that one did not have to stray far from the mountains to rid oneself of this weather.

Leave it to the Emperor to pick a battlefield commonly enshrouded in fog, Shonto thought. He had risen before first light and met with his advisors. After much discussion it had been decided that Prince Wakaro would bear an offer to his father, and though the Prince had gone off showing a brave face, Shonto did not expect him to return. Even if the Emperor answered Shonto's letter, the lord did not expect the bearer of the response to be Prince Wakaro. It is a sad family that cannibalizes its own, Shonto told himself, but Imperial families seemed to suffer this ill too commonly.

Though the fog muffled sound and played tricks on the ears, there was no doubt that an army moved upon the plain. The sounds of voices, the stamp and whinny of horses, the clanking of weapons and armor filtered up through the layers of mist to the men of Wa perched on their hillsides. This will open the Emperor's eyes, Shonto thought. I would give much to be standing beside him as the fog clears.

Guards in armor laced in the darkest blue appeared through the mist, bowing to Lord Shonto as he passed. A few paces later he came upon Lord Komawara staring out into the featureless gray.

"Can Komawara eyes part the mists?" Shonto asked.

Komawara turned and bowed low. His face lit with half a smile. "Komawara eyes fail this test as miserably as most others, Lord Shonto. But when I traveled in the desert with Brother Shuyun, he taught me not to rely on my eyes as other men do. I cannot claim to have attained the skill of the Botahist trained in this, but I am learning. It seems to be a matter of focus."

Shonto stopped at the young lord's side and looked out into the mist as Komawara did. "What do your other senses tell you, Lord Komawara?"

Komawara listened for a few seconds before answering. "An army gathers on the plain, Sire, I have heard the pounding of mallets on wood indicating that tents have been raised. Horses are being pastured," he pointed to the north. "I smell fires burning and there is a tang of tar in this odor. They burn the ships now. This close to the capital the barbarians would appear to have no expectation to return north. I hear the sounds of armor being cleaned and weapons being honed. I hear the sounds of men who are not entirely confident. So far from home—if their chieftain has misjudged the strength of this vast Empire they have crossed, they will never return to their lands, to their people."

Shonto nodded. "You have crossed swords with the men of desert, Lord Komawara, is it possible that we can win a battle against such superior numbers?"

There was a long silence then and Shonto found himself straining to hear the sounds that drifted up from the plain.

"It would depend on the place and the commander, Lord Shonto. When we attacked their supply rafts, we had the advantage of surprise and they thought they had been set upon by an entire army. I do not believe it is foolish pride to say that the men of Wa are stronger warriors. The reports from the battle for Rhojo-ma would indicate this to be true. A confident army with superior position would likely prevail—at great cost—despite smaller numbers. Confidence comes from the men's faith in their commander, Sire."

"And the Emperor? Can he meld the two armies into a force that will bear the blow this Khan will deliver?"

Komawara shrugged. "The Emperor is unknown to me, Sire. If he abandoned his position on the west side of the canal, burned the bridge, and concentrated his force and our own on the eastern hillside, the Emperor's position would be improved. But I cannot say that he could inspire the confidence required to beat a foe who is stronger in numbers. It is impossible to know."

Shonto turned and looked back toward his own position, hidden in the fog. Noises similar to those heard emanating from the enemy position echoed here.

"We will see," Shonto said quietly.

The sound of armored men approaching caused both lords to turn around. A moment later Kamu materialized out of the fog followed by guards.

He bowed low. "A rider has arrived from the north bearing news, Sire." Kamu paused for a second to catch his breath. "Lord Shonto Shokan has come down from the mountains with a small force. He hurries to join you, Sire."

Shonto remained calm at this, compared to the obvious excitement that his steward barely contained. "We must get word to him. He must not risk capture. There is no reason for him to hurry. His presence here with a small force will hardly be the deciding factor. We must warn him to stay well clear and approach from the southeast. He must take no risk of capture, Kamu-sum, absolutely none. Send messengers immediately."

The steward bowed quickly and was gone.

Prince Wakaro did not know whether to feel relief or not. The ride through the fog toward the perimeter of his father's defenses was a terrifying endeavor. Even his guard wearing the armor of the Imperial Guard was little comfort. The men of the Imperial Army knew that Jaku Katta and his rebel followers still wore their black uniforms and all the insignias of rank.

They had found a guard in the fog and finally been escorted through the lines. The feared arrow did not find him and the Prince was relieved to the point of developing a small tremor. He was not sure if Shonto or his followers would have condescended to wear armor in such situations, but the Prince had decided he did not care. To die of an arrow shot by some nervous, unknown archer did not seem like a dignified death.

He and his men stood surrounded by Imperial Guards, and though they had not been shown the courtesy due an Imperial Prince they had been treated well enough and even allowed to retain their swords. The Prince realized he had stopped trying to predict his father's reaction to this embassy from Lord Shonto—an embassy led by his own son.

Perhaps he should have refused Shonto's request that he approach the Emperor, but the Prince felt that what Shonto had said was true. This was a decisive moment in history, and he did not want to be known for all time as the prince who contributed to the fall of the Empire. So he tried to swallow his fear.

Lord Komawara had told Wakaro that he had been frightened before the attack on the barbarian supply rafts and there was something about Komawara that made the Prince believe the young lord would never stoop to lies.

A guard officer appeared then and it took a moment for the Prince to realize it was Jaku Tadamoto. The young guardsman seemed to have aged many years in the past few months.

"If it is convenient, Prince Wakaro, could you accompany me?" Tadamoto asked in the refined tones of a scholar. How did the men of the Imperial Guard respond to a commander who sounded and looked like a historian or a poet? A few weeks earlier the thought would never have occurred to him and it surprised him.

Nodding, the Prince fell into step beside the young colonel who deferred to the Imperial Prince in voice only. It was no time to demand that proper etiquette be followed, Wakaro decided.

They made their way along a deep trench behind one level of the earthworks. Bundles of arrows stood against the trench wall and, on a dirt shelf, archers stood looking out onto the fogbound plain. Prince Wakaro had become more intimate with fear recently and this had increased his sensitivity to it. He could feel the fear among these men.

They mounted a wooden stairway that brought them up a level. The effort was causing the Prince to sweat under his heavy armor, and he pulled off his helmet and tucked it under his arm as he often saw guards do, for there was no one on his staff to reach out and take this burden from him.

They progressed through various rings of guards until the sound of banners rustling in the frail breeze told Wakaro that the Emperor would be near at hand. Indeed, only a few paces farther along and they were stopped by guards. Wakaro stood trying to hold together the shreds of his failing courage. I have seen the barbarian army, the Prince reminded himself. Any death I find here will be more charitable than the death I would find on the battlefield. Stories of what the barbarians did to captured enemies had reached Wakaro through his guards. His dreams had not been the same since.

A guard appeared out of the fog and gave a hand signal. Tadamoto motioned the Prince forward. A few paces along and a small pavilion took shape before the Prince. He knelt and bowed to his father who did not offer even a nod in response.

"I am told you are a messenger for the Shonto?" the Emperor said, his voice betraying tight control—a sign of anger that the Prince dreaded.

"Despite all appearances, Sire," Wakaro said, ashamed at the quaver in his voice, "I remain the Emperor's loyal servant. The truth of this will be revealed as the fog lifts. An army of unprecedented size is before us. If the Imperial Army does not join with the forces of Lord Shonto, the Empire will be lost."

The Emperor stared at his son until the young man looked down. "You have a message from your master?" the Emperor said at last.

Wakaro reached into his sash and removed the carefully folded letter. He passed this to Tadamoto who set it on the edge of the small dais.

The Emperor looked down at it for a moment as thought the letter itself was an insult to his dignity. He picked it up suddenly, tearing it open without even glancing at the seal. After casting a final, cold eye upon his son, the Emperor turned his attention to Shonto's letter. He looked up in a moment. "This does not differ from the message Lord Shinzei conveyed," the Emperor said, his face flushing with anger.

Wakaro could only nod. He kept his eyes cast down.

The Emperor threw the letter in his son's face, startling the Prince so that he almost fell backward.

"Colonel Jaku. Take this man out of my sight," the Emperor said as though dismissing an annoying servant. "He is charged with treason and we are at war. Deal with him accordingly."

The Prince reared up, stumbling to his feet. He felt Jaku Tadamoto's hand on his sword arm and then other hands gripped him also. "I have not lied!" the Prince cried out. "I do not support your enemies. The enemy is a barbarian army that has armed itself using Imperial gold." He was dragged backward, the Emperor disappearing in the fog. "Father! You will see that I tell the truth. In just a few hours, Father!" Jerked off his feet, the Prince hit his head against something hard. He sank completely into the fog then; it swirled close about him obscuring everything, even his thoughts.

Swimming up to the surface of the fog, ever so slowly, the Prince came back to the world. He lay on his side on a surface that was soft and uneven. Nausea passed through him like a wave rushing onto the shore though it did not break but only dissipated in the smallest ripple. Two more waves moved him and he felt for a moment that he had washed ashore and was swept back and forth by the rhythms of the sea.

Finally the Prince opened his eyes. A thick, straw mat was the surface under him.

"Sire?"

It was a soft voice, not at all hostile. Wakaro tried to nod.

"Can you hear me, Sire?"

Tadamoto, Jaku Tadamoto: Wakaro recognized the voice now. He moved his head, a definite nod, he was certain.

"If you wish, I will help you to sit."

After a moment of consideration Wakaro shook his head. I must have more time, he thought. The fog will lift and then I will be vindicated. His eyes focused on a second guard who stood a few paces off. In his hands this man held a sword laid across folds of white silk. The Prince closed his eyes again.

After a few moments had passed, the voice came again. "Sire? I will do everything to preserve your dignity, but you must assist me in this."

"I am more concerned with my life, Colonel," Wakaro said, words coming with difficulty into a dry mouth.

"I am prepared to give you time to make your preparations and also your own sword. In this I defy the orders of my Emperor. Please, Prince Wakaro, I offer you the path of dignity. It is the honorable way."

The Prince shook his head softly.

"Tadamoto-sum?" he whispered, using the familiar form. "If you will grant me one request . . . I will cooperate in any way you wish."

Tadamoto did not answer immediately. "It is not my place to grant requests, Prince Wakaro. I risk the Emperor's displeasure in what I do now."

Displeasure, Wakaro thought, the word striking him like a blow. He fought to control growing panic. "I wish only to be given until the fog lifts to make my preparations. It is a small thing," he said, trying not to let his voice be reduced to the whimper that was threatening. The Prince propped himself up on his elbow then, looking up at the young guard colonel. He prayed it was compassion he saw there.

Tadamoto crouched at the edge of the mat, looking down at the Prince. Very deliberately he nodded once, then rose and walked away, leaving the Emperor's son under the eye of several guards.

The days had fallen into a pattern of fog in the morning which then lifted at virtually the same hour each afternoon. The Prince knelt on his mat facing the north, searching for the first sign of the barbarian army. The rest of the Imperial Army encampment was hidden from view by a roll in the hill and some low bushes. Undoubtedly, the Prince had been carried to the top of the hill on the canal's eastern bank.

Faint signs of blue began to appear overhead and the Prince felt his hope rise. The guard, holding what Wakaro realized was a ceremonial white robe, still stood, unmoving, at his back. Had the Prince known how to pray to Botahara, he would not have hesitated to do so.

The fog seemed to have learned considerable cruelty in the last few hours, for it kept showing signs of thinning and then blowing in as dense as it had ever been. Then the plain before the Imperial Army began to appear, a few paces at a time, the green grasses trampled but still vivid against the white of the mists.

Finally a barbarian sentry appeared, riding a dark horse. Colored banners took form, waving among the tendrils of white—gold and Imperial Crimson, and blue and spring green. Wakaro offered up an awkward prayer of thanks to powers unknown and unnamed.

The mist disappeared more quickly by the moment. A man cleared his throat at the Prince's back causing the young man to tear his eyes away from the scene being revealed before him. Jaku Tadamoto had returned.

"May I assist you with your armor, Sire? It would be my honor."

The Prince pointed out at the army that was slowly coming to light. "It is as I said, Colonel. Once I had seen this, I could not chose another course. The Empire is in grave danger. You *need* Shonto Motoru."

Tadamoto nodded. "May I begin with your shoulder pieces, Sire?"

Turning back to the north, the Prince saw that more of the army of the desert was coming into view. Fingers began working at the lacing on his shoulder pieces. *But it is there before them to see,* the Prince thought. *Could they not see?*

Tadamoto and a guard were lifting the heavy body armor over Wakaro's head when the guard happened to look up.

"Botahara save us. Colonel!" He pointed to the plain.

Tadamoto turned to look as the armor slipped over the Prince's head. He froze in position for a second and then stood up to full height, the Prince completely forgotten.

The barbarian encampment was a vast, teeming sprawl, dark against the new green, like a bloodsucker Tadamoto had once found undulating on a rush beside a pond.

"I am not a traitor, Tadamoto-sum," the Prince said as calmly as he was able, as though the sanity of his tone would make the young guard realize how mad this entire situation was. "I described this army in detail in a letter to my father. I have tried to warn him of this for some weeks. I have committed no act of treason."

Tadamoto stood staring for a moment longer. "I will speak to the Son of Heaven." He turned and hurried off, leaving the Prince to struggle against a fit of shaking that suddenly racked him.

Tadamoto made his way quickly down the path to the Emperor's pavilion. Bowing to the guard, he gave a password reserved for dire emergencies that would allow him immediately into the Emperor's presence. A guard announced his commander and Tadamoto was brought forward.

The Emperor sat in the same place under the small pavilion of crimson silk. Like everyone else, he stared out at the clearing plain as though transfixed. After a moment he spoke to Tadamoto though he did not take his eyes off the sight before him.

"Did he die well, Tadamoto-sum?"

Jaku cleared his throat. "I allowed him time to make his preparations, Sire. And then this . . ." The young officer waved a hand toward the barbarian army. "Prince Wakaro wrote the truth, Sire. . . ."

The Emperor turned to Tadamoto, his face suddenly drained of blood. "He aided a rebel lord. I will have no traitors in my House, Colonel Jaku. Carry out your orders." And with that he returned his attention to the north.

Tadamoto stood for an awkward second, then, despite being entirely ignored, bowed stiffly and retreated. *This is a murder,* Tadamoto thought, a coldhearted murder.

Fifty-seven

THE ARMY OF the barbarians and the two armies of Wa faced each other across the open fields in chilling silence. The men on either side stared out over the green grass and wondered if their death was somehow, mysteriously, taking form among the indistinguishable faces of the enemy.

After the shock of seeing the barbarian army for the first time, Akantsu II sent an embassy to speak with the representatives of Lord Shonto. Appointed to speak for the Emperor, Jaku Tadamoto rode out on a gray horse accompanied by two guards. The Son of Heaven demanded that Jaku Katta, former commander of the Imperial Guard, come forward for Lord Shonto and made it known that no other would be acceptable.

Having already helped an Imperial Prince to die that morning, Tadamoto felt like a man being slowly torn apart, for there was no doubt in his mind that Katta was also on the Emperor's list of those who would fall upon their own swords.

To Tadamoto's left the barbarian army prepared for battle at a pace that could almost be described as leisurely and this did not raise the young colonel's confidence. The Emperor would not discuss the barbarian army, and when Tadamoto dared to push him the Son of Heaven finally answered; "I am well aware that the army is larger than previously reported, Colonel." Beyond that the Son of Heaven would say nothing, knowing full well who had assured him that the barbarian force was small.

How had he been so misinformed? Tadamoto asked himself again, realizing he would quite possibly never know. But what had happened with those fools he had sent north? Katta had told the truth, he reminded himself for the thousandth time that day. Katta had told the truth and his own brother had not listened.

Jaku Katta and his two guards appeared now, coming down the last run-out of the slope that protected the Shonto position. Neither party displayed flags of truce nor did they carry banners, as would have been common under the circumstances. It was still hoped that the barbarians did not realize the armies of Wa acted separately.

The two groups rode slowly forward, like two patrols meeting and pausing to speak for a time. Katta stopped his horse first and made Tadamoto approach him. The younger brother shook his head at this tactic. With his tongue Tadamoto tried to work some moisture into his mouth. So much depended on this one conversation. . . . And Tadamoto was still not certain why the Emperor had demanded that Katta should speak for the Shonto. All of the Emperor's choices seemed to be selected to cause Tadamoto confusion and test his loyalty.

The evening before Tadamoto had played gii with Shonto's vassal-merchant, Tanaka, a practice he had taken up in the last few days. The old merchant had played a wily game, forcing the distracted Tadamoto into a foolish mistake. When the game was surely won, the old man had surrendered and pushed back from the board. Tanaka had answered the colonel's expression of surprise with a shrug. "I can see a course that will win you the game, Colonel, so I have surrendered my force to you, hoping thereby to gain your good will. In the days when I played this game with Lord Shonto, I often did the same. He is a gii master of some reputation, as you know. My alternative was to risk losing everything." The old man spread his hands in a gesture that seemed to say: *the choice is yours.*

The brothers motioned for their respective guards to stop and rode forward, Katta waiting for Tadamoto to bow and when he did not the elder brother smirked. No one dismounted.

"Brother," Katta said, and Tadamoto answered his brother's nod with the same gesture.

A moment of silence. Tadamoto thought his brother looked much the same as when they had parted months before, though now Katta had some color on his face from time in the sun, making Tadamoto wonder what things had passed in his brother's life since they had last spoken.

"Lord Shonto has asked me to inquire after Prince Wakaro. The Prince has not returned to us."

"The Prince is the concern of the Emperor only," Tadamoto said, the half-lie coming with difficulty. "Lord Shonto should not trouble himself."

Katta looked into his younger brother's eyes then, and Tadamoto found himself looking down at the leather reins in his hands, adjusting his grip on them.

Katta shook his head with some sadness. "The Emperor demands much of his servants, Tadamoto-sum. It is a sad thing. I will inform Lord Shonto."

Tadamoto swallowed. Perhaps this ability to look into the souls of others was a characteristic of all opportunists, and womanizers, too, for that matter, the young colonel thought.

Katta cocked his head to the barbarian army. "I did not lie, Tadamoto-sum. The Emperor thinks I have betrayed him, but I have merely put the safety of Wa first. There lies the end of our Empire as we have known it. We must not allow this to happen, Tadamoto-sum, don't you agree?"

Tadamoto looked into his brother's gray eyes then, wondering if there was truly some shred of honor behind the words or if this was merely part of another elaborate plot. "I have come with a message from the Son of Heaven." Tadamoto almost referred to his brother as *General Jaku,* for he still wore his Imperial Guard uniform and insignia. "You may tell Lord Shonto that the Emperor will accept the surrender of the lord's army immediately. There will be no pardons for rebels. If Lord Shonto wishes to show his great loyalty to the Empire, he will resign his command upon receiving this message. We will speak only to those who come to arrange the surrender. No other emissaries will be recognized." Tadamoto reached into his sash and removed a letter, thrusting it toward his brother. "This is the message, inscribed so that there shall be no misunderstanding. Please, deliver it to your lord."

Katta looked down at the paper in his brother's hand but made no move to accept it. "The Emperor assumes that Lord Shonto will surrender his life to the Emperor rather than allow Wa to fall. Hear me, Tado-sum, Lord Shonto will retreat in the darkness and leave you to face the barbarians alone. We will retreat toward Yankura and raise the army needed to oust these barbarian chieftains.

"This Khan, you know who he is. The Emperor paid him gold to help bring down the Shonto. He is a half-caste—born in the desert to a woman of Seh. But he is more than that. His mother was born to the House of To-kiko. He has Imperial blood in his veins, this Khan. For many years he lived in Wa, after his mother was rescued from the tribe that had abducted her. If this man takes the throne, his claim could be recognized. The barbarians think that they come to make Wa their own, but I do not believe it is to be so. This Khan does not care for their prophesies or claims or vendettas. He will make himself Emperor with the barbarian army at his back, but he will be an Emperor of Wa. The barbarian army will be split and spread across the Empire, made ineffectual, and this Khan will become a man of Wa.

"But he does not love us, Tadamoto-sum. The half-castes are barbarians to the men of Seh. His life before he returned to the desert was not such that he has gained respect for the men of Wa. He would be a danger on our throne and I cannot say what his reign would bring."

Katta stopped, glancing up for a second at his brother's eyes. Whatever he saw there seemed to give him hope. "Tado-sum. Akantsu is not a man of honor. You know this. What befell Prince Wakaro? Was it just?" Softly Katta pounded his fist on his armored thigh. "Lord Shonto has spent the last months slowing the barbarians' advance, allowing the Emperor to build an army. And yet Lord Shonto knew of the Emperor's plot against him. Knew that the Emperor would be unlikely to make peace with him even in the face of an invasion. Look at this!" Katta waved a hand at the army of the desert. "We can save the Empire, Tado-sum. The Jaku name can go down in history as the Shonto name did in the past—as saviors of Wa." Katta lowered his voice. "Exchange guards with me. Tell them it is the Emperor's wish. Return to your master with my men as though they were your own. Take them into the presence of the Emperor as witness of what was spoken here. They are the best swordsmen I have, and utterly loyal. They will not fail. Surrender the Imperial Army to Lord Shonto and there will still be a chance that we can win against this Khan."

Tadamoto still held out the Emperor's letter. It was an impossible scheme. Tadamoto knew he was being watched with great interest by the Emperor's officers. There was no chance that he and his brother could simply exchange guards—it would not go unnoticed. And even if it were possible, these guards would not be allowed, armed, into the Emperor's presence. Tadamoto knew that he was the only one who was allowed near to the Emperor wearing a sword. Yet he was loyal—loyal to the Emperor even while he had grown to hate Yamaku Akantsu.

"Brother," Katta said, reaching out and taking the letter. "Motion your guards forward. It is worth any risk to save the Empire."

Tadamoto shook his head. "Even in time of war they will not be allowed into the Emperor's presence carrying weapons of any sort."

"You carry a sword, brother. It can be snatched from your sash at the correct moment. These men understand what needs to be done. They have made their peace with Botahara. Once the Emperor falls, you must take control of the army. I know you have many loyal men in the guard, Tado-sum. They will support you. Tomorrow the Khan will have prepared his forces for the battle. There is no time, Tadamoto-sum."

Shaking his head, the younger brother reined his horse back, his gaze fixed on his brother's gray eyes. "You do not understand loyalty, Katta-sum. You think it is something one owes to another, but it is not so. Loyalty to principles is the essence of all honor." Tadamoto looked down at the reins in his hands again. "It is this difference that has led to this—meeting across the field of battle as we do. What you ask . . . it is impossible. I do not believe the Emperor will waver in his position. If you think Lord Shonto can save the Empire by retreating to raise an army, then it is a course you must recommend. But if the Khan pursues you . . . ?" Tadamoto looked into his brother's face a last time, shook his head, and turned his horse back toward the Emperor's position.

Fifty-eight

An Empire away
From distant battles
Yet there is no peace for the spirit.

When letters come,
White rice paper bearing the Dragon seal,
Old men walk out alone into rain swept fields.

FOG LAY AROUND the base of the hill and the thousand fires of the barbarian army illuminated the mist, causing it to glow like a fabric of mystical origin. Shonto stood looking out toward the plain, his hand resting lightly on the trunk of a tree. Two paces away Kamu stood watching in silence. Lord Shonto had spoken very little since sending for the steward, but this did not seem to matter to Kamu—his lord had requested his presence and it was possible that nothing more than that would be asked for. The old man did not feel it was his place to question.

Earlier in the evening Shonto had requested that his armor be brought and had then inspected it meticulously, knowing full well that Kamu had done the same. The steward did not take offense at this, for he knew that Shonto's inspection was a ritual only, something to occupy the mind. Even so, the old warrior was gratified that his lord had found the armor to be without flaw.

Now Shonto was lost in silent thought. Everyone wondered if the battle would be joined the next day, after the fog cleared. It depended on the Khan, for the men of Wa would not take the offensive.

"Shokan-sum," Shonto said suddenly, "have we word of his progress?"

Kamu cleared his throat. "The countryside is full of barbarian patrols, Sire. I instructed Lord Shonto's guides to bring him to us with all possible caution. I apologize, Sire, his present location is not known to me."

Shonto moved his hand as though he brushed away an insect though Kamu knew it was the apology his lord waved off.

Silence returned. Occasional music and singing would drift up from below—sometimes the haunting scales of a barbarian flute and sometimes the familiar tunes favored by the soldiers of Wa. Neither side seemed inclined to the drunken, boisterous singing often heard in camps. Somehow Kamu had expected it from the barbarians—curious.

Shonto shifted his position, running his hand down the smooth, white bark of the birch. "I wonder about this Emperor, Kamu. . . . Is it possible that he will sacrifice his Empire? Is Akantsu so certain I will surrender before allowing the loss of the Imperial Capital? He takes a great risk."

Kamu ran his hand through gray hair. "Undoubtedly he knows Lord Shonto is more loyal to the Empire than the Yamaku—who are only loyal to their own ambitions. If the Khan is defeated and my lord is part of the command that routs these invaders, the Emperor believes he will lose his throne for his part in bringing the barbarians into Wa. Akantsu must think that he can only survive if both Lord Shonto and the Khan fall. He will not sacrifice his House to save the Empire."

Shonto nodded. "If I were to surrender my force to the Emperor, would he fight or would he retreat?"

Kamu kneaded the stump of his missing arm and shifted his weight subtly from foot to foot. "Sire, I . . . I cannot say what is in the mind of the Emperor of Wa." Kamu considered carefully before speaking his next words. "If Akantsu stands against the barbarian on this field and does not triumph, the Imperial Army will be shattered. The barbarian army is formidable." The old steward whispered his last sentence. "Certainly the Emperor would be a fool if he did not retreat and attempt to increase his force."

Shonto nodded. "He would be a fool. I agree. The question is really very simple: who will sacrifice their House to save the Empire? Thank you, Kamu-sum."

*   *   *

The former commander of the Imperial Guard, Jaku Katta, sat on a rock with his back against a tree and examined a sketch which showed the relative positions of the armies in the field. A lamp hung from a branch to the general's right and several guards knelt on the edge of the circle of light. The fires of the barbarian army glowed in the mist gathered below, and overhead stars appeared to be immersed in liquid, points of light diffused by a high veil of the thinnest clouds.

Jaku looked up from his map and stared into the darkness. It is hopeless, he thought, the Emperor could hardly have chosen a worse field. Considering the number of ideal positions farther north, it was almost a betrayal of the Empire to have chosen this site to face the invading army. Fool! Jaku thought. If he had only listened. . . .

Rolling the map with some care, Jaku created a calm to replace his anger. His teachers had taught that anger and fear destroyed one's ability to reason, dulled the reactions, and this was a time that would demand the very best of the former kick boxer.

Jaku set the map aside. If only Tadamoto would reconsider his proposal. A dead Emperor would change the world—as surely as the change from winter to summer. Shonto could defeat this Khan, Jaku had no doubt of that, and the Jaku family would retain a position at court, for who would sit upon the throne but a member of the Shonto family—the son or Lady Nishima.

Tado-sum, the kick boxer sent his thoughts out to his brother, *why do you stay loyal to this man?*

There was no doubt in Jaku's mind that it would be worth the life of his brother to kill the Yamaku Emperor. He was not certain that his brother would agree, however.

What will Shonto do? Jaku asked himself again. He must retreat, the guardsman thought, it is the only wise choice. Akantsu was such a fool! Both armies had to be preserved if they ever hoped to stand against the barbarians.

Jaku believed it would take the Khan another day to ready his attack, which could allow the armies of Wa a chance to slip away. But if the Khan had any idea of what really transpired in the camps of his enemy, he would attack the next day. Pray that this chieftain does not understand what transpires here, Jaku thought.

As any good general, Jaku tried to consider all the possibilities, no matter how unpleasant. Defeat of the forces of Wa on this plain would put the Jaku on the run—if they survived. Nitashi or Ika Cho would be the provinces most likely to remain autonomous if the Empire fell—at least for a while. An army might be raised there. Whichever province Jaku chose, he knew that he must make his way there by the fastest method—by boat, unquestionably. Yankura would be his destination if the armies of Wa suffered defeat. From there he could go either north or south—Ika Cho or Nitashi. He would not decide before reaching Yankura. Much would depend on what occurred in the next few days—on who survived.

Calling for an inkstone and paper, Jaku shifted so he could write by the light of the lamp. Considering the uncertainty of the future, custom indicated that he must compose the required poems. There were still many hours before a battle would begin—if there was a battle at all.

A servant brought steaming bowls of cha to the two ladies who sat on grass mats looking out over the scene to the south. They were as far away from the sight of the armies as they could manage and still be within the protective perimeter of Shonto's defenses.

Once the servant had returned to the darkness, the conversation resumed.

"Do you remember, when we journeyed north on the canal," Nishima said, "my spirits fell low and you lectured me . . ."

"I never lecture, cousin," Kitsura interrupted.

"Encouraged me, then," Nishima said, slowly turning her bowl, steam rising into the air, the swirls barely visible in the starlight. "You said it was truly surprising that, considering our family histories, we had never been forced to flee before. Excuse me for saying so, cousin, but I'm not certain I truly believed that. Yet here we are. If the Emperor does not come to his senses, my uncle will take our force where? South, perhaps, or east. And will the Khan take the capital then? I believe so. Strange to think—the capital of Wa in the hands of a barbarian chieftain." She sipped her cha.

Kitsura did the same. The night was warm for the time of year and without a breeze. A waning moon would not appear until very late and the stars were suspended in a haze. The lights of the capital glowed in the south for the nightly fog did not spread south of the hills upon which the armies camped.

"I hope my family have escaped south," Kitsura said quietly. "Our estates in Nitashi should be out of reach of barbarian armies for a while." There had been no word from the Omawara family for many days and Kitsura's worst fear was that the Emperor had moved against them.

Nishima reached out and touched her cousin's arm. "I am certain they have slipped away and have been unable to send word. Your family have been well informed of the true situation, thanks to the diligence of their own daughter. The Omawara have had warning long before any other family in the capital. Do not despair, cousin, I am sure they are safely away."

Kitsura nodded—a smile of thanks for her cousin's reassurance. They sat quietly, sipping their warm cha, the aroma of the herbs blending with the complex scents of spring in Wa.

Tadamoto sat across the board from the vassal-merchant and stared at the arrangement of pieces as though he contemplated his next move, but in truth his mind was elsewhere.

Tanaka cleared his throat quietly.

Tadamoto looked up and then realized that it was indeed his turn to play. "Excuse me, Tanaka-sum, I am not a worthy opponent this evening. I apologize."

"There is no need to apologize, Colonel Jaku. Please. This battle will decide the fate of the Empire." Tanaka tried a reassuring smile. "Your brother's proposal? It unsettled you?"

Without ever intending to, Tadamoto had spent much of the evening explaining the present situation to the Shonto merchant—had even told him of the Prince's death and his meeting with his brother. It was quite likely that Tanaka was the only man Tadamoto knew who was, beyond a shadow of doubt, not an informer for the Emperor—a man to be valued for that alone. The young colonel had also come to appreciate the merchant's opinions and the unassuming manner in which they were proposed.

"Katta unsettles me simply by being Katta. He demands much." Out of frustration Tadamoto finally exchanged a piece, a move he had explored several times though he could not remember if he had decided it was a good move or bad.

Tanaka nodded. "Your brother said the same thing of the Emperor, yeh?" The merchant responded by taking a swordsman. "It seems you are caught between two men who have the same requirements but different ends in sight, Colonel." Tanaka's face contorted in a small grimace. "Most difficult."

Tadamoto stared down at the board again. Tanaka was forming a substantial attack, there was no doubt, though Tadamoto could not quite see where the effort would be concentrated. To the right side of the colonel's keep his position was weaker and to the left the board was more complex, so he moved his *Emperor* to the left, hoping the complexity would shield it.

Tanaka contemplated the shift in focus Tadamoto's move created. There was no evidence that he was having trouble concentrating nor did he appear very concerned with the situation just beyond the walls. Tadamoto had been expecting the merchant to ask what would become of him on the eve of the battle but was beginning to realize that Tanaka had no intention of asking him. This response had added to Tadamoto's feeling of anxiety and he suffered from an urge to explain the merchant's situation to him just to be rid of the tension.

"I had the honor of watching Master Myochin Ekun play gii on several occasions—years ago now. He played against my liege-lord. Those were instructive matches, Colonel Jaku, two formidable masters of gii. I must say, those were humbling matches also." Tanaka moved a *dragon ship* into the center of the fray. "Master Myochin won almost invariably—but then he had the advantage of being blind."

Tadamoto looked up at the merchant, wondering if this was meant as humor, but Tanaka stared at the board, his palms together, fingers pushing under his chin, his look serious.

"It is an unusual advantage, Tanaka-sum, one which most people would choose to be spared."

"No doubt that is true, Colonel, but the game that Master Myochin plays exists entirely within, he does not even need a board. He has also never seen any of his opponents—they are only differentiated by their styles of play. Master Myochin plays gii—we play . . ." he waved at the contest in progress, "a game on a board with another who intimidates us or is our friend or rival or lover. Our game is always caught up in the world—we cannot escape this—and it lacks . . . purity." Tanaka shrugged.

Tadamoto moved a *swordmaster* to counter the *dragon ship,* no longer caring if he made intelligent moves. "I had never considered this before, but what you say is . . . fascinating."

Tanaka removed Tadamoto's *swordmaster* with a *guard commander* and the young colonel stared at the position. His *swordmaster* had been well covered, and obviously so. Tanaka was offering a sacrifice and there seemed to be no choice but to take it. He looked further but was not sure where Tanaka's attack would concentrate. He took the *guard commander* with a *foot-soldier* and Tanaka answered without a second's contemplation, taking the *foot-soldier* with his *dragon boat* and pinning Tadamoto's own *dragon boat* in the process.

The young colonel threw up his hands and then pushed over his *Emperor* in surrender.

"The Commander of the Imperial Guard defeated by a *guard commander.*" He smiled, the tension in his face disappearing for an instant. "It could not have been more artfully done, Tanaka-sum." He gave a half bow to his opponent. "I congratulate you. For a man with the affliction of sight you play remarkably well."

Tanaka nodded, bowing lower than his opponent. "You are too kind, Colonel. Like any Emperor, I will sacrifice a guard commander without hesitation to win a battle."

Tadamoto stood abruptly, jarring the gii table as he did so, knocking some of the pieces to the floor. He looked down at the older man, his face hard with controlled anger. "You presume too much, merchant. Your instruction is neither asked for nor acceptable." Tadamoto waved toward the door. "I have much to prepare for."

Tanaka gave a low bow and rose. He was shorter than Tadamoto by half a head, so stood looking up at the younger man. "Loyalty to principles, Colonel, those were the words you used. What principles is your Emperor loyal to? Ask yourself that, for if you serve him you are, without choice, loyal to those same principles."

Tadamoto waved toward the door again, glaring at the merchant as he did so.

Tanaka turned and took a step but stopped. "There is more at stake than the honor of Colonel Jaku Tadamoto. Will you sacrifice the Empire for that?"

"Guard!" Tadamoto called and the door burst open immediately. "Take this man to his quarters, by force if necessary."

The guard bowed, but Tanaka proceeded out the door without further resistance, casting a final glance over his shoulder and though the look on the merchant's face was truly unreadable, Tadamoto felt it was an accusation.

The door closed and Tadamoto was alone. He found himself staring down at the gii board, the pieces in disarray. For a moment he could not find the *guard commander* Tanaka had sacrificed, and this was disturbing. Then he saw it and replaced it carefully on the gii board, as superstitious as any soldier on the eve of a battle.

Tadamoto slumped down on a cushion and stared at nothing. How long he sat like that he did not know, but he was eventually interrupted by a tap on the door.

"Enter," he called.

The face of an Imperial Guard appeared. "A message, Colonel, from the Emperor."

Tadamoto nodded and the guard entered, setting a small stand bearing a letter within his commander's reach. Waiting until the guard had closed the door behind him, Tadamoto picked up the letter, barely glancing at the seal as he broke it. He unfolded the pale yellow paper and found the clear hand of the Emperor's principal secretary. A single vertical line of characters:

Shonto will surrender his army to you at sunrise.

Tadamoto tried to read the message again to be sure he had not made a mistake, but his eyes would not focus. *Shonto would surrender? Shonto would allow his House to come to an end in an attempt to save the Empire?*

Tadamoto set the paper back on the stand, staring at it dumbly. He felt no joy at this news, he realized. In truth, he felt deep sadness.

Nishima paced back and forth across the small room in her tent, unable to maintain even a facade of patience or inner peace. After her conversation with Kitsura, she had sent servants to find Brother Shuyun, reasoning that a meeting with her family's Spiritual Advisor under the present circumstances would be completely natural.

A lamp flickered on a low table where Nishima had tried to write earlier—tried to create some order out of the turmoil she felt within. It had been an unsuccessful attempt. She could not find words that even approximated what she felt.

"Excuse me, Lady Nishima," her servant's voice came from close outside the tent.

"Please enter," she answered quickly, her heart lifting.

A maid pulled back the flap of the door. She bore a tray.

"Excuse me, my lady. An Imperial Guard messenger brought these." She nodded down at letters, bound together by a silk cord, lying on the silver tray.

"Please," Nishima waved at the table and the servant placed the tray there, bowing as she left. Nishima was struck by how drawn and pale the woman's face was. *Her future is as uncertain as anyone's,* the aristocrat thought.

Kneeling by the table she unknotted the cord, careful to choose the letter intended to be read first. Unfolding the crisp paper revealed a blade of spring grain and Jaku Katta's indifferent hand struggling down the page. Her view, she realized, had changed, for she had once convinced herself that the general's brushwork had qualities that could be admired—as she had once felt about the general himself.

> *Plum blossoms*
> *Cover the land*
> *In a shroud of white.*
> *Morning in the fields*
> *Grain shoots struggle up*
> *Into the season's warmth*
>   *I am not daunted by the sunrise*

"He is impossible," Nishima whispered. *Jaku cannot accept that a mere woman can resist his efforts.* She tossed the letter onto the table and found that the second letter was sealed with the Jaku family symbol and beside this a line of characters read:

> *If circumstances require.*

She was appalled. *It is his death poem,* she realized, *and he has sent it to* me. *Presumptuous fool!* On the verge of calling for a servant to have the letter returned, Nishima realized that Jaku might indeed die the next day. He was apparently estranged from his brother—who would he leave his final words to?

It is a small thing, she told herself. *In all likelihood the guardsman will survive—it will be a cuckolded husband who brings about the Black Tiger's end—and then I will have the poem returned without comment.*

She put the two poems into her sleeve and sat watching the lamp flame flicker. From beyond the thin wall of her tent the sound of a soldier's flute rose up, as light and uncertain as the flight of a butterfly. Listening not as a musician but with her heart, Nishima found the music very beautiful, evoking an image of a fragile, solitary spirit.

A rustling of the tent fabric and a soft voice. "Lady Nishima? Please excuse my intrusion."

It was Shuyun. She rose quickly to her feet and crossed toward the opening.

"Ah. My servants found you, Brother," she said quietly. "Please enter."

Shuyun slipped in through the opening. "I met no servants, Lady Nishima," he said.

He has come of his own will, Nishima thought, and this gladdened her heart. She reached out and took his hand, drawing him into the room.

"You cannot address me as Lady Nishima here, Shuyun-sum, it is not permissible." She smiled and received a smile in return.

"You sit alone, Nishima-sum. I am concerned."

She shrugged, lowering herself to a cushion. "How can one sleep? Tomorrow the world I know will change utterly. Many, many will die, perhaps some that are close to me. I feel separated from my emotions in the face of this." Nishima reached over and turned down the flame on the lamp. "When my mother died, I remember feeling much like this, as though the shock of what had occurred rendered me incapable of feeling for some time. I remember doing all the things that were required of me, appearing very controlled to everyone, but inside . . . Botahara save me.

"It was more than just the loss of my mother. A time was over suddenly and I felt that I had never given it the attention required to properly appreciate it. Everything had changed. It was as though I had been traveling in a safe canal and suddenly found myself at sea—a sea of uncertainty. I had never truly appreciated the canal and it was past."

She looked up, searching for understanding and felt the monk's warm hand squeeze her own. She smoothed a crease in her robe. "I look back at my recent journeys on the canal and think that I understand things that seemed impossible to untangle before. I realize, now, that Jaku Katta is truly the tiger, driven by instincts he can neither understand nor control, and Lord Komawara, whom I thought impossibly parochial, is thoughtful and noble and quietly very brave. Kitsura-sum and I are often spoiled and compete with each other just as we did when we were children, and my uncle is working tirelessly to preserve an Empire that the Shonto have shaped longer than any Imperial dynasty." She caught the monk's eye again. "And you, my friend . . . are out of place in this world, in the House of a great lord. Yet I sense that you are not at peace within your own Order either. Where is your place, Shuyun-sum? You . . . you look so troubled."

He shook his head. "I have been in a council. Lord Shonto did not want to wake you immediately." Shuyun took a controlled breath. "I'm sure he would rather speak to you himself, but . . . Lord Shonto has agreed to sur- render his army to the Emperor. We will join the refugees fleeing to Yankura in a few hours."

Nishima pressed her forehead with her hand, remaining like that for some time. Then she moved forward until she pressed her cheek against Shuyun's neck and he held her.

"What will become of us," Nishima whispered. "Whatever will become of us?"

Fifty-nine

A LL PREPARATIONS WERE made in the dark or the dim light of covered lamps. It was crucial that the barbarians saw nothing untoward or they might react in ways no one could predict. Nishima heard more than saw her tent come down in the dark. She was standing in the midst of total chaos, Kitsura clinging to her arm as though she feared Nishima would evaporate into the darkness at any second.

The two women were dressed in men's hunting costumes, the better for riding, and perhaps the thought of this unsettled Lady Kitsura even more—she had less experience with horses than her cousin.

Although she had spoken a few words with her uncle, the meeting had not been private and Nishima still did not know the reason for Shonto's sudden decision to surrender his army to the Emperor. Some part of her wanted to believe it was a ruse of the gii master, an apparent sacrifice that opened the gate of an elaborate trap.

Yankura was the destination everyone mentioned or the Islands of Konojii, but Shonto had said neither to her, so she was uncertain of their direction.

The great lord met with his advisors now, planning the move of the army to the Emperor's position. The Emperor was expecting the surrender of the Shonto along with the army but this was not to be so. All of those the Emperor named in his scroll would flee with the Shonto; Jaku Katta, Lord Komawara, and all of the Shonto family retainers and senior advisors. The oaths of the Shonto House Guard would never allow them to join the Yamaku. It would not be a small party able to move quickly, and this concerned Nishima.

"There is a hint of gray in the east, cousin," Kitsura said, her voice curiously high-pitched. "Should we not be on our way?"

Turning to the east, Nishima could see no signs of light. "We have time yet, Kitsu-sum. Be patient."

Servants bustled about, sorting clothing and other goods, packing trunks and bags. Much would be left behind, Nishima realized, but this did not seem important. She was concerned for her staff, and this thought brought an image of Shimeko to her mind. Where had she disappeared to, Nishima wondered? Such a troubled soul but someone Nishima had developed an affection for. I should never have allowed her aboard that infernal ship, Nishima thought.

Her last memory of the plague ship was of it passing along a side canal toward a Botanist monastery. The land there was so flat it seemed to be setting out across the fields, sails full and drawing, the terrifying green banner waving against the blue sky.

"May Botahara protect her," Nishima whispered.

"Cousin?"

"I am reduced to mumbling. Please excuse me."

She felt Kitsura's grip tighten on her arm for a moment in reassurance.

Lord Taiki rode toward the two torches, their copper light reflecting dully off black lacquered armor in the darkness and fog. Clearing his throat so that his presence would be known, Taiki whispered to a guard. "Give the signal."

A lamp opened quickly, three times, and a torch dipped once in reply, leaving an arc of flame hanging in the air for the briefest instant.

They continued forward. Shapes took form in the fog-riders in black.

"Colonel Jaku? I am the emissary of Lord Shonto Motoru." Taiki spoke quietly.

"Come forward, Lord Taiki."

A pace apart Taiki stopped and looked at the young man illuminated in the torch light. He wore an unadorned helmet and his face-mask hung open revealing a fine-boned silhouette. The green eyes could not be seen and Taiki was surprised that he would think of this.

"I have orders to conduct Lord Shonto through the lines into the presence of the Emperor, Lord Taiki."

Taiki took a long breath. "Lord Shonto slipped away with his family and senior advisors, Colonel Jaku."

Silence.

Taiki saw Tadamoto reach out and take a plait of his horse's mane into his gloved hand. "And my brother, Katta?"

"He has disappeared also along with Lord Komawara."

"I see. My Emperor's instructions were very clear: if I sense treachery, I am to cut you down and retreat."

Taiki controlled his urge to rest a hand on his sword hilt. "There is no treachery, Colonel. Lord Shonto warned the Emperor of this invasion months ago. He has done everything within his power to prepare the Empire for this war. Lord Shonto was ignored. He has now given up his army for the defense of the Empire. Do you expect him to forfeit his life as well?" Taiki realized he had raised his voice and forced his next words in the most reasonable tones. "There is no treachery, Colonel Jaku. Only a desire to save Wa. I am prepared to move our force, retreat or attack or prepare for battle as we are. I will surrender command to whomever you appoint. Do not fear, Colonel Jaku, we will not risk a war between our own army and the forces of the Emperor with a barbarian army standing ready. I await your instructions."

The sounds of clattering armor and horses stamping and calling out to each other carried across the empty field. The barbarians were stirring.

"Bring your men in an organized file down the southwest slope of your hill and form them into ranks behind the position of the Imperial Army. This must be done quickly, Lord Taiki, it is our intention to retreat under cover of morning fog. We must move south. This position is not favorable."

"You will surrender the capital, then?"

Tadamoto did not answer. "It is the Emperor's will that you retain command of Shonto's army for now," he said. "By the hour of the hare we will have begun moving south. Further orders will be sent to you."

Jaku Tadamoto turned his horse and moved back into the darkness, the torches borne by his guard were quickly consumed by the fog.

Shonto knelt on cushions set out on a flat section of stone projecting from the side of the hill. Lamps had been hung in the trees nearby, but the apparent tranquillity of the scene was belied by the sounds of an army moving in the darkness around them.

"No news could be more welcome, Lord Taiki," Shonto said, his voice calm. "It was my fear that the Emperor would make a stand upon this field, and I would have committed my troops to a slaughter. General Hojo will assist you in moving the army, Lord Taiki, and then will join my party. You have much to do, may Botahara be with you." Shonto bowed low.

"Sire. I take on this duty out of loyalty to the Empire and because you wish it," Lord Taiki said, carefully keeping emotion out of his voice. "The Emperor does not command the smallest part of my loyalty. When the Khan is defeated . . ."

Shonto held up his hand. "When the Khan is defeated, there will be much to do to restore the Empire. The commander of an Imperial Army cannot speak of civil war. Choose your words with care, Lord Taiki, even in this company. The Emperor trusts few men."

Taiki hesitated and then bowed, touching his forehead to the cool earth. He retreated three paces and rose to his feet, the company bowing to him as he turned and walked beyond the circle of light.

Shonto nodded to General Hojo who hurried after Taiki lest the lord become lost to him in the darkness.

"Kamu-sum, is our party ready to travel?"

Kamu bowed quickly. "They will be, Lord Shonto, before the hour of the hare, if need be."

Shonto gave a tight smile. "Please see to our preparations."

Kamu bowed, slipping off into the night as quietly as a Botanist monk.

Lord Komawara bowed then. Like the others present he wore full armor, his helmet tucked under his arm. "May I see to my troops, Sire? I can offer some small assistance to Lord Taiki before we depart."

Shonto nodded. "We must be gone soon after sunrise, Lord Komawara. Do what you can, but we cannot wait."

As had Lord Taiki, Komawara touched his head to the ground before retreating and hurrying off.

"General Jaku, no doubt you wish to do the same."

Jaku nodded.

Shonto gave the guardsman a half bow. "An hour after the sunrise."

Jaku, too, bowed low and disappeared into the darkness.

Shonto was left facing Lord Butto who, like Lord Taiki, was not seen as part of Shonto's rebellion and would join the Imperial Army.

Butto Joda bowed low and returned to a kneeling position, a boy in armor laced in purple.

He is no boy, Shonto reminded himself, he is a formidable strategist and ruthless when necessary.

Shonto nodded, acknowledging the young lord.

"Sire, if I may presume. . . . No one would expect you to go north. If you traveled the edge of the foothills you would come to my fief. It would be an easy thing to hide there. The Butto hunting lodge is secluded and not un-comfortable. I would send word ahead of you. And, Lord Shonto, the moun-tains could be a last resort. Even if Akantsu can defeat this Khan, he will look for you to go south or to cross the Inner Sea to the islands. You have assisted the Butto in the past, Lord Shonto, and now sacrifice much for the sake of our Empire. I would risk the displeasure of the Son of Heaven with-out hesitation if I could assist you in any way."

Shonto was silent a moment. "This is a generous offer, Lord Butto. The future is so unclear, I would hesitate to earn anyone the Yamaku's enmity. The Emperor may retain his throne yet. Do not endanger your House as I have mine. The Yamaku will not be a dynasty like the Mori—their ascen-dancy will not last. Do not be concerned, Lord Butto, the Shonto have sur-vived far worse than this. We are practiced in the art of waiting." He gave the young lord a brief smile. "Lord Taiki will need your assistance, may Botahara walk beside you."

Lord Butto bowed again. "May the Perfect Master watch over your House, Lord Shonto." Bowing low again, the tiny figure backed away and hurried off.

Shonto sat alone but for his guard who kept their distance, kneeling in perfect silence.

A whisper came from beyond the lamp light. "Uncle?"

Shonto smiled. "Lady Nishima. Please, do not be shy."

As she stepped into the light, Shonto was confronted with the sight of his daughter dressed in the clothes of a boy.

"Like Princess Shatsima, I am ready to flee to the wilds if that is your wish, Sire."

Shonto smiled, despite the gravity of the situation. "I am certain that Shatsima never looked so lovely nor faced her exile with such courage. You do honor to your House, Lady Nishima."

She came and perched on the edge of the stone. "I am certain Princess Shatsima not only exhibited but also felt more courage, Uncle." She waved a hand in the direction the Shonto army moved. "It shames me to feel such trepidation when I am not among those who will join the battle."

Shonto shook his head. "After Rohku Tadamori witnessed the fall of Rhojo-ma, he told his father that he would rather die in a thousand battles than stand by and watch others give their lives. It is a common thing to feel. There is little comfort in this knowledge, but I am certain that you would enter the battle as willingly as any man of arms, were that your part to play. Those who do not wield a sword will yet be called upon, Nishi-sum. An act of bravery may be asked of each of us before this war is over."

Nishima nodded her head, sadly it seemed. "I pray I am equal to it, Sire."

"We all have the same prayer, Nishi-sum, even the bravest."

Nishima waved toward the eastern horizon. "It grows light. Sunrise is not distant now. Is it time?"

"I wait only for the few to return who assist Lord Taiki: Jaku Katta, Hojo, and Lord Komawara. They will not be long."

The blaring of horns and the clashing of metal shook the air suddenly and Nishima and Shonto turned to look out toward the field.

"Botahara save us," Nishima whispered. "What is that?"

"An army preparing for battle. The Khan grows impatient to sit upon his throne."

"Will he attack today, then?"

"The army he seeks will be gone when the fog clears. Then this barbarian chieftain will be tested. Will he pursue the Emperor's army or will he choose to ascend the throne and declare himself Emperor of Wa? It is the question our Emperor would give half his wealth to have answered."

"No one can know, Uncle, this Khan is a great mystery. Who is he? From where did he come?"

Shonto looked at his daughter then, raising an eyebrow; "I have not told you? Jaku Katta has admitted many things now that there is no question of regaining the Emperor's favor. This Khan is your very distant cousin, Lady Nishima, a half-barbarian with Tokiko blood in his veins. He has almost as much claim to the throne as do the Yamaku or the Fanisan or the Omawara."

"Uncle, this is not possible! How can you tease at a time such as this?"

"It is the truth, Nishi-sum. His mother was of the House of Tokiko, married to a lord of Seh. Barbarian raiders abducted her and she bore a son in the desert." Shonto waved toward the north. "And now he comes to claim his birthright."

Nishima looked out into the still, dark night, where the fires of the barbarian camp glowed in the mist. "So it is he who has lived in the wilds, like Shatsima, waiting to reclaim his throne." Nishima pressed her fingers to her chin. "It is as Hakata said. During times of upheaval, when history is created daily, miracles become commonplace."

The horns echoed off the hills again and a stillness answered as the moving army paused to listen. There was no answer from the opposing camp who prepared their retreat.

Shonto reached out and took his daughter's hand. "Join Kamu-sum and Brother Shuyun, now. I will wait a while to see that all has gone well. Stay close to Brother Shuyun, Nishima-sum, he is charged with your safety."

Nishima sat for a second and then spoke in a small voice. "May I not wait with you?"

Shaking his head, Shonto squeezed her hand. "The less experienced riders should not come last. Watch over your cousin, she will find this an ordeal, I fear."

Nishima sat saying nothing, then put her arms around Shonto. Neither spoke for a moment, then Nishima released him, touching his cheek as she turned to go.

The body armor was slipped over the Emperor's head by attendants and the lacings tightened.

"Enter, Colonel," the Son of Heaven said to Tadamoto who hovered outside the entrance to the tent.

Tadamoto knelt and bowed his head to the ground, moving forward awkwardly in his armor.

"Do not keep me in suspense, Colonel. If I desire suspense, I attend a play."

"Excuse me, Emperor." Tadamoto shifted his helmet under his arm. "Lord Taiki has delivered the army of Lord Shonto Motoru, Sire, but the Shonto have fled with their advisors and other members of the rebellion."

The Emperor nodded, considering the information. "It was to be expected," the Emperor said with some finality. "Motoru will remain treacherous to the very end."

Tadamoto shifted and felt the weight of his sword against his thigh. The guardsman closed his eyes for a second, the words of both Tanaka and his brother coming back to him.

I am not loyal to his principles, Tadamoto thought. *There are no guards present—I am the only armed man in this room. It would be easy. But what would ensue?*

"Will Taiki deliver up this army as he has said, or is this a trap, Colonel?" Tadamoto placed a gloved hand on his sword.

This man. . . .

"I believe that Taiki will bring us the army and is prepared to take orders in the coming war. His loyalty to the Emperor is, however, in question."

"Once we have our march in order, Colonel Tadamoto, I will transfer the command of the Shonto army to you. After the river is crossed, we will have time to deal with the disloyal."

The disloyal, Tadamoto thought. *I remain loyal to my principles.*

The Emperor's shoulder pieces were laced into place. "Is there light, Tadamoto-sum?"

"The sky is turning gray."

The Emperor nodded. "Then let us leave this barbarian to wonder. He will take the capital, I'm certain. We move south toward Yankura."

Tadamoto nodded and retreated from the tent. Osha, he thought, I must send word to Osha.

He stepped outside to find the sky light, hinting at blue, and the fog hanging in the valley being swept away by a breeze from the north. The army of the desert could be seen in the mist, wavering, as though it lay at the bottom of a moving stream.

"Komawara. Is he not with you?" General Hojo asked Jaku Katta.

"I have not seen him since we left your company, General Hojo."

"We wait only for him." Hojo stood holding the bridle of his own horse. He kept looking north as they spoke. The barbarian position was becoming visible and the fog threatened to clear. "This will expose the Emperor's retreat," Hojo said. "The Wind Goddess will bring ruin upon us if this continues."

Jaku nodded. He dismounted. "What will the Khan do?"

Hojo did not answer. The two warriors stood looking out over the field as the sky became fully light. Horses were heard coming down the path behind them, and the two generals turned in time to bow to Lord Shonto.

They were within the protection of the trees just below the base of the hill so their view was imperfect.

"Can you see the Imperial Army?" Shonto asked. "Are they in the earthworks still?"

Hojo dropped the reins of his horse to the ground and picked his way some distance down the slope, stepping over fallen trees and bramble. Leaning out from behind the base of a tree, he scanned the Emperor's position.

Pulling himself back he shouted up the hill. "The Imperial Army appears to be retreating from their position, but this operation is not complete."

"Damn fool," Shonto said. "If this mist clears, they will be caught on an open field. Better to stay behind their earthworks and pray they can hold until dark."

Shonto came up closer to Jaku but did not dismount. Mist pushed up the hill from the valley then, enveloping Hojo in white. The lord motioned his guard forward. "Do not leave General Hojo alone in this fog."

Five guards dismounted and stumbled down the slope, disappearing before they had gone a dozen steps.

Again a braying of horns and a clash of arms, then again, and once more. The shout of hundred thousand went up, an inhuman din, and the sound of a charge shook the earth.

"General Hojo!" Shonto shouted.

There was no answer. All that could be heard was the pounding of hooves, the crying of men.

Suddenly the mist cleared, snaking off around the sides of the hill, and there, on the field, was the barbarian army in full charge.

Hojo turned and ran awkwardly up the embankment followed by his guard. "They break ranks," he said breathlessly, "the few that remain. It will be a slaughter."

"It is a rout!" Shonto shouted. "Damn that fool Emperor! Damn him for eternity. They will fall upon Lord Taiki from behind." He spurred his horse. "Come, we must save what we can. If these armies are broken, the barbarians will take the Empire."

The others were quick to follow, whipping their horses up the hillside in pursuit of their liege-lord. They came up to the shoulder of the hill in moments and Shonto stopped to survey the scene.

The first wave of barbarian warriors washed across the earthworks, taking the few who tried to stand and throwing them back like bits of flotsam.

Men of Wa were on the wooden bridge spanning the canal trying to escape to the western bank, but many fell to arrows and a fire ship was bearing down on the bridge.

Standing in his stirrups, Shonto watched with an air of detachment, the gii master surveying the board, weighing possibilities coldly. "The banners of this Khan, do you see them?"

There was a second's silence and then Hojo pointed. "There."

In the rear of the army the gold and crimson banners fluttered in the cool north wind.

"He made no offer to accept a surrender," Jaku said bitterly.

Shonto nodded, turning to Hojo. "Send guards to warn Kamu and our household. They must leave everything and move as quickly as possible."

Shonto wheeled his horse to the south and set off at a gallop, the sounds of battle growing dim as they descended the long slope of the hill. A different scene faced them as they broke out of the trees: the army of Lord Taiki was formed up, ready to march, but was not on the move, and the army of the Emperor was forming ranks to the west. Over the crest of the hill upon which the earthworks had been established men poured in disarray.

Pointing toward the Imperial Army, Jaku said, "They do not even realize what has happened."

"The barbarians will crest the hill soon enough," Hojo said, "then all will know."

"The Emperor's army will break and run," Shonto said. "Our own forces will take the blow. We must do what we are able. General Jaku, General Hojo, you will organize the rearguard action and we will march south and take our losses." He waved them forward and the small group set off at speed.

A shout went up from Lord Taiki's army before Shonto's party reached them, and men turned to the north where the vanguard of the barbarian army appeared. On the crest of the hill the army of the desert hesitated, banners fluttering, the men of Wa in flight before them. The soldiers of the Imperial Army stood looking back as the Khan's army grew, crimson riders appearing under a cloud of gold silk banners.

The Khan had taken the field and was, for the first time, seeing the distant Imperial Capital rising up above the mist. Barbarian warriors collected below the banners of their chieftain like the dark crest of a wave forming on the hillside. Like a wave crest it gathered weight and grew in size until it must rush down and spread itself across the shore. The din of horns assaulted the ears three times, and each time the barbarians answered the call with a shout and a clash of arms.

With a final shout the army of the desert surged down the hillside. The men of the Imperial Army stood looking on for a few seconds and then they broke and ran, the panic washing through the unformed ranks like wind through wheat.

Shonto's party closed with Taiki's army, standing its ground still, and a guard raised the blue silk and shinta blossom on a staff to a shout of elation from the men. A rider in Komawara blue raced along the edge of the troops, pulling open his face mask-as he came.

Hojo waved a hand at this rider. "The mystery of Lord Komawara . . . he stayed to fight with his men."

Shonto's guard met the rider with drawn swords, but Shonto waved them aside and Komawara pulled up his horse before the lord.

"The barbarians split their force to attack, Lord Shonto. My men are ready to ride out to meet them. Lord Butto will join me."

Shonto looked up the slope to the charging army and nodded to Komawara. "Their force is large, Lord Komawara. You may slow them, but be prepared to fall back quickly. General Hojo will prepare our defense. Where is Lord Taiki?"

Komawara waved a gloved hand to the south. "At the head of the army, Sire."

"May Botahara protect you," Shonto said and waved his guard to follow, setting out toward the south.

Komawara spun his mount and raced off, closing his face-mask as he went and tightening his helmet cord.

The crest of the barbarian wave broke upon the rear of the fleeing Imperial Army first, riding down the foot-soldiers. A conch sounded in the rear of Lord Shonto's force and the Komawara banner shook free in the breeze, fluttered for an instant and then the north wind faltered and died. The conch sounded again and riders in darkest blue and riders in purple set off with a shout to meet the charging barbarian cavalry.

With the dying of the north wind the cloud of fog halted in its southern retreat, reformed its ghostly ranks, and began to creep north, devouring the heads of the two armies of Wa, then drawing in the bodies.

*   *   *

Lady Nishima turned to Shuyun who stared off at the hilltop. Dark banners waved on the crest and men massed there in growing numbers.

"Those are the banners of the Khan, Lady Nishima. It would appear that the barbarians have attacked the retreating Imperial Army."

Dark stains on the green fields marked the distant armies of Wa. Horns sounded, their metallic voices borne across the land on the north wind.

Nishima looked back toward the hill they had recently departed. "Where is my father?" she said, keeping panic from her voice with an effort.

Kitsura rode up then, one hand on the reins and the other holding tight to the saddle.

"Can you see, Brother?" she asked. "What occurs?"

Rolling across the green land, the shout of the barbarian army struck like the first breath of winter.

"Botahara save us," Kitsura whispered.

The dark mass of the army of the desert poured down the slope of the hill. Nishima tore her eyes away, looking back the way they had come, searching for the signs of blue.

Near at hand a single rider jumped a low stone wall, coming toward them at a gallop from the direction of Lord Taiki's army.

"A messenger," Shuyun said.

Kamu appeared, galloping his horse down the line of Shonto retainers, his empty sleeve blowing in the wind like a banner. He stopped beside Lady Nishima, staring out toward the beginning battle.

"We cannot tarry, Lady Nishima, Brother. We must make haste," he said.

Nishima nodded. "What has become of Lord Shonto?"

The rider who came toward them waved then and no one made a move to make haste as Kamu had suggested. They waited, transfixed by the terrible scene unfolding before them.

His horse in a lather, the rider, a Shonto House Guard, reined in before Kamu, pulling open his face-mask as he did so. "I come from Lord Shonto. Our lord orders that you leave everything and flee with all haste. The barbarians have carried the attack to us."

"Where is he?" Nishima said, the fear she felt breaking through. "Where is Lord Shonto?"

"He has joined the army, Lady Nishima, to direct the defense."

Nishima turned her face away, covering her eyes with her hand.

Shuyun pointed to the north, east of the hill that had been the Shonto encampment. Barbarian riders were emerging from behind a stand of trees not far off. Turning in his saddle, Shuyun surveyed the field in all directions, then he reached over and took the reins from Kitsura's hands, pulling them over the head of her mount.

"The north wind is dying," Shuyun said, "The fog will hold for some time now. Lady Nishima?" he said with some gentleness. "Lord Shonto is a capable man surrounded by able warriors. We must look to ourselves." He tugged at the reins of Kitsura's mare. "Steward Kamu, the fog clears first in the east. May Botahara protect you."

"You must have guards, Brother," Kamu protested. "I cannot let the Ladies Nishima and Kitsura go off unprotected."

"We will be more likely to slip away undetected the fewer we are."

"I will go with Brother Shuyun, Kamu-sum," Nishima said. "Do not be concerned. In the fog Brother Shuyun can see where others are blind. Brother."

The monk turned his horse and led the two ladies south, disappearing into the cloud of white.

Lord Komawara elected to charge the barbarians, knowing from his experience that they could be thrown into confusion by a direct attack. To his left he could see the small form of Butto Joda, riding a massive stallion and outdistancing his apprehensive guard. Jaku Katta held a position to the lord's right. Arrows whistled overhead, passing both north and south.

The opposing armies met with a clash of steel that rang across the field. Komawara took his first man from the saddle with a blow from his pommel. He caught a fleeting glimpse of Jaku Katta, his sword flashing and barbarian riders falling back before the great warrior.

He fought another, one of his Hajiwara guards knee to knee with him as they both battled forward. It soon became obvious to Komawara that the momentum of their charge was being overcome. The Hajiwara guard toppled from the saddle and he saw two barbarians on foot pounce on him.

A shout came from Komawara's left and he saw Lord Butto spur toward him. "We must fall back while there are enough of us to win through."

Komawara looked around quickly and realized that, among the fallen barbarians, the field was strewn with men in Komawara colors and the Butto purple. He tore his conch from his saddle as Lord Butto fought to protect him. Sounding the retreat, he dropped the conch to the ground and went to the aid of Butto Joda. Lieutenant Narihira appeared at Lord Butto's side, unhorsing a barbarian and disarming another who retreated.

The three fell back, more barbarian raiders appearing with each passing moment.

"There is no end of them," Butto shouted.

"They are like the swarming of the Butto across my lord's fief," Narihira answered.

Butto Joda almost fell from his horse as he aimed a blow at the Komawara guard who wore the green lacing on his sleeve, but Narihira turned this aside. Komawara drove his horse between the two men as the first tongue of mist drifted past them. In a moment they were completely enveloped, the sounds of swords ringing came out of the mist around them, but they could see no others. Barbarians appeared before them, charging immediately. They were separated in the ensuing fight and lost their way, no longer certain which direction was a retreat, which a futile charge.

Despite the number of his guards the Emperor of Wa kept his hand on his sword hilt. His army was in retreat before a vastly superior force and at the crest of the hill that his army had recently abandoned he could see the gold banners of the Great Khan waving in the fitful breeze. The banners slowly descended the hill which told the Emperor more about what happened in the battle than any number of reports. The Khan had a perfect view of the situation—the scene of his triumph.

Colonel Jaku Tadamoto rode through the Emperor's guard, bowing from the saddle.

"Colonel?"

"Lord Taiki's army is holding ranks thus far, Sire, though they are cut off from us now. Our troops have broken rank, Emperor, the barbarian army sweeps all before it."

The Emperor nodded, his reaction unreadable behind the frozen features of his black face-mask. "Gather what troops remain and retreat toward the capital. If we can slip out across the lake, we may yet save some part of this frightened army. What direction does Lord Taiki go?"

"It is difficult to know, Emperor: south, generally."

The Emperor reached up and tightened his helmet cord. "Offer what resistance you can to cover our retreat, Colonel." The Emperor turned and spurred his horse toward the canal where his boat waited.

Tadamoto sat his horse watching the Emperor go. *I did not tell him that many say they saw the Shonto banner at the head of Lord Taiki's army,* Tadamoto thought—*no doubt he will find out soon enough.*

It was quickly obvious to Lord Taiki that they could not be certain of their direction in the fog and the relief he had felt at returning command of the army to Lord Shonto quickly gave way to apprehension. The knowledge that they would face a barbarian army of one hundred thousand if they were still on the field when the fog cleared kept them moving all the same.

In council with Lord Taiki, Shonto had decided to go what they hoped was southwest to meet the canal which would take them to the capital—perhaps the only destination they could be certain of.

The sounds of battle surrounded them and companies of riders would appear and disappear like apparitions. Neither General Hojo, nor the Lords Butto and Komawara, nor Jaku Katta had been heard from since the fog returned and not one member of their party found their way back to the main body of Shonto's army. The worst was feared, though no one would give voice to this, but Lord Taiki became more pessimistic about their fate by the moment.

Despite moving across level ground the army progressed at the pace of an old man on foot, a result of their uncertainty of direction, no doubt.

"This fog is both a blessing and a curse, Lord Shonto," Taiki said. Like everyone else, he found himself constantly searching the mist around him, looking for signs of the enemy or for a landmark that might tell them where they were. Patrols could not be sent out, for they would never find the army again and this made the commanders doubly blind.

"It is a blessing, do not doubt it. We should have been swept from the field, but the Khan has lost us as we have lost him. Pray it holds until we are beyond his reach. We will march by night. If we can find our way across the river, we may escape, Lord Taiki. It is the most we can hope for."

The ringing of steel sounded before them where Shonto had placed his strongest swordsmen. A rider in blue pushed through toward Lord Shonto and Taiki.

"We have met a barbarian party, Sire," he shouted as he came. "Reinforcements are being called for."

"What numbers? How large a party?"

The man rode up then, bowing from his saddle. "Large, Sire. It is impossible to tell."

Shonto turned and gave orders to an officer and there was a flurry of movement around them. Horns blared to their right, sounding far too close. Riders appeared suddenly and Taiki drew his sword at the same time as Shonto.

"They are Lord Komawara's men!" someone shouted and Taiki heard a voice thank Botahara—his voice. But then he realized these men fought barbarians.

Shonto cursed beside him. "We have ridden into the heart of the battle, Lord Taiki. Fall back in that direction." The lord waved his sword. "We must hold our force together." His words were lost in the chaos. Arrows whistled and fell among the men near him. Like any lord of Seh, Taiki did not flinch or try to cover himself.

Barbarian warriors engaged the guards around the two lords. Butto purple could be seen in the mist now, riders hard pressed and few. Taiki saw Shonto cross swords with a barbarian. The lord of the Shonto fighting like a common warrior, Taiki thought, and then he, too, was fighting for his life. More arrows fell, shot by which side Taiki could not tell. Lord Toshaki Yoshihira unseated a man to Taiki's left, shouting that he had seen the canal bank. Arrows flew and men fell around him.

Taiki took a barbarian's helmet off with a blow and then finished the stunned rider with a perfectly aimed cut. He looked around for Lord Shonto but could find him nowhere. Shouts were heard now: *the canal, they had found the canal.*

They waited in the mist, absolutely still. Nishima had lost track of the times Shuyun had made them do this, or ordered them to turn suddenly, or reverse direction all together.

"What is it, Brother? What do you hear?" Kitsura whispered.

Nishima leaned close to her cousin. "Say nothing. Shuyun-sum can sense chi at some distance. Do not destroy his focus."

Kitsura's beautiful face was pale, frightened, yet she struggled to maintain a semblance of dignity even so. She nodded at Nishima's words.

Riders had passed close to them several times and they often heard the barbarians' horns and the clash of swords. Shuyun looked up at the sky which showed some signs of the lightest blue.

"The fog is clearing to the east, we are forced toward the canal."

He tugged at the reins of Kitsura's mare and Nishima moved her horse to stay close beside him. They went perhaps a hundred feet and the mist grew thicker again. Shuyun motioned for an abrupt turn to the left, then stopped them again. Riders could be heard close by, many riders by the sounds. Kitsura mumbled the Bahitra. The riders passed.

Leading them another hundred feet, Shuyun suddenly stopped, his eyes closed. A man coughed somewhere nearby though Nishima did not know from what direction this sound came.

Shuyun spoke and his voice sounded strange, distant. "Do not move from this spot no matter what occurs." He handed the reins of Kitsura's mare to Lady Nishima, pressing her hand as he did so.

Moving his horse forward the monk slipped into the mist. Kitsura reached out and gripped her cousin's sleeve. The sound of something of weight striking the ground came to them and then a riderless horse appeared before them, causing their own horses to shy, throwing Kitsura to the ground.

Shuyun appeared then, dismounting quickly and helping Kitsura to rise. "Are you injured, Lady Kitsura?"

She shook her head. "No. . . ." Moving her arm in an arc, she tried to smile. "No, I am unharmed. The ground is soft." She remounted with the monk's assistance.

Without further hesitation they moved off, more quickly now. The fog was clearing, there was no doubt.

As the mist pushed back, Shuyun pressed the horses into a canter. Soon the sounds of battle seemed to recede and they stopped infrequently now.

There was a shout to their right. "Ride," Shuyun called out. "Stop for nothing." Saying this, he whipped Kitsura's mount with his reins and turned toward the sound of horses bearing down.

The circle of their world had drawn itself out to half a rih and in their entire world Nishima could see no moving figure. At a low stone wall time was lost while Nishima jumped both horses over, one at a time. Kitsura climbed over, one fall being enough for the day.

They rode on, seeing no one, and finally Nishima pulled their horses up, looking back over her shoulder.

"Brother Shuyun said to stop for nothing," Kitsura panted.

Nishima shook her head. "But he is alone. How many were there, did you see?"

Kitsura shrugged. "I cannot see through fog, cousin. I think the capital is showing through the mist, look."

Off to their left the white walls of the city reflected the afternoon sun.

"I am entirely turned around, Kitsu-sum." She wiped her brow with a sleeve in a most unladylike action, causing her cousin to laugh.

"It is not a time for laughter, cousin," Nishima scolded.

"Excuse me, Nishi-sum, I . . . excuse me." She forced her face into seriousness though her eyes still retained a sparkle.

The sound of a horse running over soft ground came from behind them and they both turned to see a rider jump a ditch.

"It is Brother Shuyun, cousin," Kitsura said, "I am certain."

Nishima pressed her horse forward to meet the monk. When he stopped, she rode up beside him embracing him from her saddle. Kitsura examined a tree in the distance and the beauty of the capital appearing from the shroud of mist.

Waving toward the north and west where the fog was clearing, Shuyun pulled free of Nishima's arms. She released him reluctantly and turned to look.

Among the tendrils of dissipating mist the Imperial Army straggled over the fields, making their way toward the capital in small groups, many on foot, having shed their armor to make better speed. Spread out over many rih, the silent, defeated soldiers of Wa retreated.

"Where is my father in all of this?" Nishima asked.

Shuyun shook his head. He pointed east and Nishima turned to see a large force off in the distance moving toward the river. "Lord Taiki's army?" she said.

"Barbarians," Shuyun said quietly. "That line of retreat is cut off. The Khan will force us all into the capital."

They began to move again. A flowing ditch was used to water the horses and Shuyun stopped them then to let the horses graze for a time.

Sitting on the bank in the warm spring sun it seemed to Nishima that there could hardly be a war only a few rih away. She closed her eyes and tried to make herself believe it was all a dream, but when she opened them the retreating army told her the dream was true.

Taking her reins from Shuyun as they remounted, Kitsura said, "There is no fog for me to become lost in, Brother. I must learn to ride while I may."

A group of horsemen converged with them and though Nishima's tendency was to avoid them Shuyun thought that they wore the midnight blue of the Komawara and this proved to be true.

"We became separated from our lord in the fog and confusion of battle," an officer, one Narihira Chisato explained. One of the men was obviously injured, though not bleeding. Shuyun forced him to dismount and examined his injuries—broken ribs and terrible bruises. The injured man's companions made a bundle of his armor and strapped it behind his saddle.

"Was there news of my father, Lord Shonto?" Nishima asked, almost afraid of what she might be told.

The officer turned back toward the scene of the battle as though searching for the answer to Nishima's question. "Lord Shonto joined Lord Taiki," he said, still looking out over the field, "no doubt regaining control of the army. We charged the barbarians then, Lady Nishima, to protect the retreat. Since that time we have seen no sign of Lord Shonto's force." He waved toward the thousands whose paths converged on the capital. "All we have spoken to are from the Emperor's army which was routed before they could retreat. The Son of Heaven has fled, surrendering the field to the barbarian pretender. It is a black day, Lady Nishima. The north wind blew out of the desert and brought ruin upon us." The man shook his head sadly and said no more.

The small party continued in silence, pushing their tired mounts on toward the Imperial city. As if the gods of wind and weather had not caused enough pain for one day, the western sky was lit with a sunset that caused the heart to ache.

"It is a sign of the end of a glorious empire," one warrior whispered. The others glared at him and he bowed, whispering apologies.

Darkness came slowly, the colors of the sunset lingering after the stars appeared in the east. The lights of the capital flickered to life and the night finally turned dark. Seven Imperial Guards joined them and nothing was asked or offered about the identities of the riders without armor.

Nishima and Kitsura pulled cowls over their heads and the darkness masked them well enough. Both were careful not to speak and the Komawara guard formed a protective wall between the guardsmen and the others. Little was said, at any rate, each alone with their thoughts.

The Empire had fallen; that was enough to occupy the mind.

Sixty

THE NORTHERN GATE to the Imperial Capital was open and the bridge that crossed the canal to it had not yet been destroyed. A party of Imperial Guards were stationed at the entrance, or had merely taken it upon themselves to stand guard, it was not clear which.

Lady Nishima's party was challenged as they rode up though it seemed to be mainly for the sake of form—so many fled to the capital. One of the Imperial Guards in Nishima's company identified himself as the Great Khan come looking for a good inn and in the ensuing laughter they slipped into the city of the Emperor.

The streets and canals were choked with the soldiers of the Imperial Army and panicked residents and refugees attempting to make their way toward the city's eastern gates and the Lake of the Lost Dragon. No organized defense was in evidence and robbery and looting had begun in plain view.

"Where is the Imperial Guard?" Kitsura whispered. "Will the Emperor not defend the city? Has he fled?"

Nishima shrugged, looking about, alarmed by what she saw. The guardsmen who had accompanied them into the city immediately went their separate ways and only Shuyun and the three Komawara guards remained. Among the thousands jostling in the streets this seemed little protection.

As they progressed into the city, Nishima's fear began to recede. She realized that the looting was not widespread and that, generally, people were proceeding in an organized way and often offered assistance to others. She began to relax and smiled at her cousin who looked truly frightened.

Many of the soldiers were headed in the direction of the Island Palace, as was a large part of the population. Rumors said the Emperor had not fled and that the defense was being organized from the palace.

Although horses were seldom used in the capital, a city of canals and narrow streets, they were common that evening as the retreating army arrived. The city was not designed for transport by horse, however, and they soon encountered a footbridge too narrow to pass.

Shuyun turned into a tight alley which led out onto an avenue that ran along the edge of a major canal.

"Where shall we go, Shuyun-sum?" Nishima asked. Until then there had been little hope of going anywhere but where the crowds went.

"I do not know, my lady," Shuyun answered, "your family residence will have been taken by Imperial Guards some time ago. Perhaps Lady Kitsura's family have not left the city and we could find rest there for the evening. If we want news of what has happened in the field, I suggest we go toward the palace though your name cannot be spoken there."

Nishima looked toward Kitsura. "I would like news of my family, cousin, but I understand your concern for Lord Shonto. My own family is more likely to be safe. Let us go to the palace gates at least and find out what we can."

Nishima gave her cousin a smile of thanks that dissolved immediately into a look of concern. They followed the canal, walking their tired horses across a bridge where, for the first time in their lives, the two ladies were jostled by the people in the streets.

It was late in the night when they came to the Gate of Serenity and in the square before the gate thousands gathered. A few small fires blazed on the cobbles of the square and soldiers and guards rubbed shoulders with all manner of citizens.

Atop the gate black-clad Imperial Guards stood, ignoring all questions and taunts. A single bell sounded the hour of the owl as though only one bellkeeper in the entire city stayed at his post. The hour rang through the teeming city in a strangely empty way.

Nishima's party dismounted and the Komawara guards took the animals in hand and loosened their saddle girths. One of the men walked off to see what could be learned, but when he returned he shrugged. "You can learn anything you desire here. The Emperor has fled, the Emperor has fallen on his sword. The barbarians are at the gates. The barbarians have gone toward

Yankura. Everything is being said, nothing is known." He found a wall to place his back against and fell promptly to sleep.

Jaku Tadamoto, commander of the shattered Imperial Guard, found his way into the city aboard a commandeered sampan, sculled by two river men his guards had pressed into service. He was not seriously wounded though he was bruised and battered and his once fine armor, a gift from his brother Katta, had saved his life more than once.

Scholars make poor warriors, he told himself over and over again.

The Imperial Army had been shattered and sent fleeing in disarray. The Emperor's decision to take command himself had proven the army's undoing. That and the Emperor's refusal to join forces with Lord Shonto. Had Lord Shonto escaped with his army? Tadamoto wondered. Was there hope for the Empire yet?

A group of Imperial Guards looked on as he passed, yet none made a move to bow to their commander. Tadamoto saw no animosity in their looks. It was as though he had simply lost his rank; there was no anger on their part but neither was there respect.

Scholars make poor warriors, he said to himself again.

He had but one intention now, to go to the palace and seek out his sovereign if the Emperor was not already on his way to Nitashi. Tadamoto had left his young brother, Yasata, as a guard in the palace—determined that at least one member of the Jaku would survive. They would escape. Tadamoto had a plan and gold enough. Had Osha received his message? Had she fled? He would take Yasata and find her. The three would make their way to the Islands of Konojii. It would be years before this desert-born Khan would cross a sea. It was likely that intrigue would have ended his reign before then—this chieftain did not know what would happen when he entered the Island Palace, could not imagine. He would learn to sleep lightly and listen to whispers.

The river men brought the boat alongside a set of stone steps that led to a side gate used by the Imperial Guard. Tadamoto disembarked stiffly and forced himself to stand erect to ascend the steps. The canal and the quay were thronged with people—all trying to escape the barbarians, no doubt. It was a sad sight and sadder yet when Tadamoto realized that he would soon join them. His future would become as uncertain—was as uncertain now.

A password opened the gate and Tadamoto and his guards entered. They were in a square bordered with quarters for the Imperial Guard.

"Colonel Jaku," a guard said quietly. "I will find attendants to assist you with your armor and to see to your injuries."

Tadamoto shook his head. If he kept moving, the stiffness could be worked out as long as he did not stop again. "I have duties. See to yourself now, but I will need a boat—before dawn, no doubt."

"I will arrange for the boat myself, Colonel."

Tadamoto nodded. He walked toward the central palace buildings. The grounds were quiet, deserted, almost serene in contrast to the streets beyond the walls.

Mounting a set of stairs, Tadamoto passed the hedge-maze where he had been given instructions by the Emperor—instructions and threats, as it always was with the Emperor. Two guards challenged him as he came to one of the great doors to the palace. He identified himself and gave the password needed.

"The Emperor, is he in the palace?"

"I cannot say, Colonel," one guard answered. "Perhaps the Son of Heaven attends the council in the Great Hall."

"Find my brother, Colonel Jaku Yasata." Tadamoto ordered one of them. "I will need him to attend me in my quarters within the hour."

Inside the palace, Tadamoto was met by near darkness; only a small number of the hall lamps had been lit and these smoked from lack of attention. He removed one and used it to find his way.

Few knew the palace as well as the Commander of the Guard. He took an impossibly narrow set of stairs used by servants and kicked open a door to another hall, saving himself some minutes. The Emperor, Tadamoto was certain, would flee at the first opportunity and Tadamoto did not want that to happen.

There was a stirring in the square and whispers rippled around the edge. Much pushing occurred at the mouth of the major avenue and then mounted armed men appeared, some in black and others in blue or purple.

"Shonto livery!" one of the Komawara guards exclaimed, rousing the two ladies from a near sleep.

Nishima leapt up from the cobbles, surprised by the pain from riding. "It is General Hojo," she said, and had to be restrained by Shuyun from rushing forward.

"Do nothing," Shuyun whispered in her ear, "until we know what occurs here." He kept a grip on her arm and Nishima leaned against him as others stood and vied for a view. She closed her eyes and felt the monk's warmth. Surprised to find herself fighting back tears, she forced herself to open her eyes and focus on the scene, what little of it she could see.

Jaku Katta and the diminutive Butto Joda rode at Hojo's side. All three were covered in dust and appeared very grim. They rode at the head of a substantial force of armed men, Imperial Guards and Shonto men and a few wearing purple. They stopped before the gate and silence fell in the square as ten thousand held their breath, listening.

Hojo looked up at the guard over the gate. "Open the gate," he called out. "We will speak with the Emperor."

The guard stood frozen in place and then disappeared. There was silence and then Hojo rode up to the gate, drew his sword, and pounded on the wood and bronze with his pommel. The square rang with the sound of his anger.

"Open this gate!" Hojo roared, "or we will have it down and the palace will be open to all."

A guard officer appeared above the gate. "We do not open the gate to rebels," he shouted.

Jaku Katta spurred his horse forward, pulling off his helmet as he did so. "Brother," he called out. "You must open the gate. The barbarians march toward the capital and the Emperor does nothing. The Yamaku have betrayed Wa. Open the gates! We have an Empire to defend."

There was hesitation above the gates. Other black-uniformed men appeared and there was a hasty council. Suddenly a sword flashed above the gate and then others. The crowd surged forward at this and the Shonto guards pushed them back. The black-uniformed men disappeared and a moment later the gates creaked open and Jaku Yasata appeared.

The crowd surged forward again, shouting, "Bring forth the Emperor." A chant began. "Bring forth the Emperor."

The Shonto men and Imperial Guards pushed the crowd back, but even so Nishima felt herself thrust forward and she struggled to keep her grip on Shuyun and Kitsura.

They were close to a Shonto guard now and Shuyun called out and was recognized. Nishima was squeezed through the wall of guards and found herself face to face with Hojo Masakado.

"Lady Nishima! May Botahara be praised." He almost forgot to bow.

The crowd took this up then and Nishima heard the syllables of her name pass around the square like a chanted prayer, a sound she found deeply disturbing.

"You should not be here, Lady Nishima," Hojo started but then stopped. "Come, we must go in while we may."

Dismounting his horse, Jaku Katta bowed to Lady Nishima, a standing bow but low. "The north wind has brought us together, Lady Nishima, I am grateful."

Nodding Nishima stepped away, looking for Hojo. What of my father? she thought, what has happened to him?

The general had turned toward the gate and Nishima fell into step between him and Butto Joda who performed an awkward bow.

"My father, General, I have had no word of him."

Hojo shook his head. "We were separated on the field. The main force has not reached the city though I do not doubt Lord Shonto has managed an organized retreat. Do not fear, Lady Nishima, your father is wise in the ways of the battlefield."

"And Lord Komawara—what of him?" Kitsura asked.

"Lord Komawara," Hojo said with great warmth. "He is out on the plain yet, harrying the enemy in the dark. Lord Butto tells us that, lost in the fog, Komawara encountered the Great Khan and his guard and engaged them, felling a chieftain and sending the Khan running. Lord Komawara and General Jaku," he nodded at the guardsman, "have become the great warriors of our time, Lady Nishima. Their deeds will make a thousand songs."

Lady Nishima looked away. What a terrible thing, she thought. Behind her, she heard the whispers of the Komawara guard repeating Hojo's words.

War will destroy all of our souls, Nishima thought.

The Emperor paced the length of his chamber and back again. "Hopeless fools," he muttered, "they will fall into argument over the correct color robes to wear at the surrender of the Empire."

A knock rattled the door to his chamber and made the Son of Heaven start. "Enter," he called out.

The face of a kneeling guard appeared. "We have a boat, Emperor. It is being readied as we speak.

"The palace is completely surrounded, Sire. The people . . ." he hesitated, "appear unruly, Emperor."

"They are calling for my head, is that what you mean?"

The guard said nothing but stared down at the floor before him.

"Knock when the boat is ready."

Before the door closed, the Emperor had returned to his pacing. Venturing onto the balcony, he looked out over the city. Little could be seen, but the open fires in the squares said much. They will have someone's head before the night is over, the Emperor thought. Anyone's will do—nothing less will satisfy them. Well, he almost smiled, let them have any number of ministers and palace officials.

He paced back into the room and looked down at the armor of an unranked guardsman: the disguise for his escape. It went with the uniform he wore. He crossed the room and knelt on a cushion, staying only a second before morbid curiosity drew him back to the balcony, like a man fascinated by his own fear of heights.

Where was Osha? He had sent for her an hour ago. Were the servants afraid to say that she was gone? Run off like his wife and sons the minute he left the palace to go to war. He shook his head.

From the Gate of Serenity he could hear shouting and what sounded like a crowd chanting. The words were unclear, but he found the sound unsettling all the same.

A knock sounded at the door again and it opened without the Emperor's command. Osha slipped into the room, looking around, her face like a frightened bird's.

"On the balcony, Osha-sum," came the Emperor's voice. "I am basking in the affection of my loyal subjects—who call out for my death."

Osha moved slowly toward the sound of the Emperor's voice and finally saw him, dressed in the black robes of an Imperial Guard, his dark form blotting out the stars.

"Do not be afraid, it is not your name they chant," the Emperor said.

She did not like the tone of his voice.

The Emperor stood on the balcony, his back to the rail, his arms crossed.

"It warms my heart to see that not everyone has abandoned me, Osha-sum. Loyalty has not fled the palace entirely."

She nodded.

"Here is what you must do," the Emperor said matter-of-factly. "There is no one else I would trust. I will make my escape in moments. You must bar the door to this chamber when I leave and open it to no one. Force them to break it down. I should be out of their reach by then. I had the robes of a servant brought for you. A servant will be safe enough."

I am a mistress, Osha thought. She knew what happened to the pampered mistresses of fallen Emperors.

The Emperor pointed at neatly folded cotton robes lying on a small stand. "Quickly. We will throw your robes off the balcony."

Osha nodded. She began unwinding the yards of brocade sash. Looking up, she saw the Emperor watching. I am about to die at the hands of the people he has betrayed and he stares at me as though I am a hired woman. She closed her eyes and continued.

Steeling her nerve as she finished unwinding her sash, Osha asked the question that haunted her. "I hope your officers survived, Sire, so that they may assist you in the future. Colonel Jaku, for one, would be a great loss." She turned her back to the Emperor and removed her outer robe.

"The Colonel has acted as a loyal subject should— putting himself in the path of the barbarian army so that his Emperor might escape. As for the rest, they turned and ran, trying to save their miserable lives, may they be damned for eternity."

Osha steadied herself as she felt the room spin.

"Osha-sum, shyness does not become a dancer. Do not hide your beauty."

Nishima fell in behind General Hojo as Jaku Katta led the way to the Great Hall. The tramp of soldiers behind her was disquieting and so out of place. She had been in these halls many times, but they had been filled with laughter and music and poetry on those occasions. She felt Kitsura take her sleeve, like a shy child not wanting to be left behind.

"General Hojo, what is it you intend here?" Nishima asked nervously.

Hojo did not slow his pace. "We intend to force this fool Emperor to perform his duties. He cannot leave his throne, as much as it would gladden me if he did," the general said, casting a glance at Jaku. "We cannot fight the barbarians and a civil war as well," Hojo said, pointedly.

Nishima saw Jaku shake his head. "This Emperor, in an attempt to bring down your lord's House, sold our Empire to the barbarian Khan, General Hojo," Jaku said with force. "I have not changed my opinion—the Emperor is a threat to all."

Nishima looked back at Hojo, wondering how he would respond. The two officers had obviously been arguing the point.

"We will let Lord Shonto decide the fate of Emperors, General Jaku. Soldiers will always make decisions with a sword. It is our way, but there are other ways." He said this with finality.

They reached the doors to the Great Hall and the guards stationed there drew their swords. Jaku did the same, followed by the men around him.

"Stand aside," Jaku commanded as he pulled open his face-mask. "The Emperor you serve has fallen. You cannot be loyal to a ghost. Stand aside."

The men hesitated, exchanging glances, and then gave a half bow and laid down their swords. The doors were thrown open and the members of the council turned, their eyes wide. Immediately the officials leapt to their feet and fled in every possible direction, ornate robes flapping, like a flurry of escaping moths. The Dragon Throne was empty.

Hojo stormed into the room while his guard chased down several running officials and dragged them back to him. Nishima remained outside the door, trying to hear what was said. A commotion to her right drew her attention, and she saw Jaku Katta disappearing down the hall with Lord Butto on his heels.

General Hojo came out the door then, an official in tow. "This man has kindly offered to lead us to the Emperor," Hojo said, pushing the man in front of him. Something drew his attention. "Where do they go?" Hojo waved his sword down the hall at the backs of retreating Komawara guards.

"They follow General Jaku and Lord Butto," Nishima said.

Hojo looked around as though sure he would find Jaku beside him.

Nishima pointed. "That is the way to the Imperial apartments, General."

"May the gods take them!" Hojo swore and set off at a run, followed by the entire company.

Shuyun paced the general. "Those Komawara guards wear the green lacings on their sleeve—they were Hajiwara men, General."

Hojo nodded, saving his breath. They came to stairs and the armored men lagged behind. Shuyun looked over his shoulder once and then sprinted ahead. Seeing this, Nishima pushed past General Hojo and the other men exhausted from battle. She ignored the calls of her cousin and the guard, focusing on the sound of Shuyun's running feet just ahead of her.

Tadamoto reached the head of the stairs leading to the Emperor's apartments. From the guards before the Great Hall he had learned that the Emperor was in the Imperial apartments and, though less than certain he would be allowed through the halls, Tadamoto had set out. To his surprise, he had not been challenged once. The Imperial Guard, their commander realized, had broken and run just like the army in the field.

Down the long hallway he saw lamps and the black of guards before a door, indicating the Emperor was not unprotected. Akantsu is a fine swordsman, Tadamoto reminded himself, he is never entirely unprotected. Loosening his blade in his scabbard, Tadamoto started down the hall.

As he approached the guards before the Emperor's chambers, Tadamoto heard the pounding of boots on the stairs behind. Turning, he saw a single black-clad guard crest the stairs with a leap and come running down the hall toward him. Drawing his sword, Tadamoto signaled the guards, who rose and drew their weapons as well.

Jaku Katta slid to a stop on the polished floor, facing his brother. He reached up and removed his helmet and stood regarding Tadamoto.

"It is my hope the gods have brought us here with the same purpose, brother."

Tadamoto did not lower his sword. "Do not do this, Katta-sum." He swallowed with difficulty. "Do not stain our name with this crime."

"He is a traitor, brother. You know this is the truth. Wa deserves a sovereign who understands honor. Let me pass."

The sound of running feet in the stairwell.

Jaku did not look back.

"They are my men, Tadamoto-sum. You can do nothing. Stand aside."

The colonel shook his head. "I cannot, brother."

Jaku nodded. Very slowly he tossed his helmet aside and it rattled on the floor, sliding to a stop against the wall.

Turning toward the Emperor, Osha removed a second robe, the sheer silk wafting to the floor like a falling banner. She could not stop the tears, but she did not sob. Forcing her feet to move forward, she stepped out into the cool night.

The Emperor watched her with some interest. He reached out to her as she approached and she took his hands and pressed them to her, his touch fueling her resolve.

She stood looking at the confusion in the Emperor's face for a second, realizing she could not let the instant pass. "Tadamoto-sum," she whispered, "was my lover."

Saying this, Osha pushed the Emperor, her Sonsa training giving her surprising strength. As he fell back, the Emperor's grip tightened on one of her hands and she grabbed the rail with the other, pulling against his great weight. Groping with one hand, he grasped at the balustrade, cursing her, but Osha let go of the rail and caught this hand before he could save himself. And then, without hesitation, she followed him over the railing, her motion graceful as though she took flight.

Jaku drew his sword and faced his brother who stepped back immediately, his guard faltering. Men were in the hall behind, running. Butto Joda came to a position off to Jaku Katta's right, stepping into the Tiger's line of vision but staying out of reach of his sword.

"General Katta?" the youth said. "General Hojo is correct. This is a decision for Lord Shonto or the Great Council. I beg you reconsider."

Jaku did not appear to hear. Lunging forward, he took the sword from Tadamoto's hands so that it bounced off a post and fell to the floor.

Tadamoto faced the point of his brother's blade, but his attention was drawn back over Katta's shoulder. "Brother . . ." he said, lifting a hand to point.

That second's warning saved Jaku's life. The first Hajiwara guard's blow missed Jaku's neck, the blade cutting through armor and deep into the guardsman's right arm. He raised the sword again as the Black Tiger stumbled aside. Tadamoto leapt in between and took the second blow on the side of his helmet, which drove him to the floor.

Jaku spun and landed a blow one-handed, accounting for one as the other Hajiwara men fell on him. The guardsman retreated, using a post to protect his injured right side. Lord Butto reached for his sword but, unexpectedly, a Hajiwara guard sprang at the young lord and drove the pommel of his sword into Butto's face-mask, leaving him limp on the floor.

The two guards before the Emperor's door held their places, swords at the ready. Jaku circled away from these men, unsure who they would side with. Someone else reached the stairhead and started down the hall.

"We will avenge Lord Hajiwara, General," Narihira Chisato hissed, "for it was you who placed him in the path of Lord Shonto with lies and false promises."

The injured Hajiwara man leapt at Jaku. As the guardsman cut him down, Narihira stepped in coolly, sword raised. The Black Tiger fell heavily to the floor and did not move. Narihira raised his sword for the final stroke but found himself propelled across the room, hitting the floor and sliding to the feet of the guards at the Emperor's door. One held the tip of his sword to Narihira's throat, and the Hajiwara guard lay still.

Nishima arrived to see Shuyun literally toss the Hajiwara guard aside and then bend over Jaku Katta, who lay in a growing pool of blood. The monk made a sign to Botahara and rose, looking around.

"Is there no hope, Brother?" Nishima asked. She stood across the room, frozen in place.

Shuyun shook his head. "His spirit has fled, my lady. Jaku Katta is in the hands of the Perfect Master. May Botahara protect him."

Shuyun crossed to Lord Butto who lay unmoving. Removing the youth's helmet, the monk found his eyes open, only whites showing. Coming to stand beside him, Nishima laid her hand on Shuyun's shoulder.

Katta is dead, she thought, trying to make it seem possible. But why do I feel so little now when I believed I felt so strongly before?

"He breathes," Shuyun said. "His life force is strong."

"He was knocked down with a pommel, Brother," one of the Imperial Guards said. "He cannot be badly hurt, I'm certain."

"Please, Lady Nishima. . . ." Shuyun took her hand and drew her down. "Watch Lord Butto."

The monk then rose and went to the other fallen men as Hojo and the others came into the hall.

The other Hajiwara guards were dead, but Tadamoto had raised himself to one elbow, and propped himself there with visible effort.

"My brother?" Tadamoto said in a near whisper.

"Who is your brother, Colonel?" Shuyun asked.

"Katta," he said with effort.

"Lie back, Colonel Jaku, you are injured," Shuyun said. Softly he removed the ruin of the guardsman's helmet.

Tadamoto shook him off when the monk reached out to probe the wound.

"My brother . . ." Tadamoto turned and saw the great, still form of Jaku Katta lying against the wall in a dark pool. Sobs racked him and he would let no one near.

Hojo stood looking on. He made a sign to Botahara.

"He intended to kill the Emperor, General Hojo," Shuyun said. The monk motioned at Narihira still lying at the feet of the two Imperial Guards. "It was Jaku Katta the Hajiwara men had vowed revenge against, not Butto Joda."

"The Emperor is inside?" Hojo panted, motioning to the door with his sword.

The two Imperial Guards held their positions.

"We will not harm your Emperor," General Hojo said. "Let us pass."

One guard shook his head, pushing Narihira away with his foot.

Scrambling to his feet, the Hajiwara retainer joined the other party where Shonto guards pushed him to the rear.

Hojo motioned Shonto swordsmen forward.

Lady Nishima turned away and suddenly her cousin came and knelt beside her. The ringing of swords stopped abruptly and Hojo stepped up to the now unguarded door.

"Wait," Tadamoto said, lurching to his feet. Supported by a man in Butto livery, he followed Hojo as he tried the door and found it unbarred.

Entering the room everyone stopped, searching the dim corners, looking for doors. The room was empty.

"He has hidden or made his escape," Hojo said, driving his pommel into a gloved palm.

Waving at the balcony, Tadamoto moved forward. On the balustrade a torn scrap of silk wafted in the light breeze. The guard colonel stepped out onto the balcony, looking around, confused.

One of Hojo's officers peered over the balcony and turned to his commander, inclining his head almost imperceptibly. The general hurried forward and Tadamoto did the same. A white form lay on the stones far below, a dark shadow at its side.

"There is our Emperor," Hojo whispered. Beside him Tadamoto turned slowly and spiralled to the floor.

A Shonto officer pointed out beyond the north gate where a long line of torches snaked its way south.

"And there is Lord Shonto and his army," Hojo said, his voice strangely quiet. "Inform Lady Nishima. She will have some good news this night."

Standing inside the Gate of Serenity, Nishima held tightly to Kitsura's arm. They almost leaned upon each other, their exhaustion was so great.

"Food," Nishima whispered to Kitsura. "I will greet my father and then food and perhaps a bath. If we are to escape or face a barbarian attack, let us do it fed and clean, and perhaps even rested."

"I could sleep upon the cobbles," Kitsura said.

"You did, cousin," Nishima reminded her, but her lightness of mood was entirely false, in her heart she sent up a silent prayer: *bring him to me safely. He is good and wise. Bring him safely.*

The gates were open and soldiers pushed back the crowds outside. They jostled and shouted and still called for the Emperor, his death not yet known, and then, suddenly, they cheered.

"That will be the hero, Komawara," Kitsura said. "Imagine."

Men on horses appeared in the dim light, framed by the great arch under the dark sweep of tile. Three men rode abreast, one in darkest blue, one in gray, and one in Shonto blue. Nishima let out a long sigh and another prayer to powers unnamed—a prayer of thanks.

Outside, the people in the streets fell utterly silent, and then Nishima heard a single voice—the sound of a woman crying. She found herself moving forward, Kitsura trying to restrain her. She shook off her cousin's grip and continued. Komawara was dismounting now and the rider in Shonto blue also: *her stepbrother, Shokan.* And then she was running. Shokan saw the movement and turned toward her, his face black from dust and streaked with tears. Nishima felt her body stop, as though it obeyed commands from forces more powerful than her will.

Shonto's personal guard came slowly through the gate bearing a bier of lances upon their shoulders and on it lay a form draped with a banner—the blue silk of the shinta blossom. Nishima felt her knees strike the ground. A cry of deepest agony tore at her throat. Then she felt hands lift her, and she pressed her face into the blue lacing of Shokan's armor. Kitsura's arm encircled her shoulder and she heard the soothing voice of Shuyun, chanting a prayer for the dead.

Nishima had not eaten, bathed, or slept. She sat in a strange room in the Imperial Palace turning a cold cup of cha compulsively between her hands. She stared off, deep into her memories, perhaps, and looked as if she would begin to sob again at any second.

Kitsura had left her for a few minutes, lured by a hot bath, and Shuyun was off seeing to the ceremony for her father. There was so little time; they would have to perform the rites before dawn. *They're going to burn him,* she thought, and this realization was like a blow to her heart.

A tap sounded on the door to the room and a maid's face appeared—one of Nishima's own maids!

"Tokiwa," Nishima exclaimed, "how is it that you are here?"

"Steward Kamu brought us, my lady," she bowed, hesitating, her eyes cast down. "I'm sorry, my lady."

Nishima nodded. Her mouth formed the words, *thank you,* but no sound came.

"Lord Shonto and Steward Kamu wish to speak with you, Lady Nishima."

"Please bring them to me," she said. Perhaps their company will help, she thought.

The maid disappeared.

Seconds later Shokan and Kamu entered. They bowed and knelt on the mats.

"I have no cushions, I am sorry," Nishima said, her voice small.

Shokan shrugged.

"It lifts my heart to see you safe, Kamu-sum. It is a miracle." She looked into each of the men's faces. Certainly they are able to maintain an appearance of dignity better than I, she thought. I must look a ruin.

"The miracle," Kamu answered, "is Brother Shuyun's servant, Kalam. He went out into the fog and met a horde of barbarian raiders, sending them off chasing phantoms. He led us and hid us and put his ear to the ground and lured barbarians off into the mist and even drew his sword against his own people. He will be a man of Wa yet."

Nishima's smile was pained.

"Nishi-sum," Shokan said gently, "despite all, we must prepare for the future. There are many things that must be spoken of."

Nishima nodded, a sudden coldness spread through her. "You will not marry me to this Khan, will you, Shokan?" she said, surprised by the edge of hysteria in her voice.

"Sister, I would not marry you to anyone you did not choose."

She turned her tea bowl, still focusing on nothing.

"Nishima, the Lords of Wa and the officials of the government are meeting in the Great Hall as we speak. There is no heir to the throne."

"There are sons, Shokan-sum. Have you forgotten?"

Shokan glanced over at Kamu. "Wakaro is certainly dead, and the others will follow their brother once the people learn that the Yamaku have fallen. They are a despised family, Nishima-sum. No Yamaku will sit upon the Dragon Throne again."

There was silence for a second, but Nishima did not really take this information in. She could not force herself to focus on the conversation.

"If a suitable sovereign is not found, there will be a civil war, sister."

Nishima looked up. I have lost a father, why have they come to bother me with this, she asked herself? "Shokan-sum, excuse me for saying so, but you are speaking the worst foolishness. The Khan is about to take the throne. In a few hours he will sit in the Yamaku's place. The Empire, I may remind you, has fallen."

Shokan rubbed his palm with his fingers. "If there is not a chosen sovereign, claimants will spring up all over Wa. There will never be a concerted effort to oust the barbarians, for there will be no alliance strong enough. The lords of Wa will war among themselves, making the barbarians' work easy. It will be a generation before we see the enemy gone, perhaps more."

"They are such fools," Nishima said coolly, but there was no conviction in her voice.

"Nishima-sum!" Shokan reached over and took hold of her arm, spilling cha over her hands. "You must listen."

She fixed him with a cold glare and he let go of her hands. "I am listening, brother. What is it you have come to say?"

Shokan took a deep breath.

Nishima realized he waited for eye contact before he spoke and so she looked up, not trying to hide her anger.

"There is one candidate acceptable to all," her stepbrother said, speaking with unnecessary precision. "If you will consent to become our Empress, Nishima-sum, we will avoid civil war."

Nishima started to laugh, but the laugh died in her throat. She began to speak and could not. She stared at her brother as though he had spoken words that, beyond all doubt, confirmed him mad.

"Lady Nishima," Kamu spoke gently. "Thousands of lives may be saved by your decision. There is an entire Empire to think of."

My father is dead. The Empire has fallen. Why will you not leave me in peace? "Kamu-sum," she said as reasonably as she could. "I know nothing of the ways of government. How can you seriously expect me to rule? This is madness," she said, exasperated. Again she began, trying to achieve a tone of reason. "What of Lady Kitsura? The Omawara have as much Hanama blood as the Fanisan. Perhaps she will consent to be your Empress. Please, brother. Speak no more of this . . . I cannot bear it."

"Sister, my father raised me to understand my duty." Shokan's voice was as cool as hers now. "Did he not do the same with you?"

Lady Nishima stared at Shokan. *My father is dead, how can you insult me now? Have I not paid enough?*

"Lord Shonto," she said to her stepbrother, "if I seriously believed that I could play a part in saving Wa, I would not hesitate to do so. But once this crisis is passed and we avoid civil war—then Wa will be saddled with an Empress who knows nothing of the art of ruling. If one day we do oust the barbarians, I would not know where to begin to rebuild an Empire. I would be a worse ruler than the Yamaku." She waved a hand at the door. "Bother me no more with this. We have a lord whose ceremonies must be seen to."

"I will say no more, sister," Shokan answered, "though I would ask you to come to the Great Hall and inform the gathered lords of your own decision. Then you may see the civil war begin with your own eyes."

"Shokan-sum!" Nishima cried. "You do not know what it is you ask. Please do not place this burden upon me." Her hands trembled and she dropped the cha bowl to the mat. "Please, it is my life you ask for." She covered her face with her hands but no tears came.

Oh, father, she thought, *they are not satisfied with one Shonto life, they want another.*

"Sister," Shokan said very softly, "I would spare you this if I could. I would take it upon myself, but I cannot. By midday a barbarian army will be at our gate. We must have a new sovereign and we must have made our escape. If you will not take up this duty, the Empire will dissolve into chaos. Let me tell the gathered lords that you require time to consider. That you will answer in an hour. Let us hold off calamity as long as possible. Sit and ponder the alternatives, sister. Speak with your Spiritual Advisor. Let me say you will decide within the hour?"

Nishima sat for a long moment, then nodded her head, the tiniest of movements. "I will give you my decision at dawn. Please ask Brother Shuyun if he will attend me."

Kamu looked over at Shokan who nodded toward the door. Bowing, the two men rose and left, closing the door quietly behind them, and making

Nishima think that they suddenly felt they should not disturb the grieving daughter. As though they had not thrown her already uncertain life to the wind once again.

She sat unmoving, and then Lady Kitsura entered through a screen. She was dressed in the silk robes of a peer—one of Nishima's robes, in fact.

"There is a bath, Nishi-sum, and your servants have found some of your own robes." Kitsura paused.

Nishima did not look up. "I can accept the fall of the Empire," she said in a flat voice, "more easily than I can believe that my father is gone—he seemed the greater of the two."

Kitsura nodded. Kneeling, she took Nishima's hands. "A bath will help, cousin, truly."

Nishima nodded. Servants came and led her to her bath, leaving her to soak in peace as she preferred. Carefully laid out within view were robes and combs and perfumes, and the box that belonged to her mother decorated with the warisha blossom of the Fanisan House. Nishima closed her eyes. So many had died that day. Jaku was dead, she realized. His death poem was hidden in her hunting costume. *I must have it sent to his brother, poor man.* She hugged her arms across her breasts and felt the warmth work at knotted muscles. Remembering the teaching of Brother Satake, she began an exercise to relax her muscles and calm her spirit. Her focus was so poor that this was an indifferent success.

A tap on the screen preceded a maid's voice from outside. "Brother Shuyun awaits, my lady."

Nishima fought back a sudden attack of tears and, when she felt she had mastered them, she stepped out of the bath.

Dressing without too much haste was difficult, but she forced herself to move slowly lest her servants think she rushed to meet a man. "Tokiwa," Nishima said to the maid who waited beyond the screen. "I wish to pray with Brother Shuyun, I do not want to be disturbed for any reason."

"Yes, my lady."

"Have you laid a bed for me in the adjoining room? I will try to sleep later."

"It has been done, Lady Nishima."

"Thank you, Tokiwa. You may go. I will tie my sash."

She could easily imagine the servant nodding and performing her graceful bow before hurrying off.

Nishima left her hair down and combed it carefully. She tied her sash with particular care.

Slipping into the room, Nishima was disappointed to find Shuyun not present and then she heard his voice whisper her name from the balcony.

Shuyun was standing at the rail, looking out to the north. Nishima came and stood close beside him, resting her hand on his shoulder.

"Upon the fields," he said, pointing off to the distance.

A fire burned there and then Nishima realized that it must be many rih distant—the figures moving around it were so small. The blaze was enormous.

"What is this?" Nishima asked.

Shuyun shook his head. "Even the Kalam does not know."

"They burn the fallen, certainly."

Shuyun shook his head. "Perhaps, but it is not their way, Lady Nishima."

They stood a moment longer and then Nishima took his hand and gently led Shuyun away from the spectacle, back inside. Nishima opened a screen at the room's end where an enormous bed had been made. A single lamp cast a soft glow.

Nishima stopped him at the bed's edge and embraced the monk who returned the caress with more warmth than usual. Nishima guided his hand to the knot on her sash. "Pull," she whispered.

Doing as he was instructed Shuyun felt the knot give and unravel in his hand.

"A Lover's Knot," she said.

The monk almost stepped away, but she held him.

"I am a fallen Brother," he said, an edge of anguish in his voice. "A lost one."

She held him close, afraid he would leave. "Do not despair, Shuyun-sum, I have found you. Please stay with me. Tonight I have need of a friend more than ever." She reached back and took the sash from his hand and let the heavy brocade slip to the floor, uncoiling itself around her feet.

"They have asked me to ascend the throne," she said suddenly, her voice the smallest whisper.

He nodded. "I have been told."

She stepped away, pulling the quilts back on the bed and drawing the monk in after her.

They lay close in the dim light of the lamp. "I must tell them what I will do in a few hours."

They did not speak for some minutes. "I do not think I can bear my father's death, Shuyun-sum. I have not the strength . . . and they want me to be their Empress."

"I believe Lord Shonto will be reborn in only a few days. His spirit will return, though you may never meet it or know it if you do."

Nishima did not answer immediately. "Even so, he is lost to me. I am a selfish, spoiled peer, and it is *my* loss that grieves me though it shames me to say this.

"It is not surprising that I have led you from the path, Shuyun-sum. I am so far from perfection it is a marvel I was not born an ant."

Shuyun smiled. "Be careful what you say, ants have Empresses also. It is a fate that can pursue you from lifetime to lifetime."

The sounds of distant voices reached them, the chanting of the crowd beyond the gates.

"I do not know what answer I should give the lords of Wa. My father warned that an act of bravery might be required of me, yet I do not think I am brave enough. I know nothing of ruling, Shuyun-sum. It seems a sham to ascend a throne that in a few hours will belong to this barbarian Khan."

"I am not certain the barbarian will be long for this throne," Shuyun whispered. "Perhaps only days."

Nishima pulled back so that she could see the monk's face. "Why do you say this?"

"In the mist, when I disappeared and had you and Lady Kitsura wait—do you remember the coughing? The tribesman suffered from the plague, there is no doubt. It will spread among the army of the desert more easily than the wind blows through unshuttered houses. It will be a great tragedy. Tens of thousands will die, and if the Khan takes the city the plague will spread through the capital. Barbarian patrols have crossed the river and turn back all those who hoped to make their escape. The population of the city is four times what it would be normally."

"Botahara save us," Nishima said. "We will all die-barbarians and people of Wa alike. Is there no escape?"

Shuyun nodded. "For the few, there is hope of escape."

Nishima closed her eyes. "Do the others know of this, the plague?"

"I have told only General Hojo. It is possible that others may guess what the barbarians' fires mean—they must burn the plague-dead and all of their belongings, perhaps even their horses, hoping this will save them. It will not." Shuyun paused. "I regret that General Hojo will not listen to my counsel in this."

Nishima pulled back so that she could touch the monk's cheek, tracing the outline with great tenderness. "What have you counseled?"

"To save Wa, we must save the barbarians. It is the only possibility."

Nishima froze, unable to believe what she had heard. "Even I am aghast at this suggestion. They have murdered the length our Empire."

"And so have we, my lady. You do not know how many refugees have died on the roads and the canal." Shuyun took her hand and pressed it to his heart. She felt the warmth, the tingle of chi. "When the barbarians reach the capital tomorrow, I could walk out to meet them under a flag of peace. I would offer them an exchange. My Order will save them from the plague if they will lay down their arms. Thousands of lives might be saved."

Nishima propped herself up on one arm. The people of the capital—the plague would ravage the city, while she escaped. But save invaders? No one would agree to this. She looked out the half open screen, and saw the flicker of the barbarians' pyre, far out on the plain.

Did not Botahara teach compassion? she asked herself. "Is it possible, Shuyun-sum? Will this Khan believe you?" She rolled back, staring up at the ceiling, her hand to her brow. "If not, you would be in great danger." Her mind raced through the possibilities now. "Will the Botahist Brothers perform this task? The barbarians are not followers of the True Path."

"Few are, Nishima-sum." Shuyun pushed her hair back behind her ear. "The Brothers will agree reluctantly. It saddens me to say this, but I believe it is more likely that the barbarians will listen than it is that the lords of Wa will agree to this course."

"But it is our only hope," Nishima said, convinced now that Shuyun was right. "Tens of thousands could be saved—barbarians and people of Wa alike. The lords of Wa must be convinced."

"They will not be. Their hatred of the barbarians is unreachable. Tell them that plague is about to sweep the barbarian army from the Empire and they will not care how many people of Wa will have to die so that this will occur. Sacrifice is their way. To suggest we save the invaders—they will not allow it."

Nishima rolled so that she pressed her cheek close to Shuyun's. "You make my choice difficult," she whispered in his ear.

An act of bravery, he had told her. There had been so many already.

"Shuyun-sum, tell me truthfully—if an Empress commands that this be done, will the lords of Wa obey?"

Shuyun considered for a moment. "Lord Taiki, General Hojo, and your brother control the army. No others have an organized force. Will these three obey a command from the Empress they have placed on the throne? I believe they will, Lady Nishima, though I fear it is not the answer you wish to hear."

Nishima closed her eyes for some time, breathing as Brother Satake had taught her. Oh, father, it is my greatest fear. You ask me to overcome my greatest fear. She felt her heart beating and forced it to calm. *Thousands of lives she told herself, balanced against my own desires and fears.*

Opening her eyes she whispered to the room. "If Hojo and Shokan-sum will agree to your plan, I will ascend the throne though my entire life I have vowed I would not."

She felt Shuyun draw her close. Pressing her eyes closed she said a silent prayer, though it was not to any god. Nishima spoke to Lord Shonto, praying she had chosen correctly. May this be the act of bravery, she thought, and not an act of foolishness.

She whispered close to Shuyun's ear. "What name will I take if I am to ascend the Throne of Wa?"

Shuyun drew her closer and said, *"Shigei."*

"I do not know that name."

"It is from the mountain tongue, as is my name. Shuyun—he who bears. Shigei—she who renews. It is the name of a mountain spirit. It is also the name given to fair spring winds and to the scent of new budding leaves. She who renews. Empress Shigei."

Nishima nodded slowly. "I will need the wisdom of your counsel."

"You will have the wisest of counselors, my Empress," he whispered. "You will rule with your heart as well as your reason and your subjects will come to love you as they have few others."

The lamp flickered out and they lay still in the darkness until the gray light of dawn appeared through the half-open screens.

Sixty-one

THE SUNRISE FILTERED through a long tear in the cloud, somewhere far out over the unseen sea. Among the weeping birch trees on the edge of the Pool of the Sun the Shonto guard had built the pyre. The sound of the three small falls that crossed the pond mixed with the breeze moving through the new leaves and made Nishima think of her father's private garden.

Under the silk banner that he had borne into battle, Lord Shonto Motoru lay hidden from the eyes of those who cared for him. To one side Kamu stood holding the lord's favorite stallion, a sword strapped to the saddle—the same sword the Emperor had given the lord in this very garden.

The death of his ancestor, Shokan had said, *an honorable death.*

Brother Shuyun completed a long prayer, and all present made signs to Botahara. Nishima felt Shokan release her hand as he stepped forward, a surcoat of pure white over his Shonto blue catching the light of the sun.

Removing a tiny ornate scroll from his sleeve he paused to find his voice.

Through a long winter we have awaited
The rebirth of spring.
During the cold nights
We dreamed
Of the plum tree's blossom

Along the shore of an endless canal
Cranes stand among rushes

So still
The harmony of their world
Is left untouched

The boat passes,
White against blue waters,
Its wake causing birds to fly
Rising up among blossom laden trees

Passing on the breeze, the boat
Follows the ribbon of blue,
As narrow and perfect
As the river among the clouds

Shokan and Lord Komawara had begun this poem during a sleepless night and Nishima had completed it that morning—many others would follow.

Stillness and quiet descended as all present offered their silent prayers. Nishima looked around. The more important lords of Wa, those who had not fled the capital, were present, as were the lords who had followed her father south from Seh. The senior officials of the palace were present; chancellors, ministers, and sundry advisors had come to pay respects to the Emperor's most powerful lord—the man who had given his life in an attempt to save Wa. Lord Komawara stood beside a recovered Lord Butto, the two so grim that it hurt Nishima to look at them.

She made herself breathe in careful rhythm, for her part of the ceremony was yet to come. Conscious of her new role, Nishima was determined to conduct herself accordingly though certain this would be the most difficult thing she had ever done.

At a nod from Shuyun she stepped forward, and a bowing attendant passed her a small torch, its flame guttering in the breeze. She closed her eyes for a second, certain she would be overcome by the odors of the burning oil. *I release his spirit from this world,* she reminded herself. She bowed low, holding back the sleeve of her white robe, and touched the torch to the pyre. At first nothing seemed to occur, but then the lamp oil caught and the flames rose up, spreading both left and right with a sound like a giant wing beating the air.

She stepped back then and tossed the torch into the flame. As the silk banner caught, she closed her eyes.

"Lady Nishima," the attendant said softly.

She turned and took the handful of white plum petals she was offered and these she tossed onto the flaming pyre where the rising heat took them and scattered them on the wind.

The fire crackled and roared now, too hot to be near. The mourners stepped back then and she felt Shokan take her arm. Space opened up around them and Nishima felt the distance despite the presence of her brother. Isolation, she thought, a life of isolation. Only that morning her decision had been made known and already she was set apart.

I cannot turn back, she told herself. *Tens of thousands of lives depend on the strength of my resolve.*

But Shokan and Hojo and Lord Taiki had agreed to support Shuyun's plan though they argued against it strongly. In the end they had decided that having Nishima as an Empress was more important. Then had come her first test. She discovered that the lords of Wa and the senior Ministers of the Right and Left had already selected a name for the new Empress. A name from another tongue was not acceptable, they explained; there were traditions.

Nishima had been forced to be utterly firm with them—she would ascend the throne as the Empress Shigei. Their choice was to offer the throne to someone else. They had acquiesced: a name was an important thing, no doubt, but there were certainly other matters of greater consequence.

Once she had ascended the throne, Nishima thought, this tactic would no longer be possible. There would be many more such battles of wills, Nishima thought, many, many more. Fighting them when all she felt was a need to be alone, to have time and peace to heal the wound inside her—that would be the challenge. It would be so easy to give in, but she must not. She would be an Empress and that meant she would not let ambitious counselors gain control of the government.

They ascended a flight of steps and attendants waited there with a sedan chair. Nishima looked at this with dismay.

"I will walk," she said firmly.

"But, Empress," the Minister of the Right said in his most pleasant voice, "it is unseemly for a member of the Imperial family to walk."

"I am not yet an Empress nor a member of the Imperial family. I am Shonto. I will walk."

Tugging Shokan's arm she skirted the sedan chair and ascended the next stairs as quickly as decorum would allow. The sound of the funeral pyre could still be heard and as they reached the palace doors she turned to look back. White smoke rose in a high column from the shore of the glittering pond and she thought of her father lifting up to soar among the clouds.

Movement caught her eye beyond the fire. It was the barbarian army gathering beyond the city walls. Botahara save us all, she thought.

It was the shortest and least elaborate investiture in the history of the Empire of Wa. Ceremonial meals were reduced to a few dishes being arranged to symbolize an entire part of a ceremony. Elaborate rituals involving the Imperial Governors of the Empire's nine provinces were not performed, for there was not a single governor in the capital. Swearing of oaths by lords and officials and the giving of gifts and favors and ranks—all of these things were left to another time—all present hoping there would be such a time. Only the short, final ceremony was to be performed and this was a great relief to the Empress-to-be.

Nishima was borne to the doors of the Great Audience Hall in the sedan chair she had rejected earlier and here she was allowed to step down to a carpet that stretched the length of hall to the steps of the Dragon Throne.

To each side of this knelt the counselors and senior officials and behind these men, instead of the ceremonial guard, stood men in Shonto blue. In truth, many of the members of the Great Council and of the guard had fled the city and those remaining had been forced to make do as best they could. The Major Chancellor, the second most powerful person in the Empire, had escaped some days earlier. To the dismay of the court Nishima had appointed Kamu to this position temporarily. He knelt at the foot of the steps to the dais, his ceremonial robes spreading out around him like a fan, the gold scroll of his office held in his only hand.

As Nishima entered, the assembled officials bowed their heads to the stone and remained there for some moments. A slow chant of great beauty began as the new Empress slowly progressed the length of the hall, the Ministers of the Right and Left following three paces behind on their knees.

Walk beside me, father, Nishima prayed, *I have not the courage.* She felt as though her spirit had wrenched itself free and she both walked on the carpeted floor and floated up to the heights of the hall, watching herself as she progressed, a small uncertain child in the immense hall.

Do not let my spirit escape, she prayed, *not yet.*

Shokan knelt with his forehead pressed to the stone at the end of the first row of officials and this touched some part of her and called her spirit back, for with his face hidden, Shokan looked for all the world like his father. Her father's presence seemed to be there and this gave her strength.

Before the throne a silk cushion had been set and the Ministers of the Right and Left assisted her in kneeling here and then retreated to their places. Nishima's robes spread out around her, Imperial Crimson bearing the five-clawed, golden dragon. At her insistence a tiny shinta blossom had been embroidered on her right sleeve, the flower of the warisha on her left. Kamu knelt three paces off, his head touched to the floor. Nishima bowed to her ancestors on the empty throne.

The chant continued, rising in volume, reverberating in the great hall. The Minister of the Right came forward and laid the sword of office across the arms of the throne and retreated. An ancient bronze gong was brought forward by the Minister of the Left and this was set at the foot of the throne to one side.

There were no words to be spoken by the ascending sovereign—far too many Emperors had been children barely out of the cradle—but the Major Chancellor rose to a kneeling position and recited the sovereign's oath of office. Kamu's voice gained strength and authority with each phrase.

"It is the duty of the Empress to care for her children, the people of the Empire of Wa, to care for the lands and the forests and the waterways. In time of famine the Empress will give food to her charges; in time of war, provide shelter and restore peace to the people who are the children of the Empress. In gratitude the subjects of the Empress will attend each to their duties, giving their loyalty only to the sovereign of Wa. May Botahara bless the most revered Empress, Shigei, of the Imperial line of the Fanisan House."

The courtiers rose to their knees, making a sign to Botahara. As the chant came to an end, Nishima bowed once more to the throne. She was to rise and take her place now, but she could not will her legs to move.

This is wrong, Nishima thought. What is it I do? She could not get up.

Kamu opened his mouth to whisper. She saw "Nishima" begin to form on his lips, but he stopped himself. She looked over at him, imploring him to help, and he could only stare back, unable to speak or move.

There was utter silence in the hall then, all eyes turned toward her. The carved dragon that curved around the back of the throne seemed also to stare.

I must, Nishima said, *I must.*

Willing herself to rise, Nishima found her feet under her and, with great deliberation, placed a foot upon the first jade step and then the second and finally the third. Two steps to the throne. She lifted the sword of office with both hands and turned to face her court. Stiffly she lowered herself to the cushion on the jade throne. The Great Council of State knelt before her, each official reflected in the polished stone of the floor.

And now I must rule, Nishima thought, and the realization was like waking in a cold room. The warmth of the dream she had lived had vanished and her feelings seemed distant, confused.

As one, the entire assemblage bowed again and then rose to the kneeling position. Kamu took the place of the Major Chancellor on the first step and reached over and sounded the bronze gong. It was not loud in the massive hall, but in seconds it was answered by all the bells on the grounds of the Island Palace and this in turn was echoed by the bells of the city, the bell-keepers having been found or replaced.

It was a sound of great hope and joy and as she looked down the Empress saw tears on the cheeks of the old Shonto steward. No sound could be heard above the great din of the bells, but Nishima could see that he cried freely like an unashamed child and the new Empress felt a tear streak her own cheek in response.

The ringing of bells seemed to be endless, and Nishima sat attempting an appearance of tranquillity. At last the bells ceased and Nishima took a long breath and nodded to Kamu.

He raised himself up as though the increase in height would project his voice farther. "The Empress requests the presence of the following that we may discuss a solution to the problem of the barbarian army gathering beyond the capital's gate."

The assembled officials looked stunned, but they did not understand the meaning of this and so sat, casting glances to their allies in the hall.

Kamu read a long list including General Hojo, the Lords Butto, Taiki, Komawara, most of the senior lords of Wa who remained in the city, and Initiate Brother Shuyun.

All of those listed filed in through side doors, approaching the dais on their knees and bowing low to their Empress. Lord Komawara and Lord Butto had just come from the city walls and wore armor still, their helmets tucked under one arm.

Nishima nodded again and Kamu turned to the gathering.

"Due to the machinations of the late Yamaku Emperor, a barbarian army sits beyond our walls, their intention being to place their own chieftain upon the Throne of Wa. The Empress will hear the advice of her counselors regarding this matter." To the dismay of the gathered officials, Kamu turned to the Botahist monk. "It is the wish of the Empress that the Spiritual Advisor of Lord Shonto Shokan, Brother Shuyun, make his thoughts known." Kamu nodded to Shuyun.

Performing his double bow, first to the Empress and then to the gathered officials and guests, Shuyun sat back, his hands together as though he would meditate.

"Empress," he said, his soft voice surprisingly calm in the hall full of unspoken tension and emotion. "Honored ministers. I have learned that the plague has begun to spread among the army of the Khan. The great fire seen on the fields in the night was an attempt to cleanse the barbarian army of this disease, but plague is among them and cannot be cured with fire."

Everyone present leaned forward to listen now and Nishima heard the word "plague" whispered down the length of the hall. The reaction of the council was obvious—relief, elation, joy. Many made signs to Botahara.

Shuyun continued. "It is my recommendation, Empress, that we send emissaries to the Khan bearing an offer to bring Botahist Brothers to heal the barbarians, if, in return, the invading army will lay down its arms. Only this will prevent the plague from being spread among the people of the capital."

The reaction was not so controlled this time. Nishima heard voices of protest. She looked down at Hojo and the other Shonto allies. They sat in stolid silence. Now you must keep your word, she thought, or we are lost. Shuyun had been right—they would prefer to see any number dead if it would mean the destruction of their enemies.

Nishima gave a subtle hand signal to Kamu.

"The Empress wishes to express great concern for the people who have gathered in the capital hoping that the sovereign and the Great Council would protect them. Therefore, it is the wish of the Empress that this mission be carried out immediately. Brother Shuyun, you speak the language of the tribes?"

Shuyun nodded.

The very portly Minister of the Right bowed to the throne and Kamu fixed him with a withering glare as he nodded for the man to speak.

The Minister's voice came out very small. "Certainly a decision such as this should be considered by the senior officials, Major Chancellor." He looked directly at Shokan. "The course Brother Shuyun suggests—saving those who have caused so many such grievous loss—I fear that the very people we hope to save would not choose this course."

Shokan did not make eye contact with the Minister. He sat looking toward the foot of the throne, his face composed and unreadable.

Nishima started to answer herself but stopped at a look from Kamu. Instead she whispered to the Major Chancellor. "There is no time for this," she almost hissed.

Kamu turned back to the Minister. "The barbarians prepare their attack as we speak, Minister, there can be no time lost in lengthy discussion. This embassy will be carried out immediately. If you wish to join Brother Shuyun, your wisdom and council would be welcome."

The Minister looked around attempting to gather support, but no one met his eye. To walk out onto the field before an army of eighty thousand? The Minister shook his head and then bowed low. His next words came from a dry mouth. "Certainly, the wishes of the Empress will be carried out immediately. We should, however, be proceeding to remove the Empress to safety."

"I will not leave," Nishima's voice rang out in the hall. All stared openmouthed. The voice of a woman in the Great Hall had not been heard in many years, and what it lacked in volume it made up for in sheer uniqueness. "I will not leave until Brother Shuyun has spoken to the leader of the tribes," she said quietly, "nor shall any of my council. The safety of the population is your charge." There was no mistaking the strength of her decision. The Minister of the Right cast a final look at Shokan, bowed and sat back, his dismay obvious to all.

Nishima nodded to Kamu again. "Brother Shuyun, please, there is so little time," he said.

Nishima rose from her throne, placing the sword across the arms. Stepping around the throne, she left the hall by a small door, her heart beating wildly. Shuyun came after her, followed by Shokan and several other Shonto allies.

Nishima stepped aside as the hall widened, waving the others past. "You must make all haste, Brother," she said, resisting an urge to embrace him before the others. "I will follow. May Botahara walk beside you."

The monk bowed then and turned and ran, followed by the others, each bowing as he passed.

Shonto guards fell into step around her and they passed through a door into the main hallway of the palace. Everyone in the hall dropped to their knees as she passed, pressing their foreheads to the floor.

One bowing woman caught her eye as she passed.

"Kitsura-sum? Come with me please."

Her cousin rose quickly and fell into place three paces behind. Nishima reached back and pulled her forward by her sleeve.

"Please, cousin, hurry."

The army of the desert had formed outside the capital's northern walls and this had drawn the foolish and the curious within the city. They came to see a spectacle, but once they had mounted the walls or roofs the sight left them with little to say. The men of Shonto's army who had survived the terrible retreat now busied themselves with improving the city's defenses, though the capital was never designed to weather a concerted attack, and their attempts were largely futile.

Between the barbarian army and the walls of the city a dais had been erected under a yellow silk awning. Upon this dais a large wooden chair, almost a throne, was placed and, on either side, the gold banners bearing the Khan's crimson dragons hung from standards. Frames of bamboo had been built behind the dais and crimson silk was laced to these frames, creating an effective screen.

It was not clear to anyone in the city if this seat was meant to be the place where the Khan would accept the surrender of the city or if this was merely the position from which he intended to watch the city's fall. Perhaps it was meant to perform either function, but there were many inside the capital's walls who hoped a peaceful surrender was possible.

Shuyun mounted the steps to the top of the gate he had so recently used to enter the city. Lord Shonto Shokan, Lord Komawara, and General Hojo were only a few paces behind and they all stopped to look out at the army, clearly preparing its attack not far off.

Hojo nodded. "In Denji Gorge, Brother Shuyun, I opposed your plan to scale the walls and was proven wrong. It is my hope to be proven wrong again. If the Khan does not agree to this plan, Brother, I do not think we will move our army out of the city without terrible losses. Our Empress will have no force with which to regain her throne." Hojo looked down at the small monk, the warrior's discomfiture obvious.

Shuyun said nothing for a moment. "Pray to Botahara, General Hojo. I put myself into His hands."

The monk turned and descended the stairs. He was given the green flag of peace and a guard opened a small portal in the city's wall.

Lord Komawara caught up with Shuyun as he was about to pass through. "I would go with you, Brother Shuyun. Perhaps I may be of some assistance."

The monk hesitated for a second, meeting the young lord's eye. Shaking his head, Shuyun reached out and touched Komawara's arm. "It would be my honor, Lord Komawara, but this plan is my own and has little support. It is my desire to risk as few as possible. I thank you."

Komawara bowed, the short double bow he had learned when the two had gone into the desert. Bowing in return, Shuyun stepped through the arch and heard the door close behind him.

Stairs led down to the canal where a sampan tugged at a line. Shuyun stepped aboard and sculled quickly to the other bank where a ruin of stone was all that remained of the bridge that had been torn down at first light.

Tying the sampan to a rock, Shuyun ascended the bank, unfurling his flag of peace as he went. A few paces took him beyond the plum trees that grew along the canal—in leaf now, the glory of spring blossom having been stripped from them by the winds.

The massive army of the desert did not seem distant now, and Shuyun found himself unconsciously performing a breathing exercise to calm his spirit.

So much depends upon me, the monk thought, performing an instinctive sign to Botahara. The green flag fluttered in the light breeze, as Shuyun held it high, moving it slowly back and forth so that it would be seen.

He made his way across a green field, walking deliberately but without haste toward the waving banners of the pavilion. Horsemen broke free of the great mass of humanity before Shuyun and galloped out toward him. They stopped at some distance and examined the monk, and then one turned and spurred his horse back toward the barbarian position. The remaining three riders kept their distance, matching Shuyun's pace and not taking their eyes from him.

Fifty paces from the dais Shuyun stopped and waited. As this Khan aspired to the Throne of Wa, Shuyun was unsure what protocol might be expected and so decided it was best to wait and see how the barbarian responded to his presence. He chanted quietly to himself, a prayer for tranquillity of purpose.

Perhaps an hour passed and then there was a sudden stirring on the perimeter of the barbarian position. Warriors in crimson-laced armor rode out toward the dais, forming two lines facing in. Every second rider carried the Khan's golden banner on a lance.

Time passed and then a group of horsemen appeared at the far end of the path formed by the mounted guards. In a rustling of many silk banners the riders came forward, their pace unhurried. Shuyun held his position. Meditation had focused his will and he felt no reaction to the Khan's approach. He waited.

The riders halted behind the dais and it was a moment before they emerged. Six armored men appeared from behind the awning and knelt upon the dais to either side of the throne. Guards appeared then, kneeling on the ground in straight rows. One of these took two steps toward Shuyun and waved him forward.

As he walked toward the dais, a man in a robe of Imperial Crimson and black and gold stepped around the dais and mounted the throne. All present bowed but for two guards who watched Shuyun intently as he approached their leader.

Moving closer, Shuyun could see that the men who knelt on the dais were barbarian chieftains, armored in the style of warriors of the Empire but with surcoats of tiger skins and ornate helmets.

The man who sat upon the throne was bearded and wore his hair pulled back in the style of the desert. His face was dark and lined like all men who lived in the harsh world north of the border of Seh, but as Shuyun came closer he realized this was a young man, older than Komawara, perhaps, but certainly he had not seen thirty years.

The face was handsome in its way, and not unpleasant to look at, with a strong jaw and a full mouth. A few paces more and Shuyun realized that what he thought was an ornament was in fact a patch of white hair at the temple—the sign of the Tokiko blood, the same mark that Prince Wakaro had inherited from his mother.

Sitting with a sword across his knees the Golden Khan regarded the small monk who approached, contempt obvious on the chieftain's face.

Shuyun walked until a guard signaled him to stop ten paces from the dais. As there was no mat set out, Shuyun decided that he would stand and bowed from that position, placing the butt of the flag standard on the ground at his side.

The Khan sat for some moments staring at the monk and then nodded to one of the chieftains who knelt on the dais.

The man cleared his throat and then addressed Shuyun in the language of the Empire, though heavily accented. "The Khan wishes to know why so few have come forward on such an important occasion. This displeases him."

Shuyun addressed his answer to the Khan, speaking the tongue of the tribes almost without flaw. "I have been charged to speak for the Empress of Wa. It was not thought that more than one was required—our message is simple."

The Khan looked at Shuyun for a moment and then spoke himself, his voice deep and strong and at ease in the language of the tribes. "The ringing of bells—Akantsu no longer possesses the throne?"

Shuyun shook his head.

The Khan cast a glance at one of his chieftains. "Who sits the throne now, monk—Shonto's daughter?"

Shuyun nodded again. "The Empress Shigei," he answered quietly.

Shaking his head, the Khan spat out, "The council of Wa are fools if they believe I will be satisfied to be the consort of a Shonto Empress."

The monk said nothing.

The Khan waved his scabbard at Shuyun. "Komawara—does he still live?"

"He does."

"This man is a formidable swordsman . . . for a man of Seh. He felled a warrior—a chieftain of great deeds, and drove into my own guard before disappearing into the fog. My warriors call him the Cloud Rider." The Khan fixed Shuyun with a long stare from which the monk did not flinch. "I will have Lord Komawara's head brought to me when the Empress formally surrenders the capital. Have her come to me in person to offer me her throne. I am told she is a great beauty, this Shonto daughter. Is this true?"

Shuyun said nothing but stood returning the Khan's stare.

"I have not come to arrange the surrender of the Empire," he said softly. "I have come to save you from the plague, which is silently killing the men of your army as we speak."

The Khan glanced at the men around him and then addressed Shuyun, changing to the language of Wa.

"We cleansed our army with fire, monk, unless you have been sent to carry the disease to us again as the nun was sent among us bringing disease to every man who touched her and a thousand more besides."

Tesseko, Shuyun thought, *Botahara protect you.*

Shuyun nodded to one of the men sitting to the Khan's left. "That man," he said, still speaking in the language of the tribes, "he has contracted the plague. Look at the flush on his face. He struggles to control his cough, but he will not succeed for much longer." The other chieftains cast uncertain glances at the man Shuyun singled out. "You cannot cleanse the plague by fire, it is among you and can only be stopped by the ministrations of my own Order. You may take the throne, but it will not be yours for more than a few days." Shuyun let his words have their effect, seeing the arrogance of the men around the Khan quickly dissolve. There was no honor or profit in death by disease.

"The Empress has sent me to offer you your lives, for you will certainly lose them if you do not listen. In return she asks only that you lay down your arms. Your safe conduct to the northern border is guaranteed."

The Khan pointed the tip of his sheathed sword at Shuyun. "I sent an emissary to the walls of Rhojo-ma before it fell. He carried a flag of peace as you do now—and this man was murdered with an arrow because the lords of Seh did not like to hear the truth of their own blunders. Does the Empress expect to save her throne with a simple lie? She must believe I am some barbarian huntsman who has never seen the inside of a city's walls. When I have taken all of Wa and sit upon the Dragon Throne she will know differently—will become one of my concubines willingly. I had hoped to begin my reign by sparing the Imperial Capital." The Khan shrugged. He looked over at the chieftain who had first spoken and nodded.

The chieftain hesitated for the briefest second, then rose, drawing his sword. The guards who knelt nearby did the same. Shuyun reached up and tore the banner from his staff, lifting it to a guard position, pushing himself into a meditative state.

The guards spread out to either side and then one leapt forward, aiming a blow at Shuyun's hands, but the monk's staff moved in a blur and the man lay still on the green field.

The men hesitated then and Shuyun pounced upon their doubt. "Your Khan will sacrifice you to the plague so that he may sit upon the throne for the last few days of his life. The Brotherhood can save you. . . ."

Another man lunged at Shuyun, but his attack was thwarted brutally as another guard cut him down, then turned on the man beside him. The barbarian chieftains leapt off the dais and joined the struggle. Shuyun saved the man who sided with him from a sword blow that would have meant his end. Suddenly the chieftains and the guards rushed him at once.

The flag staff hummed as it cut the air. Shuyun disarmed a man and rendered another unconscious. A barbarian stepped inside his guard and Shuyun was forced to drop the staff. He clutched the man's sword as Komawara had seen in the desert and deflected the blow, driving another man back with what appeared to be a blow that never landed. Another barbarian warrior was dealt with in this manner, and suddenly the attack came to a halt. The barbarian warriors stood staring at the monk as though he were a ghost.

A cough escaped one of the chieftains and then, as all stood frozen, this man stepped forward and drove the point of his sword into the Khan where he stood before the wooden throne. The man who had gathered the tribes sagged slowly to his knees, staring forward at Shuyun, his eyes losing focus. A guard stepped forward and plunged his own point into the Khan's chest so that he fell back and to the side, his body limp.

No one moved to avenge this action, and the chieftain who had struck the first blow was suddenly racked with a fit of coughing. The others took a step away. Several fled then and horses were heard at a gallop.

When the man had recovered, he turned to Shuyun. "That is the end of the man who brought us here to die in a strange land for his greater glory. The others may do as they choose, but my own people will lay down their arms, Brother. How will I know that the army of Lord Shonto will not fall upon us once we are defenseless?"

Shuyun did not answer for a second, and then he reached into his robe and pulled out the jade pendant on its chain. "I will swear by the Botara denu. The Empress will give you safe passage to the border of Seh." Shuyun gestured to the ground. "Bring your weapons here. Separate the sick from the well and the monks of my Order will come. Do not cleanse again with fire, it will save no one. Tomorrow Brothers will begin to arrive. Others must come from there." Shuyun gestured toward the Mountain of the Pure Spirit. "It will take some few days."

The chieftains looked on, saying nothing. An occasional glance was cast toward the Khan, but it was obvious the men were stunned into inaction by what had happened. Shuyun took a step forward, then hesitated. "I would see to your Khan," he said quietly. No one moved, so the monk knelt beside the fallen leader. Immediately, he made a sign to Botahara. "His spirit has fled," Shuyun said. Pulling the robe off the man's shoulder, he exposed the skin and pointed there to three small lesions. "Your chieftain had the plague and did not yet know it," Shuyun said and then rose slowly.

"I will return at sunrise. The Imperial Army will not be allowed onto these fields, but do not be alarmed if you see small patrols of armed riders. We must be certain that the plague is not spread." Shuyun bowed then and turned back toward the city. As he went, he chanted a long prayer of thanksgiving.

A great cry went up suddenly behind him and the monk spun around. The sounds of clashing steel echoed across the open ground and Shuyun almost covered his eyes. The barbarian fought among themselves. He could see the great army of the desert, a seething mass of horses and men writhing like a great dying beast.

Footsteps sounded behind him, but Shuyun did not turn. Komawara and Hojo arrived at his side and still others stopped nearby.

"What has happened, Brother," Hojo asked, great wonder in his voice.

"Step away, General, Lord Komawara, I have been in contact with the plague." The others did as Shuyun asked. "The Khan is dead, killed by one of his own chieftains. They war among themselves now—those who would lay down their arms and be cured and those who would avenge the death of their leader."

"At least they expend their energies upon each other," Hojo said.

"It is the saddest of days, General. The Kalam has always maintained that most of the tribesmen followed the Khan against their will." He pointed out toward the raging battle. "The innocent are dying in numbers as great as those who came to murder and burn."

Komawara waved toward the city. "We must retreat to the walls, Shuyun-sum. There is nothing we can do and it is possible they may turn against us yet."

Reluctantly Shuyun turned and followed the young lord back toward the city.

Shonto guards held boats at the canal and Shuyun waited while the others were whisked across the canal to the open door, the sound of battle echoing off the walls. He would need to bathe himself in the appropriate herbs and destroy his clothing.

The monk stood among the trees, unable to block the sounds of the fighting from his ears. He knelt upon the grass but an attempt to chant came to nothing so he was left, battered by the sounds of the terrible battle.

I have accomplished that which any warrior of Wa would have willingly sacrificed his life to achieve—I have caused the enemy to destroy themselves. Botahara forgive me, I meant only to heal them and save the people of the capital.

Shonto guards spread out around Shuyun suddenly, keeping their distance, staring out at the raging struggle. A light step stopped three paces away.

"Shuyun-sum?" the Empress said softly. "Even a selfless act of charity may bring about utter calamity. Knowing this cannot stop us from being charitable. These tribesmen have their own karma which even the Teacher may not control."

Someone came forward then and set the monk's trunk a few paces away. Shuyun looked up to see the Kalam, his face drawn as though in pain.

"Shimeko-sum," Shuyun whispered. "It was she who carried the plague to the tribes."

The Empress slowly sank to her knees, covering her mouth as she did do. "She could not have done such a thing . . . not knowingly."

Shuyun shook his head sadly. "She could hardly have acted so out of ignorance. The Botahist trained. . . ." He left the sentence unfinished.

"I cannot think what karma this will bring," Nishima said. "Life after life after life. . . ."

Shuyun nodded.

"Excuse my interruption, Empress." General Hojo stood some distance off. "This is not a secure place. The battle is spreading over the fields. We must allow Shuyun to perform his purification so that we may all find safety inside the walls."

The Empress nodded. "Shuyun-sum. Only you tried to save the tribes. Do not forget the purity of your intent. All others would have let them die, taking the population of the capital with them. Your purpose was pure."

"Thank you for your council, Empress," Shuyun said.

The woman in crimson robes stopped as she rose. "No one can hear our words, Shuyun-sum. Please, do not banish Nishi-sum from the world entirely. I—I must exist somewhere," she said, her voice growing small, "in your company, if I may." She retreated then and guards surrounded her quickly.

Shuyun went to his trunk and opened the lid.

By the time Shuyun entered the capital, the barbarian tribes had divided themselves into distinct camps and, for the most part, the fighting had ceased although it flared up again for brief moments between one group and another.

Shonto guards escorted the monk into the nearby guardhouse where he found the Empress accompanied by Lady Kitsura. Lord Komawara, Lord Shonto Shokan, Hojo, the Kalam, and Rohku Saicha had appeared, taking charge of the Empress' personal guard.

All bowed low to Shuyun as he entered and he found this disturbing, considering the results of his recent action.

"We have a boat awaiting in the nearest canal, Empress. It is a short walk. I apologize, we have no sedan chair," Hojo said.

"Apologize only when you have a sedan chair, Masakado-sum," Nishima said. "I will have the council pass an edict ordering all sedan chairs in the capital be put to the torch." She nodded toward the door.

Guards formed a tight circle around the Empress, Kitsura, and Shuyun, and the monk found himself hemmed in and close to his sovereign.

Out in the avenue two long lines of warriors held back the jostling crowds. Shuyun saw the black of Imperial Guards, Shonto blue, Butto purple—the remains of Lord Shonto's army assuring the safety of the woman they had placed on the throne.

Once the Empress was seen, the people bowed low and a whisper passed down the street like a cool breeze. Both the name of the Empress and his own became almost a chant. Suddenly flower petals of all colors were strewn before the party as they made their way to the quay.

Lord Butto stood at the head of the stairs where several boats were moored, and he knelt and bowed low as the Empress approached. Quickly the small group embarked, Kitsura and Shuyun into the same craft as the Empress, the others into boats both before and behind.

Shuyun felt Nishima breathe a sigh of relief as the boats gained the center of the canal. The banks were thick with the thousands who had hoped to flee the war, and had come to its very center. They began to cheer suddenly, their respect for their new sovereign momentarily overcome by their relief at being delivered from the barbarian army.

Shuyun heard his name chanted now as he had heard the crowds chant Komawara's name for the many lives he had taken in battle. He felt a warm hand take his own and looked over to see his young Empress turned toward him—a look of understanding, of compassion.

The lords of Wa were wise, he found himself thinking. Here sits the woman deserving to rule the Empire. And yet her subjects will never understand that she has given up her own peace so that theirs would be assured.

Sixty-two

IN A SMALL audience hall near the Imperial Apartments the Empress had gathered her closest advisors, which meant the only functionary of the Empire's government present was the Major Chancellor, Kamu.

It was late and the sounds of movement on the fields outside the city had finally ceased. For the second time an enormous fire burned outside the city as the barbarians burned all those who had fallen that day. At last light it appeared the barbarian army had split utterly and though this had caused a flood of relief throughout the capital, anxiety had not disappeared. Everyone waited to be sure the barbarians would not reform their vast army under a new leader. First light would see crowds gathered on the northern walls, there was no doubt of that.

General Hojo bowed low. "The barbarian army has split into three parts," he began, addressing his remarks to the Major Chancellor.

Nishima almost grimaced and waved a gold silk fan at the Shonto officer. "Masakado-sum, please, I cannot bear this custom. We are not in a council of state . . . do not speak to Kamu-sum as though I were not present." She tried a small smile.

"Excuse me, Empress," the soldier said bowing. He returned to the kneeling position and took a second to gather his thoughts. "Since the fall of the Khan this morning, the barbarian army has split. One company, the easternmost tribes according to Kalam, have begun to move north, some on the canal but many by foot and on horse. This is perhaps a fourth part of those who survived the battle between the tribes. A much smaller group has broken off and makes its way northeast—we are not certain of their intent, Empress, but Brother Shuyun has suggested they may make their way toward the temples on the Mountain of the Pure Spirit. They know the Botahist Brothers possess a cure for their disease. The third group—the majority by far—remain in the fields north of the city, awaiting the healers we have promised."

Nishima nodded at this. "What is your advice, General Hojo. Large armed parties wandering through our lands is a matter for concern."

Hojo considered a moment. "Combining all the men who remain from the Imperial Army and our own, Empress, gives us a force of perhaps thirty thousand men. Certainly enough to meet the threat of any of the three barbarian armies, though hardly enough men to deal with them all at once. The barbarians outside the city have disarmed, but we cannot leave them unwatched. If they do not receive assistance soon . . ." Hojo shrugged. "Thirty thousand barbarian warriors, well armed or not is a significant force. They will also need to be fed." Hojo stroked his graying beard. "The companies making their way toward the Botahist temples are of concern. We have sent messages to the Brothers so that they will be prepared, but still it would be best if these barbarians could be reasoned with, though I would prefer to send out a force of some size to emphasize the prudence of finding a solution that does not require swords.

"The army moving north is of greater concern to me, Empress. It is both larger and its intent less clear. Do they plan to take Seh and hold it as their own? Is it their wish to simply return to the desert? The Kalam believes they hope to escape the plague and do not trust the people of the Empire sufficiently to lay down their weapons. Brother Shuyun is certain the plague will begin to show its hand among these men very soon. We have sent patrols out to warn any citizens who are on the barbarian's path, but who knows what dying men might do? If the Botahist Brothers agree to minister to the barbarians, then perhaps we will be able to take some number of Brothers north in the wake of the retreating barbarians in hopes that the men of the desert will see the futility of what they do and allow the Brothers to help them." Hojo bowed and fell silent.

Nishima nodded. "I thank you, General." She looked around at the others, raising an eyebrow as they had often seen her father do.

Komawara touched his head to the mats. "Empress. I agree entirely with General Hojo. May I suggest that with the force that travels north we might send the Kalam? He is of an eastern tribe himself and may gain their trust more easily than the leader of a well armed force."

Nishima looked over to Shuyun who sat between Komawara and the tribesman. "Brother?"

Shuyun bowed low before speaking. "I will ask the Kalam, Empress, if I may?"

She nodded and the monk spoke quietly to the tribesman who responded in a whisper. Shuyun turned back to Nishima. "The Kalam asks me to say that he will do anything within his power to serve the Empress."

Nishima gave a half bow to the tribesman who touched his forehead to the floor in return, his embarrassment obvious.

"General Hojo, we remain in a state of war, so I do not feel the need to consult the Great Council in this matter. Who would you suggest to carry out each of these tasks? We must send no one who is bent on revenge upon the tribes—we have had a thousand years of raids and war because of a barbarian vendetta, let us do nothing to fuel their anger."

Hojo looked over at Kamu as though the two consulted silently. "I would send Lord Butto to pursue the barbarian army north on the canal. The lord has his own interests to consider there and I must say, Lady Ni . . . Empress, that he is a young man of great political skills. Kamu-sum has made the same assessment.

"Certainly Lord Taiki would be the correct choice to defend the temples, his devotion has been great since Brother Shuyun saved the life of his son. If I remain in the capital, I will see to the barbarians beyond the walls, with Brother Shuyun's counsel, if he will be so kind."

Nishima looked at Shuyun who nodded. Lord Butto and Lord Taiki were out in the fields patrolling beyond the barbarian encampment. "General Hojo, I will leave this in your hands. I wish to be kept constantly informed. We must restore peace and security to the Empire before we can begin to address the other ills the Yamaku have left us."

Nishima turned to Kamu who consulted a small scroll. "The matter of the Brothers, Empress," he said. The young sovereign turned to Shuyun.

"I have spoken to the Primate of the Imperial Capital, Empress." Shuyun said. "Brother Hutto and the Supreme Master of the Botahist Order sailed from Yankura recently. They should arrive in the capital very soon, perhaps tomorrow."

"The Supreme Master?" Nishima opened her fan. "Does he not sequester himself on an island in the sea?"

"He does, Empress," Shuyun answered. "Events in the Empire may have convinced him his presence would be required."

"How are we best to proceed to gain their support?" Nishima asked.

"I would speak with the Supreme Master and Brother Hutto myself, Empress, if that is acceptable."

Nishima nodded. "I will concern myself with this matter no more, Brother Shuyun, if I know that it is in your capable hands." She turned back to the Shonto steward. "Kamu-sum?"

"There is a shortage of grain in the capital, Empress, and many other things as well. Crowds have begun to gather at the gates of the palace asking for food. As of yet they have been orderly, but if they grow desperate this will change."

"They must be fed," Nishima said. "Certainly we did not destroy all the grain in the Empire as we came down the canal?"

Kamu nodded in response to this, glancing over at Hojo, whose face remained grave but whose eyes smiled. "There is perhaps someone more suited to dealing with this matter than any present, if you will excuse me for saying so," he hastened to add, addressing his remark to all present. Turning back to Nishima; "We have had word from Tanaka, Empress. He comes from Yankura even now."

Nishima greeted this news with a great smile, something her retainers had not seen in recent days. "The barbarians did not find him after all!" she said happily. "Colonel Tadamoto was mistaken."

"No, they did not," Hojo said. "Our good merchant is unscathed, or so he says. There is certainly food in the Empire despite the attempts of many to hide it away. Tanaka will know the best method to bring it forth, and he will not empty the Imperial Treasury to accomplish it, either."

Nishima looked over at Shokan who shook his head in mock dismay. "My steward, my senior general, my guard captain, and now my merchant. Will you leave my personal servants at least, and perhaps my gardener? But what do I say? Anything for my Empress."

"Lord Shonto," Nishima said gravely. "I wish only to borrow Tanaka-sum—for indeed I shall raise his rank so that he is addressed as he deserves, as my father always addressed him. In a brief time I'm sure he will have rooted out all of the corruption in my government. For this service I will pay you well, brother—and I shall pay Tanaka-sum well also. As to your gardener . . ." Nishima said, as though this thought had not occurred to her. She moved her head back and forth, weighing the idea. "Perhaps not at this time, thank you."

Shokan nodded.

Nishima turned to Kamu who became serious immediately. "My list is without end, Empress, but may I suggest that we have all done much this day. Brother Shuyun must prepare for his meeting with the senior members of his Order, for their cooperation is crucial to the peace we have arranged. We have, after all, pledged the Brotherhood's assistance without consulting them. This may please them less than we hope, Empress."

Nishima tapped the edge of the low dais with her fan. "You are no doubt correct, Major Chancellor. There are so many matters to consider and so many who have risked so much in these last days, yet I can hardly begin to think of this until we are assured of peace and the plague is contained." She nodded to all present. "I thank you. Brother Shuyun, I wish to discuss your coming audience with your superiors, if it is convenient."

Nishima rose and everyone bowed their heads to the mat as she left.

Nishima did not feel a desire to live in the apartments that had been the quarters of the Yamaku nor was she comfortable with the thought of moving into the abandoned rooms of the Hanama Emperors—ghosts or no—they had fallen to bad luck in the end and Nishima did not want be reminded of that. Fortunately the palace had any number of rooms to choose from and she was soon settled, if only temporarily, in apartments meant for visiting relatives of the Emperors. These apartments had been left in the Hanama style, uncluttered, almost austere in their simplicity and Nishima had the rugs she had brought from Seh spread over the straw-matted floors. With her own servants and retainers about, her situation did not feel as strange as she expected. Occasionally she even forgot that her father was no longer part of this present in which Nishima found herself, though these moments were brief.

A warm evening had arrived, creeping silently up the river from the sea, and with it came cloud. The sound of falling rain seemed comforting to the new Empress as though it formed a protective barrier from the world beyond. Outside her rooms a terrace with small trees situated carefully about it looked out to the west. The soft cadence of the spring rain on the terrace stones and the leaves of trees—a sound in harmony with the mood of the young aristocrat.

Nishima wore her own familiar robes, avoiding Imperial finery, though her clothing was of white—not of her choosing. She sat near a partially open screen that led onto the terrace and rubbed a resin stick over the blackened surface of her inkstone. A bead curtain of water drops had formed from the rain as it ran off the tile roof, and this caught the light from her lamp and glittered like strings of bronze colored jewels.

So many things had occurred in the past two days that Nishima did not feel as though she were part of it somehow—her life was changing more rapidly than she was able to change herself, there was little question of that. Only the day before she had been lost in the fog with Kitsura and Shuyun and the Empire had been poised on an edge, about to slide into the abyss of the complete unknown. That morning Lady Nishima Fanisan Shonto had lit a torch to the pyre of Lord Shonto Motoru. She closed her eyes tightly. And now, miraculously, the Empire had been delivered. A half-barbarian chieftain who had been destined for the throne had fallen to the sword of one of his own followers . . . and Nishima had ascended the throne left empty by the passing of the Yamaku. Ascended against her most profound desires.

"I am the Empress," she whispered, as though saying these words aloud would force her mind to accept this information, help her understand the truth, for she did not feel like an Empress, she was sure of that.

Certainly she had heard the crowds repeating her name as though it were a litany. Nishima could not remember an experience that had left her feeling so cold, so isolated.

Closing her eyes she tried to conjure up another time, and an image of walking along the cliffs above the sea on the Shonto fief came to her. She could see the bleached copper grasses, their color so carefully complimenting the blues of the summer sea and the whites of the lazy, drifting clouds that spread across the far horizon. The breeze was soft and warm, welcoming her to the shore.

Eyes still closed, Nishima rubbed her inkstone, reaching out to that time, trying to hold it—but she could not. The chanting of the crowd came back, mixed with the sound of the funeral pyre as it began to blaze.

Opening her eyes Nishima picked up her brush, dipped it in ink and with great care selected a piece of mulberry paper.

The wind blows
And the grasses bow to my passing,

Perfect golden grasses
What do they know of my thoughts?
Or of the heart
They have torn asunder.

For some time Nishima sat looking at the lines she had written, wondering, for they seemed to have come unbidden, as poetry often did. The rain washed the world outside her rooms.

A knock sounded then and Nishima swirled her brush in water and set it on its rest. "Please enter," she called out.

A woman bowed low in the opening and then rose. The round, girlish face of Lady Kento appeared, looking more serious than Nishima had ever seen it.

"Kento-sum!" Nishima broke into a smile. "It lifts my spirits to see you. Miracle after miracle has occurred this day. How is it you are here?"

Kento bowed. "It is a brief story, Empress, and less interesting than one might think especially to one who has experienced what the Empress has these past months." Kento cast a glance over her shoulder. "I would certainly tell my tale though at the moment Lord Shonto awaits your favor."

"Cha and a tale you must certainly tell me. Please, invite Shokan-sum to join me."

Nishima set a small jade paperweight on the edge of her poem and moved her cushion a pace away from the table. The screen slid aside and Shokan knelt in the opening, head bowed low. Even my stepbrother must offer obeisance, Nishima thought, for an Empress has no equals—how very sad.

"Shokan-sum, please, enter." Nishima gestured to a second cushion as her brother rose.

The lord had the powerful build of his father and a similar talent for making his presence felt in a room, even when he was not the center of the situation. Dressed in rich robes of white with the blue edges of under-robes showing at his sleeves and neck and hem, Shokan struck Nishima as a handsome figure. The sadness she could see in his face and the white robes of mourning only added to his nobility.

Taking his place, Shokan regarded his sister with a look of concern. "It has been a day that will occupy the historians for a hundred years. May I say that the Empress has begun her reign auspiciously, showing both skill and wisdom."

"You may say that but only if you will stop calling me Empress with each breath. We are in the privacy of my rooms. *Nishima,* please, Shokan-sum, *Nishi* would be preferred though I hold little hope that you will breach this foolish etiquette to such a degree, no matter how much I desire it."

Shokan gave a half bow. "Excuse me for saying so, Empress, but these formalities have been the tradition in the Imperial Palace for our entire history. It is difficult for me to ignore that."

Nishima stared at him in exasperation. "In the Great Council," she said with deadly seriousness, "I shall insist upon referring to you as *Shoki-sum.*"

The young lord broke into a smile and bowed low— the name Nishima had called him as a child. "The Empress has proffered a most convincing argument . . . excuse me—Nishima-sum."

"Nishi-sum."

"Nishi-sum," Shokan said, his voice suddenly thick.

Reaching out, Nishima took her brother's hand. They were silent for a moment.

"He saved my life, Shokan-sum—my life and my mother's also," Nishima said, addressing what was unspoken in both their minds. "It is wrong to say this, but he was more dear to me than my true father who was distant and formal. Your father—our father, did not just save the Fanisan House from destruction, he brought me into your family. I treasure the time I spent in his company, treasure it. . . ."

"You were his delight, Nishi-sum," Shokan said, his voice subdued though under control now. "It was you who were closest to his heart, who brought him joy."

Nishima looked down, she brushed her fingers over the shinta blossom embroidered in white on Shokan's sleeve.

The two sat, not speaking, listening to the rain, each lost in their own memories, comforted by the other's presence.

A bell sounded the hour of the owl and both stirred. Nishima looked up at her brother. "You are the senior lord of the Shonto now, Shokan-sum. You are a lord of great influence and wealth. I shall have to consider who it would be best for you to wed. We have alliances to think of, entire provinces of young women to consider."

Shokan smiled again. "Entire provinces . . . it gives me hope, Nishi-sum. Perhaps, with your guidance, I shall not live my life a lonely man."

Nishima laughed and squeezed his hand. "Your adventures are not as secret as you may think, brother. Never forget that every young woman in the capital pours out her heart to Kitsu-sum. And I have recently been told that you have come from the mountains in the company of young woman of the mountain race." She looked up slyly at her brother. "This cannot be true?"

Shokan shook his head. "Quinta-la."

"Quinta-la?"

"She has been sent by her elders. . . . I confess I do not know why, but she has come to the lowlands for some reason . . . perhaps she is an emissary from her people. Certainly she has come to learn all she can, there is little doubt of that."

"You have not asked her?" Nishima said, surprised.

Shokan smiled. "I have, but convincing a dweller to speak of something they are not inclined to discuss is more difficult than one might think. There is also a language problem—we understand each other imperfectly."

Nishima nodded. "Shuyun-sum speaks their tongue. Perhaps we can arrange to have them meet. I would be most curious to meet . . . Quinta-la?— to meet her myself."

"Anticipating the Empress' desire, I asked Quinta-la to wait nearby— Nishima-sum," he added.

"You have left her waiting this entire time?"

"The dwellers are very patient, sister."

"Still . . . we cannot leave her waiting like this. She is your guest, brother."

"Guest is perhaps not the word she would use herself, Nishima-sum, but certainly, I will call for her."

A maid was summoned and sent to ask Quinta-la to join them. Almost immediately the maid returned, accompanied by a young woman who bowed her head to the floor, obviously nervous, perhaps even frightened.

"You may rise and come forward, Quinta-la," Shokan said, speaking slowly and with exaggerated clarity. Nishima thought Shokan's voice warmed perceptibly when he spoke to this young woman.

Quinta-la was dressed in the robes of her people, too warm, Nishima thought, for the weather. She was very small but well formed and appeared healthy and strong. Delicate of feature could hardly be said of this woman from the mountains, but despite the roundness of her face she was fair and her mouth was beautifully formed. Nishima immediately wanted to see her smile.

"Empress," Shokan said, "it is my honor to introduce Khosi Quinta-la."

Nishima nodded.

"Quinta-la, the Empress of Wa."

The young woman bowed stiffly.

"We are honored that you would come so far, Quinta-la-sum. There is so little commerce between our peoples," Nishima said.

"La is an honorific, sister," Shokan said quietly making Nishima smile at her mistake.

Shokan gave the dweller a tiny nod.

"The honor is mine, Empress, entirely," Quinta-la said in the studied manner of a child reciting lines. "You live in a lovely village."

"You are kind," Nishima said with all seriousness. She had never heard the capital or the Island Palace referred to as a village.

Shokan shrugged. "My language lessons have not all been successful."

Cha was brought by servants and Nishima felt a pang when she realized it would not be correct for her to serve this herself—they were entertaining a guest from what amounted to a sovereign nation.

Though the mountains in which Quinta-la dwelt were contained within the Empire, only the mountain people lived there and the people of Wa did not think of the lands beyond the foothills as being their own. Only a few passes were used by the lowlanders and there was a lake here or a spring there that, due to its ease of access, was thought of as part of the Empire proper.

A servant ladled the cha into bowls, retreating a few steps when she was done and sitting absolutely still.

"I am told there are many springs in the mountains and some are very hot and healthful," Nishima said, sipping her cha.

Quinta-la smiled and darted a glance at Shokan. The lord said the word he had learned for the springs and the young dweller nodded.

"Hot," she agreed. "Shokan-li red like an Emperor's flag," she said gesturing to the lord and then touching her own chest.

Nishima cast a look at her brother who sipped his cha deliberately.

"I see," Nishima said. "I hope my brother has found suitable quarters for you?"

Shokan said another word in the mountain language and Quinta-la smiled again, which pleased Nishima. "Dragons and clouds, Empress."

"One of the rooms the Yamaku decorated," Shokan said. "She likes the painted screens."

A tap on the door frame preceded Lady Kento's reappearance. "Excuse me, my lady. Were you expecting your Spiritual Advisor?"

"Of course. Please bring him to us." Nishima turned to Shokan. "Please, brother, I'm sure Quinta-la would enjoy an opportunity to speak her own language. Stay a while. Shuyun-sum is your Spiritual Advisor now, Shokan-li. He is a remarkable young man. Someone you would do well to know."

The lord gave a half bow. "Brother Shuyun is dedicated to the Empress, there is little question of that," Shokan said and smiled, "like so many others who traveled the canal from Seh in your company."

Shuyun appeared in the doorway, saving Nishima from having to answer. "Please, Brother Shuyun, be at your ease."

At the sound of the monk's name Quinta-la's eyes went wide. She turned half around toward the approaching Brother but then prostrated herself on the rug, causing the monk to stop as though he confronted a terrible sight.

"Quinta-la," Shokan said, "please. This is unseemly. You are in the presence of the Empress."

Unaffected by the lord's entreaties the young woman remained facedown on the rug, mumbling rapidly in her own language.

Nishima looked over to Shuyun, her question unspoken.

"I do not understand, Empress." Turning to Shokan he asked, "This is the young woman from the mountains?"

Shokan nodded as he tugged gently on Quinta-la's sleeve.

Shuyun spoke softly to the woman in her own tongue. Her mumbling stopped, but she did not answer nor did she move from her position on the floor. Whispering again Shuyun reached out and touched the girl's wrist, causing a shiver to pass through her.

"Will you not rise up, Quinta-la?" Shuyun said. There was no response. "You are making the Empress and Lord Shonto most uncomfortable and I myself am somewhat disturbed. Please, will you not rise?"

A whisper so low it could almost have been a sigh escaped the young woman.

Nishima raised an eyebrow at the monk.

"She says she is not worthy, Empress," Shuyun said his face showing the tiny signs of strain that Nishima had come to recognize.

"Excuse me, Brother, Empress," Shokan said, "I had no reason to expect anything like this. I apologize."

Shuyun spoke again in the woman's tongue, a bit more forcefully this time, and very slowly she rose to a kneeling position where she sat with her eyes cast down.

"Will Quinta-la not explain this?" Nishima asked the monk.

Shuyun spoke a few words in the mountain language but the young woman only closed her eyes and remained silent.

"Quinta-la," Shokan said. "The Empress would like you to answer Brother Shuyun's question. Will you not?"

The young woman from the mountains opened her mouth as if to speak but no words came forth. After several seconds of effort she managed, "Cah Shu-yung."

Nishima looked up at Shuyun, but it was Shokan who translated. "The bearer."

The monk nodded.

"Do you understand this, Shuyun-sum?" Nishima asked. The young woman's reaction disturbed her deeply, though she was not sure why. Nishima realized she felt an inexplicable anger toward Quinta-la.

"I do not, my lady, I apologize. The bearer: that is my name, taken from the mountain tongue, as you know. What it means to Quinta-la or why she has reacted in this way, I cannot say."

"When I traveled in the mountains, Brother," Shokan said, "I met a woman—an elder of Quinta-la's village, perhaps of her people. It was my impression at the time that this woman was considered a seer among her people. They were somewhat afraid of her, though in awe would perhaps be a better description. I sensed no animosity toward her. It was very unusual. As I do not speak their tongue nor understand their ways, I did not know what to think of this woman. Alinka-sa, for that was her name, questioned me about the situation in the Empire. She also asked about you, Brother Shuyun. She knew you by name."

Shuyun sat for a moment, his face unreadable even to Nishima who believed she was learning the tiny signs that betrayed what he truly felt. "Alinka-sa," he said quietly. "Sa is an honorific: a sign of the greatest possible respect. There is no equivalent in our language.

"Alinka means ginkyo, more specifically, the leaf of the ginkyo. This tree, though common to us, does not grow in the mountains and is thought to be almost a legend to the mountain people. Alinka is also the word for fan. I remember our fortunes being cast in your garden, my lady," Shuyun said to Nishima. "The coins of Kowan-sing have descended to us from the same race that Quinta-la's people call their ancestors. The meaning of Alinka is somewhat similar to the prime Kowan, the fan: *that which is hidden.* In our world it also means temptation or desire. To know the future is one of our greatest desires." Shuyun turned to Shokan. "This woman, Lord Shonto, did she speak of what was to come?"

Shokan shook his head. "No, Brother. If she saw the future, she did not tell me of her vision." The lord fell silent, lost in thought. Finally he looked up at Nishima. "If she knew of our father's fall, she said nothing to me though now I am left to wonder. She released me from my debt—the debt I owed her people for rescuing me in the snows—but I do not know why."

Cha had grown cold in everyone's bowls and Nishima suddenly remembered the servant kneeling nearby. She gestured to the maid to leave.

Shokan looked up, slight embarrassment showing. "Excuse me, I was lost in my thoughts." He glanced over at Quinta-la. "Perhaps it would be wise for me to take Quinta-la back to her rooms for now. Alone she may speak of this."

Nishima gave a slight nod and Shokan bowed accordingly, touching Quinta-la's sleeve. She prostrated herself before Shuyun once again and backed to the door at Shokan's urging, forgetting to bow to the Empress entirely.

Nishima looked over at Shuyun. She wanted to speak of what had happened with Quinta-la, but she could not. What she might learn frightened her.

"Must everything change?" she asked quietly instead.

"Botahara taught that change was inevitable and to resist it. . . ." He did not complete the quotation. "Sadly, it appears to be so, Nishima-sum. You are an Empress now. A great empire is dependent upon your wisdom."

She almost asked the question that grew in her mind but could not. *I have become an Empress, Shuyun-sum, and what of you? What have you become?*

She reached out and took his hands in hers. I cannot bear it she thought. Let us not speak of it. Warm arms encircled her and she pushed her cheek up against Shuyun's own. Nishima closed her eyes and the image of Quinta-la, prostrated on the floor, came to mind.

That young woman was for more in awe of Shuyun than of the Empress of Wa, Nishima thought. She had been worshipful.

Sixty-three

SISTER SUTSO WALKED slowly beside the sedan chair bearing the Prioress. The scale of the halls that led through the Imperial Palace was more impressive than the largest temple she had seen and the materials and design infinitely richer.

Palace officials, Imperial Guards, lords and ladies, and soldiers in blue passed the Sisters or stood aside to let the party by, though it was hardly necessary, the halls were so wide. Looking into the faces of the people she saw, Sutso realized there was a mood in the palace that she could not quite describe. Elation and sadness seemed to dwell under the same roof and the people who inhabited the palace appeared to be caught up in both at once.

She glanced back and found Sister Gatsa watching the passage of two ladies of high birth. Gatsa-sum looks no less regal than they, Sutso thought, perhaps more: would they look as regal dressed in the plain robes of the Botahist nuns? Of all the nuns in the party Gatsa certainly looked the least out of place here.

Morima, on the other hand, looked terribly lost and at odds with all around her. Sutso cast a look at the large nun who brought up the rear of their party. Morima's appearance may not have been due entirely to her present situation, however—the nun's crisis had not yet passed and Sutso had begun to wonder if it ever would. It was a surprise to Sutso that Morima-sum had been invited at all.

Sutso resisted an urge to open the curtain to assure herself that the Prioress was well. The pretense that the Prioress was stronger than she actually was must be maintained, especially here.

The Empress had summoned the Sisters the previous evening after the Sisterhood had sent their official blessing to the new sovereign. It was only upon their arrival in the palace that they had learned the Supreme Master, Brother Hutto, and other senior members of the Botahist Brotherhood were to attend the same audience as the Sisters.

Only the Prioress had taken this information calmly, smiling her beatific smile and closing her eyes as though she would sleep and dream dreams of great peace and beauty. May Botahara walk beside her, Sutso thought.

Outside the palace wall the barbarian army, or part of it, had lain down their arms and now they waited, watched from a distance by patrols from Lord Shonto's army. Rumors flew through the city. It was said that Lord Shonto's Spiritual Advisor, Brother Shuyun, had gone out into the field and defeated the Golden Khan in single combat and the tribes had then battled among themselves, some retreating north, others surrendering. This young Initiate monk had become an even greater object of speculation among the Sisters. Sutso knew the Prioress' hopes regarding this young man and this worried the Prioress' secretary. She was concerned with the effect it might have if the Prioress' hopes were dashed entirely. *Desire,* Sutso thought, it is as Botahara said. And the Prioress is so much closer to Perfection than any I know.

The official who led them turned to the right into a hall that ended in a set of double doors. Shonto guards knelt in two rows before the doors and two young Neophyte monks swung incense burners before them.

The guards and the Neophytes all bowed as the Sisters passed. The official had the doors opened, and gestured for them to enter.

Beyond the heavy doors was an audience hall of medium size, no doubt, by palace standards, though it was as large as the largest hall of the priory. The entrance to the great room was not at the end opposite the dais, as Sutso expected, but to one side of the hall. Perhaps a dozen senior Brothers knelt in a row directly across from the opened doors and as Sutso entered she saw a single ancient monk sitting to her right, opposite the dais. Brother Nodaku, she thought, the Supreme Master of the Botahist Brotherhood. The identities of the others she could not guess.

As the official directed them to silk cushions laid out on the polished wooden floor, the Brothers bowed. Sutso returned this gesture and then tapped lightly on the sedan chair that bore her superior.

"Open my curtains, child," came the dry voice of Sister Saeja.

Sutso slid the silk curtains aside and found the Prioress propped up on her pillows. The old woman bowed to the Supreme Master and then his party who all did the same in return. Sutso moved a cushion and knelt close to her superior. The official who had brought them to the hall retreated and the doors were closed behind him. No one spoke—no one showed a sign of the surprise or resentment they felt at being forced into this situation. All waited patiently.

A door opened to one side of the dais and an official wearing the dragon fan of the Empress' staff entered. He shuffled quickly to a place directly before the dais and bowed to the assembled followers of Botahara.

"Supreme Master," he said with great dignity. "Prioress, Sisters, Brothers: the Major Chancellor of the Empire of Wa." He bowed again and moved off to one side.

Sutso watched as an old man with one arm entered. He wore the elaborate ceremonial robes of his station but somehow did not seem to belong in them. Despite his age this man would have looked more at home on horseback. To add truth to this, Sutso noticed that the man's face showed signs of having recently been exposed to the wind and sun.

Kamu, Sutso realized. This is the Shonto steward. A capable man by all reports and completely loyal to the Shonto. She wondered how many other key positions in the government were now filled by Shonto retainers. The Yamaku nightmare had come true.

Kamu bowed to all present and took up a place kneeling just before the dais as his position dictated. He produced a scroll from his empty sleeve and unrolled it with obvious skill against his thigh using his only hand.

"I regret to say that the Empress will not join us. As you might imagine, the situation in the Empire at the moment requires much of her attention." It was the closest thing to an apology one received from a sovereign. People of lesser position in the same situation would be expected to apologize for arriving when the Empress had pressing business elsewhere—despite the fact that they had been summoned.

Kamu consulted the scroll. "The Empress has instructed me to assure you that the attitude of the previous Imperial Family toward the Botahist Orders will not continue. The Empress Shigei is a devout follower of Botahara and, as you know, the Shonto have long employed Spiritual Advisors of the Botahist faith and, until recently, the Empress' personal secretary was a former Sister. There will be no untoward taxes upon property held by either Order and the Yamaku laws restricting public religious ceremonies will be re-scinded." Kamu lowered the scroll.

Brother Hutto, the Primate of Yankura, bowed to the Chancellor. "May Botahara smile upon the Empress Shigei and her line. May the Perfect Master walk beside the Daughter of Heaven in these difficult times."

Kamu acknowledged this with a half bow.

Sister Gatsa took her cue. "It was with great joy that we received the news of the investiture of the Empress, Major Chancellor. Botahara has answered our prayers for a sovereign who will protect the followers of the Way. In our prayers we will ask Botahara to bless the Empress Shigei and the reign of the Fanisan House. May we also express our regrets for the Empress' recent loss. Our prayers will not fail to ask the Perfect Master to look with favor upon the spirit of Lord Shonto Motoru who was a great lord and a friend to the Botahist Orders." She cast a cold glance toward Brother Hutto as if to say, *that is fair speech, Brother.*

Kamu nodded to Gatsa. "Both your blessings and your prayers are wel-come in this troubled time. It is the desire of the Empress to make the Em-pire secure again so that all may travel the roads and canals safely and all may come freely to the temples of your Orders with the blessing of the sovereign. This is the desire of the Empress, though it is a great task and one which cannot be accomplished without the contributions of many."

Ah, Sutso thought, they have summoned us to ask for money. She did not smile. This new Imperial family may be easier to deal with than the Sisters had hoped. Money was never given without expectations of return.

"The Empress has asked Lord Shonto's Spiritual Advisor, Initiate Brother Shuyun, to speak of the needs of the Empire."

Kamu nodded over toward a screen which opened immediately. Sutso's eyes moved there as did the gaze of everyone in the room. A small monk, almost a boy, entered. If not for his pendant chain she would certainly have mistaken him for a Neophyte. She glanced over at the Prioress, but the old woman did not notice. Her focus was on the young monk, and nothing else. The old woman made a sign to Botahara.

Sutso turned back in time to see Shuyun complete his bows and kneel before the dais, facing the Supreme Master. She glanced over at the head of the Brotherhood and then back to the boy who sat so calmly across from him. It is impossible to say whose eyes are more ancient, Sutso thought, and she felt the smallest surge of wonder.

Shuyun gave a half nod to Kamu and then began to speak. His voice was as soft as the wing of a butterfly. "It is a great honor to be here among those who are charged with the protection of the Way. If I may quote the Perfect Master to those who have studied His Words longer than I have lived this life: Lord Botahara said that the beginning of wisdom was compassion. And so I was instructed by my teachers." He gave a half bow to Brother Sotura who sat with the other senior monks.

The words Brother Shuyun speaks have been chosen for simplicity, Sutso thought, though not as a child selects from a limited vocabulary but as an artist chooses the simplest lines and yet renders complexity.

"I do not claim to have achieved wisdom, but I am learning compassion and therefore I have made a beginning. Recently Botahara tested my compassion in a manner I would never have expected. It was written in the sacred scrolls that compassion could not be limited to one's family or to one's fellow villagers. True compassion would encompass strangers. True compassion would be extended to one's enemies. Remembering this, I was able to act as Botahara had written. I was able to act compassionately toward the enemies of Wa." Shuyun looked at each face in turn, holding everyone's gaze for a second. It was an act of some disrespect from one so young, yet no one seemed to notice.

Touching his palms together as though he would pray, Shuyun continued. "Among the barbarians outside the gates of the capital the plague has begun to work its terrible destruction. In return for laying down their arms, I promised that we, the followers of Botahara, those who practice compassion, would heal them of this disease." He let his words hang in the air. "The Empress has asked that you assist me in this endeavor," he said simply.

Silence in the hall. And though many looks were exchanged, no one spoke a word. Finally, after a long awkward moment, the Supreme Master deigned to speak.

"These are not followers of the Way, Brother Shuyun. You have promised much without the consent of the seniors of your Order. Initiate monks do not speak for the Botahist Brotherhood. Even Initiates who have the ear of the Empress. You may have learned something of compassion, but you have certainly forgotten much of humility."

Before Shuyun could respond, the Prioress spoke, her voice rasping out into the tension that charged the air. "We will assist you Brother Shuyun, in any way within our power, but the cure for the plague is the guarded secret of the Brotherhood." She looked over at the Supreme Master, an eyebrow raised.

He did not respond to her but kept his attention on Shuyun as though the head of the Sisterhood had not spoken. "Brother Shuyun, we would do much to assist the new sovereign. It is our sworn duty to minister to the followers of the Way. But caring for barbarian invaders who have put many followers of the True Path to the sword. . . . This will not be a popular act of charity among the people of the Empire, let me assure you. The Empress asks much of us." The ancient monk turned his attention to Kamu, dismissing the Initiate who sat opposite him.

"Major Chancellor, the Empress understands the ways of the Empire, as do her advisors who have many years of experience in such matters. It is difficult for me to believe that the Council of the Empire expects Botahist Brothers to cure barbarians when so many of our own faith are in need of our ministrations. . . ."

Sister Sutso did not miss the fact that the Supreme Master let the sentence hang in the air, the implications clear. *What coin is the Empress willing to exchange for such a service?* And the Sisterhood has nothing to bargain with in this exchange, she thought. Only the Brothers will gain concessions from the Throne and we will sit silently and bear witness to this. What a moment of triumph for the Brothers.

Kamu did not respond or even acknowledge that he had been spoken to but only looked over to Shuyun.

"Prioress?" came the soft voice of the Initiate. "Do you mean what you say: in any way within your power?"

"Yes, Brother Shuyun, but we do not know the secret of the cure."

"I know the cure," Shuyun said simply.

"I forbid it!" the Supreme Master almost shouted. "I forbid it! You break the laws of the Botahist Order."

Shuyun stared at the old man who had gone red with anger.

"If I act according to the word of Botahara, how is it possible to break the laws of our Order? I act according to the dictates of compassion, Supreme Master."

"Where have you learned such arrogance, Shuyun-sum?" Brother Sotura asked quietly. "The well-being of all who follow the Way must be considered here. Do not attempt to make decisions that are beyond your ability. Pride,

Brother Shuyun, will hinder you on your path. Please apologize to the Supreme Master and let the Major Chancellor speak."

Sister Sutso's heart sank as she watched Shuyun bow in deference to this monk. But then Sister Saeja spoke. "They do not know who you were in your previous life, Brother Shuyun. It is unheard of that a Brother with your skill so young cannot be identified." Sutso could hear the controlled excitement in her superior's voice. "Do you know what this means, Brother?"

Shuyun turned back to the woman propped up in her sedan chair. "It could mean many things, Prioress Saeja. How quickly can you gather the Sisters to minister to the barbarians?"

"You will be expelled from our Order," the Supreme Master said loudly. "Stripped of your sash and pendant."

"Immediately, Brother," Sister Saeja answered quickly. "Some will come this very day. Two hundred will arrive tomorrow. Three hundred more in three days, if you require it."

"Expelled from our Order," the Supreme Master said with finality. "The light of Botahara will be hidden from you."

Shuyun nodded. "May Botahara walk beside you, Prioress." Saying this he lifted the pendant on its gold chain over his head.

"You will be shunned by all who follow the Way."

"Shuyun-sum," Sotura said, his voice rising. "Think what you do. . . ."

Sotura watched as Shuyun dropped the pendant and chain into the palm of one hand. The young monk stared at the gold and jade in his hand with a look of deep sadness.

"You will be cursed by the Perfect Master," the Supreme Master intoned.

Shuyun looked up at these last words. With a look of great regret he set the pendant on the floor and the chain slid out of his hand to make a pile beside it.

"I will be blessed by Botahara," Shuyun said, and Sutso felt the conviction of these words, saw even the Supreme Master hesitate when he heard them.

Shuyun rose slowly to his feet so that he stood above all the senior members of his Order. Sotura watched as he did the unthinkable: Shuyun *pointed* at the Supreme Master.

"Pray that the compassion of Botahara encompasses you, Brother, for if it does you may yet be returned to the wheel."

Brother Sotura was on his feet, lightning quick. Three blindingly fast strides toward the young monk and then suddenly he stepped back off balance for an instant as though he had been struck. Shuyun stood with his hand raised, palm out, yet he had not touched the senior Brother.

"Forgive me Sotura-sum," Shuyun said quietly, his voice full of compassion. "Separate yourself from those who have lost the Way. Do you remember the lesson you taught when I was but a child? The butterfly enclosed in your chi strong fist?" Shuyun reached into his sleeve and removed something. When he opened his hand a white blossom lay upon his palm. "Brother Sotura, your Order has lost compassion—the beginnings of wisdom. To find the True Path you must leave them."

The Senior Brother stood looking at the blossom in Shuyun's hand. "You did not touch me . . ." he said.

Shuyun nodded once.

Brother Sotura looked up from the blossom into the eyes of his former student. The chi quan master's face was deeply troubled.

Sister Sutso heard a noise to her right and then a thin hand gripped her shoulder. The Prioress stepped out of her chair and came to her knees beside Sutso. The secretary turned and saw the Prioress was crying. The old woman bowed her head to the floor and began to chant the prayer of thanksgiving.

Shuyun turned at the sound of this and Sutso thought she saw a look of horror cross the Botahist mask. The young monk turned back to his former teacher, holding his gaze for a second, and then almost fled from the hall.

Sutso looked down at her superior who still bowed her head to the floor, and then she realized that others did the same—both Sisters and Brothers.

Botahara help me, she thought, *have I been in the presence of the Teacher and not known?*

Sixty-four

THE EMPRESS OF Wa stood alone on a balcony looking north across the small part of her vast Empire that could be seen from the Island Palace. The morning's rain had let up, leaving the air clear and the sky hung with retreating clouds that twisted slowly in a clearing breeze. The shadows cast by the clouds flowed slowly across the fields and flanks of distant mountains creating an ever changing pattern no artist could hope to capture.

The barbarian encampment spread in mottled grays and browns across the green grass and came by turns into shadow and light. Outside the protective circle maintained by the Shonto soldiers, people from the capital and surrounding areas had begun to gather. Nishima could see knots of them collecting here and there, staring with fascination toward the encampment. Many brought food, Nishima had been told, and she was surprised to hear this for there was still little enough to be had in the Imperial Capital.

This sudden generosity did not necessarily indicate a great change in the attitude of the people of Wa toward their invaders: the rumor was spreading that the Shonto Spiritual Advisor, the gifted monk who had defeated the barbarian army, was the Teacher so long awaited. Only the Shonto soldiers and the fear of plague kept the people away from the man they hoped was the one foretold.

Nishima felt a deep uneasiness when she looked down at the gathering crowds as though they were another force intended to keep her and Shuyun apart.

For three days now the monk had been away tending to the barbarians and Nishima had grown more and more restive as though each day took him farther away and made his return less likely. She paced across the short balcony to its end, stopped, and looked out again. Forcing herself to give up the futile searching of tiny figures moving through the barbarian encampment, Nishima fixed her gaze on the northeast.

Kamu had said that the barbarian army that traveled there would begin to raise a dust cloud once the wind dried the land, but there was no sign of this yet nor of Lord Taiki's pursuing force. This part of the shattered barbarian army had razed a village the previous day though the villagers had fled before the tribesmen descended. Nishima pressed her fingers to her temple. No one was really certain of the purpose of these barbarians, loose upon the land as they were. The suggestion that they made their way toward the Botahist temples on the Mountain of the Pure Spirit still appeared the most likely explanation. Obviously these barbarians could not know that the Brothers would never succumb to force, nor would they be likely to simply offer a cure.

Shuyun had said that the plague would take hold among the fleeing barbarians by the third day so that only a few would remain strong when they arrived at their probable destination. Lord Taiki, she hoped, would convince these to surrender.

Her attention was taken by a line of men on foot who passed the Shonto soldiers who guarded the barbarian. Botahist Brothers, Nishima realized. A growing number were leaving their Order to come serve the one said to be the Teacher—to practice compassion rather than politics.

The Botahist Brotherhood, her advisors surmised, were locked in internal struggle. They had stripped Shuyun of his pendant and turned their backs on him, and only after this rash decision had they realized their error. They had alienated the new sovereign, surrendering the advantage of Imperial favor to the Sisterhood—and they might have forced the Teacher from their Order.

Nishima shook her head. As her father often noted, Brother Satake would never have acted so foolishly had he become the leader of the Botahist Brotherhood. It made her wonder if it was not as Shimeko said—the Brotherhood had become decadent.

A full report of the meeting between Shuyun and the seniors of the Botahist Orders had been supplied by Kamu. He spoke of Shuyun's actions and speech with pride. The Brothers made few miscalculations as great as that.

It must have been impossible for them to imagine that a young Initiate could act independently, ignoring their gravest threats, offering one of the Order's greatest secrets to their rivals. Only a few months away from Jinjoh Monastery and Initiate Brother Shuyun had rebelled against them—far more openly than Satake-sum ever had. In part, Nishima viewed this as almost a personal triumph, but it also filled her with fear. Brother Shuyun appeared to be under no one's spell.

Shokan was utterly convinced that the Brotherhood would recant their refusal to assist the barbarians and would scramble to preserve some shred of the advantage they had surrendered when the Sisters offered their services to Shuyun and the Throne. It was perhaps a sign of how fractured their Order had become that this had not yet occurred.

A knock on the screen that led from the balcony startled Nishima, and a Shonto guard appeared at her response. "The audience, Empress," he said, keeping his eyes cast down.

Nishima took a last look out to where Shuyun ministered to the army of the desert and then left the room she had begun to use so that she might look out over the barbarian encampment. Her guard fell into step around her immediately.

She had managed to break the tradition of the sedan chair, though this shocked more than just a few officials. To ameliorate this somewhat, she agreed to use the chair for ceremonies—the struggle now was focused on semantics—which events could be considered ceremonial? There was, Nishima was sure, a definite move afoot to broaden the strict definition of the word.

As Shokan had suggested, Nishima tried to view the situation with humor, but it was difficult. The officials of the Island Palace were completely obsessed with tradition and ceremony and matters too trivial to believe. It was obvious that the running of the Empire had not been their concern for a very long time—not since the days of the later Hanama Emperors. This would have to change, if it meant replacing every senior member of the government.

She descended a massive set of stairs, courtiers and officials bowing as she passed. A private audience hall off Nishima's official rooms was their destination. Until Nishima had peopled the Great Council to her liking, there were still a number of things that needed to be done beyond the view of the officials. Their interference in certain things would not be helpful. Nishima was beginning to realize that she had learned more than she ever realized about leading men from years of watching her father. There was no one more skilled than Lord Shonto at winning loyalty and achieving ends through the efforts of others. It was the intention of the new Empress to bend Imperial protocol as much as possible so that she could run her administration upon the Shonto model—something she knew was effective.

Returning the Empire to a state of stability was her immediate task and to do this she would need the assistance of many. Shokan and Kamu had pointed out that rewarding those who had followed her father from Seh, and supported him when it meant defying the Emperor, was the beginning. Let it be said that the new Empress understood and rewarded loyalty. It was the Shonto way.

She had been informed that there were rebellions in Chou, and a Yamaku cousin there had declared himself Emperor and began to gather an army—a fool's rebellion, Hojo assured her, but it indicated that speed was necessary to establish the validity of her rule beyond contesting. The previous day a report had come that the Yamaku Imperial family dwelt no more on this plane, caught by the people who fled the barbarian invasion. It was a sad thing and, though Hojo had breathed a sigh of relief, Shokan had told Nishima privately that this was not as significant as others hoped. Pretenders could easily arise claiming to be Yamaku sons or daughters or cousins—even distant relatives of the Hanama might make claims, for that was the basis of Nishima's own. Imperial blood was not terribly rare among the peers of Wa.

They reached the rooms that Nishima had made her own and the Empress nodded to bowing Shonto guards as she passed. The audience hall was empty and Nishima took her place on the low dais, arranging her robes with care—white over crimson. She was glad that she had not met resistance from Shokan or the others to this. It was customary for those who performed great deeds for the sake of the Empire to receive their rewards in great ceremony, but Nishima did not feel such a ceremony was appropriate at this time. Perhaps when the Empire was more settled. The people she would speak with this day were not courtiers or officials of the palace. They would not demand that the smallest of their actions receive public recognition. As callous as it sounded, some part of Nishima knew that to strengthen the ties to those who had supported her father she needed to treat each as a private favorite of the Empress. This knowledge embarrassed her somewhat, but it did not stop her from acting accordingly.

I have a rule to consolidate and legitimize, Nishima told herself, but may I not walk too far down the path of the cold manipulator. Botahara save me from that.

Kamu entered and knelt before the dais, bowing his head to the mat. The Empress nodded to her Major Chancellor. The officials of the palace were no doubt still stinging from Kamu's appointment but, along with the other stands she had made, this was having its desired effect—the officials were realizing that they would not rule the Empress.

"Kamu-sum. It is my hope that the constant whispers of the palace officials do not make the performance of your duties too difficult."

"The buzzing of flies, Empress. I have long since learned to ignore such things."

"Perhaps it is another of your many skills that I may one day acquire myself, for I confess this buzzing sometimes drives me to the ends of my patience."

The old man smiled, the great wrinkled raincloud of his face creasing in a thousand small lines. "Patience was not something I learned in my youth, Empress, it grew slowly as the years passed. Thus it was that, in my younger years, I fought more duels than perhaps even Lord Komawara." Kamu gestured to his empty sleeve. "Here is my great teacher of patience, Empress, otherwise I may have been too foolish by nature to have ever acquired this most valuable of traits. But you are wiser than I, my lady," he hurried to add, embarrassed suddenly by what he implied.

Nishima hid a small shudder. "Let us hope that I may learn from you, Kamu-sum. I would certainly live with my loss less skillfully and with less grace than my chancellor."

Kamu looked down, perhaps embarrassed. He consulted a scroll.

"I am ready to begin," Nishima said, giving her father's steward a small smile.

"Lord Butto Joda of the Province of Itsa, Empress," Kamu said. "The lord readies himself to go north in pursuit of the barbarian who retreat along the great canal."

Nishima nodded. Kamu clapped his hand upon his thigh once, producing a surprisingly loud sound, and the doors to the hall opened. It was a small hall, chosen intentionally so that those arriving for their audience would not have to traverse a vast room on their knees to approach the sovereign. But despite its size it was a room of some beauty. The posts here were not lacquered but left a rich natural red-brown, and the sweep of the ceiling beams that supported the massive tile roof gave the otherwise static space a feeling of motion. Painted screens of courtiers walking in the palace gardens decorated one wall, and Nishima was thankful they were not scenes of battle.

The small figure of Lord Butto bowed in the doorway and then approached the dais. At an appropriate distance he stopped and bowed again.

"Lord Butto, please be at your ease," Kamu said quietly. The old man withdrew then, slipping quietly out through a screen. Nishima was paying Lord Butto the ultimate compliment of favor and trust—meeting the sovereign of the Empire privately.

Nishima turned her attention to the young lord kneeling before her. Like a boy, Nishima thought, all of his features are small though his eyes are very fine. But belying this look of youth was the lord's great poise. He was as sure of himself as many of her officials. Here will be a great man, the Empress found herself thinking, trapped for now in the body of a child. She smiled warmly.

"Lord Butto," she began, and was surprised to find her voice become thick with emotion. She paused for a few seconds. "Lord Butto," she began again, "it is my honor to express to you and the Butto House the gratitude of the government and the people of Wa. In the recent turmoil in the Empire you have shown the greatest wisdom and exemplary judgment, placing the interests of the Province of Itsa and the Empire of Wa before those of your House. To have fought beside my father against the invading barbarian army, and to have risked being judged a rebel House for this, displayed both courage and conviction. In the subsequent battles, Lord Butto, your courage did not falter nor did the warriors of your House ever shrink from their duty." Nishima took a long breath. "If there is anything within the power of an Empress to provide, you have but to ask."

Lord Butto stared down at the floor.

The young warrior looked up, meeting his Empress' eyes for a second. "Empress. It was my greatest honor to ride at the side of Lord Shonto Motoru as he fought, unsupported by the Imperial government, to stay the barbarian invasion. It is a tale equal to any in our long history and shall be told for a thousand years. The Butto name shall ever be sung in that tale, though in truth my part was small. What greater gift could I ask? I am honored by your words, as is the Butto House."

Nishima bowed low in response. "You are fair spoken, Sire, and your words touch me. Please, Lord Butto, accept these tokens of our regard." She clapped her hands twice.

Shonto guards appeared, carrying a saddle of beautiful leather. It was not decorated with silver or stones but was a saddle a warrior would choose, perfectly made of the finest materials. Upon the right side below the pommel a shinta blossom was embossed and on the left the flower of the warisha. Resting upon the seat was a bridle, also of leather, but with silk reins woven of crimson and blue. An armor chest was borne forth on a pole and set beside the saddle. Guards opened the lid and revealed a suit of armor laced in Butto purple and trimmed in the same pattern of crimson and blue.

Finally, a guard carrying a silk cushion, upon which rested a warrior's helmet, emerged and laid this before Lord Butto.

"It is my father's helmet, Lord Butto," Lady Nishima said. "May the crimson and blue always remind you of the gratitude and loyalty of the Shonto and of the Fanisan House. May the shinta blossom and the warisha symbolize the growing bonds between our families and the great esteem in which you are held." Servants set a low table beside the Empress and from this she removed a brush.

"Lord Butto, Itsa Province needs a governor of great wisdom to repair the ravages of the invasion. I would offer this position first to you, for there is no other I would trust more." This was a formality only, for the governorship of Itsa had been offered to Lord Butto, in private by Kamu, so that he could have refused without rebuffing the Empress.

Lord Butto bowed again. "Empress, this is a great honor for the Butto House. I accept and hope only that I may prove myself worthy of your great trust."

"Lord Butto," Nishima said warmly, "of this there is no doubt." With a flourish Nishima signed the scroll of investiture, making Butto Joda the Imperial Governor of Itsa.

A memory of the Emperor speaking to his new governor of Seh in the palace garden appeared in Nishima's mind and she hesitated before setting the brush down.

Pushing this thought from her mind, she forced herself to continue.

"You will pursue the retreating barbarian army, Lord Butto?"

"I set out in the morning, Empress."

Nishima nodded. "May Botahara go with you, Lord Butto."

The young man bowed low. "I thank you, Empress," he almost whispered.

Kamu had returned almost silently, nodding to Lord Butto who retreated back to the great doors. The old man gave Nishima a smile of reassurance and then looked at his scroll. "General Hojo Masakado," he said, clapping his hand to his thigh once.

The senior Shonto general knelt in the open doorway and came forward at a gesture from Kamu.

Nishima noted that Hojo looked rather less at ease here than she had seen him appear before a battle. The general wore robes of white embroidered in the palest shades with falling cherry blossoms—a man in mourning for his liege-lord.

With his gray beard neatly trimmed and his hair drawn back Hojo was a man of great presence despite his lack of ease in such formal surroundings. This man will be less happy in the new Empire, Nishima thought, for if Botahara smiles upon us the Shonto will have little need of his warrior's skills.

"Masakado-sum," Nishima said as Kamu retreated again. "Were I a great poet, I could not find words that would convey my gratitude or do you the honor you deserve." Nishima felt her heart begin to break as she looked at the face of the man kneeling before her. These are the men who loved my father, she thought, glancing over at Kamu's retreating back. These are the people who share my loss and have walled their feelings away for the sake of the Empire and their new Empress. She remembered both these men from her arrival in the Shonto House—massive, intimidating strangers they had been then. But how quickly that had changed. They teased me as a child and indulged me and adored me as though I were a member of their own families. She closed her eyes tightly and took three slow breaths.

"General, your loyalty to Lord Shonto Motoru and the Shonto House and its causes has been as unwavering as the loyalty of Fugimori to his outcast prince—as constant as the seasons. Without your wisdom and bravery, my lord's effort to slow the barbarian advance would have faltered, I have no doubt. Anything you ask of me I will grant, Hojo Masakado-sum, for the Empire's debt to you is great."

"Empress," Hojo began but his voice came out a whisper and he cleared his throat before beginning again. "Empress, I have served two Shonto lords and it is my wish to serve a third. I believe this is what I am meant to do. If I may, I will go with Lord Shonto Shokan."

"But this is a small thing, General—it is your present position. Is there no other favor an Empress may grant?"

Hojo shook his head. "I thank you, Empress. I am honored by your words—that is enough."

"Masakado-sum, my father would never see you go unrewarded and I cannot change the tradition of my family." As before, she clapped twice and a Shonto guard appeared carrying a small stand upon which sat a single scroll. This was set before Hojo.

"It is the deed for a house in the capital near to the home of your liege-lord, General—a property I have been told you admire. This, so you may visit the capital often and so come to the palace that I may not lose the pleasure of your company." Before Hojo could respond, a second guard appeared bearing a sword in both his hands as though it were a valuable artifact.

Nishima beckoned the guard to her and, to his great surprise, took the sword into her own hands. With the grace of a Sonsa she rose and descended from the dais. Holding the sword in both her hands, she offered it to Hojo who was so taken aback he hesitated for a moment.

"It was my father's favored weapon," Nishima said as though to reassure him.

"My lady, it is the *Mitsushito*,'" Hojo said, still not reaching for it. An Empress did not descend from her dais to offer a soldier a gift from her own hands—it was unheard of.

"So it is, Masakado-sum. My brother and I hope that you will accept it." She held it out again.

Hojo took it gently from her hands, and Nishima saw him close his eyes. She thought tears would appear, but the general was a warrior and maintained control with effort. Nishima reached out for a second, touching his hard wrist, and then she returned to the dais, unable to bear his discomfort any longer.

Hojo bowed but no words came, and he retreated even before Nishima had called an end to their audience.

Nishima sat for a few moments before she would continue. Nodding to Kamu, she again followed a breathing exercise taught to her by Brother Satake.

"Captain Rohku Saicha," Kamu said quietly.

Nishima nodded. The Captain of the Shonto Guard approached. He wore the light duty armor she often saw him in and carried his helmet under his arm. A white sash was worn for Lord Shonto and in this he wore no sword, making Nishima realize that the Shonto Captain had not been granted permission to wear a sword in the presence of the Empress. A grievous oversight with a man so proud.

Except for the white sash and the missing sword Rohku had been dressed exactly so when he had argued against Nishima's decision to journey to Seh.

What a position I placed this poor man in, she thought.

"Saicha-sum," Nishima said, "though unintentional I assure you, I have paid you a terrible insult." Clapping her hands a guard appeared, for the second time bearing a sheathed sword. "Of my father's extensive collection of blades there were only three that he chose to carry into battle. The Mitsushito I have given to General Hojo. This is a Kentoka, Saicha-sum. It is my wish that you will wear it in my presence."

Rohku Saicha set his helmet gently on the floor and took the sword in both his hands. "My lady, I did not for a moment believe you had lost trust in me but only focused on affairs of the Empire and struggled with grief. I will wear this always for your protection."

Nishima nodded. "That is my hope, Captain Rohku, for I have spoken long with my brother of this very matter. Too many rulers have been deposed by disloyal guard commanders and in an unsettled Empire this is a matter of grave concern. Lord Shonto has suggested, if you would agree, that you take command of the Imperial Guard, Saicha-sum, and, if you do, I will sleep easily. It is a choice left entirely to you. If it is your wish to stay with the Shonto, it would be with my blessing." Nishima found her mouth suddenly dry. She had said *Shonto* as though they were another family—not her own.

Nishima watched the captain's face as he considered this offer. Neither she nor Shokan had been sure of his decision. Certainly she had proven a difficult charge in the past, but Nishima needed someone she could trust completely and that left very few with the proper experience—it was not enough to be a warrior or a great general, a guard captain must be born suspicious, and yet reveal this to no one. He must have the mind of an assassin for this was how security was created without weaknesses.

"Empress, I am concerned for Lord Shonto. . . . He is my liege-lord and my charge. It is difficult for me to abandon him."

"If your heart cannot, Saicha-sum, then you must stay with Shokan-sum. I will say only this—your lord has said that Shonto security could best be served by making the Imperial household completely safe. Please consider this. I will accept either decision in your own time."

Nishima waited, trying to read the look of the captain, but he kept his face hidden by staring at the floor, cradling his sword across his knees.

"Saicha-sum. My father chose to ride into the midst of a battle. You did not make this choice for him. An arrow—in a battle there is no way to guard against an arrow. No one bears responsibility for Lord Shonto Motoru's death."

Rohku nodded. "Thank you, my lady." He did not look up.

Nishima had more to say, more praise for the guard captain for his part in the war against the barbarian and compliments for his son as well but she thought these things better said at another time.

She gave a signal to Kamu, who watched through a crack in the screen and the Major Chancellor returned, clearing his throat and then nodding to Rohku who retreated.

"Kamu-sum, if giving rewards is this difficult, how will I survive making even the slightest criticism?"

"Empress, if I may say . . . this is a difficult thing you do. These men supported your father while the rest of the Empire watched the Yamaku attempt to bring about his fall. They fought a barbarian army of a size never before seen with a small force and acquitted themselves in a manner that can only be cause for awe. They have become figures in our history." Kamu gestured out at the empty hall. "This audience signals an end of sorts. How will these warriors live up to the reputations that have been created? The captain who knelt before you will be a greater figure in history than all but a few lords who live in our Empire today. Hojo Masakado-sum will be mentioned in the same breath as the Emperor Jirri. I believe that they no longer know who they are, Lady Nishima. Until only a few days ago they were the men who resisted a barbarian invasion against impossible odds. Their lives had no other purpose. And now?

"You are releasing them from the purpose that has guided them, Empress. They do not know where they will go or who they will be. Not one had previously thought of himself as becoming a character of importance in our history. You praise them, Empress, and rightly so, but also you send them into the unknown. How does one act as a living historical figure, a legend?"

Nishima nodded. "I do not know, Kamu-sum," she said quietly. "In this matter I know as little as they."

Kamu smiled. "My lady, excuse me for saying so, but Lord Shonto always said that you have long denied your place in our Empire."

Nishima nodded slowly. "If you will lecture me regularly with quotations from my father, I will give you the wealth of a province in return, Kamu-sum."

"Excuse me, Empress, I did not mean to step out of my place."

Nishima looked up at this remark, unable to hide her distress. "Kamu-sum, I did not intend to criticize. To hear my father's words spoken by a true friend. . . . It breaks my heart and is a comfort at the same time." Nishima looked over at the peaceful scene depicted in the screens. "Please, Kamu-sum, ask Lady Kento if she will join me for my meal."

Kamu bowed low and retreated almost silently.

Nishima rose from the dais and crossed the room. There was no balcony, but unshuttered windows looked out to the west as did her own rooms. The sprawling barbarian camp could not be seen from here and this bothered her. What does he do now? Nishima wondered. What are his thoughts of me? More and more the last days she had begun to admit the true question to herself. *How long will he stay?* Shuyun is no longer a Botahist monk, she told herself, but this provided little comfort. He is something more, she was forced to admit. Who am I to interfere with the course that has been set for him? It was not a question she could answer.

A knock behind her brought Lady Kento into the hall, followed by servants bearing tables and trays.

"Kento-sum," Nishima smiled at her lady-in-waiting and then held up her hand to stop the woman from her deep bow. "If you address me or treat me as an Empress in any way, I shall throw myself off the balcony."

Kento gave a slight nod. "As you wish, my lady, though may I point out that this room has no balcony?"

"I shall throw myself from the spiritual heights I have attained, then. With such a small distance to fall, I shall not risk much injury." She smiled again and then gestured suddenly to the painted screens. "We have been invited to join these fine and generous people."

Kento broke into a broad smile. "Have we, indeed? How kind of them."

Like girls playing at make-believe the two women moved their tables closer to the screen and ate their entire meal as though they were in the company of the people depicted in the painting. Many received absurd names and Nishima and Kento gossiped about them shamelessly, attributing the most shocking behavior to one and all.

In the midst of this a letter arrived from Kitsura that contained a poem, written in a mock romantic style, which made the women almost howl with laughter. The guards outside the doors must have wondered what their Empress and her lady-in-waiting could be doing.

It was as though a dam had burst in Nishima's spirit and released a flood in the form of laughter, though it was not necessarily joy at this river's source.

Only toward the end of the meal did the tone of the conversation become sober.

"When Lord Shonto was declared a rebel lord," Kento explained, "the Imperial Guards broke down the doors to the house and took the servants to be questioned. I had escaped before they arrived. The gates were guarded by the Emperor's men and it was not until it became apparent that the battle had been lost that they abandoned their post. Our own brave guards returned to the house as soon as it seemed possible to do so, Lady Nishima. I cannot criticize them—no one was certain what transpired in the capital and if they had come out of hiding too soon. . . . Less was lost than I had feared though more than I hoped. Even so, the house will soon be much as it always was." Kento toyed with her cup, looking down as she spoke. "There for your pleasure whenever the palace does not enhance your harmony, my lady."

"Kento-sum, I would move back tomorrow if I could, but it is truly Shokan-sum's home now." Nishima reached out and touched the woman's sleeve. "But Kento-sum, you are a lady-in-waiting to one Nishima Fanisan Shonto, presently masquerading as an Empress. You would be welcome to join me here, though I can say little to recommend this place." The corners of Nishima's mouth turned down. "It is devoid of humor and joy, bound by senseless conventions, inhabited by men and women whose concerns and thoughts," Nishima gestured at the painted figures, "have a depth not unlike our present companions'."

"Lady Nishima," Kento said, "I do not presume to involve myself in matters of the Empire, but as to this campaign we must wage against convention and . . ." she searched for a word, "the stultification of the spirit, I will take up my sword by your side."

Nishima clasped her companion's hand. "Kento-sum, you lift my spirit. I will make you the unofficial Minister of Joy, and for this service you will earn my undying gratitude."

"To begin, in my new capacity, I believe we should find a husband for your cousin. This will make her more joyful, I'm certain."

"Kitsura-sum?"

"Of course. She does not grow younger, my lady," Kento thought for a second, "though it does appear she grows fairer. A husband, unquestionably. She will be searching for a consort for you even as we speak. This is self-defense."

"Huh," Nishima said—her father's response. "Who would be suitable, do you think?"

Kento replaced her cup on the table. "Your brother is certainly the most appropriate of the lords I know, my lady."

"But Shokan-sum has known Lady Kitsura all her life," Nishima protested weakly.

"Does he not find her enchanting?"

Nishima weighed this for a second. "It would seem unlikely that he is the only man in the Empire unaffected by her charms. Certainly he does not confide such things to me."

"If not Lord Shonto, then perhaps Lord Komawara?"

"Really, Kento-sum, that is not likely."

"But Lady Nishima, consider—Lord Komawara is the hero of the barbarian war. Certainly he will be rewarded richly for this; larger estates, Imperial favor, a governorship one day. Every young woman in the Empire will be burning incense and chanting his name at sunrise each first day of the month. I have only met him briefly, but is he not noble and kind and quick of mind? So everyone says."

Nishima smiled. "Less than a year ago our brave hero was thought to be the most provincial lord in the capital."

"In less time one can change from a lady into an Empress, my lady. I have seen it myself."

Nishima laughed with delight.

"Then he was thought provincial, Lady Nishima, but now he is viewed as having been an innocent—noble of spirit, perhaps even pure."

"Botahara save us!"

Kento laughed now. "You do not seem disposed to let Lord Komawara go, so I return to Shokan-sum."

A bell sounded and Nishima threw up her hands, relieved to end this conversation. "I must return to my duties. I will meet with the hero of the barbarian war this very hour. It is my belief that, offered anything he would desire, rather than ask for Kitsura's hand, a sword, a suit of fine armor, and the greatest horse in the Empire will satisfy Lord Komawara."

"Certainly the Empress knows best," Kento said humbly.

Nishima favored her with a look of exasperation.

Returning to her dais as the servants cleaned away all signs of the meal, Nishima sat considering the words of both Kamu and Lady Kento. It seemed to be true—the men who followed her father and fought the barbarians when the odds were impossible had become heroes on a scale that one found only in scrolls of ancient history and tales of times beyond history. To think, she said to herself, Komawara has become the object of desire for the women of the Empire. *Komawara.*

Kamu entered and bowed, kneeling before and to one side of the dais as his office required. "A letter has come from Lady Okara, Empress." He took it from his empty sleeve and went to place it on the edge of the dais, but Nishima intercepted it. As always, she was surprised by the simplicity of the great painter's hand. Nishima slipped the letter into her sleeve pocket—my reward for completing my duties, she thought.

She raised an eyebrow at Kamu.

"Colonel Jaku Tadamoto, Empress."

Nishima nodded. Ah, yes, the brother of Katta. Tadamoto had been the subject of a lengthy debate among Nishima's advisors.

As one known to have had the ear of the Yamaku Emperor, Tadamoto certainly warranted exile from the inner provinces, or at least the capital. Yet his case was not that simple. Jaku Tadamoto had corresponded with his brother Jaku Katta when the Black Tiger was ostensibly a Shonto ally and, according to Katta, was the man who had convinced the Emperor to raise an army when the barbarians invaded. Many thought him a man loyal to the Throne, even though he had grown to despise the Emperor. In the end, Tadamoto had tried to stop his brother from committing regicide and then had thrown himself between Katta and a sword blow that was intended to end Katta's life. This Tadamoto was a man of many contradictions, Nishima realized. Rohku Saicha was of the belief that the young colonel's knowledge of the machinations of the Imperial Government alone made him too valuable to lose.

Nishima did not yet know what should be done with this man. She was not ready to trust him, yet there was no evidence that he was a threat.

Shonto guards entered and stationed themselves close about the dais just as the doors at the hall's end opened.

A man in the black uniform of the Imperial Guard knelt in the opening.

When he rose, Nishima felt a catch in her breath. She had seen Tadamoto before, the night of the Emperor's death, but he had been injured and in a daze and she had been much occupied with other things. She was surprised to find that he looked so much like his brother Katta.

But Tadamoto was Katta refined. His features were certainly not weak, but they were significantly less strong than his older brother's. His presence was also unlike his brother's. Where Katta was all instinct and desire and strength, Tadamoto appeared to be a person deep in thought, caught up in things that had little connection with the everyday world. In truth he looked like a scholar, handsome and sincere. And then there were the famous Jaku eyes: and here the difference was profound. Unlike the cold, gray gaze of his famous brother, Tadamoto's eyes were the green of the earth—warm and verdant.

He bowed low before the dais and knelt with his hands resting on his thighs. Nishima could read nothing on his face except perhaps a sense of sadness, which was so common among her subjects that it seemed normal. Here is one who has learned to wall his true self away, she thought, and she wondered if life in the palace would soon make her the same.

"Colonel Jaku Tadamoto," Kamu stated formally. The old steward stayed in his place for this audience.

Nishima hesitated a second, trying to catch the young man's eye, but she could not. He seemed like a man defeated—incongruous in one so young.

"Colonel Tadamoto," Nishima said softly, for gentleness seemed the tone needed here. "I hope you received my letter?" She had sent him the death poem, unopened, that Jaku Katta had entrusted to her.

He stirred himself to speak but did not look up. "I did, Empress. I am in your debt."

"Certainly that is not so, Colonel. General Katta was an ally of my father when few believed there was a barbarian threat at all." She paused but saw no reaction. "Colonel Jaku, may I express my regrets at your loss."

Tadamoto nodded. "You are very kind, Empress. I thank you."

"If there is anything that I may do. . . . You are the brother of my father's ally."

"Empress, I was the loyal servant of the late Emperor. I accepted the surrender of Lord Shonto's army and would certainly have fought my own brother's forces if I had been so ordered. In the end Katta-sum and I crossed swords." She saw his shoulders sag.

"Loyalty, Colonel, is something the Shonto understand. Honor and loyalty cannot be split apart, but that is not so with love. One can honor one's liege-lord but not love him—I have seen it many times. One can love one's own brother, but honor may not allow you to act in a manner that would indicate loyalty. I must ask you, Colonel—were you loyal to the Throne or to the man, Yamaku Akantsu?"

Tadamoto hesitated for some seconds. "I began with loyalty to both, Empress, but I could not maintain my loyalty to the man. In the end, I am not certain that I remained loyal to the Throne, for how can one be loyal to the Throne when the man who possesses it has thrown the Empire into ruin? What is the loyal act then?"

"When you went to the rooms of the Emperor the night he died, what did you intend?"

Tadamoto shook his head, pain written across his face. "In truth, my lady, I do not know. To face him, to face the Emperor with his treachery, his betrayal of his office. I do not know beyond that. I do not know."

Nishima regarded the young man before her. "What you have said is wise, Tadamoto-sum. Loyalty to the Throne and loyalty to the person who sits upon that throne are synonymous—until the sovereign betrays his office. I do not criticize you, Jaku Tadamoto-sum, for you acted from intentions that were honorable. Few would have acted with more wisdom."

Tadamoto bowed. "These are comforting words, Empress."

"My father's vassal-merchant has spoken highly of you, Colonel. Tanaka-sum believed that you suffered much from the Emperor's betrayal of his office. Tanaka-sum is a man whose judgment I value."

"He is a remarkable man, Empress. If the Emperor had been as wise as your merchant, the Empire would have been well governed, indeed."

This almost made Nishima smile. "I have no doubt that would be so, Colonel. I have many questions, Colonel Tadamoto, if you don't mind. Many things have occurred that are not entirely clear to me."

"I am the servant of my Empress," he replied like a reflex.

"As you are aware, no one knows the circumstances under which the Emperor died. The woman who was found with him—she was his mistress?"

Tadamoto took a long breath before answering. "Yes, Empress."

"She was a Sonsa dancer, was she not? I believe I saw her dance in a program created for Lady Okara's paintings."

"That is correct, Empress."

"How very sad," Nishima said, obviously touched by yet another death. "She was a beautiful dancer."

"Very beautiful, my lady."

"Did they go to their end together? A lovers' ending?"

Tadamoto took a long unsteady breath as though he fought down physical pain.

"Are you well, Colonel? You were badly injured."

"I am well, Empress." He paused again. "There were signs in the room that the Emperor was about to escape. A suit of Imperial Guard armor. The Emperor himself was dressed as a guard without rank. Those who guarded him said a boat was being prepared to leave the capital." Tadamoto stopped again and Nishima wondered if he indeed spoken the truth when he said he was well. "It is my belief that Osha-sum pushed the Emperor from the balcony and he dragged her after him. I do not believe that she intended to make her end with the Emperor."

Nishima was quiet for a moment. "But she was his lover, Colonel. Do you know something that my advisors are not aware of?"

Tadamoto sat stiffly, controlling pain, certainly, but Nishima realized now that it was not physical pain. He met her eye briefly and Nishima herself looked away.

"She did not love him, Empress," he said quietly but with great certainty.

Nishima gave a single nod. "I see. Her family, where are they?"

"I do not know, Empress," he moved a hand in the tiniest gesture. "The Empire is in chaos, everywhere. It is difficult to know where anyone might be."

"Sadly true, Colonel. Someone must see to her ceremony. Is there someone you might suggest? Did she have friends in the capital?"

Tadamoto clasped his hands together on his knees. "I would see to Osha-sum's final needs if that would be acceptable, Empress." He fought to keep his tone even, but it was not a successful battle.

"That would be acceptable, certainly." She looked at Kamu who gave a small nod.

Nishima gave Tadamoto a moment to recover his surface of calm. "I will tell you honestly, Colonel Jaku, that my advisors do not agree on what should be done about you. Most of those who supported the Yamaku do not pose this problem—they will be exiled to far corners of the Empire and their power stripped away. Opportunists are not to be trusted. But you, Colonel, there are some who believe you were loyal to Wa and to the Throne and, as I have said, the Shonto value loyalty. You are also a man renowned for your intellect and knowledge of the court and its intrigues. Was it you who convinced the Emperor to restore order to the roads and canals?"

Tadamoto nodded.

"Why?"

"The dynasties that provided stability have invariably held the throne longest, my lady. It is as though history has passed its own judgment, sweeping away those Imperial families that do not care for their charges, though often not quickly enough, I fear."

Nishima produced a fan from her sleeve and tapped it in slow rhythm against her palm. "If you were offered a position in the new government, Colonel, would you accept it?"

Tadamoto did not hide his surprise, though his deep sense of sadness did not lift. "I am honored that you would ask, Empress." Language failed him for a moment and Nishima spoke to cover his lapse.

"You have suffered great losses, Colonel. You have sacrificed love for loyalty to principles. Your brother. . . ." She did not complete the thought. "If the principles of the sovereign were the principles you were loyal to, it is unlikely that you would find yourself in this position again, Colonel. Let us speak of this when you have dealt with the other matters that occupy you. If you will swear loyalty to me, Colonel, I will not require guards to be present when next we speak."

Tadamoto's head rose, Nishima could see the surprise in his green eyes. The look on his face said that he had not expected the world to ever bestow another act of kindness upon him. "Empress, I have knelt before the ruler of Wa more often than I am able to count, yet only today have I heard words of wisdom and compassion. I will swear loyalty, Empress—I would lay down my life that your rule may not falter, for the people of Wa need wisdom and compassion no less than they need food and water."

Nishima gave the scholar a half bow. "We will speak again, Colonel Tadamoto. If you would offer the benefits of your experience to Captain Rohku Saicha of my guard, I would be in your debt."

"Empress, I will be in your debt, always." Bowing low, Tadamoto retreated from the room.

"She who renews," Kamu said softly, "renews honor and hope."

Nishima pretended she did not hear, but Kamu's words gave her pleasure. "This Sonsa dancer was his lover," Nishima said.

Kamu nodded.

"Have I let compassion blind me, Kamu-sum? I fear it is my weakness."

"I believe, as you have said, that Jaku Tadamoto was an honorable man torn between honor and loyalty and love. In a lifetime of service to the Shonto I have never once felt so torn." He made a sign to Botahara that would have been out of place if Nishima had not known him so long. It was for her father and she did the same.

"May I suggest that, once you have spoken to Lord Komawara, it would be appropriate to speak with others tomorrow or at a later date."

"You coddle me, Chancellor," she said.

"Not at all, Empress. One cannot rebuild an Empire in a day and, if driven to the point where one's tranquillity is destroyed, one can do no good at all."

"You sound now like Brother Satake."

"It is a compliment I shall always cherish, Empress."

She smiled. "I will meet with Lord Komawara, please, Major Chancellor."

Kamu slapped his thigh once and then retreated, the Shonto guards in his wake.

The doors opened and Lord Komawara, dressed in white robes, knelt with his head touching the floor. His hair has grown back sufficiently, Nishima thought, and then smiled at the triviality of this.

The hero of Wa came forward stiffly as though he suffered from the performance of his deeds. The agony she had seen in his face at her father's funeral had not faded and there was no doubt in Nishima's mind that this pain had no physical cause. So shaken was Nishima by what she saw that she could not speak immediately. The hero of Wa, she thought, his spirit destroyed by the horror of his own deeds. Suddenly she was ashamed of what she had said to Lady Kento—*a sword, a suit of fine armor, and the greatest horse in the Empire will satisfy Lord Komawara.* I have given up the life I dreamed of, Nishima thought, but, Botahara save him, Komawara has sacrificed his soul.

"Lord Komawara," Nishima began, intending to express the gratitude of the Empire, but suddenly she found it was a pose she could not continue. Her voice quavering unexpectedly, Nishima said, "Your spirit, Samyamu-sum, it is like a stone in water. How has this happened?"

"Have you not heard, Empress?" he answered, his voice as cool as rain, "I have become a great hero. To accomplish this I have written no poetry, played not a song, nor proposed laws indicating great wisdom. Instead I have become the greatest butcher in ten generations. And so I am honored throughout the Empire."

Nishima put her hand to her face. It will be easier to rebuild an Empire than to heal the wounds of this man, she thought. Oh, father, look what we have done.

"Samyamu-sum," she said as gently as she could, "what may I do?"

A bitter smile passed across his face like the shadow of a quick flying bird. "I am told Lord Butto prepares to pursue the barbarians who retreat north. I would accompany Lord Butto, Empress."

"Do you not feel you have done enough? Will you not leave this to others now?"

Komawara moved his shoulders. "But Empress, there is not a warrior in all of Wa more suited to this than I. There is not a trace of my humanity that has not been washed away, washed away by the blood of others."

"Lord Komawara, I would ask you to stay in the capital. Please, you have done more than any sovereign has a right to ask." Shuyun, she thought, perhaps he would know what to do for this man. But Shuyun could not be reached and Komawara knelt before her asking to be sent back to war—sent to search for his own death, she was sure.

"Empress," Komawara said firmly, meeting her eye, "it would be better if you gave me a blade, as you have the others, and sent me north."

She felt her face grow hot at this but forced herself to meet his gaze. He did not look away. Are you unreachable, then, Nishima asked silently. Is there no trace of the young man I knew that I can appeal to. "Lord Komawara," Nishima began, "I will not order you to stay in the capital . . . but I will beg you to remain."

"Empress," Komawara said, taken aback by this. "You cannot say such a thing. You do not understand— it is what I am intended to do."

Nishima shook her head, a tight gesture. "I will beg you. I do beg you. I will bow my head to the mat before you. . . ."

"My lady, you cannot!"

Nishima stepped down off the dais into the space between them, placed her hands on the floor, and began to bow.

Komawara leaned forward and caught her shoulders. "You are the Empress. This is beneath you."

Nishima came back to her knees facing him, catching his hands. "If I let you go, you might find the death you are seeking or you will complete the destruction of your spirit. I could not bear it, Samyamu-sum, I could not bear it."

As though overcome by turmoil he did not speak for a moment. "Lady Nishima, I am of no use to you here. . . ."

She felt a tear streak her cheek at these words and he stopped at the sight of this. "I will stay. If it is your wish, I will stay."

Nishima squeezed his hands. "I know you have seen terrible things. . . ."

He shook his head as though there were something he tried to cast off. "No," he said, and the word came out like a moan. "I have *done* terrible things. You should not even touch my hands."

Hearing this, she took the hand that wielded his sword and raised it to her lips and then pressed it against her cheek. "You have a fine and noble spirit—we will find it," she said, "I do not know how, but we will."

"I do not know myself, Empress," he said in a hoarse whisper.

Nishima returned his hand gently to his lap. "I do know how we will begin," she said suddenly. Turning back to the dais she removed the brush, inkstone, and brush-stand from the table.

She pressed the inkstone into his hands. "This belonged to my mother," she said.

"Lady Nishima, I could not accept this."

She stopped him as he tried to return it, saying firmly, "I am not above begging."

"But it is a treasure."

"Nonsense," she said with a sly smile, "I gave Hojo a palace and Lord Butto a province. You can certainly accept a much used inkstone."

It did not bring a smile to his lips, but there was something different about his eyes for a second as though whatever haunted them had released its grip briefly.

She held out the brush-stand on the palm of her hand— a swan, delicately carved of jade. "This was a gift from my adopted father."

Almost timidly, Komawara took it up, turning it slowly from side to side.

"And this brush," she said pushing it into his hands, "is a gift from a woman who might have been a poet had not duty forced her into other pursuits. If you write poems to me, I will answer them."

"Empress, you have more important things to do than trade verses with a poet of little ability."

"I remember your poem in my father's garden, Samyamu-sum. Do not speak to me of your lack of skill. And I have nothing I would rather do. Will you not help me keep a tiny part of my former life alive?"

Looking down at Nishima's writing implements, he nodded. "I thank you, Empress." Komawara did not look less distraught, but she thought the hard edge of bitterness and the struggle with suppressed rage were less evident.

Sadness is not destructive to the soul, she told herself. We all have reasons for sadness.

"Everything that can be restored to you, Samyamu-sum, I will restore, ten times over."

He nodded. "Thank you, Empress." His discomfort was acute, Nishima could see, but she was also sure she could see signs that he responded to her words. He cares for me, this young man, she realized. And this touched her.

"You have duties," Komawara said, quietly, bowing low. Nishima thought it best not to protest and let him go, clutching her mother's inkstone. When the doors closed, she sat staring at them for a moment before rising and crossing to the windows again. She expected Kamu to enter; when he didn't, she remembered that this was the last of her official duties.

The day's interviews had not been what she had expected. She had been so young during the Interim War that she had been shielded from its effects—had not seen the cost. I thought I would give out accolades and rewards. The faces of Tadamoto and Komawara were not easily erased from her thoughts. They were too young. Not hardened veterans like Hojo.

She wished Kamu had returned. His council had been wise. Another who must be thanked for his part in this mad war, she thought. Touching the frame of the window, she felt Lady Okara's letter in her sleeve and took it out. Returning to the cushion on the dais, Nishima broke the seal and read.

My Empress:

Upon hearing the news of your ascension my heart sang, for I knew the Empire would need the wisdom of your open heart if it was to heal. If I do not presume too much, my heart then became heavy for I was aware of your desire for a life of contemplation and art. This is a great sacrifice you have made, and greater so for it is no small talent that you have been given. How is it that fate would call a great artist to govern the Empire?

It is my belief, Empress, that Wa requires your artist's soul to heal from the betrayal of the Yamaku and from the loss and ruin of the war. Art, true art is a force for compassion and tranquillity. Let us have an Empire ruled by compassion rather than greed and warfare. Let us have art in the fabric of our lives.

And then, Empress, came the sad news of your great loss. Motoru-sum was an old and trusted friend and his passing is a loss to all of Wa. May Botahara protect his soul.

> *Out of the gray winter mists*
> *An Empire in blossom*
> *Spring*
> *Drawn from the pigments of the soul.*

May Botahara walk beside you,
Okara

Nishima folded the letter with great care, and then offered a prayer asking Botahara to protect all those she loved.

Sixty-five

BROTHER SOTURA MOVED slowly through the barbarian encampment, and though he searched with a practiced eye there were no signs that Shuyun had made even the slightest error.

He is a marvel, Sotura thought. He was never taught to manage an outbreak of plague such as this, and yet. . . . The tribesmen the senior monk saw appeared well, if somewhat underfed.

Tents off to the west housed the sick. Sotura made his way in that direction, receiving many bows from the barbarian warriors who lazed about in the warm sun. Among some crude shelters he found a Botahist Sister praying with three tribesmen. She is making converts here, he thought, not sure why this bothered him.

Nearby, men cooked by a dung fire, apparently impervious to the smoke and the smell. Horses were being moved about the area and staked where there was less-trampled grass. Nowhere was there evidence of weapons— skinning knives were all the monk saw. Quiet, Sotura realized, it is so strangely quiet here. And it was true any who spoke did so in subdued tones; there was no laughter, no calling out. A military camp and it was as silent as a temple.

The population of the camp thinned noticeably as Sotura approached the tents of the sick, but there were tribesmen standing guard here, watching him warily.

Why would they guard the tents of the sick, Sotura wondered and then realized the answer. It was Shuyun—some would brave the plague to meet the Teacher.

Many Brothers of the Faith had forsaken their vows to come to Shuyun and minister to the barbarians, so the tribesmen who stood guard did not question Sotura as a stranger in the camp.

The sound of men coughing came to the monk as he stepped over ropes guying a barbarian tent. A Sister hurried past and Brother Sotura spoke to her. "Brother Shuyun, Sister—where may I find him?"

She stopped and eyed him carefully, suspiciously even, and then pointed toward a tent across an open area. He bowed his thanks. To Sotura's surprise he found himself nervous as he crossed the sward.

Four barbarian warriors bearing staffs guarded the tent and stopped Sotura as he approached. Speaking in their tongue, he asked for Brother Shuyun.

"The Master is at his labors, Brother," one warrior answered. "If you require instructions it is best to speak to Sister Morima."

Morima! Sotura almost said aloud, she has become Shuyun's shadow.

"I have come with a message from the Botahist Brotherhood. It is important that I speak with Brother Shuyun."

The tribesmen exchanged glances. "I will ask," one offered and retreated toward the tent. In the dim light inside the door Sotura saw the man gesturing to a young Sister. She stared out at Brother Sotura for a second and then hurried off.

A moment later Shuyun appeared, drying his hands on a scrap of cotton. If he was surprised to find his former teacher, he did not show it.

"Brother Sotura," Shuyun said, bowing low. "This is a surprise and an honor. Please." Shuyun gestured off to one side and ushered the senior monk away from the tent, out of hearing of the young Sister.

A breeze ruffled the heavy fabric of the tents and overhead a plague banner fluttered on a tall staff, adding its staccato to the eerie silence of the encampment. Once assured of privacy Shuyun did not hesitate, as though matters of great importance required his attention. Yet he was unfailingly polite.

"Do you truly bear a message, Brother Sotura, or have you found compassion in your soul?"

Sotura gave a small frown, not easily adjusting to being addressed as though an equal. "I do bear a message, Shuyun-sum—a message of compassion." He met the younger man's eye. "The Supreme Master will send our Brothers to meet the barbarians who ride toward the Mountain of the Pure Spirit. We will offer to heal them if they, too, will lay down their weapons."

Shuyun gave the senior monk a deep bow. "May Botahara chant your name, Sotura-sum."

Sotura remained impassive. "I was also instructed to give you this." He held out his clenched fist. Shuyun hesitated for a moment, then extended his open hand. He half expected Sotura to release a small blue butterfly into his palm, but instead he felt the cool weight of a jade pendant and chain.

"Never before has one been returned, Shuyun-sum. It is my hope that you will not refuse."

The young monk looked down at the pendant in his palm. "Why, Brother?"

"Many felt the Supreme Master may have acted in some haste," Sotura said, embarrassed to be admitting fallibility on the part of his Order. "We have swayed him in this matter." Sotura waved a hand at the camp. "Think of the other Brothers who have followed you here. If they see you wearing your pendant, Brother Shuyun, it will cause them to reconsider their decision. I am concerned for their souls, Shuyun-sum—for theirs and yours."

The younger monk broke into a smile that seemed to arise from joy. "Your concern would be better focused elsewhere, Brother. Those who have come here to cure the barbarians of the plague live the word of the Perfect Master." He held the pendant up by its chain so that it hung between them. "No stone can change that."

"Brother Shuyun," Sotura said, his voice carrying an edge of desperation, "they come because they believe you are the Teacher. What do you tell them?"

Shuyun reached out and took the senior monk's hand, lowering the pendant into it and then closing Sotura's fingers, holding the Master's hand thus as though expressing great affection. "I tell them I do not believe I am the Teacher."

Sotura shook his head in confusion. "If this is true, what will you do? You have turned your back on the Botahist faith."

"But the Teacher is among us, Sotura-sum. I will go to him and hear the Word from one who has attained that which we can only dream of."

Sotura reached out and gripped the younger monk's shoulder, staring steadily into his eyes. "Do you know where the Teacher dwells?"

Shuyun nodded.

"Where?"

Shuyun shook his head slowly. "When the Teacher wishes you to find him, he will send you a message, Brother Sotura."

Sotura gave Shuyun a gentle shake. "You have had such a message?" he almost demanded.

"I believe I have, Brother." Shuyun, stepped back so that Sotura released him.

The older monk stared down at the grass for a moment. "How can this be true, Brother? Why has he not sent for the Supreme Master, for Brother Hutto?"

"Their karma is their own, Brother," Shuyun said with great gentleness, his face full of concern. "Ask why he has not sent for you, Sotura-sum. It is the question that will lead you to wisdom." Saying so, he bowed to the senior Brother and returned to the tent where he labored to heal the enemies of Wa.

The following day Shuyun was interrupted in his work by Sister Morima. She stood silhouetted by the sun as Shuyun bowed over a young tribesman who lay on blankets on the grass.

"Brother Shuyun?"

Like all the Botahist trained in the encampment, she still called him *Brother* though the tribesman called him the Master.

He looked up, squinting. Though he could not see her against the light, he knew and was glad that Sister Morima had returned to her previous appearance of good health. Her step had grown light as she went about her work—her crisis of spirit had been resolved by an act of compassion.

"Sister?"

"On the edge of the encampment," she waved to the south. "The Prioress, Sister Saeja, has come. She asks for you, Brother, and will come to you if you will allow her to enter the camp."

Shuyun said a few words to the tribesman and then rose quickly. "I will go to her, Sister." He hurried off across the encampment, nodding to the many bows he received.

Emerging from the edge of the camp, he saw that a small pavilion had been erected on the invisible border maintained by the Shonto guards. He set out toward this immediately, unprepared for the reaction. There was a surge among the people who had been gathering around the encampment. He heard his name over and over and people offering prayers of thanksgiv-

ing. The soldiers were not caught off guard by this, appeared to have anticipated it, in fact, so the crowd was restrained.

Steeling himself, he moved forward. Looking at the press of the crowd
and the hope in the faces Shuyun thought, this will become my life, I cannot
turn away. Approaching the Sisters, Shuyun noticed some of the faces he had
seen in the palace. The one with the strong jaw and the haughty manner, the
small one who tended the Prioress.

When Shuyun was three paces away, the Sisters knelt and bowed low.
The Prioress stayed in her sedan chair this time but managed a bow all the
same.

Before Shuyun could speak, the dry rasp of the Prioress' voice broke in.
"It is our shame to admit that we do not know how to address you."

"I would be honored if you would call me Shuyun-sum, Prioress," Shuyun
said without hesitation.

The ancient woman considered this for a moment but then rejected it as
inadequate. "Master Shuyun, we seek the Teacher," she said simply.

Shuyun looked into the ancient eyes and saw the hope there and it saddened him. "He will be found by few, Prioress," Shuyun said, his voice carrying a note of concern.

The Sisters exchanged uneasy glances.

"Master Shuyun," the old woman said, the hope in her eyes replaced by
growing uncertainty, "are you the one who was spoken of?"

Shuyun slowly shook his head, sorry that he must do so.

The Sister took a long breath, her face growing soft, like a child whose
hopes have been dashed—who would dissolve into tears. "Then how is it
that you have powers unheard of in all our history?"

Shuyun looked down at the grass and when he raised his head his eyes
seemed moist, his voice almost overcome with awe. "I am the bearer, Prioress. I will serve Him."

There was a long silence then, the nuns not taking their eyes from the
monk as though he were a myth come to life. "The few who will find the
Teacher . . . who?" the Prioress asked, her question tentative as though
she feared the answer.

"I am not certain, Prioress."

The Prioress nodded. "Master Shuyun, will you not take one of us with you?"

Shuyun looked down again, but only for a brief second, and then he raised his head, saying, "If I may, I will send word to Sister Morima, Prioress. I will ask her to join me, if it is possible."

In some of the faces Shuyun saw a hint of anger, resentment, but the Prioress smiled suddenly, like the sun emerging from behind a cloud. "I have not been wrong in all things, at least. Botahara bless you, Brother. I will pray for you."

"Prioress?" Shuyun said, deeply serious. "Shimeko-sum—the one whom you called Sister Tesseko—it is her soul in need of your prayers."

The Prioress paused for a second, her face grave. And then she nodded once and the smile returned.

The Empress sat on the balcony overlooking the vast barbarian army. She had finished reading a letter written by Tanaka—a report on the state of the Imperial Treasury. The situation was not as desperate as her worst fears had whispered it might be. Hojo had secured so much of the palace when the Yamaku fell that few officials were able to slip away with stolen fortunes. Over many years Tanaka had made an exhaustive study of corruption in the Imperial Government, though it had never been his intention. The Yamaku way of governing had forced him to it. Tanaka had paid for information, bought influence when necessary, bribed ministers and bureaucrats. As a result he had a long list of those who could not be trusted and was quickly purging the civil service. It was an irony her father would have appreciated, Nishima thought.

The Empress smiled. She had talked with Shokan regarding Tanaka and discovered the poor man was consumed by guilt. He had given Colonel Tadamoto a detailed list (though incomplete) of Shonto holdings and now felt he had betrayed every trust he had ever been given. As this ploy had quite possibly kept the merchant alive, Shokan applauded it as wisdom. But Tanaka was not reassured and suffered all the same.

Duty, Nishima thought. He thinks he has failed in his duty, though absolutely no harm came of his action and much good—he preserved his very valuable life. It occurred to her to send the merchant a charter, raising him to a minor peerage, and citing his betrayal of Shonto trust as the reason for this. She was not sure he would see the humor in this, however.

A knock on the frame of the open screens drew her attention inside.

Lady Kento knelt in the opening.

"Kento-sum," Nishima said, smiling, for pleasure came to her easily that day.

"My lady. Captain Rohku is satisfied with the security in the block of your apartments, the private Audience Halls, and the Imperial guest chambers. He feels it is perfectly safe for the Empress to move through these areas without guards."

"This is good news indeed, Kento-sum. I was going mad being followed everywhere. Please commend the Guard Commander for his diligence."

"And, Empress, Lady Kitsura has arrived."

"Please, do not keep her waiting."

Lady Kento bowed and disappeared.

Nishima quickly rolled the scroll and pushed her work table to one side. She gazed out over the fields again. A message had arrived from Shuyun earlier that morning. He would come to the palace that evening and Nishima looked forward to this visit with both excitement and dread. *How long will he stay?* she asked herself again. The question had become a litany.

Kitsura appeared, bowing in the opening to the inner rooms.

"Kitsu-sum, you are as welcome as the arrival of spring and as lovely."

"Empress, it is good to see you well." The eleventh day of mourning had passed and the only white Kitsura wore was a sash, in memory of those who were lost during the recent turmoil and for Lord Shonto, of course. Her robe was deep green embroidered with a pattern of gold-edged seashells.

"You have seen your family, I am told. I trust they are well?"

"It is kind of you to inquire, cousin. They are indeed well. My family send their highest regards to the Empress."

Nishima leaned over and squeezed her cousin's arm. "Kitsu-sum, your father—how is he truly?"

Kitsura gave her cousin a tight smile, thanking her for her concern, and began to turn a ring on a finger. "It is true that he is less well than he appeared when I left for Seh, but he is a miracle, truly, Nishi-sum. Speaking of your ascension, he told me that Wa has lost a great artist but gained a greater Empress. I think he wanted you to hear that."

"Lord Omawara is too kind." Nishima felt her heart go out to her cousin, for she had twice lost a father and knew what it meant. She did not press the matter further.

"Cha, Kitsu-sum?" Nishima asked, moving the conversation away from

the area that caused her cousin pain. "Or shall we sample some of the palace's fine wines. There is a trove of rare vintages, I am told. Shokan-sum has
said the wine cellar is of greater value than the treasury."

"Cha would be lovely, cousin, thank you—though I would gladly sample
your rare wines another time."

Nishima clapped for a servant and asked for cha.

"I was able to speak with Lady Kento when I arrived," Kitsura said casually. "She is determined to find you a suitable husband, Nishima-sum."

"Me!" Nishima said, taken aback. "It is you she is searching for."

"As I suspected," Kitsura said, laughing. "I tease, cousin. She said nothing
of husbands for you." Kitsura tried not to look too pleased with herself.
"Who has my Empress chosen for her loyal and humble servant."

"Your Empress has not yet decided." Nishima answered, shaking her head
at how easily she had been tricked. "It will depend on how loyal and humble
the Lady Kitsura is able to demonstrate herself to be."

Kitsura laughed. "I fear for the happiness of my marriage, cousin."

They both laughed.

"I will admit that we had not progressed beyond the obvious choices:
Shokan-sum and Lord Komawara." Nishima eyed her cousin as she said this,
wondering what her reaction might be, but Kitsura showed no sign of what
she felt.

Cha arrived and Nishima shooed the servant out so that she might complete the preparations herself.

"The hero of Wa, Empress? I did not realize you thought me that loyal and
humble." She considered for a moment. "Though I would have to live in Seh,
far from my beloved Empress."

". . . and the pleasures of the palace," Nishima added, ladling cha into
bowls.

Kitsura's face turned suddenly serious. "Meeting Lord Komawara here in
the palace garden only last autumn, I would never have believed his name
would one day be on everyone's lips. People kneel down and bow to him in
the streets—peers! I have seen it. Lord Toshaki, who almost forced Lord
Komawara into a duel in Seh, is now his shadow. And all the young women
of the Empire are mad to meet him. Your first social events will be attended
by more lovesick young women than either of us can imagine." She held out
open hands and shrugged. "Our shy Lord Komawara. Who ever could have

guessed?" Kitsura sipped her cha. "Of course I tell all the women who ask that I—that we—saw this in him from the beginning. I admit that I am a most shameless liar, Empress."

Nishima stared into her bowl of cha. "Does this mean that you will accept Lord Komawara, Lady Kitsura?"

Kitsura laughed, but Nishima thought it was somewhat forced. "I believe our young hero must make his own choices, Empress."

Nishima looked out over the barbarian camp. "Lord Komawara has suffered a serious wound to his spirit, Lady Kitsura. I am not quite sure what can be done for him."

"I can think of a number of things," Kitsura smiled, "if I am not being too bold."

"I was thinking of something more spiritual, Lady Kitsura."

"He is a warrior, Nishima-sum. A spiritual cure may not be what is required."

Nishima shaded her eyes and looked out toward the mountains. Was that a dust cloud? She had received news that morning: the Brothers had met the wandering barbarian army and, with Lord Taiki's assistance, convinced them to lay down their arms. Shokan had been right, the Brotherhood were scrambling to recover from their mistake.

The barbarian force retreating north on the canal was not faring so well. They were dying in numbers, leaving a trail of burial mounds behind them. There would not be a handful left when they crossed the border into their own lands. It was a terrible thing. The Kalam had returned to the capital the previous day, sent by Lord Butto. He was convinced the barbarian army would not surrender. Imagine such pride, Nishima thought.

Kitsura was speaking again, and Nishima had not been listening.

". . . everyone says it is so, Nishi-sum. Is this true?"

"I'm sorry Kitsu-sum, my thoughts wandered. Please excuse me."

Kitsura looked at Nishima with some concern but must have been reassured by what she saw, for her concern faded. "Brother Shuyun? Is it true, as everyone says, that he is the Teacher?"

Nishima took a moment to ladle more cha and stir up the embers of the burner. It was the question she had been avoiding for days, though somehow late at night it became more persistent and troubled her both waking and dreaming.

"I do not know, Kitsura-sum. Brother Shuyun denies it, but Tesseko, may Botahara rest her soul, believed he might be the Teacher and not yet know."

"What is your own belief, Nishi-sum? What does your heart tell you?"

"My heart?" Nishima said, with the tiniest hint of resentment in her voice. "I am an Empress, cousin, I am not governed by my heart."

Kitsura was quiet for a moment, watching her cousin who stared out toward the fields, her mood suddenly changed.

"Excuse me, Kitsu-sum," she said turning back, catching Kitsura looking at her closely. "Please accept my apology. It is unworthy of me to become bitter because of the part I have chosen to play."

Kitsura reached out and took Nishima's hand. Her skin was so perfect and soft. "Where will Shuyun go now? Will he go with Lord Shonto?"

Nishima shook her head. "Shokan-sum has released him."

Kitsura pressed Nishima's hand. "Then surely he will stay with you."

Nishima squeezed her eyes closed.

"Cousin?"

Nishima wanted to give a neutral answer, but she could not and she felt Kitsura move closer. A hand rested on her shoulder, stroking her gently. Then Kitsura came still closer and embraced her. They stayed like that for some time.

"If you marry, Kitsu-sum, you must promise to remain in the capital. I cannot bear to lose anyone else."

"You have my word," Kitsura whispered. "Shuyun-sum is out among the barbarians?"

"He returns this evening."

"What may I do, cousin?"

"Nothing. You have done so much already. Often, when we traveled on the canal and in Seh, you were my strength. I have not forgotten."

"Do you know," Kitsura said, and Nishima could hear the smile in her voice, "Okara-sum told me that we must learn not to compete with one another?"

"Us, cousin?"

Kitsura nodded. "But, of course, now you are the Empress and therefore have won everything. There is nothing left to compete for."

Nishima did not smile. "I feel that becoming the Empress has meant more loss than gain."

Kitsura nodded.

"Okara-sum is wise, cousin."

"I agree," Kitsura said after a few seconds, "I agree entirely."

Gently they disentangled.

"I am certain that sovereigns are not supposed to require such coddling," Nishima said.

"They require nothing but, cousin. Have you not read the histories? You are the exception in that you don't require such treatment all the time."

The tea had grown cold and what was in the cauldron was too strong. "I will call for more," Nishima said.

"Thank you, cousin, but—I know it is improper to excuse one's self from the presence of the sovereign. . . . My father often awakes in the late afternoon and is strong enough for a visitor."

"You must take him my warmest regards."

Kitsura bowed low and with a squeeze of her cousin's hand slipped into the inner rooms.

Nishima stood and paced across the balcony. She sat on the rail for a moment, looking out over the encampment, but then rose and returned to her work table suddenly. Rubbing a resin stick over her inkstone Nishima began to breathe in rhythm.

When Shokan heard that Nishima had given her mother's inkstone to Komawara, he sent her a stone that had belonged to Lord Shonto. She recognized it immediately. The inkstone was very old and had seen much use and she adored it.

Nishima added a few drops of water. Shuyun would not come for some hours. As she had not yet received a poem from Lord Komawara, she decided to force a response. The Empress would write to him.

By the time dusk arrived, Nishima was pleased with the poem she had composed. But after making many drafts she chose to send one that showed less skill than the final version. She did not want to intimidate him entirely. And then she laughed at her own vanity. A few moments later, however, she convinced herself that she was simply being considerate of Komawara's present state. In the future, when the lord had begun to heal, this would not be required of her.

Nishima read the poem a last time. She hoped her memory for the verse Komawara had composed in her father's garden so long ago was correct.

Distant horizons glimpsed in the autumn garden
Casting the ancient coins

Among the mist-lilies and new friendships.
  The Boat setting forth
  Into uncertain winds
  As unwavering as the constant heart.

Does the Open Fan of temptation
Appear to you
Spread against a white sky?
  We all stare into green water
  Seeking the passing cloud
  Knowing it appears only to the tranquil soul.

Calling for a lamp and wax Nishima folded and sealed the poem, then hesitated before she stamped the soft wax. After a moment of consideration she chose the shinta blossom rather than the five clawed dragon circling the sun—she had asked Komawara to help keep a part of her former life alive, after all.

The sun had sunk into a line of clouds above the distant mountains, appeared briefly in a blaze of copper between the cloud and the peaks, and then dissolved into embers, leaving the clouds glowing like hot coals. Nishima turned and watched the scene slowly fade.

A maid knocked on the frame to the opening, bowing low.

"Yes," Nishima said, distracted.

"Brother Shuyun, Empress."

Nishima returned from her brooding immediately, trying to hide her pleasure from the maid. "Please, I will see him here." Quickly she reached over to the cushion Kitsura had used and pulled it closer.

Although it was hardly expected of an Empress, Nishima could not stop herself from staring at the opening, waiting for a glimpse of the monk. She could barely wait to see his face, as though the answer to the question that had become her litany might be seen there even before they spoke.

Coming through the opening, kneeling, Shuyun bowed immediately, hiding his face. The last light of the day lit the room in a warm, golden light and when the monk rose, his features appeared softer, less severe than Nishima had come to expect. And the light seemed to illuminate him, light him from within.

Something has occurred, Nishima thought. Look at him—he has had a revelation. A feeling akin to panic began to rise inside her and she struggled not to give in to it.

"Shuyun-sum," she said, trying to give her voice warmth, but the words came out of a constricted throat and sounded so. "Please join me."

Shuyun came forward with the grace that always delighted her, and though his manner was as serious as usual, she sensed a lightness in him that she had not seen before. To her surprise, Shuyun reached out and took her hand in his own. For a moment she found herself carefully scrutinized by those eyes that seemed at once ancient and innocent.

"You are well, my lady?"

Nishima nodded, her voice suddenly deserting her. She did not take her gaze away from his eyes, still looking for the answer to her question.

Shuyun took her hand between both of his suddenly and she felt a warm tingle of chi-flow. "Has something distressed you?"

With effort she found her voice. "I am well, truly. Learning to govern has taken some toll, perhaps." She made a gesture as though dismissing this as minor. "The barbarians have been cured?"

"The healing takes some time, Nishi-sum. It will be many days yet. But it is not too soon to consider what will be done with them when they are well."

Although the conversation led away from the discussion she desired, Nishima found herself taking it up with some relief—the news she feared would be delayed. "Kamu-sum has begun the arrangements. We will send the barbarians north up the canal, returning them to their own lands."

Shuyun nodded. "Excuse me for saying so, but I believe we should do more. We must establish regular commerce with the tribes and open relations. We must send ambassadors and gifts when chieftains are named and allow the barbarians to trade across our border more freely. If we do not . . ." Shuyun bent his head toward the barbarian army, quickly disappearing in the growing darkness. "We shall have another Khan one day."

"I am sure you are correct, Brother," Nishima responded. "It will be difficult to convince the Council that this is the path of wisdom—the anger toward the barbarians is great—but I will speak to my advisors. There must be a way to convince the Council."

"May I also suggest, Nishima-sum, that the Kalam could become an ambassador between the tribes and Wa."

This surprised Nishima and she felt herself drawn further away from the true questions that she must ask. "Is it not true that he is obliged stay with you until death ends his servitude?"

"It is true, Tha-telor is a strict law, but so much has changed in the world now. I have spoken to the Kalam at length and he has agreed to act as I have suggested, if it is the wish of the Empress." Very quietly Shuyun continued. "The Kalam realizes now that he cannot follow me on my journey."

Nishima let out a long breath, looking down at his hands around her own. "In your eyes I see that you have made decisions, Shuyun-sum," Nishima said quietly. "You will make a journey?"

Shuyun stroked her hand. "What you see, Nishi-sum, is tranquillity of purpose. Though I have been told to seek it all my life, it is only now that I have found it. I will seek the Teacher. It is my place to serve him, as it is yours to rule an Empire."

Nishima felt her senses swirl into confusion—it was like numbness creeping through her body, but it was not lack of feeling—it was too much. Too much and all at once and she could not sort those feelings or control them. The reaction was not unfamiliar, for it felt as though she had learned of yet another death.

"Will we never meet again?" she managed to say.

"I do not know, Nishi-sum," the monk answered. Nishima could hear how gentle his tone had become. He reached out and took her into his arms, but she remained limp as though this last blow had robbed her of all remaining strength.

"You are not the Teacher, then? You know this?"

Nishima felt Shuyun's head nod, close beside her own. "When I first met Quinta-la, when she prostrated herself and recited a prayer in her own language. Later I realized some of what she said: *he who bears the Word.* Among the mountain people there is a seer—an ancient woman. Your brother spoke to her. She questioned him about me.

"In the ancient scroll that speaks of the coming of the Teacher it also says that one will come bearing the Word. Botahist scholars have long agreed that this was another reference to the Teacher, but it is not so." Nishima felt the monk take a long breath. "It is a reference to me, Nishima-sum. I will bear the Teacher's Word. He has sent for me. He sent for me some time ago and I did not realize it."

Part of Nishima wanted to offer an argument, dispute the logic of what he said but another part of her believed he could not be wrong in this matter.

He walked out into the fields alone and stopped the barbarian invasion, Nishima told herself. Among the senior Brothers he inspires both awe and fear and the Sisters have followed him since the day he arrived in Wa. And now he goes to meet one who has attained perfection—as though Botahara has been reborn. It is no wonder that I have become unimportant in his life. How could I think that he would stay with me?

"It is without question, then," Nishima said, trying to keep the feeling that she had been slighted out of her words, "you must leave to seek the Teacher."

"Perhaps I have not yet achieved perfect tranquillity of purpose," Shuyun said, his voice tender, "for I do not know how to leave when my heart is here with you."

Nishima reached up and put her arms around him now, holding him close. "Then you must stay until you know." *He wants me to release him,* she told herself in a flash of insight.

Shuyun reached up and traced the curve of her neck with a finger. He did not speak as she expected him to. Stars were beginning to appear in the sky, and even in the west the light was all but gone. Nishima began to feel a deep sadness rising out of the confusion of her emotions, overcoming all else.

It was completely dark before they spoke again and it was Shuyun who broke the silence. "I wish to take a gift to the Teacher, but the gift I desire is not within my power."

"If it is something I may provide, Shuyun-sum, you have but to name it," Nishima said without hesitation.

"Then I would ask you to write a poem."

"This is the gift you will take to the Teacher?" She pulled back slightly so she could see his face in the light of the lamp.

He smiled. "Yes. It is the gift he will desire, I am certain."

"Shuyun-sum, this man is the living evidence of the Way. He is as close to being a god as one can come. Certainly he does not want a poem from me."

Shuyun touched his forehead against her own. "A poem from you is what he desires," the monk said firmly.

"But what would I write? What words could I send to the Teacher?"

"It does not matter. Write about the sunset or becoming Empress or about your garden. It only matters that it is from you and that it is signed Nishima-sum."

"Really, Shuyun-sum, this is an unusual request, to say the least."

"Have I asked too much of you?"

This stopped Nishima for a second. "No. If it is a poem you desire, I will attempt to write a poem worthy of one who has reached perfection—as impossible as that may be."

Shuyun pressed her close to him and then, to her surprise, released her, waving toward her writing table.

"You don't expect me to do this now? Really, Shuyun-sum, I must have time to think."

"You do not need time to think. Three lines would be adequate. I would venture that one would be enough." He smiled again and she began to wonder if he was serious. This did not seem like an occasion for humor to her.

Throwing up her hands in resignation, Nishima turned to the table and began to prepare her ink. As she did so, she felt Shuyun's fingers begin to explore the intricacies of the fastenings that held her hair in place. Though this made concentration almost impossible, Nishima did not want to ask him to stop, for to her it was a sign that he felt some sense of intimacy as she always he hoped he would.

Her hair fell about her shoulders and cascaded down her back, bringing a smile to her face.

"You are not focused," Shuyun said close to her ear. "Your teacher would be disappointed."

"You are not helping, I must tell you."

He laughed. "I will leave and let you work in peace."

"You certainly will not! You must sit close to me and try not to be too much of a distraction."

"I can be as still as a stone," he said, and she felt the smile in his voice.

"Well that may be more than is required." It took a great deal of will power, but Nishima removed a piece of mulberry paper from a folder and dipped her brush in ink.

Even a few years without change
Lull the mind
And then in a day
The world changes utterly.
Heroes appear
And legends come to life.
Things immutable are transformed:

War turns to peace, despair becomes joy
The living die
And are born again.

"You are finished?" Shuyun asked.

"Finished? I have hardly begun."

"Let me see," the monk said and then leaned forward to read over her shoulder. "Nishi-sum, it is perfect."

"It is perfectly awful. I will need hours to make this a poem."

"No. Do not change a word. That is the poem I will take to the Teacher. You must sign it as I said."

"But Shuyun-sum, I would be ashamed to have anyone see this. And now you ask me to sign it in a familiar form. This seems most unconventional."

Shuyun put a hand on her shoulder. "The Teacher is not as other men. Do not judge him according to the standards of the Empire. Please, sign."

Shaking her head, Nishima did as he asked, wondering if the culture of the Botahist monks was perhaps more different than she had formerly imagined. She blew gently on the ink until it dried.

"Now you must fold it as gateway," Shuyun instructed.

Through resisting, Nishima did as she was asked, handing it to Shuyun as she finished. "I hope your Teacher will not think me as poor an Empress as I am a poet."

Shuyun smiled, putting the poem into his sleeve pocket.

The night was growing cool, as nights usually did in the late spring. Nishima reached out, touching Shuyun's wrist, then slid her hand up his sleeve past the elbow, feeling the warmth there.

"Now you must do a favor for me," she said.

"I am your servant," he answered, his tone serious.

Rising, Nishima drew the monk up with her and, taking him in tow, she walked into the inner room. She opened a screen and entered the sleeping room. There was no lamp lit here and only the starlight through the open shojis gave the scene light.

Releasing Shuyun's hand, she undid the complex knot at her back and unwound her sash. When she had done this, the monk helped her remove her outer robes until she wore only a single layer of silk. She felt the questions that consumed her being pushed aside by growing desire. When she reached out to untie Shuyun's sash, her fingers were not inclined to obey and her breath was short.

Pulling back the quilts, they almost tumbled into bed. Nishima slipped out of her robe almost immediately and pressed herself as close to him as she could manage.

"If you did not spend the night resisting me," Nishima said close to his ear, "I'm certain you would not be in such a hurry to leave. You might spend a few days more, at least."

"I fear that this is so," Shuyun answered.

They lay close for a moment more and Nishima realized that she was not alone in having lost her breath. She kissed the soft place at the corner of his eye and his mouth found hers. For the first time, he returned her kiss. Nishima thought she felt a strange sensation, almost vertigo, and then she realized that a kiss became endless and her skin was alive to the touch as it had never been before. Strong currents of emotion and energy and chi seemed to flow through her. For a second she felt panic begin to touch her, but it was swept away by a wave of tenderness and she abandoned herself to the feeling without hesitation.

Much later, Nishima lay bathed in the warmth of her companion.

"I do not want to sleep. I want to say everything that is in my heart though I do not know where to begin to find the words."

Shuyun kissed her neck. "There are no words. Everything has been said."

Despite her desire to stay awake, Nishima could not and she fell into an untroubled, dreamless sleep.

A breeze moved her hair and this finally awoke her. It was early morning, but completely light. She lay completely still for a moment, lost in memories and pleasure, and then turned to find her lover.

But Shuyun was not there. Where . . . she began to ask herself when awareness came. Burying her face in the quilt she lay very still, as though moving would alter everything for ever. If she could just not move. . . .

A bell sounded and Nishima opened her eyes to the light. On a table at the bedside lay a brocade bag containing something angular. She sat up and found the most delicate blue seashell on top of this and in the cup of the shell a bit of white paper had been placed so that it could not blow away. On this was written a single character which meant *she who renews*. My heart will break, she found herself thinking, my heart will surely break.

Setting the shell upon the pillow, Nishima took the brocade bag and opened it, finding a plain wooden box inside.

It is the blossom of the Udumbara, she realized. For a moment she did not know what to do but then, with great care, she set the box aside and rose from the bed. She found her robes and slipped them on, belting them loosely. Taking up the box in both hands, Nishima went out onto the balcony.

She perched herself on the rail with her back against a pillar and forced herself to be calm. Performing a breathing exercise taught to her by Brother Satake helped.

Finally, when her spirit was as calm as she could make it, when the pang of Shuyun's leaving was a sweet sadness not a sorrow, she opened the box.

To her great surprise she did not find a sacred blossom inside but a white butterfly, tinged with the faintest purple. It fanned its wings slowly and then, in a single motion, took to the air. It circled about the balcony once, then rose on a current, descended again, and then fluttered off into the garden where it was soon lost from sight. Nishima watched long after it had gone, hoping for a last glimpse, but it did not reappear and she leaned her head back against the pillar and closed her eyes.

My heart is both broken and full of joy, she told herself. I do not know whether to cry or laugh.

Opening her eyes she realized that a perfect paper shinta blossom lay on the silk of the wooden case and she set the case on the rail and took it up. After a moment of searching, she found the key and began to unfold the blossom. In the heart of the paper flower she found a single line of characters written in Shuyun's beautiful flowing hand.

Beyond the future lies a future in which we cannot be separated.

She thought of the butterfly flying out of the case and she smiled.

"Things are never what one expects," Nishima said to herself, and she laughed. She laughed until tears ran down her cheeks.

The guards led the Empress along a path paved in stones. They stopped at a simple wooden gate under a small arch and tile roof. Very quickly, one of the guards passed through the gate and when he returned four other guards came with him. This man nodded to the senior officer who in turn knelt and bowed to the Empress. The garden was secure.

Nishima went through the open gate and heard it close behind her.

It is a day for partings, she told herself.

A few steps into the garden Nishima stopped to look out to the north over the large encampment of the tribes. She knew he was not there, but still her eyes searched for a moment among the thousands of tiny figures before she turned away.

A few more paces brought her to the shrine and she knelt on a mat that had been placed for her. Into the face of an uncut stone had been chiseled the name character *Shimeko*.

Nishima offered up a silent prayer to Botahara and then one also to the Teacher.

We will never know, Nishima thought, *we will never know if you fell into their hands without intending to or whether you chose to take your terrible weapon out among our enemies so that others might live. When I think of your fate, Shimeko-sum, I am gripped by its horror. Among all the brave, all the heroes of this pointless war, you alone went into battle without armor, without protection. Only you risked the destruction of your spirit. May Botahara rest you and protect your soul.*

Nishima offered up a long prayer for forgiveness and then rose and went to her duties.

Sixty-six

THEY HAD SLIPPED out of the city at dawn, all three in disguise, and set out across country until they found the narrow road they sought. Only then did they throw back their hoods to the sunlight—a warrior, a monk, and a barbarian tribesman.

There was no indication that they hurried to an appointed time or place—in truth, their pace seemed almost leisurely. They stopped, it appeared, whenever whim struck and often finished their day's travel before sunset. In a time when a significant portion of the population of Wa were on the roads and canals, returning or moving to places where they would begin their lives again, these three travelers hardly stood out. Except that they did not seem to be driven to reach their destination as others did.

Of course the area the three traveled through was not flooded with refugees the way the northern canal and roads were aswarm with people returning to homes, or even the way the roads to the south and the west were filled with people seeking places to begin anew. The three set their course north by east and encountered few as they went.

Shuyun knelt cross-legged on a mat by the edge of the stream. He had spent an hour in meditation upon the sunlight falling through the leaves as the wind moved among the trees. He watched the beauty of the movement and patterns as though they were dance.

Two dozen paces up the stream bank Komawara sat bent over a letter, reading. Shuyun had seen the lord take this same paper from his sleeve several times, to pore over it as he did now, but Komawara did not speak of this and Shuyun felt it would be the worst manners to inquire.

Shuyun was certain he saw the beginnings of healing in Komawara, just a glimmer, but there, nonetheless. He carries wounds as deep as any cut by a sword, Shuyun thought. One cannot expect him to heal overnight.

What Nishima had done, the gifts that she had given the young lord, showed great wisdom, Shuyun thought. There was no question in Shuyun's mind that Nishima was the ruler that Wa needed in this time. Thinking of the Empress brought a sense of warmth and joy. She was my teacher, he thought, though she did not know it.

He turned his attention back to the light dappling the ferns and the forest floor across the stream. *The Illusion,* he had been taught and it had taken some time to learn what that truly meant. He had labored under so many misapprehensions—it made him wonder what was truly written in the scrolls of Botahara.

The sound of the lightest of footsteps sounded in the soft undergrowth and Shuyun turned to find the Kalam bearing bowls of cha. With a bow, the tribesman set one on the edge of Shuyun's mat and then turned and took a second bowl to Komawara.

Shuyun caught the lord's eye then and waved an invitation. Folding his letter, Komawara came and found a place on the corner of the monk's mat. Yes, there it was, around the eyes and the mouth, signs that Komawara was emerging through the bitterness and anger.

Shuyun noticed that the lord did not carry a sword in his sash, and had not during their journey—highly unusual for a warrior of Seh. Of course, Komawara did keep a blade strapped to his saddle, but Shuyun had not seen him touch it yet. The Kalam removed the sword at each stop and kept it close at hand for the lord's use. There were brigands abroad in Wa, and many inclined to honesty were being forced to this life. But all the same Komawara chose not to carry a blade.

"We might reach the foot of the mountain this afternoon, Brother, it is not as far off as it appears."

Shuyun nodded. "Yes. In the morning I must proceed alone, Samyamusum, though I will miss your company."

"I fear my company has been poor, Shuyun-sum. I apologize for this."

Shuyun met the lord's gaze for a moment, searching his eyes. "Lord Komawara, do you suggest that one who will serve the Teacher would speak anything but the truth?" he said, his tone mock-serious.

Komawara grinned. "Please excuse me, Brother. I meant to imply no such thing. But, in truth, I think my company has been less than joyful."

"Perhaps, but it has given me great joy even so. After our other journeys together, this one has certainly been the most pleasant."

Komawara gave a short laugh. "What, Brother, you did not feel great joy climbing the walls of Denji Gorge in the darkness? The legends will no doubt say that you did."

Shuyun grimaced. "It is your legend, Lord Komawara, that will speak of fearlessness."

"Huh," Komawara sipped his cha. "That is one of the many things I fear, Brother. On the walls of Denji Gorge I was as terrified as I can remember being, yet no song will tell that part of the tale." And then quieter. "No play will show the regret I feel for the lives I have taken."

Shuyun stared at the lord's face, watching the anguish return. "I have taken a life as well, Samyamu-sum. Lord Botahara was once a great general. The spirit can rise above all things—it is possible. Do not think that your soul will carry this stain forever—it can be cleansed. You are not a simple warrior, Samyamu-sum, able to follow the way of the sword without question. It is the terrible thing about war; it sends the most innocent into the field and strips their souls bare of this innocence. We have both seen it. Lord Shonto, Lady Nishima, Jaku Katta, you—we have all played parts in this terrible war. None have escaped unscathed.

"Duty requires much of us all. Of some it requires a life of drudgery. To rise above that is as difficult as it is to rise above what you have done in the performance of your duties. Yet souls of great enlightenment have arisen from the poorest circumstances. I have faith that you will rise above this, Samyamu-sum, though it may be as difficult as all the other feats you are celebrated for."

Komawara took a long breath. "Thank you, Shuyun-sum. It is my hope that you are right, as you have been in so many other matters."

The Kalam came and sat on a rock a pace away, sipping his cha silently. The three stayed like that into the afternoon, preserving their company as long as possible.

*   *   *

The next morning found the three travelers at the base of the Mountain of the Pure Spirit. They rode along a road that wound through a woods of birch and pine and golden slip maple.

They did not speak as they rode, for there was little left to be said. They had survived their travels in the desert and the war fought the length of the Grand Canal—words could not begin to say what these things meant. Riding out with Shuyun on the beginning of his journey said all that was required.

At length they came to a shrine at the road's edge. The road narrowed here and began to rise more steeply. As though this was a sign, Shuyun stopped and turned his horse so that he faced his companions.

"I must go alone from here, Samyamu-sum."

The monk could see the young lord struggling as he had often watched the Kalam do—looking for the correct words. In this case, Shuyun thought, none would be found.

"May Botahara journey at your side, Samyamu-sum," Shuyun said.

With an effort, Komawara managed to speak in a whisper. "May Botahara chant your name, Brother."

Shuyun reached out and touched the lord's arm. "He has, Lord Komawara. He has." The monk smiled.

Turning to the Kalam, he spoke to the tribesman in the language of the desert, the tribesman bobbing his head at almost every word. The monk reached into his sleeve then and removed something that he placed in the Kalam's hand. The final words Shuyun said left the tribesman utterly still and silent.

With a bow that the others returned, Shuyun turned his horse and began to climb up into the trees. At a point where he was about to disappear into the woods, Shuyun turned his horse and waved once to his companions. And then he was gone from sight.

It was a small gesture, but it gladdened Komawara's heart more than he could have guessed.

The lord and the tribesman turned their horses back the way they had come, riding knee to knee. It was several rih before Komawara's curiosity got the better of him.

"If I may ask," the lord said, "what was Shuyun-sum's gift?"

The barbarian dug into a pouch at his waist and held out his hand. On his palm lay a deep blue stone, the kind one might find in the bed of river—smooth and regular in shape.

"It is the soul of a butterfly, Lord Komawara," the Kalam said with apparent awe. "Brother Shuyun said to me I would one day see that this was so."

"Then that is no doubt true," Komawara responded and the two men rode on through the late spring day, lost in their own thoughts.

Shuyun gave his horse to three monks that he met, and this unexpected generosity allowed him to pass on without also giving them his name. The road wound up through the trees, past temples and monasteries belonging to both the Sisterhood and the Order to which Shuyun had once belonged. There were many shrines and, like all good seekers, Shuyun stopped at each one and offered a prayer.

Rather than sleep in the lodgings provided for seekers near the monasteries and temples Shuyun slept out under the sky, wrapped in the single blanket in which, during the day, he carried a bowl and a few things required for him to act as a healer.

With each step up the sacred mountain the monk felt he was breaking free of the earth, rising up onto a different plane. Summer clouds sailed in from the ocean and occasionally one seemed to attach itself to the mountain, clinging there until it stretched itself out in the wind like a torn banner, then it would break its bond and sail free.

They come to me, Shuyun laughed to himself, the Gatherer of Clouds. Like the Brother in the ancient play, it is my place to gather together the nebulous, the ambiguous. I will dispel the Illusion, if only for a few.

On the second day Shuyun came to the shrine he sought—the place where Botahara had given up his army and renounced all property, the place mentioned in the scroll Shuyun had received from Brother Hitara. Here the monk found a place on a large rock and began to fast and meditate. The shrine was just above the tree line and only a few of the most hardy trees survived here. Though few in number, these mountain pines were very old and each had been given a name, for they had been there a thousand years before when the Perfect Master had walked over these very stones.

Many seekers came to this shrine but few spoke to Shuyun, for most had taken vows of silence and assumed the same of others.

On the third day of Shuyun's fast, the monk he awaited appeared at last.

Seeing Shuyun, he approached, bowing in the manner of the Botahist Brothers.

"May the Perfect Master walk beside you, Brother Hitara," Shuyun said.

"May the Teacher greet you by name, Brother Shuyun."

The monk Shuyun had met in the desert perched on the edge of the rock.

"It is my hope, Brother Hitara, that you have come to show me the Way."

"Only the Teacher can do that, Brother—the Teacher and his bearer. But I will guide you some short distance."

Shuyun gave a deep bow in answer. They set off, passing between two tall stones set like gate posts on the stark landscape. The gray bones of the mountain were exposed here and interrupted only occasionally by dusky-green lichen beds.

As they passed the western shoulder of the peak itself, Shuyun was given a view of the Empire stretching off into the distance. He was above the clouds now and could see the masses of white, each trailing a shadow across the land, as they rolled off toward the western horizon. The Grand Canal was a silver thread pulled straight across the landscape and the Imperial Capital was a mound of white stones, stark against the greens of the land and the blues of the lake. Shuyun stopped for a moment, and Brother Hitara walked on a few paces to leave him in peace.

It was an easy thing to fill himself with the presence of Nishima and he did so now—her humor, her tenderness, her open spirit. Raising his hand at last as though he waved to someone far off, the monk turned and followed Hitara.

"Good-bye, my teacher," he whispered, "I go to meet another."

At dusk they had passed around the shoulder of the mountain and Shuyun felt that they were in the mountains proper now, for there was no sight of the Empire. They made a camp after dark and meditated on the stars until a moon appeared and then they continued, walking a narrow ridge that twisted and rolled like a stem of lintel vine. By daylight they had gone many rih.

Brother Hitara was also fasting, so they stopped only occasionally to drink. The late-spring sun beat down, but the air remained cool and there was always a breeze from the sea, making their relentless pace bearable. Toward the end of the second day Shuyun realized that only his Botahist-trained memory would allow him to retrace their route, so twisted was it, so devoid of distinguishing marks.

Working down a scree slope late in the day, Brother Hitara began to search along the face of a cliff. After some searching he located a break in the rock that could not be seen from even a few feet away. Through this they came upon a ledge wide enough for two to walk abreast. It wound up around the side of the cliff, its slope gradual, disappearing into a white cloud that clung to the mountain side. The stone here appeared to have seen so many generations of men pass along it that it was worn completely smooth.

Hitara stood gazing along the pathway with a look of satisfaction as though reassured somehow that it was still here or that he had been able to find it. "You must not wear your sandals here, Brother Shuyun—for you this is the beginning of the Way. Give a prayer of thanks each time your sole touches the stone, for few have walked this path."

"Brother Hitara," Shuyun said. "My gratitude cannot be expressed."

Hitara looked at him oddly then, almost quizzically. "Brother Shuyun, certainly the honor is mine. I have taken some small part in the completion of a prophesy. With each breath I thank Botahara for this. Few can say as much." He raised his hands to encompass the whole world. "What more can I ask of this life?"

He knelt down and kissed the smooth stone that began the path, then rose and bowed to Shuyun. "We shall meet again, Brother Shuyun. May the Teacher bless you."

"I must thank you for delivering His message, though I confess it took some months before I realized."

"It grows dark, Brother, will you not make camp with me until morning?" Suddenly Shuyun felt it odd to be abandoned. The path he had sought for so long seemed more daunting than he had imagined.

Hitara waved up the slope. "The moon will light my way, Brother Shuyun, for I have many tasks to perform. I would suggest you wait until daylight before you proceed, however. The Way is narrow." Bowing again, Hitara began to make his way lightly up the loose rock.

Finding a flat stone, Shuyun sat and began to meditate. Later, in the moonlight, he chanted, his voice echoing among the mountains as though he were a hundred men.

At the first hint of light he rose and removed his sandals. Like Hitara, he knelt and kissed the stone before placing a foot upon it. If there had been water, he would have bathed his feet.

The pathway led up the shoulder of the mountain until it entered a draw between that mountain and the next. Shuyun passed over the ridge that lay here, glad to find a stream of cool water. The path then followed the narrow ridge, the stone sloping off on both sides into green valleys far below. To his right Shuyun could see a small lake the color of turquoise.

At the end of the day the monk found a tiny rivulet of water that wound down the steep mountainside. A rough stone shrine stood here and Shuyun spent the night as he had before, in prayer.

He set out again at dawn and followed the narrow path as it wound its way deeper into the ancient mountains. Here and there a twisted pine sprang up impossibly from the desert of stone, and now and then he found a pond of clear water. Nowhere did he see signs that others had passed this way, no remains of fires or camps, yet the pathway remained as obvious and clear as a road in the capital. Who has passed this way? Shuyun asked himself. How could there have been so many?

On the third day, the sixth of his fast, he came into a hanging valley suspended between three mountains, and here there was enough accumulation of soil that both grass and trees grew—tall narrow firs of a type Shuyun had never seen. Rounding a massive boulder Shuyun surprised a Botahist Sister. Immediately she recovered. She smiled and bowed, making signs of welcome, but she said nothing. In a basket she gathered the cones of the pine trees and some small plant that Shuyun did not know. Obviously, she had taken a vow of silence, so the monk smiled and passed her by, following the pathway.

This valley is my destination, he realized, the awareness surfacing in him as though it was knowledge he had always possessed. The Teacher is here.

He skirted the shore of a tiny lake, and walked through a stand of trees. Here, without warning he came upon a small, roughly built house surrounded by a fence of unplaned boards.

Two Brothers knelt at the gate and they bowed low when Shuyun came into view, showing less surprise at the arrival of a stranger than had the foraging Sister. One rose immediately and slipped through the gate.

The Order's missing Brothers, Shuyun said to himself. Brother Hitara is one of these. The great mystery to the Botahist Brotherhood. They came to serve the Teacher. But how did they know? How did they find Him? Had they received messages like the one Shuyun had received from Hitara? Knowing where the Brothers had come did not solve the mystery.

Realizing the remaining monk did not intend to speak, Shuyun turned and gazed out over the lake, breathing in the scents of the valley that drifted on the cool breeze. It was a fine perfume.

I have found Him, Shuyun thought, feeling his spirit lift as though it took wing on the breeze. We have waited a thousand years. . . .

"Brother Shuyun." It was a woman's voice.

The monk turned to find a Sister regarding him with obvious interest. She was older, though nowhere near as old as the Prioress, and her bearing was that of a woman Shuyun's age.

"May you be welcome in our home," she said in a voice as youthful as her movement. "It is a place of great peace."

"I feel that I have arrived, Sister, but I do not know where."

When the woman smiled, the wrinkles at the corners of her eyes made them appear delightfully mischievous and Shuyun could not help but smile at this contrast.

"This valley, this lake, they have no names." She waved up the slope behind the house. "Nor is this mountain named. It is the home of the Teacher, kept ready for hundreds of years. And now he has come. Please, Brother, walk with me."

Shuyun followed her into a garden, stretching his time sense as he stepped through the gate to make the moment last. A gravel path led to the porch of the house but the nun did not go there. She took a second path, that wound among trees Shuyun could not name, and came to a second gate. She opened this gently, peering inside, then held it wide for her guest.

"He awaits you, Brother."

Shuyun was suddenly light-headed and he forced control over himself with great discipline. When he passed through the gate, the nun did something he did not expect—she reached out and touched him. It was not a gesture of affection or reassurance, she simply wanted to touch him. *I am the bearer of the Word,* Shuyun thought. I am part of a prophesy.

Stepping through the gate, Shuyun swept the garden with his gaze but saw no one. He stood for a moment, offering up a prayer, and then he began to walk along the path, his bare feet alive in every nerve as though the holiness of the earth flowed like chi.

The garden was small, large stones set among trees and unusual shrubs. The elevation no doubt imposed limits on what could be grown, giving the garden a sense of sparseness. All the same, this was a garden of great artistry and Shuyun drank in every detail.

Rounding a boulder, he found a man sitting on a cushion on a low, flat stone that formed a natural dais. Before this was an area of raked gravel. Shuyun stopped suddenly, unable to proceed.

The Teacher bent over a scroll. He dressed in the manner of Shuyun's own Order including a pendant and purple sash. He was not as old as many monks Shuyun had known and this was a surprise, though it should not have been. The Teacher appeared to have seen perhaps seventy-five years in this lifetime, though Shuyun was sure that was at least ten short of the truth. He was of average size with little about him, physically, to mark him. Perhaps his eyes were wider apart than most and his cheekbones higher, making his face appear less round than common among the people of Wa.

The Teacher looked up and smiled at Shuyun, a smile like the Prioress Saeja's—full of compassion, though touched by humor and the perspective of great age—many lifetimes in this case.

"Welcome," the Teacher said, his voice melodic. In that single word Shuyun was certain he heard an echo of both Lord Shonto and Lady Nishima.

Gesturing as he began to roll the scroll, the Teacher invited Shuyun to come forward.

Unsure of what was expected, Shuyun chose to walk, though he knelt and bowed three paces from the rock dais.

For several minutes the Teacher did not take his eyes off the young monk before him and his expression of great pleasure did not change. Somehow Shuyun felt like a favored son returning after a long absence.

"Brother Shuyun, it is with great joy that we welcome you into our home."

"The honor is mine entirely . . . Brother Satake."

The older man's face lit up in a great smile. "Motoru-sum would never have told you."

"He did not, Brother."

The Teacher laughed. "You will be most welcome. I only regret that I will stay but a short time."

Not quite sure what was meant by this, Shuyun searched for something to say. "I bring you a gift, Brother Satake," Shuyun said. He felt his spirit calming as though he were in the presence of someone he had known a very long time.

"It is most kind, Brother Shuyun, though I have need of nothing."

"It is a poem, Brother."

"Ah! A poem is always welcome."

Reaching into his sleeve, Shuyun found the mulberry paper. He leaned forward to place it on the dais, but Satake reached out and took it from his hand. Slowly the Teacher unfolded it and read, the look on his face made Shuyun believe that never had the Teacher received anything that delighted him more. He finished reading, and then he laughed his laugh of great joy.

"Nishi-sum, Nishi-sum," he said, as though the Empress were there in the garden with them. Brother Satake looked up. "This gift brings me great joy, Brother Shuyun. I thank you. She is well?"

Shuyun nodded.

"How I miss her at times," the Teacher said with feeling.

Shuyun nodded. "I fear I shall say the same."

The Teacher regarded him again, unembarrassed, it seemed, to do this. "It has been many centuries since a follower of the Eightfold Path walked the roads of Wa, Brother Shuyun."

Shuyun broke away from the man's gaze with some effort. "I am not sure what the Eightfold Path is, Brother Satake, but I have wandered far from the path taught by my Order."

The Teacher's face became grave. "You rode to war beside my former charge, Motoru-sum; were stripped of your pendant and ejected from your Order; met the barbarian threat; and took an Empress as your lover—all in the few months since you left Jinjoh Monastery?"

Shuyun did not know what to answer. Though the charges were most serious, the Teacher's tone seemed to lighten with each word.

Satake laughed suddenly. "I spent decades accomplishing less, Brother." He smiled his beautiful smile. "Perhaps only Botahara has lived more fully before finding His true purpose." The Teacher laughed again. "Nishi-sum, Nishi-sum," he said as though he chastised a favored child, "my own bearer."

Brother Satake regarded Shuyun again and the humor in the man's eyes seemed to shine through. "Here we have labored on other pursuits, Brother." He gestured to the scroll he had been reading. "We true-copy Botahara's great work."

Shuyun looked up, certain he had let his surprise show. "How, Brother?"

He was not sure this question did not bring a glint of pleasure to the old man's eyes. "There are Faithful even among the Botahist Brothers, Shuyun-sum. Even among the hypocrites and liars. The scrolls have been in the possession of the Faithful for some years.

"So we have labored. It is a task more difficult than one would think, for the language has changed and grown—but my special knowledge of the past has allowed us to come near to the end of this. The Word of Botahara as it must be known." He smiled at Brother Shuyun. "And the word of Satake as I have written it." He hefted the scroll he had been reading as if demonstrating its weight. "The word you will bear. Your way will be hard, Brother, never doubt it."

Shuyun stared openly at the scroll in Satake held. *The hand of Botahara, so close I could reach out and touch it.*

Suddenly his face became serious. "You have not yet stopped the sand, Brother Shuyun."

"I have not, Brother Satake," Shuyun admitted. "I confess that I am afraid."

The Teacher nodded, understanding in his eyes. "As was I, Brother Shuyun." He set the scroll down gently and wrapped it in brocade. "Tell me what it is you have learned from your teachers, the Shonto."

Yes, Shuyun thought, it is as I believed. Nishima was my teacher as was her father. "I have learned much, Brother Satake . . . and perhaps I have learned nothing. I do not know."

The Teacher did not answer but gave his full attention to the young monk, waiting.

Shuyun stared down at the gravel for a moment as though studying the patterns there, looking for order among the randomness of the world. "It is the Illusion, Brother Satake: what I was taught did not ring of truth. The world, it is not illusion, it is a plane on which our spirits take form. I was taught that believing in the Illusion would lead to great sorrow, and that joy and pleasure were not real—things meant only to trap us in an endless cycle of rebirth into the world of Illusion." He looked up suddenly. "But I now believe this was wrong. Joy and pleasure are as real as pain and sorrow and one must learn what they have to teach, just as a Neophyte Brother must learn the Form. The Illusion exists in the minds of those who do not truly believe they can progress beyond that plane onto another, who do not know that there is a lesson to be learned. To progress beyond the world one must give it up, finally. It will not disappear the day this is done—one must still come to completion before one leaves it behind. The world will exist for all the souls to come. But one must break free of the Illusion, perceive the path to the next plane. I say this though I have not done so, Brother Satake."

The Teacher smiled and Shuyun felt like a student who had pleased his Master. "You have other duties, Brother. Your time will come." He waved toward the mountains. "When I am no longer among you, Shuyun-sum, you must go to the faithful. The mountain people await you as the tribes of the desert await the rains. It will be the beginning of your long task, Brother Shuyun. Your path will eventually lead you among the hypocrites and liars—some whom you will know by name." He looked up at a passing cloud. "You will be the Bearer, Shuyun-sum, you will be the Gatherer." He smiled upon Shuyun, a smile of great peace. "Botahara will walk beside you."

I have gone to the base of the Sacred Mountain
And watched him ride up among the clouds,
He of the tranquil soul.

Turning back then,
My soul was a raging torrent
But tonight I dream of dark eyes
Above the fan's edge.
If peace can restore an Empire
Will it not a man's spirit?

Lord Komawara Samyamu,
Consort to the Empress Shigei

The End